Sharon Salvato is the co-author, with Cornelia Parkinson, of the best selling novel, THE BLACK SWAN, under the pseudonym of Day Taylor. She is married with four children and lives in Ohio.

This book is dedicated to my father, Raymond Joseph Zettler, and my brother, Raymond Jeffrey Zettler.

Sharon Salvato

Bitter Eden

A Troubadour Spectacular

Macdonald Futura Publishers

A Troubadour Book

First published in Great Britain by
Macdonald Futura Publishers in 1980
Copyright © 1979 Sharon Salvato

ISBN 0 7088 1917 6

Printed in Great Britain by
Hazell Watson & Viney Ltd
Aylesbury, Bucks

Macdonald Futura Publishers Limited
Paulton House
8 Shepherdess Walk
London N1 7LW

BOOK I

Chapter 1

The fertile rolling land of the Kent countryside was covered with a slick wet film of ice during the harsh English winter of 1829. In place of the heavily laden fruit orchards and the grand green arbors of the hop vines, there was a look of barrenness broken only by the pathetic tops of winter turnips planted along the ridges where the hops had been.

At Gardenhill House, Peter Berean alone was left outside. He finished cleaning the farm implements and replaced them in the barn. Beating his hands together, he walked slowly across the stable yard. Across his shoulders cold moisture had seeped into the fabric of his coat, leaving dark wet patches. He stopped, and tucked his gloved hands protectively against the warmth of his ribs. He stared with longing at the impressive half-timbered manor house. The timbers were bent and twisted by time; oak mellowed with age until it blended in regal antiquity with the stuccoing. Diamond-shaped lead-paned windows reflected gray winter light. Sighing, Peter turned away, looking up into the threatening, leaden sky. It would be dark within the hour and the weather was worsening.

From the protection of the house, a woman stepped into the yard. His wife. She stood, hands on hips, watching him. He didn't see her.

Peter stared up into the boiling, thunderous clouds, seeking guidance. He didn't know what was right. He felt the hurt and desperation of the Kentish peasants sharply, and with all his compassionate nature he wanted to help, but he didn't know what was right. And who was there to tell him in these troubled times?

He rubbed the back of his hand across his mouth. He had seen Nate Wheeler's rotting corpse hanging from the gibbet at the crossroads to Seven Oaks this afternoon. The vision, still too clear in his mind, had the power to bring stinging bile back into his throat. He silently asked the threatening sky, Had that been right?

Nate had been a brawling, angry man when he died, but Peter could remember a time not long ago when Nate had been cheerful, a smiling man who wanted only a mug of ale and a good laugh before going home to his wife and seven children. That had been before the common pasture and hunting grounds had been closed off and put under the control of the squires and the wealthy. It had been before machinery had taken from Nate's wife her profitable cottage industry; before Nate had no longer been able to earn enough to feed his children; and before war and weather and progress and taxes had changed England.

Peter shuddered. He was cold and more than a little afraid of the future. It wasn't difficult for him to superimpose his own features onto the purpled, bloated face of the dead Nate Wheeler. Courage was elusive when he imagined his loved ones riding the cart to

town and passing the decomposing remains of his own
hanged body.

But he knew he would ride to the laborers' meeting
tonight, because he had to. He was an honorable man,
not in the least sympathetic to politics or the machina-
tions of progress. He saw only the pain and the hunger and the fear in men he knew, men he hired to
work his own lands, and it was to that Peter Berean
responded. Tonight, once again, he'd become one of
the illegal night riders who took orders from the
phantom leader, Captain Swing.

Rosalind Berean watched her young husband, his
profile rigid and strong, look unblinking into the merciless opaque sky. Her own jaw was clenched so tight
it hurt as she willed him to turn from his thoughts and
look at her. He wouldn't. She knew he wouldn't, for
she knew what filled his mind as well as he did, and
she hated him for it. She hurried across the courtyard.
He jumped at the sound of her sharp, angry voice;
then, as always, his dark brown eyes softened at the
sight of her.

For a moment Rosalind allowed herself to be
warmed by him. Her eyes began to water and her lips
trembled with the need to smile. It was so easy to
trust him. And so horribly frightening. She looked
away from him, her eyes set on the bleak winter landscape. She'd conquer her involuntary reactions to that
gentle loving look of his, for it meant nothing when all
was said and done. For his damnable peasant laborers
he'd risk everything—his home, his life. And what did
he give to her? Long lonely hours in empty, worry-
filled nights. He knew how much she dreaded even
the thought of men like the Swing men. He knew
what hideous memories they brought back to her. But
did he consider her feelings? Did he ever once re-

member the terror or humiliation she had suffered by hands such as theirs when she was no more than a child and forced to work in her father's tavern?

"I could freeze to death and you'd never care!" she said. Her voice was shrill. "I'm sick of it, Peter." She looked at him then, and saw puzzlement flash across his face then disappear as he reached for her. She pulled away from him as he tried to enfold her more deeply in the warmth of her scarf. Fighting both herself and him, she said, "There's an end to my patience, and you've passed it. I won't have you treating me as you have been! I won't! I needn't stand for it. I left all that when I left my father to marry you. Those men are dirty! They're . . . they're horrible . . . horrible . . . things."

Her words now made sense. Fear and anger knotted inside him. He didn't know how to protect her and still do what he believed was right. He understood her hatred of the peasant men. He was aware of her pain. How could he not be? How could any man who loved a woman be unaware of what other men had done to her? He knew all these things, and the knowledge twisted and turned inside him, but he couldn't stop aiding the Swing men, not when thousands of Englishmen walked the roads hungry and unable to find work, unable to find rest or solace. One by one they would fall victim to the unreasonable justice of England's Bloody Code and die for their hunger as Nate Wheeler had. Peter couldn't be a passive audience. Why couldn't Rosalind see that? Why couldn't she take pity, knowing that the things these men suffered she'd never suffer, because he would keep her safe.

Then, as he looked at her, a great weariness crept over him. Nothing was clear to him. Sometimes he thought that it was he who needed protection. He was like any other man, wanting his wife, her love, his home.

Steamy puffs of her breath dotted the air between them. "My God, when will you learn to mind your own business?" she said. "It's not as though you haven't enough here to keep you busy."

His eyebrows, so startlingly black beneath his thatch of pale blond hair, were touched with a whitening of frost. His dark brown eyes were full of life and pain, and even now held an unquenchable warmth. "What would you have me do, Rosalind?" he asked softly. "The farm workers are starving."

"And what of me? There is more than one way to starve. Remember that, Peter. Remember who you married."

"I never forget that," he said. "Rosalind, be patient, please. Everything will be different soon. There won't be any night rides then."

She raised her chin. "Oh, yes, everything will be different, and perhaps sooner than you expect. I'm tired of promises, Peter, and I'm tired to death of being put second to those dirty, smelling peasants. They're not worthy of your help or anyone else's. I hope they all die! Every one of them! Even you!" He reached for her. "Don't touch me! Stay away from those . . . those . . . I swear to you, Peter, things will be different between us in a way you won't like. I'll never be dirtied by that scum again!" She ran from him, disappearing inside the house with a flurry of skirts and wind-whipped scarves.

Peter listened to the door close; then, head down, he followed, his anger rising. Frank had been talking to her again, he knew it. As he walked to the house, a vision of his older brother's florid, self-satisfied face mocked him. Frank had fed Rosalind's fears. He would do anything he could to make Peter give up his fight for the peasants.

The wind caught the door as Peter entered the house, slamming it shut with a ferocity that shook the leaded windows. Seven startled members of the Berean family looked up from their activities and then became attentive to the grim angry look of him.

"Frank," he said, and without preamble strode to his brother, his fists clenched. "You and I have something to settle between us right now."

Frank, secure in the presence of the rest of the family, smirked. "I suppose you're looking for a brawl."

Rosalind whirled from the glowing heat of the hearth fire. "You and Frank?"

"Yes, Frank and me. Don't tell me he wasn't filling your head with his talk before you came outside."

"What I said to you outside has nothing to do with Frank. He's right about you. You are a thoughtless, irresponsible child! You're going to bring trouble and humiliation to the whole family. You've no right to be with those horrible Swing men. You're not of them. You've nothing to do with them. If they didn't drink their wages they'd have money for their families. They don't want help or work!"

"Is that what you've been telling her?" Peter shouted at his brother. "That those men . . . what the hell is it, Frank? Can't you say what you have to say to my face? Why frighten my wife?"

Frank slowly folded his newspaper and looked with pained tolerance at his younger brother. "As the eldest in the family, Peter, I feel it is my duty to correct you when you're wrong. I have never hidden my views from you, and I have no need to use your wife. You're a bloody fool and always have been. You're playing a child's hero in a game you don't understand, and sooner or later we'll all pay the price of your stupid heroics. Riots! Demonstrations of need!" Frank snorted. "Those peasants don't want your help and don't need it. They have the dole to see them through. Let Albert Foxe tend to their ills. It's his job."

"If the magistrates did their jobs fairly there wouldn't be such a problem."

Frank shrugged. "Whatever. In any case it is not your problem."

Peter hit his shoulder, spinning Frank to look at him. "It is, damn it! It's the business of all of us. Especially us. We're educated. That gives us an obligation. If we who have learned and are supposed to be wiser don't take a hand, it'll come to a bloody confrontation between the laborers, landholders, and government. Would you prefer that? Is that what you would see happen to preserve your own precious skin?"

"Oh, blessed heaven, he's going to give another speech," Rosalind groaned.

Frank ignored her. He raised his arm, met Peter's eye, and moved sharply to slam his paper down on the table. His heavy face was marked with loathing. "You damned arrogant cock! Where in the hell did you get the idea you could cure the ills of the world? Obligation! Damn obligation. Your obligation is to this family, this hop garden. Nowhere else! No bloody where else!" Emboldened, Frank advanced on his brother, his forefinger pointing at Peter's chest. "Get it into that thick stupid skull of yours that I won't tolerate your nonsense. If you weren't my brother I'd turn you in for the damned traitor that you are! We have a reputation to uphold, and by damn we'll do it! We don't have a part in the doings of a bunch of filthy, ale-swilling laborers. Tell the bastards to stop drinking their wages, and they'll have bread on their tables."

Peter slapped Frank's hand away. "You son of a bitch," he said in a low, throaty whisper. "You damned, greedy, self-serving son of a bitch. What you mean is that Frank Berean wants to be somebody in this parish. Frank Berean wants to rub asses with the people who count, and anything to be sacrificed to that is worth it."

"You're damned right! In this world you either go up the ladder or you go down. I'm going up. And I'll look out for me and mine, because if I don't no one else will."

Peter's hands clenched into fists again. Rosalind laughed and walked over to him. "Oh, please! No brutal demonstrations in this happy family setting." She put her hands on his arms. "You should listen to Frank, Peter . . . except that he is wrong about one thing. When a man doesn't choose to look after what is his own, there is usually someone around who is *very* willing to take his place." Mockingly coy, she ran her finger along his jaw, then went upstairs to their bedroom.

Peter glared at Frank, glanced hastily after his wife; then, defeated, his eyes sought and found the understanding eyes of his younger brother Stephen. But before Peter could speak, James Berean walked into the room, assessed the situation, and gestured to his son. "Go up to her, Peter."

Frank said, "Unless he has something better to offer her than more of his shenanigans, it'll do him no good to . . ."

"You'll disrupt this family no more this evening!" James said. "Go up to her, Peter. And you, Frank, go soothe your own wife. Look at her. She's as upset by this as Rosalind is by Peter." He pointed to Anna Berean sitting quiet and huddled in a corner of the sofa. Still agitated, and wanting to reestablish order in his home, James ordered Stephen to check on the brewhouse, then began to pace the room.

Meg Berean moved to her husband's side. They looked at each other, but neither had anything to say. Meg smiled weakly at James, then went to gather mop and bucket.

Cleaning up the muddy tracks Peter's boots had made on the floor, Meg clucked over his carelessness and worried about him. He was thoughtless in small ways, but she knew this son was a man she could always count on to be kind where it counted most. It wasn't her eldest, Frank, who looked after his father. It was Peter who did his own work and took on a great portion of James's labors as well.

James settled down in his chair, his eyes closed, pretending to nap. From above he could hear Rosalind's angry voice and Peter's deep one. There was nothing so peace-shattering in a house as an unsatisfied wife, or two sons who for all their lives would never live in harmony. "Meg, my love," he said with false joviality. "Do you suppose this old man could be fed soon?"

"You can indeed. You wash up and I'll have supper laid before you're finished."

"Wash up, she says! Just like the old days when we came filthy from the fields. Ah, Frank, your mother will never change."

"It was just a manner of speaking," Meg sniffed. She added in a haughty voice, just as Stephen returned, "Dinner is served."

James took his daughter's arm and walked to the dining room, stopping before Meg. He held his hands up for inspection like a naughty school boy. Seeing his broad grin, Natalie did the same as her father. Meg gently boxed their ears and hurried them into the room.

Anna, Frank's perpetually earnest wife, squeezed Meg's arm. "He likes to tease you."

"Which of this crew doesn't?" Meg asked quickly.

Frank glanced over the table, his eyes riveting on the two empty seats. "Where are Peter and Rosalind? Why haven't they been called to . . ."

Anna gave him a nudge in the ribs. His face grew sterner. "They belong here at the table."

James caught the look of quick responsive anger on Stephen's face and said quickly, "We'll begin without them."

"It is not right that they aren't here to join us. It merely encourages Peter . . ."

"Pa said we'd begin without them," Stephen said loudly. "Why don't you mind your own business, Frank?"

Frank looked at Stephen, appalled, then glared at his father. "Well, Pa, perhaps now you'll listen to me. Out of the mouths of babes . . ."

"I'm not a babe! Why can't you leave Peter alone? At least he does something. He believes in something."

"Stephen! Frank," Meg said, then looked to James.

"You have both said enough," James said.

Frank adjusted his immaculate collar. "Ma is not the only one who cannot fathom that our position in this parish is changing. Peter will act like a common field hand till his death if something is not done about him, and now he is influencing Stephen as well."

"Peter is nothing like a common field hand," Stephen said hotly. "He . . ."

"You're right. He's worse, and all the more dangerous," Frank said, then turned his attention to James. "How long do you intend to indulge his irresponsibility at a cost to this family? Will you close your eyes until it is too late for Stephen as well?"

James concentrated on his soup, looking up momentarily from beneath craggy eyebrows. "Soup is delicious. Let's not spoil it with disagreeable talk."

"Better to allow him to spoil our good name with every important person in the district."

"He's hardly doing that," James said mildly.

"No? The first thing Mrs. Foxe asked me yesterday when I saw her was about Peter. 'Is the dear boy still consorting with the rabble?' she asks. His rides and speechmaking are the illest kept secrets hereabouts. How long do you think it will be before Albert catches him at it? Then it will be public disgrace rather than gossip."

"Albert does say that Peter will be caught and punished, Papa," Natalie said. It was the first time she had spoken since Peter had stormed into the house and the argument had begun.

"Albert Foxe has a tendency to think the worst of everyone and everything, Natalie. I wouldn't put too much faith in what he says, particularly where it concerns your brother. You must remember Peter and Albert grew up together, always competed. There may be a modicum of jealousy involved. Peter has nothing to do with rabble of any sort. Keep that in mind, and I don't expect to hear it mentioned again."

"So! You do condone his activities!" Frank said.

"I condone nothing, but neither will I have one of my sons betrayed by the loose tongue of another! I will talk with Peter. The rest of you learn to keep quiet about what is private business in this house. That applies particularly to you, Natalie. We are pleased you'll be marrying Albert, but he is the magistrate and for the moment what he does not know will help your brother."

"I know, Papa," Natalie said softly. "But please talk to Peter. I don't like lying to Albert. He will be my husband after all, and he always asks me so many questions about Peter."

"I'll talk to him," James said and changed the subject to the price of some horses Frank wanted to buy from the Foxes.

Frank's eyes glittered. Now was the time to get his father's agreement to buy. He thought of it as a well-earned bribe. Everything came easy to Peter, but Frank had to connive and maneuver for every scrap he got. He smiled. James would be pliable in order to avoid difficulty between his two oldest sons.

After dinner James and Meg lingered at the table, talking and enjoying one last cup of tea. Fretfully Meg brought up Peter's name again. "Is there so much danger in helping the laborers, James?"

"Not so much now. Frank is worried about the other landowners' opinions. No one takes kindly to having his hay ricks burned, or a horde of night riders trampling through fields."

"But Natalie says Albert questions her. Why should he be so interested if . . ."

"Albert is the magistrate, perhaps the most diligent we've ever had. We'd all be better off if Albert did not take himself so seriously." James cleared his throat and looked at Meg from under his brows. "And we have the good fortune of soon having him as a son-in-law."

"Oh, James, what a way to talk," Meg scolded. "You're as pleased as I that Natalie and Albert will marry. He's young and will make a good husband for her, and it doesn't hurt to have our daughter the mistress of Foxe Hall; you've said so yourself."

"All true. I've said it and I meant it, but do I have to like him as well?"

As the minutes passed and no strident noises were

heard from upstairs, James began to feel more kindly toward everyone, even Albert. Perhaps, he thought, hope reviving, Rosalind and Peter had reached an amicable, or better still, an amorous agreement. Perhaps for one night Peter would not ride out with the haphazardly organized laborers. "Meg, is there another piece of pie left?" He handed her his empty cup to be refilled as well.

What James hoped was taking place upstairs, however, was not. He had taken his first bite of pie when Peter came into the dining room. He hastened to his mother, kissing her cheek and whispering apologies into her ear. His face highly colored and relaxed, Peter was handsome, with a boyish impetuosity as youthful and alluring at twenty-six as it had been when he was sixteen.

James did not know from whence it came, but his children had been blessed—or cursed—with beauty. The exception was Frank, who looked much like James himself. Natalie, Stephen, and Peter had gathered their looks from some long forgotten ancestors, James concluded, for it was certain neither he nor Meg had bestowed the evenness of feature or brightness of eye these three had.

Peter chatted easily, teasing his mother. She rose to his bait, scolding and making faces of great pain. How could he talk to a lady so, even if she were his mother? Undaunted, Peter continued. Soon, in a pretense of anger, Meg hurried from the room, forgetting at least for the night her fear that he would be riding the countryside.

After Meg left the dining room, Peter rang the bell and asked the serving girl for a cold supper for himself, and then ordered her to take something upstairs for Rosalind. He ate quickly, businesslike, his mind already on the night's ride.

James sat watching the lines of concentration deepen along his son's brow and under his eyes. He knew what occupied Peter's thoughts. His own were similarly occupied far too often. He knew that his son was right, and yet he wished fervently that Peter would turn his back on the chaos of the English farm laborers. Couldn't someone else challenge the system?

In Kent and other southeastern counties, farm laborers were rioting. To the powerful landed gentry, it made revolution in England seem fearfully possible. Every minor disturbance reminded propertied Englishmen of the violence of the French revolutionaries. Perhaps because of their deep fear of mob violence, the wealthy also had an attitude of callousness toward the suffering of the poor, which couldn't be penetrated. But if the well-to-do viewed the poor lower classes with cold indifference, they viewed the vocal radicals—who stirred up the peasants with their talk of justice and equality—with the ferocity of animals protecting their lairs.

James remained silent until Peter shoved his plate aside and rose to leave. He was dressed in dark clothing. In his hands was a dark seaman's knit cap to cover his blond hair.

"Must you go tonight?" James asked, wishing he had been able to keep his silence. "All men deserve a night's sleep once in a while."

Peter's eyes met his father's and held. Slowly he shook his head; his voice was low. "One night would become two. . . . I'd like too much to stay home, Pa, to risk doing it even once."

James didn't argue. Again he understood, and chastised himself for being a coward. But he couldn't help it. He didn't want his son sacrificed for a cause that could be settled only when the time was right. A handful of farm laborers could not force that time to come.

He walked with Peter to the door and stood in the damp cold until his son had disappeared into the darkness; then he turned back to the house and sat in his chair, his heart filled with dread, his mind a jumble of worries and memories.

Peter was fighting a changing world that temporarily could not accommodate both its technical advances and its people. Unemployment was high; machines that could do the work of many were becoming common. Frank Berean looked upon the machinery as a boon: it was new, it was efficient, it meant more money in his pockets. Peter Berean deplored the rapid advance of machinery, for men he knew found themselves replaced by it, unable to feed their families. James shook his head sadly. What he could see—and neither of his sons could—was that each of them believed in progress and each had chosen a different aspect of it. Frank believed in technological advance, and Peter fought for social progress. Neither could be denied. There was no right or wrong to it, but with it came desperation. Out of the turmoil and confusion a phantom leader, Captain Swing, had emerged to lead the laborers to riot. Their hope was small—the past instructed that there would be few men of power or importance willing to listen to men of their class—but their desperation was great, and they would try anything. History deals with populations, but men die individually, and only once.

James got up to pace the room, then returned to the window. His thoughts continued worrisome and agitating. Reform was haphazard. Politics, he thought, is an erratic beast that either plods with bone grinding caution awaiting the popularity of its cause, or charges with eye dazzling speed and no thought to consequence, bringing with it revolution. After the economic collapse of 1829, the beast had gone both ways at once. The emerging nations were quick to commit themselves to the machinery that would make them great powers, and painfully slow to recognize the devastating impact the industrial revolution would have on its poor.

James wondered how much of the responsibility for Peter's restless crusading he should take on his own conscience. In some respects it had been his own life's choices that had determined Peter's choice now.

James Berean had been born the youngest son of a baronet. He had grown up with privileges and some rank, and then had acquired in his youth an idealistic, romantic love of the simple, rustic life. It was a malady common to young men of his class, but James's infatuation with the rustic was augmented by his falling in love with Meg Wharton, the daughter of a tenant farmer. There was no question of James's family's approving of the marriage, so he had married without their approval, and turned his back on wealth and position with all the cocky assurance of youth.

He became a tenant farmer like his father-in-law. He had expected to live the rest of his life as a tenant farmer just as his father had acidly predicted. That prediction had proven untrue. But his father had made another prediction, and that one had come painfully true. James began to see life as he never thought it could be. He saw for the first time that privilege came with land. Respect came with land. Dignity came with land. Without land he was nothing.

As a tenant farmer he was thought to have no opinion of value. Things that James had taken for granted while growing up were now denied him. How could he have known his education was a privilege of the rich? He hadn't—not until it had come time for his own three sons to be educated. It was believed that the poor didn't need education. It would only give them ideas. Places had to be kept, and part of the keeping was ignorance. Frank, Peter, and Stephen would never have learned their languages, history, or letters if James had not humbly returned to his family seeking their forgiveness and aid. When the opportunity came for him to buy Gardenhill House, James thankfully left the rustic life behind and moved into the landed class again.

Peasant life had been a galling experience for James, but a learning one. And it had been an experience that had, at least in part, formed the character of the son he now worried about. Peter had only been a child, but the taunts of the wealthier boys had remained with him, as had his teachers' willingness to conclude he was stupid because he was not a young lord or squire. He had been judged by what he owned and found wanting. The injustice of it was something he had never forgotten, and he would always believe that any man wanting to advance by his own labors should have the right to do so. So Peter spent his nights with the men who sought to better their positions, endangering his marriage by his absences, and his life by his presence among the outlaw workers. And James could not honestly tell him it was wrong.

Chapter 2

The night sky was opaque and black when Peter went to the stable. The horse started nervously as Peter fumbled and lit the lantern. The damp cold made his fingers stiff; the frosted metal of the lantern stung his flesh. Filled with misgivings, he harnessed and saddled his horse. Tonight, unlike other nights, he could not quell his disquieting uncertainty. Thoughts of Rosalind intruded, distracting him from his purpose. Forcibly he pushed them back, concentrating on the events before him. He extinguished the lantern and led the roan from the stable; then with a brief backward glance at James's distorted silhouette in the diamond-shaped windows, he rode out of the farmyard, across the open pasture, and into the shrouded woods.

He wound his way over familiar but unseen woodland paths. As he approached a clearing, he slowed the roan to a walk. Over the horse's head he waved a white kerchief. A man moved out from the dark mass of a tree and waved him through.

The Swing men were gathered around a small, clandestine fire. Their large work-soiled hands, fingers protruding from ragged gloves, stretched outward seeking the elusive warmth of the tiny blaze. Peter dismounted and joined them.

In spite of his efforts to dress as a laborer, he stood out from the rest. His boots were sturdy and well made. Many of the Swing men had bound their feet in rags to keep the torn shreds of their boots together. Others wore parodies of shoes—mismatched, mismade concoctions of leather and rag. Their coats were worn and thin, coarse, homemade garments. Angry once more at Frank's blindness to these people's plight, Peter shouldered his way among the men until he stood at the front of the group. He wanted to be seen by these men. He was ashamed of what his brother was. He wanted every man present to know that a Berean was there with them willing to fight by their sides for as long as reform took.

Peter listened to the speaker. He didn't know the man's name, nor did he ask. Like many of the Swing men, the man wore a dark mask over his features in a futile attempt to conceal his identity. Peter pulled up the deep collar of his black sweater, covering the lower portion of his face, but he did it only out of respect for the others. He knew too well that it made no difference. When the magistrates decided to put an end to the Swing riots, identities of men such as these would have no meaning. The arrests would be wholesale, and no one would care who they were.

Peter brought his attention back to the speaker. They were to burn the ricks of Roger Baker tonight. Peter became alert. Roger Baker was the chief tenant farmer on the Foxe property. Not only was Albert Foxe the magistrate for the parish, but the Foxe family was the most influential and the most adamantly opposed to the labor movement.

"Must it be Baker?" Peter asked.

The masked leader was silent. His cloth-covered face turned toward Peter. "If you'd rather not be with us tonight, Berean, we can see your reason. We'd not hold it against you. Foxe will be your brother-in-law. We ask no man to do harm to his own family."

"I care nothing for Albert Foxe. I was thinking of us—the movement—when I suggested another target. Thus far we've steered clear of the officials' homes. Baker's house is on the magistrate's home grounds. I am questioning the timing of the attack. Our movement has just begun to receive notice. We are slowly gaining momentum; other men are following. I am questioning the wisdom of antagonizing the magistrate now, when he is powerful enough to crush us."

"Roger Baker is one of the strongest supporters of the thresher," the leader answered. "For every threshing machine brought in, ten of us will be without work. Baker has a field of neatly stacked ricks of hay, all done by his bloody machines, and ain't the prick happy to show them off to anyone who'll look? The hop men hereabout see Baker's fields and hear him talk, and they listen. He tells them all to buy threshers. And they listen to him. We don't want the magistrate on us, but we can't let Baker speak so freely of the thresher. We'll put a bit of the fear of Swing in his belly, and see how much he talks then."

Several of the men around the fire murmured agreement. Peter merely nodded. Beyond suggestion, he never attempted to countermand the plans of the Swing men. Peter often questioned the wisdom of their decisions, for they were impatient and desperate for change to come quickly. But they spoke of children dying of fever, of children dying with cold, of children dying of hunger, and Peter could only listen and try to grasp with his mind what his experience would not allow him to feel. As the months since he had joined the Swing men passed, Peter knew that even his sympathies for them could never teach him to feel their desperation, or know what it was like to have no authority over one's own destiny, to be starving while no one cared. He could not argue with these men because he had never suffered as they suffered. He rode with them, and he talked eloquently and forcefully, encouraging them to keep their movement free of bloodshed. His voice was raised only on this one issue, and so far no man had been harmed by the Swing rioters. Their target was property.

Peter mounted his horse with the others. The masked leader came over to him. "Berean, we've heard of the talks you've made to the yeomanry on our behalf." The man seemed embarrassed. His voice was gruff. "You needn't worry about Gardenhill House. We won't touch it. Tell your pa that. We know our friends . . . and our enemies." He cleared his throat. "I just wanted you to know that. We know our friends."

The man dug his heels into his horse, wheeling the animal around. Forming the semblance of a column, the Swing men followed him through the woods, heading for the Foxe property.

The lights of Roger Baker's house winked warmly from behind the black mound of a gentle hillock. The muted thud of the horses' hooves seemed out of place among the soft sounds of the night hunters. Strange, interrupted sounds of pelting wings, agonized shrieks; fluttering, beating sounds of life-and-death struggles among the night animals.

"Willy!" the leader called in a hoarse whisper.

A small thin man rode up to him.

"When you see the ricks in flame, and we're clear,

poke this into Baker's door. Careful . . . don't be seen."

Willy looked at the scrap of paper:

Bewar of the fatel dager!
Swing.

He grinned as he stared at the note. He couldn't read a word, but he, like the others, knew the message it carried. He held the paper with pride, flattered beyond speech that he should be chosen to affix it to Roger Baker's door with his dagger.

The rest of the men went to the stable yard and broke into two groups. Dismounting, the first group went into the fields where the hay was stacked in ricks, the other into the outbuildings to remove Baker's tools and release his horses, acts calculated to wreak havoc on the operation of his farm. Systematically they spread out in the darkened barn. Peter, with the others, felt his way cautiously in the pitch-black building, searching for the location of the tools. In spite of all their efforts to move silently, tools fell to the floor, making what seemed a shattering din. Softly muttered curses cut the quiet air. Shadows of men hurried in blackness to and from the barn, carrying out farm implements and scattering them over the field, throwing them onto the fires or into the bordering woods. In the barn others continued rooting out Roger Baker's possessions. They covered the interior, climbing up into the loft, into the unused and empty stalls. They all stopped breathing as a pain-filled shriek cut through the night.

"Christ! Shut the bastard up! Who is it?"

"Kilmer . . . he fell from the loft," another voice said.

The Swing men crowded around the fallen Kilmer.

A grimy hand covered Kilmer's mouth, shutting off his cries. Another tried to straighten his leg, crumpled beneath him.

"Get him out of here! Quick, take him to his horse. Jude, you take him. Hurry!"

Two men lifted Kilmer and carried him to the door of the barn. Chaos broke out behind them. Tools clattered to the floor; men bumped into each other as they tried to regain control.

"Get out of here!" someone shouted hoarsely. "Baker's got a whole bloody army in the house. Run! He's comin'!"

"All the fires ain't set!"

"You set them!"

Hesitating, then running, their masked leader lit a dry branch and threw it into the nearest unfired rick. The dry hay sparked, snapping and smoking; then a yellow flame shot up. Incautiously the leader grabbed a handful of burning hay and tossed it onto the next rick. He was joined by Peter and two other men. Racing against time and Roger Baker, they ran through the field, throwing the burning hay.

The field lit up, glowing gold in the cold misty night, as Roger Baker and the three men who had been his dinner guests ran from the house. Baker, a rotund little barrel of a man, brandished a saber nearly as long as he was tall. The other men were better armed, two with swords and the third with a pistol.

With the leader Peter ran for the horses tethered near the woods. He nearly fell over Kilmer lying on the ground several feet from the horses. Willy knelt by the injured man's side. Peter looked behind him. Baker and the three men, momentarily distracted by the movement of the fire leaping from one rick to another, had assumed the Swing men were still setting the fires, and had run into the field. Quickly they saw their mistake and turned back. They began to run toward Peter and the horses. One man stopped, took aim, and fired the pistol. A cloud of flame burst forth. The sound was deafening. The ball thudded into the' tree trunk behind the horses. The animals, their eyes bulging, strained at their tethers, pawing the ground and rearing dangerously close to Kilmer.

"Help me get him up, Willy," Peter said. Kilmer, unconscious now, lolled across Peter's arms. The two men staggered under his weight. With Willy straining to help, Peter heaved Kilmer over the saddle. "Mount up, Will! Get him out of here. Hurry up, man! Don't look back now."

"What about you?" Willy asked, close to tears.

Peter removed his belt and strapped Kilmer's arms to the saddle. "Watch him, he's liable to spill," Peter said. "Go now!" He struck the rump of Kilmer's horse, making the animal jerk forward then run pell-mell into the fence, snorting and rearing. "Damn it, Willy! Take this lead and get out of here!"

Roger Baker and his men were only steps away. Peter flung himself onto his saddle. The tallest of the four men lunged at him, grabbing the tail of his coat. Caught off balance, with the horse in a frenzied dance, Peter slid from the saddle. Desperately he clawed at the saddle, then the horse's mane. He grabbed hold and managed to grasp the saddle horn with his left hand. The horse danced sideways. Then, at the prick of Baker's unwieldy saber, the animal shrieked, rearing and thrashing. Quivering and bucking, the roan danced into the sword, then renewed its haphazard efforts to rid itself of Peter's weight dragging its head down. Peter kicked at the men who pulled at his clothing, and maintained his death grip on the horse's mane. The animal shook his head furiously, kicking behind him. Roger Baker sprawled on the ground. The others battered at Peter with fist and sword. The man with the pistol tried awkwardly to reload in the dark.

Hemmed in by the fence and the men beating at Peter, the horse was crazed, rearing, his front legs slashing the air. Peter struggled to get one leg over the saddle. He screamed commands at the horse. The roan leaped forward, wrenching Peter against the fence. The men shouted obscenities and clawed at him. A heavy blow knifed along his arm, and then Peter was free, the roan running wildly. Unable to stop the horse, Peter was dragged across the hills and through Roger Baker's neat rows of winter turnips. His arms and shoulders were a fiery agony. Still running wildly, the horse headed into the woods that formed the boundary between the Berean property and that of the Foxes. His teeth clenched against the pain, Peter tried vainly to soothe the animal with his voice. Its head pulled to one side by Peter's weight, the roan swerved, skimming a tree. Peter hit the ground and lay motionless. Free of its burden, the animal slowed to a walk, its course now steady toward home.

James Berean had never left his post by the windows. He heard the roan enter the stable yard before he could see anything. He stuck his head out the front door. "Peter!" he called in a low whisper. Receiving no answer, James called again, then went out into the yard. Peter's horse stood, head down, exhausted. James touched the horse, felt the lathered sweat and the torn flesh of the animal's flank. He led the roan into the stable. With trembling hands he lit the lan-

tern. There was a ragged wound on the left hind-
quarters. James's throat tightened as he thought of Peter. He methodically bathed the horse's wound and
thought about his son. Should he go out to find Peter,
or should he wait? He hadn't the slightest idea of Peter's destination, nor what direction he had taken. All
he knew was that the animal had run a considerable
distance at great speed. James had never felt so helpless nor so negligent as he did now, standing in the
stable bathing a wounded horse while his son might
lay injured God knew where. James paced the stable,
then went out into the dark yard. He walked the perimeter of the yard, softly calling Peter's name.

Hours passed, and James continued his vigil, always
tempted to go in search of Peter, and knowing he was
more likely to miss him than to find him. The stiff
frosted grass bent and broke beneath his feet. False
dawn played in the eastern sky, and still there was no
sign of Peter. James had walked every inch of his
fields. He moved along the edge of the woods, trying
to peer into their dense darkness. His voice, hoarse
now and quivering with cold, sounded eerie as it
floated across the moist, frosty air. "Peter!" he cried,
no longer expecting a reply. "Peter!"

James stopped suddenly. He stood listening, his
heart pounding so hard he wasn't sure if he had heard
anything or not. Then there was a crackling of underbrush too heavy for the light tread of an animal, and
he heard his name. James plunged bull-like into the
tangle of growth at the edge of the woods. Confused,
and now hearing nothing, he stopped again, calling
Peter's name. He charged deeper into the woods, not
knowing where he was going, but merely following
intuition.

* * *

Peter wasn't sure it was his father's voice he heard, and he knew there was some reason he should be careful. He remembered he should make no sound at all, but he couldn't think why. He clung to one tree trunk, then released it, staggering, blindly reaching out for the next. Vaguely he tried to move toward the voice calling his name.

A sound of thanksgiving and fear was wrenched from James when he saw Peter, but he said nothing. With tears of relief running down his face in icy rivulets, he embraced Peter. He put his son's arm over his shoulder. "Put your weight on me. . . . I can manage with you," he said as Peter swayed then jerked forward as he tried to straighten up and take the weight from his father.

"I'm all right," Peter slurred. "The horse . . . a tree . . ."

"Hush, boy. You're home and that's enough. But we've got work to do. Albert will be here any time now . . . . We can't count on more than a couple of hours. There'll be no fooling him this time. You must listen to me, Peter, and do as I say. Can you listen? Are you able, son?"

The words echoed in Peter's head, unclear and hollow. He tried to smile, and didn't know if he had managed or not. He murmured a sound that James took for acquiescence.

Talking more to himself than to his son, James muttered, "I can't risk leaving you in the house for your brother to find. I'll have to bring you with me." He looked at Peter. "Can you stand alone?"

Peter nodded, straightened, and lost his balance.

James led him to the stable and leaned him against the stall. Then he brought the roan out. "I'm taking him to the far pasture, out of sight for awhile. Wait here, and for God's sake don't make a sound."

Thirty minutes later James returned to the stable. Peter was slumped beside the stall asleep. He awakened him and took him to the house, warning him tersely to keep quiet. In the warmth and light of the kitchen James saw the ragged, bloody sleeve of Peter's great-coat. The back of the coat was no more than torn strips of material. "My God, Peter! You said nothing . . . what . . . oh, blessed Savior, what went on tonight?"

Just beginning to recover from the grogginess of his collision with the tree, Peter looked at his sleeve as if he too just noticed it. "We . . . were at . . . Baker's."

"Baker's!" James exploded. "My God, have you no sense? He's Foxe's tenant and foreman."

Peter struggled to think. "That's why we went . . . but things went wrong . . . he had guests and—"

"And they caught you at it," James finished for him. "Pray God they didn't recognize you." He cut away Peter's coat, then stripped him of his bloodied shirt. Across Peter's left shoulder and chest was a bright red band, turning purple, where he had hit the tree. The slash on his arm was long but fortunately not deep.

"You won't be able to use this arm for much tomorrow," James said as he cleansed the wound. "There will be quite a scar, but I don't think it looks deep enough to have ruined the muscle. It should heal."

"I'll be using it tomorrow. I can't let Frank see . . ."

"You won't be here tomorrow," James snapped. "Your mother has been after me to take in that orphaned child of her cousin. Tomorrow you and I will be on our way to London to fetch the girl."

"I can't go to London, Pa," Peter said, frowning, his head still unclear and hurting murderously. "Frank wants to . . ."

"You're going to London. We'll talk no more about it. Here, drink this," James ordered, handing Peter a mug of steaming hot cider. "You're not fit to think in any case. You can barely speak clearly, and I haven't seen you keep your feet yet. You'll be lucky if your worst wound is your arm. How badly did you hit your head?"

"I'm all right. It's not so bad," he said, then was forced to cradle his head in his hands.

James shook his head morosely. "There's no way you can fool Albert this time. You've a wounded animal; you're wounded yourself, and half senseless. There's no story you can feed Albert to explain all that. You've given him exactly what he's been waiting for, Peter. Without proof he'd never touch you because of his own position and his affection for Natalie; but never doubt, Peter, that the man loathes you. He would find great satisfaction in being able to deliver you to the authorities as the elusive Captain Swing."

"That's nonsense."

"Nonsense? No one knows the identity of Captain Swing. But he is known to be an organizer, and he is educated . . . all unusual qualities in a labor leader. And what are you but educated and known for your ability to move men? Who but you handles the hop pickers in autumn? And who but you has been speaking for the laborers at every yeoman meeting of late? Open your eyes, Peter. This has become very serious business. The parish is approaching panic over this rash of fires and rick burnings. They'd like nothing better than to think Captain Swing has been captured. It would give Albert and his yeomen an excuse to round up every malcontent in the parish. It would be quite a feather in Albert's cap, and at least in this area, it would bring an end to the Swing men."

Peter rubbed his throbbing head with his good hand. "I can't hide this arm. . . ."

"Not if you're here. That is why we'll go to London. We can make up a story as to what happened . . . an accident. No one will question that. We'll collect the girl, Callie Dawson, and make your mother happy, and at the same time take you out of harm's way." Suddenly James chuckled. "Your mother will think it was her prayers that moved me to charity." He bound Peter's arm, then watched warily as Peter stood unsteadily. "Perhaps it was."

Slowly, with great care moving as though the floor too were in motion, Peter walked to the basin.

"How is your head?" James asked.

Peter made an unintelligible sound, then poured a pitcher of cold water over his head, washing the filth from his hair and face.

"Can you see properly?" James persisted.

"Yes . . ." Peter said. "I'm all right. I just had the wind knocked out of me. I'll be fine in a moment."

James put his hand on Peter's shoulder. "I'll bring you some fresh clothes," he said, walking from the room.

James climbed the stairs quietly. At the head of the upper hallway he saw Frank blinking sleepily in the dawn light. "Pa? What's wrong? What are you doing awake? What time is it anyway?"

"Go back to sleep, Frank, it's nothing."

Frank stretched and yawned. "I thought I heard . . ."

"You heard nothing but me getting a bite."

Frank smiled agreeably. "Sounds good."

James anxiously shuffled his feet, covering the noise Peter made below.

"What was that?"

"Nothing, only Peter. We're taking an early coach to London."

Awake now, Frank looked suspiciously at his father.

"I might have known. What's he done? Did they catch him at it tonight?"

Tired, strained beyond the limits of his patience, James said testily, "Your brother is going to London with me to fetch Callie Dawson, a distant cousin of your mother's."

"Albert will never believe that. No one will. Who ever heard of this Callie Dawson?"

James laughed harshly. "I'm sure Albert will have . . . at least of her father. Ian Dawson was a labor organizer, fairly well known in London circles."

"You're not bringing her here! Isn't one rabble-rouser enough? I won't have it. We'll have no reputation left. There is a limit . . ."

"The girl is an orphan, and *I* will set the limits in this house. Now go back to bed before you awaken your mother and the rest of the household."

Frank stood stubbornly in the middle of the hallway, glaring at James. "Side with Peter. You have always favored him over the rest of us, and we all accept that as our lot, but it is unfair of you to endanger the good name and prosperity of the whole family for him. He'll bring ruin to us. I'm right, Father. I know that, and although you deny it, I think you do too."

Not answering, James went into Peter's dressing room and removed clothes from his cupboard. When he came into the hall again, Frank was still standing at the entrance to his room. Smirking, Frank said, "Peter needs your aid in dressing too, Father?"

Still James did not speak. He walked down the hall to Stephen's room. He pushed the dark curling hair from Stephen's forehead and gently awakened his youngest son.

Stephen opened his eyes. Uncomprehending, he stared at James, then said softly, "Pa? Is it time to get up?"

James smiled. "I need you to drive Peter and me to the coach stop. We must make a trip into London this morning."

Stephen sat up, rubbing his eyes. "I don't remember . . ."

"Come downstairs quickly, son. I need you."

Immediately alert, Stephen looked up at his father. "It's Peter, isn't it? Is he all right?"

"He will be. Hurry, Stephen," he said and turned back to the stairs and the kitchen.

Peter dressed, then stood looking out the kitchen window at the gray, bleak new day just beginning. "I should leave until this is over, Pa," he said as James cleared away the cider mugs. "Frank is right about one thing. I am a threat to the rest of the family."

"Drivel," James snorted. "Where would you go? And what would you do about Rosalind? Will you hide her away in some little shanty while you ride the roads?"

Before Peter could answer, Stephen came into the kitchen, his boots in his hand, his hair tousled. "Peter! Are you all right? What happened?"

"Talk on the way to the coach," James said quickly. "We've got to leave. The household will be up soon. Stephen, run quickly and hitch the buggy, and hide this somewhere." He thrust the torn, bloodied shirt and coat at Stephen. "Burn them later, every shred."

Stephen paled and looked from the ragged garments to Peter. He nodded briskly. Donning his boots and flinging his coat over his shoulders, Stephen hurried from the house.

James put on his coat and handed Peter another coat to wear. "We'll meet Stephen out front. Can you walk steadily yet? Make an effort. Unless I miss my guess Frank will be watching from his window. It's best you look as normal as possible."

Peter nodded, then said, "Pa, I've got to see Rosalind first. I can't leave for London without telling her. She'll never believe I'm safe. . . . She'll be frightened unless she knows."

James began to protest, then agreed. "No more than five minutes. We must be on that early stage. We take needless chances with every moment we tarry. And we'll be out of chances entirely if we miss that coach, Peter."

With effort Peter walked up the stairs and into the bedroom he and Rosalind shared. He went to the bed and touched the side of her cheek. For a moment he let the tangle of her curls twist around his finger, then bent to kiss her. He watched as she patted the empty side of the bed, only half awake. Then her eyes opened wide, annoyance already in them. "Are you coming in or leaving again?" Her voice was deep and thick with sleep.

"I'm going to London with Pa," he said softly. "I just wanted you to know."

"You can't be serious. To London with your father? Can't he go alone?"

Peter kissed her, his lips lingering on her cheek. "No. We're to fetch home a little orphan." He laughed softly, nibbling at her ear. "Will you miss me?"

"I don't find you amusing, Peter. I want you to stay at home—with me."

He leaned over, pulling her near with his good arm. "I'd like nothing better."

"You'd be here then."

He kissed her shoulder where her nightdress had slipped down, then tugged at it to expose her breast. "Be patient. Soon I'll be home so much you'll want to be rid of me. No more laborers, no rides, no—"

"Oh, God! The laborers again! Do you think I care

about them? I hope they all rot in hell!" She shoved
him, her hand pressing hard on his left shoulder.

He winced and drew back.

"You're hurt!" she whispered. "Why won't you give
this up? I am so frightened. Oh, God, Peter . . . you
haven't been arrested? They aren't downstairs waiting
for you. Peter! Where are you going? It isn't London,
is it?"

James thumped from below with the handle of
Meg's broom. Peter glanced at the floor, then at Rosalind. "I'm going to London with Pa, just as I told
you. That's him. No magistrate, especially not Albert,
is going to thump for me when he wants me."

Rosalind put her hands over her face. Peter put her
head against his chest and sat there holding her.

The sound of James's thumping came again. Rosalind stiffened in Peter's arms. "Oh, dear God, I could
hate you, Peter. Go. Go to London. Go. Leave me.
You always leave me."

"I'll bring you something nice. What would you
like? Earrings?" He kissed her ear. "A necklace?"

"Stop! I want you with me, that's all."

"What? Surely this isn't my Rosalind refusing something new and pretty?"

She did like pretty things, and she couldn't stop him
from going. Years of longing for luxuries when she
couldn't have them made her grasp for whatever came
her way. She smiled at him. "Something pretty, but it
must be real. I don't want anything made of paste or
. . . or . . ."

"That's more like it. Am I forgiven a little then?"

She studied him for a moment and thought of the
long hours she'd be alone and unsure, temptation her
bedmate. "No," she said. "You're not forgiven, Peter,
and don't forget that I begged you to stay with me. I
won't be to blame if something happens."

"I'll only be gone one night or possibly two."

"I'll miss you."

"No more than I'll miss you," he said. "You couldn't possibly care for me more than I care for you. Think of that, Rosalind." His hands cupped her face, his eyes soft and dark-brown. "Think of how I love you."

Her eyes held his for a moment; then she looked away. "I don't know if I can, Peter. It's different with me. I'm not . . . I'm not the same person when you're gone. I need you here beside me. I can't stand being left alone."

He kissed her good-bye, his mouth lingering as he whispered his love to her again. There was no more he could say. Reassurances would only degenerate into an argument, and they had been having too many of those lately. He left her with a feeling of dissatisfaction and knew that she felt no better than he did.

James greeted him at the foot of the stairs with a scowl. "By Jupiter, Peter. Sometimes I think you want Albert to put a noose around your neck. Damn! We'll be lucky if Stephen can get us to the morning coach."

Peter hurried from the house with his father still scolding. The two men climbed into the buggy. Stephen's young face was pale with concern as he looked at Peter. His stormy blue eyes were filled with love and admiration, but he was all business as he touched the whip lightly to the horse's flank. When they were on the road to Seven Oaks he turned to ask the questions that were all but choking him. But Peter's eyes were closed, his head cushioned against the side of the buggy. Stephen remained silent and concentrated on the road, watching more carefully for potholes and ruts.

Stephen brought them to the station just as the coach pulled in. James was out on the road waving to the driver before Stephen had the horse reined in. Peter got down more slowly. Unable to stand it any longer, Stephen said, "I know we can't talk now, Peter, but tell me you are all right. They aren't out looking for you?"

Peter smiled at him. "No. No one is looking for me, and I'm fine." He grinned more broadly. "Nearly fine."

"I'll see to things at home while you're gone. Pa said you're going to fetch Ma's cousin . . . what's her name? Callie something?"

"Dawson."

"Well, I have a story about Miss Dawson that will fill Albert's ears. I can count on Ma to help me. Albert won't learn a thing about you. I told Pa I'd burn the clothes, and I'll see to the roan too. I may have to sell her, Peter. If the wound is too bad, we won't be able to hide it. I'm sorry."

"There's nothing for you to be sorry about, Stephen. Whatever happened was my doing. You'll have to take the horse a fair distance for news of the sale not to get back to Albert."

"Oh, I'll be careful. I'm getting good at covering your tracks."

Peter placed his hand on the plane of Stephen's cheek. He began to speak, then turned away and joined his father.

James and Peter took the yellow bounder into London, a C-spring coach that boasted of the speed with which it traveled. They careered along the road, jolting from side to side in mortal danger when the wheels hit a rut. The trip was a misery for Peter. He was jostled and bumped against the other passengers. His arm ached and his head throbbed. They arrived in London sore and exhausted, and unprepared to find the city ringing with the sounds of festival.

"What in the devil?" James muttered. He stopped a man on the street. "What is going on? It's no holiday."

"A hanging," the man said gleefully. "They're hanging John Robinson, the highwayman. Caught him on the Kent Road, him and two of his fellows."

James growled a reply, then looked at Peter. A mass of people moving toward the festivities swept down on them. James and Peter were caught in the pressing flow of unwashed bodies moving like a gurgling, noisy brook toward the Newgate Prison grounds. James shoved his way to the street and, battling to keep his footing, craned in all directions looking for a cab. It was hopeless; the streets were thick streams of humanity. Any vehicles that had been in the road had been firmly stopped and were now being used as perches from which the curious could see over the heads of others. Relentlessly the two men were pushed and shoved nearer to the river and the prison. Hawkers, seemingly impervious to the moving human mass, darted in and out shouting, "Penny sheet! John Robinson! Boldest rake of London! Read his life story! Penny sheet!"

James shoved one persistent urchin who had grabbed his coat sleeve.

"Buy a sheet, sir? Got his confession . . . in his own words!" the urchin whined. "Penny, sir, penny sheet."

From somewhere behind them a shrill, excited voice screamed, "It's 'is cart! 'E's comin'. The cart's comin'!"

Men held children high on their shoulders, admonishing them to look carefully at the prisoner in the cart. "He came to no good. Look at the dirty animal, and remember what you see, boy."

Women shouted at the highwayman bound and

fighting to keep his balance in the slow, unevenly moving cart. Others threw flowers and themselves at the cart, begging the condemned man's favors before he died. Bottles passed from hand to hand and were emptied and smashed in the cobbled streets. The streets smelled of gin and rum and sweat and urine. People heated and steaming in the cold air pressed tightly against one another and tried to get a clear view of John Robinson. Some shouted their hatred, others their admiration. A chant went up to the right of James and Peter. "Johnny, Johnny, Johnny!"

With another mighty surge forward the crowd came in view of Newgate. James looked up at the solid gray stone walls of the enormous prison. In front of the wall was a scaffold. The cart bearing John Robinson on his last trip through London stopped in front of the wooden structure. The prisoner looked up at the hangman and began his ascent to the platform.

James shuddered and clasped Peter's arm without thinking. "I don't care to watch this," he said weakly. He began pushing the wall of people behind him.

Fascinated and horrified, Peter stared at the man on the platform for several more seconds. The noose was placed around John Robinson's neck. With a disdainful, arrogant smile the man nodded to the crowd. His mouth puckered as he blew kisses to a group of yelling women at the foot of the scaffolding. Flowers were thrown to him. They made wilting little spots of color on the fresh wood of the platform.

"Peter!" James said loudly. "Please. I can't watch this."

Peter bowed his head. "No, neither can I." Leading the way, he forced a path for them through the crowd. The hawkers still hopped in and out among the people shouting the glories of their sheet and selling their wares.

Peter and James were still close enough to hear the snap of the platform's trap door as the crowd was momentarily silenced. Then a great roar of human awe and perverted animal pleasure rose and gained deafening proportions. Unable to resist, Peter looked back. John Robinson's body wrenched and twisted grossly. The quartering of the man had begun. Again the crowd hushed with the first rush of blood, then rose to even greater frenzy.

Peter felt the horror of fascination. James was nauseated. He wanted his son away from this place. Today the mere thought of such a death was more terrifying than James could bear. He couldn't stand to see or even think of the bits of hangman's rope being sold for souvenirs, or of the women who would battle and bargain for the dead man's clothing, later to be sold piece by piece and hung as gruesome reminders in someone's home.

Finally they broke free of the crowd and emerged on a side street nearly empty of life, for it seemed that all of London was packed into that small network of streets near the river to watch a man die.

They walked until James found a cab, then went to an inn. The George made James feel somewhat better. It had open galleries that led to the chambers, and gave James a feeling of privacy and ownership that was not easy to attain in a room one would keep only for a night or two.

Peter saw only the bed. He tested it, found it clean, and slumped onto it. His eyes half closed, he said, "If we're going to get Miss Dawson, we'd better do it quickly. It will be dark soon, and that crowd will be drinking and carrying on all night."

James silenced him with an impatient wave of his hand. "I'm not going on those streets again. Tomorrow's soon enough. Have you an objection to a good night's sleep?"

"I thought she might be expecting us, but she couldn't . . ." His words trailed off, and he fought to stay awake.

"Who knows what she expects?" James said. "I'll wager it's a good deal more than what she'll get. I imagine Ian's daughter will be thinking herself some sort of special little lady. Well, she'd better get that out of her head!" He growled. "She'll get along with the rest of us, and like it!"

"I wonder if she's pretty?" Peter mused.

"Makes no difference."

Peter laughed. "Why'd you say you'd give her a home if you don't want her?"

James looked at him with blue eyes that betrayed the soft heart beneath his rough words. "You. Your mother. All her boo-hooing about a poor homeless child did me in. I told her if it was homeless children she wanted we could collect them by the score along the roads. But no, it had to be this one. You'd think she'd known the girl all her life, the way she carried on."

"Perhaps she did."

"Bosh! The Dawsons had nothing to do with Meg's part of the family. Anyway, Ian ran off years ago. He was an ungrateful pup . . . always chasing some pipe dream. More trouble than he's worth if you ask me."

"Some claim he's Captain Swing," Peter said.

"Well, with Ian dead, Captain Swing will die too then—if he was the man. Might be a good thing. The rioting would end."

"It won't," Peter said, his eyes closed again.

"You seem sure of yourself. I've heard others claim that you're Captain Swing. It's not true, is it?"

"Would you want me to tell you if it were true, Pa?".

"My God, Peter, you're not!"

"I didn't say I was. No one knows who he is."

James started to speak, then tossed his soiled shirt onto a chair. "I don't want to talk about that. No more tonight. I'm in no mood for it." James looked over to Peter when there was no response. He was sound asleep.

Chapter 3

While Peter and James enjoyed a long and dreamless sleep brought on by exhaustion, Callie Dawson spent another fretful, disturbed waking night. The month since her father had died had been a terrible one for Callie. She now found it difficult to believe that it would ever get better again.

Her first taste of an unkind world had come with her father's death, but that was the kind of sorrow she knew to expect. People die, and though Callie would have given anything to have her father with her again, she understood that. Her introduction to less comprehensible sorrow came later.

The day after Ian was buried, Callie was alone in their flat. She had never felt so lonely or so inclined to cry and feel sorry for herself. When someone knocked on her door, she assumed it was her landlady, Mrs. Pettibone, for there was no one else likely to come to see her. She reacted with surprise and a little fright when she saw a poorly dressed, unshaven man standing in the hallway. "I . . . I'm sorry, but I think you

have the wrong address," she said hesitantly. "I don't
want to buy anything."

The man put his dirty cap in his hand and gave her
a broken-toothed grin. "I've nothing to sell. This is the
place of Ian Dawson, isn't it?"

"Yes, but . . ."

"I knew him well." The man's grin grew broader.
"Came to wish his girl well. That's you, isn't it?"

"Yes."

"Then I've got the right address, haven't I? Aren't
you going to ask me in?"

Callie stood back slightly, unsure. The man pushed
the door wider and entered the flat.

"I've never been in this part of it before," he said,
looking around. "Ian didn't do bad by himself, did
he?" He turned as Callie began to close the door.
"Don't close it," he said. "Some of my friends are coming too. I'm just the first to get here. I like being
first."

"I don't understand. Who else is coming here?
Why?"

The man smiled and placed his hand comfortingly
on her shoulder. "Don't fash yourself, girl. We're all
friends of your papa's comin' to wish him well in the
next life. Didn't he tell you anything about his
doings?"

"His doings? My father was working with members
of the House of Lords and the House of Commons for
labor reform. Is that what you mean?"

"Of course, that's what I mean. Well, miss, we're the
men your father was working to help. We're the ones
needing reforms." He laughed aloud. "And maybe a
bit of reforming."

Several other men and three women came up the
stairs and into the Dawson flat. They all seemed to
know each other, and were laughing, talking rapidly

and somewhat shyly, Callie thought, offering her their condolences. Slowly Callie lost her fear and began to enjoy these raucous and jovial people, who all seemed to have loved her father.

"Shall we have a little morsel?" one of the women asked Callie, then went with her to the pantry to help her prepare food for the guests. "Oh! Rum cakes!" the woman exclaimed. "How I love them! Shall we put them on a separate plate . . . just for you an' me, honey?" She winked at Callie.

Callie laughed, more at ease now. "Put them on a plate just for yourself. I'd like you to have them."

"You've a kind and generous heart, just like your papa. I was tellin' Jane as we came up here you'd be a good sort. I knew you would with a papa like yours."

Callie blushed with pleasure, murmuring thanks.

"Been raised to be a lady, haven't you?" the woman said through a mouth filled with cake. "That'd be Ian's way too." Laughing, she went back into the main room to rejoin her friends.

Callie brought out platters of sandwiches, biscuits, and cakes and placed them on a low table near the sofa. She was appalled, then gratified to see grubby hands grabbing the dainties from the platters and mashing them into mouths. Callie ignored the rising noise level and the crudity of her guests. They roamed freely about the apartment, poking their noses into cupboards, handling figurines and ornaments. They went into her bedroom, inspected all the rooms and cabinets of the flat. After her initial shock at such behavior wore off, she accepted these people for what they were. Inside she felt warm and pleased. They had known her father, and it was for these people he had worked every day of his life. She began to think warmly of the nights when he had talked to her of Parliament and how laws were made and why change came about. It had sounded so grand and important, and now it seemed her first opportunity had come for her to see the people her father wanted to help. In her very young, very innocent mind she tried to imagine how different these people would be after reform, when their manners would improve and their clothing would match the garments of the men her father had let her meet. She tried to place dignity on the bloated, frazzle-haired women who were now laughing too loudly in her flat.

No one paid any attention when one more voice was added to the cacophony. Then suddenly there was a sharp piercing shriek. Callie jumped to her feet.

"Out! Out of here, you scum! Go, before I beat your knotty heads in!" Mrs. Pettibone's broom swished through the air, striking heads and backs. She smacked the last ill-clad, foul-smelling man from the flat, then planted her foot on his rear end and sent him tumbling down the stairs to the landing. Breathless, she slumped into a chair. "My word, child! What possessed you to let that rabble in here?"

"You shouldn't have done that, Mrs. Pettibone. I invited them in. They came to pay their respects," Callie said excitedly. "What will they think of me?"

"Think of you? You're lucky they didn't slit your throat. You can thank your papa for that, I suppose. It's about all you can thank him for, I'll wager."

Mrs. Pettibone put her head in her hands. What was she to do with this youngster? Ian Dawson had been one of her favorite tenants. They had shared talk, an occasional pint of ale, and sometimes her bed. They hadn't agreed on everything, and she'd hate to count the number of times she had warned him to introduce Callie to some of the harsher realities of life before it was too late. He had been sure he could protect Callie, and Mrs. Pettibone had been sure he could not.

Now it was too late, and Ian was no longer here to do anything.

He had had his way, and kept his daughter innocent of the seamier inclinations of the laborers he had spent his life trying to defend. He did not pass on to her the means of protecting herself from them, for Ian never had any intention of letting Callie lead the kind of life he had led. As though Callie were part of a play, standing on a stage at a distance from the sweating audience, Ian had kept his plans for her separate from his work. Callie was raised to be trusting, to be gentle and ladylike, so that in the proper time Ian would see her married and loved by the right kind of man. That man would bear no resemblance to the laborers who frequented Ian's small study in search of help. But despite her father's good intentions, Callie was now left alone to fend for herself in a world of which she knew little.

Now she went to Mrs. Pettibone, trying to soothe the landlady. "I didn't know I shouldn't let them in," she said. "I'm sorry I've upset you."

"You haven't the sense of a chicken," Mrs. Pettibone muttered.

"Please don't scold. I'm sorry, but they knew Papa. They liked him, Mrs. Pettibone. I can tell that they liked him. He will truly be missed by them."

Mrs. Pettibone sighed. She leaned back in her chair, patting Callie's soft young hand. "Lord, yes, child. He'll be missed, by none so much as you. He was a grand man in his way, but he didn't do well by you. Those people will eat you alive. You've not a thing left in your larder." She got up, took Callie's hand, and walked through the flat, looking into the cupboards and cabinets. Callie was stunned.

"What do you think you are going to eat?" Mrs. Pettibone said angrily. "This is not a dole house, and no matter what your papa professed, he didn't run it like one."

"But I didn't see . . ."

"Nor would you! You've entertained the lightest-fingered bunch of thieves and cutthroats this house has ever seen. Why do you think your papa never let them into this part of the flat?" she snapped, then looked at Callie and felt an uncustomary softening as the girl touched the spot where a small bronze horse had stood before the mourners had cleared it away.

"Why would they do that? They said they wanted to be near the place where Papa lived," Callie said sadly.

"In their way, Callie. In their own way they mourn him, but you . . ." She paused. "Ian was a canny man. He knew their ways, and they respected his knowledge, but you . . . they'll only rob you. You can't do your father's business, Callie. Keep your door closed to all but the few you know well enough to trust."

Callie promised to be careful, and she did turn many away. Three days later a woman came to the door.

"He was so kind to me in my need," she said, "the least I can do is see to his daughter."

Callie did not know her.

"Won't you open the door to me, child? Not that I'd blame you. The way things are, it's not an easy matter to tell who can be trusted. I'll not be offended if you'd rather keep me standing out here in the cold hall."

"Oh . . . do come in, Mrs. . . . ?"

"Peach. The name is Peach. Surely you've heard your dear papa mention me." Her head was angled to one side as she watched Callie search her memory.

"I don't think so," Callie said hesitantly. "But I am forgetting my manners again. Won't you sit down, Mrs.

Peach? I was just about to have tea." Callie hurried to the pantry, wondering what she could put on the tray to make it look less meager.

As she came back to the sitting room, she noticed that Mrs. Peach's hair was of a reddish tint. She wasn't nearly so old as Callie had first thought, in fact it was difficult to discern her age. She dressed like an old woman with her shapeless dress bagging loosely over her bosom. The color was drab, a dark nondescript gray. Mrs. Peach sat in the chair Callie offered, her head forward, her shoulders rounded almost to a hunch. Her skin and hair, however, did not match the rest of her. Her face was powdered, and her skin looked soft and cared for, not the skin of an old woman. And there was her hair, reddish but pale—perhaps from gray, but also possibly from many hours of brushing, washing, and tinting. As a final touch to all her contradictions of appearance, Mrs. Peach carried a handsome silver-tipped cane, which looked to be made of ebony, but probably was not. For how, Callie reasoned, could a woman who seemed so poor own a cane so obviously expensive?

"Did you know my father well?" Callie asked, watching the pleased expression on Mrs. Peach's face broaden. Perhaps Mrs. Peach was one of those who would want to talk about Ian. Callie hoped so. No matter how sensible she tried to be, she was miserably lonely without her father.

Mrs. Peach obliged her longer than Mrs. Pettibone ever would. Whether the stories she told of Ian were true or made up, Callie did not know.

Mrs. Peach studied the girl as she spoke. The stories pleased the child, and that was all Mrs. Peach was interested in at the moment.

"What a nice visit this has been, Callie. We must do it again. I hope you will have tea at my little house. I like having young people about. It makes me feel young too." She gathered her shawl about her and picked up the impressive cane. "I must be getting home. The streets aren't safe for a lady after dark. You will come to see me soon, Callie?"

"I'd like that."

Mrs. Peach smiled. "You're no longer afraid of me?"

"Oh, no!" Callie blushed. "I wouldn't have been. It's just that Mrs. Pettibone says I'm too trusting. I promised I'd be careful."

"One can't be too careful these terrible days. Things being what they are you can't blame a man for taking what he can get, but still it makes it hard for those of us who are honest. But you needn't worry about me. I'd not take a scrap of stale bread that was not mine for the taking."

Callie walked downstairs with Mrs. Peach and watched from the door as the woman walked down the street. She liked Mrs. Peach. Mrs. Peach liked her father. She was a warm-hearted, motherly old woman—just what Callie longed for. She told Mrs. Pettibone about her visitor.

"Mrs. Peach, you say? Can't say as I know the name. Said she knew your father well? Strange. . . . I don't know the name at all. Well, I can't be expected to know everyone, but all the same. . . . Did you check your belongings? All in place?"

"Nothing was stolen. She was very nice. I'm invited to tea at her house tomorrow." Callie wanted to talk more, but Mrs. Pettibone was a busy woman and not given to patience with the young. Callie went back to her flat. She disliked being alone, but this night would not be as bad as others. She had something to look forward to the next day.

* * *

Callie dressed carefully the next morning. She wore her best: a self-striped forest green bazeen gown with puffed and banded sleeves. She stopped momentarily before the mirror, admiring the simple fitted bodice and the straight soft line of the skirt. Happy with her appearance, she confidently walked the maze of streets following Mrs. Peach's hastily spoken directions. She stopped before the house and hesitated for a moment, unsure. Mrs. Peach's home was a large one, far grander than Callie had expected. It was just the sort of place to appeal to a girl of Callie's age who had been far more accustomed to austerity than comfort.

Callie's fascination with the house and Mrs. Peach increased with every step she took into the interior. Mrs. Peach had a distinct fondness for soft multicolored pillows, overstuffed couches, and red velvet. She also seemed to like everything in abundance.

Mrs. Peach claimed she liked company. Callie could take her at her word. This was a house made and decorated to make many people comfortable at one time. As it was, when Callie entered there were several young women present. Some of them were no older than Callie, though worldly enough to deserve the name woman, while Callie was not.

Taking wide-eyed note of all the pretty girls, Callie commented on them.

"I thought I mentioned to you that I enjoy the company of the young," Mrs. Peach replied. "Did you think I meant only to put you at ease?"

"No, but . . ." Callie began, puzzled by the familiarity with which the young women treated the house and each other. "I am sure I could never feel so much at home and still be a guest," Callie said with a good deal of admiration.

Mrs. Peach looked around her, her face growing

soft and concerned. "These young women are my everlasting fountain of youth. They keep me feeling
young, so I give them what I can. We cannot take
from life without needing to return like value, can
we? Hasn't your father said something of the sort to
you, Callie?"

"Many times!"

"I was sure of it. So you understand how I feel
about my young ladies. For some this is the only
home there is, poor dears. I fear there are many not so
fortunate as you. They have no place to go but the
home I provide them." She put down her teacup and
leaned forward. "That was my true purpose in coming
to see you yesterday. I got to thinking that you might
not have anyone to provide for you. I thought perhaps you would be needing Mrs. Peach. I'm happy to
see I was wrong. And naturally I would never dream
of forcing myself on anyone. Not I, not Mrs. Peach.
I've made it my life's work to look after those who are
unable to do it themselves. It's my charity. All of us
should have a charity, is my opinion."

Callie agreed with her, but said nothing of her own
predicament. Ian had left her little, and she didn't
know if his monthly allowance from his father's estate
would come to her or not. There was no one to look
after her. She fit all the qualifications for Mrs. Peach's
charity. As Callie looked into the kindly marshmallow
softness of Mrs. Peach's face, she wished with all her
heart that Mrs. Peach would ask the magical question
that would enable Callie to say, "I'd like to come live
with you."

Mrs. Peach did not ask it that day, nor the next time
Callie came to tea. She didn't get around to it until a
week later, when Callie had given up hope. Callie met
her by accident. They both stood in a whipping winter wind as Mrs. Peach asked almost shyly if she'd be

out of place inviting Callie to join the other girls in her roomy house. "I find I have become very attached to you, child."

Callie's tongue tripped all over itself in her eagerness to accept. Her long blond hair was blown loose by the time she ran home. "Mrs. Pettibone! Mrs. Pettibone, where are you? Oh! Wait till you hear! Mrs. Pettibone?"

The entry hall had an air of emptiness that Callie would have noticed had she not been so excited. But she was excited. And she was in a hurry. If she didn't move quickly the invitation would vanish. She worried that Mrs. Peach would change her mind, or not want her after all. She longed to tell someone, to make it real. Everyone must know and be happy for her or perhaps it wouldn't come true at all.

"Mr. Jenks! Mr. Jenks!" She raced past the other tenants' flats, stopping in front of a single open door. "Mr. Jenks! I've a new home! A new, new home and someone who wants me. Oh! Mr. Jenks, say you are happy. Isn't it wonderful?" she shouted, her face beaming with a smile that made her normally somber blue eyes sparkle with inner lights. "I've a home, Mr. Jenks!"

Nearly deaf and feeble of leg, Mr. Jenks leaned precariously out of his door. "Good, good, child." Then he tottered back into his room, forgetting again to close his door.

"Good-bye, Mr. Jenks," Callie shouted at his back. "I'll come by some afternoon to see you. Would you like that?"

"Good, good, child."

She shut his door and hurried up to her own flat to write a note telling Mrs. Pettibone of her good fortune. "I will come by tomorrow for the rest of my things. I'll tell you all about it then." She folded the paper neatly, took one valise, and rushed down the stairs. She slipped the note under Mrs. Pettibone's door. For one moment just before it disappeared from view, Callie felt unsure, and sad to be leaving the flat she had shared with her father. She considered waiting to ask Mrs. Pettibone's advice, but then she thought of the night. She'd be alone again and that was awful. She could imagine Mrs. Peach's kindly voice saying, "There's no sense to spending another lonely night, dear."

Mrs. Peach was waiting at the door, and Callie ran the last few steps and fell into her arms as though it were the most natural thing she could do.

The idea of living in a house with other girls was exciting. If they seemed to have secrets, and if they considered Callie green, well, that was an understandable attitude toward a newcomer. She sat down with them, smiling more from her inner satisfaction than any communication of friendship. Mostly she listened, impressed and mildly shocked at how often their conversations were about men. However, Mrs. Peach seemed in no way averse to the girls' talk. Frequently the conversation went so far along forbidden lines it was reduced to a quivering, unintelligible whisper punctuated with quickly drawn breaths and giggles. Losing her shyness, Callie dared to speak of her father and one or two of his friends she considered handsome. They were the only men she had ever known. In spite of the laughter that greeted her innocent comments, it was comfortable sitting there, feeling herself a part of this strange, makeshift family. A cheery fire burned on the hearth, and Mrs. Peach sat all the while like a proud brooding hen, smiling at them all. Her tapping cane made a pleasantly monotonous sound in the background.

Following the example of the other girls, Callie

went to her room at six o'clock to dress for dinner. She was once again shy and self-conscious when she entered the dining room. The others looked like grown women, while Callie, in spite of her efforts, looked no older than she should at fourteen.

"Isn't she a pretty thing?" one girl said as she came in.

"Fresh, you might say," another added.

"Pure."

"And all of you having a grand time making fun of her. She's going to have a hard time of it. Don't any of you remember . . ."

"Shut up, Margot!" the first girl warned. "Let our little daisy girl enjoy herself for as long as she can." She laughed. The other girls joined in less merrily, but agreeably covered up what Margot had started and Mrs. Peach had nearly heard.

Curious, Callie glanced from one tense face to another. Some of them looked to be girls from nice families. Others might have been found wandering London streets any night. But all of them had a worldly quality that didn't seem to fit Mrs. Peach's noble philosophies about her innocents. Callie reasoned that it took time to change Mrs. Peach's waifs from worldly creatures not accustomed to a loving home into the paragons the woman had described. And Callie admitted there was something alluring about the way Mrs. Peach's girls looked.

"Perhaps one of you will teach me to do my hair as you do," Callie asked.

"Perhaps we shall. Someone had better teach you a thing or two." The girl shrugged her elegant bare shoulder. The other girls tittered nervously, glancing toward Mrs. Peach. The ebony cane came down sharply. Each girl looked straight ahead; postures became perfect. Dinner continued in relative silence, broken only by an occasional polite comment on fashion or the news of the day.

Callie relaxed again as the tense moment passed. The small French mantel clock ended the dinner hour.

"Boney's buttons are popping," Mrs. Peach said, eyeing the clock. "We are running late tonight. No time for the parlor at all." She came to stand by Callie's chair. "Time for you to go to bed, Callie."

"But Mrs. Peach, I've just finished supper and it's only eight o'clock. I never go to bed this early." She looked at the other girls, chagrined to see the knowing smiles appear on their faces. "I'm not a baby, Mrs. Peach," she whispered.

"To me you are, my dear. You must remember I am really quite ancient. Why, I imagine I could look upon Bubble and Squeaky themselves and think them babies," she said with an irreverent reference to the unfortunate Charles Wynn and his brother, who loved to speak in Parliament despite high-pitched, peculiar voices.

Callie giggled along with the others, but had lost her battle.

"Come along, dearie," Mrs. Peach said. "To bed with you. You must suffer what ministrations I deem best for you. One thing I can definitely say is that all my girls are obedient."

There was a murmured assent from the others.

Callie meekly followed Mrs. Peach to her room.

During those few minutes Mrs. Peach made up to her, agreeing with the unfairness of the early bedtime. "But you are so pale and thin, my dear! Isn't it better to retire early one or two nights than to find yourself ill for several? Of course it is! Once you've fattened up a bit and are looking healthy again, we'll reconsider this early time." She stood to the side of the room, folding Callie's clothes as they were removed.

Her attention was entirely on Callie. It was all there, just as she had thought: the good bone structure, the well-formed limbs. Callie would be slow in coming to full maturity, but Mrs. Peach was certain this young girl would be a ravishingly beautiful woman. Now she was like a young colt, all legs and energy, but a thoroughbred colt, and that was what Mrs. Peach was best at spotting.

She went to Callie and tied the small blue ribbon of her nightgown into a bow. Automatically she patted Callie's arm, and led her to the bed. "Sleep well, Callie. Everything will seem better in the morning. You have years before you and much to learn. Take my care for now, and trust that I have your future in mind." Mrs. Peach tucked her in tenderly and turned down the lamp at the side of her bed, then left the room. Callie was blissfully satisfied, all over her annoyance at being sent to bed early—until she heard the doorlock turn.

Chapter 4

Mrs. Pettibone was tired and out of sorts from a long-winded visit with her sister. She found Callie's note under the door of her flat. As soon as she read it she was certain something was wrong. But she was tired. The sheer weight of her tedious day was enough to make her see something wrong in everything. She sat down in her parlor and tried to forget all about it.

The newspaper was filled with the details of a white slavery ring. She shuddered with the horror of it, clucking a disapproving tongue at the times and conditions that led people to such things. And all the time Callie's note stayed ominously in the back of her mind.

She promised herself she would look into the matter in the morning. By then Callie would return for the rest of her things. Questions could be answered then. After all there was nothing she could do tonight. She was nearly convinced of the truth of her argument when Mr. Jenks tottered into her parlor seeking his afternoon tea.

"Well, you've missed it today, Mr. Jenks," she said,

making up her mind that she had been put upon enough today. But the old man was as dismayed with his day as she, and he was lonely. Pathetically he tried to prolong a conversation he couldn't hear so he could stay in her company a few minutes longer. She sighed and gave in.

"Sit down, Mr. Jenks. It'll take but a minute. I could do with a cup myself," she shouted into his good ear.

Warmed by the companionship and the tea, Mr. Jenks remembered Callie. "She was quite overcome with her good fortune. Poor child, I do believe she thought she'd be homeless if it weren't for that lady she met," he said grandly, feeling eloquent and competent as long as the conversation was a monologue and he needn't strain to hear the responses.

In this instance he was safe. Mrs. Pettibone had nothing to say. Her earlier fears returned. She hadn't a shred of reason, but intuition told her Callie had fallen into a regrettable situation.

Again she gave into her better nature and rose tiredly from her chair. She would not rest until she knew Callie was safe and Mrs. Peach was all she was purported to be. That was the nub of the problem. What was Mrs. Peach supposed to be? Shaking her head vigorously, she hurried Mr. Jenks from her parlor, giving him a parcel of tea cakes to keep him happy and unnoticing of the haste with which she closed him back inside his own flat.

She returned to her apartment, taking time to do something she should have done long ago. She wrote a terse note to the only people Ian had listed as family among his private papers; James and Meg Berean. Ian was dead and Callie was alone. She said nothing about Mrs. Peach, or that she suspected Callie had innocently and voluntarily placed herself in the hands of a pack of white slavers. Then Mrs. Pettibone put on her coat and stepped out into the cold foggy night, doubting her own good sense.

Muttering to herself, she hurried down one street after another, inquiring of her acquaintances if anyone knew Mrs. Peach.

"There's no one of that name that I heard of," was the most common response. Not until she was ready to give up did one woman say she knew of a Mrs. Peach. Mrs. Pettibone received the information gratefully, along with the cup of hot tea offered to warm her. Once more on her way, she went directly to the address she was given.

The house was charming; through its well-lit windows Mrs. Pettibone could see guests inside. She was certain she had been given the wrong address, but she quelled her doubts and knocked at the door.

Mrs. Peach came to the door herself. She stood haughtily in the entry, looking down at Mrs. Pettibone on the stoop. "This is the Peach residence. There is no one here by the name of Dawson. Perhaps you should check your address more carefully before you come 'round bothering decent people next time." The door closed firmly in Mrs. Pettibone's embarrassed face.

Mrs. Pettibone hurried away, then stopped confused and nonplussed at the street corner. A memory sparked and kindled. "Why! The insolent old tart," she breathed. The woman who had claimed not to know Callie stood in her doorway arrogantly tapping a distinctive ebony cane—just like the cane that had so impressed Callie. It was enough to send the landlady straight to the police station.

Mrs. Peach was certain she had humiliated Mrs. Pettibone sufficiently to send her home red-faced, but she was never one to take chances. She marched to the back rooms of her house, clearing them of the girls and their men. She didn't believe in excessive greed, and what she might lose in one night's trade would be more than made up on other nights—provided she maintained her daytime image of a respectable old woman, and her nighttime image of a madam respectful of the privacy and pleasure of her clients. She closed the house promptly, paying no attention to the remarks of the disgruntled gentlemen being sent to their homes earlier and less satisfied than usual.

She then sent for the men who transported girls to other locations for her. That very night Callie would be taken to another city. It was not an unusual procedure. Most of the girls with Mrs. Peach had come from somewhere else; otherwise it was too easy for a girl to get help from home, or for parents to cause trouble. So white slavers cooperated and all benefited by sending girls across the country and sometimes out of it. Mrs. Peach daily expected a Malaysian girl, a long-awaited prize. Patiently she sat down to wait for the coach that would remove the problem of Callie Dawson.

Callie remained locked in the little room that had looked so welcoming when she had first arrived. In the beginning she was hurt that Mrs. Peach hadn't trusted her to stay in her room and had locked the door. As the hours passed and the sounds of girlish laughter mixed with that of men, Callie began to understand. She knew little of white slavery other than what she had read secretly in the newspapers. She collected her few scraps of knowledge, putting them together in a horrifying reality. She tried to open the door, using what she could find in the room as a substitute key. Nothing worked.

She tried something simpler. She knocked lightly on the door. It was opened to her. Shyly, she said she had to tend to herself. A nodded assent, and Callie walked magnificently free toward the back staircase on the outside of the house. At the top of the staircase, Callie looked tentatively at the dark stairs, then back at the man standing guard near her room. She gathered up her long nightgown and ran, leaping downward into the darkness. The wooden steps were cold and clammy against her bare feet; the damp winter wind billowed inside the thin fabric of her nightgown.

"Where you think ye're goin', girlie?"

Callie stifled a frightened scream. At the bottom of the stairs stood a tall, burly man dressed as a footman. His big hand caressed her shoulder before he gripped her arm like a vise.

"Out back," Callie stammered.

"Mrs. P. makin' her girls go out back in the dead o' winter? Not likely, girlie. What I oughter do is let her think ya ran, an' keep ya fer myself. That's what I oughter do."

"Let me go. . . . Please, I'll only go 'round back. I . . . I promise."

He laughed. In a quick move he ducked down and grabbed her behind her knees, his shoulder jolting into her stomach as he carried her back upstairs like a bundle of potatoes.

In the upper hall he punched the man Callie had fooled into letting her free. "Ya damned fool, she nearly bolted. Hadn't been fer me, Mrs. P'd have your arse. Go get her. She'll see to this baggage."

"Don't tell her. Please, I won't try . . ."

He threw her onto the bed and leaned over her, his broad, pockmarked face thrust into hers. "Here's where you belongs, girlie—on the mattresses. Fergit it, an' next time I'll not be worryin' how fast I gits you up here."

Callie turned her head from him. He grasped her

face, spittle glistening on his lips as he pressed his mouth against hers, forcing his tongue between her teeth. The man fumbled with the placket of his trousers. His exposed flesh burned hot against her thigh. Under his groping hands Callie squirmed, kicking and clawing at him.

A sharp crack sounded. The man bellowed in quick pain and rage, arching against Callie. He rolled over her across the bed, gaining his feet. His face was red and contorted, his hands clenched and ready to attack. His trousers sagged ludicrously around his hips.

Mrs. Peach stood steely-eyed and unintimidated, staring him into docility.

Callie jumped from the bed, seeking safety anywhere. "Mrs. Peach! He tried . . ."

The cane whistled through the air and came down on the girl's shoulder. She screamed, her arms raised to protect her face and head. "Obedience, you little bitch! Defy Mrs. Peach! My girls are obedient!" She struck Callie's back and buttocks repeatedly with the ebony cane. Callie backed away, crying and stumbling, trying to put the chair between herself and her tormentor. The cane came down on her upper arm.

"Stop! Please! It hurts me!"

"Obedience! All my girls are obedient!"

"Don't! Please!" Callie screamed, tears choking her.

Twice more the cane whistled and struck, once on her back, once on her head. Then Mrs. Peach straightened her dress and hair and walked out of the room, taking the footman with her.

Callie huddled where she stood, stifling sobs, afraid to make a sound. She hurt. And there was no escape. This was to be her new life.

She had no idea how long she had been lying on the bed crying when she heard the next disturbance. Callie tensed, pressing herself against the headboard.

Then the whole house fell silent. When she heard footsteps coming down the hall, she panicked, unable to think what to do. Her mind was filled with the vision of the cane coming furiously and painfully down on her again. She scuttled under the bed. Mrs. Peach entered, accompanied by the footman.

"Where is she?" he asked. "She couldn't have gotten out again."

With knowledge born of long experience, Mrs. Peach walked directly to the bed. She lifted the coverlet and probed with the black cane. No matter how Callie squirmed and backed away from it, the black stick found her, poking and prodding and hurting.

"Leave her where she is. We know where to find her." Once more the door closed and Callie heard the lock click into place.

An hour later the door to her room opened again. This time there was no conversation, and no nonsense. Two men she had never seen before accompanied the footman and Mrs. Peach. Without a preliminary word they lifted the entire bed from over her. One man reached down and jerked her to her feet.

"Get dressed," Mrs. Peach ordered.

Callie ran to the cupboard. She grabbed the first dress her hand touched and clutched it to her. Fearfully she looked from the three men to Mrs. Peach.

Mrs. Peach smirked. "You'll get used to the likes of them oglin' you. Get on with it."

Callie stood rooted, the dress pressed harder against her. She shook her head woodenly.

Mrs. Peach raised her cane. "You'll do as I say!"

"I can't . . . make them leave . . . please."

Mrs. Peach struck the cane flat against the table top, making Callie jump and gasp in fright. "Off with that gown, girlie. You're wastin' time and my patience. We haven't all night."

Callie began to whimper. Her hands shook so violently she fumbled with the gown.

Mrs. Peach poked roughly at her with the cane. Shaking and crying, Callie managed to pull the nightgown over her head. Mrs. Peach grabbed for the gown, but Callie hung on to it. "Oh, no . . . please . . . please. Make them turn around."

With a deft stroke of the cane, Mrs. Peach tore the gown from Callie's grasp. "Well, now, that wasn't so bad, was it? It's time you started growing up, dearie. If it weren't for men takin' their pleasures, what place would a woman have? You're past old enough to know that."

Shamed, Callie tried to hide herself from their leering eyes. She quickly reached for her underthings. Involuntarily her eyes caught repeated glimpses of the lustful faces of Mrs. Peach's hired men. She crouched over, her back to the wall as she fumbled awkwardly, trying to get her feet into the waistline of her petticoat.

"Stand up straight! Be proud of what . . ." Mrs. Peach stiffened, her head and back rigid as she listened.

The doorbell jangled through the house, followed by the shrill voices of the girls. Callie hastily put on her petticoat, not bothering with ties or buttons. She dragged her dress over her head.

Warily Mrs. Peach looked at her men. "It's too soon for the coach to take the girl. Keep her quiet while I see what it is. If it's trouble, take her out the back way. Hide her, and be certain she doesn't make a sound."

Callie stood mummified, afraid of drawing the attention of the three distracted men if she made a sound. One of the men was looking out the front window. Another leaned out the door trying to hear what was going on downstairs. Then Callie heard the unmistakable, strident voice of Mrs. Pettibone in an indignant rage.

"We'll just see about this, Mrs. Peach! I've the police with me now, so none of your hoity-toity nonsense this time. Callie! Callie Dawson! Can you hear me? Are you here, child? Callie?"

Callie's captors needed no more. "Get the girl!"

Callie screamed Mrs. Pettibone's name, then ran. With the frightened eyes of a deer at bay, the girl put the table between herself and the men. She screamed wildly as the footman came for her from one side and another man stalked her from the opposite side. The oil lamp wavered and smoked dangerously as she grabbed it, holding it aloft. She thrust it first at one man, then the other. "Don't come near me! No!" Her voice was shrill and hysterical. "Stay away! Mrs. Pettibone! Help me!" She threw the lamp, missing the footman by several feet. The oil spilled across the floor, and gold and blue flames ran rapidly along its trail. Overturning the table, she ran for the door. One of the men pushed past her, fleeing as the noise downstairs became more angry and insistent. The footman lunged to put out the fire. The third man grabbed Callie by the hair, his large dirty hand closing over her mouth.

Everything became a scattered blur of panic-filled impressions as policemen raced up the stairs. Callie was flung to the floor as the white slavers thundered toward the outside stairway, and Mrs. Peach and Mrs. Pettibone and the girls alternately screamed in fright or rage. Callie crawled along the floor, seeking the shelter of the bed again.

Mrs. Pettibone was the last to make her way up the stairs to Callie's room. Callie, huddled beneath the bed, repeated hopelessly, "I'm here. I'm here. Don't leave me, please don't leave me."

When Mrs. Pettibone's sturdy shoes appeared at the edge of the bed, Callie began to cry harder. Mrs. Pettibone called to her, and still the girl did not come out. Straining, the landlady went down on her hands and knees and peered under the bed skirt. "Lord, child, what's come of you? They didn't . . ."

"Yes! Yes! He . . . he . . . touched me . . . Mrs. Pettibone . . . help me!"

Mrs. Pettibone's first instinct was to get Callie home, into warm clothes and filled with hot tea and broth. Then she would try to make some sense of the girl's ravings. God forbid the girl had been violated. Most likely the Bereans would turn her out in the cold without a hearing if that were the case. Not a decent family in England would want her for anything but a menial. There would be no future for her.

It took far more than Mrs. Pettibone had planned to calm Callie, and she got no rational response from her. At her wit's end, Mrs. Pettibone called for the doctor. Finally a draught from him and several nights' sleep began to restore Callie.

It was a week before Callie awakened without having had a nightmare tear her from sleep. Mrs. Pettibone approached her warily, not trusting this first calm morning. Callie ate a light breakfast, then fell back against the pillows wan and shaken. "Are you feeling better, Callie?" she asked.

Callie nodded.

"Well, I've some news for you if you've a mind to listen."

Callie looked at her, fear showing plainly in her blue eyes.

"Tosh, girl. All news is not bad! This is good." Mrs. Pettibone told Callie of the letter she had written to the Bereans.

Callie shuddered. "Do you know these people, Mrs. Pettibone?"

"No, I don't, but your father spoke of them often enough. He must have thought well of them. You'll be safe and sound now."

Callie's words ran together. "Are you sure though? Are they cousins? I've never met anyone named Berean. Papa said nothing to me. If they were really cousins wouldn't he have told me?"

Mrs. Pettibone sighed, not knowing what to do. She couldn't blame the girl. Mildly she wished Ian had had the good grace to die somewhere else, not leaving Callie on her hands. "They'll be giving you a home, and that's what you need. It's what you've been wanting. Well, now here it is."

"But are they really my cousins!?" Callie shouted. "How do I know they are not just like Mrs. Peach? I thought she was wonderful. She acted like it. I thought she cared. I thought . . ." She burst into tears, and Mrs. Pettibone came around to the side of the bed, gathering her into her arms.

"Hush now, Callie. It's enough. You got a long taste of wormwood, and that was all. Not all the world is as sweet as it tastes at first. Some of the sweetest things hide only the bitter root. Just like the wormwood, so good as they go down, sweet an' all. Then we find the taste was false. The real thing addles the mind and sours the stomach. That is the way of things. It's always been man's way from the beginning of time. After the fall, God left us our Eden, but it's a bitter Eden, child. It can't be helped, and it comes to us all sooner or later. But you, Callie, you've learned your lesson early on. Maybe you're lucky for the learning. Remember to look at things clearly; don't let your mind get fuddled by appearances. You remember that, and you'll be all right. Now sit up here, and dry your eyes. Tears won't help. It's faith you're needin'."

"But . . ."

"No more to be said. You'll go to the Bereans when they come for you, and you'll be grateful for the home they give you. If it isn't right, you'll know, and you can always come to me for help."

"Will they want me when they know . . ."

"They won't know! Not if I can help it. And don't you breathe a word. Even if those men never . . . harmed you, the Bereans might not believe you and . . ."

"Put me out?"

"They'll never know."

"What if they do? What if they look at me and can tell what happened? What if they want me for the same reasons Mrs. Peach did? What if I can't get back to you?" Callie was shaking as the frightful images built up in her mind.

"You're makin' up witches' tales. Stop it! I won't hear any more. The Bereans *will* be good people, and you'll go with them!"

Very late that night Callie admitted to herself that mixed with the fear and dread of what the Bereans might be, there lived a wistful hope. She was so tired and alone and afraid. If only the Bereans could be all she wished for. If only they would really want her, she would be forever grateful and willing to give of herself whatever any of them needed. If only—but *if only* were words that Ian had scoffed at, saying they were the words that made inaction seem a virtuous occupation. Words such as those were a luxury he had never let himself or his daughter indulge in. Callie turned on herself for her wishful thoughts. But underneath her good sense at squarely facing her reality, she still hoped that this one *if only* was true.

Chapter 5

James Berean was eager to be done with his business in London. Already he and Peter had been in London two days, and James was fretful. He wanted to give Peter time to recuperate safely away from the questioning, suspicious gaze of Albert Foxe, but he worried about Frank. He wasn't sure to what lengths Frank's jealousy of Peter would take him. He knew only that Frank would do what he thought was right. Frank was an honest man, but how much Frank's view was colored by the intense frustrations he lived with, James didn't know, and it worried him.

Regretfully he admitted he was getting old in mind and body. He had awakened this morning in his hired-for-the-night bed cold and stiffly cramped in all his joints, and uneasy in his mind. He missed Kent and his wife and his family and the hot brick that warmed his feet at night.

He woke Peter. "I want to get the girl and be gone from here this morning." He didn't really want Callie Dawson, he thought. She was another uncertainty to add to a new year already filled with uncertainties.

He was too old to steer ~~~~
er path. After a lifetime ~~~~
opinions, James now question ~~~~
thing. He couldn't guide his ~~~~
daughter. What was he to do w ~~~~
daughter?

Gruffly he asked, "How's your arm?"

Peter stretched slowly, cautiously loosening ~~~~
sore muscles. The bruise across his shoulder and ~~~est
was vivid and ugly. "I am feeling better than I deserve. Just don't count on me to be spritely and alert today."

"Think you'll be able to hide the damage from Albert when we get back?"

"I'll have to. But I'm not too worried about Albert. He'd have caught me long ago if he had anything but bone between his ears."

James frowned. "That kind of talk makes me wonder if you and Albert don't have something in common after all."

Irritably James pushed Peter through breakfast, then through the London streets, grumbling incessantly about everything except the problems at hand. "The damned city stinks! Too many people crammed into one place. A man can't breathe. Look at that! Brick wall grating against brick wall—no air between. Bah! Soot!" He sneezed.

Peter smiled to himself, knowing his father. James was deciding to accept Callie Dawson as one of his own children. He'd never laid eyes on the girl, didn't know who she was or what she was like, or how many more problems she'd add to those he already had, but James was thrashing out his misgivings by attacking the irrelevant. Peter loved his father heartily. James could accept anything—nearly anything—given the freedom of a few moments of irascible temper in

...er at the walls of his world and make ...for something new. Peter's laughter was soft to his father's ears. "You realize you've reduced one of the world's great cities to a rubble of people, dirt, and sweat."

James managed a smile. "Perhaps I've overlooked its finer points. I seem able to recall them only when I'm comfortably at home." James bounded into the street to hail a cab. He instructed the driver to take them to Mrs. Pettibone's establishment.

Mrs. Pettibone, in spite of talking so positively to Callie, had heard nothing from the Bereans. She had no idea if they would take Callie in or not. To Mrs. Pettibone it was no longer of consequence. Now that her better nature had recovered its practicality, she had made her decision: One way or another she was going to be rid of the responsibility of Callie. Mrs. Pettibone was not without resources. She knew of several families who would like a hand with their houses or their children. And for once that useless sister of hers could be worth something. She had traded ailments and symptoms with half the women of London. Surely one of them must be in the market for a companion. Of course, it wouldn't be quite like being taken in as part of a family, but in Callie's position there was no room to be choosy. She was fond of Callie, but only so far as her meager ability to share her life would allow. She couldn't become a surrogate mother.

Mrs. Pettibone helped Callie pack crates and boxes with her father's books, her mother's china and ornaments. These were possessions Callie treasured, and although Mrs. Pettibone recommended strongly they be sold, Callie insisted on keeping them. Defeated on that score, Mrs. Pettibone determined to have her way in all else. Systematically she sorted through the clothing, allowing Callie to select a few items of Ian's she could keep in remembrance. The rest would be given away or sold to pay the back rent Ian had owed.

Last, she examined Callie's scant wardrobe, her face crumpling in disapproval. "I've seen better in the maid's cupboard," she sniffed. "Your petticoats need mending. If you're not handy with a needle, you'd better learn. No one will be wanting a useless girl. That's what comes of bein' raised by a man." She glanced at Callie's pinched, frightened face. "Well, we'll get to that. Meantime I'll mend these for you. Come down for them in an hour. I'll leave them on the hall table for you." She snatched up the disreputable petticoats and left Callie alone in her room, fighting back tears.

Rapidly the small security Callie knew in her father's flat was being torn away from her. She knew Mrs. Pettibone liked her, was even genuinely fond of her—but didn't want her.

Callie rubbed the back of her hand across her eyes. The Bereans wouldn't want her either. No one wanted her except Mrs. Peach and her horrible men.

She couldn't count the number of times she had awakened tangled in her blankets, thinking she could hear the sound of Mrs. Peach's tapping cane in the corridor outside her room. She shivered. Still she hadn't learned to control the awful frozen feeling that came when she'd unexpectedly hear the loud sound of a man's voice in the street below her window. Mrs. Pettibone said the remembering and the fright would be washed away with time, but the fear seemed to get worse. And so did the prospect of leaving Mrs. Pettibone. Callie trusted no one else.

* * *

Peter and James arrived at Mrs. Pettibone's just as she completed mending Callie's petticoats. James introduced himself and then asked to see Callie. Mrs. Pettibone placed the neatly folded package of mending on the table, then turned her attention to the two Berean men.

"Now, what's this about wantin' to see Callie? How am I to know you are who you say you are? These days you might be anyone comin' to my door . . ."

"My dear woman . . ." James blustered.

"None of that high-falutin' 'dear woman' business, Mr. Berean. The poor child's been frightened out of her wits wondering and worrying that no one wants her. It wouldn't have hurt you to let us know you were comin' for her. And before I turn her over to you, I have a few questions I'll have answered to my satisfaction! How do you plan on usin' the girl?"

James was taken aback by this formidable, protective woman thrusting questions at him while her eyes, bold and bright as a peacock's, looked him and Peter over as though they were two stallions on the market. As Mrs. Pettibone hustled him into her parlor, James looked helplessly at Peter, who touched his injured arm, deftly sidestepped the landlady, and ambled down the hall past the other apartment doors.

Peter studied the few inexpensive prints Mrs. Pettibone had hung to make the bleak brownish wallpaper less dreary. Every now and then he heard James's or Mrs. Pettibone's voice rise as they argued about the back rent and the inconvenience James had put her to.

An old man entered the building and examined the package Mrs. Pettibone had left on the table, then walked on past Peter to his door.

Peter, bored with waiting, called a greeting to the man's retreating back. Mr. Jenks paused, tapped on his good ear, and decided he had heard nothing. He closed his door behind him. Peter sank down on a small straight-backed chair near the rear of the hall. He counted splotchy brown designs on the wallpaper, figuring how many grotesque rosettes fit across horizontally, then vertically. It was putting him to sleep when a new distraction caught his interest. From somewhere above he heard the sounds of a person moving. They were furtive sounds, not at all the kind of movement one would expect from a tenant of the building.

Callie ran down the first flight of stairs, then slowed, rounding the landing and approaching the last flight down into the hall with caution. Since her experience with the men at Mrs. Peach's, she always looked carefully into the main hall, making sure no new or unfamiliar face lurked below. She looked warily and for a long time at the empty entry square, saw the package on the table, and came down several more steps.

Peter watched the empty stairwell and listened to the stealthy approach curiously. He edged out of his chair, flattening himself against the wall so he couldn't be seen. At each step the girl paused, looking to the left and right. Peter remained quiet, seeing but unseen, waiting for this furtive creature to reveal what she had in mind.

Callie took the final step, once more looking around the hall. Reassured, she made a quick dash to the table and snatched the package with one quickly outthrust hand. Hugging it to her, she ran for the safety of the staircase.

Peter jumped out from behind the concealing wall. He grabbed her arm, roughly whirling her 'round to face him. "Thievery is a bad practice."

Ashen, Callie stared; then she began to tremble violently. Shaking her head wildly, she screamed in a maddening, senseless wail.

Peter let go of her arm. He'd never heard a shriek of such naked terror. He felt it in his own body. Her screams tore through the building. Doors on the upper floor opened. Feet raced along the corridors. Frightened, questioning faces stared over the rails. Cries for help echoed along the halls.

Mrs. Pettibone burst out of her apartment and shoved past the gathering circle of curious onlookers. Peter gave way easily as her red, work-raw hands clawed at him to move aside.

"What have you done to her?" She shook Callie until the girl's head wobbled back and forth as though her neck were made of putty. "You dirty brute! What did you do to her?" She clutched the girl close against her bosom and talked to her in a soothing way.

James finally managed to make his way to the tableau on the staircase. "What's the matter with the girl?" He got no reply from Mrs. Pettibone, so he turned to his son for an answer.

Peter's face was paper white, his dark eyes standing out like burned holes. He clutched his wounded arm. "I caught her sneaking down the stairs. She stole that package she's holding. Then she . . . she started screaming."

"You did her harm!" Mrs. Pettibone said, glaring at him. "She's tremblin' like a frightened wren. Shame be on you!"

Shame was on him. Peter reached over Mrs. Pettibone's shoulder, gently touching Callie. "What did I do to her . . ." he murmured.

"If this is the way you'll be treatin' her, she'd be better off if I find her the decent home of a Christian to work in!"

James's eyes widened with dawning comprehension. "Who is this chit? Surely she's not the Dawson girl!"

After the confusion had died down, and Mrs. Pettibone had been persuaded that the incident had been a misunderstanding, James and Peter packed Callie's boxes and baggage onto a hired coach. Sedated and quiet, Callie was seated only half conscious in the coach beside James. As dazed and sleepy as she was from the laudanum, she still watched Peter with an unsubdued, wild fright in her eyes.

Peter was tense and unhappy. Moodily he tried to keep his eyes off this quivering, doelike woman-child, whose eyes and soft trembling mouth made him feel like the most callous lout. Never in his life had he deliberately hurt a living creature. He treasured life with all its infinite variety and blessing. He let his gaze slide back to Callie. Her hurt blue eyes stared at him, the tears poised but not falling.

For all of them the trip to Kent was filled with thoughts and silence. James struggled with his misgivings. He had reluctantly given in to Meg's insistence that they give the girl a home. Now he found himself saddled with a young woman who went into hysterics at the sight of a man. James did not even consider that Peter might have brought on the hysteria by some action. He knew Peter too well for that. In a harsh age most living creatures develop an instinct of cautious wariness, but in mankind there are those few whose vision remains pure, and their defenses weak. Peter was one of the rare idealists, who saw in stumbling humanity the signs of divinity. He had not harmed Callie.

But James worried that Callie, with her instability and obvious fear, might harm his own daughter, Natalie. Fondly, he thought of his flowerlike girl child.

Her nature was as elusive as the scent of honeysuckle blown on a vagrant evening breeze. She was delicate and sensitive, and James worried about bringing a girl as distraught as Callie into his home.

Mrs. Pettibone had hinted that something terrible had happened to Callie after Ian's death, but she had adamantly refused to say what it was. Because of her reaction to Peter, James was certain it had something to do with men, but the more he thought about it, the worse his imaginings became. He had no idea if it was something the girl had brought on herself, or if she had been forced.

He wiped his hand across his face. Dear God, suppose the girl was with child! He should have left her there with Mrs. Pettibone. He should have, he insisted to himself, and avoided looking at her as Peter did. There was something too vulnerable, too hopeful, shining through Callie's frightened eyes. James again thought of the words he had used to describe his son . . . in mankind there are those few whose vision remains pure, and their defenses weak. Was Callie also such a one?

From time to time as they careened through the countryside, Callie looked out and saw knots of men standing by the roads, looking like an army on the wastelands with neither shelter nor reason to explain their gathering. They are like me, she thought. Lost. No one listening to them. No one caring about them. In spite of her efforts to fight the laudanum, her heavy eyes shut.

Peter watched her. She whimpered in her sleep. He could still feel her thin arms under the pressure of his hands, still see the look of terror in her eyes, still hear the piercing agonized screams. What had he done to her? How in God's name could he ever undo that unknown sin?

They were almost home. Wistfully Peter looked out of the carriage window at the front of the house. As he watched, the front door burst open.

A clutch of Bereans poured from the house, Meg leading them. Natalie, her sweet face lit by a dreaming smile. Anna, Frank's well-chosen, practical wife, making certain everyone had his coat on. Stephen, as always in the background, his eyes alone betraying his ardor. Still farther back, remaining in the warmth of the house, were Frank and Rosalind standing beside Albert Foxe. Those were the lost of the Berean family, but Peter loved them nonetheless. The lines of his mouth deepened into a thoughtful frown as he looked at them. How much they knew of survival and how little of life. Perhaps there was still time.

James leaned forward to open the door, but Meg, too impatient to wait, poked her anxious face through the coach window. She gaped at Callie's slumped form, her slack mouth, her sickly white complexion.

James, instantly aware that Stephen had told her what little he knew of their hasty departure, began to reassure his wife. "Now, Meg. It is nothing to worry yourself about. We're all safe and sound. We . . ." he hesitated over the lie, and she noticed. "We had a little trouble with the carriage. The girl was ill. . . ." James stopped again. He had no story. He had meant to plan what he and Peter would say, but he had never done it. He kept talking, hoping that no one would question him too closely until he could sort it all out. "Peter hurt his arm, but it was nothing serious, I assure you, dear. A couple of days' rest and we'll all be fine."

"Peter," Meg said, her own face white now too. "Is your father telling me all? You are all right . . ."

Peter looked at his mother, swallowing hard to rid himself of the paining lump in his throat. What a tangle of lies he had gotten them all into. What damage

he had done to his family, to the girl Callie, he didn't
know.

"We're all fine, just bruised and a little frightened,
that's all," James muttered, his eyes desperately sig-
naling Meg to ask nothing more.

Meg, still apprehensive, nodded and moved back
from the coach, allowing James to alight. "Bring her
into the parlor by the fire. She must be frozen."

James began to pull Callie to her feet, when Peter
gently but firmly pushed him aside.

James whispered gruffly, "You can't carry her;
you'll open that wound."

"What does it matter now? I was hurt in an accident
on the way home. Let Albert get his eyes full; let him
think what he damn well pleases. I'm going to carry
this girl into the house."

Rosalind's face was set in stony jealousy as she
watched the care with which her husband carried the
girl into the house. His eyes on Callie were filled with
tender pity to the exclusion of all else. He took her to
the parlor, laid her on the sofa, removed her gloves
and slippers, then placed a lap robe over her. Carefully he removed her bonnet, smoothing her hair from
her face.

Several minutes later Peter went to look for his
wife. Rosalind stood by the window, looking moodily
into the front yard. He came up behind her. She
didn't move, and her voice was low and flat.

"You finally got round to me, did you? What happened? Did your mother remind you that you already
have one wife?"

Peter moved so he could look at her face. "Can you
never see things as they are? She is only a poor, sick,
frightened child, Rosalind, and if you care to listen I'll
tell you my part in that."

"Don't bother to explain, Peter. I'm sure I could

guess. The story is always the same with you. If it isn't the poor starving peasants, it is the poor crippled beggars, or the poor frightened girls, and I always come last."

"Rosalind, it is my fault that . . ."

"I said that I want no explanations. What did you bring me?"

Peter slumped against the wall. He looked up at the ceiling. "There wasn't time. . . . I didn't think of it. Then Pa wanted to hurry back here, and we had the trouble with—" Peter's eyes slid back to the slender, beautiful child lying unconscious on the sofa.

Rosalind's expression grew hard and resentful. She turned quickly, crossing the room to sit beside Albert Foxe. Filled with false vivacity, she flirted and talked and charmed until she had Albert laughing and oblivious to the more serious mood of the others.

The rest of the family clustered around Callie. "Oh, Mama, will she be all right?" Natalie asked, her hand playing with a silky strand of Callie's golden hair.

"Of course, darlin', she's been—" Meg glanced at James "—ill. The trip did her no good. The first thing we'll do is fatten her up. She looks like a long piece of hop twine. Poor, poor little lambie." Meg thought her the palest, thinnest waif she'd ever seen. "I knew she needed us. Something told me as soon as I read Mrs. Pettibone's letter."

Stephen Berean, quiet and unnoticed by the others, looked at Callie and thought of what his mother was saying. Somehow he knew better than anyone that Callie needed them, needed him. He was fascinated by her, and entranced by the silent sadness of her face.

Callie slept the night on the parlor sofa. When she awakened it was afternoon of the following day. The men were already in the fields. Rosalind, Natalie, and Anna had gone to the market in Seven Oaks. Meg alone sat vigil.

Callie yawned; then her blue eyes opened wide, darting in frightened bewilderment about the strange room, finally resting on Meg. "What are you going to do with me?"

"Do with you?" Meg repeated stupidly. In all her imaginings of how she would greet Callie upon her awakening, Meg had never anticipated the girl's first words to be this despairing accusation. And there was no doubt that was what Callie meant.

"Don't hurt me."

"Heaven give me strength," Meg breathed. She looked at Callie's pinched mouth and the unshed tears in her eyes. "What sort of life have you led? You're truly afraid that I may do something dreadful to you."

With relentless kindness, Meg questioned and talked, slowly gaining Callie's trust, assuring her that no terror would be visited on her at Gardenhill House.

Callie remained silent, still doubting but hopeful. She didn't dare tell Meg the things she feared, yet she wished by some means Meg could understand what she didn't know.

To herself Meg admitted that Callie's problems, whatever they were, were beyond her. This was something for James to handle. The devils that Callie faced, only her beloved James could banish.

So Meg turned to what she was best at—making a young girl feel loved and cared for. It took less than she expected to get Callie to listen to the lovely things of life. Not half an hour after having awakened frightened and despairing, Callie's face was bright with smiles.

Meg touched her breast, fervently glad they had brought Callie home to live with them. Whatever evils

Callie had known in the past, it was obvious to Meg that she was an innocent, filled with an innate faith in the goodness of people. Cheered, Meg showed her around downstairs, and then together they examined Callie's numerous boxes and luggage to make certain James and Peter had left nothing behind.

Chapter 6

Meg was panting by the time they reached the top of the stairs and the small room she and Anna had prepared for Callie. She stepped aside letting Callie stand alone, looking through the doorway of the room that would be hers.

It was small, an unpretentious, safe nook with newly whitewashed walls. Curtains with tiny rosebuds hung translucent in the midafternoon sun. On Meg's face there was pride and hope that Callie would like what she saw. "I'll get Stephen to bring up your luggage."

Callie walked around the room and looked into the closet tucked under the wall of the roof line. A chiffonier stood endearingly dilapidated under the angle of the upcurving wall. Her bed was soft and fresh to smell. The coverlet was new, handmade.

One by one her fears were being quelled. In their place came a weak miserable hope that made her throat pain.

Callie tensed as Stephen bumped along the stairwell. Warily she looked up at the tall angular boy, whose head nearly touched the low ceiling. His unwieldy burden bumped the doorjamb and Callie. "Sorry," he mumbled. He glanced at her, then looked over his shoulder at his mother. "Where shall I put these, Ma?"

Self-consciously he continued to avoid Callie's eyes, which was all right with her because she much preferred viewing this new family member without having to respond in any way.

There was no resemblance between Stephen and his mother. Meg was plump, rosy-cheeked, and fair. Yet her son was a tall, dark, gangling mass of angles. He had the untamed look of unfinished sculpture, and the fresh-air smell of some timid, wild creature of a pine forest. His eyes, blue as a deep running stream, were as innocent of guile and the world as were a wood fawn's. His hair was the black of a starless night, unruly and curling about his face. Callie looked at him standing as though poised for flight, burdened with several of her small boxes, and nearly smiled. How was it possible that he was a child of Meg Berean?

"You can put them next to the chest," Callie said absently.

"There isn't anyplace else, is there?" he agreed, dumping the boxes gracelessly next to the chiffonier. His smile illuminated his face, taking away the shyness so obvious before. Callie smiled in return, wondering. In some indefinable way he had strengthened her dawning faith that wherever Meg Berean was, she would be safe and welcome.

Meg, as if she'd sensed these thoughts, pressed Callie to her in a gargantuan hug. "Everything is going to be all right; you'll see. Your troubles are behind you now. Bad beginnings mean happy endings."

"Did you make that up just now, Ma?" Stephen

grinned mischievously at Callie. "She thinks up an old, old saying for everything."

Meg playfully cuffed his ear. "I do indeed, and it will be so. Callie is not to fret anymore. James will have a nice long chat with her. There is nothing James can't put right, Callie."

Callie looked at Meg and Stephen with a longing so strong it could be felt. Impulsively Stephen reached out, and Callie found her tense fingers resting in his large warm hand like a trapped, trembling bird. His face reddening, Stephen released her, murmuring, "Ma's telling you the truth, Callie. There's nothing Pa can't make come right." With a flurry he vanished down the stairs to bring up the rest of her belongings.

Meg took an armful of Callie's dresses and opened the closet in the wall. "Oh, dear! There's boxes of . . . well, I don't know what all this is. It appears to be Peter's. How could Anna and I have missed this when we prepared the room? I'll have Peter come up directly to remove them."

"No!" She didn't want Peter in there. "I have plenty of room."

Meg turned sharply at the strident fearful tone that had returned to Callie's voice. She studied the girl, just beginning to form the obvious question, when Stephen, balancing boxes precariously, noisily maneuvered through the door. Meg, distracted, clucked her disapproval as she unstacked the boxes from his arms.

Another fifteen minutes of fussing and arranging by Meg, and then Callie watched the door close on mother and son. For a moment she stood where she was, alone and silent, listening to the strange sounds the wind made on the roof. To her city ears the sounds of the country house were odd and enticing.

Meg had told her to be downstairs in the parlor in an hour. She hurried with her unpacking, giving in to temptation to look out her window to see if there really were cows and sheep right outside. There were! Who ever heard of an evil person who worried to keep their cows and sheep warm? Or perhaps it was the sign of a man who cared naught for people and only for animals. Or maybe it was normal for a farm. She pushed away these thoughts and held to the first. The aching hope surged through her chest, burning her throat and eyes.

Was Stephen truly as good as he appeared? Would she be a part of this family as Meg promised? A sister to Natalie? And Peter—? She closed the thought off. She'd avoid Peter somehow. She'd wish him away. Stephen would protect her. Stephen would. . . . Callie turned from the window. There was nothing she could expect from Stephen. And there was nothing she could expect to come of Meg's promises. Her father had been right when he told her never to dream "If onlies." Hope was balm for the soul, but unfortunately Callie had learned these past months that hope seldom coincided with the reality of her life. Her mind turned to Mrs. Pettibone's warnings: never trust too easily or too completely. Life might appear as an Eden, but it was a bitter Eden. Reinforced, Callie now knew that her life with the Bereans would only be a sufferance. She'd do what she could to please, but guardedly, protective of herself. It left her feeling empty, as though again she had been abandoned. She went back to her unpacking. Slowly, methodically, she took from her boxes Ian's books, his quill pen, his smoking jacket, fondling each, drawing herself back to a lost happiness by their feel and scent. She lost track of time, never thinking of the time Meg told her the Bereans would have dinner.

Meg's family was gathered long before Callie was ready to join them. There was much curiosity about

this young girl who had come to them so suddenly
and then arrived unconscious. Albert Foxe, on the
strength of his engagement to Natalie, shared in the
curiosity and had invited himself to dinner.

Albert, in his late twenties, was handsome in a refined, highly bred fashion. His features were small
and regular. He was vain both of his looks and of his
reputation for shrewdness. Not above a bit of postur-
ing, Albert carried himself with the ramrod rigidity of
a military man. The pride of his life was the moderate,
well-waxed mustache he sported, which he fingered
with annoying regularity. Leaning back in studied re-
laxation, Albert twirled the ends of his mustache and
stated, "She seems frail, but frailty is often accompanied by an amiable disposition." He was pleased with
the sound of his words. It was almost a direct quote of
something his mother had said about Natalie, and his
mother was always eloquent.

"You make her sound dreadfully dull," Rosalind
sighed. "But what could we expect, bringing a street
waif into the house? Really, Mother Berean, I think
you have taken on far more than you know. It may be
a dreadful mistake. We know nothing of the girl. She
. . . she could be anything . . . a pickpocket . . . a
thief. Peter said he caught her stealing a package. And
now here she is, a virtual invalid. I quite frankly think
she is a superior actress."

"The package turned out to be her own property,"
Peter said.

"Then why was she sneaking around? The landlady
probably just said it was hers to make sure you took
her. I'm sure that woman didn't want to be stuck with
the girl. Anyone else would have seen through that
ruse."

Stephen shifted uncomfortably in his chair, then
rose and stirred their curiosity about Callie further.

Naturally reserved and not given to exaggeration, he amazed his family as he went into great gesturing detail describing her sweetness, her charm, and the dark blue eyes that he was unable to do justice. All he could say was that they were blue, and he tried by gesture and inadequate words to tell what feelings and emotions those eyes could impart without so much as the twitch of a facial muscle.

"I think our Callie has found her first admirer," Anna said with a tolerant, knowing smile on her face.

Several others in the room laughed as Stephen's face grew pink.

Peter remained silent, his eyes downcast, remembering what he had seen expressed by Callie's deep blue eyes. "Shame be on you," Mrs. Pettibone had said to him. He wondered if ever he would feel anything but shame when he looked at Callie. He knew he would feel it as long as it took him to make up to her in some way for the fright he had given her.

Meg looked at the staircase. "She should be down by now. Do you think I ought to go up and see what is keeping her?"

"The men are hungry after a long day's work," Rosalind said. "She might have given them a little thought. She's been here one day and already has the whole family dancing to her tune." She looked at Peter.

Peter glanced up, his dark brown eyes asking her not to complain further. "She'll be here soon."

Meg gestured helplessly. Nearly in unison the Bereans closed ranks against the complainer.

"I'd like a good mug of cider before supper," Frank said, getting to his feet and ringing for the maid. "Anyone care to join me?"

"I would like some."

"Oh, Nattie, dear, you know cider always goes

straight to your head," Meg said. "Why don't you have the apple juice? There is some ready for her, isn't there, Stephen? See, dear, Stephen makes it especially for you. Don't disappoint him by not drinking it. You'll like it better. Talk to her, Albert."

Albert smiled indulgently at Meg, then looked proudly at Natalie. Petite and delicately flowerlike, Natalie gave Albert a sense of protective masculinity he'd never known before he met her. His mother, a woman nearly indistinguishable from the blooded horses she rode so masterfully, had ridden her son all his life. The only other woman with whom he'd associated closely was Rosalind, and she, with her vixen body and her insatiable hunger, could turn him to molten steel, burning and puddling at her touch. Only with Natalie was he man, master, god. "I'll take care of her," he said softly.

Peter gave him an acid glance, then took Natalie's hand. "Let her have the cider, Ma. Nattie's no baby anymore. It's time we all treated her like the woman she is." Natalie stroked his arm and to his dismay leaned against him, her expression that of a grateful, small child.

"She hasn't been a baby for twenty years," Rosalind murmured. "Go ahead, Natalie, by all means, have your cider and maybe for once you can prove what a big girl you are to all of us."

"We don't need bickering and teasing in the family tonight, Rosalind. We shall all show Callie our better side," James warned, and accepted the mug Frank held out to him.

Callie could hear the sounds coming from the parlor. For some time she had been standing near the staircase trying to sort out the voices and gather the courage to enter the room. She heard Meg mention a second time that she should be downstairs, and she knew she couldn't put it off any longer.

It wasn't as bad as she expected. None of them stared as she thought they might. She accepted their friendly greetings, was warmed and heartened as each family member expressed his welcome. Except Peter. His eyes remained fixed on his hands resting in his lap. Callie walked hastily past him, then furtively glanced back to catch his deep, almost-black eyes studying her.

James didn't give her a chance to react. Hurriedly but tactfully he escorted her to his study, "for a talk," he said. "I have had years to get to know my other children, Callie. Could you give me a few minutes alone to get to know you?"

Meg watched Callie's expressive eyes and believed that whatever made them cloud with fear would be resolved with James's guidance.

Callie listened to the fatherly warmth of his voice. But even that soft, loving rumble wasn't enough to thaw her sufficiently to go against Mrs. Pettibone's warning. The Bereans might not understand; they might blame her for what had happened to her at Mrs. Peach's house. Callie was candid, trying to explain to James how she had felt when her father died, and how much he had meant to her, but that was all she would talk about.

James pursed his lips, wondering what the girl was withholding and why. Though what she had said had the ring of truth, it in no way explained her hysterics or her obvious aversion to Peter. He sighed and patted her shoulder, ending their brief conversation. With time, he thought, leading her into the dining room; everything will mend with time.

Meg directed her to the seat between Natalie and Stephen. It was a happy bedlam as they all sat down, still talking and occasionally lifting a heavy mug of cider to toast Callie's arrival or anything else they could think of. The two serving girls waited patiently. No one was willing to be quiet. Peter even toasted the infamous Captain Swing.

"I won't drink a drop to him." Albert set his mug down heavily. "It's treasonous."

The others drank with grumbling joviality.

"Who is Captain Swing?" Callie whispered to Natalie.

Natalie's blue-veined lids lowered over her golden cat eyes; then she looked slyly at Callie. "Ohh . . . Captain Swing is a very mysterious man . . . and evil. No one knows if he is a man at all. He may be a ghost . . . or a spirit power." Suddenly she giggled. "Don't be frightened. Spirits can't hurt you. I wouldn't let them."

Callie smiled tentatively, not certain how to distinguish between Natalie teasing and Natalie serious.

Again Natalie giggled, thrusting her chest out and clenching her tiny fists. "See what a brave defender I'll be?"

Callie burst out laughing, then pressed her hand against her lips, her eyes on Peter.

"James! Say a prayer quickly and get us started with the meal," Meg said loudly. Conversation ended. Heads bowed. James's gentle rumbling voice filled the room, thanking the Lord for their food, their family, and the bounty of their land.

Conversation began anew as soon as supper was served. Callie listened, trying to assess the family. Anna and Rosalind were talking about the house and some sewing Anna was doing for Rosalind. Natalie sat at Callie's side daydreaming. Withdrawn from the others, Natalie was rapt and intent. She was beautiful in so delicate a way that Callie had the feeling Natalie was someone she had imagined rather than a flesh and blood girl she could touch with the merest movement of her elbow.

The men returned to the subject of Captain Swing. And Callie's eyes returned, as they had all evening, to Peter Berean. It was difficult to concentrate on anything else when he was there to cloud her mind, so she was slow to realize that very real worries underlay the Bereans' merry squabbling banter.

Callie jumped as Frank slammed his mug on the table and spoke nearly in a shout. "There has never been a time when the peasants have been satisfied with their lot, and there never will be. There will always be a division between the leaders of the world and those who were meant by God to serve. It's in the nature of man, and no reform will change it. It is by Divine creation meant to be!"

Peter guffawed. "And you, of course, are among those divinely chosen to lead. Why? Because you have a patch of land?"

"I know what to do with that land! I make it produce. And I know what to do with the profits. I know how to live, and I go beyond the thinking of a man in a hovel who knows nothing but to drink every bloody penny he lays hands on. What you can't understand, Peter, is that we are in a new age. The war did that for us. The times are leaving your peasants behind. They are still as uncivilized and stupid as they were a century ago. The rest of the world is moving forward, as well we should. We were victors. We beat Napoleon, and we've proven our way is right and forward-thinking."

"Victory, Frank? Take a good look at that victory. We're a bloody victor in rags. We've debts we can't pay, taxation that is crippling all of us, and we've got more poor people in the country today than we're able to feed or clothe. What kind of victory is that?"

Albert cleared his throat. "Of course, it is true that the demobilized army and navy have created a problem in the labor market. After all, they made up nearly one sixth of our adult population. But that is being absorbed. We may have staggered a bit, but that is to be expected after a war. It doesn't change the fact that the war has caused us to look forward to new ways and methods. Machinery, world trade, and international markets are the things of today."

"Machinery, world trade, and international markets are the tools of politicians and industrialists. They don't help the farmer or the peasant," Peter said. "England still looks to her own production to feed her people. And as long as we keep having bad crop years our farmers cannot compete on the international market without subsidy, which means more money spent and more taxes gathered. It means Corn Laws, bread and food staples' prices rising so high at home they can't be purchased by the common man, which means more men on the dole, therefore more taxes to supply money to men who could make their own living if the government weren't so busy fixing everything. It's like a bloody teeter-totter. Help the industrialists, and the farmer is left begging. Help the farmer, and the industrialist is crying. We're making enemies of people who should be natural allies."

"That's nonsense. No one has been made the enemy of anyone else," Frank said. "Tell me, champion of the laborer, isn't it true right now—this very day—that the farmer is sympathetic to the laborer's problems? Wouldn't we all pay him more if we could, if we weren't already carrying the burden of taxes and duties levied on us? We don't turn to machinery to hurt our laborers, do we? No! We do it because we must, because the times and the conditions demand it."

Peter rubbed his forehead, smiling. "I think that is what I've been saying, Frank. There is no choice but to crush the laborer, because of the way our laws and systems are set up. It is the law and the harshness and inequity with which it is applied that must change. In short, gentlemen, we need reform in England in many areas, not just for the peasant, but for all of us."

"Succoring the cause of Captain Swing is certainly the wrong way to go about it, assuming *anything* you say is true," Albert said.

"What's wrong with Captain Swing? His movement has the attention of several lords, and many more local magistrates, including you, Albert. They have shed no blood. It seems to me the Swing riots have quite a lot to recommend them."

"They have one distinct quality against them," Albert replied quickly.

"Which is?"

"They must come to disaster. In the end we must enforce the law harshly and strictly, and then what happens to your peasants, Peter? They will be worse off than before. There will be mass arrests. It cannot be any other way, for if we allow them to have a say in the workings of our lives, we should all be at their mercy." Slowly he took up his wine glass, swirling the red liquid. "No, there is no question. Order must be preserved. It is the safeguard to civilization. My God, without it, we'd have another French Revolution right here in England."

"The order is wrong," Peter said softly. "It is one thing to maintain law, but quite another when the existing law is squeezing to death a large segment of your people. Then the law itself must be changed, not the people. The order must be changed or we do not

foster civilization, but stagnation." There was no need
for Peter to pound on the table or swirl wine in his
goblet for emphasis; the whole look of him was emphasis enough. He believed what he was saying with
a deep passion, and that belief could be felt throughout the room. His intensity was magnetic, attracting
every eye and ear.

It wasn't often that nature conspired to produce a
man like Peter Berean, and Albert was painfully
aware of this. Vain, and bearing the responsibility of
having to enforce the law of the parish, Albert was
too often unfavorably compared with Peter. He was
also aware that he was magistrate only because Peter
wouldn't accept the post. Though he knew he and Peter could never be friends, he seethed at the fate that
had made them competitors. Albert couldn't count the
number of times he had mentally tried to trim Peter
down to commonality. He always failed. Peter was an
intelligent man with an appetite for adventure. He
was unafraid to state his beliefs and act upon them.
The very thought of the coming confrontation between the magistrates and the Swing offenders led by
Peter made Albert's hands clammy and his armpits
itch in a way that his mother would have found disgusting and unmanly.

Callie listened with rapt attention, unable to take
her eyes from Peter as the talk went on, growing more
heated.

"You'll hear this until you know it by heart," Stephen whispered. "Neither one gives an inch, and the
next time Albert comes over, which will probably be
tomorrow, they will start all over again. If I were Albert I'd give up. Peter always wins. No one ever out-
does Peter."

"Well, I've heard more than enough for tonight,"
Meg said. "I can't see why you men always talk of

something we all hope will never happen. Please, no more tonight."

As the talk momentarily quieted, Meg took her advantage. She hurried Natalie and Callie from the room, wishing she could as easily forestall the rift that was forming in the family. Frank sided with Albert more frequently and more openly, and his hostility toward Peter was barely concealed these days. And Stephen nearly idolized Peter. Peter was as close to a hero for Stephen as anyone would ever come.

Anna and Rosalind followed Meg from the dining room into the parlor. Callie automatically turned there also, but Meg gently took her arm. "For you two there is no more talk, and no more cider or wine this evening. One of you looks as tired and sleepy as the other."

"But I haven't said good night to Albert."

"Albert will understand, Natalie. You know as well as I the men may be barricaded in James's study half the night talking their infernal politics."

"But Rosalind . . ."

"Never mind Rosalind."

"But Mama, Rosalind will talk to him. She'll wait . . . she'll say good night to him and I won't be there."

Meg made an exasperated sound through her teeth. "Natalie!"

"But Mama . . . I'm as strong as Anna or Rosalind. Why must I go to bed so early? I must be here to say goodnight. Please! Why don't you believe me? Why won't anyone ever listen to me? I know Rosalind better than any of you. She—"

Meg put her fingers firmly on Natalie's lips. "Not a word! Not a word against your brother's wife. I will not hear disloyalty in this house!"

Chapter 7

Rosalind waited what seemed an unendurably long time for the men to emerge from James's study, confident her intent would not be obvious. The others would think her a faithful and perhaps touchingly eager young wife. She could count on the Bereans to think the best, and she could also count on each of them to follow a predictable pattern for the night.

When the door to the study opened and expelled the men with a heavy cloud of cigar smoke, Rosalind smiled into the strikingly handsome face of her husband. Her hand as she touched him was possessively ladylike.

He took her hands in his, smiled at his father and Albert, showing her off a little and pleased that she was there for him. "We were long-winded tonight. You know Albert—like a bull terrier with a bone."

"Speak for yourself," Albert said.

"I know you all. The only hope we women have of seeing you is to wait for you. But in a few more minutes this woman would have been knocking to gain entrance to that smoky den."

"We're finished now and Albert has not gotten the last word for once. Now, go on up. I'll be there shortly."

"Oh, Peter—it's so late, and I've waited for you so long. You're not going to check the fields tonight, are you? Let them go this once." She pouted as he told her how necessary his nightly overseeing was; she smiled in resignation as she heard his familiar words. Her eyes sought Albert's.

As always Frank said he would join Peter. He kissed Anna on the cheek and sent her upstairs. Frank would do only as he said. He would look over the fields and return promptly to his wife's side. Rosalind knew Peter would go on, riding off into the night, not to return for several hours. She watched with detached interest as the two men put on their coats.

"Coming with us, Albert?" Peter asked. It was a taunt.

"Not tonight, old man. As you hoped your talk has worn me out. I am going home and to bed, as I would advise you to do. One of these nights I'm going to catch you at your rabble-rousing, and there won't be any more jokes."

"Good night then, Albert. Have a care on your way. Never know what you might run into."

James had already started up the stairs. "Will you be waiting for Peter, Rosalind?" he asked. "He may be a while."

"Then I shall wait—for a while."

When James's bedroom door closed, and Peter and Frank had left, Rosalind swung around on Albert. "You knew I would be waiting for you. Sometimes I think you deliberately prolong these conversations. You like to see me wait." She pouted. His hands encircled her waist.

He looked down at her, an amused expression on

his face. "Well now, Miss Rosalind, the next time the evening drags I shall excuse myself. 'A thousand pardons, Peter, old man, but I must break up this happy meeting so that I can go make love to your wife.'"

Rosalind laughed and leaned against him. "Can you think what his face would look like if you said that?"

"Not so well as I can imagine what mine would look like when he finished with me."

Rosalind forced the merriment on longer and laughed harder. She liked to laugh with Albert. It always seemed in retrospect that when they laughed together the evening had so much more meaning.

Albert placed his hand over her mouth. "Shhh! You'll have James hobbling down the stairs to see what's going on."

She couldn't force the laugh out anymore. "Why is it that you would care more than I if James did find out? That's a curious thing, don't you think?"

He kissed the tip of her nose, indulgent and determinedly gentle. "Not at all. I have far more sense than you, dear one, and what's more I look to consequences that would never enter your pretty head."

"Natalie?"

"For one."

"Do you know how it makes me feel when I know Natalie is always lurking somewhere inside your head when you are with me? You kiss me and still she is there. She is some sort of untouchable little princess, while I am nothing."

"I am going to marry her. We won't change or be changed by that. It is something that exists. That's all."

"That's all! How you lie!"

"Do I? How willing are you to have Peter walk through the door now and see us?"

"He won't. Peter isn't going to find out anything.

He doesn't look for anything." She shrugged. "Anyway he's all agog over that simpering Callie. I hate her!"

"How venomous." He grasped her clenching hands, holding them until the jealous anger in her eyes cooled. "Calm down—remember it's Peter who's infatuated, not I." He really didn't like her when she was like this. She was put out over her long wait, discontent with things he didn't understand or want to understand. He looked down at her; the self-centered look of having been wronged was firmly etched on her mouth.

"You should have married me," she said. "We'd be happy now, and not having to be snatching moments in corners. And you would have done it if you ever truly loved me."

"But I did—and I do! It wasn't a lack of love that held me back. Be reasonable. You know there was nothing I could do."

"You could have married me. You could have defied your mother. You just didn't care. You know she wouldn't have really disinherited you. You're her only son. The truth is that you never did love me. Why don't you admit it?"

He felt cramped, hemmed in by her accusing tone. He wanted to leave her as he had so often wanted to leave the sound of his mother's harping voice. But he smiled reassuringly, caressing her neck and shoulders with his fingertips. "You're a witch, Rosalind. Why do you put me through this? You know I love you. Why else would I be here every day? Why would I risk Peter finding me and blowing the brains right out my head? Only because I love you."

"Make me believe you, Albert."

He pulled her close, caressing her and kissing her repeatedly, more warmly each time to prove that he meant it. And he did in a way. "You know what you do to me. Meet me tomorrow at the cottage. Say you will."

"Maybe. I can't just leave whenever I please, Albert. What shall I say I am doing? It is a little cold for a long walk."

"Say you're going shopping. Say you have to see a dressmaker. I don't know what you should say—think of something. You can if you want. Be there, Rosalind. We'll have the whole afternoon, sweetheart. Think of it—no moments in corners—the whole afternoon." He buried his face in her shoulder. "Say yes. Say you'll come. I can't stand being without you. You know that. I need you."

"I'll be there," she whispered breathlessly. "I always come, don't I? You've only to beckon and I follow. Oh, Albert, I am a fool. I should make you suffer as you have made me."

"I have . . . I have. Every time I think of you with Peter . . . oh, God, I hate to think of his hands touching you . . . knowing what I know . . . wondering if you . . . I dream about it, am tormented by it. But we can make it up to each other, can't we? Tomorrow? Tomorrow there'll only be us."

At a sound in the upper hall, Albert glanced toward the staircase, momentarily frozen, expecting to see James—or worse, Natalie standing there viewing his guilty love. "I must leave. Frank is sure to be coming in soon. Till tomorrow, my love. Till tomorrow." He kissed her hard and hungrily, then forced himself to draw away from her warm, inviting body.

Rosalind watched from the window as he mounted his horse; then she turned down the lamps, leaving one to light the way for Frank and Peter. She went to her bedroom determined to be asleep when Peter came in. Peter could do nothing but make cow-eyes at Callie, and she hated him for it, and Albert had some-

how managed to leave her feeling used and dirty, a
tavern girl once more.

"Well, what's wrong with being a tavern girl? It was
good enough to make you look twice, Mr. Foxe," she
fumed as she fished through a pile of rumpled bed-
clothes for her robe. Her activity made her feel warmer
but no calmer, for she knew there was nothing wrong
with being a tavern girl.

It was being Rufus Hawkes's daughter that was
wrong; it was marrying the wrong man to keep a
worse fate from befalling her. She was guilty of both.

She had been born Rufus Hawkes's daughter and
couldn't help that, but she had been coldly calculating
when she had married Peter Berean without loving
him. Had she not, she would have ended up the wife
of one of the men who frequented her father's tavern.
She had sought any means of escape.

She was very young when she had learned that the
men who gathered in her father's tavern weren't nice.
At thirteen she had been embarrassed and humiliated
when they had smashed their wet, liquor-soaked
mouths against her still virginal lips. She had been
terrified as they forced their soot-stained hands down
the front of her bodice, pinching and hurting her,
their hard fingers and dirty nails digging deep into
the soft dark tips of her breasts. And she had felt de-
filed the first time one of those dirty hands found its
way up inside her full skirts to the tender moist parts
of her that her mother had said were for privacy and
love. But Rosalind, through her tears and the ragged
remains of her female pride, could look at these men
with their yellowed teeth showing like dog fangs and
know that though they had done evil things to her,
she herself was clean and good. She was only the victim, sharing in no way their lust and hatred—until one

night after the tavern closed, and Rufus came to her room.

Rosalind had started at his entrance, quickly grabbing her discarded petticoat and pressing it against her naked breasts. Rufus laughed softly, proudly. He took the petticoat from her. Without lust, his hands fondled her, not so roughly as the filthy tavern patrons', but thoroughly, with the prodding curiosity of an entrepreneur evaluating the quality of his goods. Rufus pinched and teased her nipples to hardness, then studied his daughter's face for signs of response. Satisfied, he smiled and ran his hand through her hair as he had when she was small and believed a father's love must always be kind.

"Ye're a witch born, Rosie—the devil's own. Ye'll make us a merry music with ye're band o' creakin' bedsprings and the clinkin' o' change in me till."

Rosalind had cried herself to sleep that night and many thereafter. Nightmare chasing nightmare banished her purity. The men had done dirty things to her, but she wasn't dirtied inside. Her father, however, had made her suspect that the clean soul she had been taught to nurture in church was merely a stone on which the devil had not yet carved his story. But he had begun. Rosalind couldn't forget the hot watery feeling her father's hands on her body had produced deep inside her. Nor could she forget lying that night in her bed restless and confused and wanting. Then she felt the ultimate shame when she reached beneath the sheet with her own hand to complete what her father had begun. Rosalind never again felt pure or whole or worthy. She lived with an insatiable hunger for release from the demons of doubt and desire and longing.

Her easiest outlet was her imagination. She saw beautifully coiffed women in splendid gowns riding through town in their elegant carriages. They lived in a fairy-tale world of courtesies and gallant men who adored them. Enviously Rosalind watched these women until each of them bore her own features. With all her being Rosalind longed to be a lady. She knew deep in her heart that had fate not chosen her as a devil's child, she might have been the most glamorous, most sought after of all those enchanted ladies. Her childlike dreaming led her to her second hard lesson.

Occasionally, by mistake, ignorance, or misdirection, a nicer sort of man found himself in Hawkes's Tavern. Rosalind sensed these men liked her, that some even desired her. Bravely, and with all her dreams of grandeur her only armor, she gave them what they wanted. Rufus smiled. The bedsprings creaked, and the cashbox rang. The devil's music played.

But Rosalind's hopes and dreams withered. She was someone the "nice" men wanted to fondle. Someone they wanted to bed discreetly. But no more. Even when a man thought he loved her and was willing to marry her, as Albert Foxe had been, the families of these "nice" men were not willing to allow it. No, girls like Rosalind were to be used for young men to sow their wild oats, providing, of course, the girl was "clean and of good nature," as the saying went.

Her first few lessons in this attitude were devastating. But she hardened and learned to recognize when she had the advantage and when she did not. Her dream was tarnished, but she held on to it. She could no longer enter Albert's world as the innocent she might have, but Rosalind was now equipped to enter it shrewdly and calculatingly and desperately.

She remembered clearly her one and only conversation with Albert's mother.

"The difficulty with you, Rosalind, fortunately is not characteristic of your class. You've no idea of your place. What you aspire to, by enticing my son, is a way of life for which you have no talent nor comprehension of its meaning or ways. You'll not marry my son, and you will see that it is to your benefit as well as his.

"Though you do not realize it, I am doing you a service by forbidding this marriage. You would not be happy. You'd not fit in, nor would you be able to entertain or mingle with the sort of people with whom Albert will spend his life. Find yourself a suitable man and end these yearnings after a station for which you are so totally unsuited." Mrs. Foxe had dabbed a lacy, perfumed handkerchief under her nose. Ostentatiously she had straightened her already straight back, as though rising above the atmosphere she found herself in. Her tailored mauve silk afternoon gown rustled richly at her every move. The woman's skin was milky white, her hair freshly and expertly coiffed.

Rosalind had stared at her, unwittingly rude. It was difficult to acknowledge that this woman was real. She seemed more like a character from a story book, come to life to sit and talk to Rosalind. It was several seconds before the meaning of Mrs. Foxe's words had penetrated Rosalind's consciousness, and when they did she had felt belittled. Her coarse wool dress—that fit too tightly across her bosom and pinched her already tiny waist so tightly she'd have red marks on her skin when she removed it—seemed to grow tighter and tighter, more and more obviously a garment designed to incite men's lusts. Unable to defend herself with language to match Mrs. Foxe's, and not ever thinking that she might use her father's ruthless abuse of her to gain sympathy, Rosalind had reacted in the only way she knew to defend herself against the truth.

She became hostile, her resentment coated by a sweet coyness in her speech.

"What if Albert disagrees with you, Mrs. Foxe? Suppose he sees me as suitable? Suppose he'd like his friends to see me at his table? I am not so bad to look at, you know. Suppose Albert defies you?"

"He won't," Mrs. Foxe had said with firm resolution. Her face wore an unyielding expression of self-assurance.

Rosalind's hurt had flared into hot anger. "You're so bloody sure of yourself! You don't know everything about Albert! I could tell you a thing or two!"

Mrs. Foxe's head had gone back, retreating in disgust as she looked at Rosalind through lowered lids. The lacy handkerchief slowly wafted scent as she moved it under her aristocratic nose. "I am sure you could, but it wouldn't be worth hearing, nor would it be anything the downstairs maid couldn't tell me. Let me ask you about some of the things that do count. When did you last dine out with Albert? When did you last go to the theater? What was the last party you attended together? Have you ever received so much as one invitation to any of the better houses in the parish . . . or even in London? Shall I answer for you? Shall I tell you of the invitations Albert has received, or the parties he has attended and with whom? No, I shouldn't wish to humiliate you. You see, Rosalind, you are the love of Albert's life—behind doors. That is all it is now, and all it ever could be."

There had been little Rosalind could reply, and as if in confirmation of Mrs. Foxe's accusations her anger flamed hotter, and the crude, coarse language of the tavern leapt to her mind, robbing her of her last vestige of hope to answer Albert's imperious mother.

The conversation had left her shaken. Though Rosalind had spent hours practicing before a mirror the

proper way for a lady to sit, to move her body, to talk
with her eyes and fan, and though she had read every
book she could lay hands on so she could be "educated," Mrs. Foxe had ignored the fruits of her efforts
as thoroughly as she had discounted Rosalind's natural
charms.

Rosalind had been properly chastised and numbed.
Was her dream so unattainable? Was there no one who
wanted her honorably? Would she finally be forced to
know that what Rufus said was true—that her body
alone could bring her satisfaction, and little enough at
that?

For some time after that Rosalind had been wary
and vulnerable whenever she met a man who had
come from the landed classes. Mrs. Foxe's words were
always with her. She couldn't bear the thought of another of those wealthy spoiled men saying he loved
her and yet mocking her efforts to be like him.

When she first met Peter Berean, she had thought
him a laborer. He had no pretensions, and often as not
was dressed no better than the other patrons. His only
mark of distinction was that he was always immaculately clean. She was immediately drawn to him. He
was safe—no better than she—and if she had to be
"sold" for a night's pleasure, better to a man who was
handsome to look at and sweet to smell. Before long
she had convinced herself she wanted to be known as
his woman. Not a girl she knew would fail to be
monster-green jealous. And while that was not so
good as changing her name to Foxe and riding
through town in a beautiful gown and an elegant carriage, it wasn't so bad either.

Peter's courtship, however, had thrown her into
greater self-doubt than ever. He didn't paw her. He
didn't bargain with Rufus to use the upstairs bed-

room. He behaved as she imagined gentlemen were supposed to behave: as if she were a lady.

Rosalind alternated between delight as Peter resurrected her dreams of "being someone" and fear that if he didn't pull down the bodice of her blouse it was because he didn't find her appealing.

Then, worst of all, she discovered he wasn't what he appeared to be. He was James Berean's son. Next to the Foxes, there wasn't a more secure or admired family in the parish. She panicked and tried to stay away from him. Failing that, she tried to seduce him. Failing that, she burst into tears and poured out her heart and innermost secrets to him, telling him everything except her love of Albert Foxe. That one corner of longing she kept private, but the rest of her miserable life she told to Peter, thinking to drive him away before he chose to leave her.

Peter asked her to marry him.

Two days later, after a painful attempt to convince Albert he should defy his mother and marry her, Rosalind accepted Peter's proposal in a fit of angry revenge directed at Albert. Once betrothed, she began to hunt for motives that would make Peter as crass and dishonorable as the other men she had known. She found one possibility and clung to that as though she needed the means to continue thinking herself unworthy and worthless.

After listening to the laborers talk of Peter, Rosalind decided she was a "cause" to him. She convinced herself that it had been only Peter's brash idealism that had brought him to the point of marriage. She thought she understood him, but she had drawn the wrong conclusions from the right facts.

He liked causes and claimed to hate the traditions that held a man or woman to one class or another. He was a self-styled revolutionary, picking bits and pieces

of radical thought and putting them together in his
own way. She decided he thought himself a hero and
she was to become his heroine—a fittingly pathetic
damsel for Galahad to rescue. Let him use her as he
would; she had her own reasons for marrying him.

They married and Peter took her home to a family
Rosalind trusted no better than she trusted her husband. She entered the Berean family a stranger, and
through her defensiveness remained a stranger. She
was stubbornly certain that at the back of the Bereans' pretended good nature was a quiet laugh repeated over the joke that she was Rufus Hawkes's
daughter aspiring to a station for which she had no
talent.

She suffered their imagined mockery with a bitter
pride. She had climbed from the cellar of her former
life and was now a member of the landed gentry and
secretly the mistress of the youngest magistrate in the
parish. The Mrs. Foxes and the Bereans of the world
could sneer, but Rosalind Hawkes Berean was only
one step away from being of status equal to the Foxes,
and her hold on Albert was now far stronger than
that of a downstairs maid. It gave her a dreadful sense
of accomplishment, bitter and vengeful in its headi-
ness. But still it wasn't enough. To Rosalind, the day
she'd feel proud of herself, free to be liked by herself
and others, was the day Albert Foxe recognized her as
a lady, and admitted he should have married her . . .
would marry her if she'd have him. To be whole she
had to have what he and his mother had denied her.

There were frightening times when she doubted her
own desires. Then she would wonder why she let Albert near her. He wasn't half the man her husband
was. And while Peter had not been her first true love,
he was a loving man. He cared for her and though she
hadn't been able to bring herself to trust him, he said

he loved her. He made her laugh and forget for a time the demons that plagued her. And he made her wonder what might be coming next in their lives. He talked of great plans, of sea voyages and successes. Most of all he talked of leaving the hop farm and being on his own.

So far he hadn't done anything about these dreams. There was always an excuse. His father needed him. The laborers' problems required his attention. But at other times he swore he would be off to France to learn firsthand what the Frenchies had in mind with their bourgeois monarch. Off to America to have his own hop farm, maybe a brewery too. There was no telling what was fact and what was fiction with the man.

For all she knew he really was Captain Swing. It was within belief. As Meg often said, and annoyed her by the saying, Peter liked to play at life. Rosalind knew she was included in Meg's estimate of Peter's sincerity, and that was what rankled.

Meg had an innocent way of indicting Rosalind. Had she known the hours of discomfort and soul-searching she caused, Meg might never have told Rosalind that she spent a good deal of time spiting herself with her wild impetuous actions. But she had said it, and it had struck in Rosalind a target Meg knew nothing about.

The most impetuous act Rosalind had ever committed was beginning the affair with Albert. Even to herself she could not justify continuing it. She had nothing to gain. Albert had already made that abundantly clear. And she now had a great deal to lose. She could wind up back in her father's tavern. Peter was easygoing in most things, but he was quite capable of giving her the beating of her life before he tossed her out of his home. While she counted on Peter's desire for things to be happy and cheerful, she also knew that if he ever turned his back on her, he would never look her way again.

These possibilities frightened her. Yet at the end of the thread of morbid speculation was the hard knot of decision that told her she would not end the affair. She cringed at this; she could not look beyond it. The fact that she carried it on—urging, encouraging it with an impulse that had begun when Albert rejected her and had grown since into a compulsion—was humiliating and frightening.

She did things and she didn't know why. She didn't really dislike Natalie. But why Albert intended to marry the girl, Rosalind would never understand. It negated all she knew about him. Rosalind throbbed with life; her blood coursed through her with a fury that had to be expended, and Albert liked that. Why would he choose to marry a delicate, childlike creature like Natalie and leave Rosalind behind? Surely family lineage and property and politics could not mean so much to a man that he'd deny his own love, his own body, Rosalind thought, and felt the sick sinking within at the realization that she might not know or comprehend the ways of Albert's class after all.

Was that why she had never been able to get over Albert? Was that the reason she clung to him, teased him, taunted him so that in this minor way he would never completely leave her, and always leave some hope that his mother was wrong? She had to admit she spent as much time thinking about Mrs. Foxe as she did about Albert. She was never completely sure if she was having an affair with Albert or one *against* his mother.

But then Rosalind seldom knew what she was for and what she was against. Even before she met Albert, she knew that someday she wanted to marry someone like him. Her dreams of herself, which were frequent, were all dreams of wanting, so fierce that the night didn't end them, nor the day temper them.

It was very late when Peter came to bed that night after Callie's arrival, but Rosalind was still awake wrestling with her doubts. He turned to her, stroking her hip. She lay still and he kissed her neck, then, thinking she was asleep, turned away.

It was a long night for her. Sleep wouldn't come. Peace of mind was distant. Fear of always being chained to Albert warred with her jealous fear of losing Peter's patient love. He slept untroubled the few hours left to him, and Rosalind listened and tried to take comfort in the even sound of his breathing.

"Did you really think she was that pretty?" she asked in the morning darkness as he began to stir.

"Who? What are you talking about?" he muttered groggily, and then opened his eyes peering into the murky room. "Are you still thinking about Callie?"

His humor was good, as it was most mornings. He stretched and yawned, wishing for summer months when he didn't always rise and go to bed in darkness.

"You don't think she is prettier than I am, do you?"

"She is different. Anyway she is far younger."

"And I am old!? She isn't that much younger than I!"

"She is still a child," he said and thought: *and terrified of me*.

"Everyone is going to think she is prettier than I am. They all make a fuss over her." She began to cry softly into his shoulder. He had little patience for tears. It was Albert on whom she could effectively turn her tears, but this morning Peter didn't seem to mind.

He didn't really want to put his foot down on the cold floor and wash himself in the even colder water.

Momentarily he thought enviously of Frank, whose water Anna would have warmed for him. He turned to Rosalind, lifting her chin so she looked him in the face. Gently he wiped the tears from her cheeks, kissing her as he murmured softly of her beauty. Caressingly, he told her what she wanted to hear.

"Oh, Peter, I could be all those things . . . I could be beautiful and . . ."

"You are, love, to me you are everything you've ever wanted to be." He untied the ribbons of her nightgown. She looked at him, confused, poised between helping him disrobe her, and grasping the nightgown modestly against her. He kissed her ear, wishing himself more patient. Better than she knew, Peter understood what tormented her. He knew how she was afraid to let him see her passion lest he think her cheap. He knew the damage her father had done, and he knew how the men of the tavern had misused her when she was little more than a child. Slowly, careful not to upset the balance between what she thought was "clean loving" and what she thought was "dirty loving" he made love to her.

Beneath him Rosalind lay demure and unresponsive, her head turned to one side in emulation of how she thought a lady should behave.

Easily and gently Peter stroked her, parting her legs. He kissed her, his mouth lingering on her breasts, teasing her nipples to hard buds. He waited, holding back, caressing her with his hands and eyes, patient for the moment when Rosalind, his imitation lady, would vanish, allowing Rosalind, his love, to burst free of her self-imposed prison to writhe in cat-like ecstasy in answer to his growing urgency.

Later, spent and happy, Peter lay beside her, loving better the smell of her sexuality than he did the violet water she bathed in. Their bodies were moist and sweaty under the blankets in the cold room. She snuggled close in the curve of his arm, all her fears and doubts forgotten. For these moments she was safe. Peter moved away from her slightly, knowing that any minute his father or Frank would be calling him. He was already late to breakfast.

"They don't need you this once," she murmured, warm and sleepy, "but I do."

Frank's loud voice shouting Peter's name came from below.

Peter glanced at the door, then at his wife. "Get up with me. Come downstairs. We'll have breakfast and talk."

"Stay here. Please, Peter. It's so cold . . . I'm freezing, Peter, I can't get up . . . there's no fire in the grate. Stay with me."

Half angry because she made him feel as though he were deserting her, he snapped without thinking, "Anna keeps Frank's fire going. It is she who worries that *he* might be cold."

"Anna is an old cow! You wouldn't like me to be like Anna. All she does is wait on him. She is used to all that. She had five brothers."

"And you, milady, are used to nothing but satin and silken hands attending you."

"I hate you when you talk like that!" she burst out, sitting up and clutching the blanket close against her. Then she squeezed out two more tears and flopped back down against the pillows. "You don't really love me at all. You wish you had a wife like that cow Anna. Or Callie."

He grinned and looked over at her a split second before he leaped onto the bed, pulling the blankets off her. She shrieked as the cold air and Peter hit her at the same time.

"I'll yell the house down!"

"No you won't, wife. You'll shut up and get your satin and silk backside off the sheets and downstairs with me or I'll ride you down the stairs like a piebald mare."

"I won't do it!"

"Then I'll take both Callie and Anna to wife and leave you crying at the gate."

"Ha!"

"You think Anna won't give me a hot cup of coffee? Or Callie? I could go to her room right now, and she'd be downstairs and in the kitchen before the last word was out of my mouth," he said, meaning it.

She stared at him with equal seriousness. "You are filled with conceit, Peter Berean. Not all women are madly in love with you as you think."

"You've put the wrong light on things. Get up. I've no more time to waste."

She got up, but the fun had gone from the morning. He was out of sorts and vaguely angry, and she was once again in her muddle of confusion, guilt, and indecision.

After he left she sat alone at the kitchen table. Getting up so early made the day intolerably long, filled with hours of waiting and only moments of excitement. Her thoughts traveled to Albert. She was supposed to meet him after he returned home with Natalie.

Albert thought nothing of that. He would take Natalie to tea with his mother. They would wait on the girl, fawn over her, make much of her, and then Albert would bring her back to the farm. Moments later he would leave to meet Rosalind in the hop pickers' cottage. There he would make love to her as if no comment were being made by the difference in his treatment of the two women.

Why did she go? She wouldn't. This time she

wouldn't. That would tell him something she often wished she had the nerve to say to his face. And tonight she would be extra nice to Peter. That would make up for everything.

Determined and feeling sorry for herself, Rosalind straightened the kitchen and walked with unusual speed toward the scullery. In a way it cheered her up. Meg would be completely nonplussed when she learned it was Rosalind up and about cleaning this morning.

"Most likely she'll think it was Anna, and that will be that." Rosalind, broom in hand, took another fast swish around the room and quickly passed over the idea of leaving a note informing Meg that it had been she who had been up so early and industriously.

Let her think it was Anna. Let her think anything she liked. Empty-handed now and already bored, she thought of the promised meeting late this afternoon in the cottage as she walked back to the staircase. She was safest asleep, putting off the hours of the day one at a time. She was stronger if she had less time to face all the weaknesses she didn't understand or like in herself.

Albert told her it was because she was ashamed of her father. Peter often teased her of having a chip on her shoulder. Meg said she was lazy. Natalie thought her mean and grasping. Her father said she was a slut like her mother. Rosalind didn't know what she was. They were all wrong about her, but they each had a part of the whole. She was always hungry for something. Always dissatisfied with what she had. Always worried that it wouldn't be real or lasting. Always wondering why she couldn't be like everyone else. Always hating it when she wasn't treated specially.

She slept, or let everyone think she was asleep, until

noon. Meg came down early and saw the kitchen. She promptly thanked Anna.

"But I didn't do this," Anna said, shaking her head. "It must have been Natalie."

"Nattie didn't do it." Meg laughed. "You know Nattie; she'd forget to put the broom away or she'd leave the pans out. Well, whoever it was, I thank them."

At noon Rosalind came out of her room to find Anna busy as always in her sewing room.

"Did you just get up, Rosalind?" Anna asked smiling. There was no malice in Anna or her question.

"Yes, I just got up," she answered, feeling defiant and cornered for no reason. "Peter doesn't like to see me working like a common servant all day."

"I'm sure he doesn't. Peter is very proud of his pretty wife."

"And why not! I try to make myself attractive. I think it's part of a wife's duty."

"Oh, so do I," Anna agreed quickly. "You're fortunate nature provided you with so much beauty to start. You're very lucky."

Rosalind was never sure what to make of Anna. It seemed impossible that she meant all she said, that she was never jealous or spiteful behind her perpetually nice remarks. Anna was no beauty. Her soft brown eyes were her best feature, but even they were so softly colored and placid in expression that they blended into the general plainness of her face and body. Anna *was* a cow.

Rosalind watched her methodically put away thread and chalk. How did you reply to a cow? How did one know what a cow was thinking or meaning with her amiable sounds?

"I think Callie woke up late today. Perhaps she'd have a bite to eat with you, Rosalind. She's downstairs with Mother Berean. I liked her quite well, didn't you? She's a pretty little thing. I think she'll be regal looking—just like a queen when she is grown up and can carry all that height and hair. Oh, that hair! Natalie brushed and arranged it for her this morning. Callie looked positively beautiful! Nattie has such a way with hair."

"Nattie is a pest. Maybe Callie didn't want her hair done."

"Nattie means well. She is kinder and gentler than most of us." Anna looked dreamily out the window. "Sometimes I wonder what it is like to be like Natalie. She is so appealing and helpless with her frail beauty."

"I doubt you'd like it."

"I think I might. She's so unlike me, Rosalind. All my life I'll work. I'll always be the strong, solid housewife. Someday I'll probably be called Mother Berean . . . and have a house full of grown children, and I'll still be working and worrying about Frank and the farm. I couldn't do anything else if I tried, but Natalie will never do any of that. She'll be taken care of, cosseted and cherished. She's different from you and me. Peter can look at you, and Frank at me, and know we're all right . . . capable of meeting whatever comes. But it won't be like that for Natalie. Albert will always provide for her. She won't ever meet with difficulty, because he will never let anything touch her. Don't you wonder what it would be like to have that kind of devotion poured on you? I do."

Rosalind watched Anna, aghast. Her nostrils flared, her ringlets trembled as she clenched her fists tightly at her side. "What nonsense! The only reason Natalie won't meet with difficulty is because she isn't capable of doing anything. I'm going outside for some fresh air!" She hurried down the stairs, stung and stronger in her resolve not to see Albert that afternoon.

"Let him have Natalie! Let him do without me and then see who he wants—me or his little butter lump that has to be kept at proper temperature or melt away to nothing," she muttered to herself as she walked to the stable yard. She called to Marsh, the Bereans' factotum, in no ladylike voice to hook up the carriage and bring it round for her.

"Can't drive you today, Miz Rosalind."

"And why not!?"

"Bringin' in the turnips. I've got to drive for Mr. James."

"Someone else can drive the cart. I need you to drive me to Seven Oaks. Surely you realize how annoyed Mr. Berean would be if you left me without a driver."

Marsh climbed slowly to the driver's seat. "Mr. Berean is going to be unhappy when he doesn't see me comin' across the field wi' his cart. That's what I know."

Rosalind whiled away the hours in Seven Oaks until it was impossible to make the return trip in time to meet Albert. He would go to the cabin and find it empty. He would sit there, pulling out his watch and studying it every five minutes. He would walk to the small window and peer into the woods expecting the flash of her cloak among the trees. He would be angry and disappointed and humiliated.

She smiled as Marsh started for home still complaining that she had taken him from his proper duties. She paid no attention to the old man. Her head was filled with imaginary scenes of her triumph.

"Meet you? Oh! Oh, Albert . . . how could I have forgotten?" Or: "I was tired. I didn't feel up to it." "It was too cold." "Seven Oaks is such a place for meeting people. I lost track of the time."

There were so many things, and so many ways she

would tell him that he wasn't half so important to her as he thought he was.

It wasn't until she was nearly home that she had a sobering thought. How could she know for a certainty that Albert had shown up? Suppose he hadn't gone to the cottage at all? What if he said nothing . . . didn't even know she hadn't been there? Suppose he never realized that she could turn her back on him whenever she wanted? It would ruin everything. Her whole long miserable day would be worth nothing.

In a twinkling her triumph of willpower crumpled. She returned to the house as uncertain and angry as she had been when she left.

The first person she saw was Natalie, coming eager-eyed to the door to see who had arrived.

"Where did you go, Rosalind? Albert and I had the most lovely afternoon. His mother likes me! I think if she had her way Albert and I would be married immediately. She is so kind and thoughtful. She insisted Albert take me for a long carriage ride, and then we went to see their hounds. I saw the loveliest little puppy."

"Isn't that just the nicest thing. Nice, nice, nice!" Rosalind fled up the stairs leaving Natalie standing in the hall.

Chapter 8

Natalie watched as Rosalind ran up the stairs; then she began to don her outdoor clothes. Her pale green coat fit snugly around her waist. In the hall mirror her reflection wavered in the uneven glass as she fastened the ties to her darker green bonnet. Her eyes, large and dark, stared back from the mirror, inviting her to confide to the one person who understood her— herself. As happened so often, the voices in her mind began to talk, mulling over the problems that tormented her.

She didn't blame Albert for his affair. It was Rosalind she condemned. Natalie knew her for the temptress she was. Hadn't she bewitched Peter? Hadn't she wormed her way into the bosom of Natalie's family to cause dissension and heartache?

Before Rosalind had come to live with them, Natalie had always confided in Peter. In many ways she had been closer to him than to her mother or father. She had always looked up to him, looked to him for understanding. It had always been so until Rosalind had beckoned and bewitched him. Then it was as if

Peter had forgotten Natalie existed. There were no more quiet talks or shared moments of joy or sorrow.

Natalie loathed Rosalind, but Peter now came in for his share of the blame. She had loved him, put her trust in him, and he had betrayed her. He had left her alone with no one to confide in or to lean upon for strength. For that, Natalie had no doubt, Peter would have to pay, just as all the weak and evil people of the world would one day have to atone for their wrong-doings. She wasn't sure how this would come about, but there was in her a burning certainty that it would. Too much had happened for it to be otherwise.

Mrs. Foxe had told her of the shameless way Rosalind had thrown herself at Albert before Peter had fallen prey to her wiles. More than once Natalie had been tempted to tell her brother what a cuckolded fool he was, but she was never certain that was a fitting punishment for him, so she waited and held her tongue. She would tell him only when the time was right—when he would feel the same despair and abandonment that she had known when Peter had married Rosalind. He hadn't needed to do that to her. It was cruel. He knew how much she needed him. But she would pay him in kind—when the time was right.

She smiled tightly, her bleak eyes becoming intelligent again as she forced her habitual optimism on herself. The world was supposed to be a glorious place—an Eden as God intended. It made her feel tight inside and frightened when it was not. Sometimes it was as difficult to trust God as it was to trust Peter. It didn't seem right or fair for a God to entice her with tales of Eden and then deny her their reality. Nor did it seem right that a God would bestow free will on the very creatures who would willfully destroy that Eden. But as always she laid blame where it was most easily tolerable. The world divided between evil and good.

Natalie remained heartbreakingly loyal to her wishes for a beautiful world and adamantly committed to crushing the evil interlopers whenever she could. There was beauty, she insisted to herself; it required only the faith and discipline to see it.

She looked out at the cloudy, lightless day. Her fists were clenched as she stared hard at the overcast sky. Then she relaxed, successful. She was in a world encapsulated by a silver sky, a heavy, heavenly sky.

Pleased with herself, she went to the stables. There were two new litters of pups. She had been waiting impatiently for Will, the stable hand, to tell her she could take the pups from their mothers. She greeted him cheerfully.

Will smiled broadly, shaking his head. "Just can't wait, can you, miss? Well, they're all yours now. Prettiest bunch of pups we ever had."

Natalie slid into the stall Will had set aside for the dogs, careful not to let any of the puppies out.

She sat on the straw, covering her lap with squirming pups. One, the runt, slithered off her skirt, squealing and struggling to right itself. Natalie laughed and was immediately enamored of the miserable little dog. She pushed the other puppies away and gathered the shivering frightened runt into the cradle of her arms. "Oh, ugly, ugly little pup. You must be my own. You are mine!" She held the pup up, touching her nose to the puppy's cold, wet snout. The dog sneezed, shook his head, and began licking her. His tail wagged frantically, making his small rotund body wriggle in her hands. She hugged him to her. "You are like me inside out. You're ugly on the outside and nice on the in. Perhaps you were sent to me—to remind me." She returned him to his mother, then rose to leave. At the stall gate she turned back. "Good-bye, Ugly. Remember you are mine."

For a moment Natalie stood outside the stables undecided. Perhaps the puppy really had been sent to her for a purpose. For days she'd been feeling one of her hopeless sad moods coming on. She tried to fight it, though it was difficult for she felt so totally alone. She hated those awful times when everything seemed so hopeless; people who were supposed to love her became heartless; nothing was beautiful and good. Natalie became so lost in the labyrinthine complexities of her warped reasoning, she often succeeded in hurting herself as much as others did. Even now she felt a growing anger, a temptation to walk to the hop pickers' cottage—to one particular cottage—and torment herself with the sight of the small room, the char-blackened hearth, the bed that always showed signs of having been used. The sight was painful, but it would also bring cleansing rage.

But it was wrong. There was a time when she understood why it was bad for her to go to the cottage and allow the rage to well up inside. Now she no longer knew. Reasons had become vague and confused, as had so many things. There remained only the residue of a memory that taunting herself with the cottage was taboo.

It was difficult for her to tear her eyes from the path through the woods that would lead to the cottages. Though she knew perfectly well that Rosalind was in her room, Natalie could all too well *see* her skirts swaying as she hurried down the path to Albert.

She shuddered, the mood creeping up on her. A fleeting moment of panic enveloped her, making her terrifyingly aware that she trod a narrow line between sanity and madness. She lived in dread of crossing that thin line, and now frantically pushed her confused mind toward some activity to protect herself. She began to walk, then run, to the potting shed.

Once inside its fragrant interior she felt better. Everything would be all right now. The potting shed held no fears; she had filled it with beauty. From the beams hung great bunches of flowers she had dried last summer and fall. Along the narrowly shelved walls were jars of crushed rose petals and perfumed spices. She selected several flowers. Her small delicate hands moved gracefully and nimbly as she fashioned the lovely blue and violet flowers into a pleasing arrangement. Singing now, she carried the flowers to the house.

"Callie! Callie, where are you?" Her voice sounded cheerful even to her own ears. She was surprised, for the effort to be happy was becoming more difficult. The vision of a forest path to the pickers' cottage kept intruding. The only emotion she was still able to feel honestly welled up in her, making her pulse race. With her jaw clenched she allowed the fearful hatred to seethe and flow out of her. Then she saw the image of her brother's handsome, laughing face. It took on the countenance of a jeering death's-head, and Natalie clapped her hand over her mouth to keep the wild laughter from escaping. How anxious she was to tell him of his wife's faithlessness. How good it would be not to be so alone, to have him share her deadly quiet panic. Together, she and Peter would feel nothing. Pain, hope, trust, disappointment, would die. Frightened again, Natalie hurried to the steps. The stairwell she ascended was distorted. Sounds rang in her ears too loud to bear and too soft to grasp. "Callie!?" Natalie ran the last few steps to Callie's room. She forced herself to slow down, catch her breath, and smile. Her voice was high and childish. "I have a surprise for you."

Callie looked up reluctantly from the novel she was reading, her finger holding her place. Then she dropped the book, her face lighting with pleasure. "For me?"

"Yes, for you. A gift for my new sister." Natalie held out the bouquet. "The blue flowers match your eyes and the violet . . ." Natalie paused, suddenly confused between herself and Callie; then she went on, ". . . they match the sadness of your heart. Next time I'll bring you a pink bouquet . . . or a gold one . . . for happiness. I don't know why I chose violet. It seemed . . ."

Callie buried her face in the flower petals. "They're so beautiful! My father used to bring me flowers. I'd keep them until they wilted. I never knew you could preserve them like this. Would you teach me?"

Natalie looked skeptical. The mood stirred and threatened to take over. Then it vanished again. "Would you really like to learn?"

Callie nodded, her attention on the flowers.

Natalie sighed and tried to take Callie at her word. It was so hard to believe in the goodness of others when the mood kept threatening her. "I'd like some help drying the flowers. There are always so many to be done. It's a big job and I must always do it alone. Rosalind isn't interested, and Anna and Mama say the hop picking is too important for them to take time out for my flowers; but it is important! All winter we have brightness in our house because of my flowers. You like them, don't you?"

"Oh, yes," Callie breathed. "I love flowers."

Natalie smiled. "I hoped you would. Oh, Callie—I think you are truly going to be my sister . . . and my friend. I've never really had a friend . . . not a real one." Natalie sat down on the edge of the bed. "Friends should be someone special. They should understand. You understand, I think."

"Understand what?"

"Things. How important it is to be happy . . . like my flowers. They make the house look happy even when the cold and rain and wind howl in the dark outside. It's even more important to feel happy when you're afraid inside."

"Afraid," Callie said tentatively. "You have nothing to be afraid of . . . not here. Do you?"

"There is always something to be afraid of."

Callie laughed nervously. "No—there isn't."

Natalie smiled, her eyes gleaming mischievously. "Didn't you play scaring games when you were little?"

"Oh, well, that doesn't count. That isn't real . . ." Callie jumped, scrambling off the bed as Natalie let out a bloodcurdling shriek.

"Tell me that wasn't real! You were scared." Natalie giggled. "You nearly jumped out of your skin."

Anna pounded up the stairs. Breathlessly she came into the room. "What's happened? Are you all right? I heard someone scream . . ."

Natalie laughed. "Oh, poor Anna! I'm sorry. Callie and I were trying to scare each other. You should have seen her! I thought surely she'd climb straight up the wall."

Anna laughed weakly. "Well, you girls scared me. No more. Please."

Callie's heart was still pounding wildly. She fussed with the knickknacks on her dresser, trying to rid herself of the terrible jumpy feeling.

As soon as Anna returned downstairs, Callie turned to Natalie. "Why did you do that! You screeched like a horrible old barn owl! I still feel all creepy and crawly."

"I told you there was always something to be afraid of." Natalie got up, went to Callie, and took her hand. "I'm sorry. Sit down and I'll fix your hair for you. The brushing will be soothing and I might tell you a secret."

Callie hesitated, then sat down, pulling the pins from her long honey-colored hair. "What kind of secret? No more spooky stuff?"

Natalie began to brush in slow, gentle strokes. "A good secret. But since you are such a doubter, I don't know that I'll tell you."

Slowly Callie relaxed, liking the easy pull of the brush. "Natalie! Now you have me bursting to know. If I ask you to tell me you are likely to shriek in my ear and frighten me to death, and if I don't ask it is likely to be something wonderful."

Natalie giggled. "What a dilemma you have, new little sister."

"Oh, tell me. Please, tell me now."

"Nooo . . ." Natalie said slowly, laughter in her voice. "I don't think I'd better. It's not really my secret to tell."

Callie twisted in her chair. "Whose then? Tell me! You're such an awful tease!"

"All right. I'll tell you that much. It's Peter's secret . . . and Stephen's."

"Peter's?" Callie said softly, then fell silent.

Natalie peered around at her. "What? No more questions?"

"No. It's not your secret to tell. I don't want to know anyway."

"Oh, what a nit! I think you are the most frightened little rabbit I've ever seen. Why are you afraid of Peter?"

"I am not frightened! I just don't care to know."

"You are too, frightened. Everyone knows you avoid Peter. Whatever will you do when he comes for you on Sunday?"

"What do you mean? Why—c-comes for me? Where is he taking me?"

"Wouldn't you like to know. Maybe to the dungeons."

"Natalie! This isn't funny. Tell me!"

"Sit still. I can't do your hair if you keep twisting around. You're getting all tangles."

"I don't want you to fix my hair. Tell me—what is Peter going to do?"

"I told you, it's a secret, and anyway you said you weren't interested."

"Natalie, please . . ." Callie stood up and faced her. "Tell me. I must know."

Natalie stamped her foot. "I take it all back! Every word! You are not my sister. Look what you've done. You've ruined it. I hope Peter does something awful to you that you'll never forget! I worked hard on your hair and now look!" At the door Natalie stopped and looked back. "Don't blame me for the way you look, and don't ask me to help you untangle it!"

Natalie stormed down the hall, slapping the brush against her thigh. Callie stood in the doorway indecisively. Part of her wanted to run after Natalie, yet she knew she would only annoy her further. She sat back down, picked up her book, glanced at the page, then tossed the book aside. She wrapped a scarf around her wild hair, ran down the stairs, grabbed her coat from the hall tree, and hurried out into the cold freshness of the farmyard.

Chapter 9

Callie didn't think about the mysterious secret for Sunday. She didn't allow herself to do so. Natalie's teasing had upset her badly enough despite her knowing that teasing was all that it was. Tearfully, Callie longed for the days when she had never felt afraid. They seemed so long ago. Being afraid had always meant the tantalizing wonder if witches truly rode the night sky on All Hallow's Eve, or listening to the scary imaginings of Mrs. Pettibone or her father. Never in her fourteen years had she experienced this nameless kind of fear, which seemed to magnify itself. Before her father's death, Callie remembered only pleasant days filled with security and well-being. Now all of that was gone. Its replacement had been fear. Vague, anonymous, insidious—creeping up on her from the most ordinary places and occurrences. It had become a habit with her, a habit she didn't know how to overcome.

She closed her mind against Sunday, against the habit of fear. She kept herself busy through Thursday, Friday, and Saturday helping May with the cheese making and Anna in the sewing room and doing odd chores for Meg in the house and for Stephen in the brewhouse. What little time there was left on the short wintery days she spent with Natalie, sometimes in the stables playing with the puppies, sometimes allowing Natalie to teach her to ride a horse. She wasn't overly fond of the beasts, who loved to nip at her boots when she mounted, and whose friendly, nuzzling searches for sugar treats tended to be rough and direct. But mastering the horse and herself astride the animal required all her concentration, leaving little time for her overwrought and morbid imagination to draw visions of a catastrophe awaiting her on Sunday.

When finally Sunday arrived, it had all the markings of an ordinary day. The household awakened and stirred at the normal time. The wintery March sky was leaden and heavy with unfallen rain, or perhaps snow judging from the frigid coldness of her room.

Breakfast odors wafted up the staircase tempting her to get up and dress. At the table James wasted no time in saying the morning prayers, and the nine of them ate in near silence until Meg began to fuss, urging them to hurry or they would be late for church.

All through the service and the lengthy sermon Callie kept her eyes squeezed shut, her hands clasped so tightly in prayer her knuckles hurt and her bloodless fingers were numb. She prayed to the Savior, to the Precious Blood, to His Holy Mother and the Archangels, to keep her safe. And she prayed to some nameless, personal Savior that the Father would have time to hear her pleas.

It appeared that He did, for when they returned home from church, it was already time for supper. Darkness and early bed would not be far behind, and then, with blessed sleep, the Sunday would be gone, laid to rest alongside other dead days.

Shortly after they had eaten, the family retired to the parlor. Natalie played the harpsichord, and James let his head fall back against his chair, a smile on his face as he was soothed by the sound of his daughter's music. Callie hardly noticed that Peter hadn't joined them. He often didn't, having matters of his own to attend to. But she did note that Stephen wasn't there. She had become quite close to him, counting on his willing and gentle company, basking in the affection he gave so easily and so often. She wished he were there now for she was enjoying Natalie's music and knew that he would have silently shared that pleasure with her.

The door opened, letting a cold, damp wind blow across them. Natalie looked up, her fingers poised above the keys. She smiled broadly, then played a gay little fanfare.

"Everybody put your coats on," Peter said. "Everything is ready."

Meg and James exchanged amused glances. Frank sighed, as if going along with something he thought so much silliness. Anna and Rosalind went to fetch the many coats and scarves. Natalie glowed, her soft laugh an added merriment. Only Callie remained in her seat, frozen.

Smiling, Stephen came over to her, her coat in his hands. "Come on, Callie."

"I don't want to."

"It's a surprise for you. Come along. I'll be with you."

She shook her head woodenly. "It's raining."

"Please—for me. I promise I'll stay right with you. You'll be glad you came."

Before she could answer, the rest of the family, standing by the door, chorused that she should hurry.

Still she held back, embarrassed but too frightened

to act brave. Then she wished she had, for Peter separated himself from the others. "Go on ahead. I'll bring Callie. Go on, Stephen."

Stephen handed Peter her coat and scarf. The door closed leaving her alone with Peter.

"Put your coat on, Callie."

She did as she was told, thankful he didn't touch her or try to help her.

"The surprise is for you. Stephen and I wanted you to have something special . . ." He seemed unsure of himself, but he went on. "I know—at least I suppose—things have not been easy for you, and I'm sorry for that. I'm sorry I frightened you so badly—I don't understand it. But I was hoping . . . well, perhaps our surprise will tell you what I wish for you. If I could change things for you, I would. Now come along. The others are waiting in the rain."

Callie had hardly heard him. When he took her arm it felt like wood, unresponsive and stiff. She walked at his side like a puppet, her eyes wide, fixed and staring. She was barely sensible. Whatever fears she had, they were not based on reality. They went far beyond that, and Callie lived in a tormented world of dreadful imagination. He might have been walking her to the gallows for all the anticipation she showed for the surprise. He felt tired and old, beaten and remorseful. He should have left her alone. Only a fool would have thought otherwise. A stupid gesture, such as the one he and Stephen had made with their surprise, couldn't give back to Callie the youthful zest for life she had somehow lost. He had been a naive idiot to think it could. Something had frozen the girl deep at her core. Only time could heal it, he thought, then mentally shook himself for the idiocy of that thought too. Time healed nothing.

Time hadn't healed the hunger of the laborer. Time

hadn't healed men's lust for profit. Time hadn't healed
the depraved need to exploit the helpless. Time hadn't
healed the wounds lust and abuse had left on Rosalind. Only goodness healed. Only goodness would heal
Rosalind. Only goodness would heal Callie, and that
he didn't know how to give, for it was God's gift.

At the front door he told her to close her eyes.
Again she obeyed. A puppet. Sadly Peter wondered
what kind of fear and despair could make a human
being obey anything on command. Stumbling, but
rigidly obedient, she walked across the slippery,
muddy yard, forced to cling to his arm with cold
deathlike hands.

"Callie, there's no need to be so frightened. My
brother and I built you a bower—a place filled with
the warmth and color of May. Open your eyes, Callie,
and see that even now in the rain and the cold there is
still a place of beauty. There is always such a place."
He felt like a fool. His words sounded stilted and pe-
dantic, yet he kept talking, almost desperately, wishing somehow that it was possible to make a world for
her as it should be.

Callie opened her eyes. Before her in the drizzling
rain stood the May house, a small structure built in
the cold and the wind, covered with boughs of green
and bedecked with hundreds of Natalie's dried flowers. Muted by the mist, marigolds and pinks mingled
with delicate blue-and-violet cornflowers. The flowers of the field nestled snugly against their more so-
phisticated brethren of the garden.

She took a step farther into the May house, no
longer aware of the Bereans. Inside it smelled of the
earth, a moist, rich smell. Then she smelled the pine
and the heady scent of newly moistened dried rose
petals. Bathed in the misting rain the dried flowers
came alive again. On their petals stood tiny crystal

droplets, brilliant and clean. The flowers, as dried up as Callie, softened in the moisture, their colors once more natural, their pliancy renewed for this brief moment. The March grayness disappeared in Callie's mind. She no longer noticed the cold or the wintery wind that stirred the pine boughs and occasionally threatened to dislodge the flowers from the May house walls. Inside of her spring began, its special warmth flowing through her, thawing, living.

She saw things as she hadn't been able to for months. Entwined in the branches was the Bereans' welcome. Their love was secured there as were the flowers. Caring had gone into the cold hours Stephen and Peter had spent building it after they had completed a long day's work. And Natalie's pride, her flowers, were there, given freely. In the May house she finally saw the Bereans clearly—all of them, even Peter.

Slowly the enormity of what James and Meg offered her came clear. They wanted her. The Bereans had opened their arms to her from the start. The strangeness had not been in them, it had been in her. It was she who had prayed to God to protect her from them—from Peter—and He had answered her through a loving act by the man she had feared.

The tears streamed down her face. It seemed to her that in her May house the sun shone as brightly as it might any May morning. It shone everywhere but in the one spot where she stood. She had so much to atone for.

She turned suddenly, her face wet with tears, to look at Peter. He stood at the entrance to the May house, concerned, his face lined with doubt.

"Oh, Peter, forgive me," she said, tears bursting from her. She ran to him as she might have run to her father when she needed his protective guidance in understanding some new and momentous feeling.

His arms closed around her. "Ahh, Callie, don't cry. It's nothing—just a May house. I shouldn't have forced you to come."

She shook her head against him. "No, no, I didn't understand . . . I didn't know . . . I . . . the men at Mrs. Peach's . . . I thought you were like that. I'm so sorry. Oh, Peter, I'm so awful."

He patted her, then took his handkerchief from his pocket, trying to wipe her tears and blow her nose for her. All but incoherent, Callie continued to babble out the whole tale of Mrs. Peach and her infamous business.

Rosalind took several steps backward. She watched wide-eyed, listening to a story resembling her own; then she had to turn away, her hand against the pounding pulse at her throat. She felt as though her world were crumbling. Her whole life had been peopled with men and women she couldn't trust, people who used her, who left her when she needed them. Peter had been the exception. Despite her complaining and nagging, she had believed he would always be with her. He'd be the one who would never turn from her, never leave her. Now she was frightened as though he were already gone.

She looked back to her husband and Callie with sad eyes; then her jealousy began to grow. Why had she never been able to cry as Callie was now? Why couldn't she tell her innermost shameful secrets and believe someone would listen to her and like her? Why had she always to be so alone with her doubts and fears? Rosalind had never been able to bear her soul so completely. She had always known everyone would hate her and *know* whatever evil there was, was in her.

She turned from Peter and Callie again and ran from the May house, envying Callie and hating her at the same time.

The rest of the Bereans stood stunned, helpless and moved by the wrenching outpouring. James Berean cocked his head, indicating they should leave. Peter looked at his father, seeking guidance.

"Let her talk," James said quietly. "It's what she needs. Just be patient, son. It's not important that it make sense to you. It does to her." James motioned to Stephen to join him.

Stephen stood near the rear of the May house, his own blue eyes bright with tears. He looked with longing at Callie, wishing that it had been to him she had turned. Slowly he moved past his father into the rain.

James left the May house, stopping for a moment at the entrance to look at his son and the girl. He was not certain what he had witnessed, but he knew somehow that it would affect them all. He was not a fanciful man, nor was he given to premonitions, but he had never seen anything so sad, nor anything so natural, as he watched Callie and Peter clinging to one another, drawing strength and the power to heal. He felt puzzled and uncustomarily removed from reality as he walked back through the rain to the house.

Peter watched his father leave; then his attention returned to Callie. He hardly knew what to do with her. Her whole body shook with her sobs and still she continued to explain. He listened to her tell that terrible story of ill fortune, crime, and terror, and he held her tighter. He could feel the fear and horror pouring from her, and he felt angry.

He didn't know what he was angry about, or at whom to direct it, but it was there, big and strong inside him. He wanted to fight the thing or people responsible for harming her. As he did at the laborers' meetings, he felt an urgent, surging power of idealism that made him see the simplicity of justice. Men were good. They had only to practice it. Good was simplicity itself. Yet he did not know how to give it to others. Often at the meetings he had said in his strong clear voice, "It is the abandonment of evil. It is the relinquishment of cruelty. We must not harm the farmers or any other living soul, or we can never win our battle for justice. We strive for fairness and justice for you. It cannot be gained by the perpetration of foul deeds, nor built upon the carcass of iniquity." They listened to him. Some agreed. All believed, but none practiced it, at least not fully. The striving for a better world was always relegated to a future in which it would be easier to be Christian once the laborers had gotten what they wanted. He had heard the same thing from the farmers. All of them would like to give fair wages and would—just as soon as the government gave them what they wanted.

He rocked Callie, murmuring words of comfort in her ear, and in his belly and chest there was the aching hurt that came again and again when he knew no one would stop hurting another until he himself was no longer being hurt. Who were these people depraved enough to hurt Callie? Why?

He cupped his hand beneath her chin, bringing her head up until she met his gaze. "No one will harm you again. I'd not let them."

Her eyes were the blue of the cornflowers nestled among the pines. From them shone hope and trust and love. The haunting fear might never have been. Peter's eyes held hers as he marveled at the power of the very young to begin again, knowing that was the true gift of life. "You'll come to me if you ever feel afraid again?"

She nodded, trying to smile.

He laughed in relief and hugged her fiercely. "Oh, Lord, I'd build you a May house for every day of your life if I could always keep you happy."

She laughed brokenly, hiccoughing and sniffling. "I want only this one."

Chapter 10

After the May house Sunday, the calendar lost meaning for Callie. Even in times past she couldn't remember being happier. Perhaps she'd never noticed before, but now it seemed that the Berean house constantly rang with laughter and hummed with activity. It seemed they were all emerging from a long, bitter winter.

All the work on the farm was divided casually among the members of the family. One did what one was best at. It was for Callie to find her particular niche. She set about this in a sort of frenetic joy. Her rich contralto could be heard through the house as she scrubbed like a scullery maid, polished furniture with the hired girls, learned to sew well enough to put Mrs. Pettibone's fine stitchery to shame, and mastered bread making to a fine art.

Callie grew in health and well-being with each day. She came to know each of the Bereans, feeling more and more a part of the family. Often she thought of Ian and how proud he'd be to see her now. There were few moments when Callie wasn't radiantly happy, and the Bereans in turn took to her and were warmed by her. Rosalind alone maintained a sour reserve, but she hadn't reckoned with Callie's persistence, nor her determination that Rosalind should behave as Peter deserved. The cooler Rosalind's attitude, the hotter Callie's pursuit. In time Rosalind's feeling became ambivalent. She was jealous and put out by Callie, and at the same time she wanted so badly to have the courage and freedom to do what Callie had done; she was fascinated by her. Occasionally Rosalind cooperated with Callie's constant plans, which mostly had to do with Peter.

"But what shall we do? Peter won't like this," Rosalind said in response to Callie's suggestion they take the noon meal to the fields. "He'll think we're daft . . . two silly women with their parasols." But there was a trace of excitement in her voice.

"You slice the bread while I get the fresh cheese. I think this is the best I've ever made and it's aged just right."

"Is there any pie left from last night, Callie?"

She grinned and pointed to the corner cupboard. "I baked tarts—just for the three of us. Peter's favorite—apple."

As the two of them finished packing the basket and enclosing it with a fresh cloth, Natalie entered the kitchen, her eyes hard on Rosalind, then softening as she looked at Callie. "Dinner outdoors? May I come?"

Rosalind's face fell; the lightheartedness she had just begun to feel disappeared. Callie looked sympathetically at Natalie. "Oh, Nattie, I'm sorry. I didn't think to ask you if you'd like to come. We've packed only for three, and there isn't time to change it now." Callie noted Natalie's glance at Rosalind, then at herself. "Rosalind sees so little of Peter lately, we thought we'd surprise him. Next time, I promise I'll plan for you to come too. Perhaps we could ask Albert and Stephen to join us."

Natalie said nothing, but Callie sensed her jealous anger. Quickly she suggested, "Let's go into Seven Oaks this afternoon, shall we? I'd love for you to help me select some new ribbons."

Natalie hesitated, then sauntered toward the door, looking back over her shoulder at Rosalind. "Perhaps—if Albert doesn't take me to tea with his mother."

Callie looked down at the neat white cloth-covered basket. "I'm sorry, Rosalind. I should have realized Natalie would want to go too."

Rosalind threw herself into the nearest chair. "It's all useless." She shoved the basket. "Peter doesn't care where he eats. I don't feel like going. I hate Natalie. She ruins everything. She thrives on it, the wretched bloody bitch!"

Callie cringed at the harsh savagery of Rosalind's voice. She liked Natalie and she liked Rosalind, but whenever the two women came together there was no standing either of them. Callie had tried on previous occasions to act as peacemaker and had been scolded, berated, and screamed at for her efforts.

She stood, waiting out Rosalind's tirade against Natalie. When it subsided she said calmly, "The bell's rung. The men will be going home for dinner. If we're to surprise Peter, we'd better hurry."

"Damn Peter. Let him eat with the other field hands. He prefers their company to mine. Just ask him."

"Well, if you don't want Nattie to think she spoiled your day, you'd better come anyway." Callie sighed dramatically. "But it's up to you." She began slowly to remove the white cover from the basket.

Rosalind slapped her hand. "You'll make us late," she snapped. "Come along!"

Rosalind strode to the fields, the fixed pout on her face giving Callie grave misgivings. She had been determined to give Peter a nice surprise and an unaccustomed, pleasant daytime hour with his wife. All she succeeded in doing was bringing him a waspish female, angry and ready to sting anyone in her path.

Callie felt her spirits rise momentarily as she saw Peter yelling jovially to Marsh that he'd see him in the south field after dinner; then they crashed down again as she thought of what Rosalind's greeting to him might be.

She was as unprepared as Rosalind for his loud, exultant whoop when he saw them. Like a tawny cat he raced toward them. He grabbed Rosalind by the waist, raising her into the air then down into his arms. Breathless, her pique forgotten, Rosalind dropped the basket and put her arms around his neck. "You smell like manure," she giggled, wrinkling up her nose.

"Natural-like, as they say." He nuzzled her, then put her back on the ground. "What have you brought, Callie? A bear, I hope. I'm hungry enough to eat one fur an' all."

"Callie!? *I* brought the basket."

"I know," Peter grinned, pulling her down beside him. "But we both know Callie did the work. Sit down and let me tell you both what beautiful, wonderful women you are."

Shivering in spite of coats and scarves, they laughed together, ate together, and bemoaned the passage of time when Peter had to leave to meet Marsh in the south field. Callie was sorry to see the noon hour end, and was glad to see that Rosalind was sorry too. She took the basket and walked ahead, leaving Rosalind in one of her more naturally romantic moods to linger over her leavetaking of Peter.

Callie felt warm and contented all the rest of the day and into the following morning. At breakfast, when James announced, "Tomorrow we furrow," it seemed appropriate to her. She knew as well as did the others that today the season had changed.

Spring was here although it was still cold and as miserably wet as the winter had been. The "pigging," as the furrowing was called, would be grinding work this year. Though Callie had never watched a field being prepared, she had only to look into the faces of the men to know it would be unpleasant. As had become her usual course, she asked James what she could do to help. Normally he replied she should watch, learn, and then do what she could. This time, however, he told her she would be going to the streams with Stephen to prepare the hop twine.

"Oh, James, don't give her that task. It's so cold and she isn't used . . ."

James smiled, but his voice was stern. "Hush, Meg. You'll not interfere with what I think is best. The girl wants to be of help, and she shall be. None learns so fast as the willing. Callie is not fainthearted. That so, Callie?"

Callie glanced from Meg to James. There her eyes rested. "Is it a terrible task?"

"It couldn't be any worse than the first time you tried to milk the cows, could it, Callie?" Stephen said, laughing so hard he caused her to blush as she recalled being chased terrified and screaming into the farmyard by an indignant cow.

"Let her live with us a couple of years, Meg, and then you'll hear her crying for your protection. Everything is an adventure to her now. Give me the few minutes in time when a young one wants to work."

After breakfast Callie went with James to the barn.
She gathered up the twine he showed her; then she
met Stephen in the farmyard. Together they walked to
the stream that ran through the hop garden, and began to wet and stretch the twine. They had to be
more careful this year than most for the streams were
swollen and running fast.

Stephen reached into the cold water and pulled out
a long piece of sodden twine. "I wonder whose this
was? Keep track of ours or someone further down will
benefit from our labors."

Callie nodded and continued to work. It was too
cold to feel congenial, and too wet for her to do anything but concentrate on keeping her footing on the
muddy bank. The pleasant, relatively dry afternoon
she'd spent yesterday with Rosalind and Peter seemed
in another lifetime.

Stephen threw her a coil of twine. "Ho, Callie!
Catch it."

A fraction late she dived for the twine and tumbled
down the embankment. Stephen slithered down after
her, pulling her back from the water's edge. "You
were all but fish bait," he said cheerfully. "No damage done." He brushed her coat off roughly, succeeding in smearing the mud over a larger area. "I thought
you saw me. Sorry."

"I'm all right, Stephen. Please don't brush me off
anymore. You are making a terrible mess."

"Oh, sorry." He released her. She slipped and he
grabbed her again. "Sorry."

She began to giggle, and struggled with his aid to
drier ground. "No more sorrys, please, or I'll drown
for sure." She cast a respectful glance at the stream.

Two streams of the river Medway wound through
the hop gardens of Kent. The Medway was swollen
and so were the Beult and the Teise. The little stream

on whose bank they now stood was a still smaller branch of the Beult. It was a beautiful area, and Stephen was quick to point out that beauty. "One day when it is a little warmer, I'll take you around and you'll see. There's no other place on earth like it."

But Callie was now thoroughly cold, wet, and wary of falling again. She had lost her sense of fun. She was convinced that there was nothing enticing about the stream. No matter how Stephen reassured her that it was not deep enough to be dangerous, to her it looked hungry and ominous.

"I am sure there are many such places," she said, clenching her teeth to keep them from chattering.

"Your enchantment center is frozen, that's all. Hurry up and finish this last batch. I'll return you to Ma and some hot cider."

She didn't bother to answer him, but discarded caution, following his lead as quickly as she could, the idea of hot cider and the hearth fire propelling her.

It was well that James started her out on a difficult task. As he claimed, she expected nothing easier, and that particular spring nothing was. It remained a cold, wet, miserable season for the farmers, and a frustrating riot-blighted one for the laborers.

As Callie now knew and was beginning to understand, the laborers' rioting and burning was not a thing of the moment. The cost of living had tripled, and wages had not. Economic pressures drove the laborers on.

With it all—the weather and the developing climate for trouble—James was expecting a fresh outbreak of rioting daily. He didn't question that it was coming, only how great a loss to home and crops he would suffer.

Much of what Callie heard and saw happening had been discussed in her flat when her father was alive.

There were so many times when she listened to James
or Peter speaking and remembered hearing her father
say nearly the same things. Perhaps there would never
be an end to the problems, because no one seemed
able to do anything.

What surprised Callie most was that her sympathies
had become firmly implanted on the side of the farmers. In four short months the Bereans had taken her
heart and her loyalties so completely that her father's
lifetime of work had become less meaningful to her
than the problems of a hop garden in Kent.

Still she remained loyal to her father, for she could
now see clearly what she had never been able to see
before: Ian and James and Peter were alike in spite of
their being on opposite sides of a question. All of
them wanted what was best for their country, all
wanted what was just, and all were willing to fight for
that. Ian would approve. Above all Ian had believed
in and trusted God. And to Ian God and truth and
right had been synonymous. Callie knew, with a
warmth that spread over her, that Ian would want her
to be standing beside her new family body and soul to
do what was best for them, what was right.

By April, Frank and Peter and Stephen were string-
ing the top wires for the hop vines. Callie watched in
fascination, apprehensive as the men moved along the
rows on stilts. The top wire had to be twelve feet
above the ground. The twine she and Stephen had
prepared would be strung from the top wire and anchored to the ground. The hop shoots would be trained
to grow up them.

"You've never seen the hops in bloom, have you,
Callie?" Natalie asked.

"Never. It looks so strange. Why must the wires be
so far off the ground?"

"The vines grow that tall, silly. The ropes will be

strung from the top wire to the ground, and then in another month or so we will twiddle the hop shoots around the twine to get them started properly. Before you know it this will look like a giant green tent, and it will be covered with the most delicate greenish-white flower you have ever seen. The October flower," Natalie said dreamily. "They are like flower feathers. I come out here at night sometimes in the summer after the flower has bloomed, and walk along under the rows of hops. Peter doesn't like me to, but I do it anyway. Papa used to let me come when I was little, so I think I should be able to come now that I'm grown. Peter has no business telling me what I may do. He's always going on about it being dangerous now with the laborers moving about the countryside."

"He's probably right," Callie said absently, her eyes fixed on the men on stilts.

"Gullywash. It's just his way of making himself important. After all," she said acidly, "he has to have some means of impressing Rosalind. Rosalind wants the world and when you come right down to it, what does Peter have to offer? Frank will inherit the farm."

Callie's attention shifted. She looked at Natalie, wondering why she hadn't considered this before. It was customary that the oldest son inherited. Then she looked back to Peter. How unfair. Peter *was* the hop farm. It was mostly his labor, his energetic good humor, that kept things running smoothly and quickly. Natalie watched her, easily reading the shifting expressions on Callie's face. She laughed lightly. "Actually in Kent it's the youngest son who traditionally inherits, but Papa wrote a special paper making Frank his heir. So two of my brothers—the worker and the rightful heir—won't get what they deserve. Don't you think it strangely appropriate that the Bereans cultivate the hops?"

Callie looked at her, puzzled.

Again Natalie laughed. "The flower—the hop flower is the flower of injustice and destruction. Did you know that, Callie? Don't you think it appropriate?"

The high wires went up one after another. With nimble grace Peter and Stephen went from one row to the next on stilts as Frank stood solidly on the ground shouting useless orders and words of advice.

Watching the progress of the work had lost its appeal for Callie. She felt sadness and something like anger at what Natalie had said. And the symbolism of the flower—it seemed ominous, a herald of things preordained. "You didn't truly mean that about the flower?"

"Being the flower of injustice and destruction? Certainly I meant it. I know my flowers—all about them."

"Maybe you got it mixed up with another . . ."

"I didn't," Natalie said impatiently. "And I'm tired of talking about it. Are you going to stand here all day? I'm bored, and so will you be before the season is over. All we'll hear about is hops."

"Oh, but it is so fascinating. I've never seen it before."

"Well, I want to do something else."

"Oh, I'm sorry. You don't need to stay here with me. Go ahead—don't let me keep you."

Natalie stamped her foot. "You do anything anyone in this family asks of you, but let me ask the simplest thing and you'll have no part of it!"

Callie stared open-mouthed at her.

"I want to take a walk—and have dinner in the woods. But of course, it would be only Rosalind you'd do that for."

"Natalie! You said nothing about it."

"I did!"

"You didn't . . . I didn't hear you. I'm sure . . . anyway Peter said we weren't to go to the woods alone. It's not safe because . . ."

"Oh, Peter! I'll scream if I hear his name once more!"

"Why are you so angry? What has Peter done to you?"

Natalie laughed bitterly. "Things you'd never understand, sweet Callie. If he were any man at all—" she shrugged. "But he isn't."

"That's an awful thing to say! Peter is the nicest, kindest man alive. He treats you as most sisters only wish their brothers treated them. Who takes you for trips to Seven Oaks and drives you all over the parish so you can collect the flowers you want for your drying?"

"To make up for other things," Natalie snapped.

Callie walked several steps away from her but Natalie followed doggedly. "Who turned you against me? Rosalind? Peter? What has he said about me?"

"That he loves you!" Callie shouted, then lowering her voice glanced at the men in the fields. "He thinks you're dear and sweet."

Natalie had the grace to look momentarily ashamed. "Then it must have been Rosalind."

"She doesn't say anything about you," Callie said, still angry.

Natalie was silent. Finally she said, "Then I'm sorry. But we never do things together anymore. I thought you and I would be close—sisters and friends."

"We are."

"Show me. May will pack a basket for us. Say you'll come, Callie."

"We're not supposed to be in the woods alone."

"The men are right here. No one would be lurking around with them so near. We'd need only to call out.

And the almond is in bloom now. Please—I'd love to find one of the bushes. The blooms won't last long."

Callie remained reluctant, but Natalie sounded so earnest and apologetic. "We shouldn't."

"We won't go far. I promise. Please say you'll come. It would mean so much to me, and it's true you and I have not enjoyed an afternoon together for a long time."

With the dinner May packed for them, the two girls set out. Natalie walked to the far edge of the field and took the long way around to the woods, as if she thought no one would notice them. Callie knew they had been seen and wondered just how she would explain this disobedience to Peter this evening.

Peter had been very firm in warning them. Dangerous bands of laborers wandered the neighborhood, and the women were not to go near the woods even for berry picking unless one of the men went with them. He was sure to ask her about today's venture.

Her misgivings growing stronger, she called to Natalie who had run gaily ahead. Natalie looked back, laughing, then ran along the woods path. Callie hurried to catch up. Natalie remained several steps in front. Callie shifted the dinner basket to her other arm and ran a few more steps, then stopped. They were already deep in the woods. It was too late to protest. "Natalie, wait. I want to rest. The basket is heavy."

The sounds of the woods closed around her. But no human sound. "Natalie!" Callie called, alarmed. She was still not familiar with the woods, and fearful of becoming hopelessly lost. "Natalie! Where are you?"

Callie stood still as stone, her ears straining, already edgy at her disobedience to Peter for coming into the woods at all. Every sound became ominous, a possibility that a band of men could leap out at her from the cover of any clump of underbrush. Leaves rustled; a twig snapped. Callie dropped the basket and ran pell-mell into the thicket.

Natalie raced after her, finally catching the sleeve of her gown. Breathlessly she gasped, "Why are you running away? I found the almond bush. Come see."

Callie sank to the ground. "Oh, Nattie, you scared me. I thought you were a band of those men."

"Me!? A whole band of them?"

Callie laughed weakly. "Yes."

Natalie put her hand out, helping Callie to her feet. "Come see the almond. There's not a living soul in these woods but you and me. I *know*. I can sense these things."

Natalie led Callie to the small lovely almond, its pale pinkish flowers delicate and fragile-looking like small confections set deep in the green woods. Callie's eyes shone with as much pleasure as Natalie's. "Let's eat here."

Natalie agreed, saying she could use the emptied basket to carry the blooms home. They nibbled on cold shepherd's pie and thick chunks of bread and cheese. Callie wrapped up what was left and tucked it into one end of the basket. "It's so beautiful here. I'm glad we came . . . even if Peter will be angry." She lay back and stared dreamily up into the laden green boughs. She loved these woods. The sounds of the trees in the wind, and the animals scurrying unseen around her, were like symphonies far more exhilarating than any she had heard in London concert halls.

With great reluctance she got up and reminded Natalie they had to get back to the house. She had no idea how long they had been gone, but from the angle of the sun she knew it was well into the afternoon.

They started back, Natalie leading, for Callie no longer had any idea which path to take or where she was.

Callie stopped in surprise. "What is this place?" She pointed to a neat row of small cottages. Where the ground had allowed them to sink, they leaned against each other as though for comfort.

Natalie stood for a long time staring at the cabins. Her face was sad; then slowly the sadness became anger. She spat on the ground.

"Natalie!"

Rigid, Natalie tore her eyes from one particular cabin and faced Callie, turning so she could no longer see the hated place. Her lips barely moved; her eyes blazed as she said, "They are goatherd's cottages—when we have need of goatherds. They are shepherd's cottages—when we have need of shepherds. Mostly they are for the hop pickers when we have need of hop pickers. And they are for Rosalind and Albert—when they have need to . . . to . . . of each other."

"Natalie Berean! I truly don't know what is wrong with you today. God forgive you. The terrible things you've said about Peter and now Rosalind and Albert. You can't say things like that. Truly you can't. It's a grave sin."

"Good Callie. Everyone knows how good you are . . . and how sweet. Why, you've probably never even committed a sin, have you? Do you do any wrong?"

"Nattie!"

"Oh, Nattie what? You make me sick sometimes. What do you know? How do you know I'm not telling the truth? Truth doesn't always have to be nice."

Callie said nothing, and Natalie went on. "What would you say if Rosalind and Albert really did meet here?"

Callie remained silent, walking a little faster away from the cabins.

"Why don't you answer? You can't admit you're wrong! You're afraid!"

"I am not afraid!"

"Then answer me."

"All right," Callie sighed. "It would be different if Rosalind and Albert really met here, but they don't. Rosalind is Peter's wife. She'd never do something like that. She loves him and Albert loves you. You're wrong and it's terrible of you to say such things. Think of what something like that could do to the people you are slandering."

"It could be true."

"It could not! Maybe with other people, but not with our family."

"You could prove it—one way or another," Natalie said slyly. "Rosalind is always taking walks. Don't you think that is strange for someone who thinks lifting the fork to her mouth is work? Follow her. See if she doesn't come straight here."

"I'll do no such thing! And to accuse Albert—your own fiancé! How can you claim to care a fig for him? You don't even trust him!"

"It's because I do love him," Natalie said airily. "But you wouldn't understand. You're too young."

"I'm fifteen—old enough."

"You just turned fifteen. I'm still four and a half years older than you. I should know far more than you, and I do."

"I'm not going to talk to you anymore about this. It's hateful. I'm going back to the house."

"Go back and I shall tell Mama and Papa that you asked me to come to the woods then ran off and left me!"

"Tell them! Go ahead! And I'll tell them the awful things you said."

Stalemated, they stared at each other, neither willing to take another step until the other gave in.

Finally Natalie smiled. "Oh, let's forget it. You

know I didn't really mean anything. I was just teasing."

"Teasing?"

Natalie shrugged. "You'll never know for sure, will you?"

"I don't want to know."

"Are you still going to tell Mama and Papa?"

Callie hesitated, then shook her head. Once again she walked by Natalie's side, but she was no longer sure she liked Natalie. As delightful as the girl could be, there was an inexplicably vengeful side to her that Callie despised. Natalie called it teasing, but Callie thought it malicious.

Sideways Callie looked at Natalie. She was in much better humor now, smiling and humming softly to herself. Catching Callie's look, her smile broadened. "Am I forgiven?"

Callie's lips pursed. Her impulse was to say no, but she couldn't make the word come out.

Natalie sighed. "Well, I wish I could take it all back, but I can't. Surely you know I didn't mean it. Rosalind just makes me so angry. She's so flirtatious and syrupy around Albert. She has her own husband; why must she fall all over Albert?"

Callie said nothing. It was just Rosalind's way—but Natalie would never listen to that.

"Say something," Natalie prompted, feeling frightened for reasons she didn't understand fully. She knew only that she regretted heartily the honesty she had exposed to Callie. "I said I was sorry. I didn't mean those things I said about Peter. Don't you believe me? Don't you?"

Callie looked at her. "Honest? You'll never say them again?"

"Never."

Chapter 11

By midsummer of 1830 it was apparent that the threshing machine, which had been used primarily in the north, would be coming to the southern counties. The year had been bad and the crops had to be brought in. One threshing machine would do the work of many men.

Callie heard the news as she did nearly all the rumors that passed through the Berean farm. She did not realize its importance until August, when four hundred Kentish laborers began to smash the hated machines.

The sporadic disturbances had been exciting and a little frightening, but not quite real. The Bereans had observed certain basic precautions, but even those had not seemed connected with anything too serious or imminent. The disturbances hadn't touched them directly. Now, with a rising lump of apprehension, Callie stood at the entry to the barn watching Peter clean his gun.

Sensing her presence, he said, "Come in, Callie."

She walked over to where he sat. The gun was no longer in sight.

"What were you doing, Peter?"

"Oh, not much. Just sitting here and thinking about getting the hay into the loft."

"Why did you hide the gun?"

"You saw, then. Well, it's a good thing you weren't Ma." He leaned down, pulling the gun from the hay. "Ma would worry needlessly, so keep it between us, will you, Callie?"

"But why do you have it out?"

Peter's serious expression lightened immediately. "Because, little one, there is trouble afoot. Where have you had your head and ears? In some cloud of daydreams where they belong, I guess."

"I have heard—but you are in sympathy with the laborers. They wouldn't hurt you. You're one of them!"

"Desperate men are rarely true friends, Callie. They can't be. Nor am I so much in sympathy that I will let them ruin my thresher or burn my fields. There are four hundred or more of them wandering about. Do you comprehend what they could do?"

Callie did not comprehend.

The following morning Albert appeared at the front door before breakfast. The usually immaculately groomed Albert was untidy, his face pale, the meticulously neat mustache in need of a trim and waxing. Brushing past Callie without a greeting he went directly to James's study. "Tell James I must see him immediately!" he called as he went to the liquor cabinet. Albert never drank in the day and only moderately at night.

Callie hurried needlessly in search of James; Albert's urgent voice had carried. James was already coming, with Meg close behind. Natalie was at the foot of the stairs. "Albert? Did I hear Albert? Where is he?"

"Have you firearms at ready?" Albert demanded from the doorway.

"Firearms! James! What is happening?" Meg wrung her hands.

"Did you come to see me, Albert?" Natalie asked, slithering down the final two steps toward him.

"Always dear, I always come to see you, but at the moment there is an emergency. Your father and I have important business to discuss."

"James, what is he talking about?" Meg cried.

"Albert, for the love of heaven," James said. "You have the entire family in alarm. What the devil's gotten into you? What's this about firearms? Have we declared war?"

He turned and shoved Albert, who had come to the door, back into the depths of the study. "Now, what is all this?" James asked severely.

Within a few minutes the door to the study reopened. "Callie! Callie! Call my sons in from the fields!"

Albert stood in the middle of the floor, his third glass of rye in his hand, holding in the other a ragged piece of paper. James looked at the note. "Bewar of the fatel dager!" He read the signature, "Swing."

"Have you an idea of how many of these notes we've collected?" Albert asked. "Swing is everywhere, I tell you. The man has spread his agents throughout the country. The attack is planned. Wellington himself has received several notes threatening an invasion of London, and death if reform is not made law. We've been up all night recruiting and preparing for what is coming."

"Just how far has it spread?" Frank asked.

"We've had reports from Northhamptonshire, Dorset,

Norfolk, Lincolnshire . . . and of course all of the south."

"And how bad is it?"

"We don't know. How can we separate rumor from fact in a situation like this? We've had reports of the streets running in blood. One market town claims to have dead bodies piled in front of the town hall. It may all be true."

"Sit down. You look ready to drop." James rang for food to be brought in.

Slowly they pieced together Albert's disjointed story. Several things were clear. Pressure was being put on the local magistrates to control the situation. There would be no help on a national level. The men in Parliament were still convinced that the problem wasn't serious. The Duke of Wellington ignored Captain Swing. He also discounted the fears of the Kentish landowners. Wellington had written to a friend, "The gentlemen in Kent, so bold in Parliament, are terrified out of their wits with the burning of a few cornstalks and the breaking of a few threshing machines." There would be no help from London.

Albert slumped deeply in his chair, his head nodding with fatigue and the effect of the rye. "We must organize immediately. Everything must be organized. Can't do anything until then . . ."

"I suggest you go home, Albert," James said. "And get some rest. Come back this evening and tell us what we need to do to be prepared. Better still, I'll have Meg prepare a guest room. You can rest here, and please my daughter. She would like nothing better than to care for you today."

The problem Albert and the other magistrates faced was clear. The southern counties were infected with a virulent tide of righteous rebellion. There was going to be no help from the army, and the magistrates were having difficulty assembling local men. They had the power to increase their yeomanry to enforce the law, but the yeomanry was a voluntary, unpaid, thankless job. Many of the tradesmen and farmers were in sympathy with the laborers and didn't want to join a force designed to quell them. At the same time there was panic and fear as to what could happen to any individual farm or community. They wanted protection from the very forces whose ranks they refused to fill.

There was no unity of purpose in the effort to quell the rebellion, only a massive atmosphere of panic.

The Bereans, sympathetic to the laborers and to the difficulties Albert faced, turned to their first and primary concern: the hops. The hops had to be gathered and taken to the oast house in Seven Oaks. Callie saw the Berean house empty for the first time.

Everyone in the family, and hordes of temporary laborers from other communities as well as London, poured onto the fields to gather the hops. The little cottages that Callie and Natalie had seen were nearly filled. Around them were the tents and caravans of other families. The gypsies with their bow-topped and gaily painted wagons were in a group of their own away from the others.

The hop harvesting was like a fairy-tale world to Callie. With the people and the colorful costumes, everyone was in a festive mood. Everything was better for they had worked hard all day and were excited by the odd blending of music and dancing and story telling at night. It could be forgotten that the reddish night skies were caused by the destruction of other fields or machinery. It was easier to believe that the flames were the gypsy campfires glowing, and that the smells permeating the air were of campers' bread being baked, and not of scorching grain.

The hop picking began at the end of August and

continued until the first week in October. Callie went
out each morning with the rest of the family. Natalie
was her picking partner, though she did more dreaming and chattering than picking. By the end of the
first week Callie had become an expert with the pole
used to bring down the hop vines from the top wire.
As the vines tumbled Callie stripped away the clusters
of greenish-white flowers that left her fingers stained.
She filled up cart after cart with them, and as she did
she tucked away thoughts and sights of these days,
savoring them and rethinking them in her room at
night.

The sight of Peter's blond hair glinting in the sun as
he rode through the long rows on the brightly colored
farm wagon was something she never wanted to forget. He gathered the carts of hops from each group of
pickers, praising their work and making them laugh as
he clowned and showed off his strength, dumping the
hop carts into the larger wagon as though they
weighed nothing. He was tireless, and for all his good
cheer no one doubted the seriousness of his business
or his attention to it as he took the hops to the oast
house.

No matter how tired anyone was by nightfall, the
sight of the people dancing among the fallen vines
was something to revive the most weary hands and
feet. All of them acting the wag—happily twining the
hop vines around their heads to keep the flies away,
but mostly for fun—added to the pleasurable feeling
of a long holiday.

The sounds of Romany music and the gypsies themselves fascinated Natalie the most. The woods were all
around them at the perimeter of the fields. The coolness of the trees was enticing to everyone, but particularly the children. Natalie would watch.

"That is the child of a Romany," she said as a stray

child fled into the green shadows. "Let's visit the gypsies, Callie."

"Aunt Meg would skin us alive. Hurry up, Natalie. Our cart isn't filled. Peter will be back to collect them soon."

Natalie dropped a few more hops into the cart and returned to her musing. "They'll be dukkering."

"Natalie!" Callie breathed in exasperation. "Pick the hops. We won't be finished if you don't help."

"Wouldn't you like to have your fortune told?"

"No! Pick! You aren't picking your share, and I'm tired."

"You probably don't know anything about gypsy dukkering."

"I don't and neither do you. Aunt Meg would be very angry if she knew the gypsies were telling fortunes while they were here."

"Mama never finds out about it. Let's go. Say you'll go with me and have your fortune told too."

"Nattie, we can't go. Stop talking about it and get done with this cart. Please, it's the last one."

Natalie did as Callie asked, but she clung to the idea of going to the gypsy. She had gone every year for the past four. That was how she knew Rosalind was an evil influence.

Each time the gypsy had told her only the best of things—until the year before last, the year Peter got married. Then the gypsy told her to beware of a dark-haired woman who heralded danger. Aside from herself, Rosalind was the only dark-haired woman she knew well.

All her misfortunes dated from Rosalind's arrival at the farm. Last year the gypsy had predicted she would be unlucky in love. She had expected to be married by the end of the year, but Albert had said nothing. Things between them remained as always.

Nothing progressed. Nothing was settled. Always it was the future he spoke of, some time so far beyond Natalie she wasn't sure it was there at all. And the card showing the dark female influence had still been there, blocking her happiness and her future. This year she was certain that if only she could get to the gypsy, she would find that her own card would be the dominant one. This year she would be more powerful than the card of the evil woman.

Out of loyalty to Meg, Callie refused Natalie's regular requests to sneak out at night to visit the gypsy. It was difficult. Callie was as curious as Natalie, but for far more innocent reasons. As the hop season wore on her resolve weakened. She could think of nothing more exciting than to sit by the firelight of a Romany camp as an old woman read her future in the cards.

She decided she would go the day Peter took her to the oast house.

"You've never been to the oast house?" he exclaimed one evening at supper. "How could we all have neglected that? Have you never noticed the buildings with the cone-shaped roofs when you went to Seven Oaks?"

"Oh, yes, I have, but Aunt Meg said they were oast houses so matter-of-factly . . . I just didn't ask any more about them."

"Ma!"

"I'm sorry, Peter. I'm so accustomed to them I didn't think of them being new and interesting to Callie."

"Well, you can't live on a hop farm without going to the oast house at least once," Peter said.

"I've never been inside an oast house either," Rosalind said. "And I can tell you I never will. From what I hear they are hot, smelling old places."

"Callie's different from you. She really likes the

farm," Stephen said. "She'd like to go, smell or no, I'll bet."

"I would. May I go sometime?"

Riding at Peter's side atop the wagon was enough to make the day special, but Peter, with a sure instinct, made the day unforgettable. He gave Callie the one thing she treasured most: his confidence. He talked to her as he might to Stephen or James.

"You like it here with us, Callie?"

"I've never been happier. Sometimes it seems. I've never lived anywhere else."

"Then you don't miss London at all? Not the noise or the excitement? You must have been used to a much livelier life."

"Not so much. I think about it sometimes . . . the concerts and the theater, but truthfully most of the time I lived in London I was cold and frightened. Even when Papa was alive it wasn't safe for me to go anywhere alone. I don't think I miss London in a good way at all."

"You're lucky to know that. It's useful knowledge."

"I don't understand."

"I mean, I talk about leaving Kent, even England. I have talked about it since I was your age. I was going to sea first; then I was going to book passage on a timber ship to Canada. Or go to America. I have never done any of it, because I hold fast to the life I know now."

"But this is a good life. You have reason to hold fast to it."

"Does that mean there is no better? Wasn't your life in London the best until you came here and saw that it wasn't?"

"Yes, but . . ."

"I have always yearned to go . . . to be on my

own, to see a world that is new and alive with ideas and people doing things their own way with no tradition to hold them, no limits to what they can attempt. I would be like Absalom and take for myself a kingdom. Should I not think such thoughts? Should I let all that dry up and die inside of me?"

"I don't know."

"But I think you do know. That is why I talk to you, Callie Dawson. What would you do if you were I? Shall I answer for you?"

"I can answer for myself. If I were a man and wanted to go as you do, I think I would do it."

"No matter what you had to leave behind?"

"No matter."

"Without fear of what you would find in an unknown world?"

She giggled. "Perhaps with fear, I think, but I would still find out."

"And what of me, Callie? What do you think I should do?"

Callie said nothing for a time. "I don't want to answer that."

"Why not?" He looked at her pensive, stubborn face. A smile played at the corners of his mouth.

"What I think is not important. I know nothing, and I don't want you to leave," she said in a tight little voice. "I would never see you again. It wouldn't be the same being left behind and knowing you were somewhere else."

He touched her cheek, smiling as he did. "You'd miss me then?"

"I'd miss you both . . . you and Rosalind."

"Ah, well, there's little cause to worry. I've been talking for eleven years and done nothing."

"But things are different now," she said softly. He didn't hear her, for the oast house and its attendant confusion with wagons coming and going claimed his attention. He called out to several men and went to talk to a group of them.

Callie looked up at the top of the strangely shaped building. From it came a curl of smoke that signaled to all who could see the cloud on the horizon that the hops were drying.

Peter returned to help Callie down. She stood aside as he and the other men unloaded the wagon; then he took her inside. The smoke stung her eyes; the whole place was filled with the odor of the drying hops. He took her to the top, showing her each and every stage they went through. For once she agreed with Rosalind. An oast house was not the most pleasant place to be.

But she would ever after think of the oast house as a part of her idea of Peter. Time would erase the stinging of her eyes and the odor that assaulted her nose, leaving only the picturesque look of it and the happy memory of a happy day.

Of all the Bereans, James and Peter were dominant in her life. Frank was a kind man, but like Anna he was quiet and reserved, and somewhat stuffy. He did what had to be done, showing little pleasure in its accomplishment. Stephen was like her brother, her friend, someone near her own age. She loved him, but she never thought of turning to him for guidance or strength. Alone he might have caught her attention, but standing next to the steady, ponderous Frank, and Peter as handsome as any man could be, Stephen remained the image of youth and no more.

Peter was a man, and in him Callie could imagine all the things she wished. Peter would do the impractical things girls thought of sometimes and knew would never happen to them. She would like to travel on the sea. She would like to board some great ship and ride on top of the endless ocean. And she would like to be able to put her foot down in a new land and say it was hers. She never would, but someday Peter would.

She returned home with her whole being filled with the excitement of unknown places and adventures. She was bursting with pent-up desire to do things, see things, experience new ideas and places. Natalie found fertile ground when she asked Callie again to go see the gypsy. It was a very small adventure, but at least it was an adventure.

Chapter 12

It was the right kind of night for their visit. After a rain the skies cleared, leaving the way open for the light of the moon. On the ground was only the slightest covering of mist. Through it Callie and Natalie, their skirts swaying in the soft breeze, dashed from the shelter of the barn to the shroud of the shadowed woods.

Both of them were breathing quickly and giggling softly in their excitement. They kept their eyes fixed on the spot in the woods that glowed golden and red with the gypsies' campfire. As Natalie had claimed the old woman was seated before the fire. She looked to be asleep, but Natalie knew that without opening her eyes the old Romany would know they were there and why.

"Sit down before me," the gypsy woman said, eyes still closed. Her hand extended to Callie. "You are new to this place. You will be first."

Callie looked up at Natalie. Natalie smiled and nodded. From inside the fold of her gown the gypsy brought out a pack of frayed, much-used cards. Callie was shivering and thinking she should have remained sensibly in her warm bed; but her heart was beating furiously in anticipation.

The first strangely marked card would tell of her past. The old woman spoke softly to herself in a language Callie could not understand, and then the card was placed.

"What do you wish to know from the cards?"

"Ask her a question, Callie," Natalie whispered.

"What kind of question?"

"Anything. Anything you want to know."

"Will I ever take a long journey?" Callie asked and sat back chewing on her lip. The old woman separated one group of cards from the others. She sat back studying the configurations, then looked into Callie's firelit face. She tapped the card that lay in the center of the configuration. "It is you, this card. A good card."

"What of her journey? Will she take the journey?" Natalie asked.

"It is not time to tell of the future. You are too young."

"You told mine. Why won't you tell Callie's?" Natalie moved closer. "There is something in her future that is bad, isn't there? You don't want her to know! What is it?"

"Why won't you tell my future? Is it bad, as Natalie says?"

"There are many difficulties ahead for you. It is so."

"But what?" Callie asked.

Natalie stood directly in front of the gypsy and peered down at the cards. "The card of the moon . . . the madhouse, and the hanged man too. They are all cards of misfortune. Is that why you won't tell her?"

The old woman shrugged. "There are cards of great strength as well, and of good fortune. The querier is a good and true woman. Those who do not know the secrets of the cards are misled by them. The young lady has a gentleman who will never lose faith or leave her side. All through her life she can count on this man. There are not many who know such a love."

"And will she take her journey?"

"It is for her to ask."

"Will I?" Callie asked.

"You will take your journey, and come to live in a foreign land beyond the sea. This will happen in the near future. There you will find happiness for a time; but there will be difficulties and sorrows as well in this new land. You return to me, young lady, another year. It is better we tell of the future then. Not now."

"But if I'm in a foreign land, I can never come back. You said I wouldn't be here."

"You will return. It is there in the cards." She pointed to a grouping of cards. "You will return to Kent, back to this place, and I will be here. You will need me then."

"Is that all you will tell me?"

"Of the future. You are a strong lady, of good mind and great love, and you are a wise lady with these gifts. But there will be times in your life when you will regret your nature. It will lead you to obligations that are difficult. But do not fear. The strength is there, and the man who stands faithfully by your side. He is there."

"But I don't understand . . . what is going to happen to me? What does the devil card mean? Can't you tell me more? Natalie said you told her everything . . . and answered all her questions." Callie was near tears and wishing she hadn't come.

"All questions are never answered. Only a fool would think so. Do not worry yourself. You will learn from your trials and benefit from the suffering."

"But . . . why is this in my fortune? I just wanted to have fun. Natalie told me . . ."

"A lady of dark passions . . ." the old woman began and scowled at Natalie; then she looked back to Callie more kindly, placing a hand on the girl's shoulder. "For some it is as it is with you. It has been ordained. There are trials for all of us. Yours has come now. For others it is another time. It comes to us all sometime. For you the wormwood star of the Apocalypse shall fall into the waters of your life when you are young, turning the sweet to bitter of error and disappointment."

"Wormwood?" Callie sniffed and wiped her eyes. "Why did you say wormwood?"

"It is the name of the star."

"But someone else, not so long ago, told me I had drunk from a wormwood cup."

The old woman nodded wisely. "That was during the time of grief for you when you lost someone very close to you. Perhaps your father . . . or brother."

"My father," Callie breathed. "How did you know?"

"The cards," she said, making a simple gesture toward them.

"I don't believe all this. They are only cards. They can't tell the future or the past. Natalie told you my father died. This is all a joke . . . isn't it?"

"I told her nothing!" Natalie protested, then turned to the gypsy. "If you won't tell Callie anything else, tell my fortune now."

"No more tonight. I cannot tell any more tonight."

"But you have done nothing! You've not even begun mine. Lay out the cards."

"Not tonight. You come another time. Come alone. Tomorrow."

"Tonight! I want to know tonight."

"No more tonight."

"What's wrong with you, old woman? You never did this before."

From out of the shadows of the caravan a man came and stood in the light of the fire. "She is tired. There will be no more dukkering tonight."

Callie got up, leaving her money on the ground near the old woman as Natalie had instructed her earlier. "Thank you," she said softly. "I'm sorry I spoke in anger. But I do hope you are wrong about my fortune."

The old woman nodded. "You come back when you return from the new land. Perhaps the evil woman who shadows your life and brings the bitter star from the sky will no longer be so powerful when you return. Perhaps then too you will no longer be tied to the man who shares the bitterness of the wormwood star. Perhaps things will change for you."

Callie nodded and turned to Natalie who was still arguing with the man.

"I'll have you put out of here! You'll never work these fields again after I tell my father you've been dukkering," she yelled.

"Natalie, let's go back to the house."

"I want my fortune told."

Callie sighed, tired and dispirited. "Then come tomorrow. She said she would do your fortune tomorrow night. I'll come with you. I can wait at the edge of the woods."

"Will you tell my fortune tomorrow night if I do as you say?" she asked the old woman. Her head nodded downward, and again she appeared to be asleep. "Answer me!" She looked up at the man. "Will she?"

"Her head is nodded. Answer enough."

Natalie looked doubtful, but moved a few paces toward Callie. "I'll be back, and you tell her she better read my fortune. And not like Callie's. She told her nothing!" She swooped down and picked up the coins Callie had left on the ground. The man moved forward, taking hold of her wrist, forcing her to drop the coins into his open palm.

"Natalie, please, I want to go home," Callie said again. Natalie took a few steps and stopped. "I'm leaving, Natalie. I don't want to stay here any longer."

"I'm coming," she said and caught up with Callie. "You shouldn't have paid her. I wouldn't have. Not for that mumbo-jumbo she told you about stars falling from the sky and bitter waters. What nonsense! I think I *will* tell Papa. She deserves it."

"Don't tell him. He has enough to worry about and anyway all you'll do is get us into trouble. What will he say when he finds out you and I were in the woods at night . . . alone. We aren't allowed near the woods in the daytime."

"It would be worth it just to pay that old harridan back for what she did to me."

"She didn't do anything to you. It was my fortune that was horrible."

"She wouldn't even lay the cards out for me."

"She will tomorrow. Mine probably upset her and she didn't want it to affect yours."

Natalie brightened. "Maybe! Then it's all your fault that I didn't get my fortune told."

"Yes," Callie said softly.

"She did say that you had a good faithful man in your future," Natalie went on, her spirits restored. "It wasn't all bad."

"Yes."

"I wonder who? Why didn't you ask her who he was?"

"Be quiet, Natalie. We are too near the house. Someone will hear us. Peter has been keeping a watch . . ." she said, and no sooner had the words come out when Peter appeared behind them, gun on his arm as he made a final night check.

"Natalie? Callie! What are you two doing out here?" he asked gruffly.

"We were taking a walk," Natalie said hastily.

"Don't you realize what could happen to you? You were not to leave the yard without someone to escort you."

"Callie is escorting me, and we are safe anyway," Natalie said lightly and skipped toward the house. "Good night, Peter." She ran through the front door.

"What do you mean going out this time of night?" he asked, turning his frustration and anger on Callie. She glanced up at him, trying to think what she could say, and burst into tears. Peter's arm went around her. Aside from that day in the May house, he had never seen her give in to tears. "What happened? Are you all right? You didn't . . . no one came on you as you walked? Are you all right, Callie!?" He grew more worried over her tears. "Callie, tell me what happened."

Gradually he succeeded in comforting her, and slowly the night's adventures loosed from their tension as she told him where they had gone and what had happened.

"You went to the Romany fortune teller," he said matter-of-factly; but in the darkness he was smiling as he looked down at her head resting against his chest. "That had to be my sister's idea."

"She said it would be fun. It wasn't fun at all. It was horrible."

"But not so horrible that it deserves all these tears. What can a few moldy old cards have to say that we would listen to?"

"Then you think it is nonsense?"

"Don't you?"

She nodded, realizing in the same moment that she was snuggled close against him seeking comfort and protection. The man the gypsy had spoken of came to her mind and she moved away, blushing unseen in the darkness. "Are you very angry with me?" She tried to make her voice normal.

"I am angry with you," he said and began to walk slowly with her to the house. He couldn't help feeling flattered and amused at her sudden move away from him. "You put yourself and Natalie in danger. It was a very stupid thing you did."

"Peter . . ."

"Yes?"

"I promised Natalie I would go back with her tomorrow night. The gypsy wouldn't tell her fortune tonight. Mine was so awful I think she was afraid it would disturb Natalie's. What should I do?"

"You won't go."

"But I promised! And Natalie . . . you know she'll be furious if I tell her I won't go after I promised."

He sighed, then put his arm across her shoulders. "Then keep your promise."

"I can go? You mean you'll permit it?"

"Don't worry, I'll be following you. Natalie will never know I'm there. Keep this promise, but make no more. At night you stay in the house where I can be certain you are safe."

She hugged him and ran into the house.

Natalie was waiting for her in her bedroom. "Are you still going tomorrow night? Or did you let Peter frighten you off?"

"I'm going. I promised, didn't I?"

Natalie stood back, her eyes narrowed and distrustful. "You'd better keep it, or you'll be sorry, Callie."

"Go to bed, Natalie. I said I'd go and I will. Leave me alone."

* * *

When Callie came down to breakfast the following morning both James and Meg looked at her with concern. "Aren't you feeling well, Callie?"

"You look pale," Meg added and came over to her, placing her hand on Callie's forehead. "You seem all right, but you'd better take it easy. Stay in today. The hops are nearly in; we can get along without you in the fields."

"She is my partner. She can't stay in. Anyway Callie is fine, aren't you?" Natalie hissed.

Callie looked over at James. "Take care of yourself, Callie," he said. "We can't be having anyone getting sick. Natalie, you will go with Anna."

"But Papa!"

"Show a little concern for your cousin, Natalie. Do you want her working when she is not fit for it?"

"She is fine! There is nothing wrong with her. She just doesn't want to go with me!"

"Natalie! I'll hear no more of this. Meg, speak to your daughter. Callie, you are to remain close to the house today, and not another word from either of you." He wiped his mouth decisively with the napkin and left the room.

She was glad for the day of freedom from Natalie, and glad to be alone for a time. She hadn't slept well last night. As often as she would tell herself it was all nonsense, she seemed to hear the gypsy's voice telling her about the wormwood star, the man whose misfortunes she would share, and the man who would remain faithfully at her side all her life. And then she would think of Peter and the quiet night and his arm around her. Would the sound of his heart beating never stop in her ears?

Most of the morning she spent alone in the house straightening the scullery and the kitchen. It hadn't been properly tended for weeks while everyone was busy with the hops. From August to October nothing took precedence over the hops, not even the condition of Meg's normally immaculate scullery. It took Callie the greater part of the morning; but she had it nearly at its best when Anna came in from the fields.

"Are you feeling better, Callie?"

"I'm all right. I'm just a little tired, that's all."

"Cleaning the scullery is not the best sort of rest. Why don't you lie down for a while?"

Callie went to her room as Anna suggested, but she couldn't rest. As soon as her head touched the pillow she began to think again. She thought of Ian, and of Mrs. Peach, of coming to the Berean farm, and then of the gypsy. Every time she seemed happy and things were going well something came along to spoil it.

She got up and wandered into the gallery where she knew she would find Anna sewing or preparing wool.

"Do you need any help?" she asked as she entered the room and sat down.

"No. What is wrong, Callie? You look so unhappy."

"I'm not," Callie said dispiritedly. The afternoon passed slowly. With nothing to do Callie slumped down into inertia, and Anna began to worry in earnest.

"Something certainly is wrong. Won't you tell me? Or are you afraid it is something I would not want to hear?"

"It is nothing, Anna, honestly. I am fine. I'm just tired."

"Callie—is it that you don't like it here? I thought you did, but perhaps . . ."

"Oh, I do! Honestly, Anna, I am not unhappy. I think I should have gone to the fields. I don't have anything to do."

"Then how about taking a walk with me?" a mascu-

line voice asked from behind them. Both Callie and
Anna started. Stephen stood in the doorway, his head
nearly touching the lintel.

"You could knock, Stephen," Anna said sternly.

"But then I couldn't startle you." He smiled. "Will
you come, Callie?"

"Go with him, Callie. Perhaps a little fresh air will
perk you up." Anna gave her a gentle shove in Stephen's direction.

"You don't feel well?" he asked as they went down
the stairs and out into the farmyard.

"I feel fine. I don't know why everyone keeps asking me," she replied irritably.

"Well, I know just the place to take you."

"Where?"

"My mountain."

"Your mountain?" Callie said and then thought of
the hill that all of them called Stephen's mountain. It
was a smallish sort of a mountain, but no one argued
with his designation.

Stephen awakened each morning to the view of that
hill and watched the sun rise over it, bringing with it
news of the kind of day that was dawning. Some days
it was so mist-enshrouded that he couldn't be certain
it was still there. Other days dawned with the sun
glowing so strongly on its gorse-covered slopes that he
wanted only to be up and out of the house.

"There is no better place from which to view the
world favorably than the top of my mountain. Come
with me and I'll show you. You'll be surprised how
everything changes. All kinds of ordinary things become beautiful from up there."

"Oh, do they?" Callie followed him as he walked
along the side of the sloe hedge. She touched the
nearly ripe sloes, thinking how soon they would be
busy making the sloe gin.

"Yes, it's the detachment, I think. You go high up there and it's a new world you look down on. I love the mountain for that. You will too," Stephen said with great certainty and then immediately fell into a self-conscious silence. He seldom had much to say, and never so vibrantly as that. So they walked along in silence, Callie with her momentary need for reserve and privacy, Stephen overwhelmed by the rush of thoughts that he had put into words for her.

To add to his amazement and embarrassment, an unaccustomed feeling of wonder touched him. He was aware of her as he had never been aware of another human being. He had always been able to shut himself off from others, and now he felt the warmth of her and noticed for the first time her distinctive gait. He hoped she would awaken from her pensive mood so he could hear her lively voice. He wished she would laugh so he could hear the sound. It left him with nothing to say of the common world, and he began to long for the top of the mountain for himself even more than to cheer Callie.

Callie was paying little attention to where they were going, and less to Stephen. They had entered a section of the woods with which she was not familiar. She kept pace with him, turning when he turned, following paths that only he could see. They began climbing the hill, and once more Callie awakened to the world around her.

At the top Stephen stopped, crossing his arms over his chest. He looked out, pleased, over the valley and the house below. Never before had he felt such a sharp poignant possessiveness and pride in this world of his, and in his own being.

He had spoken the truth when he told Callie that the world became a different place from the vantage point of the mountain.

Callie looked down at the Berean farmhouse with its thatched roof, and saw its mellow beauty as the setting sun washed the half-timbered house in gold. She sat down on one of the larger boulders and lost herself in the sights and sounds of the closing day, thinking again about her father and the gypsy woman. And just as Stephen had promised, each began to take on a different light. Her mood shifted with the shifting colors of the sunset.

She was staring at the deep rich ochre of the roof, letting her eyes focus dimly and then with clarity as the sun made the colors change in warmth and depth, going deep into the blackness of shadow, when from the side of the house came a man. He became a part of her scene, like a new actor coming out on stage. Then she drew in her breath, and not knowing she did so, leaned forward to see better. She became rapt in the looking, and felt the tight-chested elation that comes with knowing one is looking at something naturally beautiful.

He didn't know he was being watched as he strode to the well and splashed water on his sun-bronzed face. His hair was like wheat, silvery in moonlight, and he moved with the suppleness of a green tree shoot. As though he had to, moved by some inner joy, he threw his arms into the air, his head back as he watched the droplets of sunstruck water tumble down on him.

He stripped off his work shirt and splashed water all over himself. Callie didn't move, nor did she want to. She was far too enchanted by the magic the mountain could work. For just this one moment, she was a Venus, a Minerva, a Diana looking down upon her suitor, and she was beautiful because he was beautiful to see.

At first Stephen hadn't noticed Peter standing by

the well. His eyes roved over Callie's young body and the rapt, thoroughly lovely expression on her face that drank in the rosy hues of sunset. Though she wasn't finished, still, being but the promise of a woman, he didn't notice, for neither was he quite a man yet, and to him she seemed perfect. While Callie dreamed of being a momentary Venus, she became one in Stephen's eyes. Such were his visions of a future and the sights of glories to come. How close they all were this day when he was seventeen with a young girl who made his head whirl and his heart pound.

He glanced away from her long enough to let Peter's form catch his eye. The Venus disappeared, and his thoughts traveled back to a time when he was younger and Peter would race him from the base of the hill back to the house. He smiled as he looked at his brother, and wondered if Peter would remember.

"Peter!" he called in a voice that carried across the valley.

Peter Berean, shaking his wet hair like a tawny young lion, stopped and looked to the top of the hill at Stephen. He raised his arm, waving and smiling. Then he sprinted toward the hill and was lost from sight, but Stephen waited, poised—and listening.

"I'll race you!"

Callie was forgotten, and Stephen began to run down the hillside in a long-legged sprint. Peter waited at the base until his younger brother neared him. Then, taking a good headstart, he ran along the turning paths through the woods to the farmhouse, his heavier, well-formed body losing a little ground to Stephen at each stride.

Callie watched from the hillside as she walked slowly down. Her thoughts were not for the race or its winner. Stephen belonged, like all mortal creatures, to that world of ordinary plainness, and she was putting that off a moment at a time. She knew that by the time she reached the bottom of the hill and went back inside the farmhouse Peter would also look like everyone else. But for a few minutes from the top of the hill Peter Berean had looked as she had never seen any man or woman look.

When she made her leisurely way down the hill, Peter and Stephen had disappeared into the house. No one was left in the farmyard. The well stood alone, a solitary stone monument with only the puddles of water at its base giving testimony that Peter had been there at all. But Callie knew. She had only to close her eyes against the setting sun, and there in the red brilliance she would see him over and over standing at the well with the water pouring over him making his torso glisten in the light. She wrapped herself in the fleeting and delight-filled moments of a girl's first romantic love.

She had never felt this before, but then she had never seen a man like Peter before, and never from the top of a mountain. Mountains were made to make men know what it was to soar, and Callie had been captured in flight, caught and held far above the earth. She went back to the house smiling both inside and out. She ran to her room, not stopping to look in at the others gathered happily and noisily in the kitchen. Her bed smelled sweet and freshly aired as she flung herself onto it, pulling the pillow close against her hot face.

The transformation in Callie should have been apparent to both Anna and Meg. But as usual the supper hour was filled with the talk of the day and the relaying of stories. No one noticed Callie at all.

"You are going with me tonight, aren't you?" Natalie asked as soon as the table was cleared and the dishes done.

"I told you I would. Don't fret so." Callie laughed.

"What are you so happy about? I thought you really didn't want to go, especially after Peter caught us last night."

"I want to now; and anyway, it isn't likely that we could get in trouble two nights in a row," Callie said and felt a shiver of anticipation as she thought of Peter moving unseen and unheard, watching out for them and protecting them as they made their visit to the gypsy. Natalie would be livid if she knew about it. Even that pleased Callie, and she laughed aloud.

"What *is* wrong with you? You're plain giddy," Natalie hissed. "Stop it, or someone will wonder. Mama will put you right to bed if she thinks something is wrong with you."

It was nearly midnight before the house quieted down and Natalie and Callie could think of going. Twice Peter tried to get everyone to retire for the night, but they were all having a good time. Finally James made a great show of looking at his watch and yawning. "We're going to pay for this night's fun tomorrow," he said and looked pointedly at each of them. Cards were put back in their place, the backgammon board put on its shelf, and the room emptied and darkened.

"It's about time," Natalie whispered in Callie's ear as they climbed the stairs ostensibly to go to bed. "I thought they'd stay up all night."

Half an hour later they were making their way through the woods. Callie could neither see nor hear Peter. Several times she wondered if he had changed his mind. Perhaps he thought they would have better sense than to go so late. He should know his sister better than that.

Natalie was so excited she could barely talk. Her whole body trembled with tension. "She'll not refuse me tonight. She can't. If I have to camp in front of her wagon, I will. That old hag . . . what business has she to refuse me my own fortune?"

"She said she would tell you, Natalie," Callie panted. "Don't run so. I can't keep up, and the last thing I want to do is get lost in these woods."

Within minutes they came to the clearing. The campfire was cold. The ashes were already scattered by the wind. Where the gaily colored wagon had stood were only the tracks it had made in leaving. The gypsy woman was gone.

Chapter 13

As though the gypsy had, by leaving, put all her predictions into motion, the world of the Bereans began to crumble. The hop picking season was nearly over. The nights were no longer pierced with the sounds of the music makers and dancers. It was late October and growing cold again. Some of the seasonal workers had already left; the ones remaining were tired, and the fires burned low and went out earlier than before.

James was pleased with his year considering its bad beginning. It wasn't the crop he could expect in a good or even a fair year, but neither was it a disaster. They would manage. Frugality was no stranger to them. Meg knew how to run a household on little, and she would. For that he was thankful.

For the end of the season he was thankful as well. He was tired and not feeling well. He almost looked forward to a long cold winter that would force him to stay indoors. Perhaps it would also help quell the continuing burnings and riots. There comes a time when even the most patient of men needs a moment's peace. For James the time was now. He no longer wanted to think of Peter riding with these men, or of Frank trying to remain uninvolved and secure with his farm.

Each night Peter and Frank walked the fields and checked each of the barns and cottages—a necessary procedure and one that kept them constantly aware of the uncertainty of the times. No one had bothered the farm so far, and with a little luck no one would. That was mostly due to Peter's efforts, as they all knew. Peter continued to ride periodically with the laborers, going out into the night and accompanying them on their search for threshing machines brought down from the north. He liked to think he was helpful not only to his own family, but to all concerned.

His intentions, however, did not lessen the danger to himself. If he were caught, he would be arrested with the others. If that should happen there was nothing any of them could do to help him. But he continued for the sake of both the farm and the laborers—and because he enjoyed the danger and the excitement.

Albert was his worst critic and his greatest threat. Though he couldn't prove that Peter rode with the Swing men, his suspicions were all but certainties. Peter didn't deceive himself that Albert wanted to see him caught and punished. Peter's activities pricked Albert's pride, and there was a certain jealous hostility of Albert's that Peter didn't understand completely, but recognized.

"What will you do when you end up locked in prison, Peter?" Albert had said with a certain relish one evening when the family had gathered in the parlor. "You can't count on me to get you out, you know. As magistrate I'm bound to do my duty. Lord, man, give a thought to what you are risking. I am responsible to this parish. I must see the riots quelled. Shall

you force me to arrest my own future brother-in-law?
How would that look?"

"What shall you arrest me for, Albert? My sympathies?"

"You know damned well what I'll arrest you for!
Why pretend? We all know of your night rides. Everyone knows. You don't go to much trouble to keep
them a secret. The whole neighborhood sees you making a fool of me."

"They think. They don't *know* anything, and so long
as I have made no night rides—with my family to back
me up, of course—that is all they will do."

"Until you are caught."

"If you're so damned sure I'm a Swing rider, catch
me!" Peter said and left Albert chewing the end of his
mustache.

However flippant and confident Peter was when
talking to Albert, he was quite patient and pliant later
when his father and two brothers spoke of the dangers
involved. It was agreed that for the time being Peter
would remain safe and easily seen inside the house at
night.

"You should never have challenged him," Frank
said. "Albert does not like being made to look a fool,
and in his opinion that is exactly what you are doing.
You know his next move will be to come here and
find you gone."

"I know," Peter muttered, annoyed. "He's like a bull
dog. He's not going to give up until he knows for certain if I ride or not. He'll be knocking at the door in
the middle of the night before the week's out. Why
can't the damned fool mind his own business?"

"It is his business," James said reasonably.

"Whose side are you on?"

"Yours, of course, but let's give Albert his due. It is
his business to stop the rioting, and that is no small

task. No matter what our sympathies, none of us truly thinks these uprisings can go on. None of the farmers hereabouts can stand a continuing loss of crops and machinery."

"So we do nothing?" Peter asked belligerently.

"My God, you're a bullheaded ass! You know it can't go on," Frank said.

"It will."

"If hotheads like you have anything to say, it will; but I'll tell you, Peter, I sometimes wonder if you care at all about the cause. Isn't it the restless urge for excitement that keeps you agitating?" Frank walked to the end of the room. "It isn't anything new to you. Ever since you've been old enough to be on your own, you've been wanting newness, excitement. You'd have been better to take to the road years ago and gotten it out of your system instead of threatening our livelihood and good name with your wildness now."

"You sound put out, Frank," Peter said grinning. "Is it that you want me to leave?"

Frank gave a fleeting glance to his father, then looked down at the floor. "It may as well be said openly, and without the heat of an argument. That is what I mean. It would be better for all of us if you went."

"And what do you think you'd do without me?"

"I'd manage."

"You may find you have to."

James stirred in his seat. He had heard enough bickering. It wasn't the first time this had come up, and it wouldn't be the last, but it was enough for to-night. "Peter is not leaving, and you cannot get along without him, Frank. Shall we retire for the night with the understanding that for now Peter will not ride with the Swing men? Let's see how serious Albert is with his intention of ending the disturbances. Good night to you both."

Albert was very serious. He showed up unexpectedly at the Berean house several times, and always during the evening. Peter was always present, which Albert attributed smugly to his own efforts. Angry and tense, Peter was tempted to leave the house and join the Swing riders right under Albert's ferret nose. But he remained at home, and for the next few nights the Bereans were all together.

Peter walked the fields twice as frequently. He became short-tempered with Rosalind. More often than not he went off alone to stand by the weir, gazing at it as though the season were spring and he would at any moment see a trout dash itself against the barricades.

It was a nerve-wracking time for all of them. Every night they would stand in front of the house and see the night sky turn colors as it glowed from the light of fires. It was all around them, and sooner or later it would have to reach the Bereans or by their exclusion the Swing rioters would condemn Peter as one of them.

"If we only knew what was going to happen and when," Meg cried, wringing her plump hands together.

"We would if you'd agree to let me meet with them. We could even arrange for them to fire a rick with dry grass. There'd be no loss at all."

"No. You stay here," James said flatly.

"Don't take any more chances," Meg added. "Things are so bad as it is, we want no more brought down on our heads."

Peter looked at both of them. "If you had more faith in me you'd trust me to ride out unseen and do what must be done without incident."

"You'll stay here," James repeated.

The days marched on, the nights continued to be reddened by the fires, and Albert organized his forces in earnest.

Hourly the parish officers visited the farms checking for anything amiss and relaying the information to the variety of other petty officers Albert had rounded up. It looked as though they were preparing for invasion: men trooped by in regiments; carts of soldiers were transported day and night.

Rumors, rampant before, became wilder and more frequent than ever. Panic was beginning to seep in, where before there had been respectful fear. The high roads were reportedly blocked off by the rioters. Travelers were being murdered and soldiers defeated at every turn. There was no one left unarmed, and no one who did not at least half believe the stories being circulated.

On the tenth night after Peter ended the rides, the family was gathered in the parlor after supper.

"I'm going to check the hay fields," Peter said.

"You went not an hour ago. Sit down and relax a bit, dear," Meg said and patted the seat next to her.

"Oh, let him go!" Rosalind pouted. "That's all he thinks of anyway. Look at him. Just look at him. If he isn't pacing he is staring out the windows. He might as well be outside for all he cares about what is going on in here."

"I think I'll come with you," Frank said. "I don't know what it is, but I have been feeling edgy myself tonight."

Peter and Frank went outside. The parlor was completely silent as though they were all waiting and listening. Stephen finally stood up. "I think I'll join them."

"Be sure you call out so they know who you are,"

Meg said, her hands automatically beginning to twist in her lap.

"I will. I have no desire to meet Peter in the dark with him thinking me the enemy. He is bad enough when he is playing." He laughed and put his jacket on, then stopped still, listening as they all did. First there was the sound of the gun, then of men yelling. All of them ran from the house, crowding through the door and spilling into the front yard.

At first they saw nothing, and then a column of flame wriggled up at the south end of the hay field. Peter's and Frank's forms could be seen in relief as the fire took hold. Little columns of thin brilliance shot up in various sections of the field; then it all seemed to blaze.

James ordered Meg to get anything that would hold water, and all the blankets and sheets they could wet down.

"Callie, you and Stephen go to the well. Fill everything; wet everything. Rosalind, go to the barn and get all the receptacles from there. Anna, you come with me."

Callie and Stephen drew bucket after bucket of water to be thrown on those parts of the field that hadn't yet caught fire, in hopes that the flames could be contained and then controlled. Stephen was doing the heavy work, but both were panting and straining.

"It's turned," Stephen shouted. "It's going toward the cow shed. You'll have to do this alone, Callie. I've got to get the animals out of there."

It was all confusion for the better part of the night; but slowly the fire was reduced to a smoldering mass of sodden hay and burnt earth. The outbuilding steamed, reeking of acrid smoke. It would take weeks to repair the damage; but the buildings still stood. Meg, who had come to take Stephen's place at the well, leaned heavily on the stone ledge, looking around her; then she slumped to the ground. "I am too tired to move," she sighed, but Callie heard relief in her voice. The fire was under control and they had come through it. "Are the others coming in?"

"Peter, Anna, and Frank are, but I don't see Uncle James, Stephen, or Rosalind."

"They'll be coming soon, I expect. Help me up, dear."

Callie helped Meg back to the house and into a chair in the parlor. Rosalind was already there, looking remarkably fresh.

"All over?" she asked brightly.

"Where have you been?" Callie demanded.

"The smell of the smoke was making me ill. I think . . ." Rosalind stopped as Peter, Anna, and Frank came in followed closely by Stephen.

"Rosalind, give us a hand with Peter. He's burned his arm," Frank said and motioned toward the kitchen. "Did anyone see to the animals?"

"The animals are all right," Stephen said.

"You got them out?"

Stephen nodded and Frank seemed satisfied, but only for a moment. "You didn't put them back in the shed, did you?"

"No. The smell of smoke and ash was too strong. They are grazing over near my hill. They'll be all right for now."

"Good. Where's Pa? Hasn't he come in yet?"

"I haven't seen him since the beginning," Anna said. "He was with me when we first went out. I thought he went after the animals. Didn't you see him, Stephen?"

"He wasn't there," Stephen said. Each of them looked at the other, but not fast enough for Meg to miss the concern registering among them. Bone weary and unsteady on her feet, Meg rose and went to the door.

"We'll go, Ma. Nothing has happened. Sit down."

"Something has happened to him. He's out there and I'm going . . ."

"Ma, he's all right. Stay here. Anna, take care of her. We'll go. Pa knows how to take care of himself. He's probably seeing to something we overlooked," Stephen insisted and thrust Meg into Anna's capable hands. "We'll find him."

"I want to come with you, Stephen. I want to see where James is."

"You'll only slow them down, Mother Berean," Anna said, and put her arm around Meg. "If something has happened the men can help him far better and faster than you could." She nodded for Frank and Stephen to go.

Callie slipped out the door just steps ahead of them, hurrying across the barnyard toward the smoldering field. Behind her firelights flickered in the darkness once more as they lit torches. From time to time she looked up from the search and could see the dots of flame marking the passage of the men through the field. After making a complete circuit they all met at the entrance to the field. None of them had seen James. Their concern was now real and deep. Not one of them thought to tell Callie to go inside or wondered why she was wandering around alone. All of them thought only of James. He answered no call. No one had heard any noise or seen any sign of his having been there.

Separating, they each took a section of the farm where the disturbance was seen or heard. It covered a lot of ground and promised the rest of the night would be spent searching if James did not call out to guide them, or come back on his own. Since he was the most familiar with them, Peter searched the woods. Frank covered the fields that were not yet threshed and the one that had burned that night.

Stephen retraced his steps from where he had left Callie at the well and went to the cow shed and the horse barn. Although Stephen had not seen him, it was possible that James had been there, perhaps fallen or hurt and Stephen hadn't known. Inch by inch he searched inside and out of the cow shed and then the horses' stalls and the stable and barn.

Peter was having the same ill luck in the woods. It would take him all night and longer to cover one section of the woods. Frank found the same to be true of the fields. A man could lie on the ground and not be seen in the darkness unless his seeker had the dubious fortune of tripping over him.

Callie was looking in the tool shed and all the smaller buildings nearest to the house. Her way was darker for she had no torch, but she was thorough. Her search, however, was equally fruitless. Finally she heard one of them call, and all ran to meet at their designated spot at the opening of the field.

As they each told of their failures, Anna ran across the yard. She was panting and struggling to catch her breath as she clung to Frank. "Mother Berean doesn't know it yet, but Natalie is missing too. I went to her room . . . no one thought about her when the fire started. . . . Did she go out with any of you? I don't recall seeing her."

One after another they affirmed that Natalie had not been in any of the twosomes that had gone to help.

"What about Rosalind? Did she see Natalie? She went back to the house sooner than the rest of us," Callie said.

"She hasn't seen Natalie . . . before or after. She

thinks Natalie left before the fire started. Do any of you remember if she was in the parlor before Frank and Peter went out?"

"No," they said in unison. Then Peter sighed, winced a little as he touched his burned arm. "You'd better get Rosalind out here too, Anna. We're all going to have to search. If Natalie is missing, it could mean that Pa saw her and went after her. I just hope none of the rioters saw her. In any case, our best bet is the woods."

"But if Papa is with her, why wouldn't he call out or answer us?" Anna asked.

"How should I know?" Peter said irritably.

"Maybe she was hurt," Callie said.

"He would come for help." Stephen looked toward the woods. "Let's begin or we'll never find them."

Once more they set out in pairs, each looking to one side or the other of the network of paths through the woods.

"Let's go to the pickers' cottages, Stephen," Callie said. "She was very upset that the gypsy had left. Maybe she went back to the campsite again."

"We can look. One place is as good as another," Stephen said grimly and hurried along, forcing Callie to run to keep up with him.

It was so unlike her first trip to the gypsy camp when she and Natalie had been laughing with excitement. There was no laughter in any of the Bereans tonight. As the minutes slipped away from them and there was no sign of James or Natalie, Callie's foreboding grew.

They came to the campsite, walking more slowly and cautiously, their eyes straining to see into the dark shadows of the overhanging trees and brush. Quickly Stephen put his hand out, stopping Callie. He raised the torch.

Natalie sat on the log where the old gypsy crone had sat. Slowly a golden arc of light from Stephen's torch crept over the log and over her. She stared at the darker patch of earth within the wavering arc of light. Dark and smelling of scorched wood, the spot showed her where the gypsy's fire had been. Truly she had been there. Otherwise the fire couldn't have been. Oblivious to the noises, the voices around her, Natalie was pleased with her mental gymnastics. The gypsy was real because the fire had been real. She began to hum. One tiny piece at a time her shattered thoughts began to emerge from the haze of nothingness that had overcome her today and then had reached an unbearable white-hot brilliance that night. It had been so bright inside her head it pained her, drove her, blinded her so nothing else could get in.

She reached down. The ashes of the Romany woman's long-dead fire funneled through her fingers like the sands of an exhausted hourglass.

"Natalie!" The voice sounded far away. She looked at Callie's hand on her arm, but it didn't feel right. It seemed that Callie was touching someone other than herself. From the corner of her eye she watched Callie's long, graceful fingers make the material of her gown crinkle. Natalie thought of shadowy snakes coiling around Callie's fingers. She fixed her eyes on the ashes. Only they were real.

"Nattie . . . Nattie, do you hear me? Are you all right?" Her voice sounded shrill to Natalie. Sharp and loud enough to pierce her eardrum, burst her head.

"Stephen! Her gown! Look, the hem is burned. Oh, Nattie, say something—please! Are you hurt? Did . . . did those men find you?"

Natalie put her hand to her ears. Her skull was splintering, the sounds distorting and ripping the bone from her brain. Then she began to cry. She couldn't keep her hands on her ears and still touch the real ashes. She leaned over, digging her fingers deep into the blackened ashes, clutching a fistful of them, then watching the black stream fall to the ground.

Someone was crying. Then Stephen stood in front of her. Stephen her brother. Stephen worried. She closed him out, staring hard at the ashes. Dark ashes. A dark-haired woman.

"Are you all right?" Stephen's voice shook. The torch he held, making the wavering golden circle, wavered more. The circle jiggled and shook. The earth looked as though it were falling apart. They would fall through the molten gold ellipse.

Stephen's free hand ran over her shoulder. He moved the light about, forcing her chin up, making her hold out her arms, making her stand. "We'll go home now, Natalie."

"No! I'm waiting for the gypsy."

Callie knelt on the ground, her skirts in the ashes. "She's gone, Nattie. She's not coming back."

"She promised!"

Stephen walked impatiently from the clearing, taking the light with him.

Callie pleaded with Natalie.

Natalie shook her head frantically, her hands pressed tight to her skull. "She must come back! She must! I need her! I need her to help me!"

"Nattie, you don't need her. We're all here. We'll help you. We . . ." Callie's mouth opened on the next word, but no sound came. Stephen had returned. He strode up to Natalie, his face marked with anger, his body rigid. "Why didn't you come for us? At least answer our calls?"

Natalie hummed and stared at the ashes.

Stephen grabbed her small wrist, making her cry out.

"Stephen!" Callie jumped to her feet, her hand restraining his.

Tightly he said, "They've found Papa. Not ten feet from here. In the woods. She knew. She had to know."

Callie looked from one to the other. "Is he . . ."

"I don't know," Stephen snapped, then pulled again at Natalie's arm. "Get up."

Natalie whimpered, lowering her head and curling her back as if by bringing herself nearer the ground she could avoid Stephen.

"I said get up!" He jerked her arm so hard she staggered to her feet off balance and screaming in fright. He grabbed hold of her shoulders, spun her to face him, and shook her until she gasped for breath.

"Stephen, stop! You're hurting her."

"She knew he was there! Damn it, she had to know. Why? Why didn't you call for help?"

Callie clung to his arm as Natalie's mouth opened in a silent scream. Her arms swung disjointedly in a macabre doll's dance. Her tongue curled, blocking her mouth; her eyes rolled up deep into her skull. "Answer me! Tell me what happened! I'll shake it from you if I must!"

"Stephen!" Callie screamed, pounding on his arms and back.

Blinking, his face a rigid mask, he stopped all motion. He stared at his limp, unconscious sister, his arms slowly lowering her raglike to the ground. Tears spurted from his eyes; his chest heaved with ripping, inarticulate sounds of rage and pain and shock.

Callie, choked by her own fear and tears, knelt between Natalie and Stephen. With one hand she held Natalie's hand on her lap. The other gripped Stephen's coat lapel, holding fast as though she could keep the tension and fear from growing if she could only anchor both of them.

Callie was afraid to speak to him on the way back. Stephen carried Natalie back to the house.

Callie followed him up the stairs to Natalie's room. He laid her on the bed, then stood back staring at her. His face was still etched with pain and bitter sadness. His dark eyes glittered like sparking coals. Almost inaudibly he spoke to his unconscious sister. "I don't know what part you had in this, Nat, or why, but it's been a bad night's work."

Chapter 14

Stunned and bewildered, Meg took her place at the side of James's bed. His lips were nearly blue, his face ashen. For once Meg had no idea what to do for her husband. She had no means by which to bring comfort to him. She looked helplessly at the faces of her family, who came and went from the room hoping to see some improvement.

Meg followed the doctor's instructions faithfully, but each small improvement in James's health was secured by hours of worry and nursing and sleeplessness. And it was Meg who paid the price of those long hours. Aware now of the fragility of life as she had never been before—not even when she had watched two babies, born between Frank and Peter, waste away and die—Meg drew in the boundaries of her life closer to herself and James. She'd never given much thought to how much she counted on James. With cruel suddenness it was pressed on her that the air she breathed was only pure when it carried his scent. The food he ate pleased her palate. Her thoughts, loves, opinions, desires were founded on James.

She sluffed off responsibility for the rest of the house as though she had never welcomed its homey weight. The small unnoticed chores that keep a house warm and hospitable were now left to take care of themselves, or to be recognized and taken care of by the other family members. Meg's entire attention focused on James, for he was helpless and needed her, and she was helpless and needed him.

It took the other members of the family some time to realize that Meg had relinquished the general family concerns to whomever would accept them. Anna was worried about Natalie, and expected Meg to be as well.

"Mother Berean," Anna called, hurrying to the kitchen to talk with Meg as she fixed James's tea tray. "I don't know what is to be done with Natalie. Callie and I are quite worried."

Meg looked up from her task, maternal concern quickly clouding her eyes. "She's not ill?"

Anna hesitated. "No . . . that is, I don't know."

Meg raised her eyebrows. "You don't know?"

Anna, accustomed to Meg's placid, inquisitive way of sitting down to discuss any problem, was nonplussed by this quick, almost brusque Meg who was obviously more interested in arranging the china on James's tray than she was in Anna's worries. Awkwardly Anna raised her hands, helpless to explain succinctly what she sensed. "I don't understand her. Since the fire, she's changed."

"Changed? How?"

"She . . . as often as I've criticized Rosalind for her lack of charity, I can't say I blame her now. Natalie has become impossible."

Meg sighed, touching the side of the teapot. "I do wish they would simply stay away from one another.

James's health must come before all else. You tell them, Anna."

"Rosalind is trying, Mother Berean! But Natalie has taken to following her around. She dogs her every step. It has been like that for two days. Every place she goes when Peter is not around, Natalie is steps behind her. It's . . . it's . . . eerie."

"Bosh! Tell Peter to do something about it."

In one of her rare critical moments Anna frowned. "Oh, Peter! No one tells him anything. He never listens."

"Well, where is Callie? Why doesn't she help? Natalie is quite fond of Callie. I'm sure Nattie is just lonely and worried about her father." Meg patted Anna's shoulder. "We all are, dear. You must make allowances. None of us is himself—not without James to guide us. You talk to Callie. Things will be back to normal soon."

"Mother Berean, I don't think you understand . . ."

Meg smiled sweetly, her mind only on James. "Tea's getting cold. We'll talk later, Anna."

Ploddingly stubborn, Anna stepped forward. "I . . . I'm not certain Callie should be asked to . . . to look after Natalie. You don't understand. Something happened to her the night of the fire. It's as if she entered a different world. She . . . she frightens me sometimes. She's so single-minded . . . she thinks only of Rosalind."

"I might expect such fantasies from Rosalind, but not from you, Anna."

"Come see for yourself. Please." Anna moved toward the garden door. Reluctantly Meg followed.

"They were standing here just a few minutes ago," Anna said, bewildered.

"Well, they aren't now. Perhaps they took a walk." Anna ran a few steps, looking to each side. Then she went toward the herb garden. "Please try this one last spot. If they're not here, I shall say no more."

They entered the gate of the walled garden. Meg stopped short, staring in disbelief.

Rosalind was backed against the far wall. "Go away!" she cried at Natalie.

Natalie stood immediately, whirling to face Meg. She ran to her mother and hugged her. The tinkling sound of her laughter filled the garden. "How is Papa? Better I hope."

"He is much better, Natalie. What were you doing when I entered the garden?"

She laughed again, the pitch a bit higher; then she moved closer to Rosalind. "We were playing a game. That is all. Rosalind is the deer, and I am the hound. It is a silly child's game, but I like it. Only Rosalind will never remember that deer cannot talk. She always talks when she gets trapped."

"She sounded very frightened to me, Nattie."

"But of course! She is the hart! The hound had her trapped. She is supposed to be frightened. That is part of the game. You must act . . . like we do in charades. I do love to play games, Mama. You know, I shall always be part little girl. Even when I am an old woman I shall still be a little girl sometimes, and sometimes play games as I do now."

"It is no game!" Rosalind gasped. Her eyes never leaving Natalie, she stepped onto the path. "She is playing no game. She means it. You haven't seen her or been victimized by her. She'd tear me to pieces. She would! Lock her up or she'll bring me to harm, and it'll be on your head. I'm going to talk to Peter. Someone has to do something about her. Keep her away from me!"

"Harm you?" Natalie asked, all innocence and hurt. "Why do you say such cruel things about me in front of Mama? It was your idea to play, and we were having such a good time until they came. Why are you telling lies now? You're just ashamed to admit you like to play too. Why do you want to hurt me?" Tears formed in Natalie's eyes.

Confused, Anna retreated. "You were playing hart and hounds?"

Rosalind looked frantically from Meg to Anna. "You don't believe her! Surely you can't! You couldn't! I'm telling you she's a lunatic. She . . . she . . ."

"Go inside, Rosalind," Meg said. "We are all too bestirred to know what to believe. No harm came to you."

"Only because you came into the garden. What will happen next time when no one comes?"

"Nonsense!"

"I see," Rosalind said. She smoothed the front of her dress, her chin rising to its normal haughty angle. "Well, *Mrs. Berean,* let me tell you something and you'd better listen well. Don't you let that loony daughter of yours near me again, or I'll take proper care of her. It's only because she is Peter's sister that I didn't strike back at her today. Let her follow me again and I won't think about who she is, only *what* she is. Remember that, *Mrs. Berean!*"

"How dare you speak to me in such a manner!"

"And what manner is that, *Mrs. Berean?*"

"Why! You impudent piece of baggage."

"You just keep her away from me. You can be assured Peter will listen to the truth of what happened today, and not some story about a game of hart and hounds. She has gone too far this time."

But Rosalind did not get her opportunity to tell Peter of Natalie's new game that night. Albert was pounding on the door shortly after they finished supper.

"Peter!" he said breathlessly as he hurried into the

dining room. "You have got to let me sign you as one of the yeomanry immediately."

"You've lost the little sense you were born with. I want nothing to do with your little army, Albert. You know how I feel. You'll have to play general all by yourself. And I don't discuss business in the dining room."

Albert dogged Peter's steps, talking as the man walked to the study. "It's too late in the day for sympathies and principles; listen to me! For once, shut your mouth and listen! The whole thing is over. It's done. The arrests are being made now . . . hundreds of them as I speak to you. We'll not have an inch of space left in the jails with all of them being rounded up. You're likely to be one of them if you don't start listening to me."

"You want me to assist you in arresting these men? The same men I've been trying to help?" Peter asked incredulously. He broke into a wide grin. "Sit down and we'll have a game of dice, Albert. You've been working too hard."

"I didn't come here for my own pleasure," Albert said seriously. "I'm trying to help you. The Swing riots are over. They are finished; get that into your head. There is nothing you can do now except protect yourself. My men are arresting everyone connected with them right now. I told you this was coming. This time you'd better heed my warning, if not for yourself then for the sake of your family."

"Listen to him, Peter," Frank said, mopping his forehead. "He should know what is happening. God! The last thing we need is for a Berean to be locked up with a bunch of rabble. My God, can you imagine the damage it would do to our name?"

"I am not going to take part in arresting these men."

"Then let me swear you in as a yeoman. You can

find some excuse for being absent, but sign up. Protect yourself."

"Sign it, Peter! You owe us that much. We've put up with your damned nonsense; now do something for your family," Frank shouted.

Glaring at his brother, Peter refused to sign the paper, then suddenly he agreed. "Make me a part of your little army, Albert."

Albert looked at him suspiciously. Peter looked too cocky, too sure of himself standing with his hands on his hips. Albert didn't trust him, but Peter had called his bluff and he couldn't back down.

"Now I am a yeoman. Is everyone satisfied?" Peter looked around the room. "Just remember not to ask me to do your dirty work. I'm only your prize—for show only."

Frank clasped Peter's shoulder. "We all know how you feel about this, but you're really not compromising your principles, Peter. Your first duty is to the family . . . and Rosalind. Can't you look at it that way?"

Peter glanced away from Frank, suppressing a bitter smile at the degree to which his principles had grown in nobility now that they were to be laid aside and Frank had his own way. "A family call must always be heeded, eh, Frank? The family name preserved. Well, all that is settled. Albert has me safe and sound, family calls heard and not a principle bent. Let's say no more about it. Anyone for cards?"

Albert had remained quiet. Now he walked slowly toward Peter. "If you have it in your mind to use your position as yeoman for other than its rightful purpose, Peter, *don't.*"

"You wrong me, Albert. What could I have in mind?"

"Perhaps freeing men already arrested."

"Come now, who would have the audacity?"

"I won't bite at your bait tonight, Peter. Just remember what I've said. I take my responsibilities seriously. To you they may seem of little consequence, but to me they are important." He turned to face Frank. He shook his head and smiled as though about to discuss a naughty child, but his eyes were hard and held a warning Frank understood. "He'll never change, Frank. You'll have to keep a steady hand on him. I've got to be off. There's more to be done, and little time."

"Watch yourself, Albert." Peter shook his hand as he left.

He waited a quarter of an hour, plenty of time for Albert to be off the property, before he said, "I'd better check the fields."

"I'll come with you," Frank said.

"Don't bother. It's late and I don't mind going alone."

Frank hesitated, wondering as Albert had if Peter would be so brash as to swear loyalty to the yeomanry one minute and betray it the next by riding to the aid of the Swing rioters.

Peter grinned, clapping his hand on his brother's thick shoulder. "There'll be no trouble tonight. General Albert's out there with his army."

They both laughed and Frank gave in without a murmur of protest. It was late. Anna was waiting. And he was tired.

Peter fussed with a lantern until Frank ponderously mounted the stairs. Then he went out the door, leaving the unlit lantern on the front stoop.

Only Callie saw Peter leave. She was sitting at her window seat looking down into the stable yard. She watched him walk stealthily, distinguishable only as a darker form in the darkness. He entered the stable, then emerged leading his horse slowly, quietly away from the house until he was lost in the inky black barrier of the woods. She might never have noticed had he not been staying close to the farm of late. Nor would she have been alarmed had she not heard it said so often that it was vitally important that he not be seen with the laborers now.

She sat for several minutes wondering what she should do. Then she heard Frank's heavy tread in the hallway. Instantly fear leaped in her. Perhaps she had misguessed Peter's night errand. She ran from the room, nearly colliding with Frank.

"Frank! What's wrong? Is Uncle James worse?"

Frank looked puzzled. "What made you think that? Having bad dreams?"

"I . . ." Callie stammered, confused and not knowing how best to help Peter now that she knew the truth.

Frank watched her, then began to frown. "What made you ask about Pa?"

"Nothing," she blurted too quickly.

"Peter," Frank whispered, his face paling, then suffusing with blood. "The fool! The bloody irresponsible fool! He'll get himself hanged for sure."

Callie grew woodenly quiet, her heart thumping hard against her ribs. Then she asked calmly, "He went with the Swing men tonight?"

"The bloody liar! He just gave his word to stay out of it."

"Peter?"

"Albert swore him in as a yeoman. They're rounding up the scoundrels tonight. Albert has every ablebodied man out for the task. It was damned decent of him to give Peter the chance to align himself on the right side. And this is the thanks my brother gives him! Damn Peter for his deceit. He'll bring ruin to

this family yet! I should have known better than to
trust him. He gave in too easily."

"What will you do now?"

"Nothing. Hope the fool gets away safely."

"Shouldn't we . . . you . . ."

Frank scowled, his face set and hard. "No other Berean will take part in this. Pa forbids us to side against
Peter, and I forbid this family to side against the law.
Peter will have to pay the whole price of his arro-
gance alone."

She forced herself to smile. "He'll be safe. Good
night, Frank."

"Good night, Callie, and mind—no waiting."

"Oh, no. Waiting won't help. Good night."

Callie slipped inside her bedroom and closed the
door softly. Soundlessly she dressed; then, carrying
her boots, she slipped barefooted down the stairs.

She had been on a horse no more than a dozen
times in her life and Natalie hadn't been the best of
teachers. But what Natalie lacked in pedagogic talents, necessity provided. From the moment she had
seen Peter lead his horse across the darkened stable
yard, a cold lump of knowing fear had been growing
in her chest. As she had seen him do, she led her horse
across the yard until she reached the woods. Taking a
deep breath and saying a quick prayer that she had
the cinch tight, she placed her foot in the stirrup. As
always the horse moved and Callie hopped awkwardly, trying to get purchase with which to mount.
Somehow she did, and sat unsteadily astride the man's
saddle.

Before her loomed the blackened woods with its
endless twisting, interconnecting paths. Peter could
have taken any one of them, heading in any direction.
Overwhelmed with sudden despair, she knew she'd
never find him in the woods. For several minutes she

sat undecided, clinging to the reins. The horse, restive and aware of the uncertainty of its rider, tossed its head, sidling until Callie's leg was pressed uncomfortably against a tree trunk.

All her attention on the horse now, Callie poked futilely at the beast. From a distance she heard noises. Horses. The crashing of brush. Men's voices. The crack of gunfire. Trembling, she leaned low against the horse's neck. "Come on, Gent, live up to your name, please," she whispered. The accompanying kick she gave him was gentle, but Gent raised his big head, listening as Callie was to the sounds coming nearer.

Her heart pounding in fright, Callie erred in giving Gent a mighty kick at the same time the crossing horsemen thundered past. With a great toss of his head Gent bolted forward, plunging off the path and through the low brush toward the other horses. Having lost the small control she had, Callie clung to the animal's mane, her knees pressed tightly to the saddle, her arms and fingers aching with the effort to stay seated. She didn't dare to lift her head.

Around her men shouted wildly. "Halt!" "Flank them!" Horses snorted; some crashed through the brush. The yeoman and the Swing men shoved at each other wielding great sticks like cudgels. Others slashed at their adversaries with spades and shovels, matching their crude implements against swords and muskets.

Amid the straining grunts of men fighting in the pitch-dark forest, Callie pressed harder against Gent's neck. He lunged forward as he was hit on the rump, only to slam into another horse. An enraged cry came from the rider. He brought his crop down hard on Gent's flank. "Hah!" Again the crop came down as he lashed at the seemingly riderless horse. Gent took off in an erratic twisting canter, brushing past trees with Callie plastered to his back holding back cries of pain and fright. Not until the sounds were fading behind them did Callie even attempt to gain control of the horse.

Finally she let out the cramped, hurting sobs she'd been holding back. Albert's men were everywhere. They were rounding up the laborers. Had Peter been one of those shouting, cursing, battling men whose ragged ranks she'd just passed through? She didn't even know how to control her horse. How could she help? Why had she ever come out tonight? What could she do?

Dry sobs caught at her chest and stomach with each breath. She was terrified. And alone. And she didn't know how to help Peter. The sounds of the fight grew more distant. Without seeing, or even understanding how she knew, Callie was sure the Swing men had lost. They were being taken to the village.

She shuddered. It was over. Her fear of the horse forgotten, she sat straight in the saddle, her hands firmer on the reins. She looked around her, her eyes fixing in the direction of the farm. Almost roughly she pulled Gent up short. She wouldn't give up. With a firm tug on the reins she turned the horse to the road leading to Seven Oaks. She'd risk no more encounters along the woods path.

She would find Peter in the open. She should have realized from the beginning that all she could do was wait in the village to see if the yeomen brought him in as a prisoner. She jogged along the narrow row of cottages, coming as near to the town square as she dared.

She waited in the shadows there for nearly two hours. Groups of men came in, some passing right by her. Loud triumphant voices cut through the night as other, quiet, beaten men were herded toward the square. Callie tensed as each new group came, her ears alert, her eyes straining to recognize one face among the many. Tired and frightened, her neck and back aching from tension, she nearly cried out as she saw one man with hair lighter than the others. He wore no hat. Peter seldom did, even in the worst weather. She bit her lip, racked with fear and indecision. She wasn't sure. It was dark. Was it Peter?

She began to smooth her dress, torn by branches and filthy with dirt and bits of twigs and burrs. Then she thought better. She took a stick and added a fresh scratch to the others on her face. She rubbed dirt into her forehead and on the shoulders and front of her coat. Satisfied that she looked sufficiently disheveled to have fallen from a horse, she wandered up to the town square.

"Can you tell me where I'll find Mr. Albert Foxe?" she asked one of the yeomen. "He is a friend of my family's . . . I've had an accident . . . please."

Callie carefully avoided looking at the line of men being shoved into some kind of order on the far side of the square. If he were not with them, she would lose heart when she saw Albert, not to mention the trouble she'd be in. If he were there, she would be frightened witless. She followed the man, keeping her eyes down.

The streets were filled with men milling about, and yeomen shouting orders, obscenities, and threats at the laborers. There was a carnival air in the night, the same sadistic glee attendant at a bear baiting. She was taken to a building and told to wait in the entry.

"Callie?" Albert didn't try to hide his surprise as he walked out of one of the rooms toward her. "What in mercy's name are you doing here? Does anyone know you are out? Who is with you? What's happened?"

"Peter . . . Peter knows, but that is all," she whispered, cowering from the sight and sound of the activity around her.

"Here, here, come inside with me where we can talk." He led her into the room he had just left. "You'll have to excuse the clutter. We've been at this day and night," he said, indicating the makeshift cots and pallets. "Now, what's all this? Here! You're hurt. Let me clean your face and see to that scratch."

"I'm all right. I scratched it when I fell. In the confusion Peter and I got separated. I mean we were out for a ride, and then all these people were everywhere and I got lost. I can't find him. Do you know where he is?"

Albert tugged at his mustache. "What made you come here? Why should I know of Peter's whereabouts?"

Callie sat speechless for a moment, her mouth working but no thought coming to fill it with words. "I didn't know who else to ask," she said finally, then looked up at him imploringly. "Do you know where he is?"

"I might. You got separated, you say? Where?"

"I fell off my horse. I don't ride very well. Peter was helping me when it happened."

"What happened?"

"Horsemen! All around us and the next thing I knew I was all alone and I couldn't find Peter. You said you know where he is. Will you take me to him?"

He watched her carefully. She was embarrassed and uncomfortable. "He's been arrested, Callie. I suppose you didn't know that."

A great shudder ran through her making it difficult to speak. "Oh, no! No, I didn't know, but it's a mistake! Surely you can see that. Could he please take me home now, Albert? I am very tired. Aunt Meg will be so angry."

"I should think so. It is nearly two in the morning. Do you and Peter often go for midnight rides?"

Callie stared at him dry-mouthed. "Just this once," she said softly. "Will you take me to Peter now, please?"

"Perhaps. But there is one thing, Callie. You understand that Peter was arrested in the midst of a band of Swing men? Since you claim he was with you and not where we found him, you will be willing to testify in court to that effect, will you not?"

"Testify?"

"Yes. Of course, my men will have to tell the opposite story from yours so it will involve a risk on your part. The judges will have to see that someone is lying. A man cannot be in two places at one time doing two different things. But if your story is the true one, you have nothing to fear. Are you still willing to challenge the word of my men, Callie? Bear false witness?"

Callie's face was as white as the wall behind her. She trembled so, her head shook like that of an old woman. But her eyes, so filled with purpose, looked steadily at Albert. "I'll testify."

Sighing, Albert shook his head. "Shall we go see if Peter recalls having lost you this evening? Perhaps if he is as smart as he is lucky you may be able to get him out of this mess after all. That is if he doesn't make you a liar with the first words out of his mouth."

She walked by Albert's side as they crossed the square, afraid to utter another word. When they were within a few feet of the group of prisoners, Callie spotted Peter. She bolted free of Albert and ran to him. "Oh! After we got lost, I thought I'd never find you again. All those people yelling and running about! I was so frightened of the horses," she cried, clinging to the front of his coat. His arms closed around her.

He looked up, angry eyes blazing at Albert. "What are you doing with her?"

Albert smiled catlike. He moved a step nearer. "I'm not with her. She claims *you* were. Let's hear it, Peter. What were you doing tonight? Make it good. I'd hate to see all her efforts go for naught. She's willing to risk perjury for you."

Peter's arms tightened around Callie. With a hard, cold-eyed smile, he said, "Didn't you hear her, Albert, I was busy being a fool and losing track of Callie. She might never have found me again."

"But where were you?"

"I already told you, Albert! We'd gone for a ride and I got lost from him in a crowd of your men," Callie said quickly. Peter grinned and repeated what she had said.

Albert looked from one of them to the other, undecided, tempted. A half-smile crossed his face; his tongue licked his partially open lips.

Callie clung tighter to Peter's coat, the material bunched in her fists. "Albert . . ." she whispered, "please . . . let us go home."

He looked at Peter again, his eyes hard and filled with dislike. Then he glanced about angrily until he spotted one of his men. Roughly he pulled Peter out of the line of prisoners. "Don't you know better than to arrest one of our own men!" he shouted angrily at the deputy. His eyes still cold, he said to Peter, "Take her home before someone else hears her cockeyed tale."

"Albert—she wouldn't lie. Just look at her," Peter said, his lips twitching in amusement, his eyes sparkling as though what he and Albert played was after all a game.

"I have," Albert said curtly and walked away from them.

"Peter, please hurry. Don't stay here any longer. I'm afraid." Callie pulled at his hand, urging him from the square and back to the row of cottages where she had tethered Gent.

"Wait a minute, you little devil's spawn! What do you think you are doing out on a night like this, alone? What do I have to do to keep you safe? Tie you to your bed nights?" Peter's voice was low as he turned her toward him.

"You needed . . ."

He laughed out loud and swung her up into his arms, whirling her around and around until she was dizzy. "Do you know what you did? What you risked? Is my life worth trading your own for?"

"Albert said I will have to testify that you were with me. What shall I do if they don't believe me, Peter? What will happen to us?"

"Not a thing," he whispered into her ear. "Because Albert is never going to have you testify to anything. I'd kill him with my bare hands before I'd let him harm you. There are too few like you on this earth, Callie. Even idiots like me know something special when we see it."

She was not very steady when he released her, but she was speechless, and remained so most of the way home.

"Would Albert have let you go if I hadn't come?" she asked as they neared the farm.

"I doubt it. Albert is a duty-bound man, and he's been wanting to catch me out for a long time." Peter laughed mirthlessly. "Even if he'd wanted to release me, which he didn't, Albert never does anything improper if he can help it. If it isn't in the book, Albert won't do it. Poor Albert; he was probably as relieved as I was to see you. What a tale! A midnight ride in the middle of the Swing riot arrests . . . with you."

She wriggled on the saddle behind him. "Well, it wasn't so easy trying to think up a reason that I should be there, you know. It was the best I could do."

"It worked. That makes it good enough; and anyway it will give us all a good story to laugh about."

"You're not going to tell everyone!"

"Of course. Why not? They'd enjoy a laugh over it."

"But Peter! I'm not supposed to be out. They think I am asleep. Aunt Meg will be terribly angry. I only came because Frank said it would kill Uncle James if he found out you were gone."

"You didn't come for me?"

She blushed and remained silent.

"I think you came for me," he said.

"Please—I don't want you to tell them."

"You're a heroine, Callie. It's not every day a man's life is saved by a pretty girl. You can't make me keep that a secret, can you? You alone made an effort to help me. You think my family shouldn't be told that? I suppose they'd see me hang before they'd risk a hair off their own heads. No, Callie darling, I'm going to tell them."

Frank had been no more honest with Callie than she had been with him. The difference between the two was Frank's lethargic patience. About an hour after Peter had left, Frank went to the stables. He found not one, but two of the riding horses missing. He raced to Callie's room. In his agitation, he awakened the entire household.

They gathered one by one, coming sleepy-eyed from their rooms into the hallway. The confusion and hushed talk, as plans were made for Stephen and Frank to take the carriage, wakened James.

"What is going on out there?" he called from his room.

"It's nothing, Pa," Frank answered and shushed everyone, but not enough. James was too alert.

"It's twelve thirty. What's happened? Meg! Meg!" He struggled from his bed, clinging to the furniture. He stumbled and bumped the table. His face contorted as he grabbed for the chair and fell.

Frank and the others stood in shocked stillness, then ran to his bedroom.

James had suffered a second attack.

The carriage was put to use to fetch the doctor.

Meg again took up her vigil by his side. She sat in the darkness and wondered if she were to lose both her husband and her son tonight. And where was Callie? What had happened to the child?

Anna went down to the kitchen and made hot chocolate. No one except Rosalind and Natalie had been able to go back to sleep. They all sat waiting to hear what had taken place, hoping for the best and dreading the worst.

It was to a quiet, saddened house that Callie and Peter returned. Peter's high spirits were out of tempo with the tense drawn faces that greeted him. Their anxiety turned quickly to anger. Callie fled to her room as Peter lashed back at his brothers with anger of his own. Only when he was told of James did he quiet. Then he took the stairs two at a time. Meg, nodding sleepily, roused as he came into the room.

"Peter? It's you . . . you're safe . . . and Callie?" She began to cry softly.

Peter remained with her that night, watching over James more carefully than she, if that was possible. As always, after he had stepped out of the bounds of good sense, he was mortified and repentant. Primarily he was frightened. It was as though someone had caught him from behind when all his concentration was in front of him. By an appalling lack of prudence he had endangered the lives of three people: himself, Callie, and James. Two of them he loved dearly.

James recovered slowly and unsatisfactorily. His mind no longer responded with the quick clarity of old. But his first fear was allayed when he was told immediately that his son was safe and unharmed. James was the one person in the family who approved Callie's rash action, so Meg's scolding was mild. Instead Anna kindly and mildly reminded her of the dangers she had faced. Nice girls were not known to go riding out in the middle of the night for any reason whatever.

The arrested men did not have such good fortune on their side. By December it was bitingly cold again, and the rioting in Kent was a thing of the past. Hundreds of prisoners awaited trial. Most of them were poor and illiterate. In spite of a touted and prized system of justice, there would be no justice for them.

No man was able to testify in his own defense without implicating himself or his friends in the riots. There was no counsel for the defense. It was a desperate situation for them, and for the magistrates who had to see the matter cleared up. Bribes were offered to any person who could be persuaded to testify against his fellow rioters. The offers were tempting, for over the heads of the rioters loomed the Act of 1827, which prescribed penalties. Destruction of threshing machines could mean being transported for seven years. One of the most common offenses was the firing of ricks. For that the penalty was death.

Peter began to realize how closely he had courted real trouble. The causes of the riots—the poverty, joblessness, hunger, injustice—were all disregarded in the ensuing trials. Evidence given about background was ruled out. Most of the laborers' problems were attributed to drink. Through drinking a man would suffer distress. Wages and conditions had nothing to do with it. In the end all extenuating circumstances became irrelevant. The prejudices and preconceptions of the judges and lawyers were the ultimate evidence.

The single factor favorable to the laborers was the reluctance of the juries to convict them. That quickly became an embarrassment. So Special Commissions convicted the prisoners. The Special Commission at Winchester convicted one hundred prisoners. Six were sentenced to hang; the others were to be transported for life. A second Commission sat at Salisbury. Two men were sentenced to death. One hundred and fifty were transported for life. Some of those convicted were young; one was seven years old.

The Special Commissions and the trials moved throughout the countryside to Dorchester, Reading, Aylesbury, and Abingdon. Fortunately, as they went their inclination toward leniency increased. Winchester and Salisbury had served to produce the desired effect. Everyone knew how far into tragedy the Swing riots had plunged them.

The riots reached every home of every hamlet. Daily, families of the men involved stood at the prison gates begging for leniency. There was sympathy for these destitute people, but no help. People talked in the comfort of their homes of a situation that was "heartbreaking." The men were convicted heartbreakingly.

By the end of the trials four hundred and fifty-seven men had been transported for some designated

period of time. The length of the term mattered little,
for, having served his term, a man then had to pay his
way back to England. Few of those transported would
ever see their families again.

It was agreed generally that wages should now be
raised. People were still anxious. Perhaps the riots
would start up again. It had been frightening to see
the quiet countryside become a raging mass of determined, hungry mobs. With the transported rioters on
their way to Van Diemen's Land or Australia, wages
went up, and remained high as long as people remained anxious and worried. But as soon as memories
dimmed and things became normal, the wages returned to seven shillings a week.

The Bereans said little about the trials. There were
still too many raw feelings about the night Peter had
been arrested, and no one wanted any more division
in the family than already existed.

Peter was both relieved and ashamed at his narrow
escape. Somewhere inside himself he continued to
think that it would have turned out differently if the
educated, landed people had dared to stand beside
those illiterate masses who could neither defend themselves nor avoid being sacrificed to the fear of the
times.

It had been a long time since Peter had turned to
his father. But since James had had his second attack,
Peter had felt a closeness for him and a need to be
near him.

"I might as well be dead," James complained. "What
good am I now? I can't eat proper food, nor even get
out of bed." He roughly shoved aside his glass of chalybeate water. "I'll not swallow any more of that. What
I need is a glass of Stephen's best cider. Put me right
back on my feet again." He looked at Peter. "What is

it you have on your mind? Certainly hope it isn't my chalybeate water. Damned abominable stuff." Peter did not respond to James's effort at humor. He watched Peter's thoughtful progress to a chair. He wiped his mouth with his handkerchief. He could not speak as well as he once could. "I've got more sores on my behind than if I'd been riding for a month," James said, again trying to make Peter laugh and not notice that he sometimes drooled. One side of his face was worse than the other, he thought. He angled his head so Peter could not see so much of his left side. "What is it, Peter? What's on your mind? Or must I pry it out of you a word at a time?"

"They've transported nearly five hundred men. Nine hanged. Do you remember the Cooks, Pa?"

James was relieved to learn that Peter's serious mood had nothing to do with his illness or the look of his deformed left side. "Yes . . . son a little older than Stephen . . . don't they?"

"Henry. He knocked off the hat of one of the Boring family, I don't know who, but it doesn't matter. It was in the midst of one of the free-for-alls. They hanged him, Pa. He was nineteen years old and had done nothing."

James shook his head. "Snow will never lie upon his innocent grave."

"How do we live with things like that?"

"We don't. We die with them, and we die of them. They are man's disease."

"My disease," Peter said morosely.

"I suppose you're thinking you should have stood by their side. I can understand the feeling."

Peter laughed harshly. "Can you also understand that I feel glad it was them who were hanged and imprisoned and transported and not me?"

"Well now, which is it? Are you bothered that you

weren't hanged, or that you wanted a better fate for yourself?"

Peter rose, gesturing helplessly. "Both."

James stared at him, his mind suddenly blank. "You're leaving?"

"I shouldn't bother you with this kind of talk. I guess I wanted to see if you would despise me as I do myself. Confirmation of sorts. It's a bad day when you discover you are a coward."

"You're not a coward, Peter."

"Aren't I?"

"No. You haven't found what you believe in. You thought you knew, but it wasn't so. Perhaps your sympathies were with the laborers, but did you ever really understand what your part was? Or was it just a lark? A good cause and a good reason to be out riding and playing the hero? Knowledge is but a small part of reality, Peter. It requires understanding and wisdom as well. We all know that what was being done to the laborers was wrong, but how to change it—that required more than just the mere recognition of a wrong."

"I think I prefer cowardice to what you describe."

"It is youth."

"I am no youth. You can't call my failings the result of youth."

"You argue everything and gather no insight," James said irritably. He knew what he wanted to say to Peter to make him understand, but the words that came were words of habit. His mind would touch only the edge of the problem without letting him cut to the quick. Peter slowly moved through the door. James watched. There were some children about whom one would always worry no matter what their age. James wondered if he should have made one last attempt to talk to Peter. He sighed and tried to adjust himself more comfortably in his bed. It was so simple to think things out in his mind. It was amazing how difficult it had become to make those thoughts come out in words.

Peter's ideas of cowardice were the opposite of useless heroism. Neither had true meaning, for they both rode the surface of the problem and never gathered depth. To be a revolutionary, one first had to know the most pivotal spot in which one could be of use. Peter had never been able to see beyond the glamor and apparent success of the night rides. Innocently, enthusiastically, he had aided in leading the rioters to an inevitable slaughter, and himself with them. Except for Callie's intervention, he thought.

"Meg! Where are you, woman? I'm dying of thirst, and not a soul to care," James shouted and felt better for having done it. Anger was nearly all he had these days. And far better than the nameless fear he felt for Peter. And for Callie. He couldn't fathom why he had these strange feelings about them, nor could he rid himself of them. They needed him just at the time he'd never felt weaker or worse in his life.

A man knows when life begins to ebb. He was not getting better. And he was running out of time and the ability to tell his children all the bits of wisdom his years of living had given him. He wished now that he had called Peter back. He should have tried harder to make himself understood. He laid back on the pillows, seeing only the ceiling. He vowed he would be up and out of bed for the planting of the hops—or he would be dead with the trying.

Chapter 15

Callie wandered through the grounds bundled in her coat with her scarf wrapped tightly around her, hoping to keep the frost from nipping her nose and making it redder than it already was. She felt like a lost soul, abandoned by all guiding hands, seeking her way in an abysmal, endless maze. Longingly she looked back, wishing for the return of the days before the magistrates had moved to end the riots.

They had all been so happy, each of them looking forward to the warm, comfortable, laughter-filled nights in the parlor after supper. It didn't seem possible that those days were gone. More, it didn't seem fair.

Very little seemed fair when she thought about it. Nothing was right. Meg, always busy, was never to be seen. When she wasn't with James she was trying to soothe Natalie.

Natalie had not been herself since the night of the fire. They hadn't been able to find out what had happened to her that night. Natalie had never told them, and James either remembered nothing or would not tell them. Like so many things, it seemed there would never be an answer to it; and one more bit of strangeness was felt among them. Callie no longer knew Natalie. The harpsichord was silent, for Natalie no longer played. Her flowers hadn't been dried that fall and the house was bleak without the summer colors they had always provided. She had changed and Callie found it frightening. The animosity between Natalie and Rosalind was unbearable, and no one seemed able to help. The last time Callie had tried to intervene, Natalie had run forward, butting Callie out of her room and slamming the door.

Callie had tried to keep it from Meg, but somehow she knew. Callie stood helpless and hurting as Meg's eyes filled with tears. "Everyone is at one another's throat and poor dear James is helpless. It is killing him. Please keep trying to bring Natalie and Rosalind to an understanding, Callie. Please . . . for James's sake."

Callie had promised to try. That had been yesterday, and still she hadn't found the courage or the ingenuity to change Natalie's mood or Rosalind's sullenness. She rewrapped her scarf and headed determinedly for the brewhouse and the comfort of the person she counted on most.

"Are you terribly busy, Stephen?"

He was standing on the planked walkway high above her head, stirring the brew. "I'll be with you in a minute. Sit down and get warmed by the fire. You look frozen."

Callie moved close to the sweet-smelling fire and put one stiff hand out, feeling the warmth creep slowly across her skin and into her bones. Stephen, stirring and watching her from the corner of his eye, finished his task, climbed halfway down the ladder, then leaped to land dramatically in front of her. "What brings you out in the cold today?"

"I've been trying to think."

"That's a bad sign. One should never try to do anything too strenuous for oneself. What else?"

"Don't tease me, Stephen. Aunt Meg wants me to talk to Natalie and Rosalind, but I don't know what to say. Aunt Meg doesn't really understand how different Natalie is . . . and Rosalind . . . Nothing I say . . ."

"How did you get saddled with this task?"

"Because Aunt Meg says I am good for Natalie, that she likes me. She did, but not now. She's so unhappy; I don't think she likes anyone. And she doesn't want me around. She has a secret. Stephen, would Aunt Meg be angry if Nattie had a dog?"

"Of course not. We have dogs running all over the fields."

"I mean a dog of her own. A pet . . . for inside."

"I don't see why she should. Ma likes dogs and so does Papa. Is that what you want to do, get a dog for Natalie?"

"No. I think that's her secret. She won't let me in her room, but I have thought several times that I have heard a dog whining."

Stephen looked at her with a disbelieving grin. "In her room with none of us seeing it? Why would she hide it?"

Callie shook her head. "It sounds silly, doesn't it. I'm probably wrong."

"There's only one way to find out," Stephen said, clapping his hand against his knee as he got up. "Come along . . . we'll ask my naughty sister if she is hiding a dog."

"If it isn't true, she'll think we're daft," Callie said.

"You never know. She might be right. Are you coming?"

"Wait a minute . . . I've got to fix my scarf," she said, struggling to get it back on as neatly and effectively as it had been. Laughing, Stephen took the end of the scarf and wound it around her head mummy-fashion.

"Stephen! I can't see. Undo me!"

He took the end of the scarf, gave her a push, making her twirl around as the scarf unwound, laughing and teasing until he had her laughing too.

"Let's find Natalie. I want to see this dog or whatever it is she's got."

Stephen knocked lustily at Natalie's door. "Nattie, are you in there? I want to talk to you. Open the door."

"What do you want? I am busy."

"Open the door, Nattie, or I'll raise a ruckus even you can't top."

"Go away, Stephen."

He banged on the door again, louder and more determined. Callie backed to the other side of the hall, her hands over her ears. Suddenly he began to laugh, and sat down cross-legged in front of the door. "I am sitting in front of your door until you talk to me, Nat, so you might as well give up now."

"You are odious, Stephen! Go away!"

He put his fingers to his lips and looked at Callie. By gestures, he told her to walk toward the stairs. Callie did, clumping to make her tread sound more like Stephen's heavier one.

"Ha! Got you," Stephen said triumphantly as Natalie's door opened a crack. Like lightning he put his foot inside and grabbed hold of the door, forcing it open the rest of the way. "Come on, Callie, we can talk to my unfriendly sister now."

"I am going to tell Mama about this. You can't just force your way into my room!"

"You wouldn't answer when I knocked."

"I answered. I told you you are odious! Now go away."

"Not until you tell us your secret. What are you hiding? Is it furry?"

Natalie glanced quickly at her chiffonier. "I am hiding nothing. You can see . . . there is nothing hidden. Now go away. I have a headache. I don't feel well."

"What's that noise?" Stephen asked. Both Natalie and Callie listened. "It sounds like a dog to me. You wouldn't have a dog, would you, Nattie?"

She ran over and hit him on the chest. "Sneak! Spy! How dare you spy on me?"

"She does! She really has one. Why hide him?" Stephen laughed, fending off her glancing blows. "Let's see him. No need to keep it a secret."

"I'll make him bite you!"

"Not if you value him. It'd be a short-lived dog."

"All right. I won't make him bite you, but don't tell anyone about him yet. I don't want anyone to know until I am ready." She opened the door to her chiffonier, and a scrawny little dog crept out, bellying up to her.

"That's a dog? That's the ugliest looking thing I've seen."

"That's his name. Ugly."

"Hello, Ugly," Callie said softly and got down on her knees, reaching for the dog. Ugly inched back toward Natalie, and then began to growl. "Don't be afraid. I won't hurt you. Come here, Ugly." Ugly displayed a small uneven row of teeth and growled a little louder.

Natalie laughed and nudged the dog with her toe. "Ugly is afraid of nothing and no one, and he does exactly what I tell him."

"He's a stupid mutt," Stephen said.

Natalie touched Callie's hair. "Be nice to Callie, Ugly." The dog's tail began to wag, and he walked over to Callie and placed his head on her lap. "Ugly is not stupid, Stephen. He'll do whatever I say. Anything at all!"

Stephen silently watched, wondering still why Natalie had kept the dog a secret. "Tell it to come to me."

"As your friend or as my protector?" she asked with raised eyebrows.

"What do you think?"

"Since I don't want you to wring his neck, I guess it had better be as a friend—this time. Go to Stephen, Ugly," she said as she touched her brother. The dog cocked his head looking from his mistress to the tall stranger. He ambled toward Stephen. Standing on his hind legs, he placed his head on Stephen's lap as he had Callie's.

"You've trained him well," Stephen said, scratching the contented dog.

"He is my servant, my slave. My devoted slave who obeys my every command, serves my every wish, cares for me, and acts for me. He is my friend. My very special, faithful friend."

"I think it is wonderful, Natalie. I wish you had let me know though. I would like to have helped you with him," Callie said and moved to Stephen's side, patting the dog.

"I don't think you would have liked it." Natalie laughed as only she could with the tinkling bell-like sound that carried an air of secret thoughts and sights.

"But you are wrong. I love little animals."

"Why have you kept him a secret, Nattie?"

She looked at Stephen. "I haven't completed his training. He will know so many cute tricks when I am finished. I want to surprise everyone . . . especially Albert. You know I sometimes think he believes I am an empty-witted helpless creature. Won't he be surprised when he sees what I've accomplished with Ugly?"

Everyone was surprised. Meg was pleased. "Why Nattie, I do think you have quite a way with animals; but I don't see why you plagued the poor little creature with such a name as Ugly." She bent down to give the dog a tidbit of meat. "You know, Natalie, so many silly townspeople want dogs . . . for lap dogs and show and the like. You may be able to breed dogs for them. After you and Albert are married it could be quite an occupation for you. I do think it is important for women to have their hand in something."

Natalie picked Ugly up. The little dog nuzzled the side of her neck. "Do you think people would want to buy dogs that look like Ugly?"

"Well, perhaps not Ugly, but there are other dogs. You could choose whatever breed you wished. Albert is well enough off to give you a start."

"But it is Ugly that I like."

"You would," Rosalind said as she came into the room. She walked past Natalie and Meg and went to the pantry.

"What are you looking for, dear?" Meg asked.

"I missed dinner. There must be something left."

"You wouldn't have if you hadn't been out walking," Natalie said softly.

"I was asleep."

"I saw you walking."

Rosalind stopped her search and turned to look at the back of Natalie's head. "You're daft."

"I saw you."

"You did not." She turned back to the pantry.

"Oh, but I did, Rosalind. I always know where you are and what you are doing. You can't hide from me. I saw you and I saw Albert."

Paling, Rosalind looked dubiously at Natalie, then at Meg. "I . . . I don't know what you're talking about. I was asleep . . . I wasn't walking with Albert. Tell her, Mother Berean."

"If you didn't get so upset at every mention of you and Albert, she wouldn't tease you about it," Meg said, and laughed a little.

"I'm not teasing," Natalie said in a thoroughly teasing voice. "And for being such a bad girl and walking out with my young man, I think Ugly should give you a little bite. Bite her, Ugly."

With small jagged teeth bared, Ugly jumped from Natalie's lap and dashed to Rosalind, who stood stock still in fear and disbelief. Rosalind shrieked as the small dog tried vainly to bite through her abundance of skirts and petticoats.

"Natalie!" Meg dumped the bowl of turnips on the floor as she ran to help Rosalind. "Call this little monster off. Hurry! Stop that laughing and do as I say. He'll hurt her!"

Still laughing, Natalie clapped her hands twice and the small dog ran over to her, tail wagging and looking hopefully to her for a reward. "Oh, such a good doggy, such a good little doggy," she said, patting at him and holding him close.

"Don't let him near your face!" Meg cried, shaking from the last experience and afraid of another. Rosalind was sobbing, slumped down where she had stood. "We must get rid of him. He's liable to hurt you."

"Don't be silly, Mama. Ugly is as gentle as a lamb. He does exactly what I tell him and he doesn't like Rosalind."

"You are a beast . . . a mad, mad beast who ought to be locked up!" Rosalind gasped. She backed from the room.

Natalie smiled cunningly at her, glanced at Ugly, and said, "Would you like to bite her again, Ugly?"

Rosalind ran from the kitchen, slamming the door behind her.

"Natalie Berean, I don't believe my ears. Surely you didn't set that dog on her deliberately . . . with the intention of having Ugly bite her."

"Of course I did. She deserved it."

"She could have been seriously hurt!"

"She wasn't hurt at all. Any fool would know she couldn't have been. Ugly can't bite through all those petticoats; Rosalind knows it as well as I. Can't you see, Mama? She was making a scene just like she always does," Natalie said nonchalantly. "He does have pretty fur, don't you think? It is the only pretty thing about him."

"Natalie, I am going to have to speak to your father about this. If you have trained that dog to attack people he may not remain here. I just can't believe it of you."

"It was just play. Rosalind wasn't hurt." Natalie moved agitatedly around the kitchen.

"Once a dog turns—I won't have it, dear, and most certainly James will be displeased. Put Ugly outside, Natalie."

"You're not going to take Ugly away from me. You're not!"

"If he is vicious I certainly will. James will never permit such a thing in the house."

"You can't take him! He's mine. He's all I've got and he loves me. He is the only one in the world who truly loves just me. I'll kill myself! I'll have him bite you, I will. I will!"

Meg began to shake her; the dog alternately growled at Meg and whined as Natalie clutched him too tightly. Freeing one hand, Natalie angrily slapped her mother.

"Natalie!"

Natalie spun and ran from the room. Meg ran after her. As Natalie raced up the stairs and made the turn that would take her to her room, Meg slumped down on the bottom stair, shaken. Her hands cradled her throbbing head. She was sure every hair on her body stood on end when she heard the sudden screaming scuffle from upstairs.

"I hate you! I hate you! You won't take my dog! Bite him, Ugly! Bite! Get him!"

James at first stood confused and weak, holding on to the edge of his door, having come to the hall to see what was causing the commotion. He didn't know what Natalie was talking about. He didn't even know Ugly existed. Natalie was talking too fast for him to follow her, and the look on her face appalled and frightened him.

She was wild looking, not at all his sweet Natalie. He paid no attention to the small orange ball of hair that flew from her arms and darted straight for him until Ugly's teeth sank deep into his bared ankle.

Everything became confusion with Natalie and James screaming. Meg, breathless, began to run up the stairs heavily. "I'm coming James!"

Blinded with pain and the agonizing throb in his head and chest, James stumbled toward the sound of Meg's voice and over the edge of the staircase. Meg grabbed hold of the rail. Only her very solid form blocked him from falling all the way to the bottom.

"Natalie, get the boys from the field!"

"He was going to take Ugly," Natalie said. She picked up the dog from the top stair and returned to her own room.

"Natalie! Oh, Almighty Father . . . someone help me," Meg sobbed, trying to get James up. "Rosalind! Anna!"

Frightened, Rosalind would not come out of her room. She had no intention of coming anywhere near Ugly. Peter, she had decided, was taking her out of this house tonight. Anyplace would be better than staying here with Natalie. She put her hands over her ears and blocked out Meg's pleading.

Callie, coming in from the brewhouse, saw Meg helplessly bracing James on the staircase and wiping his forehead with her handkerchief. She turned and ran for Stephen.

"Let me take him, Ma," Stephen said.

"Be gentle with him, Stephen. Be very gentle."

"I will, Ma. I will hold him like he was a newborn."

Meg moved aside. James was so wasted Stephen had no difficulty lifting him and carrying him back to his room. "I'll go for the others," he said, not sure how much his mother understood of his father's condition at that moment.

She surprised him. "Yes. Hurry, dear. Your father has always wished that his family be near him when it was his time. He may have a message for us."

Callie began to leave the room quietly. "Come here, Callie," Meg said. "You are a part of James's family too, dear. He loves you dearly, you know."

"I love him too," Callie said and the tears slipped out. "Is he really . . ."

"Yes," Meg said simply. "Please fetch Rosalind, Anna, and Natalie.

"And Callie . . . if Natalie . . . doesn't want to come . . . don't try to force her."

Within minutes the house was filled with noise and confusion as Peter and Frank ran in from the fields and Rosalind came guardedly from her room, not having grasped the whole of the situation for Callie had been all but incoherent in her message. Rosalind's eyes darted about, searching for Ugly or Natalie. Then she saw Peter coming up the stairs. "Peter! You must take me away from here tonight. I won't stay here with that loony woman another night."

"What are you talking about?" he asked irritably. "What happened to Pa?"

"I don't know what happened to him. I'm trying to tell you what happened to *me*! Listen to me! She had that creature attack me. Peter! You must take me out of here."

"Why aren't you helping my mother?"

"Peter! Listen to me!"

"Oh, get out of my way." Roughly he shoved her aside, hurrying into his father's room.

James died within minutes of his family's gathering around him. In spite of Meg's fervent hopes, he never regained consciousness. The precious and all-wise deathbed message was never given.

"Perhaps he has written it down somewhere. You know how important you all were to your father. He often thought about what he should tell you if it were his last thought. Perhaps he has written it down somewhere."

"He has given us a lifetime of wisdom, Ma," Stephen said gently and motioned to Callie. "Go with

Callie now, and rest. Anna will be back soon and she will take care of Pa."

"No, I must prepare James myself."

"But Ma . . . all right. You shall, but first you rest. Lie down for just a time . . . a short time. Callie, take her to the guest room."

Once Meg had been led from James's bedroom, the others left as well, going to the parlor. Natalie remained in her room, refusing to come when Callie called her.

Peter paced back and forth across the room, trying to stem the tide of feeling that boiled and churned inside. "What happened? Surely someone saw . . ."

"I didn't see it, but I can certainly tell you what happened," Rosalind said. "Perhaps now you will all believe me when I say that horrible sister of yours should be locked up. She is a murderess now along with being mad."

"Rosalind!"

"Don't bother trying to defend her, Frank. You can't," Rosalind said sharply. "She trained that dog of hers to attack. First she set him on me in the pantry. Your mother saw it. Later I heard a commotion in the hallway. I was afraid to leave my room. Natalie was screaming at the top of her lungs. I heard her set that vicious cur of hers on her own father. It was horrible."

"It's ridiculous," Frank said. "We knew his condition was poor. He has had another attack and that is all. He probably hurt his leg when he fell."

Peter went to Rosalind. When he tried to put his arm around her, she drew away, looking at him with accusing eyes. "I told you! I told you she hated me. Now will you listen?"

Peter looked puzzled. "I thought you said she set the dog on Pa . . ."

"She did!"

Frank stood up, his face grave. "Enough talk. There's been a terrible accident. There is no sense in any of us hurling ridiculous accusations at each other. As head of the family now, I think—"

"But suppose Natalie did set the dog on him—on both Rosalind and Pa . . ." Peter said, his eyes moving from Frank to the others. "My God—if it's true . . ."

Privately he seldom heeded Rosalind's complaints about Natalie. And of late he had heard rumors about his wife and Albert Foxe that had made him wonder if all his sister's fantasies were actually imagined. But today he felt only confusion and doubt. "Do we dare ignore what Rosalind says? I don't know how the rest of you feel, but Nat has changed—in my opinion. She hasn't been herself since the night of the fire, and we never did find out what happened that night."

"I agree with you, Peter. She has changed, but she certainly isn't the maniac that Rosalind describes."

"What are you saying?" Frank demanded. "That our sister is mad and deliberately caused the death of her own father!"

"No, of course not," Peter said quickly.

"What then?"

"I don't know, damn it, Frank. I just don't know."

"Well, I do, and I demand an end to it. I won't have our family name dragged through the mud because some of us go off half cocked at every turn. There will be no more said of this!"

"No more said?" Rosalind demanded shrilly.

Peter quieted her, then looked steadily at Frank. "We'll get Ma to tell us what happened; then we'll decide."

None of them moved. It was as if they had all been

frozen in place. The house was eerily quiet. Though each of them thought only of James, none mentioned his name aloud, as if they were holding off the truth by keeping it a secret from each other.

It was too soon for grief to flood in. It had been too shocking. None of them was ready, nor would they be ready when the dam of grief began to crack and the aching loss seeped through to wash away the protective numbness they felt now. They sat in idleness, Meg alone having something of importance to do. And she would permit no one to help in the preparation of James's body.

It was late when Meg came downstairs that evening. "Your father's body is prepared. Frank, will you and Stephen put him in the special parlor?" Her face showed no emotion. The nervous bustle of Meg's personality was missing.

She followed Frank and Stephen, making certain things were arranged as she wanted.

While they were gone, Anna said, "Peter, don't say anything to her tonight about Natalie and the dog. It is a terrible time for her. Worse than it is for us."

"It won't be better tomorrow," Peter said.

"Then be kind to her."

"You don't need to tell me to be kind to my own mother, Anna," Peter snapped.

"You know all you need to know. Why must you make her say it?" Anna for once showed a touch of temper.

"Because I need to hear it said! I don't know the answers. Did that miserable cur of Natalie's attack Pa, or was it an accident? Ma knows. She is the only one who knows."

"Natalie does," Anna said.

Meg came back into the room with Stephen and

Frank as Peter began to answer Anna. "I don't want to talk about it," Meg said.

"Ma! My wife is begging me to take her from the house tonight because of that dog and my sister. My father is lying in one room in death, and all you can say is that you don't want to talk about it?"

"It can do no good, Peter. James is dead. Shall you take my daughter too?"

Peter's face registered the hurt. His mother wept silently. It was there. Her admission was there, but he refused to grasp the meaning of Meg's words. He raised his arms, then let them drop helplessly to his side. He continued his nervous march around the room.

"Do sit down, Peter. You are making us all edgy," Rosalind said.

"*Someone* tell me something. Tell me about the dog. Say it!" he implored and looked at each of them in turn. "It's true, isn't it? Ma? It was the dog, wasn't it? The dog caused the accident. Why are you protecting that dog?"

"She's not protecting the dog. How stupid can you be, Peter? It is Natalie she is protecting. That dog does Natalie's bidding. I've told you time on end that Natalie suffers from a nervous disorder of the mind," Rosalind said.

"Yes, Doctor Berean. We thank you," he said acidly, coming close to hating her. His father was dead. He loved his sister.

Sobbing, Meg looked up at him. "Nattie thinks the dog is obedient to her, but he isn't, Peter. He isn't. The dog is bad. Nattie isn't capable of training a dog . . . you know her. Poor Nattie . . . she couldn't . . . Nattie couldn't do . . ." Meg's eyes reddened, pleading for answers much as Peter was. "She adored James, didn't she, Peter? She would never . . ."

Peter hugged her tightly, his eyes squeezed shut. "It was the dog, Ma. We all know that. Nattie loved Pa very much. Remember—she was his little girl, his only daughter."

Chapter 16

"Dear Nattie is a sly vicious minx capable of anything, and I am sick to death of hearing about dear sweet little Nattie!" Rosalind burst out. "All of you make me sick the way you protect her and hide from the truth." She walked quickly from the room to stand for a moment by the staircase. "Are you coming with me, Peter?"

Peter looked strangely at her, almost as if he were asking her to take back the damning statements. When he spoke, the words were wrung from him. His eyes were wide and filled with pain and confusion. "No, I'll be up later."

"By all means, stay with them and think of ways to whitewash dear Nattie. After all she managed to murder her father. It might take some thought to excuse her this time."

"Go upstairs, and wait until I come up," Peter said, angry and torn between his wife and his family. But now the hurt had found something to focus on, something to fight. Rosalind disappeared from sight. He turned back to his family huddling close to one another, seeking comfort. "I want that dog. It killed Pa, and I want it. Where is it?"

In the suddenly silent room their breathing sounded loud.

"I want that dog!" Peter shouted. He stalked the room, waiting for one of them to speak.

"The dog is with Natalie," Anna whispered.

Meg got up slowly, looking sadly at her son. She walked to the far end of the parlor, opened the doors that led to the Sunday parlor where James now lay. "Don't be cruel, Peter. You are hurt and unhappy . . . it isn't Natalie's fault."

"It's the dog! The damned, bloody dog!" he shouted; then, uninvited, the horrible question he had been keeping at bay pressed forward. Miserably he looked at his mother, fighting within himself the conflicting loyalties that kept boiling to the surface. "Are you certain, Ma? I have always sided with Natalie— even against my own wife. I've told Rosalind she is wrong about Nat, even jealous, but I don't know anymore. Do you? Do any of you know? Are you really sure it wasn't Nattie's fault?"

Meg said nothing. She went into the small cold parlor, closing the door behind her. The light of two small candles guttered, dimming and then straightening as the draft passed. She went to her husband's side, sitting still as stone, wishing as she had always done when there was trouble, that James was there to guide her.

She didn't know the truth about Natalie. Meg knew she had lied to Peter though. Natalie was capable of training the dog. She had, and had done an excellent job. But wasn't the dog naturally vicious as well? Wasn't it the dog who had caused the harm? Natalie couldn't deliberately harm someone, surely not her own father. Meg thought of the child she had given birth to and raised. Natalie was a kind, gentle girl. Meg knew that to be true. She was never cruel. Cruelty was not in her.

As Meg thought, Rosalind's face kept coming to mind. Natalie had never had any difficulties before Rosalind's arrival. And Meg remembered Natalie begging her to listen when she said Rosalind was evil . . . bad for Peter . . . bad for the family. Perhaps she was. When one laid blame for a tragedy, where did one begin? Surely not with the last and final incident in a series of events. Neither Natalie nor the dog would have been upset if Rosalind had not started it in the kitchen when Natalie accused her of going off with Albert. And why would Rosalind have been with Albert? Oh, dear God, Meg sobbed, her mind a tangle of pain and worry for Peter, for Natalie, and for her lost and beloved James.

"James . . . " Meg whispered into the murky, smoking light of the candles. "If you are anywhere that you can hear me, James, please tell me what to do now."

Peter stood with his hands jammed into his pockets for several minutes after his mother left the room. "I don't know what possessed me to speak to her so."

"You would have done it sooner or later," Frank muttered under his breath. "This is no worse than tomorrow or the day after."

Peter grimaced, but showed no sign of having heard his brother. "I was wrong. I should have taken care of things and said nothing. It isn't the same now, with Pa gone. We can't say things we once did. Ma without him . . . well, it is different. I am going to get the dog. Get it over with." He didn't move, but stood staring at the staircase. His forehead glistened with sweat.

Reluctantly, his movements stiff and awkward, he walked into the hall.

They listened as he went up the stairs and knocked on Natalie's door.

"Who is it?" she called.

"It's Peter, Natalie."

"What do you want? I am resting."

"Natalie, open the door now. I want to see you."

"I am resting!" she screeched. "Go away!"

"Natalie, I've come for the dog. Open the door immediately."

There was no response. "Nattie, either you open the door or I'll break it in. You know me, Nat, I mean what I say. Open it before I count to five." He began to count.

Natalie began to scream behind the closed door. Obscenities, mixed with nonsense and rambling accusations, streamed from her. Peter finished counting. With all his weight he slammed against the door. It gave a little on the first assault and opened on the third.

Natalie, with streaming black hair loosed in disarray, stood wild-eyed, pointing her finger at him and screaming for Ugly to attack. For once the little dog did not obey. He cringed in the corner of the room as far as possible from his mistress. Peter scooped the small dog up in one hand, fighting Natalie off with the other. Screaming, she pursued him to the door. He shoved her back, slammed the splintered door, and leaned against it, shaking.

That could not have been his sister. Not that wild-haired, wild-eyed creature with the distorted features and the clawing hands. He touched his neck where thin streaks of blood ran from the welting scratches.

He felt sick at his stomach. Nothing was real. James wasn't dead. Couldn't be. That hadn't been his sister.

Rosalind wasn't unfaithful. Nothing was true! Peter wiped his hand across his wet, sweating brow. He'd come so close to believing the rumors, Natalie's wild hints. His own wife—his father—his mind closed down on the jumble. He glanced at the small homely animal cradled trustingly against his chest, and felt sick again.

He went back down the stairs, walking quickly past the parlor.

"Oh, poor little Ugly," Callie cried and ran to the hallway. "What are you going to do with him, Peter? Don't hurt him!"

"He'll be destroyed," Peter said through stiff, white lips.

"You can't! Peter, you can't hurt him. He only did what he was told. Please don't hurt him. Give him away . . . or let him run with the field dogs. Please! Please!"

Peter struggled into his coat trying to look neither at Callie nor the dog, wishing somehow he could stop her pleading. His head was going to burst—he was going to burst.

Peter almost groaned aloud as Stephen joined them, taking Callie's hand and trying to soothe her. Stephen looked sympathetically at Peter, then said, "Let me come with you. I can help."

"I don't need help destroying one bloody little dog!"

Peter looked at his brother, his head pounding. Stephen with his quiet honesty would make him face everything. Everything. Nothing hidden. Nothing avoided. Peter shut his eyes for a minute wishing he could turn the clock back, wanting to be as sure of himself now as he had been at the outset of the Swing riots. Everything had seemed so clear then, and so well-defined. He had known where his duty lay. He had believed so easily and trusted so fully. Stephen and Callie still had that faith. But he did not. He needed someone to take the blame, something to clarify what had happened. "I started this whole thing. I'll finish it."

"Peter, no! Please. Think what you are doing. It won't help. Please!"

He grimaced and shoved her aside. "Get out of my way, Callie. Let me do what must be done."

Callie tore free of Stephen's embrace, pulling at Peter's coat. "You can't! It's cruel! You're mean and hateful. Ugly never did anything. It wasn't his fault. You know that, Peter! You know that!"

"Leave me alone!" Peter shouted, wrenching past them.

He was shaking like a man in a fever by the time he walked to the area where Meg killed her chickens. He didn't dare look at the dog in his hands. It had to be done. James was dead. The dog had killed him. Not his sister. Not Natalie. Dear God, not his sister. The dog.

As though he had seen it all, visions of Natalie commanding the dog flashed before his eyes. Ugly obeying every command, every wish she uttered. His father. . . . Peter shook. He couldn't breathe. It had to be the dog. The vicious dog. Mocking him, the dog moved in his hands, so small, so trusting, trembling as Peter was. He clenched his jaw against the sickness that pushed up into his throat. Eyes shut tightly, he strangled the dog.

Callie was waiting with her face pressed to the glass of the front mullioned window. Everyone else had gone to bed.

"Did you do it?" she asked coldly as he came through the door.

He didn't look at her. He couldn't. "He's buried be-hind the stables," he murmured.

Stricken and unable to let go of it, Callie followed him as he hung up his coat. "It was wrong, and horri-ble. He was a poor little dog, wanting to be loved by someone. He was a good little dog. I'll never forgive you, Peter. Never."

He turned to her. "Callie . . ." Her face was closed, and he turned away. "Go to bed where you belong, and leave things that don't concern you to those they do concern." He brushed past her and went up the stairs.

He felt dirty and tired. Callie's accusing eyes were the worst of all, because she was right. He knew she was right and he couldn't stand the knowing. It had seemed that with the death of the dog, James's . . . accident would seem more understandable. It wasn't.

Peter's fondest wish had always been to be away and free; now it was something, a thought, a longing, that would stay with him night and day. Everything had become cramped and dirtied. He didn't dare think or question what had happened. He no longer had the pure vision that could provide him with truthful an-swers, and he couldn't stand the muddied thinking that would lead him from one question to another without the courage to accept any of the answers. So he longed for the dream of a new start, a new life that was clean and unblemished. It was a hard despairing dream for nothing had gone right, from his part in the Swing riots to this day when his father died.

He held on to the railing as though he might not make it up the flight of stairs if he let go. Natalie heard him coming. She stood at the head of the stairs clad in her nightdress, her hair loose and flowing but somewhat neater than before.

"What are you doing here, Natalie? Go to bed. You'll catch cold," he said tiredly.

"I want to talk to you, Peter."

"We'll talk tomorrow."

"Not tomorrow. Now, Peter! I want to talk to you now, while you still have Ugly's blood on your hands, and his smell in your nose!"

"Quiet!"

"What did you do to Ugly? How did you do it?"

"Ugly is gone."

"You killed him and took away what I loved! Do you know what it is to lose someone you love?"

"I said he was gone. Leave it at that," Peter snapped.

"I pray I see your immortal soul in Hell . . . burning. I'll hate it and hate it for all eternity."

Peter's dark brown eyes opened wide.

Natalie's face was tense with the effort it took to keep her mind on what she wanted to say. She shook her head wildly. "Oh, Peter," she gasped. "You destroyed what I loved, but what you did to Ugly is nothing compared to what I can do to you."

He tried to touch her. She shrank back, crossing her arms protectively over her chest. "Oh, no . . . no comfort . . . not for me . . . not for you. Not tonight. Not ever. You are as alone as I am, and just as bereft of love."

"Natalie," he said with an overtone of awe. "I don't know you. What has happened to you? It's not just the dog. It's more . . . worse. I did what had to be done."

"And what I am about to do must be done. We both have our reasons, don't we, Peter?"

He was trembling again. He didn't know why. He wished she'd smile. Come to him for comfort as she had when she was younger. Her pain was so raw. Everything was slipping away from him.

"Do you remember the gypsy, Peter?"

He nodded, then wiped his hands across his eyes. He was tired, so tired his mind would work no more. "Good night, Natalie."

"Oh, no! You'll listen!"

"Tomorrow . . ."

"No! Now! Indulge me, Peter. That much you owe me."

Peter slumped into the chair by her door. "Be quick then. I'm tired."

"Of course," she smiled. "The last time I saw the gypsy, before Callie went with me, she told of the future. Now, I'll tell you, for it concerns you as much as it does me."

"I don't care what the old woman said, Nat." He straightened in his chair, looking at her curiously. "Natalie . . . do you know . . . do you realize what happened here today . . . about Pa?"

"Your wife is not your wife alone, Peter."

"Natalie, for the love of God! Listen to me! Pa is dead!"

"She lies in your bed only at night," Natalie shouted.

It all flooded back. He thought perhaps it was he who was mad. The confusion, the unreality, the sickness and dreadful suspicions. "My wife lies in my bed at night, and in my bed alone. In the day she is in the house with my mother. There is no more than that."

"And when she gives birth to a child—the image of his father—then will you admit I have spoken the truth? Will you then see that she loves Albert? Not you! Never you! She loves Albert! She wants him! Goes to him! Albert! My Albert!"

The ruined door slammed crookedly as Peter fled the room.

Peter slowed when he reached the door to his own room. It was quiet. There were no small rustlings of the sheet to indicate Rosalind was awake waiting for him. But he needed her. She had to make him believe again. Surely she'd know, be able to sense the chaotic tumult that raged inside him. She *was* his wife. None other's.

Peter was not a man who cried. He had always believed it was a sign of weakness. But as he lay beneath the sheets that night tears stung his eyes. Rosalind's still form lying beside him seemed to confirm the hate-filled accusations Natalie had hurled at him. Though he wouldn't turn to his wife—couldn't—he was tense, despair making his chest and stomach hurt as he waited hopelessly for her hand to bridge the chasm he couldn't. He waited for the slightest movement of contact that would free him.

He remembered as clearly as if it had been yesterday, the day, during their courtship, that he had taken Rosalind to Seven Oaks the first time. She had worn a simple white organdy gown she had designed and made herself. It accentuated the sweet innocence that should have been hers had her father not robbed her of it. Her long hair fell softly to her shoulders. Her hazel eyes, almost blue that day, with the golden flecks sparkling, looked to him trustingly. He had never been prouder than he was that day to have her by his side. Perhaps it was the first time he realized she was his in every sense of the word. She needed him. She loved him. And he loved her.

He remembered the shy, shocked surprise in her eyes when he had boldly introduced her as his future wife. She had expected him to be ashamed of her. But he hadn't been. Never had been. He had introduced her to Mr. Richards at the oast house, and then to Mr. and Mrs. Beggs, proprietors of the inn where he boarded when business kept him overnight in Seven Oaks. How she had looked at him! And how beautiful she was. All he had been able to think was, "She's mine!" His thoughts had begun and ended with that. Away from her father and the tavern, she was the softest, most loving creature God had created.

He had been so sure he could keep her that way. And yet, tonight, he lay in his bed beside her and ached with doubts and bitterness, no longer certain that she was faithful to him or loved him.

Again the salty tears stung his eyes. If only they were free, away from everything, everyone. Rosalind in the white virginal gown, the soft adoring smile on her parted lips, the love glowing on her face, floated tantalizingly close, yet disappeared before his eyes.

Not daring to find out if his longing hopes or his despairing doubts were the truth of his marriage, Peter stayed as far from his wife as he could. He lay awake, aware of her sleeping warmth beside him until it was dawn.

Before Peter could escape the house the following morning, Stephen came in to have his breakfast. "You are certainly a lie-abed today," he said testily. "I needed you to help prepare the wagon."

"I will." Peter pushed his plate aside.

"'Will' is a useful word. It's been done," Stephen said. He looked disinterestedly at his food.

"You've finished it, Stephen? I'm sorry . . . I hadn't meant to shirk."

Stephen shook his head. "Forgive me. Nothing is right this morning. Even the sky is gray like a lead shield." Stephen looked out the window into the gloom of a rainy day. "For once I understand your desire to leave. I never really have, you know, but I do now. It isn't so much like home as it was."

"Since yesterday," Peter muttered.

"Before that. Papa died before that, I think. It hasn't been the same since the night of the fire. Something . . . the spirit of things has gone out of us. I don't know what I'm talking about. It is the day and the funeral coming that has me this way. I'm going to see to the last touches on the wagon."

Peter nodded and went back to his morose thoughts.

James, with all the regalia of a farm funeral, was buried two days later. With great disapproval his London friends followed after the simple procession bereft of their normal splendored phaetons and carriages. Meg had insisted. She and James had started out humbly in spite of James's superior birth, and he would go to his reward with the same humble simplicity. So it was a gaily bedecked and freshly painted farm wagon that carried her husband. Gallantly she ignored the appalled looks of some of the mourners and turned a deaf ear to the titters that spoke of her quaintness, and the ever present reminder that James had married beneath himself when he married Meg.

She supposed it was true. But one other thing was true. Without beauty of face, or accomplishment or family name, Meg was the one James had chosen to be his wife, and he had been happy with her. To be sure there were times when he had tried to convince her they would do well with a house in London to spend the winters, and that she should allow her cook and servants to take over her chores in the kitchen and house. She had tried but it never took. Within days she was back in her kitchen. She loved it there and felt both useful and sure of herself. The kitchen and the nursery were her natural domains, and after several futile attempts James had given up trying to reform her. He had settled for a farmer's wife dressed in a lady's clothing and loved her all the more for it.

She wouldn't change now. All the sniggers and comments in the world would not stop her from giving James the kind of final send-off he would know he could expect from Meg. Laugh though they might now, she would lead them down the hill behind the wagon. They would march to the graveside and, in the country way, walk three times with the sun around the churchyard cross before laying James to rest. They would follow in the procession, having to admire James's carefully tended fields and the tall straight-backed sons who would carry on for him. And they would follow her back to the house and be pleased for her talents as they ate her food, prepared that morning and the night before.

Meg left her guests when they came back to the house. Not many of them stayed for long, and those who did would understand that she wanted to be alone. It was so much easier for her to feel close to James when she was alone. She went to the bedroom that was hers alone now and tried once more to reach him somehow, so that he could tell her how to deal with the problems ahead.

Chapter 17

Callie could never remember feeling more saddened or oppressed than she did those days after James's death. It was not like when her father had died. That had been a deep knife wound that had cut hard and cruelly, making her hurt and afraid, but this—this was far different and much worse. A knife wound healed. The Bereans showed no sign of wound or healing.

Perhaps too much had happened and too much had gone unanswered for any of them to come to terms with James's death. She didn't know, but she felt alone and more alienated than she ever had.

Stephen, upon whom she could always count for a good talk or a romp along the gentle ridges of his mountain, had buried himself in the brewery. For once he closed her out. She missed him. She missed them all.

Each of the Bereans had vanished to live solitary lives and struggle with solitary suffering in the private houses of their own minds. She missed them and went off, wondering if in solitude it was possible to reach upward to touch God, who alone touches each life. Could He ever bring them all back together again? She went to Stephen's mountain; from there she could look back on happier days and remember scenes from a warmer time.

Peter waited for a month before he told anyone of his plans. He waited and looked on as Meg settled into listless sadness. She had turned to Natalie, pouring on the girl her affection and attention until she was bone-dry for the rest of them. By January he knew that if he were ever to speak, the time had come.

"I've given it full consideration, Rosalind. We'll be leaving the farm," Peter said too loudly, the words seeming strange on his tongue. He had thought about leaving for so long and had done nothing, that now it sounded as though someone else had said it.

"Peter! Do you mean it?" She rose from the bed, going to him. "When? Where will we be living? London? No, not London . . . Manchester maybe, or the Cotswolds. Tell me!" she cried, putting her arms around his neck. "I am so happy. I thought we might always live here . . . in this house. Peter, I'm so happy."

He leaned back and gloried in her approval. "It pleases you that much?"

"I've wanted it for so long. I know you'll do much better on your own. Frank is not half so bright as you," she said, kissing him. "And we'll live as people of our station should. We can entertain and go places . . . and our house will be the pride of the town. It will be the prettiest, most fashionable house you've ever seen. Peter, I'll make you proud of it . . . and me."

He frowned as he listened to her go on. "Rosalind, it won't be here."

She looked blankly at him. "We would leave England? Where is there to go?"

He laughed. "There's a whole world to choose from. I was thinking of the colonies. I'd like to begin anew, start fresh."

"Colonies? India! Oh, yes . . . yes! Arimintha Dowling has recently returned from there. She says one can live like royalty. She has three servants for herself, Peter. Oh, we could be quite something. Why, I'd never have to lift a finger. Oh, and I'm sure Albert's family would be pleased to help you get a position with the East India Company. Why, we would never have to see another field or pig or cow again. It would be heaven!"

"My life is those pigs and fields and cows you speak of. It's all I know, and all I care to know. I am a hop man, Rosalind. It's the American colonies I have in mind."

"That's a wilderness . . . whatever would we do there? They're not even British now."

"I've been corresponding with a man in New York State. He says the hop gardens there are as fine as they are here."

"Corresponding? And not a word to me! For how long?" she asked, then shook her head before he had a chance to answer. "I don't want to go there. It would be worse than going nowhere. The women work like field hands. You can't expect it of me. I won't go."

"We're going, Rosalind. As soon as the hops are planted," he said firmly and a little sadly as he realized that once again they were not going to agree. He got up from his chair and moved toward the door. Rosalind stood at the window, her arms folded around herself. "Rosalind—I wish you'd try to see it differently. There are cities in America as great as London.

You'll be mistress of your own home, and it will be a fine one, I promise you."

Silently she shook her head.

He left the room with his enthusiasm dampened but his resolve firm. He went to see Meg. She showed no surprise, and seemed only to be waiting for him to announce what she already knew.

At the beginning of February Peter went to London to book passage. When he returned home, he had the passage contracts in his pocket.

"You finally did it, did you?" Frank laughed, clapping him on the back. "It's a good thing. You'd never be happy here until you gave this a try. Now, when you come back we'll all be ready to go on. It's a great move you're making, Peter."

"I won't be coming back, Frank. When I go, it is for good."

"You say that now, but you'll be home soon enough. I'll wager you'll begin to see sense and be longing for home before the year's out. I know my little brother," Frank insisted as he settled down in James's chair. He lit his pipe, looked around the room. He sighed through his ring of pipe smoke, blowing it askew.

"I wish I were coming with you," Stephen said thoughtfully. "There's no chance you'd be needing an extra hand, is there, Peter?"

"Stephen? You'd like to come?"

"I would . . . could you use me?"

Peter let out a whoop, then leaned forward, his face happy and excited. "I've been writing to a man in New York State. He tells me there's good soil along the Hudson River. Some of it cleared already . . . some not. It would be hard work, Stephen, and no guarantee of success."

"There's no guarantee in anything. But if you'd

rather I didn't come—I understand. There are some things a man wants to do alone. This is your venture, and I . . ."

"No! You madman. You'd be a blessing. I want you to come. Truth is, I need you, but it's a hell of a thing to ask . . . I can't let you agree unless I'm sure you know what you're getting into."

"I want to go."

Peter threw his head back laughing with the sheer joy and promise of it. "Ah, Steve, it will be good. The Berean Brothers' Brewery—finest in the new world . . . whole world."

"You're planning a brewery too?" Stephen asked agog. Instantly his mind caught fire, blazing in a whirl of thoughts. "Then I must come. What the hell do you know about brewing beer? I'm the expert here."

"What a team we'll make."

The evening wound to an end with the family content, toasting Peter, Rosalind, and Stephen.

Lulled and sleepy from the cider she had drunk, Callie said, "I think it would be wonderful to be going."

"You can have it. Believe me when I tell you it will be nothing like Peter describes," Rosalind said. "Why, it isn't even English! They haven't a king . . . not even a queen. What sort of place can it be? How would one behave?"

Peter cocked his head toward Rosalind, grinning. "Listen to her. If there is no king and no queen, it must be nothing. You're a narrow little chit, Rosalind. They have a president, which is something on the order of a king, except that the people have a great deal to say about his activities . . . and the taxes."

"You should fit in there," Frank said.

"We shall," Peter said, rising and taking Rosalind's

hand. He looked at Stephen. "I'm glad you'll be going with us. Good night, everyone."

Rosalind's disapproval did not lessen as the days passed, and her temper reflected it. Peter wisely gave her wide berth. But Callie could hardly contain her excitement because they were going and she loved them. It was a little like going herself to be near them and help with the preparations.

"May I help you pack? You'll need to take just everything. You are so lucky. Imagine what it will be like . . . it will be so much your own. Everything you build there and have will be yours and Peter's."

Rosalind watched her for a moment, then rolled her eyes into her head. "You are the most naive, stupid creature I have ever had the misfortune to run across. Will you kindly shut up."

Callie backed away from her. "I'm sorry. I only wanted to help. I'm sorry you don't want to go. It sounds so nice."

"Sorry, sorry, sorry! What have you to be sorry for? Just go away. Let me be, you little ninny."

"I will. I'm going." She went to her room and indulged in satisfying tears. She wanted to go so badly she could taste it. It hurt more for Rosalind to express her dislike of the trip than it did to be left behind.

Rosalind shut and locked her door behind Callie. She dressed, taking particular care, and hurried unseen from the house. It was a bad time of year to be going to the hop pickers' cottages. The men were in the fields and might see her. She took the long way around, and was breathless when she arrived.

"Thank heaven, you are here," she said as soon as she opened the door. Albert sat stiffly on one rough-hewn chair. He always looked so out of place in this barren cottage, and that pleased her. She took off her cloak and gloves, tossing them carelessly on the table.

"Peter won't listen. He is going ahead with his ludicrous plans."

"I never doubted it." Albert stood, his arms open for her to come to him. "But I would rather you keep your mind on me for now." He kissed her.

She pulled away. "You don't understand. He's going to take me away from here—forever! It will mean an end to this—to us. I need your help. You've got to talk him out of it! You must. I can't go there. If you care anything for me, tell him what a foolish, rash move it is. You know about these things."

"He wouldn't listen to me. Peter is going, Rosalind. Must we talk about him all afternoon?" He sat down, pulling her onto his lap. "Be quiet. Let me look at you. Before long I'll need my memory to see you."

"What do you care?" she pouted. "You would never let him take me away to that awful place if I meant anything to you."

"I care," he whispered. Rosalind smiled and leaned back as he loosened her bodice. She was light and easy to carry to the bed. It pleased her to see Albert's well-practiced, deft fingers fumble with her hooks this afternoon. She lay back, uninvolved for once, as he became more urgent and clumsy with his own clothing. "You're a damned beautiful bitch, Rosalind," he murmured, looking at her lying there, waiting for him. She teased, taunted, gave in, moved away, then grasped at him as he did her. She prolonged their lovemaking as much as it was in her power to do that day. He lay back, covered with a thin layer of perspiration, tired and very satisfied.

"Keep me here," she whispered.

He wagged his head from side to side, too content to make the effort to talk.

"Keep me here. Don't let me go."

"Can't," he murmured and wrapped his arms

around her again, nuzzling against the soft warmth of her skin.

"If I were going to have your child?" she asked, nipping at him as she spoke.

"That would be different," he breathed.

"Then you'd better begin to think of a way to keep me here. I am quick with your child this very minute."

Albert lay still. Then he raised up on one elbow to look down into her small triangular face.

"It's true," she said.

"It can't be true. We agreed . . . you know how to prevent these things . . ." he stammered. "My God . . . the talk . . . my mother . . ."

She put her fingers to his lips. "Don't you know better than to trust a woman scorned, Albert?"

"For the love of God, Rosalind, this is no time for levity. It'll be a bloody scandal!"

"No joke. Your child will sail when I do. He will be raised as Peter Berean's son if you don't do something to prevent it. Just think of it, Albert . . . your bastard heir."

He sat on the side of the bed, not able to resist the impulse to look at her belly. "You're lying."

She got up and began to dress. "I'm not lying, Albert. It is your child. As you said, I know how to prevent these things, so I know whose child it is."

He looked at her baffled and disbelieving. "How could you let this happen? What am I supposed to do? What'll it do to Natalie?" he asked softly.

Rosalind backed away from him. "Natalie? You think of Natalie while I stand here and tell you I carry your child? What are you? You're no man at all!" she screamed and moved for the door, stumbling as she went. The chair overturned. She glared at him, accusing him with her eyes of everything that had ever gone wrong in her life.

"Rosalind! Wait!" He leapt up to grab her arm. "Wait . . . I'm sorry. I didn't mean that the way it sounded. You know I must marry Natalie. Mother expects it and . . ."

"Damn your mother for the bloody interfering bitch she is!"

"You don't understand. I need the dowry she'll bring. Don't you see, I'm the only Foxe left . . . the last of the line. I must have a wife with position and wealth. And I must have heirs. Try to understand. I can't help it. You know I love you. God above, I don't think I know how to live without you," he said and began to pull his own clothes on.

Rosalind waited, her face a hard little mask of hurt and anger. "You are a bloody pig! How could I ever have loved you?"

He came over to her and touched her cheek. "For the same reasons I love you. I do love you. You know that, don't you? What is poor Nattie compared to you?"

"I don't know what she is, Albert. But she *will* be your wife, because she has the money to buy you. And me? I'll bear your bastard son. What does that make me compared to poor little Nattie?"

"I'll talk to Peter. I'll do whatever you ask. Somehow we'll find a way out of this. Have you told him yet . . . about the child?"

"No."

"Tell him."

"Tell him I am carrying your child?"

"Rosalind, please!" he begged, running his fingers through his hair. "This is difficult enough."

"Poor Albert."

That night Rosalind told Peter she was having his child. He was as happy as if she had told him she wanted to go to America, which was quite a lot for

Peter, for only there, free, did he see hope for them. And he was ashamed as he listened to her. He had doubted her. And she had been carrying his child. As always, when he was contrite, Peter blamed himself for her petulance and unhappiness. He'd left her alone too often. He'd not been gentle when he might have been. He hadn't understood the anxiety Natalie caused her. But he knew he would be able to make it up to her in America. There it would be different.

He took her hands in his, his eyes admiring her, and as he expected, she responded. The hazel eyes, golden this evening, lit from within. She smiled at him. He saw the love there again.

He thought of her and the child. A delightful shiver of wanting what had been missing for a long time ran through him. He pulled her quickly into his arms. His kiss was long, searching and hungry.

"I love you," he murmured, his lips pressed to her temple. "Lord, you are beautiful. What would I do without you?"

She laughed, her body taut and impatient as he undressed her leisurely, pausing to kiss her and whisper his love for each newly exposed part of her body.

He hadn't made love to her like this since the first days of their marriage. She had forgotten how tantalizing it was to see the light of discovery in a man's eyes. He made her feel like wife and wanton at one time. And he believed her. More than believed her: he was ecstatic at the prospect of the coming child. Surely now, with his passions newly fired, he'd do whatever she asked.

The thoughts fragmented as Peter's hands and lips continued their hot hungry search of her body. There was no room left for thought. Only wanting. She forgot Albert and the baby and America. She forgot that Meg or Frank or Anna might hear the impassioned animal cries of joy emanating from her throat. She bit at him, nipping at his neck and ears. She clawed at his back, matching his urgency with her own lusty unsated needs.

When it was over, she still longed for more. For something. She felt like laughing or crying. And he knew. Quieter than she, he turned to her, making love again with his hands, his words, and finally his body. And still, as she writhed in pleasure beneath him, she felt like crying like a madwoman, screaming at God: What was wrong with her? Why couldn't she love him? Why?

Finally quiet, Rosalind rested in his arms. He kissed her damp hair. "When will he be born?"

"He will be born this autumn. September," she said, smiling and curling into the curve of his body.

"By September we'll be there. He'll be an American citizen, Rosalind. The first of our family born on that soil."

The fears returned, drumming in her head. The loss of Albert. Being alone with Peter. Perhaps for the first time having to truly become his wife for there'd be no one else in the distant lost land of America.

He didn't notice her silence. He was too caught up in his own thoughts until she began to cry with heartbreaking softness. "I'll die there, Peter. I'll never see the new land or my house. If you make me travel in my condition, I'll die."

"Little love, you'll not die. I'll see you have the best cabin on the ship. You'll have everything you need. Maybe we can talk Ma into going with us. She could look after you."

"She won't come. She wants Natalie . . . only Natalie."

He didn't argue that. "We'll hire someone . . . a

nurse. She'll take care of you, watch over you every minute."

"Peter, I don't want to leave England."

"Sweetheart, you will. You're frightened and worried now, but you'll change your mind." He caressed her shoulder, then leaned over to kiss her.

Rosalind grimaced, pushing him away. "I won't."

He turned away from her. He lay without moving or speaking. She could see only the broad muscles of his back expand and contract with his breathing.

"You will," he said determinedly.

Rosalind rolled on to her side, pulling the sheet up over her shoulders.

Chapter 18

Peter made the trip to London again. He returned buoyant and happy. He couldn't keep his hands off the two additional passage tickets he had purchased for Stephen and the as yet unhired nurse. He touched the edges, felt the texture of the paper, put them into and out of his pocket so many times they were dog-eared and wrinkled. He looked around the house for Rosalind, then found her sitting listlessly on the stone bench in the herb garden.

Proudly he thrust the two tickets in front of her. "You've only to hire your nurse now. It's real. We're on our way."

She turned her face from him. "I don't want to see those, and I don't want a nurse."

"Hire a nurse, Rosalind, or you'll go without one."

"Such concern."

"It is."

"Then hire her yourself! I'm not going to do one thing to help you drag me from my rightful home." She jumped up from the bench and ran into the house.

Peter looked down at the two tickets, then up at the brewhouse beyond the garden wall. The smile returned to his face.

"Stephen! Ho, Stephen! I've got them." Peter stopped at the door, holding on to the sides and leaning in.

"What the hell?" Stephen grinned as he saw his brother swinging forward on the doorjamb like a monkey. "What's the simple smile for?"

"See that?" Peter again pulled the much-handled tickets from his pocket. "That is the great Atlantic Ocean to us. Miles and miles of endless water."

Stephen touched them reverently. "I can't believe it's true. A brewery of our own." He turned and walked back into the main room of the brewhouse, a worried frown on his face. "We can't take the equipment with us. I talked to Frank and he says he intends to keep the brewhouse going."

"We don't need it," Peter said grandly. "For what we'll build we'll need the very best commercial vats made. We'll come back here and buy the best when we're ready for it."

"Come here for it?"

"Naturally. We'll be wanting to visit, so we'll combine business and pleasure. Think of it, Stephen . . . we're going to do it all. We'll do anything we damned please. We'll take a look at the whole bloody world, and see if we like it."

Stephen drew two mugs of ale. "You're off your head, Peter—but here's to the whole bloody world!" He raised his mug.

"To the whole Atlantic Ocean—one mile at a time!"

"To Berean Brothers' fine beer!"

The more they drank, the more reason they found to continue.

* * *

Anna looked concerned at the two empty seats at the supper table. "Shall I get them?" she asked Meg, doubtfully. "I'm not certain they're in any condition to come to the table."

Meg listened for a moment to the raucous sounds of laughter and snatches of song drifting on the night air. "Let them be."

"I'll leave something for them in the scullery," Anna said with a baleful glance toward the brewhouse. "Perhaps they will be more themselves later." Callie smothered a giggle in her napkin.

The evening passed without sight of Peter or Stephen. Later, Callie lay in bed listening as the revelry continued far into the night.

They did not come in at all that night. They weren't seen at the table until late the following afternoon as each, pale and subdued, nursed an oversized, sensitive head.

By the end of March the hop shoots were well out of the ground, and the wires strung. Peter's attention turned to the practical matter of packing the necessities they would take with them. Larger items of furniture, he stored, asking Frank to ship them once they found their house. "The man I told you about, Sam Tolbert, thinks I may be able to purchase a working farm. If this Grampe place is suitable for hops as Sam has led me to believe, I'll send for the furniture immediately."

He organized the packing easily. His one remaining concern was Rosalind. Her pregnancy was beginning to show, and she had made no effort to hire a maid or a nurse to accompany her.

With their departure only two weeks away, he put an ad in the local paper. Only three girls came in answer to it. One changed her mind before she was interviewed. The second one made such cow-eyes at her prospective employer that Meg sent her packing. The third was an anemic little thing who couldn't be trusted to survive the voyage. When she left, Peter slumped over the kitchen table, his head propped in his hands. "What do I do now?"

"I think the only solution for you is to take Callie with you."

"Callie? Good Lord, Ma, she's just a girl. She wouldn't have any idea of how to care for Rosalind. Suppose something happened . . . went wrong. What could Callie do?"

"A lot more than those ninnies you interviewed today, and what's more Callie would care. She'd love to go. It's written all over her face for those not too blind to see."

Peter looked hopeful for a minute, then looked down at his hands, finally saying aloud what he loathed to think about. "You're wrong, Ma. Callie would never want to come with me . . . not after . . . not after what I did to the dog. She hated that . . . hated me for it."

"Oh, Peter, will you never learn? She can overcome nearly anything if you give her the time. It is you who have not forgiven yourself, not Callie."

He looked at Meg for a long time, then said, "Callie . . ." testing the idea.

Meg smiled and patted his hand. "I'll send her to you."

"Outside, Ma. Ask her to meet me outside."

Callie went hesitantly down the stairs. She and Peter had been cordial, but had had little to say to one another since the night Ugly had been done away with. She hadn't liked it being that way, but there was no taking back the things she had said to him, and there hadn't seemed a way for her to reestablish the friendship that had once been between them. She didn't know what she could say now. But what was worse, she knew that what she wanted him to say was beyond the realm of possibility. After the horrible things she had said to him, he'd never want her near him by choice. Nevertheless her heart pounded an erratic rhythm. She came to stand in front of him, her eyes wide and questioning.

She was sixteen this spring. He looked down at her and saw cheekbones beginning to come into prominence. Her face was maturing and rapidly losing the overfleshed look of a child. Her eyes were deep and blue, still filled with the crystal-clear innocence that he had found appealing in the girl. In a woman, it made her tempting. He cleared his throat. He remembered her hurt fury when she had begged for Ugly's life. Had she forgiven him? She said she never would. He wasn't prepared for how much that hurt. When he managed to speak, his voice was thick and husky. "Could you see your way to coming to New York with us? I'd understand if you said no, but . . . I hope you'll come."

She stood before him, the wind blowing her hair and whipping color into her cheeks, speechless.

He shifted his weight, gesturing helplessly. "You'd be Rosalind's companion. And then when the baby came . . . she'll need someone . . . say something, please."

"I can't," she whispered and put her hands over her mouth.

"Do you want to come with us?"

She nodded deeply, laughing and crying at once. "I thought I'd die from the wanting," she whispered. "Are you sure? I think I'd go mad if you didn't mean it."

"I mean it. Lord, do I mean it!" He grinned, taking a deep breath and laughing as he exhaled. "If you had said no . . . I . . . we might not have gone at all. I couldn't find anyone for Rosalind, and I thought . . ." He stopped, let out a whoop, tossing his cap into the air. "We're going!"

She stood where she was, hands still covering her mouth, laughing and crying. "We're going. We're going."

Callie was still not certain she believed it would come true until that final morning when they went to the docks. She gazed at the masts, so many and so close that they blocked out the sky. They walked from the carriage to the Blackwall frigate that would carry them to America. Her stomach remained in a tight knot, tensed for disappointment when it came.

"What's the matter with you, Callie? You're the eager one . . . why are you hanging back now?" Peter asked and gave her a gentle shove forward.

"I still can't believe it. The ship is sure to vanish before my eyes. I know it will." She squeezed her eyes shut and quickly reopened them. She looked at Stephen, afraid to glance back to the ship. "Is it still there?"

He took her arm. "Come along, you simpleton; it's there." He laughed. "You've got everyone on the dock looking at you."

"Are they?" she breathed and craned around to see the smiling, work-hardened faces of the men near the customs quay staring at her. "Oh, Stephen, do hurry! I've made a spectacle of us."

The hard solid feeling of earth was left behind as they stepped onto the gangplank.

Meg waved good-bye to her sons and Callie, waiting at the dock until there was no sight of them. They disappeared into the mist and the distance. She stood for a long time wondering if she should not be experiencing some guilt for the relief she felt when they vanished from sight. She felt nothing. Without a word needing to be said, Frank took her arm and helped her into the carriage.

BOOK II

Chapter 19

Their first view of New York Harbor surprised them.
It was a bustling, active port, as filled with ships and
the evidence of trade as the British ports had been.
Persuaded to come on deck, Rosalind stared agog at
the activity on the dock below. Vehicles of all descrip-
tions moved in a swift and busy tangle on West Street.
Drays, expresswagons, butcher's carts, beer-skids, carriages, hansoms, trolleys, and garbage carts moved in
all directions, their drivers all screaming to be heard
above the roar of the dock. The waters were crowded
with canal boats, freight ships being loaded and unloaded, barges and ferries taking on cargo and passengers and moving about the river in as frantic a bustle
as the horses and carts moving on land. Grudgingly,
Rosalind admitted to a stir of curiosity and excitement.

"I told you you would like it," Peter said.

"I would like anything that would relieve me of the
taste of ship's food and the stench," she said, her eyes
going back to the store fronts and the constant activ-

ity of the street. "Anyway, appearances can be deceiving."

He put his arm around her waist, squeezing her to him. "Say what you will. I don't care what changes your mind, as long as something does. I want you to be happy here." She glanced up at him, but he didn't give her a chance to say anything. He excused himself to go off to talk to a group of men standing on the quay. He was smiling broadly when he returned.

"Come along; our cab is waiting."

Jauntily he told the driver to take them to the Saint Nicholas Hotel. "He's the patron saint of the city," he explained to Rosalind. "I thought it best we begin by getting on the right side of the patron. We may need his assistance."

"Indeed," Rosalind breathed and looked from one side of the carriage, leaning across Peter to see from the other side of the street. "It is far more of a city than I had thought."

Peter grinned, pleased. "That's more like it."

"How was I to know what it would look like? Anyway it may still be nothing."

Peter took her hand. "Not this time. You're free here, Rosalind, there are no taverns or Rufus Hawkeses or Mrs. Foxes with long nasty memories. You'll be happy here," he said in a low voice.

Rosalind looked at him, thinking about him rather than herself, and for a fleeting moment knew that he had understood her from the beginning. Then the moment passed and Rosalind's eyes went back to the busy, crowded streets that sped by through the window of her carriage.

"When will we be seeing Sam Tolbert, Peter? Will he be meeting us here?" Stephen asked.

"I'll send a message as soon as we're settled in the hotel. I thought we'd take a day or two to see the town. We'll be doing a great deal of our business in New York. The more we know about it, the. . . . What are we stopping for?" Peter asked suddenly as the carriage halted at the intersection of Third Avenue and Fifteenth Street.

"What is going on?" Peter leaned out and asked the driver. "Why are we stopping?"

"Nothing to alarm you, sir. Just a race."

"Race? In the middle of the street?"

"Yes, sir! You'll see it often on Third. It'll only hold us up for a moment."

He pulled back into the body of the carriage, grinning at Stephen. "Did you hear what the man said, Steve? It's a bloody throughway and they use it for sport. This is some town. I'll have to write to Frank about this."

"Peter . . . look at the women," Rosalind said. Along the street were throngs of people, shops, restaurants, and oyster bars, all with counters full and doors opening and closing as people came and went. Many of them were women, well-dressed in gay vibrant-colored gowns, going about their business.

Rosalind couldn't take her eyes from them. "They're dressed to the height of fashion, Peter. I've never seen such an array of color on . . . I mean they must be ordinary people. There can't be that many nobility here, can there?"

"None, my dear; we are as noble as the lot of them."

"Are we truly?"

"Truly," he said and took her hand. Impishly he looked at her and put her hand to his lips.

She sat straighter, her chin going up just a bit. "We will do well here. I admit, Peter, I was wrong about coming here."

Callie, Stephen, and Rosalind spent the afternoon in their hotel rooms. Rosalind, searching through her wardrobe, tried to select the most becoming gown that would still fit her, and Callie sewed frantically to let out seams and put in strategic tucks to accommodate Rosalind's cumbersome belly.

"I do wish my time would come."

"It won't be long now," Callie said. "And you look lovely. You always do." She threaded the needle yet again.

Rosalind looked into her mirror, studying herself disapprovingly from all angles. One dress after another she tried and rejected. Callie kept altering and sewing, and Rosalind disapproving. It took the entire afternoon for her to select the gown she would wear to dinner that evening.

"You can hardly tell with this dress, can you?" she asked. "And if I wear my dark-blue cape—why, I won't look as though I am to have a child at all. I'll just look fat!" she fumed and tossed the cape onto the pile of clothes on the bed. "I shall have but one child," she said firmly. "One is all any woman should be asked to suffer. Months of looking so . . . pregnant women are *not* attractive. It is all talk. Something to say when no true compliment can be forthcoming." She walked to Callie, bowing awkwardly. "You are so radiant, Madame Cow. When will the happy event take place?"

Callie giggled, and Rosalind frowned. "It is not funny. I didn't mean it to be funny at all. It is true! I wish I wasn't going to have this child."

"Aunt Meg told me she felt like that with her first. Frank was more nuisance than joy while she carried him. Then she said the morning he was born and she first held him everything changed. Maybe it will be the same for you."

"You are comparing me to Meg Berean? Dear me!" Rosalind walked grandly to the chaise longue, arranging herself artfully over its curving surface. "You have managed to make a dull day intolerable. I think I had better rest before we go out. Bring me a wet cloth soaked in my violet water, Callie. I think you've brought on one of my headaches."

Callie continued her care of Rosalind throughout the afternoon. Her own unpacking went neglected. She was still wearing the same travel-stained suit when Peter and Stephen returned to the hotel to take them to dinner.

Peter had scoured the city asking questions and talking to people. He already knew the location of the best oyster bars, the best restaurants, and had had his first conversation with the men who lunched daily at the Tontine restaurant to transact business.

"It has been an informative day," he said to Stephen as they sat down to wait for Callie. "We are going to have to learn a whole new language here, it seems. English alone will not suffice. There is quite a mixture of Indian and Dutch and German and Danish and other languages all combined to make up this American English. My tongue has been twisted around itself half the day."

"But did you find out anything about the hop production?"

"Certainly. We've come at the most opportune time. A fortune can be made right now. There is a great demand for good beer and ale, and few able suppliers. And the Erie Canal opened just five years ago. With it the way to the West is clear. We can send hops to Chicago, Cinc'nnati, Detroit . . . all over. The brewery industry has been very slow in starting here, and production is low. It was made for us, Stephen. We have a wide-open field. Berean Brothers' Brewery is not so much a vision as we thought. It is very possible, and something that is needed here."

"If it's so needed, why hasn't someone done it?"

Peter shrugged. "Be glad they haven't. And there are many who are starting. We'll not be alone. We'll have to work harder and longer than our competition. But we'll succeed. There are plenty of raw materials. Can you imagine that hops grow wild along the Hudson Valley and yet no one grew them commercially until 1808? It is unbelievable."

"Or maybe it is believable and we just don't know the reason. Perhaps it is not good land, or maybe the climate is wrong for hops."

"Ahh, Steve, you're looking for trouble where none is to be found. There are hop gardens—yards they call them here—all over the northern part of the state, but they are small. They are still importing English hops. From what I've been told today, and I trust the information can be relied upon, the favored type of hop is Farnham. That's what we'll grow. And we'll not make the mistake of starting out small. We'll put everything we've got into it. We'll start with the idea that we will be supplying the hops for the brewery industry. Now that they have imported the Englishmen, they can refrain from importing the hops."

"When can we see the farm? And where is this place, Peter? Is it in the midst of the hop country you speak of? I'll never get used to these Yankee names. Where are these counties?"

Peter's eyebrows shot up as he grinned. "Watch your name calling. I was told today we would be Yorkers, not Yankees. Some kind of an old holdover, . . . Who knows, but these people may be as touchy as we are about the Kents and the Kentish. Scratch deeply enough and I guess we are all similar under the skin." Then, as Rosalind appeared: "Whenever will Callie be ready? I am near to starving. What have you two been doing all day, Rosalind? Didn't she unpack at all?"

"I unpacked all my things. As you can see I am ready and just as impatient as you to be on our way."

"Well, go see if you can help her."

"I'll do no such thing. You'll have to hire someone. We can't manage here without help."

Peter shook his head and got up to pace the room for the remaining fifteen minutes it took Callie to get ready. They dined at Fraunces Tavern. Peter had been told it was the best restaurant in town. Just as he had registered them in the hotel named after the patron of the city, so he would take them to the finest restaurants.

Among the other things Peter had learned from his afternoon of talk and sightseeing was that New Yorkers above all else admired success and all of its attendant evidences. There was no point in attempting to achieve success when one could begin at that level with no class structure to bar one from it. Never would he enter the second-best restaurant when the first-best was open to him.

The following day he took Stephen with him on his tramp through the city. Rosalind made her first trip to the shops that lined the streets, carefully garbed so that she was satisfied no one would know how close to her time she was. It annoyed her that her efforts resulted in making her look like a heavyset matron, but even that was preferable to the other.

Friday afternoon Sam Tolbert took the steamship from Poughkeepsie to meet the Bereans in New York. Already feeling that he was an old, favored customer by virtue of the two days he had been in New York, Peter arranged for Sam to meet him and Stephen at the Tontine.

Sam was a squat bull of a man. His manners were

correct, but his voice and mannerisms made him seem as uncultured and rough-edged as the toughest of the laborers in Kent.

Peter had seen him and another man come into the Tontine and talk to the headwaiter, but he had paid little attention. He didn't know what Sam looked like, but expected someone like the sleek, well-dressed businessmen Peter had grown accustomed to seeing on the streets. If nothing else Sam would be wearing fashionable clothes similar to those Peter had ordered for himself the previous day.

He was momentarily at a loss for words when that gruff, hearty man strode across the dining room, cheerfully and loudly prepared to introduce Peter to the glories of *his* land.

"I'm Sam Tolbert. This is my brother, Jack. Pleased to meet you, Berean," he said, and Peter shook the broadest, hardest hand he had ever felt.

He introduced Stephen and all of them sat down to eat and talk. Sam expressed only delight when he found Peter already well-entrenched and by now fairly familiar and knowledgeable about the past, present, and probable future of New York.

He laughed in his deep jovial way, clapping Peter on the back. "No need to welcome you then; you've already found your spot."

After they had finished their lunch, Sam said, "Well, what say we take a trip upriver and see the Grampe place. It seems to me you fellows are anxious to get started with this brewery of yours, and I can tell you now who is going to be your first customer." He laughed, thumping his chest.

"You don't have much to say," Jack said to Stephen as they boarded the ship.

"Not much," Stephen agreed. Jack was slightly

taller than Sam, but the resemblance between them was strong. Dark snappy eyes peered out from his sun-toughened face. Stephen smiled and looked away. Jack was as homely as a mud fence, but he had a rare, appealing quality. His eyes seemed to say there was fun and deviltry to be had just around the corner.

"Have you seen any of the sights yet?" Jack asked.

"Some of them. Mostly the monuments you have erected to the revolution. They are everywhere. Looks a little like we're still the archenemy," Stephen said, grinning.

"Can't blame us now, can you, Stevie? You fellows gave us a hell of a time. We just got rid of you once and back you came again in '12. Maybe you're an advance invasion party right now, eh?"

Stephen glanced at Peter's excited face. "You have a point. We may be."

Jack too looked over at Peter, shaking his head. "He's too pretty."

"Pretty!?" Stephen barked, laughing. "Peter?"

"Yeah. If I looked like that, man, I'd have a harem escorting me everywhere I went. All them pretty ladies, bowing and blushing and calling me magnificent."

"You're daft."

"Yeah . . . I am. But His Magnificence there . . . think he'd go for a little bit of fun at the gaming tables?"

"Not if he hears you call him pretty."

"How about you, Stevie? You like a good game of chance from time to time?"

"From time to time."

"Good. I'll take you to the Abbey. Best place around here. We'll meet some of the ladies and have a good old time. Of course, it won't be like having His Magnificence by my side, but you'll do all right. You bring the little pretties over to us, and I'll tell you what to do with them once we get them."

"I think I might be able to figure that out for myself."

Jack ignored him and looked back to Peter. "Think we could get him to go with us?"

"I doubt that his wife would like it much—not with what you have in mind."

"That's a pity. He's just too damned pretty to waste on one woman. My God, Stevie, with his looks he could keep us all in supply just with his overflow."

Stephen shook his head, bemused. "Don't you ever work around this town? I've seen horse races down the main street, bets waged on every corner, men stacked five deep at oyster bars midafternoon, and talk about harems. Not much to indicate serious business of any kind."

"It's all serious, Stevie. We just do our serious thinking in the most pleasurable of ways, and the most novel. It's that kind of town. What's the point of being rich and old when you can just as well be rich and young? There's fortunes to be made on every street corner here. This is a town for a day and the man who is awake on that day. I'll show it all to you before we're done. I've a feeling ours will be a long, happy relationship . . . maybe even a partnership."

"In what?" Stephen asked suspiciously.

"The harem, of course."

"Somehow I have the feeling that you'll end up with the best of the bargain."

"Never doubt it," Jack said, looking out across the Hudson to the wooded hills beyond the bank. "Sam tells me His Magnificence is thinking of buying the farm next to ours. Want to put in hops? Well, we've got the finest barley crop you'll ever see. Seems as though your hops and our grain combined might make a pretty good brew with a brewery not far behind."

Stephen looked at him, but said nothing.

"See, business slips in pretty neatly. Now you've got a proposition all nice and fixed in your mind. Next time I see you, you'll be filled to the top with a yes or a no to the idea."

Jack chattered all the way, never once referring to Peter as anything but His Magnificence. Later he shortened it to "old H.M." Stephen liked him. He had no idea why. The man never closed his mouth, and mostly talked of silly things and crazy ideas he had for having fun or wooing women.

Sam and Peter went below to the lounge to talk. Stephen and Jack remained on the deck with Stephen leaning over its side watching the water and the landscape rush past. The great cliffs on the western bank stood out against the sky, multihued and regal. The forest lands on the other bank were overwhelming. It looked to him as England must have looked when the great forests of Kent were all around and dense. Inside their hidden glades then lived the dark forest animals and the Cantii, according to the stories he'd read. To Stephen, to be traveling through this river valley was to be seeing something for the first time, before it had been touched and altered by time and the efforts of man. Of course, those efforts of ambitious men were already in evidence, but not so much that they obliterated the natural beauty. The sky suddenly filled with eagle screams. Stephen looked from the giant birds above down to the water rushing by the sides of the ship.

"It was called the Shatemuc by the Algonquins," Jack said solemnly. "Whatever name you call it, it is glorious. You'll never be able to forget this river once you have known it."

"So you do have a serious side," Stephen said.

"Well, there are two different worlds here. One is God's and one is man's. It's easy to make fun of man's world. It fair begs that you do, but God's . . . well, it isn't so easy to make fun of that."

"No," Stephen said, looking dreamily up at the hills. "I didn't realize it would be so mountainous. Is there a mountain or hill near our property?—I mean the farm we are to look at?"

"Well, it's not on the main part . . . it won't hinder your hop yard."

Stephen laughed. "I have no objection. All land should have at least one decent hill that a man can call a mountain when the mood strikes."

Jack's eyes lit up again. "I'll take you to the highlands . . . way up. Maybe we'll even go up to the source of the river. You've never in all your days seen water purer or colder than it is up there. In the Catskills it is truly paradise. There's places around here that would start your heart to thrumming. I can't let you miss seeing the Lake of Tears. Not you. I can see you're the man for this."

"Perhaps I am."

Chapter 20

The Grampe house sat at the top of a gentle ridge, three white stories with shuttered windows staring out over the Hudson. Paul Grampe had built his house thirty years before, during his prime. He had raised two sons in that house. The cholera took one, and in the last year a sleighing accident had taken the other. With the death of his last son, Paul Grampe lost his zest for his home and his fields. He was as anxious for the Bereans to like his piece of land as they were.

Sam introduced Peter and Stephen to Paul Grampe. After exchanging niceties, Paul stood scratching his gray head.

"Seems to me the best way to get a feel of the land is for me to leave you free to walk it. Go ahead, Berean. Feel free to poke about all you wish. I'll see you up at the house later."

Peter thanked him and left with Sam as companion and guide to walk every inch of the Grampe farm, mentally clearing new fields and erecting hop wires as he went. At every rod he stooped to dig his fingers into the soil, smelling it, feeling it, noting its color and texture. He looked out over Paul Grampe's fields of ripening wheat, and they began to seem his own.

"Well, what do you think?" Sam asked.

Peter looked down at the soil in the palm of his hand. "Think he'd throw in the wheat crop if I pay his asking price?"

Sam considered a moment, then shrugged. "Don't know till you ask. Paul's a fair man though, and he does want out. He just doesn't have the heart for it these days. He might. He just might be glad to throw the crop in with the rest of the deal. You want it then?"

Peter nodded, brushing his hands free of soil. He turned to look at the house. "Let's go."

Mr. Grampe took Peter alone into his study. He placed a bottle of applejack on the table between them. "This is the way my son and I used to do our dickerin'. Let's see if it works for us, Berean."

It worked. Peter paid more for the farm than he had intended. Paul Grampe sold the wheat he had intended to harvest himself. Each had struck a bargain he considered advantageous.

Peter emerged from the study smiling. "Come here, Stephen. I want you to see something." He walked out onto the front porch with Stephen. "Look all around you. Everything you see is ours. We've done it, Steve. This is the first Berean hop yard of the great state of New York in the United States of America."

"Said like that, it's damned awesome."

"It *is* awesome."

Sam came out on the porch to join them. He placed his hand on Peter's shoulder. "You two seem pleased enough and well you should be. This is a fine piece of land. Let me greet you now as neighbor."

Peter leaned forward with both hands placed on the porch rail. "I hate to leave, but I suppose we should."

"Aren't you forgetting something?" Sam laughed.

"What is that?"

"Well now, I know it's land you're buying, but don't you think your wife will want to know there's a house on it as well?"

Stephen stared at Peter. "You mean you didn't even look the house over?"

"No. I didn't think of it. Did you?"

"Sure, of course, I did. Hey, Peter, come on. Rosalind will have your head if you don't tell her about this house. It's a beauty."

Peter followed Stephen inside. The four men, led by Mrs. Grampe, walked through the library, gun room, and drawing room. Peter was trying his best to fix in his mind the details of carved mantel pieces, woodwork, and windows. All the small things that would mean something to Rosalind and nothing to him. It was the feel of the house that held his interest. It was like the farm in Kent had once been. He felt as though he had always lived there. He belonged in this house. That it had a spacious dairy, pantry, and scullery meant nothing to him, and in this instance would probably mean little to Rosalind. What would matter was that it was spacious, would easily lend itself to gracious living and entertaining. After Mrs. Grampe had taken him through the upstairs rooms and shown him the one she had used as a nursery for her own sons, he decided his son *had* to be born there.

He wanted to be living in the house before his son was born. It would be quite a feat, for Rosalind was due shortly. Mr. and Mrs. Grampe looked bewildered at one another. Who was to know these two nice young Englishmen would become so pushy once the bargain was struck. Peter, who had been so steady and serious-minded as they worked out the sale, was now as eager and erratic as a summer storm. Paul Grampe was moved more by his enthusiasm and youth than any logic, but even another glass of apple-jack, poured from his own bottle, could not make him agree to move before the end of the month.

It was less than what Peter wanted, but he was certain with Rosalind's cooperation everything would be fine. After he had managed to get them to New York, found the right place for them to live, delaying the arrival of one small baby seemed no problem at all.

"You're crazy," Stephen muttered and then laughed. "But I'm not fool enough to say you won't make it happen."

James Hawkes Berean was born in New York City. His first act was one of disobedience to his father's wishes. If Peter was disappointed that his son didn't wait to be born in the new farmhouse, he was pleased that the infant showed such distinctive independence of spirit.

"He defied me! Damn it, the kid defied me right out of the hatch!" Peter cried, wildly joyful as he stomped around Rosalind, who lay like a limp violet on her bed. The midwife had taken the baby out of the room, away from his noisy father.

"Peter, please! Don't shout so. Tell me again quietly how wonderful the baby and I are," Rosalind smiled wanly, putting her arms up for him to come to her.

Peter sat gingerly on the edge of the bed, leaning over to kiss her. "I don't think I can be quiet. I want to shout and paint signs and hang them in the streets so everyone will know herein lives the most beautiful woman and the most beautiful child the world has known."

Callie wrote home to tell Meg of the news:

We all agreed that the baby should be named James, but it was Peter who insisted that Rosalind remember her own father as well. She does not care for the name Rufus, but I think she is rather pleased for Jamie's middle name to be Hawkes. It is difficult to say whom he resembles at the moment. He is such a tiny babylike thing, but very beautiful. And very determined according to Peter. He may well be for there is no doubt that he makes known his wishes loudly and clearly.

Peter has found us a grand home. It is near a village called Poughkeepsie. I doubt that we shall ever become accustomed to the names here; so many of them come from the Algonquin language. Otherwise it is a thoroughly lovely place, and we have so many of the same things here that we had in Kent that we do not become homesick. There is a great hill on the property, and of course, it has already been named Stephen's mountain. It is not the same though, and he says there is only one mountain for him and that is in Kent. I must say I agree with him, but it is still nice to have a hill here as well. Maybe this one can become Jamie's mountain. . . .

She wrote as many letters as she could those first few months, and received news from Meg on nearly every incoming packet ship. In so many ways the letters going back and forth revealed the similarity of their lives: Frank was harvesting hops; Peter and Stephen were harvesting wheat. All three men raced against time, the weather, and the market. The letters also showed where the similarities ended. Frank continued to be beset with the problems of an old country in the throes of reform, and Peter's life reflected the vigor of a new country not yet hemmed in by laws and limitations. For once Peter had as much to do as he was able, and he stretched the days until there were no more hours to fill, with all the variety of enterprise he could. With fearless audacity and the fortune of a beginner, he plunged the inheritance he had received from James into the games that were becoming a part of New York—speculations, gold markets, railroads, shipping, and the buying and selling of cargoes on the chance his ship would come into port laden with spices and silks and hand-crafted furnishings status-greedy New Yorkers would buy before the ships were unloaded.

Some called New York the City of Ships, and it was true that one could barely see the sky for the masts that stretched upward all along South Street. But it was not only the hustle and traffic-clogged streets that fascinated Peter; nor was his interest merely in making money. The longshoremen held his interest and admiration. They were plain men, ordinary men, not unlike the laborers in Kent, but as early as 1825 these men understood the strategic position they held on the New York docks, and had staged a strike. And here, in America, they had succeeded without an army of magistrates arresting all in sight, without hangings and unreasonable punishments. The laborer here was valued, and Peter felt a joy that he tried to describe in letters to Frank.

Callie also dutifully reported all these things to Meg and Frank and Anna, and received in return news that Frank thought Peter a fool who would end up penniless and begging for passage money home once the truth of the situation in America was known.

As Callie read the most recent letter from Frank aloud after supper, Peter and Stephen laughed.

"Frank never has any view but one," Peter said.

"Would you like to wager, Stephen, that he has been talking to Mrs. Foxe lately? If those aren't the words of that old horse blanket, I'll eat them. Wait until he hears we will be expanding the size of our fields this year. Be sure to tell him that in your next letter, Callie. See if he still thinks we need passage money home."

Stephen laughed then. "I can tell you now what he'll say. He won't believe it. It's too near winter to be able to prepare additional fields."

"Oh, no, it isn't. We'll do it."

Peter, true to his boast, insisted on clearing more of the land. He and Stephen worked with the field hands from sunup to sundown. By the end of that first harvest season, they had, by determination, grinding work, additional hired help, and sweat, cleared twenty-five acres in addition to the thirty-five-acre field Paul Grampe had put into wheat. Sixty acres would be ready for planting the following spring.

But even with this, Stephen was not completely satisfied. Brewing season was well underway when they had arrived in America, and it was the first year he could not recall not having brewed at least small beer for the house. Paul Grampe had once thought himself of brewing and had the beginnings of a modest brewhouse, but he had never equipped it. The building stood empty and idle, a thorn in Stephen's side until he could stand it no more.

He gathered up what odds and ends he could find and began his brewing as though it had never been interrupted. Peter walked into the brewhouse to see him industriously fidgeting with the fire, trying to get the wort, a mixture of fermented malt, boiling properly. Peter looked at the oddities Stephen had collected. Hogshead barrels were serving as mash tuns and back coolers. For the copper needed to boil the wort, a suspicious-looking object served. Peter touched it with the tip of his boot.

"Where did you come across that? It isn't what I think it is, is it?"

Stephen looked up from his awkward position on the floor. "Oh, don't mention it. Don't say a word about it, even to me. Callie will have my skin. It's her best kettle, but I had to have it. For the moment I have her believing there are thieving Indians about."

Peter laughed and gave the conglomeration of barrels and kettles another look. "What's this stuff going to taste like?"

"Well, it can only be small beer. Maybe a bit of stronger if I'm lucky."

"What are you using for hops?"

"A few of the wild . . . but mostly I'm not using them at all." Stephen beamed. "Jack told me of a way to use corn or molasses as substitutes. I've been experimenting, and have a pretty good mix. Jack says it's pretty good."

Peter made a sour face, sitting down on the ground beside Stephen. Idly he fanned the fire. "If this is the stuff they drink, there's little wonder that the brewery industry is slow in growth here. It makes me all the more certain that we must get your brewery going as soon as possible. That's all there is to it. Even if it's only a few barrels at a time in the beginning we've got to get started. Callie can take it to market when she takes her butter and eggs. Once we give people a taste of real beer, we'll have so many orders we'll never fill them fast enough." He stood up, brushing himself off, and glanced back at the boiling wort. "And for God's sake go buy yourself another kettle before she finds out that you have this one."

"Ahh, she'll never find out. She doesn't come in here."

Peter shrugged. "It's your neck, but don't say I didn't warn you."

"Leave it to me. I can talk Callie out of anything."

Peter shook his head, eyes twinkling. "I hope like hell I'm around to hear that."

Stephen grimaced at his brother and continued working.

When Jack came later that afternoon, his first question was, "How's the brew? Any ready for a thirsty friend?" He lounged gracelessly across three barrels. "Any luck with the different mixes yet?"

Stephen shrugged, looking doubtful. "So far I haven't come up with anything that Peter will even try. No matter what I do it's never going to match a good ale—not even a good small beer. It's all second rate . . . maybe not even that. About the best I can say for it is that it is drinkable."

"That should count for something. Maybe I'd better sample it again. My judgment is always good on these things."

"You'd do damn near anything for a free beer." Stephen laughed, drawing Jack his mug. He got up and handed Jack the beer and a mash oar. "Keep the mash stirring for me, will you? I want to catch Henry before he goes into town. I need some supplies. I'll be back in a few minutes."

"Hey! Wait a minute. I came over to see if you're going to the dance Saturday night."

"I haven't thought about it. Maybe."

Jack hesitated. "Think Callie would go with me?"

"Callie? No."

"Why the hell not? What is it with that girl? I don't think she likes men. Every time I get around her she's as skitterish as a new colt. Why don't you think she'd go with me?"

"I didn't say she wouldn't go with you. Just that she

isn't," Stephen said gruffly. "Keep that mix stirring. I'll be back shortly."

"Wait a minute! What do you mean, she isn't? You'd better tell me what's what. Do you want her for yourself? Is that it?"

"Just leave her alone. That's all."

"Oh no, it isn't. That's not enough. If you want her, well, then I'll step back as a good friend, but otherwise . . ."

"Otherwise just never step in. Stir!" Stephen said and left.

Stephen had been gone about twenty minutes when Callie stormed into the brewhouse. "There it is! I wouldn't have believed it!"

"Hello, Callie darlin'," Jack drawled.

"Where is he?"

"Gone. You don't need Stevie, not when I'm here." He grinned happily and put his arms around her waist, cuddling her playfully.

"Let me go, Jack."

"Don't be like that. I just want to have a little fun."

"Jack! Let me go."

He aimed for her lips and got the sharp edge of her jawbone. "Let me go!" she breathed through clenched teeth. As his grasp tightened, she reached for the mash oar.

"Ouch! Damn woman!" he cried, hand over his ear. She swung again, catching him across the rear end. "I let you go! Be damned, you banshee—leave a man his healthy limbs!"

"Get! Out! Go!" she cried, swinging wildly as she chased him from the brewhouse.

Stephen stopped at the edge of the walk, but too late.

"You! Stephen! Indians indeed. The Berean tribe it was!"

"Callie—I'll give it back. Callie, calm down. For God's sake, watch what you do with that oar! Callie!— look, look I've got another kettle. You can have yours." He backed away from the oar whizzing past him. "Callie!" he cried as he tripped over the garden border, falling hard on his back.

She walked toward him and then began to laugh. She placed the oar gently across the flat of his belly. "Seeing you flat on your back in the poison ivy makes it all worthwhile—thieving Indians and all."

Stephen didn't have the courage to look to see if he was really lying in poison ivy. He just lay there thinking about Jack running down the path, and began to laugh again.

Chapter 21

The first months in Poughkeepsie were the busiest and most exciting Callie had ever known. There were never enough hours in the day for any of the Bereans. Peter had been right when he had told them that everything for which they labored here would be theirs in a special way. Each of them had a sense of pride and accomplishment that seemed unique to them, and each of them changed in accordance with the new state of well-being.

Rosalind had come into her own after Jamie was born. She was slim again, and could fit into the most daring and beautiful gowns. And for once she found she had as many outlets as she wished for all her pent-up energies and her dreams. Here they could be real. Peter bought her a small, shiny black buggy, which she could drive herself. From the moment of the buggy's arrival, Rosalind was off on her round of visiting their neighbors and becoming involved in the local ladies' societies. Somewhat sheepishly she admitted to having learned to quilt, giving them all a good laugh and Rosalind a feeling of warmth and belonging to the family she'd never had before.

By a steady process, in direct proportion to Rosalind's success at becoming what she considered a "lady," Callie was eased out of the task of being Rosalind's companion. Rosalind had become far too grand and independent to tolerate Callie's haphazard interest in clothes, committees, and charities. So Callie's first concern was now Jamie alone. But she also cared for the dairy. For all intents and purposes, Callie ran the house. She was housekeeper, governess, and scullery maid all in one. It was no small relief when a maid was hired to assist Rosalind in sorting out the complexities of how a "lady" should spend her day.

It was a hard year, but one Callie would always look back on as one of the happiest of her life. It was not only filled with work, but fun as well. And with the fun came a feeling new to her. Shyly she felt a tremulous stirring in Stephen's presence. It was a strange and confusing feeling, and she found herself avoiding him at times she might otherwise have felt free to enter his male world. And then there were times she seemed to be compelled to be around him no matter what. As her desire to be nearer him grew, her ability to act naturally, as she always had, became more difficult. Uncomfortable with her confusion over Stephen, Callie sought reasons outside of him for the cause, and she found them, unsatisfactory as they were. She was changing because her life was changing. All of them were becoming happier and more attuned to each other as their life developed.

The farm was taking shape. It was an exciting process to live through. It was no longer Peter alone who could see what it would become. Outlines of future fields were clearly visible. The stakes had been driven into the ground marking the place and shape of the first brewery site—Stephen's brewery. Day by day they were taking pieces of dreams and turning them into something real, something to be touched and seen. And best of all, they were happy doing it. As it had been when she had first come to live with the Bereans, the supper hour was again a raucous, happy time, filled with stories and laughter. She even enjoyed Jack Tolbert's jokes as long as he kept his hands and his intentions under control, which wasn't often. If he couldn't stir up trouble, he just wasn't happy. But he was a part of this new place, and without him it wouldn't be the same. So she liked Jack after a fashion, and sometimes admitted to herself she would be happy if Stephen were as bold as Jack.

The winter came on with a snowy blast, but it was nothing like the damp winters she had spent in Kent. There were none of the tensions to keep them worried and strained. Peter was home every night with Rosalind. Slowly the strain that had been present in their marriage began to lessen, and Rosalind was more often than not a cheerful, active participant in their fun. She even took part in some of the winter sports that seemed to abound. The people along the Hudson looked upon their winters as a time for great fun. With Jack leading them, they all took to the ice. The river the Indians called the Shatemuc, which seemed so powerful that nothing could stem its flow, froze over. At first there were only the skaters who dared to move on the ice, but as the winter went on, sleighs and sleds began to make their appearances.

Jack was Poughkeepsie's official bonfire builder. He had claimed the title for himself, just as he bragged furiously that he could build a fire so warm and so large that it would keep the whole town warm till spring. No one disputed his claims. They were happy to let him do the work. In his own random way, he was as reliable as the rising sun. The bonfire was always roaring when everyone appeared at the river for a day of racing and skating.

It was Jack who introduced them to the people at the sleighing races. As a result Peter, in accordance with his habit of wanting the best ever since they had come to New York, purchased the finest and brightest sleigh made. His horses were matched and of good bloodline. It was difficult to know who was prouder of his new possessions, Rosalind or himself. In any case the tempo of the city and the constant community activity of Poughkeepsie gave him adequate outlet for his energies and the need for excitement he had been hard-pressed to control in Kent. Winter Sunday afternoons were filled with talk of sleighs, horses, races, and competitors. Jack often popped into the dining room just in time for lunch, usually on the pretext of having "Great news!"

"There's going to be a grand race today. Fellow by the name of Bates is visiting from Cooperstown. Thinks he can beat anything we can move on ice." He paused for a moment, letting Peter think. "Going to let him get away with that, Peter?"

"What do you say, Stephen?" Peter asked, his eyes glinting with the challenge.

"I'd end up with my head in a snowbank, is what I think," Stephen said. Peter made a face and Stephen went on. "But then maybe I'll give both you and Bates a run myself."

Jack nodded his approval. "The more the better. If we can't beat him fair, we can always squeeze him in between us." He chuckled. "That might make for more fun anyway . . . most likely it'll cause one hell of a brawl. Damn, I wish I could run too. The runner on my sleigh is bad from last week."

"If you didn't run over every damned thing on the

ice you'd still have your sleigh. But why don't you ride with me?" Stephen said.

"Can't. I already promised I'd hold all the bets. I knew I couldn't run so . . ." He glanced over at Callie. "Seeing as how I am going to be free all afternoon except for a minute or two at the start and a minute or so at the end, Callie, what about you coming down with me?" Ever since he had had time to reconsider the incident with the mash oar, he had been leaning toward the theory that Callie's reaction had really been a display of abandoned affection. His only concession to reason was that he decided to approach her in a more gentlemanly fashion than he had previously. "I'd be more than happy to escort you to the races today," he said sweetly.

Stephen hid his smile behind his napkin. "She's riding with me, Jack. Sorry. Maybe some other time."

"I'm not riding with anyone," Callie said.

"Yes, you are. I need the weight on that side."

"How nice to be needed," she spat, and excused herself from the table. "Get yourself a rock."

She was upstairs in Jamie's room supporting his back as he made his first round-bottomed attempts to sit up alone. He was a dauntless little creature, growing angry and red-faced each time he recovered from the surprise of falling over. Stephen came into the room, leaning over the crib.

"Watch him, Stephen. He's almost got it. He starts out beautifully, but he rolls right over on his face. See—look what effort, and he never stops trying."

Stephen's entrance distracted the baby for a moment, as did the bright scarf around his neck. Jamie reached up and grabbed the scarf, immediately stuffing it into his mouth.

"Mary Anne will be up as soon as she has cleared

away downstairs. She is going to look after the little
lord of the manor until you and I come home from a
trip on the ice."

"Oh, Stephen, I'd dearly love to provide the weight
for your sled . . . it was such a nice thing for you to
suggest, but I can't."

"I didn't mean that, and you know it."

She grinned. "Well, I can't anyway. Honestly. Jamie
is so used to my being here, and no one else knows
what to do for him. He needs me."

"He'll manage without you, and I won't. I take what
I said back. I do need the weight. I'll turn over for
sure unless you're there."

"Stephen, no, I can't go."

But Stephen wasn't listening.

"Good! There's Mary Anne now. No more talk from
you. Go dress warmly and meet me outside in fifteen
minutes."

"Fifteen minutes! Oh, Stephen, at least let me get
him to sleep."

"Not a second longer, and you needn't give Mary
Anne any instructions. I am as good a mother as you,
and I have told her all she needs to know. Hurry up;
you have only fourteen minutes now."

"Yes, sir!" Callie saluted, then ran from the room.

They got into the sleigh and Stephen headed toward the river.

"I've only watched the races before. It is a little
frightening to think of really being in one," she said
warily. She loved the ice, and she loved sleighing, but
she had never seen a race yet that didn't end with
someone spilled all over the ice. That did not seem
like it would be fun.

"We'll watch the first one and see how rough it is
going to be."

They sat in the sleigh at the edge of the bank.

There were three sleighs lined up on the river waiting for the starting gun. At either end of the half-mile length, barrels marked the turn in the track. At the sound of the gun they came down the straightaway toward the first turn, where Stephen and Callie were sitting. Stephen began to frown as soon as the first turn was completed. By the second lap it was clear that it was a two-team race. The third man dropped out, leaving Peter and Bates to finish.

"That Bates fellow has his sleigh weighted somehow. Look how he takes those turns."

"Maybe he really did put rocks in the back," Callie said.

"I don't know what he did, but Peter is going to lose this race on the turns. Damn!" He sat for a second longer and then leaped out of the sleigh.

"Where are you going? Stephen! What are you going to do?"

"Turn the sleigh for him," Stephen shouted as he ran, slipping onto the ice. He crouched at the end of the straightaway, waiting for them to come down for the beginning of the final lap. Callie squeezed her eyes closed as the sleigh came speeding toward him. He leapt, flinging his weight to the outside as he scrabbled to get a hold on the back of Peter's sleigh. The sleigh swung 'round, righting itself to take the straightaway back. As he had throughout the race, Peter began to gain on the straightaway.

Callie peeked through gloved fingers to see Stephen safely, if precariously, straddling the open space between the runners as the sleigh whizzed toward the final turn. Stephen jumped from the runners, running along behind while holding onto the back of the sleigh. As they came to the turn, he again leapt, slamming his body against the outside of the sleigh. The race was Peter's by no more than the length of the horse's head, but a win is a win all the same. There could not have been much more jubilation if it had been a grand national championship. Stephen and Peter were both mobbed by the onlookers. Next to the bonfire Jack leapt up and down like a frog on a lily pad. Bottles were passed, congratulations were offered, and already tall tales of the race were being formulated. It was some time before Stephen freed himself to come back to Callie.

"That's enough racing for me today. How about you?"

"I don't think I ever want to be in another."

"Another?"

"Watching you . . . it was awful. You could have been hurt, Stephen Berean. Don't you ever think?"

"Not often." He grinned, pleased at what he could see in her eyes. She looked away from him. "Anyway we won, and I wasn't hurt." He reached over and pulled the scarf from her head. Immediately the wind caught her long hair and whipped it around her face.

She scrambled to get the scarf back in place. "Look what you've done! I'll never get it untangled now!"

"You're getting bad-tempered," he said cheerfully. "I'm going to have to do something to improve that."

"I am not bad-tempered!"

"You are. And getting worse." He liked the rosy coloring coming into her cheeks, and the blazing liveliness of her eyes. And it was because of him. She cared. Though she expressed it in anger, he knew she had been frightened today because she cared about him. He didn't say anything else to her, but drove along, winding in and out of the narrow paths that best showed the rolling, snow-covered hills patterned and slashed with black, silhouetted trees. He turned toward her again. She had become fascinated by the countryside as he knew she would.

"I have a place I want to show you," he said.

"The mountain?"

"No. I've given up on the mountain—it isn't the same as the one at home. This is another place." He turned the horses back to the east. She was surprised when he halted in view of the house.

"Where is this place?"

"I'll show you. We can't take the sleigh back there yet. We'll have to walk until I've cut the path wide enough for the horses."

She climbed down holding on to his hand, and he took her into the woods at the edge of the new field. There was a small frozen stream that cut through the woods. Forty yards into the woods was a clearing, where the stream widened to make a small pool. With the snow and the barren trees in black relief against the whiteness, it was a fairyland heavily draped with ice formations dripping from the limbs. The total silence there folded them within itself and held them bound by its own eerie power.

Neither spoke a word. It wouldn't have been fitting to mar such pristine elegance. Stephen had been there often. He had seen it decorated with the wild flurry of autumnal color and the dripping cloak of a rain shroud. He had seen it in snow before, but he knew the feelings that filled one the first time it was viewed, and he waited for Callie to fill herself with it.

Snow fell gently, white flakes on her scarf, framing her face and fringing her long eyelashes. Stephen's lips on hers were warm and sweet.

Chapter 22

During the next year Peter found himself the bewildered and pleased possessor of the Midas touch. He was not alone with his success or his feeling that it could never end. The tenor of the times was jubilant optimism. Americans, particularly New Yorkers, felt that they lived in a world devoid of failure. Men bought heavily on credit; the amounts of money they borrowed and spent were staggering, and yet they continued their upward climb. Peter followed the lead of others. He dared anything and risked everything. He backed enterprises which in England would have been considered most foolhardy. But New York had already acquired a reputation for commerce, and in accordance with the city's nature, entertainment, ice cream parlors, races, and theater had become big and profitable businesses. There was no end to what Peter could do with his money, and there were no rules or laws to keep him from daring what he pleased. His speculations ranged from the most solid to the most frivolous, but his constant love was the hop farm in Poughkeepsie. However extravagant his behavior became on Wall Street, he was solidly conservative when it came to the farm. Not one penny of the money needed for the farm or the brewery was risked in speculation.

He put his heart and body into the clearing and planting of the land. The fields cleared too late for planting hops were sown with vegetables that could be sold at market along with Callie's dairy produce and Stephen's brew. Nothing was wasted. Nothing was too small for Peter's attention. He was adamant that the hop farm should be a profit-making business in its own right. He allowed no one, least of all himself, to consider the idea that they could operate at a loss and pick up the margin elsewhere. As a result the farm did better than Peter and Stephen had hoped on their most optimistic days.

Occasionally they worried that they had overestimated the market for their hops and brew, but they hadn't. If anything the market was greater than they thought, and the customers recognized immediately that Stephen and Peter Berean were men who knew their business well. The most pressing problem they faced was finding enough hours in the day to accomplish all they had set for themselves.

Peter was now spending more and more time setting up and working with accounts. They were well into business before the entire acreage of the Grampe farm was cleared. The task of working the farm was falling to Stephen now while Peter tended the business end of it. The current crop was already sold, and Stephen had not yet begun the harvesting.

The two brothers saw little of each other during the day. It was only in the evenings that they had time for talk, and even then it revolved around business.

* * *

Peter was writing in his account book in his study when Stephen came in. Peter waved him to come nearer. Stephen looked over his brother's shoulder.

"Chicago?" Stephen asked as he looked down the list of names and locations. "When did you get that order?"

"Last week. Sam put me in touch with him—what's his name?"

Stephen looked at the list. "Marcus, says here."

"Yes, William Marcus. He's got the beginnings of a big brewery on the outskirts of Chicago. He doesn't believe in starting small. We'll be supplying him with forty percent of his hops to start, and he'll be taking some of Sam's barley. I'm hoping that in the next year or so we can increase that figure to one hundred percent."

"Have you forgotten that we're going to start a brewery of our own? At the rate you're going we'll be supplying the whole country with hops, but what happens to the plans for Berean Brothers' Beer? Are we to forget that?" Stephen asked with deceptive calm.

Peter looked up at him. He put his quill down on the desk. Stephen stood thoughtfully tapping the paper with the names of the customers. A look of satisfaction spread over Peter's face. "Look around you, Stephen. What do you see?"

Stephen stared at him for a moment, then looked at the room. He didn't know how long it had been since he had really looked at his brother or the house. Peter's study had slowly been filled with the mementos of passing triumphs until it had become a room bespeaking wealth. Stephen began to smile. He plucked at his own faded blue work shirt, then glanced pointedly at the stylish, well-fitting suit Peter wore.

"By the end of the year we will have cleared all three hundred arable acres. The cultivated fields are already yielding two thousand bushels to the acre. You can begin plans for the brewery whenever you're ready."

Stephen sat down limp-legged. "When?"

"Now." Peter laughed, and Stephen agitatedly excused himself, making a sprint to the brewhouse for the drawings and requirements he had made for the brewery. He had been designing it, and redesigning it, ever since they had come to Poughkeepsie.

They spent the afternoon trying to concentrate on the plans. Little of lasting value was accomplished, however, for Peter, caught up in his exuberance, kept increasing and expanding the capacity of the prospective brewery as Stephen struggled to accommodate his brother's ideas with practical refinements. Finally he threw his arms up in dismay. Peter leaned forward, placing his hand on Stephen's arm.

"There's not a brewery in this country to compare with the production capacity of an English brewhouse—but the market is here. The largest brewery in Albany is turning out only four thousand barrels a year. Stephen, there's not a man alive better able to fill that void than you. If I didn't think you could, I wouldn't be asking it of you; but you know more about brewing than anyone I have spoken to over here. You're the best. With your experience and all those gadgets you use to regulate your temperatures and quality, we've got to look far ahead. Before you know it this brewery we're planning now will be too small for you, and you'll be complaining that we didn't make it large enough."

"But the cost! Peter, we'll be out of business before we've begun."

"Bother the cost. You spend too much time in the fields and brewhouse." Peter shoved the books at him. "Look at them. It's there, Stephen. Orders. Money. Income from contracted crops. We've been operating at a profit for months. Next year's crop is already spoken for." Peter sat back again with the confident look of merriment that was so much a part of him now. "Build your brewery. Now. It's time. Already I've had tavern owners and suppliers asking for beer—and that coming from the miserable stuff Callie peddles at the market. They're begging for you, Stephen."

"I am not going to attempt to fill orders commercially from Paul Grampe's brewhouse. No! Don't even consider it. I can't control the quality of the beer properly, and I haven't got the right equipment. I don't want to start out that way. When someone drinks Berean ale or brew, I want them to know they can count on the best—consistently the best."

"We'll enlarge it . . . equip it however you want."

Stephen listened as Peter talked on. His enthusiasm was catching. Stephen rubbed his forehead, then gave up, smiling. "Perhaps," he said. Peter's smile was triumphant. "Perhaps" from Stephen was as good as a promise.

"Then we'll celebrate. We'll take Callie and Rosalind to Buffalo. We'll stay a whole week . . . make it a real holiday. I don't know anyone more deserving than ourselves. What do you say?"

"You're off your head. You take a week to play if you want. I can't."

"It won't hurt you. You need some fun."

"I can't leave the brewing for that long. I haven't got anyone to step in for me."

"I told you to start training someone. We've plenty of good lads who could learn. What about the McHenry boy? He seems eager."

"He isn't ready yet. Next time."

"Whatever you say," Peter said and shrugged his disappointment.

"I say I'll be ready next time."

"All right. I can see it will do no good to argue with you. I have to go to Buffalo on business anyway. There's a power-driven brewery up there. I thought you might like to see it . . . I just thought we could make a trip of it."

"The brewery will keep, but my brew won't unless I tend it." Stephen stood up. "Have a good time."

Peter went to his bedroom. Rosalind sat at the vanity he had bought for her the last time he had sold a big order of hops. If she sat before the mirror overmuch, it was excusable. She had changed so much since coming here. She enjoyed herself, and for once had no fear that she would be looked down upon. She was far easier to love here than she had been in Kent.

Rosalind's world had opened up when they left England, as had Peter's. No one knew or cared about Rufus Hawkes. Rosalind presented herself as a refined, cultured English lady. Whenever she was in doubt she dredged out of her mind the mannerisms of Mrs. Foxe, and that served her well. People accepted her for exactly what she wanted them to; more, they seemed to like and admire her. In a remarkably short time Rosalind no longer looked upon herself as an imitation. She felt completely real and confident as a lady.

Peter came up behind her, placing his hands on her bare shoulders.

"You look very pleased with yourself," she said to his image in the mirror.

"At the moment I am pleased with you."

"Oh? How so? What marvelous thing have I done?"

He turned her to face him. "It's not what you have done, but what you are about to do." He grinned wickedly.

"You're crass," she said, but took his hand as he led her to their bed.

"As long as you sit before your mirror half naked, I shall continue to be—crass." He picked her up and placed her in the middle of the four-poster bed. He drew the drapery, enclosing them in a tiny disheveled world.

It was nearly time for supper when he told her of the trip to Buffalo. She was pleased, as he knew she would be. He took her to New York City often, but seldom anywhere else. She liked new things, especially if they sounded important.

"Will we be going with a party? Whom?" she asked, her eyes glistening. Whom they went with made all the difference in what she would wear and who she would concentrate on pleasing.

"No party. Just the two of us."

"The two of us?" she repeated. "What shall we do by ourselves?"

He touched her lips with the tips of his fingers. "We'll make a party of our own," he said softly.

She began to protest, then looked at him quite seriously, a new thought obvious in her eyes. "We've never taken a trip together, Peter—alone, I mean."

Peter and Rosalind left at the end of that week. They boarded the canal boat, which looked like a floating box rocking gently in the water. Rosalind was pleased from the start when she saw that several well-dressed women would be traveling with them. Peter took her below to see the accommodations in the cabin section. At one time all a passenger could count on was a piece of crude tenting hung to divide the men's section from the women's. That was no longer the case, and Rosalind was satisfied with the attempts to make the rooms look livable. There were curtains at the cabin windows, and tastefully arranged settees and writing desks.

As the barge moved along slowly, pulled by horses on the bank, Rosalind seated herself on the deck with the other passengers.

It was a precarious deck, higher in the center and sloping gently to the outside, presumably to keep water from collecting. It managed, however, to give inexperienced passengers some feelings of insecurity, as there was no netting or rail to prevent one from sliding off the edge of the boat. After the first small jiggle of the barge, Rosalind clutched Peter's coat sleeve. "I'll fall in. I very nearly did then . . ."

Peter pulled his seat nearer hers. "I'll hold you to the deck as snugly as if you were nailed down."

She looked at him doubtfully and then at the other people. One woman was sewing, another was reading; a man had his fishing pole in the water without a concern for anything but the success of his baited hook.

"If you're really afraid of falling, we can go below."

"No. I'm being silly. No one else seems worried, and it is nice to sit here in the sun for a while."

He nodded, knowing that very soon Rosalind would be heading for the cabin anyway. It was best they enjoy the fresh air as long as they could.

The canal had been dug through many small towns and individual farms, sometimes cutting through the transportation routes. As a result, farmers and townspeople had built bridges at close intervals across the canal to provide crossings. The bridges were very low, with only the depth of the canal bank as headroom for the passengers on the boats.

Peter knew they would soon be coming to a grouping of these bridges, but on a nice day with nothing to bother him, he became interested in his newspaper and lost track of the miles. He was surprised when he heard the bridgeman sing his song.

> Low bridge! Everybody down!
> Low bridge! We're coming to a town!

Rosalind smiled. "Isn't that nice that he sings."

Peter grabbed her hastily, tumbling her from her seat.

"Peter!"

"Get down!" he yelled and forced her flat on the deck.

"Low bridge! Everybody down!" was a precise and definite warning. The unheeding were fished out of the canal afterwards with a hook that all the boats carried.

"Peter!" Rosalind gasped, trying to straighten herself and locate her parasol. "What was wrong with that bridge? Was it falling? We could have been hurt."

"Most are that low," he said, hoping she wouldn't realize how many of them they were likely to pass under.

"Low bridge! Everybody down!"

"Oh, no!" she cried, flattening herself again, both hands over her head protecting her new hat. Peter lay at her side laughing until he thought his sides would burst at the travails of his wife dealing with a world that didn't work by her rules.

"This is terrible!" she fumed. "Imagine what we must look like to somone passing over that bridge. Why don't they raise these bridges! I will *not* be made to lay on this filthy deck again!"

"Let's go below. We can come up when we've passed the town. There aren't so many bridges when we come to the open land. Hurry! We're coming to another."

She had just seated herself on one of the settees in the cabin when she heard her archenemy sing out again in his clear angelic voice, "Low bridge! Everybody down!"

Throughout the canal boat trip, Rosalind had looked forward to seeing Buffalo, but found she didn't care for it after they got there. She had expected it to be like New York City, and it wasn't. In her eyes it was no place at all, offering her few shopping delights, and fewer opportunities for nightlife. She was restless and irritable long before Peter was ready to leave.

For him Buffalo had everything to offer. He received two orders for hops and one for Sam's barley. While he was there he made a point to see the brewery that boasted a steam engine to power its water supply. There were several types of steam engines being made and used for all manner of things; but the one he deemed best and most adaptable for a brewery was the Evans steam engine he saw in operation in Buffalo. By the time he returned to Poughkeepsie, he had decided to order one.

When she greeted him at the front door, Callie had a letter from Meg in her hand, and the steam engine was forgotten momentarily.

"It's so good to have you back! It's been too quiet around here without you, and Jamie has missed his mama and papa."

"Where is the little fellow?" Peter asked.

"Mary Anne is giving him a bath. He made some delicious mud pies. She'll bring him down to you in a few minutes. I thought we'd give you enough time to take your coats off and catch your breath. Did you have a good time?"

"The best—at least I did. It turned out to be a poor trip for Rosalind."

Rosalind said nothing for a moment. She was looking at Peter as though seeing him for the first time. "I did like the trip," she said a little bewildered, realizing that the terrible canal boat trip had been a time of closeness and fun between Peter and herself. It had been Peter's company she had liked so. She wondered when that had happened. When had she begun looking forward to the moments she could spend alone with him? "Isn't it funny . . . it was a horrible, uncomfortable trip . . . and I had nothing to do in Buffalo . . . but I liked it. Isn't that the strangest thing?"

Callie and Peter both laughed. Rosalind looked at them critically, then uncertainly, before she smiled and began to laugh with them.

"I have some news from home. Would you like to hear?" Callie asked, her eyes sparkling.

"Shall you tell us or shall we guess?" Peter asked.

"Oh, yes—do! Guess. You'll never get it right. But I'll give you one hint. It is not about . . . no, I won't give you any hint at all."

"Anna has finally had a child," Peter said.

"No."

"What then?"

"Guess! Just one more. Think hard."

Peter shook his head. "I don't know. It can't be something ordinary, or you wouldn't be . . . I know! Frank has run off with the milkmaid."

"Tell us," Rosalind begged, laughing. "He'll never guess it."

"It's Natalie—she and Albert were married. Aunt Meg says she wrote to us before it happened, but we never got the letter. She guessed it must have gotten lost when I didn't mention it in my letter to her, so she wrote again. They've been married about four months."

Peter sat down. "She must be well then," he said. "Married."

Rosalind said nothing. She didn't know what was wrong with her. Everything seemed so different. She really didn't care that Albert had married Natalie . . . it didn't seem to matter. "I think I'll go see Jamie," she said.

Callie glanced at her, then at Peter. Subdued, she handed the letter to Peter. "Would you like to read it? Aunt Meg describes the wedding and all. Nattie must have made a beautiful bride."

He smiled, shaking his head. "I can't believe she's married. Nattie always seemed such a child to me."

"You are pleased, aren't you?" Callie asked uncertainly.

"Pleased? Of course, I'm pleased. If she's well and happy, that's all anyone can ask. I'm just shocked. Yes!" he said more brightly, opening the letter. "I am pleased."

Later that evening Peter told Stephen about the trip and the steam-driven engine that could power the water and work elevators as well.

"Stephen, I simply do not have the patience that you do, and in this instance I feel that you are wrong in being patient. I know that it's a little sooner than we'd planned and it will mean another god-awfully busy year, but Steve, I hope you'll agree with me that the time to build the brewery is now. I want to start breaking ground."

Stephen grinned. "Would you like to go over my plans again? I've been collecting a few facts and figures here and there. All we need to begin is a crew and some bricks and mortar."

Peter shuffled through the blueprints and fact

sheets. "Good God! You've even figured out to the ounce how many bushels of malt and hops you need to the barrel. Three and one-eighth bushels of malt, two pounds seven and one-half ounces of hops—you haven't been idle."

"Those figures will vary a bit from time to time depending on quality and what it is we brew, but it is a guide. Now, as to the buildings—I feel we must have a malthouse of brick with at least two cisterns and two kilns to start. We may be able to use your steam engine in the maltmill, but I still think we should plan on a horse-drawn mill."

"You don't trust my machinery," Peter said, frowning. "Have you no faith in the future?"

"It isn't that. Neither of us is familiar with it. I'd hate like hell to have to move those iron rollers by some improvisation if the engine should break down. Without the barley being milled into the malt, I can't do a thing. There must be some way to arrange it so we can alternate systems if need be. The important thing is that we can keep the water coming and the malt milling with the minimum of labor—especially mine."

"Agreed. Go on. What about the brewhouse?"

"Large storage cellar, and we can probably get away with two coppers to start. One of about two-hundred-gallon capacity and the other smaller. Otherwise just the regular equipment we've always used—fermenting tubs, mash tuns and all." Stephen handed him the list and specifications.

Peter studied them for some time, then looked up. "Do you ever think of home?"

"Often."

"Of late, I find that I do too. Perhaps it was Ma's letter about Nattie's wedding," Peter mused. "Before we came here we said when it came time to equip the brewery we'd go back and get everything we needed there."

"I know, but it isn't necessary. Everything can be gotten right here."

Peter agreed, his fingers tapping on his desk. "But I'd like to go home." He looked at Stephen's surprised face. "Not to stay," he added hastily. "Just for a visit. We could still get the equipment there. Sam can manage the farm for me. The only problem is your brewhouse."

"We'll close it," Stephen said quickly. "I don't produce enough to speak of, and if we're going to begin the brewery, I don't mind leaving the brewhouse idle. I'll have other things to keep me occupied."

"Then you'd like to go back for a visit?"

"Like to? I've considered going myself several times. There never seemed a time when I could leave. We were too busy."

"Then it's settled. We're going back."

Chapter 23

They arrived in Kent just before the start of the hop-picking season. All around them as they drove over once-familiar roads were the green arches of the hop vines, orchards heavy with fruit to be harvested in the months to come. In another two weeks the pickers would fill the cottages, and the night fires and music would begin.

"It's beautiful," Callie said, hugging Jamie close to her. "See there, Jamie—that's part of your Uncle Frank's hop yard." Jamie looked around contentedly, babbling in his own language.

"He doesn't seem too impressed," Peter commented. "Sounds like his standard 'what's to eat' speech."

"It's nice that nothing has changed much," Stephen said. "I was afraid that it might have."

"What would change?" Peter asked.

"I don't know. Things do though."

The driver turned the horses onto the farm road. Ahead of them they could see the house. It was home, just as it had always been. Meg's roses climbed over the front entrance wildly profuse with pink and red blooms. The small gate to the herb garden stood open as it always did, because none of them could ever remember to close it.

As soon as she heard the field dogs barking at the approaching carriage, Meg flung open the front door. Her squat little figure rushing out to meet them reminded Callie of those first days when she had been alone and frightened. Meg had overwhelmed her with warmth and goodness. Callie's eyes filled as she looked at Meg's happy face. "That's your grandma. You're a lucky lad, Jamie Berean," she said softly to the child.

"Peter! Stephen!" Meg cried, rushing to hug first one and then the other, and back to the first again like a demented moth. "Oh, Callie—Rosalind!" Suddenly she stopped, her eyes wide, her hands trembling as she reached for Jamie. "Let me see my grandson."

"Here he is, Ma. All yours." Peter proudly took Jamie from Callie, placing him in Meg's arms. "You should see how he's grown in just the last month."

"So big," she crooned, then turned to the others. "Anna has thought of nothing but feeding you. She should have the table all ready by now. Marsh will bring your luggage in. Come along now, wash up."

"I was wondering where Anna was," Stephen said.

"Anna is where she belongs. . . . A woman after my heart," Peter said, leading the way into the house. "I haven't had anything to eat since early this morning, and I'm famished. Where's Frank? Will he be here?"

"He's still in the fields, but he'll be in shortly. You know Frank—doesn't like anything to change his routine. He claims it upsets his digestion. But don't worry; he's not likely to miss a meal."

Peter laughed. "That's Frank. I told you nothing could change around here, Steve."

Anna entered the hallway as Peter spoke. "Welcome back. Oh, my! For all we've not changed, look at you! There's not a one of you that is as I remembered. So grand. Rosalind, you look lovely. I can see America agrees with you. And Stephen . . . where's that young boy who left here? You're grown so handsome and strong . . . I am speechless. Callie . . ."

Stephen, blushing—one of the things he had never outgrown—edged toward Callie and helped Anna keep her attention focused there. But Anna was as flighty in trying to spread her affection and greetings to everyone as Meg had been; then she saw Jamie, and as Meg had, she made a beeline for him. "Ohhh!" she said, trying and failing to wrest him from Meg's possessive grip.

Jamie was content where he was as well. He was learning rapidly of the delicious wonders to be found in a grandma's house.

"I see you've done well, Peter," Frank said as he came in. "Or is it all show?" He laughed, touching the lapel of Peter's suit.

"There's a bit behind what's seen," Peter said.

Frank greeted the rest of then, but wasted no time in sentimentality over the baby. He walked to the head of the table and seated himself. Without looking up, he tucked his napkin in under his chin.

The others took their seats at the table.

"How has it been going with you, Frank?" Peter asked.

"I can't complain too badly. We're a bit busy at the moment. Hop pickers will be coming in before we know it. It's a rowdier bunch that turns up every year."

"I always enjoyed the hop pickers," Stephen said.

Frank shrugged and looked back to Peter. "How

were you able to leave your hops this time of year? Or have you given up hops? Living on Pa's legacy?"

"You have quite an opinion of me, don't you Frank?"

"You're looking pretty prosperous, and a man doesn't leave a farm to idle during harvest if he's got one."

Stephen laughed uncomfortably. "Things aren't quite the same in Poughkeepsie as they are here, Frank. If you want to know the truth, he works as though a demon rode his back, which isn't so bad, but he works the rest of us as hard. Ask Callie if Peter has given up on hops, and remember to duck when she answers," he said, smiling as he nudged Callie.

"Then you must be daft to leave at harvest time. You'll end up with no crop to speak of."

"We'll harvest five hundred thousand bushels this season," Peter said, anger niggling at him. "There is a piece of land adjoining ours we've taken an option on. That'll give us another hundred acres to plant. We'll be the leading hop yard in the area then. Personally I believe we are now."

Frank emptied his mug before looking at Peter. "Sounds like a fairy tale to me. It would take years to build up a farm like that."

"Not in the United States," Stephen snapped. "I told you things were different there. Fortunes are made every day. In railroads and mining and hops and any new product a man can think up and market. Nothing moves slowly there. You keep up with the times and the competition, or you get lost in the shuffle. Peter and I gambled everything we had to keep ahead of the others, and we've done it."

"It is that good there, huh?"

"It is very good, and there's a ready market for anything we can grow."

"I never would have believed it. I always thought you'd be coming home to stay. I thought perhaps this visit . . . this is just a visit, isn't it?"

"Just a visit," Peter said. "We'll stay until mid-September. Stephen is going to buy the equipment for the brewery. We'll have just the right time for seeing each other and tending to business. Then we're going home. Our home."

"You've got the brewery underway, as well? So soon?" Frank asked, filling his mug with porter again. He sat quietly, studying the liquid. "Well, it must be a different sort of place. Changed you. Changed you a lot."

Peter sat back sipping his brew contentedly as Stephen eagerly leaned forward to tell Frank about their property and the new brewery.

As the men talked, Callie asked Meg, "When will we see Natalie? I was so hoping she would be here when we arrived. I keep thinking of this as her home. I don't suppose the Foxes would thank me for that thought."

"They'll be coming for supper tonight. Albert had some business in Seven Oaks this afternoon. He thought it better if Natalie waited for him to bring her. He is so careful with her. I do think he tends to overdo it a bit. He won't let her do a thing that might tire her or upset her. But Nattie seems to thrive on the attention so I suppose it is all right after all. She is terribly happy."

"But why should he worry about her tiring? She isn't ill, is she?" Callie asked.

"Oh, dear me! Why, of course, you wouldn't know. Her letter is probably waiting for you in Poughkeepsie."

"Know what?" Rosalind asked.

"Oh, dear—I don't know if I should tell you," Meg

sputtered. "It's Nattie's surprise. Perhaps . . . Anna, what do you think? Should I tell them or should I let Nattie tell them?"

Anna looked at Callie for a long time, noting the change the last year and a half had made in her. She was so little of the child Anna had known. Callie had fulfilled all the promise of beauty of her youth, but she was very much a poised woman and no longer the excitable child who could be counted on to play along with Natalie's mysterious games. "I think Callie would do better with Nattie if she knew. After all, Nattie needn't be told the letter arrived too late."

Meg smiled happily, rubbing her plump hands together. "Nattie is with child," she said breathlessly.

"Natalie?" Rosalind asked in disbelief. Not only was it difficult to imagine Natalie the mother of anything so touchingly human as Jamie, but it was disgusting and annoying to think of her as the mother of Albert's child. "She's not really going to have a child."

"At the beginning of the year. Don't you think that is nice? A new Foxe and a new year. We are all hoping it will arrive on the very day." Meg beamed. "Now all we have to do is get Anna started, and all my girls, but you, Callie, shall have given me a grandchild."

Anna shifted uncomfortably in her chair and changed the subject hastily. "I've been sewing clothes for the baby. If you'd like I'll show them to you, Callie."

"I'd love to see them. Perhaps I could make something while I am here. I'd like Nattie to have something that I had made too."

"Oh, she'd like that," Anna said. "Perhaps we should wait until she comes. She'd like to show you the little things herself. Many of them she designed."

There was no hurry now that Meg had left the uncomfortable subject of Anna's barrenness. No one felt

it more sorely than Anna herself. She had always believed that God compensated each of his creatures
with something the others had not. Rosalind and Nat-
talie and Callie had beauty. Anna believed her lot
would be children, and yet first Rosalind and now
Natalie had a child, and she had nothing. It was not
that she begrudged them their good fortune, but it
did seem unfair that the balance should swing so
heavily against her. She excused herself from the table
and helped the serving girls clear. Frank had gotten
her a new set of china she trusted only to her own
careful hands in the washwater.

Callie was in the herb garden with Rosalind when
the Foxes arrived. The dogs began to bark and then
Callie heard Natalie's soft voice and bell-like laughter
again. She and Rosalind moved together toward the
garden gate.

Natalie looked more delicate and ethereal than
ever. She was dressed in filmy white. Along the hem
of her dress were embroidered the most delicate lilies
of the valley. Her abdomen swelled just enough to
show she was with child, while her hair, worn loose
and flowing around her pale hollow-eyed face, made
her look no more than a child herself. She reached up
and removed the wide-brimmed hat that had shielded
her from the sun. She stared at Callie as she walked to
the garden.

"You've changed, Callie. You don't look the same at
all. Have you changed inside as well?" she asked in a
soft quizzical voice.

"Oh, Nattie!" Callie embraced her. "Not a bit. I am
just the same. It is so good to see you again, and you
look lovely."

"But you've become beautiful," Natalie said.

"Don't be silly. Come sit with me and tell me all

about the baby and your plans. Shall it be a boy or a girl?"

"Didn't you read all that in my letter?"

"I want to hear you say it, so I can hear your voice and see you smile as you talk. It is so much better to be with someone than to have to learn things from a letter. Tell me everything—again."

Albert followed his wife, more slowly, and his eyes rested on Rosalind, not Callie. If anything he found her more alluring now than ever. She had an air of calm and self-confidence he didn't remember in her. He hadn't expected to miss her when she left. In fact her departure had been a relief to him. But once she was gone, he had missed her dreadfully, far beyond what he could ever have imagined. She crept into his thoughts and dreams at the worst times, unspeakable times, crowding Natalie out of his mind and heart when she had the most right to him.

"Hello, Rosalind," he said, placing his hand on the open gate so near hers that their fingers touched. She glanced at their hands, but did not move her own. Once she would have been content, even eager for so small a display of affection as the brush of his hand. It was amusing and enlightening that the action had been Albert's and not hers. Perhaps he didn't know that the tone of his voice, the look in his eyes, his very posture, was telling her that now he was the beggar at the gate, while it was she who would determine if her affections would ever be opened to him again.

"How have you been, Albert? I hear you are to be a father. It seems to agree with you; you are looking well."

"Yes," he said and looked away from her for a moment. "Rosalind . . ."

"Are you happy, Albert?"

"I want to talk to you. There is so much I must say to you."

"Oh, do! Tell me!" she said brightly.

"Not like this. It's been so long—and yet, here you are teasing as you always did. It doesn't seem you've been gone from me for a minute now that you're here again where I can see you and touch you."

"What a nice compliment. It does every lady good to know she's been missed."

"Don't be like that, please."

"Don't be a boor. Shall we go in? I am sure Peter will be anxious to see you. You two always used to have so much to talk about."

"What's wrong with you? I thought you'd be happy to see me."

"I am, Albert."

Peter opened the door as Rosalind and Albert came to the stoop. He hesitated for a moment, then smiled broadly, "Albert! How've you been, old man? I hear I owe you congratulations on two counts."

Rosalind smiled, her arm slipping around Peter's waist for a moment as she passed him in the doorway; then she left Albert to deal with her husband.

Rosalind enjoyed supper that night. Anna was unabashedly impressed with her new finery. Frank treated her with an interest and respect he had never given her while she lived there. Albert was uncomfortable and fidgety, trying to get her attention without appearing to. As for Natalie, nothing had changed. From the first moment the two women had seen each other in the garden and chosen not to speak, the old animosity had flared.

After supper, Callie and Natalie went with Anna to the sewing room to see the baby clothes Anna had been making. Anna laid the little garments on the table one by one for Callie to see.

Peter, Frank, and Stephen got out the cards.

"It's so nice to see you boys sitting together again," Meg said contentedly. Jamie lay back on her lap, sleepily limp as she rocked. "Time for bed, little one," she said, taking him on her shoulder. She got up ponderously and went toward the nursery. "Stay where you are, Rosalind. Let me see to the child tonight. I won't have so many times to see him while he is young."

"Aren't you going to play, Albert?" Frank asked as Albert continued his restless patrol of the perimeter of the room.

"Uhh—no. It's stuffy in here. I think I'll walk around outside for a bit. Anyone care to join me?"

No one said anything. Nervously licking his lips, Albert finally looked at her. "Would you care to join me, Rosalind?"

She walked across the room to stand behind Peter. She put both arms around his neck. He leaned his cheek against her hand.

"Then no one wants to take a walk?" Albert turned to go out alone.

"I didn't say I didn't want to walk, Albert," Rosalind said. She kissed Peter in the cheek, then went with Albert.

Frank watched Peter's eyes follow them as they left the house. "It didn't take long for that, did it?"

Peter looked sharply at him. "What do you mean by that?"

"Albert. He always did have an eye for Rosalind. Hardly could sit a minute tonight. Didn't you notice? It always surprised me that he didn't marry her that time years ago."

"It is my wife you are speaking of."

"Well, she wasn't your wife then—not when I meant."

"I don't give a damn when you meant, Frank."

"Well, now, Peter, for someone who just sent his wife out with another man, you are mighty touchy about an innocent observation. Why? Could it be things are not so well in America as you let on—at least in certain quarters?"

"Wait a minute," Stephen said, placing a restraining hand on each brother's arm. "Peter didn't send Rosalind out with just any other man. That's Natalie's husband. What's the matter with you, Frank? You don't worry when Peter takes Anna to town. Why should Peter worry that Rosalind walks in the garden with Albert. We're all the same family, and it's best we don't forget it. Deal the cards."

Peter and Frank sat rigidly facing each other like two fighting cocks, held back from a battle they would both relish.

"Don't ever hint or say anything like that to me again, Frank," Peter said with quiet fury.

"Seems to me that much anger indicates—"

"Shut up!" Peter stood, the chair crashing to the floor behind him. Stephen jumped to his feet as well.

Anna hurried into the parlor from the kitchen. "What was that I heard?"

There was silence for a tense moment; then Peter looked at her. "I was merely clumsy, Anna. The chair fell . . . bull in the china shop."

Stephen sat down slowly. He said again in a low voice, "Deal the cards."

Anna stayed where she was, her face perplexed as she tried to figure out what had taken place.

"I don't feel like playing cards," Peter said finally.

"Neither do I." Frank pushed his chair from the table, getting up to hunt for his newspaper.

Peter walked to the window; Stephen followed.

"What are you going to do?"

"I don't know. Nothing. Let me alone, Stephen."

"Don't go outside, Peter. You know Frank is all hot wind. Don't give him the satisfaction. He's been eating his heart out because you haven't come running home beaten. You do know why he said it . . . ?"

"Do I?"

"Yes, you do, and so do I. Come on, Peter, you know he wanted you to come home like a whipped pup. You didn't and you've made him feel small. Frank may be slow an' all, but he doesn't like being bested . . . especially not by you. He's always been jealous, Peter, and he's a proud man as well."

Peter looked down at his feet. He nodded slightly, but said nothing.

"Look, Peter, I can't speak for what went on between Rosalind and Albert before, but it would take a blind man not to see she's never been happier than she's been since we left here. Come on, be reasonable . . . you know it's true. She's the only one of us who wasn't anxious to come home for a visit. Is that the way of a woman longing for another man? My God, Peter, think! It's you she watches. Have some faith in her, man. She's your wife."

Peter smiled faintly. "I never used to doubt her."

"Then don't now. It's that bloody Frank . . . it's his way of paying you back for being the success he's not."

Peter glanced over at Frank.

Stephen placed his hand on Peter's arm. "Beat me in a game of chess? Come along, please. Rosalind will be back in no time. And when she does come in, give Frank a demonstration of his error."

Peter laughed silently, and went with him.

* * *

The window of Anna's sewing room overlooked the herb garden. Callie and Natalie excitedly talked about Anna's patterns. The room had become a confusion of baby dresses, crib blankets, and paper patterns and drawings. Callie was trying to decide what special thing she would make for the baby.

"Which do you think, Natalie? I love this little dress, but perhaps another blanket. You don't really have anything for warmer weather. Mostly these are winter blankets. Nattie?"

Natalie stood at the window, her hand holding the curtain open.

"Nattie, you haven't heard a word I've said. What are you looking at? You've been staring out that window for the last ten minutes."

"I like the sunset," she said. There was an edge to her voice, however, and Callie went to the window. The sky was golden red with dark shadowy clouds puffing and shredding across the horizon like great moving stone ridges. In the garden below Albert was talking earnestly to Rosalind. The gestures he made rendered the hearing of his words unnecessary. Callie felt a trill of apprehension move through her. She had forgotten the tension she had once lived with and considered a part of her day. Now it was back. One day, and all the feelings of foreboding had returned.

"I've been happy since she left," Natalie said, dropping the curtain and turning toward Callie. Her eyes had a burning far-away look in them. Callie could hardly bear to meet her gaze. She remembered seeing that look after the night of the fire. It had frightened her then, and it frightened her now.

Slowly, Natalie looked away from her, her eyes fixing on the window. "I wonder if I will be now."

Callie mentally shook herself. Things were not the same as they had been then. She wasn't the same. She wasn't sixteen now, and Natalie was a married woman. If Natalie was all right when Rosalind wasn't here, then she could also be fine in Rosalind's presence. "Of course you'll be happy. You have more reason than ever now."

"I'm not afraid of her anymore."

"Who?"

Natalie smiled knowingly. "Rosalind, Callie. Must you pretend to misunderstand everything I say? You never used to be so stupid."

Callie exhaled deeply. "Neither am I now; so I want you to listen to me. Don't start looking for things that aren't there. I know how you feel about Rosalind, but you're wrong. Peter and Rosalind have been very happy in Poughkeepsie. I know, and you'll have to take my word for it. I'd not lie to you, and if you could have seen them yourself, you'd know too that she loves him very much."

"They aren't in Poughkeepsie now. Here it is different," she said mysteriously. "They will never be happy here."

"That's ridiculous! Don't even begin to think of it. There is nothing to alarm you about Rosalind and Albert. Do you understand? Keep remembering we'll be leaving in September. We'll be gone, and I doubt very much we'll return for a long time. Rosalind didn't even want to come this time. So there can be nothing. Whatever you do, don't start imagining things now," she ended a little desperately.

"I know or I don't know. I *never* imagine," Natalie said and walked from the room.

Albert paced back and forth in front of Rosalind. "Why? Why for the love of heaven won't you let me see you? I just want to talk to you. Is it so much to ask? If he is my son, haven't I at least the right to talk to you?"

"This is the second time today we've talked, Albert. We are alone. Whatever you have to say can be said now."

"No! No, damn it, it can't. I *need* to see you—alone. Meet me. Just one time. Please. I have to see you. Isn't that satisfaction enough for you? Must I continue to beg?"

"Albert, really, if this is what marriage has done to you, you should have remained single. You are really very tedious today."

"It's marriage to the wrong woman. That is what's wrong. I'll admit it. You were right. I should have defied my mother. I should have married you. I should have. . . . I can think of nothing, no one but you. You must meet me."

"Sometime, perhaps," she said, smiling contentedly.

"When?"

"I don't know. Sometime. When it's warmer."

"Warmer!?"

"Yes."

"Damn it! That means never. The hop pickers will be coming at the end of this month, and in another month you'll be leaving. It must be now."

"Don't be ridiculous, Albert. We've only just arrived. I can't go off with you. I'm not even sure I want to," she said and looked at his reddish-gold hair muted in the soft twilight. He was as distinguished looking and meticulous as ever. Whatever Peter made of himself, he would always be too broad of shoulder and heavy of frame to look as Albert did. Peter, with his ruggedness and vital power, was a man among men in New York; but here—here Albert was still the English gentleman as one ought to be. And yet, for

the first time, she felt a loyalty to Peter. Albert was
again asking her to choose between the two men, and
Rosalind was no longer sure her choice was Albert.

His eyes narrowed as he looked at her. "We've managed to reverse positions, haven't we?"

"Yes," she said honestly.

"Then remember, I never refused you. I never
made you go through what you are putting me
through now."

"Didn't you? I don't recall that you were so kind to
me."

"I should have been kinder. I was blind and stupid
about us—I've admitted that—but I wasn't deliberately
cruel."

"Are you saying that I am?"

"I'm only asking to see you alone—one time when
we can talk freely. I won't touch you unless you wish
it. You have my word."

She shrugged, but she wavered. Her curiosity was
aroused as was her vanity. It was heady to feel the
power she now had over this man who had once been
able to make her grovel.

"Will you come?"

"I don't know."

"Day after tomorrow. I'm supposed to go to Seven
Oaks. I'll send my deputy in my place."

"And of course, I shall begin my long lonely jaunts
again."

"Oh, no. I think you've become far too grand for
walking. But milady does ride, doesn't she?" he asked
sarcastically.

"Milady does."

Chapter 24

Peter got up from the chess table when Rosalind came in. On his face was the anxious look that told her he knew Albert had not merely wanted to walk. She took his hand, smiling reassuringly at him. And she found she was speaking honestly when she said, "It is a beautiful night. I wish you had come with us, or better still that you and I had gone alone."

There was a time when she would have teased him, made him jealous as she did with Albert. She couldn't say when or why, but sometime during the last year her zest for that kind of sport with Peter had left her. She wanted him to know Albert meant nothing to her now and he, Peter, meant everything.

The afternoon she was to meet Albert, she was confused and worried. She wasn't certain what Albert might do if she didn't meet him. Once she would have been wildly joyous to have Albert bear the humiliation of declaring his love for her, but that time had passed. She now wanted desperately to keep it forever a secret and forgotten.

She would have to meet him. That much she could

see. He had to be made to understand that it was finished between them. Her decision made, she felt a perverse titillation in the danger that Peter might find out about them in this last meeting. Albert was acting so much the desperate lover. It gave the situation an air of adventure. For a moment Rosalind reverted to the daydreaming woman she had been before they left for Poughkeepsie. She saw in herself a little of a Cleopatra or a Josephine. It made her feel vibrantly alive to think of being so desired. There was still in her, she recognized, a recklessness that made her court disaster, made her want to tempt fate by meeting Albert this one last time.

Not that she would let anything happen. She was finished with Albert. But she would confront him one last time and let it be ended dramatically and for always.

Another part of her coldly said there was no need for a final meeting. There was no place left in her life for Albert. She didn't know what to do. It was all so confusing. If only there were some way to guarantee that Albert would behave, be able to do nothing; then she would be strong enough to be sure nothing would happen.

She turned to Callie.

"Callie, would you like to ride with me this afternoon? There is so little to do here . . . I thought perhaps a ride would wake us up."

Callie agreed readily. They left with Rosalind leading, heading directly to the woods path that would take them to the pickers' cottages. Neither spoke. Each was wrapped in her own thoughts and memories.

Albert was waiting for her inside the cabin. He burst through the door as soon as he heard the horse

"Rosalind!" He stopped short when he saw Callie beside her. Both were speechless.

"Why, Albert! Imagine running into you out here. What can you be doing?" She glanced at Callie. It had been a simple-minded plan and an even simpler comment, fooling no one, least of all Callie. Realization and dismay were written all over her face.

Nonplussed, Albert looked from one woman to the other; then the fiery, angry look Rosalind was so unfamiliar with came into Albert's eyes, and he darted forward, pulling the reins from her grasp. Roughly he led the horse to the side of the cottage away from Callie.

"Albert! What are you doing! Stop it! Let go of my horse."

"I am going to talk to you. You brought her, not I," he rasped. His free hand agitatedly messed his hair until it stood in loose waves, making him look more appealing than she had ever seen him.

She shook her head. "Albert, what has come over you? I can't come with you . . . not with Callie right . . ."

"Why did you bring her?"

"I was wrong. I shouldn't have."

"Get down from the horse. Come with me—just for a moment."

"I'll meet you. Tomorrow I'll come alone. I promise. I'll be here."

"It must be today. You won't come tomorrow if I let you go."

"I will come. I gave you my word. You can come to the house and drag me out if I don't. I *will* be here. Oh, Albert, please!"

He stared at her for a moment, then tossed the reins back at her. "I will come after you, Rosalind. I no longer care who knows, so you'd best be here and alone."

* * *

Callie had turned away from them, waiting at the edge of the clearing. She supposed she had always known and not really wanted to. She couldn't block out the sounds of their voices, but she could the words. She didn't want to know now what was being said anymore than she had once wanted to know if Albert and Rosalind did meet. She wished somehow she could again know nothing. Think nothing. Soon she heard Albert ride off.

"Callie, I'm sorry. I didn't realize that would happen," Rosalind said when she rode up to Callie's side.

"Why? I don't understand. You and Peter are happy. You have been given everything a woman could ever want. Why did you meet him! Oh, Rosalind, whyever did you have to make me a part of it?"

Rosalind put her hand to her head. "I don't know what to say. Albert was the first man I ever loved. . . . I needed someone . . . then. Callie, I didn't think he would act this way today if someone were with me. He is always so proper and . . ."

Callie shook her head, biting her lip to keep the tears back. The horses pawed as the two women continued to keep them standing.

"You won't tell Peter, will you, Callie?"

Callie let out a sobbing laugh. "Tell him? Oh, dear Lord, Rosalind—how could I tell him? I don't have the courage . . . he trusted you. I just don't understand. How could you have done it?"

Rosalind looked helplessly at her. "I don't know," she whispered. "It started so long ago . . . I wouldn't even begin to know how to tell you. I'm not sure I understand myself. Callie . . . don't hate me."

Callie was no longer trying to hide her tears. "I wish we had never come back to England."

"So do I. Callie . . . ?"

"Don't you know what this would do to them if Natalie and Peter find out? Natalie already believes that you and Albert meet. And there has been talk. We never paid attention to it, but . . . people have gossiped. Oh, Rosalind, Peter trusted you so. He believes in you. If he didn't love you, I could—"

"Callie, don't! You can say nothing to me that I haven't said to myself a hundred times a day. I know what I am, but I meant to end it. Truly I did. That's why I agreed to see him this last time. I just don't know what came over Albert. He's been like a madman ever since we returned. I didn't want to meet him today—I wouldn't have asked you to come if I had wanted to see him. Please believe me. I thought nothing would happen if you were along."

"What will you do now?"

"I don't know. Something. Somehow I must make him understand I never want to see him again. You must believe me, Callie. I love Peter. No matter what I did before—I love him."

Rosalind wrestled with her problem all that evening. She thought perhaps she would be unable to slip away the following day. Perhaps Peter would want to take her into Rochester or Seven Oaks. *Anything* that would give her an idea of what to do about Albert. Nothing occurred. After they had returned to the house, Rosalind was left alone to do as she pleased. Callie found Anna and continued making the blanket she had decided upon for Natalie's baby. Meg was with Jamie, as she had been every minute since they had arrived.

Peter had left the house early that morning, chagrined at having thought such foul thoughts about his wife the night before, and sorry he had let those fears precipitate an ugly argument between himself and Frank the first night he was back. He made amends with Frank by offering to help prepare for the hop pickers, and spent the day accompanying Frank around the farm, careful not to refer to his own hop yard as Frank told of the improvements he had made since they'd left.

"The brewhouse isn't in such good shape. I haven't your touch, Stephen," Frank admitted graciously and hopefully.

"I can give you a hand. Who do you have working it?" Stephen asked.

"Jem Bonner. He's able enough, but he hasn't the experience. He still comes out with a brew that is hit or miss."

"If that is all, I can have you straight in no time. If he's got the feel for it, I can teach him the rest."

"I'd appreciate it."

"All right, Frank, you've got Stephen occupied. What about me?" Peter asked.

"You're here for a holiday—both of you."

"Holidays don't seem to agree. I'd rather be busy."

"I've not had time to check out the pickers' cottages. One needs a patch on its roof. I'm not sure what shape the others are in. And the cows have to be taken to the hill pasture."

"That'll give me a pleasant day's work," Peter said happily.

Stephen was already on his way to the brewhouse. Peter went to herd the cattle to the upper pasture. He would see to the pickers' cottages on the way back.

Natalie sat in her sumptuous bedroom in Foxe Hall, staring at the tokens to femininity that Albert constantly brought home to her and placed in pink and white profusion all about her room. He gave her too much of everything and too little of himself. She loved him with a possessive desperation and felt him slip-

ping away from her a little more each day. It had
been bad enough when Rosalind was in Poughkeepsie, but now that she had returned, her relationship
with Albert was impossible. She had only the shell of
him. Someone else held the core of his being captive.
She thought about that for a long time—his captivity.

She made a circle in the moire bedcover with her
finger, then smoothed it all out. She repeated the motion until the feeling cemented itself in her mind that
she had freed the circle by the erasure. Then she got
up, dressed quietly, put on her walking boots, and left
the house unnoticed.

Rosalind rode to the cottage as she had the day before. This time, however, she was alone, and very
aware of that aloneness.

Albert was standing outside the cottage waiting for
her. Long before she could see his features clearly, she
knew by his stance that he was angry. As she came
nearer the cottage and dismounted, she was frightened.

"I'm here," she said nervously. "What is it you absolutely must talk to me about, Albert? I really can't
stay long."

"Come inside," he said and waited until she entered
the cottage first. He didn't close the door. "Why did
you bring Callie with you yesterday?"

"I didn't want to come alone. Surely you can see
that by now. I don't love you anymore, Albert. We're
both married and . . ."

"It's all neatly wrapped up for you now."

"Yes."

"Well, it isn't for me."

"Albert, please. I don't know what's happened to
you. You're so different. I don't know you," she said,
backing away from him.

"Is Jamie my son?"

"I don't know."

"You said he was."

"I know, but that was a long time ago. How could I know? I wanted to hurt you then. You had hurt me and I wanted to strike back at you. It meant nothing," she stammered.

He laughed harshly. "Nothing? It meant everything to me. You'd never see that, would you, Rosalind?"

"That isn't true! You made no effort to keep me here. You didn't want me to stay. I know that now, and I know you were right. Leave it there, Albert. Please. We were wrong."

"No. I was wrong. I was afraid . . . of everyone. Afraid of Peter. I couldn't bring myself to confront him then, but I loved you. I love you now. And I'm no longer afraid. We'll leave together. I want to make it up to both you and Jamie. We'll go anywhere you want—India, France, the West Indies—name it, Rosalind. I'll take you anywhere in the world."

Rosalind stared at him, bewildered and afraid. "Albert, you're not thinking clearly. You . . . you can't mean what you say. It makes no sense. You're married. . . . Natalie is expecting your child. Even if I wanted it there is nothing you can do for Jamie and me now."

He took a step toward her, the anger gone from his eyes, replaced by a hungry lustful look unfamiliar to Rosalind. He placed his hand on her throat, feeling the lively pulse throb beneath his fingertips. "I remember everything about you," he said in a low husky voice. "Every inch of flesh on your body." He took off her hat and placed it on the battered table beside them. "Let me see you again."

Rosalind was breathing in shallow, quick gasps. She was both tantalized and scared as he unbuttoned her riding jacket. One of the things she had always loved best about him was his ability to move with the even precision of a man who knew what he was about and needn't hurry. He took off her blouse, caressing and fondling her breasts until the nipples stood hard and she was swimming through a haze of feelings and desires whose end was only Albert, hard and waiting.

Her back was toward the open door. She neither saw the shocked terror on Albert's face nor felt the bullet that entered at the base of her skull, exploding all thought and feeling in one thundering moment.

She was thrust against him. Albert clung to her slumping body helpless to so much as cry out before the second pistol went off, crashing through his own skull and leaving him in Rosalind's lifeless arms for all eternity.

Peter had gathered some new thatch and tools. He walked happily through the woods to the cottages. He heard the shots, but shots were nothing to be alarmed at in a woods where poachers were often more numerous than the game.

It had been the most relaxing day he'd spent since they had left Poughkeepsie. He was wearing a blue work shirt that he had left behind. He felt as young as he had been before he ever dreamed of leaving Kent. He liked his life in America, but it had been a long time since he had been mentally free to enjoy the physical exhilaration of a task without being burdened with the responsibilities of the farm. He was happy that summer afternoon.

He came to the tidy row of brightly whitewashed cottages, which leaned comfortably against each other. The door to the last cabin stood open, swinging crazily against the wall whenever the wind blew.

As he came nearer, he saw two dueling pistols laid

neatly at the lip of the door, the barrels touching, nose to nose. Puzzled, he walked to the cottage, shoving the door open the rest of the way. Albert and Rosalind lay together across the bed where they had fallen.

He stood for a dazed, shocked moment, staring at them. Blood stood like a huge coagulating ruby on Albert's forehead, but nothing showed on Rosalind. Her sleek black hair hid everything. Confused and shocked, he felt like an intruder, and backed out the door. He wandered around the clearing, putting down his thatch, then picking it up, not knowing what he meant to do. He stopped, stood still, then went back to the cottage. He picked Rosalind's jacket up from the floor and went over to her.

"Rosalind," he said softly as though he were afraid to awaken her from her sleep. He picked her up gently, covered her nakedness, and carried her from the cottage.

Chapter 25

Peter struggled back to the house awkwardly bearing Rosalind's body. He kicked open the kitchen door, slamming it against the wall.

The scullery maid glanced up scowling from her scrubbing and saw him standing there, leaning heavily against the door, and began screaming. The entire household was alerted by her terrified noise and Peter's own alarmed, anguished voice as he cursed her and demanded a silence she couldn't maintain.

Anna clutched Callie's hand as they came to the entry of the scullery and saw him there with Rosalind draped in his arms. The scullery maid was down on her knees moaning her way through a litany. Seeing the look on Peter's face, Anna rushed over, shaking the girl until she was a chattering blob ready to obey whatever she was commanded.

"Get Mr. Berean . . . Mr. Frank. Hurry! Run to the fields and find him," Anna said tensely and in as low a voice as she could manage, keeping her eye on Peter as she spoke. "Go!" Anna repeated.

The girl moved forward, then stopped, pleading with her eyes on Anna. Peter blocked the doorway.

"You can get past him. Now hurry! Go!"

The girl squeezed her eyes shut, flattened herself against the wall, skirting Peter without touching him.

He stood stunned and confused. Once the noise had stopped, he didn't notice the scullery girl at all. He kept his eyes steadily on Rosalind.

Anna took a step forward, as afraid as any of them to go near him looking as he did. Callie cowered at the entry, not knowing what was wrong, knowing only that it was terrible.

"Peter," Anna began as she approached him. He didn't move or indicate that he had heard her. "Peter," she said louder. "Peter!"

He looked up. The dark brown eyes she looked into showed the tortured dullness of disbelief without intelligence. He opened his mouth, but no words came.

"Take her to her room. Take her to the bedroom, Peter." For a moment Anna's voice took on a depth and authority unknown to her. Callie glanced from Peter back to Anna, and then to Peter once more. He didn't seem to understand anything she said to him. Anna kept repeating herself and saying in a prayerful voice, "Bring Frank quickly. Peter—listen to me—please hurry, Frank. Peter, take her to your bedroom. Dear Almighty Father, help me. Help us all."

She placed her hand on his arm, pushing gently at him. He took a step forward only to stop again. He looked down at Rosalind's face.

Frank and Stephen had also heard the shots, but it had been difficult to tell where they had come from.

Frank's attitude was not so easygoing as Peter's had been. "Damned poachers!" he had muttered and motioned Stephen to follow him. "Got to get rid of the bloody nuisances before the pickers come . . . someone will get hurt with those jackanapes around here."

They ran into the woods, thrashing about then standing still to see if they could hear a noise that would indicate where the poachers had gone. Eventually they made their way to the hop pickers' cottages. Frank began to run. He had sent Peter there to work on the roof. His first thought was that perhaps there had already been a hunting accident. The bale of thatch was lying in the clearing. Fear shooting through him, Stephen sprinted past Frank the last few yards to the cottage. Its door was partially open.

He flung the door wide, then stood stonelike at the entry as Frank pounded up behind him.

"What is it? What do you see? Is it Peter?"

"Albert . . ."

Frank's feet hit one of the dueling pistols as he tried to push Stephen from the door so he could see. Both men looked down at the pistols.

"Oh, my God!" Frank breathed, hunching down to pick up the guns. "These are Pa's guns. What's happened here? Get out of the way, Stephen," he said and peered into the room. Albert still lay across the bed, the wound ugly on his forehead. "Oh, God, no! Why did I send him here?" he muttered, stuffing the guns into the belt of his pants.

"What are you doing? What happened? You mean you know!" Stephen asked.

"I might," Frank said grimly. "Go outside and look around. See if you can find Peter."

"Peter?"

Frank walked over to the table and picked up Rosalind's hat from where Albert had placed it. He waved it in Stephen's face. "Yes, go and see if you can find him. This is Rosalind's hat. These are Pa's guns.

They came from our house. Use your head, man, think what he is likely to have walked in on!"

"Is he dead?" Stephen asked.

"Of course, he's dead. Snap out of it, and find Peter."

Stephen backed from the cottage. He found Rosalind's horse, but not Albert's. There was no sign of Peter except for the bundle of thatch. He returned to the cottage to tell Frank. "What should we do? Why should Rosalind's horse be left here?"

"I don't know. Oh, God. I don't know what to do. It's nothing we can hide. We should send for the magistrate. Oh, God!" Frank searched the cottage, trying to think what should be done. He wanted to protect someone . . . maybe it was Rosalind who had done it and not Peter. He didn't know what to do or think, or which was the worst thought.

He was still in his quandary when the fear-crazed little scullery maid ran up the path to the cottage, babbling an incoherent tale of a man coming to the house bearing a dead girl. His mind, racing into blankness, made no connection between what she said and what he had already seen. Fear for Anna replaced all his worries about Albert, Peter, and Rosalind. "Go notify the authorities, Stephen. We've got a madman running loose."

"Frank—wait. We don't know what happened . . ."

"Do as I tell you! You're not in Poughkeepsie now. This is my home, and I'll protect it as I see best! Hurry! We've no time to waste. I've got to see to Anna." He ran from the cottage, pounding his way back through the woods to the main house.

Anna managed to get Peter to carry Rosalind upstairs, but she succeeded in little else. The cook, who had heard the scullery maid's cries, came to view the episode and took to screaming where the other had left off.

Peter moved with his dead wife toward their room. The shrill sounds of the cook's voice accompanied him like an unearthly dirge.

Anna saw Frank running toward the house from the bedroom window. She sank down on a chair. It seemed like hours that she had been trying to get Peter the short distance from the scullery to the bedroom. She could deal no more with Peter's stupefied silence than she could with the cook's mad lament. She ran down the stairs and lunged for the protection of Frank's arms, trembling against him.

His chest felt like it would burst. The sounds, the fear, the sight of his house flashed and shuddered inside him as he was assured that Anna was all right. Everything that Peter had touched in passing bore the faint markings of Rosalind's blood.

"Are you sure you are all right? You haven't been hurt? Do you know what happened?"

He listened as Anna tried to sort out the happenings of the last half hour. When she finished, his face was the color of the well-scrubbed scullery floor. "Has Peter told you anything?"

"Not a word. Frank," she began in a quaking voice, "Frank, why did you ask that? Surely, you can't think . . ."

He walked to the foot of the staircase. "Isn't there some way to quiet that woman? God alive, she's stirring the demons. Can't you do something?"

"Frank! Answer me, please. Why did you ask about Peter? Please, I have to know."

"Albert is dead as well. He was shot . . . Oh, my God!"

"What is it? *What?*"

"I sent Stephen for the deputy magistrate. Anna, run. Get someone to stop him!"

"We can't hide it . . . not Albert's death. No matter who—"

"We can give ourselves some time. Do as I say, woman, or he'll hang with no questions asked. Do you want that?" He stormed past her, headed for the stairs and Rosalind and Peter's bedroom.

Peter was sitting on the side of the bed, Rosalind across his lap. He was staring at her in the same senseless way he had before. The tears sprang to Frank's eyes as he looked on the broken sight of his brother. He reminded Frank in this moment of Natalie, so vulnerable and fragile no matter how ferocious her temper was. But Peter was anything but fragile.

Frank brushed his big, work-hardened hand across his face, wiping the sentiment from his mind as he wiped the tears from his eyes.

He asked nothing of Peter then. He lifted Rosalind from Peter's lap and placed her on the bed, arranging her riding habit as best he could. He pulled her riding jacket across her. Then he led Peter from the room, steering him down the stairs to the study. He put a glass of brandy into Peter's hands and guided it to his lips. "Drink it. All of it."

Peter drank the liquid, felt it burn down into his stomach. He slumped into a chair, holding his head in both hands. The brandy glass rolled on the floor.

"Oh, my God, Frank, she's dead." His shoulders began to heave, and without another sound Peter Berean began to grieve for his wife, not yet considering how or with whom he had found her.

Frank watched and waited at the far end of the room. He turned away, not able to bear the sight of Peter without breaking down himself.

self. She watched as he hesitated at the study door, then closed it softly behind him.

Frank, slow by nature, was a workman unused to prodding shocked, silent men. He was near the end of his patience and pacing the floor nervously when Stephen came into the room.

"Did you find out what happened?" Stephen asked, and then looked toward the hearth of the shadow-ridden room and saw Peter gazing into the blackness of the dead ash fire. "It's true then?"

"It's true. Both of them are dead. Peter brought Rosalind here."

Stephen's face softened in compassion. He no longer listened to Frank talking, but went to Peter's side, hunching down on the hearth rug. Neither said anything and Frank left the room.

Meg came home while Stephen was with Peter.

"I'll go to him. Let me see my boy!" she cried after Anna told her what had happened.

"Let Stephen tend to him, Mother Berean. Peter is so dazed I don't believe he knows what is going on."

"But he's my son."

"He is no one's son right now. Leave him to Stephen. He seems to take comfort from Stephen."

"But . . ." Meg began anxiously.

"Mother Berean—Natalie . . . think of Natalie. She has not been told yet. She doesn't know anything. We thought it best to wait for you, but we must hurry. Both the scullery maid and the cook were here and saw everything. It will be all over the village before long. We don't want her hearing from someone else."

Meg sat down unsteadily. "Natalie," she breathed. "Dear merciful Lord, what will come of my precious little Natalie?"

"Albert's mother must be told as well."

Meg nodded. She went first to the study. She laid

her hand on Peter's white-blond hair, but he made no response. He clung as he had been to Stephen. She went upstairs to Anna.

"Gather up Jamie's things. We'll take him with us. Callie can't manage everything here."

"But do you think we should?"

"Yes. There will be two of us there, and the Foxes have servants to help us. We can't leave it all on Callie. And I don't want the child out of my sight for a moment now," she said firmly.

Marsh drove them to the Foxe house. All the rooms were lighted. Inside Mrs. Foxe was annoyed and irritable that Albert was late for supper. The Foxe servants knew what had happened, but none had the courage to tell their mistress. Mrs. Foxe knew only that Rosalind Hawkes had returned to the Berean farm, and since her arrival Albert had been unreliable and short-tempered with Natalie and herself.

As Meg and Anna and Jamie were ushered into the house by the butler, Mrs. Foxe stood arrogant and regal at the end of her hallway.

Meg bustled past her without greeting, leaving to Anna the unpleasant task of telling Mrs. Foxe her son was dead. She went straight to Natalie's room, clutching Jamie against her.

Natalie was in her bed, surrounded by billows of white pillows and lace. Her face was like a cameo framed by the dark clouds of her hair. "Hello, Mama," she said sweetly. "I didn't know you were coming to visit this evening."

Meg stopped short. Natalie smiled. "Oh, you brought Jamie to see me too. What a nice surprise. I hope Albert comes in soon. I'd like him to see me holding a baby."

Meg could hardly speak. She cleared her throat and concentrated on the lacy cuffs of her daughter's nightdress. "Nattie, I haven't come here for a visit exactly."

"Why then?" Natalie asked, her head cocked to one side.

"Natalie . . ."

She frowned. "Did you come because you knew I didn't feel well today, Mama? But how did you know? The doctor said I had overdone yesterday. Did he stop by to see you too? There's nothing he's keeping hidden from me, is there, Mama?"

"I haven't seen the doctor, Natalie. I didn't know anything about your feeling unwell. Natalie . . ."

"I've been having horrible dreams, Mama. Awful, terrible dreams. Sinful dreams."

Meg squeezed her eyes shut for a moment. "Oh, Nattie," she cried. She got up hastily, closed the door, and put Jamie on the floor to scoot about.

"Mama, I'm so afraid something is going to happen to Albert. I feel it all around me. I see it when I close my eyes. Mama . . . !"

Meg darted awkwardly to Natalie's side, side-stepping Jamie. Crying and kissing Natalie, she smoothed the girl's hair. "It will be all right now, I'll be right by your side."

Natalie frowned, touching her head as though it hurt. "What is it, Mama? What is wrong with me? Why do I see these terrible things? Nothing really happened today, did it, Mama?"

"Albert is dead, Natalie," Meg whispered, wiping the tears from her face.

"Oh, no." Natalie smiled. "Albert isn't dead. Albert is free. Rosalind can never take him from me now."

Meg sobbed convulsively, blowing her nose with fury. "Lie back, Natalie dear. Rest now. It will be all right. Somehow it will be all right."

Natalie did as she was told, the sweet smile still on

her face. "I always feel better when you are here, Mama. I think I can sleep now. You won't leave?"

"No, Nattie. I'll stay right here as long as you need me."

Within minutes Natalie's eyes closed. She slept with a look of peaceful innocence on her face.

Meg gathered up Jamie, pushed aside Natalie's shoes, which he had pulled from the cupboard, and went downstairs to find Anna alone in the parlor. Anna jumped to her feet as soon as Meg came in.

"Mrs. Foxe is prostrate. She keeled over when I told her about Albert. They've sent for Doctor Potts. He should be here any time now. How is Natalie? How did she take it?"

Meg shook her head. "I don't believe she even understood what I was saying. She hasn't been feeling well today, but she is sleeping like a baby now. Watch Jamie for a minute, Anna. I am going to find the housekeeper. Jamie is hungry and tired and we'll all be staying the night. If Doctor Potts comes before I've returned, tell him to look in on Natalie as well as Mrs. Foxe."

It was more than an hour before Stephen emerged from the now darkened study at the Berean farm. His eyes were red-rimmed, his face sad and drawn. He went to the kitchen where he knew he would find Frank.

Callie had taken over in the kitchen after cook had screamed herself into a state of exhaustion and been sent home. She handed Stephen a cup of broth and some bread and cheese. He pushed the bread and cheese away, but drank the broth. Frank sat at the table weary and preoccupied. Stephen gathered himself and moved his chair closer to Frank's.

"I wasn't sure what to make of this whole thing, so

when you sent John after me, I told him to go into town tonight. He's to bring Albert's deputy sometime late tomorrow. I gave him all the money I had with me and told him to have a night on the town. I doubt that he'll be in any hurry to tell the law anything given natural reluctance and the liquor."

"We've got some time then. Bless you, Stevie. Did Peter tell you anything?"

"There wasn't much to tell. He went to fix the roof. He heard the shots as we did. The cottage door was open, so he went in to look." Stephen stopped, anger and sadness mingled on his face. "Rosalind was there with Albert. At first he didn't realize what happened. He says he doesn't know what he did then. Later he carried her here to the house."

"Then he says he didn't do it."

"God, yes, Frank! Where's your head to ask a question like that? My God, can you imagine how he felt? He loves her. Peter wouldn't hurt anyone no matter what. You know that."

"Who then?"

"I don't know. Anyone! But not Peter. Never him."

Callie listened and prepared a tray for Peter as she had for Stephen and Frank. She didn't expect that he would eat anything, but he shouldn't be left alone as though no one cared. Neither Frank nor Stephen paid any attention to her as she moved quietly from the kitchen.

The study was in darkness when she entered, except for the slice of moonlight that cut across the carpet where the drapes were not completely drawn.

The three of them—Callie, Stephen, and Peter—met more often than not in silence, each sensing the attention of the others without the need of words. She went to Peter's side as Stephen had, kneeling close to him.

He reached out, touching her hair. Slowly he lowered himself to the floor beside her. "Rosalind," he whispered into the darkness. Callie remained quiet and listened to the sounds of tears spilled in darkness. When he reached for her, murmuring his wife's name, she put her arms around him, answering the seeking warmth of his lips with that of her own. She rocked him as she did his son, with his head on her breast, humming to him in a low throaty voice. Slowly she felt the tautness leave his body. She brushed the hair from his face and wiped away the moisture from his eyes.

Much later Stephen found her there, Peter cradled in her arms as she continued to rock him.

"Build the fire, Stephen. He's asleep. We'll get blankets and pillows and leave him here for the night."

After Meg had made certain Jamie would be cared for and that she and Anna had a place to sleep, she returned to the Foxes' parlor. She and Anna both sat rigidly as if waiting for something. Neither knew what it was they expected, but neither was prepared when the knife-edged screams came from Natalie's room and cut through the silence of the house.

Meg, straining and clutching at her thudding chest, ran the long flight of curving stairs to her daughter.

"Mama!" Natalie shrilled, her voice quivering and high. Her eyes were wild and unfocused. She wasn't truly awake, but trapped in some nightmare. "Mama! Where are you? Albert! Albert!"

Meg, gasping, ran to Natalie, clutching her against herself. "Nattie, I'm here. I'm here, my loved one. I'm right here. You're safe now."

Natalie thrashed and fought. "Mama! Stop her, Mama! She killed him! I knew it. I knew! Damn her! Damn her! Mama! Where are you? Albert!" she screamed, breaking Meg's hold on her. She leapt from the bed, looking wildly around the room. *"Albert!"* She turned, running from her bedroom.

"Stop her!" Meg cried. The servants of the Foxe household stood immobilized at the foot of the gracefully curving stairs and listened to Natalie's screaming laughter as they watched her run frantically back and forth across the upper hall.

"Help me!" Meg shouted as time after time she reached for Natalie, only to have her break free again.

Anna came running from the other end of the hall where she had gone to make certain Jamie was all right.

"Stop her, Anna. Stop her before she hurts herself."

Anna stood mulishly at one end of the hall, waiting for Natalie to turn and run toward her.

Natalie hesitated, poised midway between Anna and Meg. Her hair was disheveled, a black aura encircling her head. She spread her arms wide, looking straight at Anna. Her fingers bent slowly to make talons of her hands. She grimaced, her teeth bared.

"Rosalind!" she shrieked, and charged Anna.

Both Anna and Natalie fell with the impact of Natalie's hurtling body. Stunned, Anna lay still for a moment. Her cheeks stung just below her eyes, where Natalie had clawed her. She didn't know what had happened for a moment; then Meg was standing over her trying to lift Natalie's inert weight from her.

"Get up here, you bloody fools!" Meg yelled to the servants still standing safely below. "Get her to her room."

Slowly the butler detached himself from the others and came up the stairs to carry Natalie, limp and unconscious, back to her bed.

She lost her baby that night.

* * *

The Berean house was quiet. Stephen took Callie's hand. Together they went out into a star-studded night. He took her to the top of his mountain. They sat close together on a large boulder overlooking the farm, the house, and the fields.

"I hate her tonight," Stephen said, looking up into the velvety heavens. "You shouldn't hate the dead, but I do tonight."

"You hate Peter being hurt," Callie replied flatly.

"Do you believe in God, Callie?"

"Yes."

"Things like this wouldn't happen if there were a God."

"God didn't do this."

"He let it happen."

"Someone *made* it happen," she said harshly, then added in a choked voice, "and I know who it was."

Stephen said nothing, but removed his hand from hers.

She looked at him in the darkness. "You do too, don't you, Stephen?"

"I only know who didn't do it."

"It was Natalie," she said, unwilling to leave it unsaid between them.

"Don't say that, Callie."

"Sometime it has to be said."

"It could have been anyone—a poacher. A highwayman. An accident."

"What's the point in hiding from it, Stephen? It was Peter or it was Natalie, and we both know Peter didn't—"

"Callie, please . . . don't ask me . . . he turned completely from her, then got up and walked several feet away until she could barely see him in the faint moonlight. "Don't you see?" he said finally. "I can't choose between my brother and my sister. There must be someone else."

She got up and walked to him. She slipped her hand into his and stood looking into the starry darkness. "What is going to happen to us, Stephen?"

Chapter 26

The night's sleep did Frank no good for there was no rest in it. His world was upside down and moving too swiftly for him to comprehend or cope with it. Anna was not there to warm his bed or see to it that he had warm water to bathe in that morning. His clothes were not laid out for him.

It would have been one thing for Peter to have killed Rosalind in a fit of jealous rage. A man could understand that, and even the law provided a certain latitude where unfaithful wives were concerned. But Albert was the magistrate of the parish. His family was important and well-respected. An arrest in such a case would be fast, and the trial a formality.

He fumbled about his bedroom, unaccustomed to dealing with anything that did not grow on a vine. It was regrettable he had made such a hasty statement to Anna about spiriting Peter out of the country. Words spoken in the heat of the moment were mostly regrettable in the end. And he did regret these. He could not help Peter escape. My God, it wasn't as if his brother were innocent. And Frank had his own reputation to consider. He'd be ruined. At least it had been Anna and not the others to whom he had said it. In the cold dawning light of day, she too would see that it was obvious he couldn't risk that sort of impetuosity. With all the sensational circumstances, word of Albert's demise would spread through the parish like flame in tinder.

He looked into the study when he came downstairs. Peter still slept in his makeshift bed by the hearth. He stared at his brother for a long time. In a sense it was better to say good-bye like this, without words or emotions to clutter up what must be. There was no point in playing the hypocrite. He and Peter had never lost any love over each other. Frank walked closer to where Peter slept. He was sorry it had happened here in Kent, but he had little sympathy for his brother. To Frank, Rosalind wasn't worth sorrow, so it didn't occur to him that Peter might mourn her. Aside from the hideous scandal and difficulty the murder would cause both him and the Berean name, Frank might have been able to dismiss the whole incident from his mind.

He went to his fields. They would always be there, demanding of him with the passing seasons only that which he was capable of giving.

Albert's mother recovered sufficiently from her shock and grief to rise from her bed and give two orders. Meg, Anna, Natalie, and Jamie must leave her house immediately. She had been appalled at Natalie's shocking tantrum. No matter how she stretched her mind, Natalie's method of grief did not fit any proper form of mourning she knew.

"That girl is deranged. You tricked us . . . you duped my poor, darling Albert into marrying her when you knew she wasn't right. It is you, Meg Berean, you and that entire family of yours that is responsible for my son's death. He always said you were a nest of treasonous revolutionaries. There has been trouble since the first day you took ownership of the hop garden. If it is the last act of my life, I'll see that the Bereans pay for this!"

Meg held her tongue and packed Natalie's things. They went back to Gardenhill House.

Mrs. Foxe's second order was a demand for the immediate arrest of the "harlot's keeper" for the murder of her son. The deputy magistrate stayed at the Foxe house to gather all the information and gossip he could. That afternoon, he and three yeomen came to the farm for Peter.

Callie stood dumbfounded and helpless as they entered the house to arrest him. Stephen stood by her side. "Stephen, we must do something. Tell them it was Natalie. Tell them!"

"Callie, no! Peter has made me promise not to say anything!"

"I don't care what he said. He doesn't even fully realize what's happened yet!"

"He knows enough to know what will happen to Natalie if she is taken."

"I won't let him do it! I won't! It's wrong." She moved to the kitchen, watching in disbelief as Peter walked between the yeomen to the cart that would take him to prison. "There must be something we can do," she whispered.

Peter heard her and turned to look at her. He smiled for the first time since he had found Rosalind. He watched Callie's face and remembered how she had ridden out to find him the night of the Swing riots, and understood that she wanted to save him again this afternoon. He touched her cheek gently. "You can't do it this time, little one." He paused for a moment and then went on. "And I don't want you to try, Callie. It can only make things worse and hurt more people. There's been enough of that." He climbed into the cart.

"Stephen!" Callie cried and ran to him, burying her face in his coat. "Don't let them take him. Please! Do something, but don't let him do this!"

"We can't stop them, Callie. But we'll do something. We'll find someone who knows what happened. Someone must know Peter didn't do this, and I promise you, Callie, even if I find that it was Natalie . . . if . . . if there is evidence, I'll . . . report it."

Callie watched as the cart rumbled down the far road with Peter in it. "There'll be no witnesses. Peter says no one was around."

"Peter doesn't know what he's saying. We'll have to think for him. Right now all he can think about is protecting Natalie. He thinks she did it too, and he's got some idea that he is the cause of it. Callie, he's wrong, and somehow I'll prove it. Believe me, Callie. You can't fall apart now. He needs you."

She looked into Stephen's eyes, her own brimming with unshed tears. "Stephen, I'm so frightened."

"We'll be all right," he said, putting his arm around her. He hated the reassuring, confident sound in his voice, hated her for needing that reassurance, and hated himself for needing to give it. Callie had taken his own thoughts from out of his very heart and put them into words. He was afraid. He didn't know what could be done or where to begin attacking the mesh of law that was as strong as steel and as debilitating as disease.

An Englishman held on a capital offense was allowed no counsel. Prisoners conducted their own defense with the disadvantage of not being permitted to give evidence in their own behalf.

There was one other horror that Stephen saw clearly even though Callie did not: She had been able to say openly that she believed Natalie had killed Rosalind and Albert, while he had not; but Stephen, deep inside himself, admitted it was true. What was also true—and Stephen recognized it—was that no one else, last of all judges and a jury, would ever believe it. Peter might think he was protecting Natalie by refusing to proclaim his own innocence, but what little evidence there was all pointed to Peter, and popular opinion had it that he was guilty.

Stephen was painfully aware that the only hope Peter had was for Stephen to find someone who had actually seen the crime, or something that would prove Peter hadn't committed the murder—or more unlikely still, for the murderer to step forward and admit guilt. None of these possibilities seemed likely, and no one was more aware of that than Stephen. He also knew there was very little time in which to search for a witness. If English justice tended to be harsh, it was also unquestionably swift.

Stephen was correct. Peter's trial, to be held in London at Mrs. Foxe's request, was scheduled just three days after his arrest.

Stephen left Callie at the house, then rode off searching for someone or something to prove Peter innocent. He dared not think what he might find, or what it would mean to Natalie. He still could not find it in himself to choose between the love he felt for his sister and the love he felt for his brother. Instead he prayed and left the decision to a higher order.

He rode back to the farm late that evening. When he took the horse to the stables, Frank was there watering and feeding the plow horses. "Where were you? I could have used your help today."

"I was looking for someone to testify for Peter," Stephen said tiredly.

"You're wasting your time," Frank grumbled as they

walked back to the house. "No one is going to stand up for him. Listen to the talk around."

Stephen stood silent and dejected just inside the study, gazing at the spot where Peter had been last night.

It was true what Frank said. No one was going to stand up for Peter. He was going to stand alone in that courtroom, and there was no one who could help. Even the truth would not help. There was no way of proving it.

All day long he had heard talk of the murder. Mouths overflowed with half-truths and scandal. Eyes lighted with curiosity; people all over the parish had been on Peter's side, but in such a fashion that their very support would help to convict him. He had every right, they all said, to do away with an adulterous wife, no matter how imprudent he had been in shooting Albert as well. They didn't believe him innocent, only justified.

Stephen walked fully into the room and took Peter's seat. He leaned forward, tired deep inside, propping his head up with his hands. It was all so painfully clear why Peter had always longed to leave England, why he had always felt hemmed in and trapped. Peter had always associated with the people who came most under the law's thumb. He understood the fear and futility that Stephen was only now learning. But why, if there were a God, had it to be Peter who became trapped by this thing called justice?

And then he remembered the morning prayer James used to say to begin each day of their lives. "Teach us to be just to those dependent on us."

He stared into the blackness so long and so hard that it seemed to undulate before his eyes, shaping and reshaping itself into human forms, some dependent, and some who prayed to be just. It was the whole essence of the Bloody Code to him that night. One group of people praying faithfully to a god, knowing he was there to answer because he was of their own making. And the others never praying at all, never knowing that God was there because they didn't know they were of His making.

That night he spent hating England and her Bloody Code, which could boast nearly two hundred thirty offenses for which a man could be hanged. English justice!

"What are you doing, Stephen? I've been looking all over for you," Callie said as she came into the study.

"Nothing. Thinking," he said moodily.

She fumbled at the table, trying to light a rush lamp. "Did you find someone to testify?"

"No."

"You're not giving up? There must be someone. We must keep looking." She turned away from him, biting her lip. "Oh, why did we ever come back here? None of this would have happened if we had just stayed in America."

"Shut up, Callie. Stop talking about it."

"I can't! I can't just sit here and do nothing. How can you? You know who did it. Why won't you just admit it, and do something about it?"

He glared at her. "Shut up, Callie. You're talking like a bloody fool. You want to drag it out of me that I think Natalie killed them? All right, I think it. I think she did it. But get this through that block you call a head, my opinion doesn't mean a bloody thing in a court of law, and neither does yours."

"Stephen—"

"I've ridden this whole parish today and found not one soul outside this house who believes in Peter's innocence, or who has seen or heard anything that would help. I've heard plenty that would hang him, but not one word that might save him."

"Stephen, no."

"Yes. If you still believe in that God of yours, you might pray he gets a compassionate jury," he said and strode out of the room.

Chapter 27

The following Friday, Stephen, Callie, and Frank went to the courtroom. Curiosity seekers crowded in among those present as witnesses or because of a connection with the trial. Stephen was surprised to see so many farm laborers there. It was a strange mixture of people, he thought. Ragged, soil-dirtied clothing rubbed against fur-trimmed velvets. Plumed bonnets waggled in the air over the flat caps of neighboring spectators. There were so many there, but none of them gave Stephen hope. He felt as though he was about to view something that had been preordained, and nothing would change Peter's fate or help Callie or him to accept it.

He looked around at the room itself. Golden, oiled panels of wood covered the walls. The judge's seat, high so that one had to look up to him, the lawyers' boxes, all carved and carefully crafted of the finest wood, lined up on opposite sides. The prisoner's box was set back and also built high so that the spectators could view it. Everything Stephen looked at seemed to be enclosed in wood, and while he thought that it was probably to provide a sense of permanence, it gave him only the apprehensive sense of impenetrability. He couldn't help but feel the truth could never be arrived at in this place, which was already so set in centuries of rules and laws. A man's life meant so little when it was pitted against fixed minds and rigid principles.

There was a stir in the room as people adjusted their seats for better views and the judge's gavel hammered. Robed lawyers moved papers, straightened wigs, and tugged at their robes in a final ritual of preparedness.

Stephen looked up and fixed his eyes on the ceiling, unable and unwilling to watch the final stages of what amounted to the ceremonies of righteousness. He didn't listen to the opening statements, nor to the first few witnesses.

Callie and Frank listened to every word spoken, their hopes rising and dashing as one witness after another told of having known about Rosalind and Albert's affair. Peter's part in the Swing riots came out and was discussed at length. His temper, his impetuosity, his recklessness in years past were repeated so often and with such enthusiastic vigor that it sounded as though he had spent his life riding the highways and stirring up trouble. It was also made clear that he and Albert had been in opposition to one another on several occasions. Mrs. Foxe was having her revenge on the "harlot's keeper" and would forever be satisfied that she had been right.

Callie sat stiffly in her seat. An idea formed as she heard a witness verify that Albert had once arrested Peter during the Swing riots. As the witness stepped down, and there was a lull in the courtroom, Callie kept remembering Albert asking her if she were willing to take the witness stand in Peter's behalf then.

She had been, but it hadn't been necessary. Now it was.

Quite suddenly, before Stephen could realize what she was doing, Callie stood up. "May I speak, Your Honor?"

A hum of motion filled the room as people shifted in their seats to look at the young woman who stood pale and frightened asking to speak to the court.

"I . . . I have testimony pertinent to the defendant's case, sir," she said, her voice shaking.

Stephen grasped her hand. More than anything he wanted to pull her down into her seat, but he didn't. She'd never forgive him; nor would she rest until she had tried her best to save Peter and to tell the truth. Most of all he dreaded what it would do to her when she discovered the truth did not always prevail. He increased the pressure on her hand, gently, reassuringly, letting her know he was there.

"I wish to speak, please," she said louder, her voice firmer.

The judge rapped his gavel as the barristers began objecting to her request.

Quickly she took her hand from Stephen's, stepped past Frank, and boldly walked to the witness box. Stiffly, not daring to look at anyone, she sat there waiting for the argument to abate, or for them to forcibly remove her.

When all was quiet and the proceedings resumed, the barrister, his white wig impeccably straight on his head, walked toward Callie. After a sarcastic comment about her audacity, he asked preliminary questions about her place of residence and her connection with the defendant. "Cousin," he repeated her answer. "A close cousin?"

"No, sir, distant. I'm not sure of the connection, only that it comes from Aunt Meg's side of the family."

"And were you not the *cousin* that the witness"—he glanced down at the notes in his hand—"Job MacBride told us about?"

"I don't know, sir. I don't know who Job MacBride is."

"Were you the woman who came into Albert Foxe's headquarters the night of the Swing arrests and claimed to have been out riding in the middle of the night with Peter Berean?"

Callie hesitated, then spoke in a low but clear voice. "Yes, sir."

"Cousin, are you? More likely that you'd be the reason he had no use for his wife." He strutted around the immediate area for some seconds, a smile on his arrogant face. "Well, Miss Dawson, shall we now get to the present problem? Here we have Mr. Berean embroiled in another misadventure, and again we have you sitting here telling us he is innocent. Why this time are you so certain of his innocence? Were you also out riding with him on this occasion?"

"No, sir."

"No, sir? Well, well, Miss Dawson, I am pleased to see that you have sufficient respect for this court not to foist that same story on us again."

"I have no desire to tell this court anything but the truth," Callie said quietly.

"The truth. Ah, yes, the truth. The truth will set him free, something like that, Miss Dawson?"

Callie began to stammer. "Y-yes, sir."

Stephen cringed in his seat, barely able to hold still as he watched the predatory barrister stalk back toward the witness box. He glanced up at Peter. The guard had his hands on Peter's shoulders holding him seated. On Peter's face was a mixture of grief and anger.

"Were you present at the farm the day the murder took place?"

"Yes, sir."

"Did you see anything of note—unusual that day?"

"No, sir, but . . ."

"Were you witness to the crime? Do you know anyone who was? Is there any reason we should waste our valuable time listening to you, Miss Dawson?"

"He didn't murder his wife . . . or Albert! I know he didn't. It was . . . it was someone else!"

"Who, Miss Dawson? Can you tell us that, or has it slipped your mind?"

"Must I say?"

The barrister glanced up at the judge, barely able to stifle his laughter. "Why, yes, Miss Dawson. You do want to free the accused on the basis of your testimony, do you not? Isn't it reasonable, and why, yes, even fair, that you should tell us whom we are to try in his place?"

"It was Natalie," Callie whispered. "It wasn't her fault. She couldn't help herself. She isn't well. She . . ."

"Repeat your statement, Miss Dawson. Aloud. So all can hear. Whom do you claim committed the crimes?"

Callie was ghost-white, her eyes wide with pain and fright. "Natalie Berean Foxe."

The barrister laughed aloud, turning his arms outspread to the spectators. "Natalie Foxe! Do you realize, Miss Dawson, that your testimony contradicts that of the elder Mrs. Foxe and her household servants? Natalie Foxe was confined to her bedroom all day under doctor's orders. You weren't at Foxe Hall, were you? And yet you presume to tell us that you know more about Natalie Foxe's whereabouts than those people who were with her all that day and night as well."

Callie sat straight and rigid in the seat. "They're

wrong! Natalie went to the pickers' cottages. She knew about Albert and Rosalind. She had told me just the night before. And . . . and why was Albert's horse found in the field behind his house if someone didn't ride it there?"

"Most horses can find their way back to their stalls, Miss Dawson."

"Rosalind's horse didn't run back to his stall. Only Albert's was gone."

"Perhaps he had a more intelligent horse?" The barrister guffawed, then turned to look at the spectators. "Well, Miss Dawson, you've had your moment of glory, but I'm afraid we have indulged you enough." He turned back to Callie, his head lowered. "The truth is, Miss Dawson, that you *want* the murderer to be someone other than Peter Berean. You want that badly, and are willing to sacrifice anyone to achieve that end. Even this man's sister, a dangerously ill woman who has just lost her husband and her child. A woman who at this moment lies at death's door! It is this woman you want us to believe tramped through a mile of dense woods, entered the Berean farmhouse unnoticed, stole her father's dueling pistols unseen, tramped across the yard of the Berean farm—unseen— back through the woods, intercepted her husband and his lover and coldly shot both of them, then returned to her sickbed to await the news. Of course, I might add that in addition to this diabolical piece of story telling, we must also in that case believe that this same woman wished the death of her unborn child and perhaps herself; for otherwise we would have to accept her behavior as hysterical grief, and we cannot do that if we take your story as the truth. Can we, Miss Dawson?"

"It's true!" Callie sobbed, standing in the box, pounding on the front panel. "You have twisted it all around. But it's true! It is a simple matter for Natalie to come from Foxe Hall. She does so all the time."

Stephen held to his seat white-knuckled, one fist pressed hard against his teeth. He couldn't bear to see her, nor could he stand hearing her voice, but he watched her and listened to her plead, cry, and beg the sneering, cynical barrister to listen. He called her every name but whore, and he implied that; and still she kept telling them the truth, stating Peter's innocence over and over, until she had no voice left and they forcibly took her from the witness box.

Peter leaned forward, his hand outstretched toward her until the guard pulled him back. The prosecution called Frank Berean, whom they didn't actually need, for the trial was already over.

Frank, his jowls quivering with rage and resentment at Callie, swore his testimony was true, then neatly placed Peter at the scene of the crime, identified the dueling pistols as his father's, and claimed that Peter, like all the members of the family, had access to them. Then, unasked, he volunteered information of the argument that had occurred the night before the murders—the night, Frank said, that Peter had nearly attacked him because he had made bold to tell Peter to watch better over the activities of his wife.

After having been warned that she would either be quiet or be expelled from the courtroom, Callie pressed her handkerchief into her mouth to silence her sobbing. Stephen had tried to get her to leave, to wait outside, but she wouldn't. She'd stay to the end. He held her close, no longer caring what they thought of him or of her. All the name calling had been done; so he held her and glared defiantly at the curious who persisted in staring and pointing and talking.

They listened to the final business of the trial being argued and decided.

There were three means considered sufficient to deter a murderer. One was hanging. To the poor it was the most satisfactory. Since the time of George III they were given eight holidays a year to attend the hanging days. If there were no hangings, there would be no frivolity and gaiety at the Tyburn Tree and at Newgate.

If the jury was not in a hanging mood—and they might not be, for hangings were more often for villainous men, or property offenders—Peter might expect to live his life chained within the frame of one of the hulks that crowded the Thames near Newgate, or he might be transported halfway around the world to live the rest of his life in servitude in one of the penal colonies.

While Stephen prayed to his tarnished God for a miracle, Frank sat two seats away from him, hoping that Peter would be hanged. Hanging had the single advantage of being relatively quick, and there would come a day when Peter, and Stephen too, would see the virtue in that.

Peter remained like a stone in the dock as he waited for sentence to be pronounced. He didn't know what he had expected, but somehow the reality of it hadn't reached him until he had heard Callie take the stand and tell the truth. It had been one thing for Peter to feel that he was keeping his sister from suffering prison, or worse, incarceration in a madhouse where she'd most likely be chained to a wall and treated like an animal for the rest of her life. It was another to stand there and hear the truth laughed at, to know that he was being condemned because the judge and the jurors "knew" they were condemning a murderer.

Now, for the first time, Peter felt like proclaiming his innocence, and he knew it was too late. Beyond that, he knew it had always been too late. His knuckles were white as he clutched the front panel of the dock for support. His head buzzed with the shuffling sounds of people leaving the courtroom. He had never known such terror. No matter what a man may sacrifice for another human being, or for a cause, there lives in him the certainty that behind all the pain and fear there is the solid rock of right, truth, and God. But Peter had just seen that fortress crumble in a welter of sarcasm, name calling, and cynicism. He looked out at the judge from the void that was now inside him.

The bewigged, black-garbed judge looked over at the prisoner. His flat, unspeaking eyes prolonged the moment. Then he said, "You shall be sentenced to the Crown colony of Van Diemen's Land to serve for the term of your natural life."

Peter heard it, then froze into blankness as he had after he had found Rosalind. The guard came and forced his hands free of their grip on the dock. Stiffly he was led away.

"He'd have been better off with a hanging sentence," Frank said.

"No!" Callie cried, near hysterical. "No!" Stephen took her in his arms again, pressing her face against his chest.

"He won't go, Callie. We'll do something."

Frank sat stolidly in his seat; then he turned looking at the staring people. He tapped Stephen on the shoulder. "Let's go. We've made enough of a show for them already today. And stop feeding her that pap about doing something, unless you have a Royal pardon up your sleeve. Start facing things as they are."

"Just how are they, Frank? Perhaps if his own brother hadn't been so damned anxious to get up there and condemn him with every word out of his mouth he wouldn't be where he is now."

"I'll not lie for any man."

"*Lie?*"

"Yes, lie. Are you so damned sure he didn't do it, Stephen? It's just the sort of hotheaded thing he would do."

"I *am* damned sure he didn't. And so would you be if you were any brother to Peter or to me."

Frank looked at him, but said nothing. They rode back to Kent in silence. Anna met them at the door. Jamie clung to her skirts, trying his best to stand alone.

Sobbing, Callie picked the child up, hugging him close to her.

"It went bad," Anna said.

"It went as expected," Frank snapped and headed for the study and the liquor cabinet.

"Oh, Frank! What shall we do? What can be done?" Anna asked, following him into the room.

"Damn it!" he shouted, slamming down the decanter. "Will you all shut up! There is nothing to be done. He's dead! Get it into your heads. Peter is dead. He died today when sentence was passed. We'll never see him again, and there's nothing you or I or any one save the king can do. That's the last I ever want to hear about it. Now get out—all of you. I want to be alone."

Anna shut the door, leaving Frank. She put her hands out, speaking quietly. "He doesn't mean it. You know he doesn't mean it. It's just his way. Let him be for a time, and you'll hear a different tune. Now—let me fix something for you to eat before I take Jamie up to bed. Mother Berean will want to be told what happened. She will need me to stay with her for a while after this."

"We're not hungry, Anna. Thanks anyway. How is Natalie?" Stephen asked.

"She is doing fairly well. The doctor says she should

recover if she doesn't get childbed fever. If Mrs. Foxe hadn't put her out of Foxe Hall, I'm sure she'd be stronger. But after the horrible things that woman said, I suppose we are all better off here. You can just never tell about people. Mrs. Foxe didn't consider Natalie's condition at all. Her own daughter-in-law. . . . the drive did her no good, but she is quiet now. Doctor Potts says we'll just have to wait and see how she improves."

Stephen nodded but said nothing. He began to walk to the front door. Anna took Jamie from Callie's arms and started up the stairs.

"Stephen, don't leave me," Callie cried and ran after him. "Stay with me, please."

He turned and waited for her. As soon as her reaching fingers touched the warmth of his outstretched hand, she felt safe. Stephen was like bedrock to her. Where he stood the ground would never shift under her.

Chapter 28

The great dirty stone walls of Newgate Prison contained a world unto itself, a world Peter had never thought he'd see let alone live in. He was put with others like him—those who had been rightfully or wrongfully convicted of offending English law—to await transportation to Van Diemen's Land.

Peter had always prided himself on his ability to work. He was an energetic man who enjoyed not only the sense of accomplishment work gave him, but also the physical invigoration that was part of it. In Newgate he learned what it was to expend pointless energy hour after hour to no purpose but humiliation and endless punishment.

Along with the other prisoners he was given tasks to perform most of the day. The most favored of these was the separating of oakum, a fiber from old rope, encrusted with pitch that had to be picked out by hand. He sat in a long line of men slowly and monotonously untangling and separating the oakum from the pitch. It remained his favorite job, however, for at least there was a purpose to it. It didn't prevent boredom, but he could imagine the oakum later being used to caulk ships, perhaps the very ship that would carry him to Van Dieman's Land. The separating of oakum ceased from time to time so the prisoners could pound logwood into the small pieces used to make dyes. These were the tasks that redeemed to some degree his time spent in Newgate. The other hours were those he dreaded most.

The prisoners spent time on the treadmill, a contraption of twenty-four steps like the floats of a paddle wheel fixed to a wooden cylinder sixteen feet in circumference. The wheel revolved two times each minute. There was a device by which a bell rang every thirty revolutions. At that time twelve men stepped off and twelve other men took their places. Occasionally the treadmill was used to grind corn or cayenne pepper. Sometimes it was used to pump water. Mostly it was used for punishment, not the punishment earned by insolence or bad behavior, but the punishment that was a part of being unfortunate enough to land in Newgate.

The treadmill turned endlessly, moving around and around in man-powered circles as twenty-four men mindlessly struggled to keep their footing on the narrow steps, each time lifting the equivalent of their own weight. At the end of each treadmill period, the men who were used to it learned to nap on their short rest periods. They needed it. It was an exhausting effort, a man lifting his own weight once every thirty seconds and doing so for thirty-minute periods. Peter was too new and too sore to be wise, still too incensed at the treatment of prisoners, still not able to think of himself as one of them, and still wondering what diabolical twist of fate had brought him to this.

The remaining part of the day he spent in his cell, save thirty minutes in an exercise yard with walls so high he was never certain he was really outside. In his cell he found the time and the silence he learned to dread. He could reflect without respite that this was the way he would live·his life from this time forward, unless Van Diemen's Land could offer something better.

Slowly the hope began to emerge and grow. As one day passed and blended into another, he believed nothing could be worse than the constant agonies of physical strain broken by hideously lonely, quiet isolation which could not be tempered even in conversation with other prisoners.

Peter's original sense of outrage was quickly gone. There was no place for it in Newgate, where cries of innocence and agony fell on deaf ears as did cries of rage and death. One thing that was quickly learned in prison was that no convict's life was as highly valued as that of the most lowly beast of burden. Every other feeling soon became secondary to a claustrophobic fear of abandonment that grew hourly.

It was during those long lonely hours in his cell that he began to think of Callie. He couldn't think of Rosalind. That day in the cottage always crept in, tainting every good moment of their marriage. He no longer knew if he had ever had an honest moment with Rosalind. And he didn't dare to think of Natalie. In those thoughts were guilt over the things he had not done for her, those times when he hadn't listened and hadn't believed her. And there was bitterness. No matter how badly he might have wanted to save her from the horrors of an asylum, he had not wanted to bring this relentless punishment down on himself. Though Peter knew—if it ever came to be—that he would refuse any help Natalie might offer him, it still hurt deeply that without a word she had allowed him to accept the burden of her crimes. Rosalind, Na-

talie—thoughts of them brought him nothing but pain.
But his memories of Callie were pure and clear.

There were so many times he could think of with
Callie; she had marred none of them with lies or longings to be someone else or someplace else. He remembered the May house, the first time she had ever
really turned to him. It was like the birch trees being
a signal of spring: pheasants begin to crow; the thrush
lends its song to the air again; then the oak begins to
bud and the finch to sing. All of it was tied with his
thoughts of Callie and what had begun with the
building of her first May house. He thought of the
trust and the love she had given him that wintery Sunday. She had taken his hand for the first time then, as
she did so often when she felt the need to touch someone she knew to be real. "It's too beautiful, Peter.
It's too beautiful." He had held her that day, kissing
her on her cheek, trying to comfort.

Now he clung to that memory as he would to a
floating log in a raging river. He began to long to see
her, to be able to touch her and know she was real, as
she had once reached for his hand because she was
afraid happy times would never be real.

The Bereans said little about Peter while they were
all gathered together. The mere mention of Peter's
name sent Frank into an ill-tempered tirade. It was
the most grim reminder of all, forcing them to see
how hopeless the situation was. But Stephen, fighting
his feelings of resentment against Frank, had kept silent about Peter as long as he could.

"There is no way to know how long Peter will be
kept at Newgate," he said at dinner several days after
the trial. "I've asked around, and we can see him—
take him food and clothes—as long as we pay the

turnkey. I've been told they are quite amenable as long as they get paid enough."

"I have no brother named Peter," Frank said, reaching for the ale. "He died."

Stephen sat silent for a moment, controlling the anger that boiled inside. Finally he said calmly, "I have a brother in Newgate Prison. I would like to do whatever I can for him."

"Do as you wish," Frank said.

"I need to borrow some money. I've already sent to New York instructing Jack to make payment to the bank here, but there isn't time. We never expected—"

Frank burst out with a harsh laugh. "Money!"

Stephen gritted his teeth. "Yes, money. You'll get it back, and you never need ask for what it is being used. I am still your brother, aren't I? Or do you consider me dead too?"

"Don't be an ass."

"Then lend me what I need, Frank."

"You want me to do something I believe is useless, more than useless—I think it is bloody wrong. No matter what words you use, it is still the same. If I give it to you, it is the same as giving it to Peter. Peter is dead to us. The dead don't need comfort; the living do. Learn to accept it. One day you'll thank me for making you see it now."

Stephen took a deep breath, his eyes darting around the room in frustration. The plate before him was untouched. Finally his eyes rested on Frank again. "Frank, please, lend me the money I ask. I'll have to get it some other way if you don't. You can't stop me, you can only make it more difficult."

"Get it elsewhere. I haven't got it to give even if I were inclined to do so."

"You haven't got it," Stephen repeated disbelievingly.

"You heard me. I haven't got it. I'm not your rich brother; I'm the poor fool who got left behind in Kent. Remember? The one who shouldered the responsibilities for the family while you and Peter made a new life." Frank shoved his chair from the table and left the room.

The following day Stephen took the postechaise into London. He found a larcenous turnkey without difficulty and visited Peter for the first time since his arrest.

"My God, you're here!" Peter cried. "How did you do it? Blessed Heaven, you're a welcome sight." He laughed, hugging Stephen, then stood back to look at him, then hugged him close again, needing to be touched.

"Are you all right, Peter? You're well? They haven't . . . haven't hurt you? Do you need anything?"

"No, nothing. I'm well. God, it's good to see you. How did you do it?"

Stephen rubbed his fingers together. "It's not difficult if you oil the hinges properly. Ma sends her love. And Anna."

"And Callie?"

Stephen shrugged, smiling. "You know Callie. She'd dig through the walls of this place given the chance."

Peter looked pensively at the tiny grated window at the top of his cell wall. "Will she come?" he asked hesitantly.

"Here?"

Peter looked down at his feet. "You're right, of course. This is no place for her. I've just been thinking about her lately. She's so—fresh, you know. She makes you think of spring and—well, it's no matter. A prison is not the place for spring, is it?"

"No, it wasn't that. I wasn't sure you'd want to see

her . . . here. She wants to come. She wanted me to ask you, but . . ."

"She will come!?"

"Next visit," Stephen said, standing. "That's a promise. I'll bring her myself."

Callie came to London with Stephen the next trip. It was the last trip Stephen could pay for without jeopardizing their return to America. He took her to Newgate, saw her safely inside, and then went to the Old Bailey Boiled Beef House to wait for her.

The turnkey took her to Peter's cell, letting her inside with a leering wink in Peter's direction. She stood just inside the heavy door. He looked at her as though he was afraid to touch her.

"Peter?" she said softly. "Is it all right that I am here?"

Still he said nothing and did not move. She walked close to him. "Oh, Peter." She stood near, her eyes roving over his face. "Are you all right? They haven't hurt you?"

He touched her hair, then her cheek. His arms went around her, pressing her tight against him as he swayed back and forth, burying his face in her hair, smelling the sweet scent of fresh country herbs she carried with her wherever she went.

She sat down beside him on his cot, holding his hand in both of hers as she told him about Jamie and Meg. Jamie had a new tooth and three new words. Peter had avoided thinking of Jamie. He came too close to other questions Peter would still not consider. But from Callie's lips Jamie seemed entirely his son, because he seemed to be Callie's. She had always been more mother to Jamie than Rosalind had. He wondered why he hadn't seen that before.

"Will you come back again?" he asked as she got ready to leave.

"I'll try."

He took hold of her arms, looking anxiously into her eyes. "You must come back. Promise you will. I need to see you again. Without you here, there's . . . don't leave me alone, Callie," he ended and turned from her.

It was her first and only glimpse of how he truly felt there, perhaps because such a request was so unlike him, or perhaps because of the look of fright that he hadn't been able to hide. "I'll be back, Peter. Stephen and I both will. We'd never leave you or stop believing in you. You know that. It is only the truth."

He looked at her intently and then rushed over to her. He held her head in the vise of his hands, burning the impression of her face and eyes deep into his memory so that he wouldn't be alone again that night.

Stephen went to work on the neighboring farms to earn the money for them to use in bribing the turnkey until Jack managed to send funds to them from New York. In the beginning he and Callie took turns seeing Peter. As it grew nearer the time when he would be taken to the hulks before transportation, it became obvious that it was Callie he wanted and needed to see more often than the one day a week she and Stephen had been visiting him.

With each visit the demands of the turnkey became greater, and the money harder to come by. Step by step Stephen began to do more and more menial labor for less pay. Many times he found himself working for families who had worked for Frank. He would take any work he could find and with it he took the humbling so many people seemed to want to give.

"Will we be able to visit Peter this week?" Callie asked. "There won't be many more times, and he does seem to take comfort when we're there. It's your turn to go, Stephen. Will you have the money in time? Perhaps we could ask Frank again. It wouldn't be much this time."

"Don't think about the money. We'll have it."

"Then you'll go!"

"It's you he wants to see, Callie."

"And you. You take your turn. I want you to."

Stephen pressed the money into her hand. "This isn't all of it, but I'll have the rest in time. You go."

"It isn't right, Stephen. You do all the work to get us there. You take your turn. I know you want to see him as much as I do."

"I said, you go! No more argument, Callie. The decision is made and as you have said, I earned the right to make it." He was angry at himself for urging her, at Peter for depending so much on her, and at the look on her face that told him how much it had cost her to urge him to take his turn. She was beginning to want to see Peter as much as he wanted her to be there.

His lips were pressed shut so no sound would burst out unbidden, so he wouldn't take hold of her shoulders and shake her as he told her in fierce torrents of words that there were dreadful moments when he wished Peter were already gone, safely away from their lives. Tell her of nights he had cried as bitterly and harshly as he had heard her cry for Peter; but that his tears were those of shame and loathing guilt born out of the awful, fearful thoughts when he was glad of what had befallen his best-loved brother, because he loved and wanted the woman he saw falling in love with that brother.

He stood before Callie tall and angry. Shame poured from him like sweat as he thought of her. His voice quivered as he forced it into softness. "I want you to go, Callie. You can do far more for my brother now than I."

Callie's eyes filled with tears. "Oh, Stephen, you are truly one of God's children." She moved close to him, kissing his cheek. "I don't understand you, or your angry moods, but I couldn't go on if you weren't there. You are my courage, Stephen."

He took a deep breath, placing his hands on her shoulders, pushing her away from him. "You would go on, and so must I. As long as the jailer keeps demanding more money, we're hard-pressed to keep a shilling ahead of him. I'll be back sometime tomorrow or the next day."

"You can't! Where . . . you can't leave me . . . not now. Peter . . ."

He put his finger to her lips. "There is no work near here. I am merely going farther afield. If you're going to comfort Peter, we must have the money. I'll go where I can get it."

She smiled apologetically. "I should have known."

"Yes. You should have known," he said quietly and left her.

Stephen walked. He and Frank barely spoke now, and Stephen would take nothing from him he didn't consider a necessity. A horse was not a necessity. It made his chore all the more difficult, but it made him feel a little cleaner inside.

Everywhere he went he became a curiosity as soon as his name was known. A few times he had given a false name, but he was too well known throughout the parish. The false name discovered, elicited more excitement and suspicion than when he simply said who he was and faced the questions and innuendos.

He had learned a great deal about people, none of it particularly favorable. Too many of them enjoyed knowing a person suffered, just as they enjoyed acting the bright sympathetic role that would encourage their victim to talk so they could enjoy his suffering all the more.

Half the day passed before Stephen found any work at all, or anyone who would hire him. Finally a woman offered him three shillings to cut her wood. It was quite a lot to pay a laborer, and no matter what his name, or how wealthy he and Peter were in America, at this time Stephen was a laborer and learning what it meant to work at anything and live on nothing.

"Mind you stack it properly. I'll not pay for any job not well done."

Stephen touched his cap. "Yes, ma'am. It'll be cut and stacked to your liking."

"Umm," she said, standing back, hands on ample hips, watching him. "You're the brother of that murderer they caught some weeks back, aren't you? I must be daft letting you come around here. No telling what might happen . . . having a brother like that an' all. They say things like that run in families. You like he is?"

"Yes, ma'am, I am like him. But he committed no murder," Stephen said, driving the head of the axe down on the wedge and splitting the wood.

"Why's he locked up then, eh?"

Stephen said nothing. He continued with his work.

"Not very talkative, are you? Guess you wouldn't be with a brother like that." To his relief she returned to the house.

It was very late in the afternoon when she came back. He was nearly finished with the wood.

"Well now, looks like you do know how to put in a day's work. I didn't think you would. Didn't think any Berean would know how to do much of anything, from what I hear. Your family's got money, don't they? How come you're out here workin' like this?"

"I like to earn my own way," he said shortly. His back hurt and he was tired, too tired to listen dispassionately to any more of her suggestive talk.

"Wouldn't let you throw good money after bad, more'n likely. Can't say I blame them much. It isn't just your brother they talk about, you know. I heard about you as well. I heard about you sendin' that young girl into that murderer's cell an' leavin' them there all alone. God knows what the brute's done to her. You men are all alike. I shouldn't have let you near my place. Just shows what a soft touch I am for a handsome face, just like most women. I can't help feelin' sorry for that girl though." She moved a little closer to him, her head thrust forward. "Or maybe I'm wastin' my sympathy, am I? They say she's been chasin' after him for years. That so? She just like the rest of you? Don't care?"

Stephen placed the last of the wood into the pile and put the axe down. He straightened and asked to be paid.

"You cryin'?" she guffawed.

"No, ma'am." He immediately put his hand to the side of his eye, digging his thumbnail into the flesh. "A wood chip caught the side of my eye."

She glanced at the angry reddened mark and took the coins from her apron pocket and placed them in his hand.

"You can wash up over there. Best be more cautious. A bit more and it would have hurt your eye. You may be a fool, young man, and maybe a lot worse, but you're a good worker. You can tell your mother Joan Burke said so, and I don't say it often."

"I'll tell her, Mrs. Burke. Will you have any more work for me?"

"You come by tomorrow. I'll have something for you. I got some fences needin' mending, and the barn needs some attention." She guffawed again. "You keep workin' like this young man, and you'll end up rich."

Stephen felt the meager shillings growing hot in his hand. "Yes, ma'am."

He slept in her field that night so he could be at her door with the rising sun. He worked for her all that day. By the time he returned home, he had the money. Peter would see Callie at least one more time.

Chapter 29

Time was growing short and all three of them sensed it. Before Stephen and Callie made the last trip to London, she was certain they wouldn't be able to visit Peter again. It seemed of the utmost importance that she and Stephen be there when he was moved to the hulks. For days she tried to think of some way to accomplish it.

"Stephen, could we stay in London overnight this time?"

He looked at her questioningly. "Why?"

"It's only a feeling, but I don't think we will be able to see Peter again. It's probably foolish, but it is such a strong feeling."

"It would also be expensive . . . I don't know, Callie. We haven't the money."

"But couldn't we use our passage money? Would it really matter if we have to stay here a little longer? Jack will be sending money soon . . . as soon as another packet ship arrives. Couldn't we?"

Stephen looked down at his feet, then directly at her. "I've been using it right along. There wasn't any other way . . . I couldn't earn what the turnkey was asking."

"Oh . . . well, then. . . ." Flustered, she looked away, then turned to him again, her eyes pleading. "Perhaps we wouldn't need money. Mrs. Pettibone once told me if I ever needed her to come to her for help. I'm sure she would let us stay with her one night. I lived there an awfully long time. Oh, Stephen, surely she'd see I'm never likely to need help more than I do now."

"Suppose this isn't the day he'll be transferred?"

"I don't know. We'll have to think of that when it comes, if it comes. But I feel . . ." Her voice trailed off. "I'm being ridiculous, aren't I?"

Stephen had little doubt that she was accurate in her feeling. He had heard talk of a ship that would be leaving for Van Diemen's Land later in the month. But he didn't like what he saw happening to Callie. With amazing speed she was committing herself to Peter. She was associating herself with him in every thought she had, every word she spoke. Not only was Stephen jealous of that single-minded devotion, he hated what it would do to her. And to him.

She had said often enough that she would do anything in her power to help Peter, but Callie was an idealist with the strength to carry out those ideals no matter what it cost her. And Peter was a disillusioned man, stunned and hurt, grasping for anything he could believe in. He had found Callie. Stephen's Callie.

Stephen had no idea what to do about it. But there was Callie, young, beautiful, and loving, wanting only to give her strength to a man who needed it, and that man was his brother. He couldn't tell her she was wrong. Nor could he deny Peter the one remaining person who seemed to give him hope. And yet somehow it still seemed wrong. He could not say why, except that he knew he needed Callie as much as he loved her. He felt guilty and selfish; but there were times when he thought he couldn't bear anymore to watch her chain her life to Peter's just as Peter had chained her life to his. He pushed down his own feelings once more, but he couldn't look at her as he said, "We'll talk to Mrs. Pettibone."

"You don't want to do it," she said slowly. "Why, Stephen?"

"I want to," he said.

"Something is wrong."

"No, it isn't. I'm just tired."

"Are you sure?"

He looked at her then. Her look of concern was entirely for him. She would go back to Kent as they always did at the end of the day, never seeing Mrs. Pettibone if he asked it of her now. She trusted him completely. It was her blind faith in him that defeated him for he would never be certain his decision hadn't been based on his own wanting her, and not on what was right.

"I'm sure," he said and knew he had made a decision far more important than the words indicated.

Peter was nervous and tense that day when she saw him. She came into the cell as she always did, but he was not as always. He couldn't sit still. He paced the cell looking everywhere but at her. He couldn't keep his concentration on anything she said. She sat quietly, her hands folded on her lap, watching him. "Peter, what is it? Would you rather I hadn't come today?"

He walked to the wall with the tiny grated window at the top, looking up at the dull trace of light coming through. Both his hands were braced against the wall.

He put his forehead on the cold stone between his hands.

She came up behind him, her arms locking around his waist, her head resting on his back. "Tell me what you are thinking."

He raised his head, once more looking toward the weak light of the window. "I can't stand being locked in here any longer," he said more to the window than to her. "Do you know what it is to be haunted by a breeze on a summer's evening and never be able to feel one?"

"No."

"There's nothing here. Nothing but time, endless, empty time. I can't breathe anymore. I can't think. I can't . . . stay here any longer."

"You won't be here forever, Peter. It will be better."

"Will it?"

"It must be."

"There is nothing that says anything must be," he said harshly.

"Oh, Peter, don't talk like that. I hate to see you this way. If you don't keep believing and hoping then nothing can happen. You must believe that everything will be good again. You must."

He touched his head against the stone of the wall again, then turned, taking her in his arms. He kissed the top of her head. "You've never given up, have you, Callie? No matter what they said to you, or what they did to you, you never gave up."

"No."

"That counts for something." He smiled, holding her away from him so he could look at her face. "It is what I love best about you, little one. You believe in the impossible, and somehow make it so."

"Peter, someday you will be free again. I know they say no appeal can be made, and I'm not very knowl-

edgeable about these things, but you will be free.
Something will happen."

"You are very young and very innocent, Callie.
Sometimes it happens that nothing will change. And
this time, it isn't likely that anything will happen no
matter how hard you and I wish it. It will be too bad
when the day comes that you face that, and this belief
of yours will stop."

"I would never stop! And neither will you, Peter Berean! You'll keep right on believing, and so will I. Stephen and Jamie and I will be waiting for you just like
always when you come home. We'll keep the hop yard
going, and the brewery will be built. And those apple
trees that you planted will be bearing fruit, Peter. Everything will happen as you planned it."

"But I'll never see it."

"Oh, but you will. Peter, do you remember the May
house you and Stephen built for me?"

He laughed. "I remember it far better than you'd
ever guess."

"When you took me to see the May house, I knew it
couldn't be real. It was beautiful, and I had just
learned that the world was an ugly cruel place to be.
It was filled with people like Mrs. Peach and those
men who stole and lied and did terrible things to get
what they wanted. I didn't believe anyone could be
trusted, and I thought never to see beauty or joy
again. Then Uncle James took me away from London,
and you and Stephen built the May house and you
brought me to it. I knew then that the awful time I
had lived through was just a time, and not the whole
world. Peter, write to me about the May house. Just
put it in one special letter, and then I'll know you are
coming home to Poughkeepsie where you belong.
Promise me that. I want to know the day you see that
this is a bad time, and not the world."

"I promise you that, should it happen."

"It will. You'll see."

He laughed, tolerant and wanting to believe it was more than childish wistfulness. "Will you be writing to me then?"

"Always," she said.

With her standing so near to him, looking like a fresh-picked flower with her golden hair and milk-white skin, everything took on a clean brightness that he knew would disappear as soon as she walked out of the door. With her leaving all the gray dirtiness of the prison would close in on him again. "Oh, God, Callie, why did it all happen?" he asked, his arms wrapped tightly around her. His breath caught. He shuddered and trembled against her. "Don't ever stop believing, Callie. I need you." He buried his face in her neck, kissed her on the cheek as he always did. Then he looked into her eyes and gently sought her mouth.

Except for the night Peter had thought she was Rosalind, Callie had never been kissed like this. His mouth was both soft and hard. His beard was rough, making her skin tingle. But most important of all, this time, she knew it was her he kissed and she could feel the lonely hunger that was inside her. He needed her as no one had ever needed her before. Within his arms in the space of a kiss, Peter Berean changed from a man Callie had idolized from afar, to a man she cared deeply about and who sought in her all the love and devotion she so wanted to give the right man.

He stepped away from her, breathing rapidly. His expression was soft and loving. "My little dreamer of dreams." He smiled down on her. "Never stop dreaming for me, Callie. As long as you believe, perhaps I can too."

"Then you'll always believe, Peter, for I'll never stop."

* * *

Stephen had sent Callie's note to Mrs. Pettibone while Callie went to see Peter. Then he went to the Old Bailey Boiled Beef House to wait for her as usual. She wasn't there at the regular time. He went outside, looking anxiously down the street for her. When finally he saw her, he felt irrationally angry. A bitter jealousy stirred inside him, and he didn't know how to deal with it for he had never felt that way before.

She was radiant when she came up to his side. Her cheeks were flushed and her eyes sparkling.

"How was Peter?" he asked brusquely, but she didn't even notice the strained tone of his voice.

"He was distraught at first, but he seemed better when I left. Did you send the note to Mrs. Pettibone?"

He looked at her oddly. Jealousy was not a nice feeling; it curled him up inside and made him think things that should never be thought. The seeds of ideas that Joan Burke had placed in his mind with her insinuating talk haunted him. Nothing had happened in that cell in Newgate. Nothing could, he told himself, and remembered his own trips through those bleak corridors, past those cells, and knew that anything could and did happen within the walls of Newgate, and no one cared. He looked over at Callie. She was so different today. She was always so talkative, telling him everything she and Peter had said without his having to ask. Today she was reticent, and he didn't know why. He just knew something had happened, because she was different. "I sent the message," he said finally. "Did Peter say anything about the hulks?"

"He doesn't know when it will be, but he thinks it is soon too. Perhaps tomorrow. One of the other prisoners told him that in line. We will come—just to be sure?"

"We'll come, but you know I have nothing to give to the turnkey. We can't see him in Newgate tomorrow."

"I know. We'd better hurry, Stephen. Mrs. Pettibone will be expecting us. What time is it?"

"It's four o'clock. Callie . . . ?"

"Oh dear, that's the time I said we'd be there. Now we're going to be late."

"Callie!"

"What is it, Stephen? What is wrong with you? We're late."

"How . . . how completely are you promised to Peter?"

She avoided his eyes. "Promised? I don't know what you're talking about, and I don't see why we have to talk about everything right now. We have to hurry."

"Something happened today. It shows all over you. What was it?"

"Nothing. Just nothing. He was very unhappy and I gave him what little comfort I could. I talked to him about Poughkeepsie, that's all." She looked at him belligerently. "I promised him we would go home and do all the things he had planned to do himself. We decided that was best. Remember? You told me we were going back, so I told him."

"And that was all?"

"Yes! And I told him we'd always be there. We'd wait for him to come back. He *is* coming back, Stephen."

Stephen looked at her knowing and not wanting to know that Callie would wait for Peter for as long as it took. He'd never be able to touch her as long as Peter was in prison, without denying his brother the one person he still believed in.

"What is wrong with you, Stephen? You've been acting strangely since yesterday. Don't you want to go to Mrs. Pettibone's?"

Stephen breathed deeply, the path ahead already laid for him. He forced a smile and took her arm, walking fast and turning the wrong direction at the first corner.

"You'd better follow me, or we won't get there at all," she giggled.

They hurried along the streets, Callie leading through a tangle of house-lined roads that all looked the same to Stephen. "This is where you used to live?" he asked. "Yes."

"It's hard for me to picture you here. I always think of you in the fields and around the hop yard."

Callie glanced around. Black soot clung to brick and window. "It's hard for me to imagine living here now too. It is this one. That window up there is the window to our flat. Papa and I used to think it was a grand place to live then. It was, while he was here." She climbed the steps to Mrs. Pettibone's house. She stopped at the top and looked back at him. "Why did you ask me if I were promised to Peter? What did you mean? Not marriage, surely. What then?"

"I meant nothing," he said lightly. "You just seemed so intense . . . different than usual. I . . . I don't know."

"I promised I would wait for him to come home. He needs us, Stephen. I wanted him to know we'd be there."

Stephen nodded, then indicated the door. "We're going to be late."

She rapped at the door only once, and Mrs. Pettibone's broad, anxious face peered out from the window at the side of the door. She flung the door wide. "Callie? Is it really you, child? All grown up! I never thought to see it, silly little goose that you were. I was afraid the world would swallow you whole. Come in. Come in, child, and make yourself at home."

Callie hugged her, then took Stephen's hand. "This is my cousin, Stephen Berean, Mrs. Pettibone."

"How do you do, Mr. Berean," she said and looked approvingly at him. She turned to Callie, unconsciously tugging at the stays of her corset as her eyebrows went madly high on her brow, her eyes slanting back toward Stephen. "You found yourself a well-favored family, didn't you, child?"

Callie laughed as Stephen blushed. "Oh, I did indeed."

"What can I do for you then? You said in your note that you needed my help."

Callie explained what had happened to Peter, and why they were there. Mrs. Pettibone was the first person who had heard the story who did not look knowingly and eagerly for scandal. Stephen sat back and relaxed. She had his approval.

"Well, all the flats are let. If Mr. Berean wouldn't mind sleeping on the sofa, you could sleep in with me, Callie," she said. "It's the best I can do."

"It is all that is needed, and we're grateful," Stephen said quickly. "I'd be happy for the couch. I'd be thankful for it."

They had supper, and Stephen fell asleep soon after. Mrs. Pettibone went over to him and took off his boots with the expertise and tolerance of a woman with much practice and love of the nature of men. She put his legs on the sofa, then covered him with a blanket. She motioned Callie into her bedroom. "We can talk in here and not disturb him," she said, closing the door. "My, he is a handsome one! Such an awful lot of man. He's your cousin? Not too close, I hope."

Callie giggled. "Not too close, but still the dearest friend and brother I could ever have hoped for. I love him with all my heart for the kindness and affection he never fails to give."

Mrs. Pettibone made a face as she stood in front of Callie, letting out her corset. "Brother? You are still a silly goose. He does not look at you like a brother, and if you had a grain of sense you'd see that. The man is in love with you, child. If you can't see that, then it must be your own feelings do not match his."

Callie looked at her, her eyes wide; then she began to cry.

Mrs. Pettibone sat on the bed beside her and put her arms around her. "Tell me what it is, Callie. You're not still frightened by all men, are you? Tell me what it is."

"It's Peter," Callie sniffed.

"You are in love with him?"

"No . . . no . . . yes. Oh, Mrs. Pettibone, I love Stephen. I love them both. I don't know what I mean. I'd die for Peter . . . I would if I could help him. He's so kind and so good. I'd do anything." Callie stopped talking. She stared at the wall, and her face softened. "But it's Stephen who makes me feel alive. I love him. I . . ."

"I understand, child; you needn't say more. But you've never told him?"

Callie began to cry again, slow, pain-filled tears. "No, and now I can't. I promised Peter I'd wait until he was free, and I will do that, Mrs. Pettibone. He needs someone."

"But must it be you, Callie?"

"I don't know. I don't know."

Callie and Mrs. Pettibone talked far into the night, Callie telling her everything she could remember about her life with the Bereans. She talked about Peter and Rosalind and Jamie and Stephen.

Mrs. Pettibone sighed as it became obvious Callie was too tired to talk anymore. "If it isn't tomorrow that they transfer Peter to the hulks, you can stay here as long as Stephen doesn't mind sleeping on the sofa." She looked sadly at Callie. "You've had a difficult life, Callie. I wish I could say something to you that would make it all right and proper as it should be. But, you love that man sleeping in the other room, and he loves you, child. Whatever you decide, don't lose sight of that. It's a rare gift, Callie, and it doesn't come often."

"I won't. As soon as Peter is free . . ."

Mrs. Pettibone looked down. "Yes, then," she said as she climbed into her bed beside Callie.

The hulks were blackened relics of naval man-of-war ships no longer being used. They were moored in the Thames as prison ships during their last days. Peter was taken aboard the hulk *Justitia* early the following morning.

There were guards and warders everywhere. As Peter passed over the gangplank one of the guards came up to him immediately, roughly searching through his clothes for money or anything of value. The first guard passed over the silver-buckled belt he wore. The second did not.

Peter was then led below with the other prisoners. Many knew what was coming. Some had been here before. Their perpetually sullen faces and leaden eyes drooped as they walked along. Peter followed in the line not knowing where he was being taken or what would happen.

All of the men were stripped of their clothing, then washed down with an ablution to kill the pests that lived happily on so many of them.

As this took place, one of the guards read from a manual. "No person other than convicts and their guards shall be permitted on board ship."

Peter was scrubbed, shoved, and pushed from one area to another. He was given over to another warder, who cut his hair off.

"Visitors may stand on the designated platform by the side of the hulk. Prisoners may be spoken to only in the presence of an officer," the guard said, clearly marking the lines whereby the men now being processed would be cut off almost entirely from the normal world.

Peter was given the prison garb that would mark him as something less than human and make him open to any brutality any guard wished to inflict upon him.

"Any articles of value or money given to a prisoner will be handed over to the chief mate. All letters written or received by a convict will be opened by the captain to be sent or not at his discretion," the guard droned on.

Peter was taken finally to a room from which he had been hearing the ominous sounds of hammered metal ever since he had come aboard. He knew it would happen, but knowing is nothing like having it done. Irons were placed on his legs held fast by rivets driven well. It would require a tool to take them off again, if indeed they would ever come off. The last rivet was like the closing of a door to Peter, blocking out the possibility of light ever coming through.

To avoid Hell, children are taught the "awful doctrine of man's depravity." Peter stood looking at the warder who had just fastened the leg irons on him. The man looked back and thought Peter arrogant. Another prisoner who would have to be taught the hard road to repentance. As they stood staring at one another, each thought he knew what was meant by the depravity of man. One man on wholesome ground thinking he looked in on depravity, and the other in Hell thinking he looked out on it. A child's lesson, learned by men and understood by none.

Callie and Stephen arrived at Newgate later in the morning and were told that Peter had been taken aboard the *Justitia*. They reached the hulk just in time to see him, part of a chain gang, being led up the quay amid jeering urchins, at his first day of hard labor. It was a routine he'd follow every one of the twenty-one days he'd be aboard the *Justitia*.

Stephen and Callie waited in London until Peter returned to the hulk and the officer aboard said Callie could mount the platform to speak to him.

Peter didn't want to see her, or rather he didn't want her to see him with his head shaved, his legs in irons, and in the prison garb. But he came and stood on deck as he was ordered. He had learned quickly that disobedience was punished quickly and severely. He did as he was told, but he didn't look at her. His eyes remained downcast.

"You're wasting your time with this one, miss," the officer said. "He'll not talk to you. He's a hard one." He gave Peter a shove. "Come on, if you'll not speak to her, get below."

Peter looked up then, the deep humiliation written on his face, but that was as it should be, the officer thought, satisfied. The first function of a prison ship and the penal colonies was humiliation. The criminal spirit had to be broken before a man could sincerely repent. For men to be saved they first had to recognize they were sinners, unfit to be thought of as men. Humiliation and the erasure of pride were primary, all-important steps to this recognition. Conversion would surely follow.

"Callie," was all he said, and she knew he wanted something of her so he could remember that someone would be there for him even when he couldn't see her and when it was hard to believe there would ever be anything better than what he lived through now. She took off the paisley scarf Mrs. Pettibone had given her. "May I give this to him?"

The officer nodded, shrugged, and took it from her. He turned it over in his hand, then gave it to Peter.

He buried his face in the scarf, then turned to go as
the guard tapped him on the arm.

"Peter . . ."

"Yes?"

"I'll wait."

He nodded.

"The May house, Peter. Remember it."

"The May house," he repeated and looked at the
brightly colored scarf in his hand.

Chapter 30

Callie and Stephen returned to Mrs. Pettibone's apartment. They couldn't face going back to Kent that night. Meg would be waiting for news, hoping it would be good news just once. Neither Callie nor Stephen wanted to remember the day or talk about it.

They kept their minds on other things. They had been in England long enough. It had been planned as a visit home, but it had been one long nightmare from which none of them seemed able to awaken.

When the morning dawned, nothing had changed but that they could no longer put off returning to Kent and to Meg.

The house was quiet with an unhealthy stillness over it. Natalie was slowly recuperating from her miscarriage. Physically she would be completely recovered soon, but the family no longer tried to hide from the fact that mentally Natalie was not normal in any sense. Her peculiarities grew deeper and more serious. It had begun when she cut herself off from Meg. There had been an argument over Jamie, when Nat-

alie insisted Jamie stay in her room. She had ordered
the nurse to move his crib and playthings to her bedroom.

When Meg had come upstairs, Jamie's crib was beside Natalie's bed. She had called the nurse and ordered her to take Jamie back to his nursery. "Why,
neither of you would get a decent night's rest, and you
need your rest if you're to get well, Natalie," Meg had
said, turning her attention to her angry daughter.

"I want him *here*—with me."

"In the morning, darling. He'll be brought to you
first thing."

"You're not going to keep me away from him. I
won't have it, Mother. I am not a child any longer.
I am a married woman with a child. I know what I
want and how to get it. Don't get in my way. Do you
understand? I won't stand for my baby being kept
from me."

"Yes, dear, you'll see Jamie; but the nursery is the
place for a child. You know that, Nattie. You planned
your own nursery—remember? Now, do lie back and
rest, dear. The sooner you do as the doctor asks, the
sooner you will be well again. Then you can take Jamie for nice long walks and play with him as much as
you like."

Natalie had done as she was asked that day, and
Meg had been much encouraged. She became a model
patient, and was soon on her feet again. From that
time on, however, it quickly became apparent that her
reliance on Meg was broken. She did as she wished
and what she wished was to spend every waking hour
with Jamie.

Callie first realized something was wrong with Natalie's sudden devotion to the child after one of her
trips to visit Peter.

"Oh, what do you have in the package?" Natalie asked as soon as she saw it lying on Callie's bed.

"It's a ball for Jamie. Peter asked that I get him something as a gift from his papa."

"May I have it?"

"No, Natalie. I told you, it's a gift from Peter to Jamie."

"But I want it! I need it!"

Callie took her hat off. She tried to straighten her hair and gave up. It had been a long, tiring day, and she was in no mood to listen to Natalie. "What would you need a ball for?" she said with a long sigh. "Stop being ridiculous, Natalie. It's a child's toy and meant for Jamie."

"Bertie wants it," she said angrily. "Give it to me, Callie."

Callie turned slowly from the mirror. "Who is Bertie?"

"You know perfectly well who Bertie is. Give me the ball!"

"Your child?"

"He wants the ball. Give it to me! I'll take it if you don't."

Callie put the ball behind her back. "Where is Bertie, Natalie? Can I see him?" she asked softly.

"He's in the nursery where all good children belong," she said gruffly, then brightened. "Would you really like to see him? He's the very image of Albert. I do wish Albert would hurry and come home. You know how fast babies grow. He's missing all the cute things Bertie is learning."

"That's too bad. Why don't you take me to Bertie now? I'd like to see him," Callie said, and prayed that it was a doll Natalie spoke of, or some imaginary being Natalie was calling Bertie.

"Oh, silly! You know him," Natalie said, taking her

to the doorway of Jamie's nursery. Jamie dropped the blocks Stephen had made for him and ran to Callie.

Callie stooped down to take him in her arms. "Do you know who I saw today, Jamie?"

"Papapapapapa!" He laughed and clapped in their usual ritual. Callie gave him the wrapped ball and put him on the floor to tear the colored papers that hid the treasure.

"Papa sent this to you."

"I wanted to give it to him," Natalie said, pouting.

"It was Peter's gift to *Jamie*, Natalie."

Natalie stared at her, then went to Jamie and kneeled down on the floor with him as she crooned about the pretty ball Papa had sent to Bertie.

Callie took Natalie by the arm and pulled her to her feet. "Get out of here! Stay away from him, and never let me hear you call him Bertie again!"

Natalie slapped her, trying to break Callie's hold on her arm.

"Natalie, I don't want to hurt you, but you're going to leave this room, or I am going to remove you from it," Callie warned, and began pulling her toward the door.

"I can go by myself!" Natalie hissed, pulling her arm free and walking from the room.

Callie went directly to Meg. "Do you realize she is trying to convince herself that Jamie is the child she lost?"

Meg had lost weight. She was tired and haggard. "I don't know what to do about it. She'll not listen to me. I've tried to talk to her. The last time she threw her hand mirror at me," Meg said and raised her sleeve to reveal an ugly bruise on her forearm.

"This can't continue. It's not good for Jamie, and certainly no good for Natalie."

Meg remained silent and defeated, slowly rubbing the bruised arm.

"Aunt Meg . . ."

"I don't know what to tell you, Callie. I know what you want me to say, but I can't. She's my child, no matter what she's done or what she is. I am too old and too tired," she said brokenly. "I don't know what to do."

Callie sat looking at Meg. She *was* old. Meg had never seemed to be any age before, always bustling about, keeping everything in order and smiling as she did. The last month had taken its toll of her and left her showing her years. She had abandoned her household chores to Anna and the housekeeper, something unheard of when James was alive. Anna and a hired cook reigned supreme in the pride of Meg's life, her kitchen.

Callie looked down at her hands on her lap, sorry she hadn't the good sense to realize all this before she had spoken. It was plain to see: Aunt Meg was no longer the Meg Berean Callie had once known. "I shouldn't have come to you with this. I'm sorry, Aunt Meg."

Meg sighed. "Oh, you should, Callie, and you should be able to trust me to remedy it, but I can't. I don't know how. I'm just not up to it anymore."

"Well, you're not to worry about it. You've been handling problems for this family for years. It's time some of the rest of us did our share. You're tired, and it isn't much of a problem anyway."

Callie had left Meg then, still disturbed, not knowing whom to turn to. She could say nothing to Stephen. He had as much to do and think about as he could manage trying to find enough work to keep her going to see Peter. All she could do was to give strict instructions to the nurse for Jamie's schedule, keeping

Natalie away from him part of the time. It annoyed Natalie and resulted in another scene between them.

"His name is Jamie, Natalie. I will not permit you to call him by any other name."

"Is that why you won't let me see him?"

"Yes, it is."

"He's mine. You can't keep me away. Albert is the magistrate. He'll have you put in prison," she said with steely determination.

Callie said slowly and precisely. "Jamie is Peter's child. Peter and Rosalind's. Not yours."

"Don't! Don't! Don't! Don't say her name! Don't, don't ever say her name!"

"She is his mother, Natalie."

"You're hateful! Horrible and hateful. Why do you torment me?" she cried.

"I don't. I have never wanted to hurt you. But you must stop pretending, Nattie. It is very bad for both you and Jamie. He doesn't even know his own name anymore, you've called him Bertie so often. Think of Peter. You don't want to take your brother's child from him, do you?"

"Peter was never kind to me. Why should I care about him? Anyway Peter is gone. Frank told me he is dead."

"Well, he isn't. That was a lie. Peter is alive and very unhappy. Jamie is important to him."

Natalie frowned. "Where is Peter?"

"In prison," Callie said shortly.

"In prison? Why? What did he do? Did Albert arrest him?"

"You don't know?"

"I think I did . . . I must have forgotten. What did he do?"

"He was accused of shooting Rosalind and Albert,"

Callie said and waited for whatever violent reaction that would bring from Natalie.

Natalie shook her head. "But that's not true. Peter wouldn't do it. He never listened to any of the things I told him. I told him they were all true, but he wouldn't listen to me." Her voice rose as she spoke.

"Who did do it, Natalie?" Callie asked, holding her breath.

Natalie put her hands to her head, pressing so hard her features were distorted. She choked, nearly strangling; but as Callie reached to help her, Natalie pulled away. Her body was rigid, yet she was trembling. Her voice was no more than a thin wail. "Peter did it! He killed them! I saw him. He went to the cottage, and he had Papa's pistols. He took one and aimed it and shot. I saw him! I saw him . . . and then he took the other pistol. Albert looked so surprised. He looked so funny . . . he was afraid. And then the other pistol shot . . . and . . ."

"Natalie!" Callie took her in her arms. Natalie was stiff and hard to her touch. "Natalie, it's all right. Calm down. Look! I'm here. Nothing is happening. Natalie!" Callie screamed. "Look at me!"

Slowly Natalie looked at her, her eyes still filled with horror.

"Peter is gone now, isn't he? You don't see him now. I'm here. Just me." Callie petted at her, turning her face so she could look at nothing but Callie.

"He can't come and get me, Callie?" Natalie said pathetically. "He'll be so angry. He'd never believe me. I couldn't make him do what I wanted him to. Oh, Callie, I want Albert and Bertie. Why was Albert with Rosalind? Why did he have to be there? I thought she'd be alone. He left late. I thought . . ." She began to sob. "Please, I want to see Bertie."

Callie had had her confrontation with Natalie just two days before she saw Peter for the last time. The evening they returned to Kent, Callie remained in the parlor until the others had gone to bed. Then she went to find Stephen, who never seemed to sleep these days. Together they walked back to the house from his mountain.

"We've done all we can for Peter, Stephen. He doesn't like us seeing him now," she said thoughtfully.

"I know. If there was just some way we could do something . . . if only we knew what had happened."

Callie thought for a moment about the horrified words that had poured from Natalie's mouth. She was certain she now understood what had happened that day, but nothing in what Natalie had said would help Peter. No one would understand. They would blame Peter again, never considering the twisted substitutions Natalie's sick mind could make. "There is nothing," she said aloud. "Not now anyway. All I know is that we shouldn't go back to the hulks again."

"Callie, I've been thinking . . ."

"About going home?" she asked hopefully.

"Yes."

"So have I," she said and then told him about Natalie's fixation on Jamie, and about Meg, omitting only that part about Rosalind and Albert's death.

"Why didn't you tell me before?"

"There was nothing you could do, and you have enough on your mind."

"You should have told me. I could have helped you."

"Well, I have now, and our leaving will take care of that. Jamie is young. He'll forget. How soon could we leave, Stephen?"

"Peter's ship sails in less than three weeks. I think we should wait until he is gone, even if we don't see him. I . . . oh, Callie, I don't know. Sometimes I think if we just keep going to London we can ward off the inevitable. But we can't, can we? There's a ship sailing for New York a week after Peter sails. It's American, so if Jack hasn't sent us the money, I can talk to the captain. We can sail on that ship."

Callie and Stephen talked to Meg the next morning and told her of their plans. Meg had spent most of the morning closed in her room. Boxes of papers and letters that James had written and received were strewn about. She hardly seemed to care about what Callie and Stephen had to say. She held one of James's ledgers on her lap.

"What are you doing with these, Ma? Checking up on the family fortunes?" Stephen asked, taking her hand in his.

"Remembering," she said.

"With a book of accounts?"

"James wrote them."

"Are you all right, Ma?"

"Oh, yes. I'm just fine. I was thinking about the house your papa wanted to buy in London. He has the expenditure he planned to make all worked out in this ledger. I wouldn't let him buy it. I didn't want to be in London. Do you think things would have been different if I had let him buy that house?"

"No, Ma, I don't. We were happy here for a long time. You did the right thing."

"We *were* happy, weren't we?"

"Yes," Stephen said in a barely audible voice.

Callie slipped out of the room and went to her own.

Meg didn't come to supper that night, and Natalie ate in the nursery with Jamie. Stephen told Anna and Frank of their plans to leave.

"We have a good ship going back. We should be there by the end of harvest. The only thing I am wor-

ried about is Ma. She doesn't seem very good to me. I
don't like to leave her like this."

"Well, you needn't worry about her. You just run
along home. I've always taken care of Ma, and I'll
continue," Frank said gruffly.

"Don't be so quick to speak, Frank. It isn't just
Mother Berean," Anna said. "It is Natalie as well,
Frank. I can do nothing with her, and Mother Berean
will no longer try. Natalie wanders around the house
at all hours. She nearly caused a fire the other night
. . . when you were in London, Callie. She came
down sometime during the night and lit lamps
throughout the house. One she left too near her nee-
dlework. It was all singed and browned when I found
it. I don't mean to be cruel, but I think the loss of
Albert and her child coming so close together has
completely unbalanced her. The doctor says that this
sometimes happens after a woman loses a child, and
that she may get better. But he has not heard her talking to herself as I have, and today Callie told me she
has taken to calling Jamie 'Bertie.' It is frightening . . .
the hateful things she says."

"Then we'll have her put away," Frank said.

"You can't do that. It would kill Ma," Stephen said.

"It's not your problem. It's mine."

"She's Stephen's sister as well as yours, Frank," Callie said.

"She may be, but I don't see him doing anything
but giving advice. As long as I have to provide for
Natalie, I'll decide what must be done for the good of
all."

"You're not providing for Natalie. Papa did that for
her as he did all of us," Stephen said.

"That went when she married Albert. You don't
suppose she went to him empty-handed. We'd have
never married her off without a dowry. And if you're

thinking she'll get something from Albert's estate, think again. Not only did Albert have virtually nothing in his own name, Mrs. Foxe and her brother are trying to get that marriage annulled because Mrs. Foxe claims Nat was not sane when she married Albert," Frank said.

"That's nonsense. Albert knew Natalie for years. They grew up together." Stephen looked angrily at Frank. "If he thought something was wrong with her why did he marry her?"

Frank shrugged. "He's not here to say, is he? But Mrs. Foxe is, and she has plenty to say to whoever will listen."

"Including you," Stephen snapped.

"Yes, including me. I have to live here and don't you forget it. Her brother is one of the most important men in the parish. I've got no place to run off to as you have. The two of you may feel you are doing a fine piece of charity by parading into London and making spectacles of yourselves, but you won't be here to face the talk and the resentment stirred up against the Berean name. I've got a convicted murderer for a brother and a loony for a sister. They are calling Callie Peter's whore; and you, Stephen, do you know what they call you?"

"That's enough, Frank!"

"Enough! It's nowhere near enough! How much abuse do you think a man can take? What do you think that does to my name and business? How do you think I feel?"

"Who in the hell cares! You don't begin to know the meaning of abuse, Frank. And I'm wondering how much and who you are willing to sacrifice for your name and business."

"Nothing worth anything, I'll guarantee you, Stephen."

"First it was Peter, and now it is Natalie, but you say nothing worth anything. What about Ma, Frank? Will she go too, after she's worth nothing?"

"While we're hurling abuse, little brother, what are you willing to do? You're so damned almighty high and noble, what is it you're willing to take on your back?"

"I've already got Peter and Jamie."

Frank snorted. "Peter!? And a baby. What you've got is a lot of mouth." Frank threw his napkin down in disgust and left the dining room.

Stephen got up and walked out of the house.

Anna looked down at the table. "Maybe you should go after him, Callie."

"Not now. Let me help you clear the table. He'll come back when he's ready."

"Don't judge Frank too harshly. It is I who don't want Natalie here any longer. She never did pay much attention to what I said, but I can do nothing with her now that Mother Berean doesn't help. I am afraid of Natalie in truth, and I think she knows it and takes deliberate advantage."

They cleared the table, and Callie waited up in the parlor long after Anna and Frank had gone to bed.

Stephen paced across the stable yard, his mind a blinding storm of conflicting thoughts and feelings. He was shaking with anger at Frank, and yet the problems that faced him were far too important to allow him to vent that anger by lashing out at his brother. He thought of Peter and the life term he would serve for something his sister had done. And he thought of Natalie and wondered how far back her derangement went. Why hadn't they seen it? Had they all refused to see what was before their eyes, or had it been well-hidden in her strange but enticing personality. Even if they had seen what was happening to her, what could they have done? There were no medicines to help her. They could have kept her locked in the attic as other families did. They could have committed her to Bedlam and let her be chained to a wall to live like a savage, to become hopelessly insane. What was he to do now? He had no answers, no cures, no solutions that he had not already considered with horror.

His anger grew and with it the pain of what was happening to his family. As he thought of each of them, with his hate and his frustration shouted at the cold, impassive moon, one certainty came to rest equally cold and impassive: He would not let Natalie be put away, or left to Frank's charity. Frank didn't care. Stephen wondered now if Frank had ever cared about anyone other than himself and his good name.

For another hour Stephen fought with himself, seeking a way to take care of Natalie without having to chain his life to hers as he had already to Peter's. The cold certainty that he would not leave her here stirred. He did not feel impassive on the surface; there he boiled, his hatred for Natalie something he could almost touch. There were times he avoided her, thinking that if he were left in the same room with her he'd put his hands around her slender neck and choke from her an admission of guilt. But beyond those hot, seething emotions, far below the surface, Stephen loved her. She lived in torment. He had only to look at her to know. The hell she lived in was a part of his own. She was his sister.

When Stephen walked into the house, he saw the light of Callie's rush lamp and strode defiantly into the parlor. "We're taking Natalie back with us," he said quickly and harshly, his mouth set, his eyes cold.

"I know. It would have been that or never return at all."

"I won't let them lock her up and forget her someplace. Ma could never stand that, not after Peter."

"I understand that, Stephen."

"My mind is made up," Stephen said, ready to argue. Callie sighed and smiled. "You don't mind?"

"Ahh, you silly," she said, smiling and walking into his arms. "Whatever you decide is always best. That's one thing I know of you, Stephen, and I hope I never forget it. I only worry about Jamie, but that will come right too."

He laughed in relief, hugging her. "Callie, Callie, what would I do without you?"

They walked together to the sofa and sat down next to each other, Callie's hand in Stephen's. He stretched out, resting his head against the sofa back, his mind returning to its tortured thinking. All the old doubts flooded back and new ones were added to them. What was he doing to Callie? It was she who would care for Natalie. It was Callie who would bear the burden of the house and the child and his sister and his brother . . . and him too. He sat up suddenly, ripping his hand away from hers. He buried his face in his hands. "Ohh, my God, I don't know . . . I don't know what's right anymore."

Callie's voice was soft and coolly soothing. Stephen drank it in, letting its sound flow over him. She spoke of so many of his own doubts, but as they came through Callie's pure and trusting view, he began to see them differently. The life he and Callie faced was no easier, but it once more seemed good. As long as she was there, he'd live through anything.

Callie began the packing. She sorted through all of Rosalind's clothes, leaving most of them for Anna to alter for herself. The petticoats and few practical garments she packed to take with her. Peter's clothes she folded and packed with care. All of them would be taken to Poughkeepsie for that sometime day when he would return.

Stephen received the bank draft from Jack and purchased the passage tickets, and all that was left was the waiting to leave. During that last week, the nights came alive with the sounds of music and revelry as the hop pickers came back to Kent. The campfires glowed against the midnight blue sky and Callie thought of the gypsy woman and wondered if she'd be there in her camp as she had been that night long ago.

The old woman had told her to come back when she returned to England, that she would need her then. But the old gypsy had been too late. What Callie needed now was not to be found in a gypsy camp, or in the deck of tarot cards. She would not go to see the gypsy again, then or ever.

But the sounds of the eerie music and the campfires glowing brought back visions of an old woman staring at her cards as she recited words from the Apocalypse telling of the bitter wormwood that would touch Callie's life.

They set sail for New York on a bright September day. It would still be warm when they returned home. The Hudson valley would be a blaze of autumnal color when they saw it next. Once they had stepped foot on the frigate, Callie's feeling of strength returned to her. They were leaving behind all the bitterness and sorrow she had ever known. With their return home would come hope.

BOOK III

Chapter 31

Moving like an oily stream of filth from the hulks, an irregular line of men, each chained to the man in front of him, was led by guards to a day of hard labor. Some days, as if to taunt them with that which they no longer possessed, the sun shone bright and symbolic of the gift of the earth which God had given so freely to men. Along the roads were the people of London, some going about their business, so inured to misery, the convicts stirring nothing in their hearts, neither pity nor contempt. For others it was a sight to provide some mean entertainment in a life filled with few pleasures.

Peter soon learned the women were the worst of all the roadside taunters. Idle women, who worked by night and drank away their suffering by day, paraded near the lines of chained men, laughing in their hoarse, abused voices. Some had come to see their men, slipping up to the line to thrust a gin bottle into a quickly opened mouth. Others had come to blame them for having been caught at whatever felony or misdemeanor had caused them to end in this rotting line of humanity. Others pranced and yelled their taunts for the sport of it.

For the most part the guards ignored them, wanting no part of the consequences that might come of trying to quell them. There were few men, even of the worst sort, who were bolder or less fearing of attacking an offending guard than these women. Little better than rabid animals, the lowly women who followed the chain gangs had been known to down a full-grown man, strip the clothing from his back along with his flesh when he dared interfere with them.

In the evening when they returned to the hulks, the same scene was repeated; only by nightfall the women were far gone with drink, and feeling meaner. Some of the faces grew familiar to Peter. He looked for them, knowing at what dirty corner or from what mouldering doorway they would appear.

For most of the convicts, the morning and evening circus performed for them by the women was welcome. They were, in truth, their compatriots, and the women's shameful behavior was understood and accepted as a part of the "good" life they had left behind. The convicts were, in the main, small men, most not over five feet four, who had been raised in hunger and squalor. They were men who had breathed the fetid gin-soaked air of the back streets of St. Giles and Clerkenwell and Wapping since they had first drawn breath. They had grown up learning the age-old professions of their forebears, training as pickpockets, footpads, robbers, and thieves. Their women all seemed to have the same names; Doll and Peg and Mag with only an attending adjective to distinguish them from each other. Some were known by Polecat, some by Tantrum, some by Hell. There were Bloody Lizzies and Doll Tantrums, and Hellcat Maggies and Sadie the Goats. These were their women, their larcenous, calloused, and understanding women, who knew what it was to live as they did, and who had the bloody courage to say "Be damned!" to the guards. They thrust their gin bottles into the guards' faces, lifted their dirty petticoats in obscene defiance, laughed their bawdy laughter, sang their bawdy songs.

During the first days aboard the hulks, Peter had been horrified by these women and their men, and more than a little afraid of their raw, unfettered viciousness. He had never seen people like this, not so many and not so close at hand. He had heard of them. He knew, as all gentlemen knew, that the streets of London were not safe because of people like these; but now, living among them, seeing them both in prison and clustered in groups along the way to the stone barges, it was different. He thought, rather bewildered, of the people in Kent he had tried to help. Were they like these people? Had he been among them, spoken to them of justice, freedom, hope, and not known their true nature? No, he knew the Kent workers had not been as were these Londoners. They had not, for all their poverty, been crowded like so many dead herrings into tenements not suited to hold half their number. They had not been raised in the atmosphere and the expectancy of crime that these men and women had been. Poverty and injustice and hate had fallen unexpectedly on the rich Kent countryside, the fault of innumerable unforeseen events. These city people had had violence and cruelty bred into their bones. It was like a permanent barrier they no longer had the stature to see over or beyond.

With some admiration Peter thought of Ian Dawson, who had had the fortitude and the audacity to challenge the morass of poverty that afflicted these people. It was almost incomprehensible to Peter that a man would dare to try to undo what centuries had done. Yet Ian had. Callie had told him often of her father and the kind of man he was. Peter wished he had known Ian, for he had possessed a strength that Peter knew he didn't possess. It was a strength that Peter couldn't even understand, and he staggered beneath the weight of his need for it. He was afraid, and faced a lightless future with a trembling soul and a heart that knew hope only by the scrap of colored cloth a young girl had given him.

Peter was held on the convict hulks for twenty-one days. Most of the time he stayed with the prisoners who were more like himself, men of some education, men able to talk of principles and philosophies. But the talk of such things served only to emphasize the callous injustice of the convicts' treatment. And while he said nothing aloud, inside of Peter welled up the cry, "I don't belong here! I'm innocent! I did nothing!" making him feel reckless and hopeless and driven. Then Peter would listen to the other convicts, hearing their constant chatter, allowing their chronicles of age-old injustice to become a part of the bitterness he felt.

After twenty-one days aboard the *Justitia* Peter came to look upon the men who guarded him as a different breed, separate from him, his enemy. It seemed ridiculous and humiliating to him that he had once been naive enough to believe the guards and officers would accept him, even like him for who he was. He had been a friendly man, a man willing to work, and if he hadn't willingly resigned himself to the necessity of serving a term for a crime he hadn't committed, he was at least resigned to the fact that he couldn't change it.

He had quickly learned that none of this made the slightest impression on the guards. Innocence or guilt meant nothing to them. The quality of one prisoner or another meant even less. They had a mass of resentful humanity to control, and control it they did. With few exceptions the soldiers and guards detailed to the hulks were as miserable and of as beggarly a disposition as were the convicts. Most of them were men unfit for finer duty, sentenced much as the convicts were to a wretched life, blighted by the pestilence of hopelessness and frustration. Their pride and sense of accomplishment came not from their position, but from the degree of difference they could create between their wretched lot and the far greater misery they inflicted on the prisoners. They were men only because the humans they guarded were reduced to depraved beasts.

From the beginning the credo of degradation was forced on Peter by the guards and the soldiers and the people in the streets. He was a convict and convicts were to be despised. Mentally he chafed at this. He thought about it and dredged up all the history he knew, thought of Plato and Aristotle and Socrates and knew that the bitter, godless hate that was thrust on him was wrong.

But reason has no voice to penetrate the deaf ear of despair. From the outset, had he but seen it, Peter had had to choose to live in the solitary isolation of his own memory, or join with the other prisoners as enemies of society. He joined with the others, hesitantly at first, then with greater relish as they made life more difficult for the guards, stealing biscuits, rations, handkerchiefs, taking gin from the women, any small infraction possible. Playing the clown, falling and holding up a chain gang, often worked well to annoy, providing the warder wasn't one too free with the use of his whip or stick.

These were the childish ways of tormenting the tormentors that made no sense, yet somehow eased the despair by giving the illusion of protest. Peter learned them all and allowed himself to be dragged down into the confused morass of tortured humanity who danced devillike around him, their mouths stretched taut in smiles revealing their rotting teeth, their faces pocked with disease, their minds bent and twisted by a life of degradation. His one hold on life as it had been was the scarf that Callie had given him and the memories he conjured into visions during the night, when the demon world was asleep and unable to plague him.

On September 3, 1832, one week before Callie and Stephen were due to sail for America, Peter Berean was taken in chains aboard the *George III*, the transport ship that would carry the convicts to Van Diemen's Land, or Tasmania as it was sometimes called.

The sun lighted the September sky as the ship moved slowly down the Thames, but there was no accompanying lightening of Peter's spirit. Only months before he had believed, as did most Englishmen, that transportation was an easy sentence. All Englishmen knew of the horrors of Newgate, Fleet Street Prison, and others, and no one who had been to London could doubt the wretchedness of life aboard the hulks; but of transportation little was known.

Convicts were sent to new unsettled lands. Once it had been America, until England had lost this fertile dumping ground, and then it was Australia, and now it was Van Diemen's Land. To most it seemed a fair chance for a man to redeem himself by helping to settle an unsettled land, an opportunity to extend the might and glory of England. The worst aspect of transportation appeared to be that of exile, the terrible pain of being deprived of life in Mother England, the fairest land on earth. Now, boarding the *George III*, Peter no longer knew.

He was embarking on a voyage into the unknown aboard a ship the convicts had told him was called a "floating hell." His name was already in the logbook as a known troublemaker from the hulks. Whatever inconvenience he had caused his captors, he was certain they would repay him tenfold. He found it hard to see hope in anything that might come from Van Diemen's Land, for Peter now knew the quality of all imprisonment depended on those who administered it. Each step of his confinement had been an experience worse than the one preceding it. He no longer knew what the word *lenient* meant, though he heard it often enough when he was given rations of brackish water and hard bread instead of lashes. To him this life was a descent into the Pit, a consummation of spirit whose pain grew greater and more unbearable with every agonized kindness. He never dreamed that kindness could be a cruelty, but now he knew better. It hurt far more than the lashes when its touch meant only the memory of what had been and would never again be.

Many times he would look at Callie's scarf, hating it as though it had been his betrayer. At least once each day he'd want to tear the scarf to shreds, drop it over the side of the ship, and watch it sink far below the water, drowning it, and with it his aching hope. But he never could.

For all its betrayal, with each succeeding day the scarf remained a symbol of promise for the next. He couldn't stop the craving he had for one more bright, free day. He kept Callie's scarf, hating it by day and putting his faith in the strength it symbolized by night.

The *George III* carried one hundred and eighty men and boys to transportation in Van Diemen's Land this voyage. The boys from eight years upward in age would be taken to Point Puer if they survived the trip. The men would be landed at Hobart Town to be sent from there to a variety of penal colonies on the island, depending on the seriousness of their crime and whether they were classified as good-conduct men or incorrigibles.

The *George III*, specially rigged for her human cargo, still bore the rank, acrid odors of the convicts who had gone before. The first special structure that Peter saw when he boarded was a cattle pen. It was a strong wooden barricade at the foot of the foremast and at the quarterdeck, extending from bulwark to bulwark.

Though that first morning he had not even liked looking at the cattle pen, Peter shortly learned to look upon it as an El Dorado, a place of golden, blessed light. For two hours a day the prisoners, under armed guard, were led to the exercise pen. Two hours in which to see the sky, in which to breathe. Two hours in which to relieve themselves of the claustrophobic oppression of the prisoner's quarters.

Even the most hardened felons dreaded the return to the prisoners' quarters. No man likes facing death, and it was death the prisoners faced 'tween decks. The barricade walls of the cattle pen extended down the main hatchway forming the side walls of the ship's prison on the 'tween decks.

The convicts were prodded along the passageway down into the room where they lived for twenty-two hours every day. Each man was counted and identified as he entered the prison. The men bumped into each other, tempers flared, curses muttered by some were shouted by others. The stench of urine, refuse, and disease was imbedded in the walls, thick in the poor air. Peter's stomach rolled; hot bile burning in his throat threatened to spill from his mouth. His head reeled as he tried to hold his breath and adjust to the pitch of the ship and the overpowering odors. That first day he had looked dazedly over the shoulders of the other convicts, pushing at one another as they moved to their bunks.

The prison was a fifty-foot cage. In it were pressed one hundred and eighty men and boys. Peter and some of the other men were stooped, their necks bent as the height of the cage was only five feet ten inches, four inches too low to accommodate Peter's height. The only ventilation came through the loop holes, and where the planks of oak didn't fit tightly. Otherwise it was little better than being sealed in a communal coffin. What light there was came from two candle stubs hanging from the roof. The candles smoked and guttered, barely able to remain lit in the airless hole. Some of the younger children whimpered and cried. Men swore and fought each other as panic joined the medley of convict emotions. Twenty-two hours a day trapped and guarded in this airless pen was more than most could comprehend. Hunger seemed nothing, thirst but a minor discomfort; it was air they wanted, air to fill lungs that barely moved, air to cleanse the room of the damp moistness of the coughing sick.

Peter climbed into his bunk and lay on his side, his head and feet hanging over the edge. His face was but inches away from the man in front of him, and he could feel the hot, panting breath of the man in the bunk behind him. The prison berths were five feet three inches long, and the space allotted to each man was sixteen inches. Six men were assigned to each berth to sleep in triple-tiered bunks. Peter and his bunkmates lay on the hard surfaces as long as they could; then as one they moved to take their turn pacing about the narrow confines of the room. As they got up from their bunks other men were asked, then threatened into their bunks. It was the only way to make enough space on the open floor for any of them to move around.

As Peter, hunched over, walked back and forth along the space between the bunks, he looked at the miserable, crowded prison. In the walls were ports, tightly shut now, but easily opened from the outside should there be a riot or mutiny among the prisoners. From that vantage the guards could have an excellent record of marksmanship. A gun fired into this crowded room could hardly miss. Irritated, he doubled his fist and slammed it into one of the ports. Almost immediately it was opened to show the face of a smooth-cheeked sentinel. Peter laughed bitterly, making an obscene gesture with his finger; then he walked on, hunching down the row of bunks. Some of the convicts played cards with a deck that better resembled a collection of limp rags. With sly glintings in their eyes, the men gambled away what small possessions they had. One had a small wad of tobacco, another had a few shillings, one wagered his shirt— "almost new," he said, "brought by my ma at the parting." One man clutched a bottle of gin, which he was sharing with no one. And though there were other men in tremors and desperate enough to risk nearly anything for a sip of gin, he was left alone for he was under the protection of the seaman who had given it to him. Peter shot a look of revulsion at the man, who for services rendered to his seaman would enjoy a far better voyage than would the rest of them.

Soon another man scrambled over the body of his mate to reach the prison floor. He tapped Peter on the shoulder, asking with his eyes for Peter to return to his hard bunk. Peter didn't move; then from the sides of the room several men began to get up, each pushing at the others. The floor would be held by the

meanest, the strongest, the men most willing to fight.
Peter glanced at the group who had emerged from
their foul bunks together. Their faces were lit with vicious smiles. In less than a minute the first convict
fight would occur aboard the *George III*.

As the sixteen-thousand-mile voyage continued, tempers grew shorter, nerves were constantly on edge,
fights common, and lethargy more frequent. Men lay
for hours, their heads hanging out of the narrow, short
bunks, staring at nothing. Eyes glazed, skin pasty-
white and sickly, faces expressionless, they thought of
the great nothingness surrounding them.

Men maliciously began to think of the inevitable.
Seasickness. Fever. Scurvy. Death. A bunk with one
less man in it. Clothes the dead man wouldn't need.
Food the dead man wouldn't eat—if his body could be
kept hidden for a time.

The two-hour exercise period in the cattle pen became something Peter lived for. For that short time he
could forget where he was, and see in the clouds
above the configurations that he could turn into the
sights of days he could remember in Kent when he
was very young and burning to see the world. In the
subtle fusion of sea and sky there was a doorway to
the good things that had touched his life: Callie and
her clear-eyed belief in him that never seemed to fal-
ter; Stephen, whom he had teased about his seriousness, and who had stayed with him each step of the
way making their victories all the greater and their
defeats small.

He stayed to himself in the cattle pen, resenting any
intrusion on his reverie. It was the single bright moment in his day, and perhaps the time he inflicted the
worst of mental tortures on himself. By contrast to his
memories, the guards' treatment was all the more
hateful. His memories opened him time and again to

reach out for personal communication and understanding. Each time it was forced on him by the guards that he was despicable, unworthy of being considered a man as decent men were. It was not long before he too questioned the worth of himself. To think of touching Callie as an outcast, as the brute he was fast becoming, depraved and deserving of loathing, was hard. He soon became unable to think of himself with her without feeling ashamed. He saw himself clearly as a man reeking with his own filth, unwashed, smelling of his own dried sweat, condemned, unwanted, and he saw Callie with her creamy white skin, her cheeks touched by healthy rose, her skin clean and smelling of sunshine and herbs. It had become nearly impossible for him to see himself as he had once been; always the vision of the convict, the despised, filthy convict, intruded and made his fantasies revolting, humiliating nightmares.

Self-degradation was only one of the mental tolls each convict would pay in his own time. Physically, the worst toll of the ship would be taken by men contracting both typhus and typhoid due to unhealthy conditions, bad water, and little food. The best insurance they had of arriving in Van Diemen's Land alive was the one-half guinea the ship's surgeon was paid for every man delivered alive at Hobart Town.

Peter seldom gave thought to Van Diemen's Land. He heard the other convicts talking and speculating about their destination. Some optimistically told tales of men they had known who had been transported to Australia in earlier years. It didn't sound so bad, and Sydney was a thriving settlement now. Perhaps the same could be hoped for Van Diemen's Land. To Peter it seemed something beyond his reckoning. He couldn't think of a new, unsettled land without his imagination soaring and his mind groping for ways to clear and plant the soil. And yet he could see none of this as remotely possible while standing in the cattle pen, no better than a prize steer exhibited for the curious civilian passengers carried aboard the *George III*.

From the corner of his eye, Peter often watched the passengers as they sat comfortably on deck shaded from the hot sun by a canvas raised for their benefit. Occasionally, attended by the amused smiles of his fellows, one of the passengers would make his way to the cattle pen, laced kerchief daintily held to his prim nose, to make conversation with one of the convicts. It provided entertainment for the spoiled, bored Englishmen on their way to settle in Van Diemen's Land. Oftentimes the man bold enough to talk to the convict beasts was considered daring and brave by the prettily gowned and perfumed ladies in the party.

Peter stayed as far from their reach as he was able. Men who would once have taken their hats off to him and been flattered had he spoken to them waited now in affected impatient boredom as he touched his forelock in deference to them. Peter couldn't count the number of times he had felt the quick surge of anger make his face red with blood before humiliation swept it away as he tugged his forelock, his eyes sliding away shamefully from the well-dressed tormentor. How often he had wanted to smash his fist into those supercilious faces, only to glance aside and see the sentry with his ever present gun butt there, poised and ready to see that the convicts gave signs of respect to free citizens with alacrity and humility. The voyage had barely begun before Peter was deemed hostile and sullen to his betters.

Once England's shore had vanished and Land's End was but a smudge indistinguishable on the seascape, the voyage was truly underway. The sailors played cards, fished, talked, and sang together. The sounds wafted down to the prisoners crammed 'tween decks, who answered with their own bawdy songs.

Tiny sparrow-sized petrels followed the wake of the *George III* feasting on crumbs and leavings from the galley. There wasn't a seaman aboard who didn't watch for the presence of the petrels. As long as they were about, the superstitious crew were happy and confident. The ship petrels followed was a ship with good wind to fill her sails. Legend had it that the birds, each representing the soul of a mariner, were under the protection of the Virgin Mary.

In October they were hit by their first storm. The *George III* wallowed in the heavy seas, her timbers creaking so loudly the trapped prisoners feared each heave of the ship was the last they were to know. The candles were put out and the prisoners huddled, clinging to their bunks so as not to be tossed upon each other. The sounds of raging winds and the harsh crash of the green water sea on the *George III*'s hull were magnified in the prison chamber. Mingled with the horrifying sounds of rampaging nature were the belly-twisting moans of men sick, sick with the rolling sea and sick with the fetid air and the poor grade of salt pork and water they subsisted on. The horrible odors emanating from the prison engulfed the ship. Alarmed and fearful of losing his half guineas, the ship's surgeon ordered the convicts taken to the cattle pen more frequently. Carefully counting as the ragged beasts were led from the prison barricade, the surgeon toted the guineas he'd receive from those still living at the end of the voyage.

The reason he was sent on deck did not matter to Peter. He threw his head back, his eyes and mouth open to the tumultuous sky, breathing as deeply and fully as he could. Then the sea itself caught his eye, and he stared in awe-filled fascination. The ocean was alight with phosphorescent patches glowing eerily in evidence of nature's mysterious powers.

Though the sight of the ocean entranced Peter, this was one of the most dangerous parts of the voyage. Squalls were frequent and often followed by dead calms. In a powerless ship, sitting on an endless expanse with the pitch softening in the hull seams, and the ship creaking as though she must break apart at any moment, the crew's watch for the tiny wind-bearing petrels was conducted in earnest.

By the end of October, the heat and the stench preyed heavily on the tempers of the men cooped up in prison. Peter was in his hunched position, pacing the small room. His hands were across his stomach in an effort to alleviate the nauseating cramping that afflicted them all. He seemed better when he moved about. Taller than the cage, and not feeling well to start, he was tense and angry with frustration.

Jemmy Ripley, a wizened, mean little man transported for life for thievery, and for practicing a poor hand of forgery, had a quill he had sharpened to a needle-fine point. For the mean sport that boredom gives birth to, he jabbed the quill into Peter's ribs at each passing. With the fifth passage and unheeded warning, Peter grabbed the man by his ragged shirt-front, propelling him from his bunk. He shook the man furiously like a squalling pup, then took the quill, scratching Jemmy with it until he had raised bloody welts on the man's face and arms. He let the man go, dropping him to the planking in a screaming heap. Peter took the quill and returned to his bunk. Jemmy lay on the floor, a stream of sobbing curses coming from his thin lips. Peter shoved the quill into one of the cracks of the oak planks and closed his eyes and ears against the sight and sound of the wretched man.

Once Peter was safely tucked away and out of arm's

reach, Jemmy ran to the cage loop shouting and moaning for the sentry.

The sentry peeked into the cage to see what the commotion was. He had orders from the surgeon to take any man from the prison if he seemed too weak or ill, but it was difficult to tell which of the sly creatures was truly ill and which was feigning to get himself an easy stay in the ship's hospital. At first the sentry thought the babbling little man was just another malingerer.

"Thievery! There's been a thievery in here!" Jemmy cried.

The sentry gave him a baleful look and began to close the port. Jemmy let out a howl of pure agony. "Owww, sir! The bloody bastard has done me harm. Me arm. Don't think I can move it, sir. Help! He attacked me. Can't breathe, sir!"

The sentry turned away, but the port remained open. He stood immobile and silent outside the prison until a commissioned officer granted him permission to speak to the convict.

The wizened little Jemmy, his eyes sly and hateful, waited patiently, moaning pathetically on occasion to keep the sentry's attention. He knew his game; it was a brutal one the prisoners often played against one another. Finally the sentry received permission to speak to the convict, and the story he heard was a fantastic exaggeration of the truth. Without question the sentry accepted Jemmy's version of the brutish attack by the prisoner Berean, and the subsequent theft of the precious quill—Jemmy's only possession, a gift from his dear ailing father, no doubt the last gift he'd ever receive for the old man was not long for this earth.

Jemmy's friends laughingly confirmed his tale. Peter refused to speak. The quill was found where Jemmy said Peter had hidden it.

The sentry took the quill from the planking, then looked critically at the comparative size of Peter and Jemmy, who was hunched up to make himself look near to a dwarf. The sentry knew, as did all the soldiers and guards, that Peter was marked as a bad conduct man from the hulks. He had also been involved in several mass fights aboard ship, and had once struck at a sentry through a closed port.

The offense was considered serious, more so because of the man involved. Word was passed to the proper authorities. Both the ship's master and the surgeon agreed that Peter had committed a punishable crime that should be noted on his record. They also acknowledged, privately and to themselves, that he had committed it at the most propitious time. Due to the poor wind conditions and the tense atmosphere mutiny was a thing to be feared by the ship's master. It was time the crew, the convicts, and even the passengers were diverted from their fearful imaginings of being stuck forever upon a vast sea. It was particularly important that the convicts should see what could come to them should they be inclined to turn their brutish minds to riot or pirating of the ship.

On the advice of the ship's surgeon and the ship's mate—all that was required to have a man flogged—the punishment of Peter Berean was ordered.

All the convicts knew what was afoot long before it happened. The close-packed prison hummed with speculation as to what would be done with Peter. On deck during the exercise period men gathered in clusters, more animated than at any other time since they had boarded ship. Small wagers of tobacco and treasure they had managed to secure were placed. Others made tentative plans. Should the Berean man get off free for his offense, perhaps the captain was a man from whom privilege could be extracted. Some made so bold as to suggest that he might be a man from whom a ship could be wrested. Ahead of them lay South America, a vast land in which to disappear provided one could land there.

Four mornings after the incident, Peter was called from the prison and held in the ship's hospital as the other convicts were herded out on deck. His arms secured behind him, he stood waiting between two armed sentries. No one had told him what was going to be done to him, but from the talk in the prison he knew it could be anything from hanging to flogging. There were moments when he hoped it would be hanging. It would be over then. No more endless days. No more hoping for what could never be again. No more humiliation. No more fear.

Then, as if to mock himself, he began to shiver. Neither his pride nor his willpower could stem the quaking that shook him. He didn't want to die. He was young and strong and he loved life. It wasn't fair and it wasn't right that it should all be taken from him. He wanted to live with such a hunger that it shivered inside of him and made him cry at night for just one more day.

At a signal from the deck, the guards took his arms. Peter was surprised to find that they were dragging him. His body was no longer his own. He pulled back against the pressure of the guards, his mind telling him there was no point in fighting it; and yet his body fought on its own, detaching itself from good sense, recoiling from whatever abuse would soon befall it.

Peter was stood near the main mast facing the gathered assembly: the crew, the passengers, and the convicts. Above him the tropic sun blazed. The deck shimmered, and the faces he saw in the crowd glistened and swam before him. He heard the voice of the captain reading the accusation and the punishment, and yet he didn't hear. It was all a buzz, loud and melting with the sensual impressions of the coarse rope around his wrists, and the hot fiery sun and the rocking motion of the deck beneath his feet.

One of the crewmen detached himself from the others. In his hand he held the cat-o'-nine-tails used for such punishments. He said something, and the sentries moved. One untied Peter's wrists and placed some new kind of attachment on them. Peter looked from one gawking face to another. Convicts he had known looked back at him, sympathy in their eyes. Others had smirks on their faces, pleased. Lacy kerchiefs daintily covered the noses and mouths of some of the gentlemen settlers. Women tittered, watching from the corners of their eyes, but watching nonetheless with an eagerness that was feral and primitive.

The other sentry walked around Peter, placed his hand on his shoulder indicating Peter should face the mast. Peter stood dumbly, staring at the sentry; then all of it came rushing together in one great, blinding rage—Rosalind's death, Natalie, the trial, Newgate, the hulks, the prison ship. In a quick reasonless flash he saw the similarity to the bear baitings at county fairs, the dancing, shouting revelers at the Tyburn Tree while men hanged, the greedy crowds who fought over the hanged man's clothes and bought pieces of the rope with which he was hanged. He jerked his arms tight against himself, breaking the guard's hold. He knew he was shouting, but he didn't know what words he said. He screamed at them, his anger ferocious and righteous although all but unintelligible.

The sentries were joined by several soldiers. They surrounded the single man in the middle, squared off by the main mast shouting that he was a man, made by God, not to be put on exhibition like a crazed animal. Yet to all he looked like a crazed animal. His eyes were wild; his pale flaxen hair swirled like a battle flag around his head as he leapt and dodged, his fists swinging at any who came near him. His dark eyes were animal eyes, trapped and vicious, wanting to kill his pursuers.

The guards milled about, under orders not to shoot him, yet not knowing quite how to seize the flailing, angered man. Much as Peter did, they darted in and out, trying to grab hold of the ropes that flew wildly from his arms, and missing as he kicked them, or swung a huge fist with all the force of his body.

The passengers of the *George III* were vastly amused. They hadn't expected such a grand entertainment. The ladies squealed in prettily designed yelps of fear. The men puffed up their lace-bedecked chests ready to defend their women. The convicts whooped and hollered, some with encouragement, some with abuse at the ineffectual military, some at the world in general.

Finally it was a seaman who solved the problem. Quietly and with little ado he and the second mate took an old fishing net and slung it over Peter. Quickly other men grabbed the ends of the net and wound it around him. Peter was bound like a great fighting fish beached and struggling on the deck.

With a great deal more care this time, the guards held him hand and foot. They moved him back to the main mast. He was hauled to his feet, his arms stretched until he was standing on tiptoe; then he was secured to the mast. His feet were spread wide and fastened. Behind him he heard the whoops and cat-calls of the convicts all but drowning out the bravos and polite clapping of the passengers.

And then there was quiet. Into the stillness came the captain's voice. Twenty lashes would be added to the twenty he had already prescribed for the theft of

see the Hudson River. Then one day it was gone, no more substantial than a soap bubble flying up from Callie's washboard to die in the air. What had he done to deserve such punishment? He had never intended to be an evil man. He didn't think he had been, yet he must have done something. He looked out across the hard, steely ocean. Trinidad was growing hazy in the distance, a darker blue smudge on the gray of the sea, the blue-gray sky, a landmark pointing the way to nowhere.

Peter moved across the cattle pen, where he wouldn't have to see Trinidad. He stared out at the nothingness and listened with little interest to the sailors talking about laying over at Rio de Janeiro. Such an out-of-the-way stop made little sense to Peter, so he discounted it. But Peter was ignorant of the well-established, profitable practices of the sea captains who transported convicts by contract for the Crown.

Most of the ships coming from England stopped over at Rio or at the Cape of Good Hope. The Cape required less loss of time and was en route, but Rio was the preferred stop for other reasons. While it delayed the voyage by at least three weeks—usually longer if the crew was given leave—and further endangered the lives of the convicts, rum, tobacco, and silk could be obtained cheaply and then sold at a good profit in Hobart or Sydney. So far from England and the civilized world, the settlers in Van Diemen's Land and Australia were always eager to buy luxuries from incoming ships. Both the surgeon and the captain stood to gain a handsome profit. And though each prisoner delivered alive meant half a guinea to the surgeon, convict ships had been known to lose as many as twenty percent of their human cargo before arrival and more after they had landed. The half guinea on the head of a convict was worth risking for the less perishable cargo of silk and rum.

The convicts were left aboard ship under heavy guard as the crew and officers went ashore to more comfortable lodgings and a bit of merriment and civilized living with Rio society. With the ship riding at anchor, then tied up at the wharf, the slow listless movement and the slap and bump against the dock became a constant irritant to the convicts spending most of every hot stifling day in the prison. Predictably tempers flared, and the usual squabbling and petty meanness turned to more malicious things. Thefts of small treasures of cards, tobacco, and little caches of pence and shillings increased. Fights, always a daily occurrence, became hourly events. Most were not serious and disregarded by the guards, who were as bored as the prisoners. So as not to appear to be slighting their responsibilities, they chose altercations at random and those men were recorded as deserving of special attention or punishment. Peter's name was entered in the logbook four times during the layover. Once for insolence, twice for fighting, and once for theft. By the time the *George III* set sail again, Peter was listed as one of the incorrigible prisoners.

The crew sighted the African coast about four and a half months after leaving England. Again they ran into bad weather. Sudden squalls and storms struck the ship and were often as not followed by deadly calms. Tension and fear mounted among the passengers and crew. The stop in Rio had been a pleasant diversion, but it had also served to remind of the long voyage and increase the need to finally stop traveling upon this empty ocean. Even those practical stalwarts who decried superstition and such airy things as luck found they could not control the primitive within them. At night they looked into the great blackened bowl of the heavens and saw no boundaries to its vastness. At dawn the sun began its ascent from the left, moving precisely across the brilliant tropic skies, pressing down on the ship that now seemed so tiny in an empty universe.

The men and women aboard the *George III* had traveled long and through seas that were little traveled. They were tired and apprehensive of the ending to this trip. The talk among the new settlers was not so readily spiced with braggadocio dreams of great success now; it was beginning to be tempered with fear of the unknown. A storm sounded to them that all the old and ancient gods rose before them shouting their wrath. The calms became so bright and airless it was difficult to think that they were real at all. This far into the voyage any delay was bad. One that carried fear with it was demoralizing.

Apprehension brought on by a deadly silver sea heaving against a creaking wind-dependent ship brought an end to the weak thread of common sense that still held aboard ship. One woman, the wife of a settler hoping to make his fortune in Van Diemen's Land, watched her son be wrapped in a sheet of canvas to be thrown overboard. He had succumbed to typhoid. Clutching her husband's arm, she stared out over the water, not daring to look at the grim activity. She didn't cry or make a move. Then in that silence following a prayer, the mute woman broke free of her husband, clawing at the seamen trying to wrap her son for a proper sea burial. Held back by her husband and two crewmen, she strained against him, then fell limp, only to revive and race for the side of the ship to follow her son to his watery grave.

The civilian passengers held meetings on deck, most of them refusing to remain in their cabins because of the fear of typhoid. They blamed the convicts for the illness that beset them. They also blamed the convicts and their evil influence for their abandonment by God's grace. They petitioned the captain to improve conditions. He looked helplessly to the sky, ominously devoid of the little wind-bearing petrels; he had no idea what might come of them, or what he might do to change things.

Below in the prison the convicts lay listlessly, unable to help themselves. Crowding and the odors emanating from the sick-ridden prison quarters and the ship's hospital added fervor to the idea that it was the fault of the convicts that the ship was threatened with disease. The ship's officers took up the cry, certain that their cargo was not of human variety, but some complex animal the Devil had created to torment the good people of this earth. It was due to the depravity of these two-legged beasts that the *George III* sat becalmed. For those demons decent people were suffering, becoming ill, dying while God vented his wrath on the evil ones.

Righteous indignation surfaced among the crew. If God wanted the convicts punished, it was their duty as good Christians to see the punishment was carried out. One of the passengers suggested that the ship was becalmed because the captain had been negligent of his duties. After all he was known to be easy on his prisoners—during this entire voyage they could count on one hand the number of convicts who had been flogged, and none had been hanged or keelhauled.

Two more days of calm and the continuing rise of fear and discontent among passengers and crew, and the captain considered the few options he had. He chose the quickest, most expedient method of satisfying the primitive urge for a sacrifice to the gods. He would punish the prisoners.

He was selective. He chose the worst of the lot,

those who were not likely to survive the voyage anyway, and those about whom no one cared. These men, ten of them, were taken to the bowels of the ship. Peter, because of his murder conviction and designation as an incorrigible, was one of the ten.

The convicts were lined up on the ladder descending into the lower holds. One by one they were taken to the hold, the same area where irons were taken off or put on. Sweat stood out in beads all over Peter's body, grouping and running down in rivulets as screams and the sweet, sickening odors of cooking meat wafted toward him. Panicking, sensing what was to come, he backed away when the guard came for him. He grasped the ladder, trying to force his way over the other convicts as he managed to climb two rungs up the hatchway. With guards above and below the convicts couldn't move. His sweating grip loosening, Peter slipped back down the ladder. The guards grasped him by the shoulders. He struck out blindly, wrenching free of one guard as he leapt to the side, once more trying to climb the hatchway over the other convicts.

The guard shouted for help. Three men came to his assistance. The largest pushed through. He grabbed hold of Peter's hair, forcing his head back, then pressed on his windpipe until he had Peter on his knees.

Peter twisted, grasping the guard's hands, pulling with all his strength to free himself. The guard laughed, his knee coming hard into Peter's stomach. The other guards stepped forward, each taking one of Peter's arms. The rest followed behind as he was dragged to the hold.

He was thrust onto his back across a wooden beam six inches wide, and secured there so he couldn't move. His shirt was opened from the front and pulled back so it would not be in the way. Next to him, so close he could feel its heat, was the forge fire with the brands glowing red in its pit.

The burly, soot-encrusted custodian of the fire pulled out one of the brands bearing the letter *M*. The man held the brand close to Peter's face until he could feel his skin tighten and dry with the heat.

The forgeman laughed. "'T'would make a mess o' your purty face now, wouldn't it?" Then he looked up at the guards. "Our captain's a soft-hearted bastard, he is. Last one I shipped with branded 'em all. The whole bloody lot of 'em. Right there . . ." He pressed his thick, blunt finger into Peter's forehead.

The thought of that searing hot iron coming down on his brow was more than Peter could bear. His body tightened inside to a tight coil. He shuddered, turning his head from side to side, avoiding the sight and the heat coming from the brand. With a strong filthy hand, the forgeman roughly forced Peter to keep his head still, staring straight into the glowing iron. He brought the brand closer to Peter's eyes.

"I leave it there long enough, it'll blind you. Want that? Eh? Like that?" He looked up at the guards. "He doesn't seem to like the sight o' it, does he?" The guards laughed. "Well, take a good look for it's all yours. Your name's right on it. Murderer. Look at it!" He plunged the brand back into the fire and brought out a fresh one that glowed white, then red as it cooled before Peter's eyes.

Fear-crazed, no longer able to think of the brand falling, Peter struggled, straining against the chains that bound him to the beam until the muscles of his arms, chest, and neck stood out in tight corded knots.

"He's not lookin' so grand an' brave now, is he? They're all alike in the end. Every bloody one o' the bloody gaolbirds is a coward at heart. They all sweat blood and mess their pants when they finally get what's comin' of their evil ways," the guard said.

Trembling, knowing there was nothing he could do, no compassion or mercy to be accorded, no pleas or reason he might call upon, Peter spat into the face of the leering guard hovering over him to better enjoy what was taking place.

The forgeman laughed, hitting the guard jovially on the shoulder as he reached into the pit again exchanging the brand for a fresh white hot one.

The brand came down like perpetual fire on Peter's chest, held in place until the sizzling sounds and the stench of his own flesh combined with the inescapable, burning pain and melted into a vast graceless blackness.

He awakened in his bunk in the prison confine. The scent of burnt hair and flesh were still in his nostrils; the pain still ate his flesh, fiery and encompassing. He turned his face to the wall trying to blot out a memory that could never be erased.

A deep sense of degradation engulfed him even worse than the pain. He shivered in the airless bunk. He squeezed his eyes shut and then opened them, wondering if he still had his sight. For a moment he stared into the oak panel of the wall; then he looked down at his mutilated chest to see the *M* of a murderer emblazoned there for all his life.

Prison was more than just punishment for a crime committed. It had become the outlet for the deep and primitive hatreds of men; an outlet for yearnings of power, exercised in sadism by the powerless. What had been done to Peter and the other convicts was not unusual. But neither was it necessary or a part of their prison sentence.

Branding was no longer an acceptable practice. In polite London circles and in Parliament it was declaimed loudly. But it had been the order of the day aboard prison ships for a long time. A general rule, outlawed, was now practiced at will and without record. Its exercise depended on the captains, who ran their ships with absolute authority.

Technically Peter had the right to register a complaint. But his evaluation as a prisoner was dependent upon the same man responsible for the branding, and any complaint he might make would be processed through that man. With the ship's surgeon always ready to agree with the captain and the mate, there was no one to whom Peter could speak and not expect reprisal.

Reformers were the only ones who professed to care. But unfortunately reformers tended to think in terms of laws. They spent their time before the Houses of Parliament and celebrated their success when a scrap of paper was signed by prime ministers and kings. But aboard the vessels, the floating hells, the branding went on, and there were no kings or prime ministers there to stop their wordy laws from being broken. Van Diemen's Land was sixteen thousand miles away from England, and there was no paper law in the middle of an ocean, unless it was carried in the hearts of the people.

Peter cringed against the wall of the prison, trying to bury himself in its rough-planked sides, knowing abandonment. He would not expect to reach out as one man to another again. Only men were fit to have communion with other men. He was no longer a man. He was a convict.

Among the thoughts that devastated him, then burned into his mind the fears that the brand had burned into his flesh, was that the men who tortured him were very like other men he had known and liked. He had called some of them friends. But he had always been different from them. He had thought he was right, had thought he was trying to foster good. But if he were evil, he wouldn't even have known what good was. Had they seen that in him? Had they always sensed that one day he would wind up as he had, a convict, a branded murderer?

The humiliation drove so deeply inside him, and the confusion was so great, he no longer thought of his innocence. Innocence was a clouded, abstract concept he no longer understood.

As he stood at the edge of the cattle pen the following day, he placed Callie's scarf on the burn. It was soft and could be kept wet and cool. He guarded his chest, which the other prisoners were likely to bump or touch. He watched the officers and passengers lounging under the striped canopy on deck fretfully fanning themselves as they talked or played cards. He could be called insolent for looking at them as he was, but he no longer cared. He continued to stare from over the rail of the pen. Some of the crew fished, others laughed now that a breeze was again blowing, and some of the passengers had begun again to talk optimistically of their business ventures. They spoke in the same excited but courteous way he once had. These men, of whom he had been one, were the same men who kept him bound, in pain, always aware that he was not fit to so much as cast his eye upon them without permission.

Was there any difference between these men and Sam Tolbert, Rufus Hawkes, or even his brother, Frank Berean? What would they have done to him given the chance? What hidden hatreds had his own wife felt when she turned from him to seek Albert Foxe? He remembered when Albert had arrested him during the Swing riots. Albert hadn't wanted to release him. Peter had known it then. He had been freed only because of Callie. Now he wondered if Albert would have enjoyed watching him hang if Callie hadn't come along. He thought he would have.

One hundred and sixty-seven days after leaving England, they came in sight of Van Diemen's Land. It had been nearly a six-month voyage during which many men and young boys had died, and at whose end no man held in the prison cage of the 'tween decks would be the same man who had begun the voyage in England. They were far nearer to being the beasts their captors called them.

Van Diemen's Land was discovered in 1642 by Abel Jansen Tasman. He believed it to be a part of the Australian continent, and named it after Anthony Van Diemen, the governor general of the Dutch possessions in the East Indies. No one realized it was an island until 1798, five years before the English took possession of it. During the early 1820s it was first used as a penal colony, being dubbed "the Botany Bay of Botany Bay."

As they approached the island, the Mewstone, a great conical rock a few miles from the ruggedly mountainous south shore, came into view. Patches of snow lay on lofty peaks. Great basaltic cliffs rose up from the jutting, jagged shoreline.

They passed the dangerous Actean Reef, rounded the rocky straits of Tasman's Head, going up Storm Bay along the east side of Bruny Island. All along they passed massive columns of basalt, regally primitive sentries of a regally primitive land of fern and pine.

The ship was guided by a pilot boat up the treacherous river Derwent to anchor in Sullivan's Cove. All the prisoners were brought on deck in irons as the ship was brought in.

Hobart Town, the capital of Van Diemen's Land, sat on the Derwent on beautifully undulating ground. The streets were spacious and laid out at right angles. Most of the houses were sturdily built of brick and slatelike shingles. Gardens graced most of the houses. It was a picture of peace and contentment, a testament to the efforts of convicts enslaved by settlers in a land so new and so far from England.

On their arrival the convicts were questioned and categorized.

"What was the nature of your crime?"

"I committed no crime," Peter said.

The man looked at him, waiting, warning with his eyes that insolence should not be tolerated once, and would not be twice. "What was the nature of your crime?"

"Murder."

"How many times were you apprehended previously?"

"None."

"Has it been necessary to take disciplinary action against you at any time during this voyage?"

Peter hesitated. "Yes, sir."

"Your parents' names?"

"James and Margaret Berean of Kent."

"Can they read and write?"

"Yes, sir."

"Their occupation?"

"My father is dead. My mother lives on my brother's hop garden in Kent."

Each piece of information was written into a record book. As the convicts were brought into the square, the colonists looked the men over, asking questions and examining them. Requests were put in for the best, strongest looking of them, and those who were most highly skilled to be assigned to the settlers as laborers. Some of the men were separated from the group immediately. They would go to the settlers after they had been processed and their status as convicts established.

Men being transported for the second time, incorrigibles, and those considered dangerous, life-termers, or murderers, were to be sent to penal colonies of harsher security and discipline. Heated words were exchanged over the commandant's refusal to allow Peter to be taken for free labor.

"He's the biggest damned buck you've shipped. I don't want no ninny who can't lift the water bucket. Why, that man's worth two mules working."

Coolly, the commandant looked over Peter's record, and then at the irate colonist. "Would you risk having your throat slit in your own bed for the sake of a well-drawn bucket of water? This man is one of the worst of this shipment. His size makes him all the more dangerous to handle. When he has been controlled and taught to obey, he'll be made accessible to any settler who wishes to take him on."

Peter was returned to the ship to be sent to Sarah Island. They set sail for Macquarie Harbor, a short but tortuous, wind-blown distance. The ship was anchored for three days as the storms that buffeted the rocky shores made it too hazardous to chance going on. In this area of the island it rained ten months of the year.

Sarah Island lay about twenty miles from the sea up the inlet leading to Macquarie Harbor. In spite of the storms and rain there were magnificent snow-covered mountain ranges. Frenchman's Cap, forming half a sphere, rose perpendicular five thousand feet above sea level.

Peter saw Huon pines, Forest Tea trees, black swans, gulls—raw, striking, primordial majesty wherever he looked. One year ago he would have longed to walk this island, touching its soil, spiritually possessing its mountains and unexpectedly lush valleys. The sin, he decided, was not in his inability to ever come to know it as he might wish, but that it had ever been used to such a purpose as this.

He stood, still in irons, on the deck of the *George III*, wind-driven rain lashing cleanly at his face, realizing how long it had been since he had been able to feel anything but hate and anger. For those few minutes that he stood there alone he looked upon nature in all her awesome glory, and he was free, breathing crisply cold air.

Chapter 33

As they approached New York Harbor, Callie and Stephen stood on deck searching the horizon for familiar landmarks that meant welcome home.

Natalie hovered at Stephen's side. The voyage had been exhausting for her. She had been seasick, and the tossing frigate had done nothing to dispel the nightmares that afflicted her. Fleetingly she looked at the clutter of masts and buildings. "Is this where you live, Stephen?"

"This is New York City. We live up river."

"I'm glad you don't live here. I wouldn't like it. It looks like London. I'd be afraid here."

"It's nothing like London, Nat. You don't know what you're talking about." He still couldn't keep the angry edge from his voice when he talked to her. He left her, thankful that he had the excuse of the brewery equipment to see to.

Callie, Jamie, and Natalie waited on the deck until he came back to get them. As they stepped off the gangplank, Stephen spun at the sound of a friendly, familiar voice.

"Hello, Stevie! Welcome home!"

Standing tall, Stephen could just see the top of Jack Tolbert's head as he threaded through the crowd, leaping to wave over the shoulder of the man in front of him. The man stepped aside, letting Jack push through. He pulled off his hat, beaming with smiles.

"Hello, Callie darlin' . . . pretty as ever and just as sweet, eh? Did you miss me, darlin'?" he asked impishly as she greeted him. He clapped Stephen on the back, then noticed Natalie standing somewhat behind and to the side of Stephen and Callie. "Ah, Stevie! You did it! You brought me home a fair English flower for my very own."

Stephen shook his head, beginning helplessly to laugh as Jack pranced and chattered about them. Callie gave Stephen a healthy elbow to his ribs. He glanced at Natalie and became serious. "Jack—shut up. This is my sister, Natalie Foxe—Mrs. Foxe," he said meaningfully, hoping Jack would remember the letters he had written to him.

Jack was planning rather than remembering. "Mrs. . . . Oh, well, she's here and lovely and so am I. I don't see any husband lurking about. You won't mind her having a new and thoroughly harmless admirer, will you, Stevie?"

"Natalie is a widow." Then firmly and slowly he hissed, "Think, you damned monkey!"

Jack's impish expression disappeared. "Oh, blessed heaven . . . damn my mouth. I'm sorry, Steve—forgive me. I'm such a damned fool. Callie, forgive me. Mrs. Foxe . . ."

Stephen put his hand on Jack's shoulder. "Enough, for God's sake. You're no good as a penitent. See if you can find us a carriage."

"Yes, oh, yes. That's why I came. I have a carriage. I'll never say another foolish word as long as I live. I swear it!" he declared, pounding his chest. "The carriage is right over here. Follow me. You do forgive me? I am such a damned fool. It's just that I was so glad to see you. Forgive?"

"Yes, you damned ass. Stop your braying. Take us to the carriage." Stephen grinned.

"Damned ass!? That's a singularly rotten thing to call your best friend. God alive, it's good to see you again. Nobody's called me a lousy name since you've left."

"Tell me what's happened. What was the final harvest? Is it all in? Was it what we hoped it'd be?" Stephen walked ahead with Jack talking animatedly.

Walking at a more leisurely pace, Callie said uncertainly, "You'll get used to Jack in time, Nattie. He isn't half so bad as he first seems."

"Why should I care about Mr. Tolbert? Is he someone important? Did Albert know him?"

"No. He's not particularly important, I don't suppose. He sort of comes with the house though," she said, then climbed into the carriage, neatly avoiding Jack's helpfully extended hand.

Natalie showed no interest as they drove to the steamship landing. She boarded the ship without comment.

"We live on this river, Nattie. Isn't it beautiful?" Callie said, trying to stir some response and not seeing how anyone could resist the Hudson in autumn.

Natalie said nothing. She wore a perpetually worried and distracted expression that disturbed Callie. She did not look well, and Callie worried about her quiet withdrawal. "You can see this river from the front windows on the second floor, and in the winter when the trees are bare, you can see it from Peter's study."

Natalie looked sharply at Callie. "Is Peter there?"

"Not now," Callie said, and went on. "Would you like a room overlooking the Hudson?"

"No . . . no . . . I don't want to be near Peter's river. Take me far away."

Callie said nothing. She no longer knew what Natalie did and didn't understand. She seemed to have everything in a jumble, some of it fantasy, some of it real. Callie worried often about having her live with them. But what was one to do with a relative afflicted as Natalie was? There was no place to put her. No doctor to cure her. It was the family's duty to see to its own regardless of their personal feelings. There was no other acceptable choice, and Callie repeated to herself a vow to resign herself to what had to be.

She shifted Jamie's weight to her other arm, then put him down and walked the deck with him. Natalie remained where she was as if rooted in place. She looked frightened and lost. "Are you tired, Natalie?"

Natalie took a fearful backward glance at the black smoke and cinder billowing from the smokestack. The deck was hot and beginning to vibrate as the steamship gained speed. She moved closer to Callie. "The . . . ship . . ." she quavered. "He . . . he's going to do something . . . to the ship."

"Natalie . . . this isn't the same ship we were on before. Nothing is wrong. You are feeling its engines, that's all."

"It's . . . it's on fire . . ."

Callie smiled reassuringly. "Here—take Jamie's other hand. We'll go to the salon. You should have told me the ship makes you nervous. But there is nothing to worry about. All the steamships shake when the engine works hard. Ask Stephen about it. He knows all there is to tell."

They remained in the elegant salon the rest of the hour-long trip. Just before their stop, Stephen and

Jack joined them. "I looked for you on deck," Stephen said as he plucked Jamie from Callie's lap and held him high over his head. "We're almost home, little man. Come along with your Uncle Stephen and see your country. Why have you got him down here, Callie? It's a beautiful day."

"We were a little tired," she said.

He glanced at Natalie. "I see. Well, Jamie, you're going to have to learn to go on your own steam if you're going to wear everyone out. He is getting heavy," Stephen commented, surprised, and then offered to carry the little boy the rest of the way for her.

Jack drove them home. He and Stephen had apparently talked, and were now both ablaze with altruistic ideas of helping Callie with her two charges and getting the house in order. Fortunately their good intentions lasted long enough to carry into the house the boxes, valises, and baggage they had brought with them on the steamship. The rest would come later.

The farm looked the same as it had last spring. When they had left the hops were not yet full grown; in returning the hops had been harvested and once more the wires stood barren at the top. The one difference in the landscape was the tall brick building being constructed on the far boundary of the farm.

Though Stephen tried valiantly to keep his mind on organizing the household, no intentions, good or saintly, were enough to keep him from inspecting the new brewery.

Callie took Jamie upstairs, handing him over to Mary Anne. She hugged him tightly. "It's good to have you back, Miss Dawson." Jamie poked an exploratory finger at her face. "He hasn't forgotten me! See, miss—he knows me." Then Mary Anne's long face grew solemn. "I'm sorry—we're all of us sorry, Miss Dawson, about what happened to Mrs. Berean. Poor little tyke without a mama." She hugged Jamie again. "Will *he* be coming back—ever?"

"I don't believe I like the tone of your questions, Mary Anne."

"Did he do what they say he did? Did he really slaughter them both in cold blood? I could just see him doin' it. He was the kind that could, you know."

"Mary Anne! He did nothing of the sort," Callie said shortly.

"Well, he *is* in prison . . . he must have done something. Poor Mrs. Berean . . . such a pretty little lady. Seems like it always happens to them who have everything to live for, don't it?"

"Give Jamie a bath, Mary Anne, and there'll be no more gossip about this. I can see tongues are already wagging falsehoods. Jack Tolbert should learn to keep his mouth shut. And so should you. Peter Berean pays your wages, and I won't stand another word said against him. If you plan to say here, you'll remember that. He was always good to you; you might keep that in mind the next time you feel like slandering him. Make certain Jamie has a good nap this afternoon. No excitement—it's been a long trip."

She went downstairs, more disturbed than she liked, to show Natalie the house. Natalie was vague and disoriented. She kept looking for the familiar rooms of the house in Kent. Callie had to explain two and three times what each room was and how it connected to the others. Natalie looked confused and unhappy.

"I'll take you to your rooms, Nattie. You'll feel better after you've put some of your own things in the house."

Callie led Natalie upstairs. She had decided to give Natalie the rooms farthest from Jamie's. There was also a sitting room adjoining the bedroom, and Callie had no doubt that there would be times when she and

Stephen would have to confine Natalie to her rooms for Jamie's safety as well as Natalie's. The luggage Stephen had brought up earlier was outside Natalie's door. Natalie accepted the rooms without comment; then she went back to the hall, touching the boxes she had marked herself. She paid no attention to the valises that held her clothing; she wanted only the boxes that contained the figurines and trinkets that Albert had given her. Callie removed the packing tissues, handing each figurine to Natalie. Soon she was frowning. "Did you realize you have two of everything?"

"Yes."

"But why?"

"That is the way I like them. Albert does too. It makes it so nice to arrange them. One was never alone as long as I had two." Natalie took two small china shepherds and placed them on the mantel facing one another. She arranged each set of figurines precisely; always together, and always facing.

Callie found it disturbing, her mind going back to Peter and Stephen's description of the two guns placed so precisely on the door lip, nose to nose, Stephen had said. She wondered briefly if Natalie ever had meant to kill Rosalind. Had it been herself and Albert she had meant to "free," as she put it? The pair of them. Together. Face to face.

Natalie stood back to admire her handiwork. "Don't they look lovely? They each have a place of their own. They are in their proper places, aren't they? I wish Albert were here. He always knows where to put them . . . where they'd be happiest."

"Maybe if you mixed them up a bit . . . turned them, or put the lamb with the shepherd . . . like this." Callie rearranged two of the pairs. "Isn't that better?"

"No!" Natalie screamed and grabbed the offending

figurines, hurling them against the marble fireplace. She stepped on the shards, grinding them into the soft stone.

"Nattie! Why did you do that!?" Callie stooped, picking up the tiny colored pieces of the lamb. The shepherd was beyond reclamation. "Oh, Nattie . . ."

"They belong in their own places. Never anywhere else. Never! You made them tainted and dirty!"

"All right," Callie said, getting up and moving cautiously to the door. "All right, Nattie. You put them wherever you want. I'm sorry I touched them. I won't ever again."

"Albert likes everything neatly ordered," Natalie said positively.

"Then you have done everything just right," Callie said and left Natalie talking to herself about Albert and the pairs and order.

When Callie went downstairs she was upset and grumpy. She was itching to complain to Stephen for having run off to the brewery, leaving her alone to deal with Natalie. She knew he was somewhere in the house. She had heard him come in earlier, moving about, singing to himself in the best of spirits while she watched Natalie destroy four perfectly lovely figurines because they had not been placed to stare at one another nose to nose. She turned at the landing and saw him.

He was standing in front of the hall mirror struggling with his cravat.

"Where are you going?" she asked harshly, surprised to see him dressed in his best. Unconsciously she pushed at her tumbling hair and smoothed her gown.

"There are doings in Kingston tonight. Jack and I thought we'd go." He untied the cravat again. "Can you do something with this?"

He turned so she could work on the tie. "It didn't

take you long to fall in with Jack's ways. How long will you be out?"

"Not long, I guess. Unless Jack has improved in the last few months; these things are never as much fun as he thinks. You don't mind if I go, do you?"

"Why should I? You do as you like," she said off-handedly.

"I could stay home." He put his hands on her shoulders. "I wouldn't mind if you'd rather I stayed. Shall I?"

"Of course not!" She said it too heatedly. "Why should you? I've . . . I've got work to do. This house is still in an upheaval. I suppose you'll be wanting the cook to put your supper on early?"

Stephen's hands dropped to his sides. "No. Bea is an understanding woman as well as a good cook. She let me eat in the kitchen while she prepared it."

"How thoughtful."

"Don't be like that. Smile. Blame me. Bea didn't upset your supper; I did."

"You've upset nothing. It makes no difference to me where you eat," Callie said, annoyed as she walked back toward the staircase. "I do hope you have a lovely time."

"Thanks." Stephen waved as he went out the front door.

Callie sat down on the step. "Drat! Just drat to you, Stephen Berean. Have a good time . . . see if I care where you go."

She ate alone with Natalie. There was nothing to do or talk about. Natalie was in one of her quiet moods, and went to her room as soon as she had eaten. The house was empty and Callie was idle.

She undressed and climbed into bed soon after supper, determined not to care when or if Stephen came home that night. She lay in her bed, her hands folded

neatly on her chest, her eyes shut, patiently waiting
for sleep. She saw Stephen standing before the mirror
adjusting his cravat. She felt the quick rush of resentment and rejection she had felt earlier. And then her
magical mind rearranged events for her. Stephen
turned from the mirror smiling, his eyes bright on her.
He asked her to join him. She refused demurely. He
begged her to go with him. He said his evening would
be spoiled if she stayed behind. And then she said . . .
the magic wore off. She could carry the fantasy no
farther. She again felt resentful and angry with him.
Yet she wouldn't permit herself to examine the reasons
for her feelings any more than she'd permit herself to
carry her fantasy on.

She began to think of all the acidly clever remarks
she might have made to him had she just thought
quickly enough. In her mind she verbally abused him
and left him bloodied, and then disliked herself for
having thought those things.

Restless, she turned to her side, curling her legs up
close to her chest. Her eyelids trembled, unwilling to
stay closed. Frustrated and discontent, she sat up,
slapping angrily at her coverlet. She got up, rearranged the toilette articles on her vanity, and still the
restlessness lingered.

She went to Peter's study and hunted through his
books until she found a volume on soil preparation
she was sure would put her to sleep. She carried it to
her room and began to read one dreary page after another. She remained wide awake. The fast ticking
clock with the slow moving hands held her attention.

It was well past midnight when she heard him
trying to work the front door lock. She waited, listening, but the door didn't open. Finally she could stand
it no more. She padded barefoot down the stairs. She

peeked out the side window and saw nothing. She opened the door. He was sitting on the stoop.

"I knew you'd come." He grinned.

"I was asleep."

"No," he said, getting up slowly. "You couldn't have been asleep. I've been thinking too hard about you. Callie . . ."

She stepped aside for him, getting a strong whiff of whiskey as he passed. "You've been drinking!" she said, sniffing. "And . . . and that's perfume I smell! Where have you been!?"

"With Jack," he said sheepishly.

His hair was damp from the night air, and curling about his face. It made her angrier. "Jack indeed! He doesn't wear perfume as far as I know. You smell like . . . like you've been in . . . in a bawdy house!" she sputtered, bristling with indignation and something else.

"It was all because of you." He laughed, stumbling toward her as he tried to remove his coat. "Help me get out of this damned thing. I'm stuck."

She yanked the coat halfway down his arms, leaving him in a worse fix. "You should be ashamed coming home like this."

"Callie . . . get me out of this thing."

"You got yourself in, you get out. I never thought I'd see the day when you'd be like Jack," she scolded, leaving him tangled in his coat sleeves.

"But I had fun." He smiled at her as she began to climb the stairs.

"As if that makes everything all right. You never think of anyone but yourself!" She ran to her room.

She still couldn't sleep. How could she have gotten so angry with him? She wasn't even sure what he had done that was so wrong. She hid her face in her pillow, letting hot tears scorch her eyes. She felt better crying. She didn't know why, but now at last she was beginning to feel safe and very sleepy.

In the following weeks Natalie became even more nervous. There were certain rooms she refused to enter. When Callie tried to persuade her that nothing was peculiar about the rooms, Natalie accused her of trying to help Peter trap her. Callie didn't mention the rooms again.

Natalie continued her strange ways. She slept too much, ate too much, and remained inclined to prefer her own company to anyone but Jamie's. Outside she patrolled the yard as though she guarded it while Jamie played. She wouldn't go near the barns or the brewhouse. The fields didn't exist for her, and the mere mention of taking her to see the hop yard sent her into a tizzy of unintelligible protest.

By the time winter came and there was little to show her in any case, Callie and Stephen had given up on trying to make her feel at home. Beyond the play yard and the confines of her own rooms, Natalie was uncomfortable. They left her to find her own incomprehensible satisfactions with her figurines, dreams, and private conversations with an imaginary Albert.

Callie was far too busy with the house, Jamie, and the dairy to continue worrying about Natalie when Natalie was both quiet and happy in her own way.

For Stephen, it was easy to put Natalie out of mind. He was discovering that Peter's end of the business was more involved than he had thought. He found it necessary to be in New York and Albany more often than he expected. The accounts were taskmasters that demanded to be served. Their one advantage over some of the clerical tasks was that tending to them combined easily with pleasure. Stephen was too honest not to admit that he welcomed a chance to get away from the house, Natalie, and even Callie.

Stephen had one advantage that Peter hadn't had. He was a bachelor. Often he found prospective clients welcomed him into their homes for purposes other than the sale of hops and grain and brew. While he didn't take it too seriously, he enjoyed meeting a variety of unmarried female cousins, daughters, and sisters. And he thought one day perhaps Callie would notice him, not as a brother, or someone she counted on, but as a man, the way other women did.

Callie broodingly continued to adjust his cravat for him, and to his dismay had stopped complaining about his late hours or asking where he had been.

Callie had never felt so ashamed. She had no idea how to control the terrible anger that welled up in her toward Stephen. But she did now admit to its cause. She was miserably, horribly jealous and lonely for him. The thoughts she had of him now brought her nothing but shame. She had pledged herself to wait for Peter, and she watched Stephen working sixteen or more hours every day to try to keep Peter's business flourishing. That she had somehow allowed her feelings for him to continue to develop into something that was never meant to be, she couldn't bear. She thought of Natalie, and of Jamie, and most of all, she thought of Peter. All this she and Stephen had accepted as a part of their lives. At the end of it, she would have Peter, but if she ever dared let Stephen know her feelings, he'd remain faithful to her. She knew he would. And then when it was over, Stephen would be left with nothing. She'd die before she'd do that to him.

She helped him get ready to go out, and listened as patiently as she could manage when he talked about the people he met. But she kept seeing him, tall, hand-

some, and appealing, and in someone else's arms. He'd
be with people she really knew nothing about and
had never met. There were times when she was so
overwhelmed with her thoughts, she was sure everyone he ever met was female and reeked of perfume for
as often as not Stephen did when he came home.
Then, sternly, she would tell herself that is what she
wanted. He had to meet someone one day and marry.

If Callie felt at a low ebb, Jack was riding the high
tide. Naturally reserved, Stephen had never before
been so willing to meet people, attend the theater,
dances, and gaming houses as he was now. Jack didn't
question, though he suspected he knew the cause of
Stephen's sudden gregariousness. He lived one glorious day at a time. For the moment he had the best
of companions and an endless stream of cold winter
nights to warm and fill with all manner of frivolity.

Callie remained generally resentful of the entire situation. She felt cut off from Stephen and lonely. It
seemed to her that her whole life was duties and obligations, when all she wanted was fun and gaiety. At
night while Stephen was out and she was upstairs in
her room unable to sleep, she often imagined herself
dressed in a magnificent gown, walking queenlike beside Stephen as she charmed all his clients and devastated the hopes of the women who had set their caps
for him.

But all Stephen had to do was to ask her to join
him, and her conscience betrayed her. She had a bas-
ketful of excuses. There were Jamie and Natalie to care
for. She had to be up early to tend to the dairy. She
succeeded at last in convincing Stephen that she cared
less for him than she did for Natalie and Jamie.

By the end of January, Stephen was tired of seeing
her mope about the house, and he was angry. He ordered her to have fun. "I don't give a damn if your

face cracks like crazed china, you're going to smile and laugh and dance or I'm going to dump you in the bloody river. They still have dunking stools for women, you know!"

She agreed to attend one of the local Saturday night socials. It was a disaster. Callie couldn't make the two warring halves of herself merge. She could neither relax and have fun with him, nor close off the girl inside her who wanted to shed her responsibilities and dance in the moonlight.

She behaved as though she were Stephen's sister, constantly at his side, shying away from all young men who showed an interest in her. Every spark of response that rose in her seemed a vague betrayal of faith. No matter what, she wouldn't let Peter down. She couldn't forget what Rosalind had done to him, and whatever it cost her she would never become the sort of woman Rosalind had been. She just wished she knew how to become a woman at all.

Suddenly she felt like crying. She couldn't. Not here, not in front of all these people. She moved closer to Stephen, slipping her hand under his arm.

He smiled. "Will you dance with me now?"

She shook her head. "I like watching the others." She looked out at the dance floor, then she looked contritely at Stephen. "Don't let me keep you, if you'd like to ask someone to dance."

"I did ask the lady I want to dance with. She said no."

She didn't hear the annoyance in his voice beneath his lighthearted delivery. "Oh, Stephen . . . really, you don't have to look after me like this. I'm fine. I really like to watch. You don't need to cosset me."

Stephen removed her hand from his arm. "For God's sake, Callie, shut up. I can't stand to hear you talk. You sound like a damned saint bragging about her martyrdom."

Hurt, Callie blinked back tears. "You never used to talk to me like that. What have I done?"

Stephen laughed mirthlessly. "You haven't done a damned thing. Sometimes I wonder if you ever will."

"What? I don't understand . . ."

"Oh, you understand! You just won't . . ." he began, then fell silent, looking at her pensively. Then he sighed, saying, "I only meant there's no point in your coming to the social if you refuse to enjoy yourself. Did you ever think that it might be natural to want to meet people and dance and have fun?"

"But it isn't the same for me now. I can't be silly and . . . you know. I gave my word . . ." She stopped talking, having to look out across the crowd, push the longings and the threatening tears back. She lowered her eyes and spoke in a whisper. "I told you I shouldn't come. Maybe you'd better take me home."

"Maybe I'd better." He stood up, impatient for her to rise from her seat. "Come on. I'll take you home. You want to leave."

Callie's heart sank. She didn't know what she wanted from him. What did she expect from him? She didn't want to leave, and she looked up, hoping he would see the denial of her words in her eyes. "I don't—not if you'll stay with me."

Stephen didn't even want to look at her. His eyes were looking somewhere over her shoulder. "And keep you safe? No, thank you. I'm not in the mood to play your guardian angel, Callie—not even for Peter." He walked her to the back of the meeting hall to get their coats.

She began to protest, ready to tell him she wanted to dance. She wanted to stay. But the words wouldn't come. They were locked inside, fighting to be said,

yet she couldn't say them. She felt heavy and sad
when she said, "I'm sorry I spoiled your evening, Stephen."

"So am I."

She was quiet on the way home, and he didn't dare
say anything because he felt like hitting her.

The ride seemed twice as long as it really was. She
had made a fool of herself. When she had tried to be
loyal to Peter she sounded too pious to stomach. And
Stephen despised her for it. She despised herself.

She crossed her arms over her chest, her face severe
and determined. This romantic tomfoolery of hers had
to stop. And she would stop it! These strange disturbing feelings she was giving into were ruining everything. Stephen was barely talking to her, and she was
miserable. For everyone's sake it was important for
her to keep her mind fixed firmly on her duties at
home, on Jamie, and on the man for whom she'd
promised to wait.

Chapter 34

In 1826, when the convict barracks were completed at Hobart Town, a system of classifying the convicts was devised. It attempted to evaluate the character of the prisoner and encourage those most likely to become a part of the growing settlement once their prison terms were served.

England did not want her native soil cluttered with petty thieves, forgers, and highwaymen; but she had learned from experiences in America, Jamaica, and Australia that some men who leaned toward crime in England often made admirable and durable settlers once rehabilitated. And England did need settlers. Van Diemen's Land was still unconquered. Aside from Hobart Town, it could boast little real civilization.

To this end it was made easy for a reformed convict to settle after his sentence was served, but nearly impossible for him to return to England. He seldom had the cost of transportation back, and the Crown provided him with a one-way ticket only. Not all ships entering the ports in Van Diemen's Land were authorized to carry ex-convict passengers. And more often than not, the only life to which a convict could return in England was the same one which had caused his arrest and imprisonment. From the beginning of a man's term, it was made clear that he would most likely never see England again.

Those prisoners sentenced only to seven years and whose conduct record was good were entered into the first class of convicts. These men were as nearly free as a convict could be. They were permitted to sleep outside the barracks and to work for themselves on Saturday nights. At the end of his term a man could expect to have a little money, be familiar with life and work in the settlement, and, of course, be prepared to enter fully into that life when he was freed. The second and third classifications of prisoners were given less freedom and privileges, but their lots could be considered lives of ease compared to the classifications that followed theirs.

Beginning with the fourth classification, the convicts were considered refractory and disorderly. They worked in irons.

The sixth class was for those convicts considered socially dead. They were a collection of murderers, bandits, and villians untamed by chain or lash. These men were shipped to Hell's Gate at Macquarie Harbor, or to Maria Island.

There was little in Peter's record to recommend him to the first few classifications. He was a convicted murderer; his record aboard the hulks and later aboard the *George III* was poor. And last, but perhaps most important in the determination of his prison class assignment, Peter was educated. It was firmly held by prison and clergical authorities that an educated man who had turned to crime had abused his advantages more than the uneducated man and was more depraved and degraded as a result.

Most of the educated prisoners were sent to Port Arthur, a penal settlement established only the year before. At first it seemed the proper place for Peter Berean, but a controversy arose. Peter was not the usual educated convict. He was also considered an incorrigible. While there was little question that the educated prisoners were debased, flawed creatures of the Devil, they were not usually violent. Peter Berean was considered violent by nature.

After some deliberation, it was decided that Peter's prison record dictated he be placed in the sixth classification. He would be sent to Sarah Island, and if he proved too difficult to handle there, he would be sent to the most severe of all the penal settlements, Norfolk Island, a place of no hope and no return. For the moment the commandant decided to look on the brighter side of things. Perhaps this Berean man could be reclaimed. Sarah Island had broken many hardened criminals. It might do the same for Peter Berean.

Sarah Island was at the southeast corner of Macquarie Harbor. When Peter first saw it, the prison complex looked like a fortified town with its lines of palisades encircling the settlement. He assumed the palisades were built to keep the prisoners from escaping. All the complexes had their own means of security. Port Arthur's was considered among the best—a guard of soldiers at Eagle Hawk Neck, only one hundred twenty feet wide at high tide, a barrier made more secure by nine watch dogs with nine lamps between them at even intervals. Only the most rebellious or suicidal dared attempt running that gauntlet. By comparison, Peter considered the Sarah Island palisades tame.

As the prisoners were taken from the ship each of the buildings was identified. While the Port Arthur convicts were still living in primitive bark huts, Sarah boasted a barracks, a jail, and two penitentiaries. The commandant's house stood in the center of the complex. The chaplain's house and the prison barracks stood between the commandant's house and the jail. To the west, near the shore, was the hospital, flanked by the two penitentiaries. Attached to the penitentiary was a treadmill, a replica of the one Peter remembered too well at Newgate.

On Peter's first night on the island the wind raked the land, howling like an animal in pain over the sea and the rocks. The palisades were never constructed as a barrier to the prisoners, but as a barrier against the brutal wind. The rocks surrounding Sarah, with waves roaring and dashing them with primal force, were guarantee that no man would ever leave the island without a boat to carry him. Nature was Sarah Island's fortress.

Furious gales made navigation dangerous. The entrance to Hell's Gate in Macquarie Harbor was not attempted except in calm weather. Sarah's shores and Macquarie Harbor were marked with the carcasses of wrecks. Sunken rocks bore the names of ships they had ripped asunder. Icy winds from the South Pole lashed the island. From the northwest the wind churned and blew toward Sarah and Macquarie, driving salt as far as twelve miles up the river Gordon. The turbulent Gordon, indigo blue and undrinkable, was fed by several rivulets that oozed through swampy ground and decaying vegetation. Sarah Island was not the most hospitable land for either the settler or the convict, yet it had its own harsh beauty.

By the time Peter was assigned to his place in the barracks, he was too tired to give thought to what life would be like on this raw, windswept island. That it would be unpleasant, he had no doubt. Already he was in chains again, and the older prisoners told him he would wear them permanently. He'd eat, sleep, and work with the irons on his body. He fell asleep thinking of the irons, but it was the barren, inhospitable land he dreamed of.

At five thirty Peter was awakened. He opened his eyes to the dreary morning light, sleepy and irritated at the clanking of his fellow convicts' chains as they shuffled toward the dining hall. He was among the last to eat. A bowl of colorless, tasteless mash was given him. He looked at the men on either side of him slurping the mess as quickly as they could. The man to his right ran his dirty finger around the bowl, then lifted it to his face, licking it clean. Peter stared at the bowl, then began to eat the skilly, a mixture of flour, water, and salt. It all but made him sick, but he didn't need anyone to tell him it was all he was going to get.

After breakfast, there was a forty-five-minute period. The week's food rations were given to each prisoner. Peter took his packet thankfully and went off alone to search through it for something to add to his meager breakfast. He had just bitten into a piece of hardtack when the shadow of another prisoner fell across him.

"You're one o' the new ones they brung in, ain't you?"

Peter ignored him, taking another bite of the hardtack.

"Allus can tell the new ones. They eat up their rations the first days. They're allus the fat happy ones on Monday an' the lean hungry ones t'rest o' t'week. Take some friendly advice. It's best to be hungry seven days than starvin' for two or three." The man spat at Peter's feet, then walked back to his friend before Peter could answer.

Peter watched the man sit down and begin to mend his torn trousers. Then he looked around at the other convicts. It was easy to pick out the newcomers. Without exception they were raiding their ration packets. The older convicts used the time to wash their clothes or mend. Many of them gathered in groups talking, their voices gruff, their laughter coarse and too loud. With one last look into his rations packet, Peter closed it up, keeping out the piece of hardtack he had started to eat. Still hungry, he put the packet in his bunk.

He came back outside just as the guards ordered the chain gangs formed. Each gang was comprised of a hundred men. They were lined up, boarded on boats, and ordered to row to the woodcutting station near the mainland. A section of Huon pine was to be cleared there.

Peter looked at the virgin forest and marveled at giant-trunked ancient trees. What ships these pines would build! For a moment he forgot why he was there and felt the surging challenge that nature gives to some men. He staggered as the guard butted him in the small of the back for holding up the gang as he gazed at the trees.

Trees felled by yesterday's work gang lay waiting to be launched into the river. Peter touched the weather-beaten bark fondly, then put his daydreams aside and bent his back to the task. Men stationed themselves along the log. At the unison call of "heave!" they lifted the log to their shoulders. Stumbling through the marshy ground, cursing as they tramped through tangled scrub and underbrush, they carried the logs to the water's edge, placing them carefully. One log at a time they began to build a road a quarter mile long.

Before noon the muscles in Peter's back were on fire. His shoulder was raw and his empty stomach gnawed at him like a rabid rat. He stripped the trees of branches, carried them, and placed them in the roadway until a "slide" was formed. Once the slide was made, the heavier logs were shunted down it into the water. Then they were floated into an arrangement to be transported to Hobart Town where they would be used in construction and the building of ships.

With the last log finally placed in the slide, Peter and several other men were assigned to the log launch. Reluctantly they waded into the icy river, awkward in their chains. The water closed over knee, then thigh, creeping up to his waist, and finally Peter stood in the river, the water cold and tight across his chest. He looked up at the slide. From his new vantage point in the river, it appeared as tall as a mountain, its angle steep and precipitous like the side of a great pyramid.

His anxieties rose as he watched the men at the top of the slide put into position the first giant log to be sent careening down to the men in the river. Erratically the great trunk rolled downward, bouncing and bumping, sometimes catapulting off the uneven slide surface into the air. Peter and his crew scrambled frantically, their movements hampered by their leg irons, their footing uncertain on the slippery river bottom. Peter submerged, shoving himself away from the hurtling log. The crash of the log exploded the water around him. He came up blowing water and shouting imprecations at the grinning men at the top of the slide. His words were drowned out by the thunderous roll of the next log.

Hour after hour the logs tumbled into the water. The river crew maneuvered and shoved them into formation. Peter had never been so painfully cold in his life. The frigid water ate through his skin and muscle and bit deep into the bone. His feet were raw from the rocks in the river bottom. His hands and upper torso were cut and scraped and bruised from the logs.

At six o'clock that evening work ended at the wood station. In that instant when the river crew looked to the top of the slide and saw no more logs being positioned, their leaden arms dropped immobile. Peter looked longingly at the dry river bank and wondered if he'd be able to climb it. With the work stopped, he seemed to have no strength left.

But only the logging had stopped. There was still the long rowing back to Sarah Island and the march to the barracks with their chains dragging, becoming heavier with each step. Peter set his mind on the food rations that awaited him in the barracks, not permitting himself to think of the pain in his back or the hot agony of his shoulders or his feet that looked like the Union Jack; white skin mottled with blue bruises and ragged streaks of blood.

He fell into his bunk, not even able to reach for the ration packet. His eyes shut, but he could only doze. The hunger cried and tormented him, yet the deep cold of the river was still in his bones and demanded he seek the warmth of unconsciousness.

Finally, unable to stand it any longer, he reached for his rations. He brought up the pouch from his hidey-hole. Empty. He stared at the pouch. There would be no more food for a week save his skilly in the morning. One day on Sarah Island and already Peter knew he'd die there. Most likely he couldn't last the week with no more to eat than skilly. He might survive if he could beg or steal or bargain for rations from the other convicts, but he'd never survive the cold of the river or have the agility to handle the deadly logs that hurtled down the slide to him. His mind clouded with quick visions of himself being crushed among the weighty lumber, being pressed beneath the foaming river, and then he was blank. Only a deep immovable sorrow worked up from his loins, pressing through his stomach and chest and invading his throat and eyes.

He didn't notice the convict who sat on his bunk beside him, nor did he seem to understand or move when the man held out the contents of his looted ration pouch.

The man put his hand on Peter's shoulder. "Cheer up, mate. I tol' you this morning not to be eatin' your rations too soon. But you didn't listen, so I thought I'd best show you what comes of a man who don't keep his ration pouch in sight." He pushed the rations into Peter's empty pouch. "I didn't take none. Damn if you didn't tempt me though, but I didn't touch a bloody crumb. Here—take it. Come on, now, mate—it ain't the end yet."

Peter's hand clenched the pouch. Suddenly he leapt from the bunk, wheeling to face the man. "You damned, bloody interfering bastard!"

The man guffawed. "So you are still canny!"

Peter charged at him, the pouch still clenched in one fist, the other doubled and poised to drive into the man's belly.

Darting lightly from side to side, the smaller man seemed to enjoy Peter's rage. "This be thanks? After I saved your dinner for you?"

Peter lunged at him, missed, and staggered forward on legs that were still numb with cold.

"Come on, mate, I did you a good turn. Don't make me lay you flat on your back for bein' a fool again." The man put his hands out.

Peter, his face twisted with anger, came at him once more.

The man shrugged. "Seems like you're determined to be a donkey's ass, mate." He shouted at another man. The convict met Peter's attack, butting him in the diaphragm as his friend came from behind Peter hitting his legs.

In seconds Peter was flat on the floor, the small convict sitting on his belly, a knee firmly planted on each arm. His friend stood nearby.

"Quiet now, mate. We don't want the guards in on this. I'm John the Pocket. This is my friend Walter Wheeler. We mean you no harm."

"No harm? Never turn your back on me, bastard."

Wheeler's expression turned ugly. "Don't you talk to John like that. He fought two men to save your bloody rations for you. I say he keeps 'em."

"Naww, we don't want 'em, Berean. They're yours, but you've got to learn, man, or you'll not survive the month on Sarah. Now, can I let you up without you comin' at me like a crazed bull?"

Peter did poorly with his rations that week and the next. Despite the lessons his two new friends had tried to teach him, the gnawing hunger drove him time and again to the pouch. He found it almost impossible to work as he did and live on the rations he was given. Too often he found himself with nothing to eat at the end of the week. He was constantly hungry, often dreaming of what one bite of fresh meat would taste like. He could hardly remember the taste, and now it seemed terribly important that he should, for he feared he would never taste it again. No fresh meat rations were permitted on Sarah Island. The craving for food became an obsession even greater than his longing to be free.

"By God, Wheeler, we must do something for this donkey's ass before he turns cannibal on us. Did you see how he looked at that plump-bottomed little minister today? I thought the commandant would be writin' to the poor soul's mother tellin' her how her son was et by a vicious convict."

Wheeler and John the Pocket laughed, but it was not all in fun. Beneath their jokes was a serious concern. They stole for Peter and taught him to be one of the lightest-fingered men in the barracks. John bragged that he could steal a man's false teeth between the bites of an apple. That other men went hungry because their rations had been pilfered was no consideration. The three of them stuck together and took care of their own.

Peter didn't realize how important this was until one day in line when he saw a settler slip a piece of tobacco to a convict in front of him. That evening word spread that in exchange for a favor from a guard someone had reported the gift of tobacco. The convict was given fifty lashes and the settler fined.

For a month Peter enjoyed a friendship with John the Pocket and Walter Wheeler. John had told Peter of his life and bragged of being the best pickpocket London had ever known. Walter, the milder of the two, and a worshiper of John, had little to say. As far as Peter could tell, Walter had been a fence for John's stolen goods, and the two of them had been caught trying to sell the engraved pocket watch of an important lord. Since neither of them could read, they had paid little attention to the inscription, taking only the precaution of trying to sell the jeweled watch to a Dutchman. They had been sentenced and transported together four years ago.

During the interval Peter told them of himself and even dared to tell them of Callie's scarf, and what it meant to him in his dreams. As he had hoped, neither of them laughed. In fact they had envied him the ownership of such a fine talisman.

In the midst of Sarah Island's bleak, brutal life it was good to have these two men to talk and occasionally laugh with. At first Peter listened, then began to join in, talking about women, places they had been, great exaggerated adventures they had had, successes they had known. To hear John, he had all but had Big Ben in his pocket when caught, and Walter had fenced a king's ransom in jewels. Peter's brewery had grown to the biggest and finest in the world. His fields stretched farther than a horse could walk in a fortnight. Callie became the most beautiful woman ever born, and as faithful as Penelope awaiting the return of Odysseus.

With the companionship of friends, talk of escape and return in triumph, dreams shared and magnified by hope, life on Sarah Island became at least tolerable. It eased the most unbearable ache of all: loneliness.

Peter, John, and Walter managed to get on the same river crew. They talked about it often and knew it was only a matter of time before someone on that crew would be hurt by one of the logs coming off the slide. But they were not prepared for it to happen to one of them.

The three of them stood in the cold river with the other men, shouting ribald remarks to the slide crew as they waited for the first log. The shouts changed from bantering ribaldry to frightened, angry screams as a man at the top slipped and released his log. Not one, but three logs, and the man, lunged down, jamming and tumbling over one another. The men in the water dived for safety. Walter seemed to be stunned, staring at the bloody pulp of the man hurtling down the slide, crushed by the logs. Peter grabbed him by the hair, dragging him away from the plunging logs. When they surfaced there was a telltale, expanding splotch of red staining the river. Peter dived and brought from under the floating logs the body of a convict who had been working the river crew for only a week. His head and shoulder were crushed. Peter took the man to the river bank and laid him beside the body of the man who had come down the slide.

Walter covered his eyes, hiding the gratitude he felt that it hadn't been John the Pocket. Then he walked through the water hunting for sight of John. The convicts shouted their condition to the guards on shore. As Walter came toward Peter, standing on the shore, two men struggled to the bank further down river. One of them was John the Pocket, his left arm dangling useless and bloody.

John was taken to the prison hospital. His left hand was amputated and his broken arm and shoulder set. Walter cried like a baby, as though his life were over as well as John the left-handed pickpocket's. No dreams could come true if they were impossible. As long as John had his hand, escape from Sarah was something to talk about because John could take care of them in the world outside. Now he no longer could, and Sarah Island could no longer be escaped, even in dreams.

When John returned to the barracks, he was a different man. He was grim, determined to escape in a way Peter had never heard him speak of before. He asked for his old job on the river crew again, and took chances no man could rightly expect to survive. The logs, however, seemed perverse. If John stood directly in their path, the logs swerved, leaving him untouched.

Peter and Walter tried to cheer him up, make him laugh and plan and dream again. John merely became quieter and more introspective. His one desire was to be released from Sarah Island. He looked lovingly and sorrowfully at the two friends he had already decided to leave behind. "Can't you find it in you to see I can't take no more? I want my Maker. He can be no harsher than a man, and surely I think He'll judge me kinder."

Peter didn't understand. He still throbbed with life and though it was of a bitter sort, he had hope. Walter did understand. But for Walter, understanding wasn't necessary. He knew that where John went he would go too. John had always been the leader. He would remain so.

At the river the great logs tumbled down the slide. Peter, John, and Walter stood in the water waiting, their eyes fixed on the logs, their minds and hearts centered on God. Would He forgive? Was there truly a place on His right hand for the good thief?

As the log plunged deep into the river, the rushing swirl of water pounded against Peter's legs. John the Pocket went under without a struggle against the strong hand that held him down until the log had been pushed over him and replaced the hand. Shortly Peter shouted there was a man under.

John was replaced on the crew by a new convict. The following week another convict replaced Walter Wheeler, and Peter was once again alone on Sarah Island.

For two months Peter went out each morning, rowing to the woodcutting station, silent and ignoring the others around him. The less he had to do with anyone the better it seemed to be. At least that way he had only himself to fight and be responsible for, and not the kindness and hatred of others.

Because he caused no trouble, Peter was reclassified within the confines of Sarah. He was termed a good-conduct man within the sixth classification. At the end of June his job was changed. He would, starting in July, be sent to the island's sawmill. Each step in good conduct was a step up the classification. If it continued, he would soon be classed as a fifth-level convict. It seemed a good thing as well as a relief to be sent to the sawmill. There was no icy water to stand in for twelve hours a day, and there would be no more of the backbreaking weight of the logs on his shoulders.

The mill stood in a large clearing, rolling scrub land around it. On the hillsides he saw guards, whips in hand, shouting and directing heavy sleds of wood being dragged toward the sawmill. They shouted, geeing and hawing as they would any horse or ox, except that there were no horses or oxen or asses on Sarah. No beast of burden was allowed.

The guard assigned to Peter took him to the sled he was to pull. The man reached to the top of the loaded wood stack, hauling down the harness thrown there. Peter stood straight and rigid as the guard came toward him.

"You're not putting that on me," he said in a low voice.

"Get over here. Raise your arms." The guard jabbed him with the whip handle. He took Peter's arm, slipping the harness onto one shoulder.

"Get your bloody hands off me!" Peter grabbed the whip. He hurled it into the brush. As he stretched out, the guard hit him in the stomach, doubling him over, and quickly tossed the harness across Peter's back. Peter reared up, taking hold of the harness and the guard, shaking them both with a savage fury.

The other prisoners sat down on the ground, glad to be ignored. Other guards rushed over. The convicts watched as five guards closed in on Peter. It happened to them all at sometime, but they would enjoy watching it now. It was quite a show to see the tall blond man in irons wildly swinging the harness like a weapon at all comers.

"A man is no beast, damn you!"

The guards formed a circle and began to move in. To whichever of the five Peter turned his attention, the other four flicked at him with their whips.

Slowly the circle closed. Peter lashed at them, his face and body covered with sweat, tears streaming down his cheeks. "A man is no beast! I am a man . . . a *man*." His voice was smothered with the scuffling and grunting of the guards as they bore down on him driving his face into the ground.

The other convicts got up, going back to work. It had been good while it lasted, but it was too short a test. They knew it was probably the last show of rebellion they would see from Peter Berean. Men who had not been to the triangles were always more outspoken than those who had. Those bearing the scars might be recklessly revengeful, but "A man is no beast" were the words of a newcomer.

The triangles, wooden staves fastened together to form a triangle, stood in an open area. They were constructed atop a wooden structure, making it easier for onlookers to view the punishment. The bell was rung and a crowd began to form. Peter stood on the platform, his shirt taken off him and tossed to the plank floor. A stir of interest rippled through the people at the sight of the brand on his chest.

"Who'd he murder?" one woman asked her neighbor.

"His wife, I heard, and the local magistrate . . . found them together and had done with them both. I heard tell he's a real brute, this one is."

The first woman shook her head. "A magistrate . . . well, it's often the way with these 'andsome ones. They don't have two corn kernels in their heads to call brains."

More people trickled up to stand at the base of the triangles. Men and women from the settlement, some with their children, convicts, guards, and officers forming a waiting sea of eager, anticipatory faces all around him.

"What'd he do?" a man asked.

"Attacked a guard, they say."

"He's lucky they didn't hang him."

"Mmmm. They'll skin the back off 'im. You watch. He'll take at least a hundred."

His body was extended to full length as his hands were lashed to the apex of the triangle at the same time his legs were spread wide and lashed to the angular braces. He hung there naked to the waist, listening to the murmuring talk around him. The chaplain, probably a disgraced minister sent to Van Diemen's Land to rid himself of his own demons of drink or lust or hate, mounted the platform with Peter. He thrust the Bible into Peter's face. "Sin has a dreadful hold on your immortal soul. Keep your mind turned toward the Lord lest you be lost to the legions of evil."

The crowd mumbled amens piously, then raised their eyes to stare at the prisoner hanging half naked before them.

Peter hung his head, trying to avoid the sight of the minister, if not the sound of his voice.

"Repent, dear soul, that your depravity may not destroy all hope for the salvation of your soul. Repent! Lest you be cast into the everlasting sulphurous fires of Hell," he concluded, the spittle standing in white flecks on his lips. Ponderously, clutching the Bible to his breast, the minister left the platform to join the crowd below.

Another convict stepped forward. He took the cat-o'-nine-tails and stepped into position behind Peter.

Peter remembered the flogging he had received aboard the *George III* and thought that with mercy he'd be unconscious before this one was half over. With the slow regularity of a metronome the lashes were called out. Peter hadn't reckoned with the thirty-second delay between strokes. The time seemed an eternity. His nerves were flayed raw along with his back. He was screaming long before the lash ever touched him, and when it came it thudded into his back driving the breath from his body, making him choke and strangle on his own saliva and blood as he bit through his lip and tongue. He was insensible to everything but terror and pain. There was no sound on heaven or earth but the swishing scream of the scourge and the dull impact on yielding flesh. The platform was lined with armies of red ants carrying off the torn slices of Peter's back. At every stroke blood sprayed.

Thoughts of withstanding the whip were gone after twenty lashes. He couldn't stand it. But he couldn't escape it. He couldn't move from it. He couldn't beg, though he would have, for there was no mercy. He couldn't think with that fiery lightning coming down on him again and again eating away his flesh and his soul. All he could do was endure. Survive because neither was there a way to die. He thought he knew then what it meant to want to die. He thought he understood John's despair and longing for death. But he didn't.

With each lash his body jerked spasmodically. The blue sky leapt; the wood of the triangles wavered against the blue like brown worms in the heavens. The blur of faces bobbed and weaved. Grotesqueries. Ascending and descending in sickening revolution.

When the lash began to cut muscle, the commandant ordered it stopped. They needed the man to work the sled. There was no value in a cripple.

Peter's hands and legs were cut free. He fell to the planking, his face cushioned on his own blood and flesh. An inch from his half-opened eyes the red ants carried the red flesh through his red blood. He thought he'd never move again, thought he no longer cared what they did to him. But he screamed till he thought he'd torn his throat out, and arched his back as the guard threw a bucket of saltwater over his open wounds.

"Pick up your shirt, Berean. There's still a sled to be hauled."

Peter struggled to his feet, falling twice before he could stand wobbling and dizzy. He staggered across the platform, nearly falling again as he went down the steps.

"Now we'll see if that harness doesn't suit you better."

No concern for his back was exercised as the harness was placed on him. The straps were affixed just as securely. Peter stood weakly letting his tormentor do as he would, never once allowing his eyes to meet the guard's. It was the most satisfying evidence the guard had seen that Peter Berean was beginning to acquire the proper attitude for a convict.

He kept his eyes downcast as the guard hooked the harness to the sled and told Peter to test the fastenings before moving the lumber. Peter pulled against the straps, the leather biting deep into his flayed shoulders and back.

The guard didn't expect him to be able to pull the sled. Peter was far too weak and sick after the triangles, but the guard kept him at it the remainder of the work day. He watched as Peter tried to pull the heavy weight and fell under it, struggling to his feet, flinching and straining under the shouted commands of *gee!* and *haw!* The entire day he managed to pull one load of lumber.

From that day on he was worked and treated like a brute, prodded with a whip, attending to his commands.

Chapter 35

That spring Stephen had to prepare the hop fields without his brother for the first time. The crew of men Peter had hired and trained before they left for England knew their work well. Without them Stephen would never have been able to manage.

Jack had lost his boon companion. Stephen was working from dawn to dusk. By the time the fields were plowed, the hop wires strung, and the young shoots twiddled, Stephen was dreaming confusedly of work-filled days.

There was so much that had to be done all at the same time. He and Peter had planned a two-man operation, and it was. There was more to be accomplished than either could have managed alone, yet Stephen was determined to try. He too had some of Callie's determined faith that some day Peter would come home.

The brewery was nearly completed and Stephen was needed there daily to direct the installation and placement of the new equipment. In the malthouse it was the steam-powered engine that required his attention. In the fields it was the varieties of hops and the selection of new fields to clear. In the office it was the ledgers. Daily he was reminded of how much he missed Peter. This farm was their dream, and Stephen couldn't find the delight in it that he would have, had he been able to share it with his brother. If only Peter were home. Had he been there, the completion of the brewery would have been a day Peter would have celebrated. Stephen could almost hear his laughter and the extravagant plans he would have made for a party, no doubt inviting every man and his family who had worked on the brewery to join them. Stephen sighed. He would never have the quality of shared joy that came to Peter so naturally.

Peter was on his mind a great deal that spring. He had never before realized how much a part of his life his brother was, or how much he loved him. Stephen wrote frequently, not really expecting a reply. Peter was not a likely correspondent to start, and with a new land to explore and become excited about, Stephen thought, he probably wouldn't be heard from until he was brimming with news and wanted to share it. For no matter how lonely Stephen was without Peter, he didn't doubt that Peter would do well, even as a convict. He had no reason to think otherwise for life on that lonely, distant penal colony was a secret to the outside world. And Stephen knew his brother was a born leader of men. He was bold and he was honest. He was sure those qualities would be recognized and valued. Anyone would realize Peter wasn't a criminal. All they had to do was listen to him.

By July, when there still had been no word from Peter, Stephen began to worry. What disturbed him most was not that he had heard nothing, but that Callie had not. In some ways it made Stephen feel more at ease, taking it as a sign that Peter no longer depended on her so much. On the other hand, he wished Peter would at least write making it clear to Callie that he was all right. She worried constantly.

Her feelings for Peter, and the uncertainty of his well-being, had opened a rift between himself and Callie he didn't know how to heal. Inside he ached with longing for his brother, yet he couldn't keep from feeling hurt and jealous as Callie continued to talk about Peter. In her own way she was as bad as Natalie was about Albert. Between them Stephen was often made to feel like a piece of farm machinery—used, but unnoticed until he wasn't there when they wanted something of him.

Jack added his own persuasive views to Stephen's general feeling of being taken for granted. "You're off your head," Jack fumed. "Callie's a good girl, but she doesn't know you're alive, Stevie. When are you going to wake up and see it?"

"I don't know," Stephen said dispiritedly.

"It's not like she's the only girl in the world, you know. There's easily half a dozen that'd run for you if you give 'em a little encouragement. And their Papa's business wouldn't do you harm either. I don't understand you. I don't understand Callie. Hell, I don't understand any of you! You're a damned crazy family if you ask me. What is it? Is she in love with Peter, or what?"

"She loves him," Stephen said.

"Then what in the hell are you doing dying on the vine waiting for her?"

Stephen sat back, playing with his glass. "I'm not dying on any vine."

"What do you call it?"

"How the hell should I know? I love her, that's all."

"Did you ever think of getting over it?"

Stephen laughed. "Get the tooth extracted, eh?"

"Yeah, something like that."

"You have a pair of pliers handy?"

"No, but I'll put my money on Agnes Wharton having something a lot softer than pliers to cure you. She's just holding her breath for you to give her the chance. And—I got that straight from her brother's mouth."

"Agnes . . .?" Stephen tried the name speculatively.

"Yeah, Agnes, and even you got to admit she's got everything Callie has and more."

"She's different from Callie."

"She sure is! *She* loves you. I'm sorry, Stevie, but I get damned tired of seeing you hankering after that little piece of ice day after day, and she doesn't think of anyone but Peter. I like His Magnificence, you know that, but sweet Jesus where does that leave you?"

Stephen shrugged, shifting his weight uncomfortably. "You want another drink?"

"No, I want you to smarten up. Go see Agnes. Give her a chance."

"Maybe . . . after harvest."

"Not after harvest. Now."

Stephen shook his head uncertainly.

"All right, you don't want to give up hoping Callie will finally see you—tell me this, what does His Magnificence think about all this? Is it a one-way thing with Callie, or is he thinkin' the same way about her?"

"I don't know. I really don't. He needs her—needed her, but we haven't heard from him. I don't know what Peter feels."

"I can't say I'm too surprised you haven't heard from him," Jack said cryptically, making knowing faces as he spoke.

"What's that mean?"

"Never mind that now, you're not going to sidetrack

me. If what you say is true—that he needs her and she loves him—you gonna tell me you're gonna step in between them?"

Stephen downed his beer. "Let's go home. I've got to be up early."

"You're not," Jack said.

"Five o'clock. I call that early."

"I didn't mean that. You're never gonna come between Callie and Peter. It just ain't in ya, friend. And you're gonna see Agnes Wharton if I have to hit you on the head and carry you to her door myself."

"Shut up, Jack."

"You shut up! I know what's good for you."

Stephen went to see Agnes. By the end of autumn both Agnes and her family anticipated the announcement of an engagement to follow.

During the month of October, Stephen was once more aware he hadn't heard from Peter. The brewery was complete. Once the hops were gathered, Stephen would fire up the new steam engine in the malt house and begin the first official batch of Berean Beer.

It had been a year since Peter had sailed from England. Stephen was uneasy; he should have heard from his brother by now, no matter what the conditions. The mail delivery became the most important event of the week for Stephen. It was easy to disguise his interest; he told Callie he was waiting for verification of an important hop order.

By the end of November, when still no letter had come, he mentioned it to Callie, and was immediately sorry. Everything Jack had said seemed all the clearer as he listened to her pour out her own fears and worries about Peter's silence.

Resigned, he decided Jack had been right all along. Love her or not, she didn't love him, and he didn't want to spend his life watching her raise Jamie and long for Peter. As it was they were nearly a family now. Callie filled every function of a dutiful, faithful wife, save one, and that was obviously due only to Peter's absence. She tended his house, raised his child, and loved him.

Stephen sat down patiently listening to her and then tried to comfort her. "Just one lost letter can mean a delay of months before we hear from him, Callie."

"We don't even know if he's alive. Maybe his ship. . . . Do you think he has gotten my letters?"

"He must have," Stephen said simply.

She looked up at him, worried. "Then what is wrong, Stephen? It isn't like Peter to be silent. He . . . he always is so happy about everything, and wanting to talk about what he is doing. Even in Newgate . . . he talked . . . he wanted company. He'd answer my letters if he could, Stephen. I know he would. Oh, Stephen, if only we knew something. Where is he?"

"He's alive, Callie. We would have heard . . . if the ship went down or something happened to him. He'll write soon, I'm sure. By now he probably has started a new hop yard."

"As a prisoner?"

"It's possible; many Australian transportees did it. They say transportation is a light sentence. Even though they're prisoners, they have a life."

"Then perhaps he's just too busy to write. Maybe he's making plans for us to go out there? Do you think . . ."

"I'd think that was it," he said with less certainty than he wished for.

Stephen had no idea of what a term at Van Diemen's Land was like, and no idea how to get information. The penal colonies were a world to themselves, secretive, controlled, and closed off from all but the settlers who lived there. There were no ties to the outside world, for to a convict there was no outside world.

In order to write, Peter had to ask permission of the commandant. His letter would be handed unsealed to the commandant for censoring and approval. Whether the letter would actually be sent, Peter was never told. The task of writing a letter that would be approved was in itself a risky business. Any criticism, direct or implied, of the penal colony would earn him another flogging on the triangles. Any mention of his life in Van Diemen's Land that could be construed as implying a lack of mercy was considered blasphemy. If found in violation of any of these restrictions the least Peter could expect was flagellation or a long time in solitary confinement. At worst he could be tried and condemned to death; blasphemy was a capital offense. As a result, convict's letters to home and families were religiously tinted, glowing accounts. They fostered the idea that transportation was a light sentence.

In the beginning Peter had been too tired and too depressed to figure out the intricacies of a letter filled with phrases of repentance and sprinkled with passages from the Bible he was to study and think about every day. After he had been sent to the triangles, thoughts of Callie and Stephen were as painful as were the faces of the people who had watched him being flogged. He didn't want them to know who he was now. He didn't want to reach out to or be known by anyone, not even them.

Stephen wrote to Meg asking if she had heard from Peter. He hoped Peter's silence meant he was permitted only a limited number of letters and had chosen to write to Meg rather than himself or Callie. It wasn't likely, however, for Meg wrote frequently and had never mentioned Peter.

He sat with Jack in a tavern in Poughkeepsie one evening in early December, his beer in front of him untouched.

"What's eating at you?" Jack asked disgruntled. "You're about as much fun as a wet towel tonight."

"That's about the way I feel. Jack, there has to be a way we can find out about Peter. He didn't drop off the end of the earth. But I don't know how to reach him."

"Are you sure you want to? Let's go see Agnes and forget about this."

"Goddamn it! Of course I want to know about him. He's my brother—remember?"

"You've got a one-track mind."

"If you don't like it, you can always go somewhere else. There's the door. No one is barring it."

"Don't get angry. There's always talk around . . . I don't know how true it is, mind, but I listen and learn things now and then."

"About Van Diemen's Land? What would you know about it?"

"From the sounds of it, a hell of a lot more than you do."

"Such as?"

"It's a hellhole."

Stephen sat back in disgust. "So was Newgate." He went back to brooding about a way to find out about Peter. Jack leaned forward, hurt and annoyed that Stephen should dismiss him so easily.

"Listen, I know plenty. I was trying to be nice to you and Callie by keeping my mouth shut. I didn't think you'd really want to know."

"Well, we do, so if you do know anything, tell me."

"I know some whalers . . . I've talked to them a couple of times. I was curious too, you know. I wanted to know how His Magnificence was coming along. These whalers re-rig in Hobart Town. It's right in the middle of one of those penal colonies. They tell me no convict's life is worth spit. They die like flies, Stevie. Tell the truth, more'n likely Peter isn't alive."

"We would have heard."

"If they felt like telling you! He was sent there for life, wasn't he?"

"So?"

"So what difference does it make when he dies? How are you gonna know different from what they tell you? Stevie, I'm tellin' you those commandants out there are little kings. They do what they want and say sorry to no man."

"Oh God, Jack . . . you're wrong . . . you . . ."

"You told me you wanted to know. I'm tellin' you straight, Stevie, honest."

"Where'd you hear this?"

"I told you—some whalers I met."

"Will you introduce me to them?"

"If that's what you want; but Stevie, you're not gonna like what you hear, and there's not a blessed thing you can do. I wish you'd take my advice and forget it."

Jack took Stephen to the docks, wending through narrow streets stacked high with barrels and crates all marked with signs of travel and the wear of a sea journey. Jack tried several pubs frequented by the whalers before he found the man he sought, Tom Baker.

Tom Baker was a burly, gruff man with a short temper. He was a hard man well suited to the lack of comfort of the whaling life. Until he had begun whaling on his own, Baker had worked as part of a fleet, leaving New York and not returning to port for two years or better. Once he had been gone for four years. His body was marked with the scars of his profession; his mind was marked with harsh and often violent memories of long years with only his mates and the sea for companionship.

He looked Stephen over as Jack introduced them and told Tom that Stephen wanted to know about Van Diemen's Land. Tom twisted back in his chair, his thick arm thrown over the back as he studied the slender, well-built young man Jack had introduced. Without exchanging a word, Tom decided Stephen was a sensitive, bleeding-heart type, as ignorant of the ways of Van Diemen's Land as most of the well dressed young gentlemen from England he had met.

He shot a walloping spew of tobacco into the brass spittoon by the bar. "What t'hell he want t'know fer?"

Jack explained. Tom squinted until his one eye became a slit. He decided he'd tell this clean-minded young dandy what he asked for. It would give him pleasure to watch him squirm inside his expensive clothes. Anyway he liked telling these Englishers what their government did to the men they didn't want. Not that he blamed them—if it were up to Tom Baker, he'd beat them all senseless, and if they didn't shape up he'd hang the lot of 'em. He wouldn't be letting it drag on for years like the Limeys did. If this man's brother were in Van Diemen's Land it'd serve him right to know what it was like.

Tom began to thoroughly enjoy himself. His mates joined in the telling of stories they had heard in Hobart Town of convicts who had tried to escape turning cannibal and eating one another until there was only one starving man left. They told of floggings and deaths as a result, and of men working like animals when they could barely stand from weakness, illness, and fatigue.

Their laughter rose, as did their storehouse of tales as they watched Stephen's eyes widen in horror as he placed his hand on his roiling stomach.

By the time they finished telling of the atrocities they had either seen or heard about, Stephen was trembling in a cold sweat, his face ashen. "Oh, my God . . . oh, my God . . ."

Jack grasped Stephen's shoulder. "You all right? Take a drink, Steve . . . come on . . . come on, please. Don't pass out on me. You all right?"

Stephen pushed the glass away. "I've got to get him out of there," he said shakily. "Why the hell didn't we hear this in England? I asked everyone."

The whalers laughed. "How you gonna hear? Who's to tell? Those convicts can't breathe hard or they're gonna taste the cat. Why risk it? What fer?"

"But . . ."

Once more Tom squinted, evaluating Stephen. Slowly he said, "Course there've been escapes. Not many, but they've been done. I got a man out once."

Stephen grabbed the man's beefy arm. "Could you get my brother out?"

"Maybe. Depends on a couple of things." He looked at the palm of his hands, then rubbed his fingers together.

"I'll pay whatever you ask . . . anything I have. Can you get him out?"

Tom laughed loudly. "Anything I ask, will ya? Maybe yer brother ain't worth what you think. Trip like that'll cost you."

"I don't give a damn about the cost. Can you do it?"

"Where is he?"

"Van Diemen's Land," Stephen said weakly.

"Where?" Tom asked, knowing Stephen had no answer. "Port Arthur? Hobart? Sarah? Norfolk? Maria? Where?"

"I don't know. I've never heard from him . . . or the authorities."

"You come talk price when you find out where he is. If they've got him at Maria or Sarah, you can forget about getting him off. Otherwise maybe we can make a deal."

"What's the best place for him to be?"

"Hobart's easiest. Once a convict has a good classification, he's a little freer . . . can get around a bit. Thing is, I gotta be able to talk to him without a guard listenin' in. I can't walk in, ya know, and ask the commandant where I can find Peter Berean. Your brother's gotta know when we're comin' and get to us. We can't get to him."

"Then there's no way."

"Sit tight till he writes."

"Will he?"

Tom shrugged. "Most do if they have someone, and if life ain't too hard."

"Then that means . . ."

"Your brother's probably not at Hobart. He'd be writing if he were. Tell him to work his way to Hobart if you find a way to reach him."

"I will."

"Watch what you say. You can't do it direct. Them commandants know all the tricks. If they catch wind you're thinkin' to spring him, your brother'll pay with every piece of meat he's got on his back an' then some. I've seen those bastards turn 'em around an' slice off their chests when there weren't no back left."

"Nothing direct," Stephen repeated, stunned and sickened. He got up unsteadily. Jack hovered near him. The whaler finished his beer.

"There's one more thing you might wanna think about. Are you sure you want him out? He was sent away fer murder?"

"Yes, but he didn't do it."

"Don't matter. He maybe couldn't kill when you knew him, but if he's been there a year already and he ain't in Hobart, trust me to know you got a killer for a brother now. They send 'em there with hearts o' men, and turn 'em out with hearts o' beasts. I've seen it happen. They're animals . . . wild animals."

"No . . . not Peter. You don't know him. Peter is . . . he's gentle and fun loving. Tell him, Jack," Stephen said anxiously.

Jack nodded enthusiastically. "Yeah, he's all that and more. His Magnificence is one grand man."

"Just thought I'd let you know. You ain't gonna get the same man back that went. Tell the truth, if it were my brother, I'd shoot him myself, like any other beast. One more thing . . . you ain't gettin' no promise from me to bring him back alive neither. If he's as mean a bastard as most, I'll treat him like one o' my seamen when they's outter line."

"The man's a gentleman," Jack said huffily.

Tom sent a brown tobacco wash ringing in the spittoon. "He's a bloody convict. You don't get put away for kissin' ladies' hands."

Stephen, his voice still shaking, said, "Peter would give you no trouble, Mr. Baker. You don't know him. He's . . . please, Mr. Baker, you must help me . . . I've got to get him out. I'll pay whatever you ask . . . I'll get in touch with him. Somehow. He'll answer. He must answer!"

Stephen rode home with Jack early that evening. Callie looked up from her sewing in surprise. Alarmed, she went to him. "Stephen—are you all right? You look ill. Come sit down. Jack, what happened? What's wrong with him?"

"I think he'd better tell you himself. Good night, Callie."

"Stephen?"

"Callie, I want you to write to Peter every day, and I will too."

"What is it, Stephen? What's wrong—did you get news of him?"

"Every day. Write to him."

"Stephen, you're frightening me! Please, tell me what it is. Where were you tonight?"

"I talked to some men who've been to Van Diemen's Land. Whalers."

"And they saw Peter?"

"No. It's an awful place, Callie. We've got to get him out. Oh, my God, why didn't I know before? The whalers can get him out, but not until I get in touch with Peter. He has to know . . . and play his part. He must write!"

Callie went limply to her knees on the floor beside Stephen's chair. "You mean you're going to bring Peter home, Stephen?"

"I'm going to try."

Tears welled up in her eyes; her hands shook as she touched him. "I've prayed and prayed for a miracle, and . . . and it's you. You're the miracle."

He drove his fist into the palm of his hand. "Somehow we've got to get him to write. If only there were some sort of signal. Nothing can be said straight out. Oh, God, Callie, I don't know how to begin. I don't know what to do."

"But I do! Oh, see, Stephen . . . there is a God and He does look after us. Peter and I *do* have a signal."

Stephen looked at her smiling face. "You do? But how . . . why would you and Peter have a signal . . . ?"

"It was never intended to be used as such, but it could be. I asked him to write to me of the May house. It was to be a . . . a special message to me so I'd know the minute he began believing again. He was to write of it the day he knew he'd be coming home. If only he remembers, we could use that."

"Thank God. He'll remember. He'll have to. Write to him about it, Callie. Now! Hurry, sit down. I'll get paper for you."

"No . . . you write it. If I do, he'll think it is me wishing. If you write it he'll realize we're trying to tell him something."

"All right . . . good . . . I'll write about the May house. You write about Hobart Town. That's where the whalers told me it was best for him to be. It'll have to be up to Peter to get there, and Callie, none of this will be easy."

"I keep remembering that last day we saw him at the hulks. I can't forget that day. He was so unhappy—it was killing him. It's been so long . . . how much longer will it be?"

Stephen looked away from her. He had told her almost nothing of what the whalers had revealed. In some ways Callie knew Peter better than anyone, and Newgate seemed enough to her to put him in agony. He felt a physical pain claw at him as he began to realize what the whalers had tried to tell him. What was he bringing home to Callie?

Floggings and brutality and starvation would eat deeply into a man like his brother. Peter was proud and he had an idealist's sense of justice. How many times would Peter have tried to fight the cruelty and injustice, and what would they have done to him as a result? Stephen began to wonder just what his brother was now. What remained of the man he and Callie loved?

They wrote several letters that night. The next day Stephen took the letters to Tom Baker.

"We'll get 'em there. That's all I can promise."

"I know. You will see if you can find out anything about him?"

"I'll do my best. Understand it's got to be done sneaky like. One thing you don't want in a penal colony is to be noticed."

Stephen took another packet of letters to be sent aboard freighters and commercial ships; then he returned home to wait. He and Callie continued to write daily, constructing each letter carefully, making sure it held the proper clues and yet was different enough from other letters to arouse no suspicion. Each one they wrote seemed to be the most important, and the one deserving the most thought and care, for it might be the one Peter received.

They knew most of the letters would never arrive, but they sent off each one with a prayer. If only one letter could get through!

Chapter 36

Peter received a letter from Callie, not one of those
Stephen had frantically begun to have her write, but
one she had written seven months before that he had
not been given until now. It was a letter typical of
Callie, telling him about Jamie and the things he had
learned to do. It was filled with talk of Stephen and
the brewery. In his mind Peter could see exactly the
point to which the construction had come. He was
shaking as he held the letter, his eyes tearing as he
began to feel the things he no longer had the strength
to feel. Longing was the most dangerous emotion. It
opened the door through which other feelings
flooded: anger he wasn't permitted to express, ideas
that made him prone to talk when all that was wanted
of him was dumb obedience, fears from which he had
no release, shame that was now his ever-present companion.

He crumpled the letter, not reading the last page as
he laid on his bunk trying to force his mind closed
again. He succeeded in stemming the tears that had
begun, but it was impossible to cut off memory com-

pletely, especially after a year of utter loneliness when he could still remember the feeling of her soft skin and the scent of her hair.

He pulled the faded, stained scarf from the waist of his trousers. It was no longer brightly colored. Its edges were frayed and it bore many stains of his own blood. He looked at the scarf, holding it up before him. It was no longer fresh, and the thoughts he had of Callie, when he dared to think, were not pure either. He folded the scarf into a triangle and put it around his neck. One day, sometime in the past year, everything had lost its purity. There was no reason to treasure a scrap of silk that meant nothing. Around his neck it was a talisman. A sign that said plainly that he had someone somewhere. A woman.

He need never tell the scarf had been given to him a long time ago and had since lost its meaning—if indeed he had ever truly known what it meant. He could remember many women passing out symbols of affection, none of them lasting longer than the moment of giving. Rosalind had given him many things, little tokens, and none of them had meaning.

He still worked at the sawmill, but there was no more fight in him about the harness. He did what he was asked, and for the most part he avoided trouble. He had been sent to the triangles one other time, and that for refusing to flog another convict. Peter was given the man's lashes, and then had to flog the man anyway. Fortunately it had been a settler's convict and the number of lashes only twenty.

Otherwise one day was much the same as another. He listened to the convicts talk during breakfast and dinner, but he kept mostly to himself. Several times he had been asked to participate in death pacts so common among the convicts. One would enter into an agreement to murder the other thus freeing them both. While one man would die kindly and quickly at the hands of his companion, the murderer would be hanged, a relatively quick end. Straws were drawn to see which man would be the most fortunate and die at his fellow convict's hand, and which would be left behind to face the commandant and hanging.

In one year eighty-five men died, only thirty by natural causes. Of the remaining, eight were killed accidentally, three were shot by soldiers, twenty-seven drowned, and twelve were known to be killed by other convicts.

Twice Peter had honored such a request. At the time it had been easy for him, and it seemed simple and right. With his assignment on the river crew, all he had to do was to step into a deeper pool of water. Taller than John or Walter, he stood in the deep pool long enough for the heavy irons to hold them under— long enough to drown. Then he pushed a log over them and called the alarm, "man under."

He had ended the lives of the only two convicts who had befriended him, and he had done it because they were friends. He was never accused of their deaths, however, for accidental drownings were not unusual, and Peter had never been able to bring himself to kill in any other way. He couldn't have hit them with a log or strangled them or sent a knife into their hearts. All he had been able to bring himself to do was to find the deep water and let it do the killing. He thought bitterly, however, that he now deserved the branded *M* on his chest. He was a murderer now. Twice over.

Few of the convicts seriously considered suicide, for it condemned them. While they seemed to be forgotten by God, and their God bore no resemblance to the one the ministers hammered into their minds with exhortations of evil and repentance, the hope that He was there lived on. He might forgive a man for ending the tortured life of a fellow man, releasing him from what they considered Hell, but one could not take one's own life. Expected death at another's hand gave time for the victim to repent and beg salvation. A man dying by his own hand died in the process of sin. What they would do to help another man to reach God, they could not do for themselves for fear of losing their chance of salvation.

On the way to the sawmill one day, Peter passed Holiday Island, the convicts' burial ground. It had originally been Halliday's Island, named after the first convict to die here. It soon became and remained Holiday Island. At a glance Peter could pick out the two pieces of wood that marked his friends' graves. He had come to look forward to that walk to the sawmill. He liked seeing those markers, knowing that neither John nor Walter would ever be flogged or put in harness again.

The next morning as he walked past, he touched the scarf at his neck. They would have liked knowing he still had it. They would have made lewd jokes and teased, but they would have liked him having the scarf. He wondered why he hadn't thought of wearing it before.

The guard strapped the harness in place. Peter stood still or moved appropriately to augment its proper fastening. Once he had considered writing to Stephen to tell him never to use a whip on the field horses. He hadn't written the letter, but each time the harness was strapped on him and he heard the crack of the whip behind him, he thought of it.

That evening the convicts were given time to wash and repair their clothes. It was never a time Peter liked. The convicts spent most of the hour quarreling among themselves, choosing sides, picking on the weakest, and generally letting out aggressions for which there was no other outlet. Peter sat away from the main body of them trying to repair the tear in his pants leg. He had never been able to mend well; consequently it was the third time he had had to repair the same tear. When he was finished, he took the scarf from around his neck, dipping it into the wash water. He laid it out on a rock to dry, and a quarreling convict named Roush saw it and came over to him.

"Where'd you get that?"

"It was given to me."

The man picked it up.

"Put it down," Peter said.

"I want to see it."

"Put it down."

"Look at this, mates. He's got somethin' goin' we don't know about."

Peter stood up. Roush was his equal in height, and one of the few convicts Peter couldn't intimidate merely by size and reputation. He put his hand out for the scarf. Roush danced away, waving the scarf and laughing. Peter started after him. The man darted back, laughing loudly and drawing the guard's attention. Peter turned and sat down on the rock again, leaning forward, relaxed. His hands were folded in front of him.

Roush stopped his prancing, watching Peter with canny wariness. Then he came forward, holding the scarf by two fingers.

"What's the matter, Berean? Don't you want the pretty scarf?"

"I want it," Peter said quietly.

"Come and get it."

"No. You give it to me."

"Like this?" Roush darted in, lowering the scarf so it touched Peter's cheek. Peter didn't move. "Hah!

Like this? Or this!" Roush said, thoroughly enjoying himself as he bobbed in and out, toward and away from Peter.

Watching Roush's moving feet, Peter got the timing, then moved like a springing cat, thrusting upward with his clasped hands.

He caught Roush directly under his jaw, snapping his head back. The man lay dazed on the ground, shaking his head to clear it. Peter bent to pick up the scarf. Roush kicked him just below the rib cage. Scarf in hand Peter whirled, jumping on Roush, pummeling until his fists were covered with blood.

The guards looked on with moderate interest. The two men were a fair match. If they came out with a few bruises, it meant nothing. Money changed hands between them as each chose his favorite. They did nothing until Roush lay motionless and Peter continued to pound his fists into him.

Then both guards ran, shouting orders for Peter to stop. He did not hear; he would not have obeyed if he had. His eyes were crazed, his powerful body taut and flexed as one muscle. His fists moved like pistons, beating and pounding Roush's inert body.

"Stop him! He's killing Roush!" a convict shouted.

Neither guard was willing to touch him in the frenzy he was in.

"Do something, you bloody bastards! He's killin' 'im!"

The guard raised his rifle and pointed it at Peter's head. The other pushed the rifle aside. Taking his own weapon and turning it butt forward, he brought it down on Peter's shoulder. Peter's back straightened, but he did not get off Roush. The guard hit him again and again, finally driving the rifle butt into Peter's cheek and knocking him off balance.

"Get him now!" the guard shouted. "Tie his hands. Good God, be quick before he starts again."

Peter was locked in a gaol cell. The scarf was still crumpled in his hand, once more stained and bloodied.

The chaplain came in an hour later. "Get on your knees."

Peter fell to his knees. He spent the night there, his mind blank, his back aching and straining until he was trembling from the effort to stay upright. The indefatigible minister droned on reading passages from the Bible and his book of prayers. Intermittently he stopped, placing his hand on Peter's clammy brow. "Repent."

"I repent."

"Beg forgiveness of the Lord God, thy Savior."

"I beg forgiveness."

The minister looked at the barred window and saw finally the first muted shades of dawn. "I have spent the night with you, sinner, doing my best to make you aware of your depravity. Your immortal soul has been so blackened by the influence of Lucifer you were driven to take the life of a fellow Christian, loved by the Almighty Father."

"He is dead?" Peter asked in a flat voice not really caring, except that he would hang if Roush died, and then it would be finished.

"He is not dead, but very nearly so. You have been blessed with another opportunity to release yourself from the vicious evil of your sinful life. Repent," he said, hand on Peter's brow again, waiting.

"Repent!" he repeated.

"I repent." Peter's head was down so the minister would not see his eyes grow watery and think he had been touched either by God or Lucifer. "I repent," he said again, barely audible.

"Are you now willing to attend to the convictions of the Holy Spirit?"

"I am."

"May God see fit to bless your efforts to walk in holiness before the Lord. Fill the sense of vacuity of your mind with thoughts of Heavenly good."

The minister ended his night's vigil. He turned with gravity toward the watchful sentry. "Sin has a dreadful hold on this man's soul. He cannot keep his thoughts toward the Lord, but perhaps we can take some comfort in faith that this night has made him see the error of his ways. I shall speak to the commandant after I have seen the other man involved. Perhaps God will grant that a glimmer of blessed enlightenment shall come of this night's work."

The following morning Peter was taken to Grummet Rock. Grummet was one of several large rocks that dotted the area. Its dark craggy bulk protruded from the sea some distance from the mainland, solitary and stark. The guards shoved Peter ahead of them. He stood listlessly staring out at a flat slate ocean, drained of all thought and feeling. He paid little attention to the guards, but moved obediently when they ordered him. They fastened two iron rings connected by a short heavy chain around Peter's legs. In the middle of the chain was a leather strap, which split to form a T, buckling around his waist. The entire contraption was affixed by another longer chain to an iron ring deeply set in the rock. Checking supplies from a list, they gave him an iron pot, and some wood and food rations for a week, then beleaguered him with tales of other men's experiences on Grummet Rock. Satisfied their assignment was duly discharged, they left him.

Solitary confinement was not given lightly, as it kept a convict from working. Its duration was never less than one week and usually longer. It was used as a punishment only when flogging did not seem sufficient to quell the criminal spirit of a man.

To the layman and the uninitiated, it seemed hardly credible that there were cells into which sane men could be solitarily confined from which they would emerge idiots. But it was true. Grummet Rock was one of them. One recalcitrant convict was chained to Grummet Rock for two years; a forgotten man who finally learned to forget.

Either by man's design or nature's quirk, cell-like caves were gouged into the the rock side. It was into one of these Peter was put and left.

Solitary meant little to him the first few hours. He watched the slow massive movements of the sea, then became mesmerized by the smaller swells within the larger heaving motions. He lay back relaxing against the warmth of the rock, his attention turning to the sky as the morning sun crept upward.

Later he began to notice the heat of that sun. He walked around the rock as far as the chain would allow. The sun climbed higher. He removed his blue-striped prison shirt, then as the sun became merciless, put it on again. The surface of the dry rock glowed white. The sun blazed overhead shooting shards of blinding light off every wave. It beat down on his bare head, making his scalp prickle with sweat, then itch as it dried.

The few thoughts and memories that haltingly began to form in his weary mind withered and died in the sun's unrelenting assault. Peter moved restlessly, searching his surroundings, for what he knew not. He covered his throbbing head with his hands. Unable to stand still, wanting shelter from the sun, he continued his wandering around the rock, like a captive animal moving as far as the chain would allow. The heat made him irrationally angry. He attacked the chain, pulling on it in a determined rage to yank it from the rock. He was sweating, his head throbbing, his hands raw when he finally gave up, sinking to the hard, hot surface. He looked up into the painfully blue sky until his eyes hurt and teared. Alone on the rock there seemed to be nothing. He had no past. Living this day meant being consumed by a sun and a sky that had no end and no relation to man as he conceives living. To think of tomorrow was unendurable. To think at all was unendurable. He turned to his stomach, pressing his forehead against the hot surface, his eyes focusing mindlessly on the intricate grain of the rock. He fell asleep only to awaken from a dream that he was being branded again. The sun-hot metal of the irons burned into his ankles and wrists. Automatically he pulled at them, rubbing swollen welts from the heat and strain. Frustrated, feeling desperately trapped, he shouted obscenities at the sun and the sky. He stood on the rock screaming with an outraged soul until he had no voice left. Defeated and beaten, he crept inside to the cool dampness of the cave.

The heat of the day vanished so quickly Peter thought he had only imagined it. Darkness fell over the rock and the ocean blinded him to the possibility that anything existed outside himself and the rock. Throughout the night the wind howled, roaring over the rock. He was sleepless, shivering from fright and cold as he guarded the small fire that the guards had started for him. The cold wet winds made the fire flicker, sending mad, hideous shadows dancing about the cave walls.

Civilization was sheared from Peter. His disorientation was so complete he couldn't think what was real and what was not. Had he ever lived among people?

Had he? Or had he dreamed it? Was it part of the longing dreams that tortured him?

He was no longer sure. The enormity of his isolation on the rock filled his mind and terrorized his senses. The turbulent water had lost the sound of peaceful rhythm he had always associated with the sea. Wave after wind-driven wave thudded against the rock, showering water over the surface. The rock's surface was now black, its great bulk looking alive, its shiny slippery skin glowing in the darkness. Peter thought he could feel it move with the motion of the sea. Common sense told him he could see nothing outside the small golden circle of his fire, nor could he feel it move. But still he felt it, and his mind went mad imagining himself chained within the gaping mouth of a giant sea beast.

In the morning, with the sun gentle and reliable in the sky, he felt better, even able to laugh at himself for his self-created nightmare monsters. He felt foolish, as though he had reverted back to childhood days when as a little boy he would imagine goblins in the night shadows of his bedroom. But as the day wore on and the sun climbed to scorch him once more, and when his head began to pound with the heat, the goblins and monsters seemed more real than did his reasoned thinking. By afternoon despair had consumed him. He knew now what "alone" meant. It was not being lonely, nor was it merely being cut off from natural communication. It was this. It was being put on a solitary rock in the midst of a white watered sea beyond sight or sound of land or men. It was the greatest and deepest of all humiliations he had suffered. Thrust down on him was nature's total superiority to a lone man. He was less significant in the scheme of the universe than the rock on which he was chained. And he was made aware of his insignificance day and night.

God had meant man to band with others of his kind. But Peter had been condemned to survive outside the family of man. And now he stood naked in the knowledge that he was nothing. He had been left to the wind and the elements, unwanted and undeserving of participation with humanity. To the civilized world he was as unnecessary as he was to nature. No one would gaze on him as they had when he was flogged on the triangles. Cruel though he had thought it then, their jeering curiosity had been a form of caring. They looked. They laughed at him. They exhorted his sinfulness. They had cared. Here, he was put away for no one to look at him, no one to care, no one to think of him, no one to know if he lived or died.

Far in the distance Peter could see whales periodically. The great shining black beasts were beautiful at first sight. But, as with all his surroundings, they soon became threatening and fearsome, accentuating his isolation on the rock.

That night his primitive imagination took hold of him again. Try as he would he couldn't keep hold of rational thought. He became certain the rock was being beaten away by the crashing angry sea. Every roaring sound became a piece of Grummet tumbling away into the ocean. In the pitch blank blackness of a starless night, he was sure there was nothing left but the small ledge of his cave. Cursing himself for his primitive fears, he cowered at the back of the cave afraid to go to its edge to prove his fears false.

The third day he spent his time outside the cave, not watching the movement of the water which now frightened him, but peering instead at the surface of the sea. He searched the horizon for anything that moved, any sight that meant someone was near. He saw nothing all that day.

By nightfall he was claustrophobic and nearly hysterical. The monsters came nearer. The walls of the cave closed in on him, and the sea terrified him. He prayed that night, begging to be allowed to write the letters he had never written, pleading to be allowed to see another human being, promising to repent in any way anyone asked of him. He dredged up every sin of his life, hating himself, fearing that he had forgotten some evil of his character that would prevent him from being absolved. He cried and prayed throughout the night until the words he spoke were not words at all.

The fourth day was as empty as the preceding one. And he feared that God too had abandoned him. Not one ship was seen, no rowing boat, no man, no whale, nothing. Nothing. For as far as he could see there was nothing. He couldn't stop trembling. The blazing heat of the sun no longer bothered him. He didn't even realize it was there. He was cold so deep inside that no heat could touch him. He stared at the edge of the rock considering throwing himself over its side, no longer able to reason that it couldn't be done due to the chain that anchored him to the rock.

That night Peter felt an inner agony he couldn't begin to identify for it touched too deep within. He hurt physically and mentally for the presence of another human being. He could endure the knowledge of his worthlessness. His strength had no meaning for it was too puny to meet the challenge of wind, sea, or sun. His mind and language were useless for there was no one and nothing to understand. He needed someone to understand with a passion so deep and driven it was beyond thought. He needed someone in order to be real himself. He clawed at the sky, then at the cave

walls, his body writhing in the pain of loneliness.
Crying, he lay flat on the floor of the cave, touching
every part of his body, trying to imagine it was someone other than himself he touched and who touched
him.

The fifth day he spent like an animal on all fours,
trying to seek out any warm spot on the rock, imagining it was the warmth of human skin. He kissed the
rock, his hands roving over the grain, feeling the
curves of its rough surface sensual and pleasurable
against his own pliant body.

During the night he was cold. The fire had gone
out. He couldn't see anything inside the cave. The sea
lashed with a cold heartless fury. Peter curled in a
tight ball against the back of the cave wall, going
mad.

On the sixth day two guards came to drop off new
supplies. Peter sprang from the cave as the guard
climbed up the edge of the rock. He grabbed hold of
the man's hand, laughing and kissing it. The guard
slapped him back-handed across the mouth. Peter fell
to the rock kissing the man's feet.

From below in the boat, the other guard called to
his partner. "He all right?"

"Berean?" The guard laughed.

"Yes . . . is he alive?"

"Sure he's alive. Bonkers as a loon in May. C'mon
up here and take a look. I'd never have thought Berean would take solitary this way."

The other man began to climb the rock. Once his
head and shoulders were above the surface, he
stopped. He made a face of disgust at Peter groveling
at the guard's feet. "Get in the boat. We'll report it to
the commandant."

"Shouldn't we take him back? They're never going
to get him back to work if we don't get him off this

rock. They say he can work like a team of oxen if they give him enough of the lash. They're not going to want to lose him."

"We've got no orders to release him. Get back in the boat."

The other guard stood for a moment, fascinated by Peter. "Funny which ones solitary breaks. Take Berean here, a loner from the start. The triangles didn't do a thing to him. The arrogant son of a bitch just took his medicine and went back to work as unrepentant as ever. Six days on Grummet and look at him. He's a pussycat. Come here, Berean. Let Gene get a good look at you."

Like an obedient dog Peter got to his feet, standing as near the rock's edge as his chain would allow.

"Don't stand near him, you fool. You don't know what he'll do. He damn near killed the last man he attacked," Gene said.

"Ahhh, he's not going to do anything, are you, Berean? Look, he loves me." The guard reached out touching Peter. Peter stood, his eyes closed in ecstasy. The guard jumped down to the ledge of the rock and got back into the boat.

Peter opened his eyes, staring in horror. "Don't leave me! Please! Don't leave me."

They could hear him screaming as they rowed back to the mainland.

Four days later they returned for Peter. The commandant had finally ordered his release and considered it a favor, for his solitary was to have lasted two weeks. He was being released after ten days.

By the time the guards returned for Peter, he was afraid of them. He was afraid they weren't real. He was afraid they were more of the strange creatures who had begun to haunt him, airy men and women who danced before his eyes and reached out with warm hands until he leapt to his feet trying to embrace them; and then they disappeared, leaving him alone grasping the air.

He had learned the air people would stay with him as long as he didn't attempt to touch them. Any company was better than none. He forced down the desire to be touched, taking comfort in the fact that the air people at least shared his solitude by being there.

As the guards came forward to release Peter's chains, he backed fearfully away from them. He didn't dare let them touch him. By their touch they would vanish, and he'd be alone. He could no longer stand being alone. He'd give up anything rather than be alone. With disorderly speed, thoughts flashed through his mind. The air people were trying to trick him into touching them. They wanted release from this loneliness as he did. They wanted release. Only he had the power to release them. He wouldn't give it. Power exercised by the powerless. He laughed, delighting in his newfound eminence. Cunningly he sat back and watched the guards from the corner of his eye so they wouldn't know he saw. As long as they didn't know how badly he wanted them near him, they wouldn't be so likely to leave him.

The guards finally had to rush him, pinning him to the ground. One held him screaming and writhing as the other took the chains from him. To make him manageable they had to bind him hand and foot and carry him to the boat. Peter lay in the bottom of the boat raving and crying in rage and despair all the way back to Sarah Island.

The doctor sedated him and put him in one of the solitary cells in the prison hospital. When they had him reasonably calm, he was examined by the doctor and found to be sound of body considering that he had eaten virtually nothing. He had hoarded his food fearing the day he would have no more and no one would ever return to him. As to his mind, the doctor shrugged, unconcerned. "Most of them get over it sooner or later. He is a life-term man, isn't he? Well, then, you've no worry. He's better off as he is. He obeys what he's told, so he understands. You'll get many a good day's work from him."

When Peter returned to the barracks there were three letters waiting for him. Two were from Stephen telling him of the May house, and one was from Callie telling him about Hobart Town, but he was incapable of reading them. He stared at the letters, not even daring to pick them up. He was as frightened of them as he was of everything else.

The criminal spirit of Peter Berean was broken. It was hoped that conversion would follow.

Peter was sent back to the sawmill the next day. In the harness he found security. In the work he found a mindless solidity that helped camouflage the deep despair of being despicable and alone.

Chapter 37

It seemed to Stephen that it had been weeks since he had had the time to be young, and he longed for it. Though he saw her every day, watched her work by his side and put out every bit as much energy and effort as he, he missed having free moments with Callie. Moments when she would shrug free of the responsibilities of Jamie, Natalie, the farm, moments when she would forget Peter and run like a wood sprite through his newly plowed fields, laughing with a sound that was like a song on the wind to him.

He counted the days of his life by those moments when the smell of freshly turned earth and flowers and grass all swelled and enveloped him, whispering her name in his ears. Those were the moments when she was his. Those were the days he worked for and longed for when he didn't have the time to be with her.

He had known for some time he would never marry Agnes Wharton. He just hadn't found a way of breaking free without hurting her. Jack had called him a damned fool, and was probably right. Agnes would make him a good wife, but he loved Callie. He expected to die a very old man still loving Callie.

For months, however, Stephen had struggled with his decision, trying to be fair. Jack's constant warnings and his own logic told him to marry Agnes Wharton, to settle down and begin to raise a family. He would be happy with Agnes; he didn't doubt that. But the yearning inside him to be near one particular woman would never be satisfied.

Stephen knew that all his arguments against marrying Agnes were the romantic tomfoolery that Jack labeled them, but he questioned that men ever achieved anything extraordinary by being objective. The heights and nadirs of life were achieved only subjectively. Stephen never mentioned this line of thinking to Jack, knowing it would bring forth a barrage of sarcastic teasing. But he made his decision on it. He'd wait for Callie.

Even with the decision made, he didn't rest easy. There were too many questions and uncertainties. There was Callie herself to complicate it. Though he believed that a desire as great as his could not go unrecognized by her forever, she had not given any indication since they had returned from Kent that she would ever consider him as anything more than a loving brother.

The other consideration that made him doubt himself was Peter. He knew he would never step between Callie and Peter if things were as bad with his brother as he suspected. No matter how much he wanted to, he could never interfere if Peter truly needed her. But if he should be wrong and Peter returned home healthy and well, then he'd be free to court Callie openly and on an equal footing with Peter. So much of his life depended on Peter. The waiting to bring him home became more difficult for Stephen with each passing day.

After brooding about it and arguing with Jack for a solid week, Stephen decided the time to break with Agnes had come, and it must be done with complete honesty. Jack waited for him in the carriage as Stephen went to tell her they would never marry, that while he cared greatly for her he loved someone else and he would marry that woman or none.

Jack scowled as Stephen climbed back into the carriage. "Do you feel like the heel you are?" he asked.

"I've felt better," Stephen said shortly.

"I don't know what you're going to do now, but I'm going out to get drunk."

"I don't feel like drinking," Stephen said. "And I don't want to see anyone tonight."

Jack looked disgustedly at him. "I didn't mean I was going with you. I'm going alone and forget I ever introduced you to that girl."

Stephen looked somberly from the carriage window. He said nothing, and felt about as low as Jack thought he was. "Good night, Jack," he said as the carriage stopped to let him out at the house.

Jack leaned out of the window. He looked at Stephen standing on the side of the driveway. "Change your mind, Stevie. Don't be such a damned fool all the time."

Stephen shook his head. "I can't, Jack. I am a damned fool about this."

"Ahhh, shit," Jack said and whacked at the top of the carriage for the driver to go on.

Stephen walked down to the spot he loved in the woods. He wandered aimlessly along the side of the stream, then sat down staring into the water. Slowly the tension and the sadness of his meeting with Agnes washed away, and he was left with a sense of relief.

Though it had been difficult, he didn't doubt now that his decision had been right—at least for him. And then his thoughts turned, as they always seemed to turn, to Callie.

Tomorrow was Sunday. His fields were plowed. Her creamery was in order, butter churned and the room cleaned. He would take her all to himself to this wooded spot near the stream. He imagined how she would look standing against the backdrop of the trees and the sky and the water. He pretended to know what she would say and what he would respond. She could bring Jamie if she liked and they could laugh and play and watch the child together.

It was very late when he finally left his place by the stream and returned to the house. He went to sleep still making plans for the morning and trying to imagine how it would all be. But when he awakened he found the house quiet and empty of all but Natalie.

"Callie's made them all go to church," Natalie said when he asked.

"Everyone?"

"Yes, even cook, who says she hates sermons."

He laughed and went to the pantry, pulling bread and cheese from the shelves and wrapping it to go into the basket. He finished packing the basket with a crock of beer for himself and the cider Callie preferred. "Have you eaten?" he asked as Natalie stood watching him.

"No one fixed it for me. Callie took everyone with her."

"Sit down. If you want the best breakfast you'll ever get, wait until you taste what I can do with an egg."

Natalie sat down, waiting.

"You can set the table, Nat."

"I don't know where the dishes are kept."

"Try looking on the shelf." He pointed to the neatly stacked dishes.

She looked at them but didn't move. He walked over, took two dishes, and put them on the table, then put knives and forks on top of them. "You can arrange them on the table?"

"Yes."

Stephen scrambled their eggs and browned two pieces of bread. He sat down opposite her and began to eat. "You've got to stop your daydreaming about Albert, Nat. You do it too much. It's no good for you. I know you loved him, but he's gone and you're still young. You've no business acting the way you do."

"I must be careful."

"Of what?"

"He might see me."

"Who might? What the hell are you talking about?"

"Peter. He knows that I know he killed Albert."

Stephen put down his fork, staring at her.

She looked earnestly at him. "Peter's here . . . looking for me. He thinks he can kill me too, but he can't . . ." She looked around the room warily. "I'm always on guard. I see him sometimes. He has terrible eyes and he hates me, but I guard. . . . He'll not find me."

"You're imagining things. You keep yourself closed in that room of yours too much." He tossed his bread onto the plate, disgusted.

Natalie stiffened, her head cocked, listening. "He's coming," she whispered and jumped up from the table, running all the way to her room.

"She's crazy as a loon," Stephen muttered as he cleared the table. He finished cleaning the dishes, then dismissed thoughts of Natalie when a happy crew of household help, Jamie, and Callie came in the back door.

"Good morning, sleepy heathen," Callie said cheerfully.

"Good morning to you. Go change your clothes. We're going to the stream, and don't try to give me an argument," he said.

"Me too?" Jamie piped.

"You too."

"Uncle Stephen, will you teach me to swim some more?"

"Uhh—well then, I'd better change my clothes too if that's what you have in mind."

"I do!"

"All right—go! Get ready."

Jamie came downstairs again with cutoff pants and more equipment to entertain himself with than he could carry. Behind him he left a trail of balls, toy trains that Stephen had carved for him, and a bag of marbles that spilled as they dropped, rolling over the hallway.

"Jamie!" Callie scolded as she came down the stairs.

"He didn't drop his hoop or towel, Callie." Stephen laughed, ruffling Jamie's hair. "Come on, I'll help you pick them up."

They reached the clearing in the woods half an hour later.

Stephen stripped off his shirt and, wearing an old pair of pants cut off at the knee in similar fashion to Jamie's, dived into the deepest part of the stream. Callie stood on the bank holding the undershirt she insisted he wear while swimming.

It wasn't that she wasn't used to seeing him bare-chested. She was, and it was that that kept her insisting on the shirt. There were some proper social customs that Stephen would not adhere to no matter what. Keeping the upper part of his body covered was one of them. He even refused to wear a nightshirt in bed, and might be seen by anyone, including the servants, as he tramped through the upper hall in the morning, stretching and yawning without a care to propriety. She dangled the shirt at him. "Put it on."

He reached for it. She tossed it to him, and he dunked it beneath the water, then threw it back to her dripping. "I can't," he said sincerely, "It's all wet. I'll catch my death in wet clothes. You told me so yourself."

Callie stamped her foot. "Ohh, you'd catch your death if I could get my hands on you!"

"Jump in."

"I would drown."

"I'd save you."

Jamie came to the bank. "Save me, Uncle Stephen!" he cried and flew frog-style in Stephen's direction, paddling frantically. Squeals of delight and laughter pierced the air. Callie, smiling, looked wistfully at the two of them playing in the water. Stephen dived and came up near to the bank where she stood. His smile was wide, his teeth strikingly white in his darkly tanned face. "Come in with us, Callie."

"I can't. I have no bathing outfit."

"Wear your bloomers. You do wear bloomers?" He grinned, bobbing up and down.

"Stephen Berean! You're not to know what I wear."

He laughed and tossed Jamie into the air. "Come in," he whispered. "I won't tell anyone."

Her eyes sparkled. She looked at the tempting blue stream, her lower lip caught between her teeth. "Would I dare?"

He shook his head and turned his back. "Hurry up."

"Suppose someone comes."

"No one will."

"But suppose they do."

"Stay under water."

"Stephen! I'd drown."

"Well, nobody'd better come then. Are you ready?"

"No! Stay turned around until I get in the water." Cautiously she stepped off the bank, inching her way along the bottom until she stepped into a deeper hole and the water closed over her chest.

"*Stephen!*"

"What?"

"I'm sinking! I can't swim."

He dived and came up with his arms around her. "I'll teach you. If Jamie can paddle around, you can too. Just do as I tell you. I'll hold you up till you get the idea."

"I'll absolutely die if someone comes and sees me in my undergarments."

"Definitely if you stay underwater."

"You are a rotten tease with no morals whatever."

"But I'm lovable."

"Is that what all your lady friends tell you?" she asked, paddling as he instructed.

With his arms around her waist, he was minutely aware of the soft curving body he supported. "Some of them."

"They don't know you. Ignorance is bliss."

He laughed and let go of her.

"Stephen! Stephen, I'm sinking!"

"Say something nice."

"Stephen!"

"Nice."

"You're lovable! Oh, Stephen, help!"

"That's nice," he said, taking hold of her again. She turned in his arms, clinging to him. The gentle motion of the water pushed her against him and away. He put his arms around her waist and pulled her closer along the length of him. She looked up in mock anger.

"Do you have to drown all your admirers to make them say something nice?"

"Only a few." He laughed and let her struggle free of his grasp. "Hold my hands and kick while I pull you along. Watch how Jamie does it."

They stayed in the water until the sun went behind the clouds and they felt the coolness of the wind. Callie got out first, shivering as she ran behind the bushes. Stephen and Jamie turned away.

"Oh, Stephen!"

"What's wrong now?"

"I don't know what to do . . . my bloomers . . . they're all wet."

He began to laugh until tears were in his eyes. She came out from behind the bushes, her skirt and bodice already showing wet spots from her hair and wet undergarments. Stephen and Jamie both got out, flopping down on the warm earth to dry in the air and the sun as it made its way out of the clouds.

They ate and Jamie went off to play with his trains, building a station with rocks and sticks he had gathered. Callie shook out the cloth Stephen had laid on the ground before they ate. She folded it neatly, standing straight-backed and looking toward the stream. "That was fun."

He was lying on the ground, his head propped up by a fallen tree trunk. He smiled up at her, thinking she looked pretty with her still-wet hair drying in the wind. Her dress was splotched with patches of moisture, and her feet were bare. He didn't remember seeing her look so relaxed or natural since they had returned from England. He put his hand out to her. "Come sit with me."

"You're half naked. Get dressed and I'll sit with you."

He raised his eyebrows looking pointedly at her

skirt. "Do you think it any more proper that a fully dressed man should sit beside a woman who's wet her bloomers?"

She ran to him, pulling his hair, tumbling to the ground with him as he grabbed her. He rolled with her. Callie was flat on her back, both hands full of Stephen's damp, curling hair, looking straight into his deep blue eyes. He lowered himself down on her. His hands held the sides of her head as he looked at her wonderingly. As he said her name in a low, husky voice, she felt his breath touch her lips and cheek. Then he kissed her long and hard on the mouth. Her lips separated as his tongue slipped easily between her teeth, searching, seeking, filling her with hot, tingling feelings, emptying her of all thoughts except those of him.

"Whaddya doing, Uncle Stephen?" Jamie asked.

Callie lay motionless, looking at him, hardly aware Jamie was there. Stephen kissed her again, very gently on her parted lips. "Kissing your Aunt Callie," he said and smiled. He touched her hair and moved slightly so his weight was no longer on her.

"Well, if you're done, could you help me build my train station?"

"Yes, let's build a train station, Jamie." He got up and went off with Jamie, acting as he always did.

Callie sat up, brushing the dust from herself, wondering if she'd ever breathe normally again. She should be both angry and offended, she thought, but she was neither. She sat there in a daze, remembering the feelings his kiss had evoked. Then quite suddenly her breathing returned to its normal, even rhythm, and she began to think clearly. She thought of herself rolling over in the dirt like a common . . . and she thought of Peter. Last, she remembered Agnes Wharton.

She picked up everything that was left in the clearing, packing it back into the basket. She hurried over to where Jamie played. "Come on, Jamie. It's time to go home."

"But Aunt Callie . . . Uncle Stephen just built me a train station."

Cross-legged on the ground, Stephen grinned up at her, looking as pleased as Jamie. "Pretty good, eh?"

"It's time to go," she said severely.

His smile faded. He reached for her hand, which she hastily withdrew. He took a handful of her skirt, keeping her from running off. "Are you angry?"

"Yes," she hissed.

He stood up. "Why? Callie . . ." Taking hold of her arm, he pushed her until she walked with him away from Jamie. He placed both hands on her shoulder, holding her fast against a tree. "Because I kissed you?"

"Yes."

He tried to laugh, but even as a gesture, it wouldn't come out. "I always kiss you."

She glared at him; then her lip began to tremble. She turned her head away as though she couldn't bear the sight of him. "Not like that."

"Oh," he sighed. "I thought . . ."

Her words came out in an angry torrent. She wanted to hurt him, because in some way that she refused to examine he had hurt her. "I suppose you do that all the time. All those women. . . . I suppose you think I'm just like that."

"No." Tears were coming to her eyes. "Callie, I didn't mean to hurt you. Please, don't cry. Don't you underst—"

"I'm not crying!" she shrieked. "Let me go! I know all about . . . about men like you. You're almost engaged to Agnes. I'm not so dumb as you think. I know about you."

"I'm not engaged to Agnes."

"That isn't what I hear."

"Callie . . ."

"Don't talk to me, Stephen. You shouldn't have done that. I'm not one of . . . of your women."

"Callie, listen to me." He touched her cheek.

She turned her head. "Don't!"

His fingers tenderly traced the line of her cheek-bone and jaw; then he walked back to Jamie. "Come on, little man, it's time to go." Jamie looked up with great round imploring eyes. Stephen shook his head. "Get on my back; I'll give you a ride home."

To Stephen the most magnificent feeling he knew had come from walking to the top of his mountain in Kent. Being with Callie gave him the same feeling. She made the air seem fresher to him. Her presence took him above the scurrying, wearying bustle of work. He felt whole and larger than himself with her. And because she was so much a part of his life there lived in him a belief that hidden within her she had a special love for him as well. Yet there was another side to Callie. Her sense of duty and loyalty was as hard as granite. Today he had let down his guard and kissed her as he wished he always could. She had responded. He was sure she had, and yet to look at her now, walking ahead of him, her back rigid, so remote and cold, it was difficult for him to recall anything but her angry hurt and her cold withdrawal from him. Unhappily Stephen realized the chances of him beating himself bloody against the granite wall of Callie's sense of right were just as great as his chances that she would ever love him as he loved her.

* * *

Later that week Stephen received a letter from Peter. It was the first he had written. The chaplain had suggested it, and Peter, much to the prison authorities' delight, now did everything he was told without question.

Callie and Stephen sat on the sofa, reading the letter together. Callie kept so respectable a distance between them, she was strained to see the writing. The script was cramped and irregular, that of an old or infirm man. Stephen read two or three lines, then flipped the single page over to see the signature at the bottom. It was signed with Peter's name.

"Who wrote this? It isn't Peter's handwriting," Callie said, forgetting her vow to avoid Stephen and moving closer.

"Peter," Stephen said absently. "I'm sure he wrote it, but . . ."

"What's wrong with him? Does he say? Is he ill?"

Stephen scanned the letter, his eyes stopping at a paragraph midway down the first page. Peter wrote asking Stephen's forgiveness for having hit him. Stephen pointed it out to Callie. "That happened when I was six. Peter and I were walking around the edge of the well, and he hit me. I was afraid I'd fall in, so I told Pa on him. Peter got a good thrashing for that. But why bring it up now? And why in heaven's name ask my forgiveness? He sure didn't care for it then. He beat the stuffings out of me next day in the woods for telling on him." Stephen sat puzzling over the letter. "Maybe he is trying to tell us something . . . maybe it means he is sorry he can't get to Hobart."

"No . . . there is something all wrong with this, Stephen. Look at his handwriting, and what he says; it barely makes sense. Even if he meant to tell us something secretly, he'd never choose this method. I think he means just what he says. He wants your forgiveness."

"That's nonsense. There's never been anything to forgive between Peter and me. He knows that."

"Well, we'll just have to keep writing until he sends a letter we understand. At least he is writing. That is something, isn't it?"

Stephen nodded, folding the letter and tucking it into his pocket. He went outdoors to finish plowing the field he had interrupted to come in and check the mail.

Late that afternoon Callie was waiting for him as he walked in from the fields. He was surprised to see her there. She used to wait for him, but since he had kissed her she had stopped. He smiled and ran to her. "What brings you out here?"

A hundred thoughts crowded her, then merged in a rush of warmth. "I just wanted to see you coming home. I like to, you know." She began to laugh. "You've never learned not to blush."

He reddened all the deeper and took her hand, walking her over to the stone bench where he had put in a flower garden for her.

Stephen stretched out on the ground, looking up into the sky. "Did you play at making figures in the clouds when you were a child?"

Callie sat back, contented, her legs tucked under her. "I think everyone does."

"Well, I see Zeus right now."

"Do you? Is he handsome and awesome?"

"No, he's bumpy and disintegrating."

Suddenly she felt like crying. She wished nothing would ever change. Zeus should always stay in the sky. "Oh, Stephen, I'll miss you so."

"Miss me?"

"When you marry Agnes. Jack came over while you were out. He told me about it."

"Don't rush me into anything," he said, laughing as he wondered what Jack was up to now. He knew perfectly well Stephen wasn't going to marry Agnes. Then, understanding Jack had given him the opportunity to discover Callie's feelings, he asked, "Do you think I should marry her?"

"Only you would know that, but I will miss you."

"I'd still live here."

Callie smiled and shrugged in embarrassment. "Well, I know that, but . . . but things would be different. You know what I mean. I couldn't be with you—not the way we are now."

"You value that?"

"Of course I do. You know—oh, Stephen, what would I do without you? I mean, everything I know is you. The farm, Jamie, my whole life is part you. Of course, I value that, and I will miss it dearly. That's natural, isn't it?"

He was very sober, looking down into the heart of one of her border marigolds. He didn't answer her.

"Don't look so serious. I'm sorry. I shouldn't have said all that. All I really want is for you to be happy. That will make me happy too . . . when you marry. I was just talking . . . silly talk . . . little girl talk. I guess I don't want you and me to grow up no matter how old we are. I am trying to keep us as we were. See—I am a silly goose, trying to keep everything from changing. And I *am* happy you'll marry Agnes. She is a wonderful girl."

He looked up at her then. "Are you really?"

"Yes, I am. Honestly. I am happy for you." She leaned forward, taking his hands in hers and kissing him on the forehead. "I think I was feeling a little left out, that's all. When Peter comes home the four of us will have fun together. There will be so many things we can do, and times when the four of us will be happy. Oh, we'll be such a large family."

He removed his hands from hers and stood up. He walked to the edge of the garden and looked out toward the newly plowed field where he had worked all day. His back still ached between his shoulder blades. He rubbed at the back of his neck, sighing deeply. He had never really believed that he would never be with Callie. There had always been his feeling that it was only compassion that drove her to Peter, but leave it to Jack to set him up so there was no way that he could do anything but face things as they were. He wondered how many times and in how many ways she would have to tell him she didn't want him before he finally accepted it. She had all but said she wanted to be Peter's wife. She wasn't likely to dream of marriage out of compassion. And she wanted him married to Agnes. That wasn't the wish of a woman who loved a man.

"I'm not getting married, Callie," he said harshly, with his back to her. "Not to Agnes or to anyone else. I've already told her."

"But Stephen—"

"Forget it, Callie. I'm not marrying. Leave it at that."

"*Why?* You said you cared for her and . . ."

He turned on her angry-eyed, lips pressed thin. "Forget about it. Don't you ever know when to leave a thing alone? I don't want to talk about it."

His sudden angers always startled her and left her mildly frightened, but today she felt a lightness.

He walked swiftly to the well. It seemed strange to Callie that he should have done that at this particular moment, for as she watched him stride to the well and strip off the sweat-sodden work shirt, she was reminded of another place, another day, and another man she had seen do the same thing.

It was no golden-haired young lion of a man she watched washing himself with the cool sparkling water today in the fading brilliance of a setting sun, but a tall, dark-haired, work-hardened man who carried his responsibilities with all his heart, and who had, for all her familiarity with him, remained unknown to her.

She knew well what made Stephen laugh, but had no idea of what brought joy to him. She had seen him sad but never known the cause. She had seen him troubled and had brought her own troubles to him, but she had never shared in his.

She watched him until he finished and turned, water still glistening on his chest, to return to where she sat on the garden bench, her arms locked around her knees.

The anger had left his face. He knew she would have no idea why he had been angry, and it didn't matter now. He'd have to remember to tell Jack his tactic had been successful. Things couldn't be changed by wishing. A "sister" was all she'd ever be. He smiled as he came near to her.

Callie kept watching him, wanting for the first time to have him talk of himself. He never had, and she had never tried to make him. She wanted to now.

"Let's take a walk before we go in," he said, and put his hand out for her.

She got up, returning his smile, relieved he was no longer angry. "What is it that makes you happy, Stephen?"

He glanced at her quizzically. "Ummm . . . I don't know. When I mix the right brew and the beer is good, I'm pleased."

"I don't mean pleased. Happy."

"A nice day."

She looked up at him. His eyes were friendly and warm as always, but she sensed Stephen's withdrawal. He would tell her nothing of himself now. The moment had passed. She took his hand, walking at his side, leaving things unchanged between them.

Chapter 38

As the months passed Peter collected the letters Stephen and Callie wrote. He had them all—unopened and tucked as securely as anything a convict owned could be secured in his bed.

He was no longer afraid to touch them as he had once been, but neither was he interested in reading them. They spoke of a world he would never see again, and of normal emotions that had been taken away from him. The thing he feared most was wanting anything as much as he had wanted someone on Grummet Rock. He would gladly have walked unbidden to the triangles or placed the brand on his own chest rather than ever again be left so totally alone.

In recovering from the shock of solitary, Peter acquired a protective cunning. He could not gain approval for himself, but instant obedience to his masters gave him some of the rewards of approval, just as meanness gave him approval from the convicts. While he would never be spoken to in friendship, there were those who spoke to him, thinking they instructed. He learned to base the actions of his life on deceit. That it left a coldness inside of him mattered little. It was far better than the agony of hope.

He couldn't have said why he kept the letters, except that he liked owning something. He liked the other convicts to think someone cared about him even though he knew no one did. Few convicts could boast of letters as he could, and none of them had so many as he.

To the authorities he gave the appearance of being a model prisoner. He could recite passages from the Bible so long and so varied that the chaplain was sent into fits of blessed delight over his conversion.

Only the convicts knew differently. None dared tease or annoy him anymore. He wasn't afraid of them, and where he once would have grown angry at their pranks, fighting back openly, Peter was now as cold as the winds that swept across the settlement. They let him alone. And with it they had taught him a new and different sense of pride. There were ways of reducing the "decent" world to the level of the debased, if one considered oneself so worthless as to make it necessary.

Because of Peter's miraculous conversion, the touching of his criminal spirit with the need to be good, he would now become a settler's convict. He was to be transferred to Hobart Town with the next ship. He wasn't pleased about the transfer. It would mean he had to leave the barracks. As he had found security in the harness, so did he find it in the familiarity of the barracks.

The night before he was due to leave for Hobart Town, he was more tense than usual. He never slept well, waking up two and three times each night, but this night he couldn't sleep at all. When the barracks grew quiet, when the last-minute whisperings faded away and the nighttime coughs subsided, he got up.

Stealing as quietly as he could, he went from bed to bed. At one he stood, looking down into the sleeping face of its occupant. He moved down the room, stopping at another bed. He took the man's hand, holding it in his own. The convict murmured in his sleep. Peter drew back, his breathing quick with fright. He stood rigidly in the shadows until the man settled back into a motionless slumber. Peter hunkered down on the floor, his forearm resting on the bed, touching the man's back. Later he moved and knelt beside another bed, his arm just touching the occupant. At dawn he went back to his own bunk.

The next morning as he prepared to leave, gathering up the letters and few belongings he had collected, demanded, or stolen, he turned to see one of the older convicts sitting dejectedly alone, watching him.

"What are you looking at?" he demanded harshly.

"You got a lot of letters."

"So what?"

"Nothin'. I just never got one."

"What would *you* do with a letter?"

"I'd keep it— like you do."

Peter pulled one off the stack, tossing it to the floor. The old man picked it up, holding it against his chest.

"May I open it?"

"Eat it for all I care."

With tedious care taken not to damage the envelope, the old convict broke the seal and opened the letter from Stephen. He touched it, moving his hands over its surface. He looked at Peter. "Thank you."

"It meant nothing to me," he said, lying down on his bunk with his bundle, ready to go whenever he was called.

"Berean?"

"What?"

"Would you read it to me?"

"Read it yourself."

"Can't you read?"

"I can read," Peter said, irritated.

"I can't read. Never learned."

Peter ignored him.

"Berean?"

"Oh, Christ—bring it here."

The man came over to Peter, his expression that of a small child about to be told a marvelous fairy tale. He sat on the edge of the bunk as Peter took the letter and began to read:

> Callie has long had a deep desire to be given a special May House. As always fond wishes are those that should be granted. We gathered the green boughs, and the flowers, and built the May house exactly as she wanted it.

He read, then his voice trailed off. He squinted at the clear bold writing and read the first few lines silently to himself again.

"Go on—there's more. Tell me about the May house. What did our Callie do? Was she happy?" the convict asked.

> The building of the May house such as this one meant more to her than I can tell you in one short letter. I shall confess, I too found it a moving experience, as one always must when an entire family can be brought together through the performance of such a pleasant task.

The rest of the letter was normal, telling of the hop yard and news of the neighbors, and a man named Tom Baker.

The convict reached for the letter as Peter finished reading. Peter jerked it beyond his reach.

"My letter!"

"Get out of here!" Peter shoved him to the floor. He tore open his packet of letters. He ripped them open one after the other, looking at dates that went back over the year. Each one of Stephen's letters had some mention of May or the May house. Each one of Callie's mentioned Hobart Town. Other bits of information were put in each of the letters. Together they told Peter he had not been forgotten—at least not by Callie and Stephen.

He knew Tom Baker's name, and had a reasonable certainty he was an American whaler due to Stephen's explicit and rather encyclopedic discussion of the black whale in one of his letters. Callie had also given a very accurate account of the wreck of the *George III*, the ship on which Peter had sailed to Van Diemen's Land. Unless she or Stephen had spoken to someone who had come to Van Diemen's Land, they could not have known the details in the letter.

Worried that he had already waited too long to answer the letters, Peter requested permission to write a letter that morning.

He wrote in frantic haste, fearful he wouldn't have it completed before he had to board ship for Hobart Town. He knew the commandant here and had his trust, but he knew nothing of the commandant at Hobart Town. He might not give a new man permission to write. Dutifully and time consumingly Peter quoted profusely from the Bible, giving each text an interpretation of his own that would indicate he was spending his days in prayerful concentration of heavenly good. The last he quoted was the Prodigal Son.

Duty fulfilled, he wrote on:

I was gratified to know you built the May house for Callie. I once promised her to build one myself; however, due to a life wasted by sin for which I am repenting, I was unable to do so. I am grateful to know that my depravity did not prevent her from having what she desired. Please tell her that in my heart, I too have begun to build her May house.

If you would be so kind, you might also thank her for writing to me of Hobart Town. I will be leaving for that settlement this afternoon. I am thankful that she thought to write to me of its beauty and pleasant aspects. I am sure to feel at home there immediately, due to her efforts.

> Sincerely,
> Your Christian brother,
> Peter Berean

He laughed nervously as he signed his name. He gave the letter to the guard, handing him a small amount of money he had stolen from a settler to whom he had been sent to deliver lumber. It would help insure the letter would be given to the commandant immediately.

No longer needing them, Peter picked the least informative letter of the bunch and tossed it to the old convict. Then he picked up another, scanned it, and tossed that to him as well. "Here—have two."

He lay down on the bunk again, his eyes narrowed as he allowed himself for the first time in months to think about *his* farm. It was no longer the soil or the brewery that filled his thoughts. It was the idea of owning it that held him in thrall. He remembered his study and the heavily tufted chair in which he sat while he worked at his accounts. He thought of putting his feet up on the shining mahogany desk. He thought of spending money, giving orders, doing anything he pleased at any time. They were hard thoughts, unrealistically void of people.

Rebecca Ward stood on the jetty, waiting to choose the convict the commandant had promised she could have.

Rebecca was a large woman, domineering and far too iron-willed to have done well in London's marriage market, not that she wanted to. She had never met a man she considered equal to herself, and she would die a spinster rather than submit to a weaker one. She was, however, suited to the colony at Hobart Town. She would withstand the rigors better than most, and make a good teacher as well. She was both sure enough and bold enough to keep error-prone little boys in line.

The idea of a convict slave had appealed to Rebecca from the start. She had never met an animal yet she couldn't train, two-legged or four.

She spotted Peter as soon as he stepped off the gangplank. He towered above the others. His hair, unkempt as it was, shone nearly white in the sun; and despite his hardened, closed expression, she sensed the underlying vulnerability.

She appraised him as she had her father's hunting dogs, her eyes keen for straight bones, well-formed muscle, proper proportion, coordination, and alertness. "There is the man I want," she said firmly to the commandant, indicating Peter.

The commandant hesitated, then said, "He's not your best choice."

Rebecca laughed. "He is *my* best choice. What is your objection?"

"His record."

She shrugged. "How bad can it be? Would he be here if it were felt he is incorrigible?"

"They say he has lost his rebellious spirit, but—"

"Then we should assume he has."

"Perhaps," the commandant conceded doubtfully.

"Then I shall have him."

The commandant looked at Rebecca, the fiery red hair, the determined jaw, and the shrewd, intelligent cat's eyes that left no doubt of the will they cloaked. At least he could count on her not to be soft with the man. He motioned to a guard, then in a low voice issued several orders.

Rebecca insisted on waiting where she was, and she stood in the hot sun for nearly half an hour until Peter was brought to stand before her. She looked him over again, checking teeth and muscle and prodding at his knees and back; then she seconded her first approval. "What is your name?"

"Peter Berean, ma'am."

"May I take him with me now, John?" she asked, turning to the commandant.

"Whenever you wish. We're finished with him. I anticipated your haste in the matter, Rebecca," he said, smiling.

"In that case the sooner he learns what is expected of him, the better. Follow me, Berean. Mind you keep proper distance." She looked critically at him. "Stand up straight! I'll not tolerate slovenly posture." She tapped him briskly on the shoulders with the end of her parasol.

Peter shrugged his shoulders back, walking nearly as straight as he once had. The sway given to his shoulders by his long-strided step brought back traces of what had once been called insolence in him.

The commandant looked at the two of them marching down the wide, house-lined street. He shook his head knowingly. He didn't believe in Peter's supposed conversion. Peter, he expected, would be sent from Rebecca's house regularly with a note to be given lashes for insolence and insubordination. He didn't like the look of the man, nor his walk, nor anything else about him. But for the moment, Peter was not his concern.

Peter was nervously aware that in order to gain the freedom he required to make contact with Tom Baker, he had to please Rebecca. He was apprehensive and frightened at the thought of being the only convict at her house, not knowing what would be demanded of him. His hands and body were clammy with doubt and fear as he tortured himself with questions of what Rebecca would want of him. He looked back on Sarah Island with a feeling almost of longing. There he had had a certain kind of security. He knew what was wanted. His job, though loathsome, held no surprises, and he knew and had survived the worst they could do to him. With Rebecca there was the awful uncertainty of not knowing.

She lived on the outskirts of the main settlement in an area just built to accommodate newcomers. Her house was minimal and not ready for the quartering of a convict. For the most part convicts slept in the outbuildings. Rebecca's plot did not yet have the outbuildings constructed. It was one of the reasons she wanted Peter. That she had taken a man with no means of sheltering him, meant nothing to her. Rebecca vowed she'd never be like other settlers, living with suspicions and fears about being able to trust their convicts. Her convict would be so well-trained she would be free to have him in her house once proper accommodations could be made. He would be near at hand to do her bidding at whatever time of the day or night she chose.

As they turned into the pathway to the house, she asked, "Have you ever been a carpenter?"

"No, ma'am."

"Well, you will now. If you are reasonably intelligent there should be no difficulty. Can you read?"

"Yes, ma'am."

He followed her as she motioned him into the house. In an austere room, as devoid of warmth as was Rebecca, she handed him a crude blueprint. "I want a room built to these specifications. The dimensions must be accurate. It will be your room. Be certain it is as well built as the rest of the house, or you will tear it down and begin again. You will build the room as often as it takes for you to get it right."

"Yes, ma'am."

"You may begin today. There's no purpose in wasting time."

Peter looked, confused, at the stacks of lumber at the back of the house. He had built things before, but that had been in Kent and Poughkeepsie, with no one to decide whether he had met all the requirements they wished. Then too it had been assumed that he was competent and capable; now he would be judged with the expectation that he would commit errors. Without confidence he began the room, never relying on his own judgment or ingenuity, but carefully checking each bit of progress against the blueprint.

At night she chained him outside, leaving him some straw to sleep on until the room was finished. As the room progressed, Peter realized he was building an airless, boxed-in cell into which he would be put. He worked, closing it in board by board, because he could do nothing else. He completed it without error one week after he had started. The original back door to Rebecca's house became the only entrance to his room. She would keep it locked from her side. She had planned a single window for him, a high slit in the back wall.

Rebecca ordered him into the room the evening he finished it. He didn't realize how much he had been dreading this night until the blood rushed from his head. He didn't think he could breathe as he stared at the tight bare walls. In panic he stood where he was, feeling sick to his stomach and fearing he'd scream, bringing Rebecca and all of her mighty wrath down on him. In order to be given the freedom settlers could grant their convicts, Peter had to keep silent his terror of being closed in and alone.

Trying to hold off what he had experienced in the cave, he paced the floor, repeating to himself everything he had done that day, trying to mentally rebuild the room. For a while in the early hours it worked, but as the hours passed, he was mentally and physically exhausted. He sat down on the built-in bunk, and the night slowly began to come alive. The horrible apparitions of the Grummet Rock cave crept into the black silence. The air people danced about him, and the monsters that had once come out of the sea now emerged in spiraling dark shadows from the knots in the wood. Repeatedly he fled to the slit window, standing on the edge of his bed to look out into the darkness. When the moon was out he could see the trees and be reassured, but when it was not, he saw nothing. When it rained he heard the sea pelting at the outside of the rock, washing it away into the sea again.

Rebecca followed a schedule that was rigid to the minute. In the mornings she opened the door to let him eat. Afterward she locked him in again while she went to the schoolhouse. At noon when she returned she came to the room, each time putting him through some sort of confusing test she devised to no end he understood.

"Do the garden fencing today," she ordered.

"Yes, ma'am."

"What are you waiting for, Berean? I gave you a command," she said, a full glass of rum in her hand as she stood in the doorway blocking his exit.

Rebecca watched as Peter stood indecisively, his eyes fastened on the glass of rum.

He didn't know what she expected him to do. He remained mute, and Rebecca waited until the annoyance showed on his face. "Can't you speak?" she asked irritably.

"I can, ma'am."

"Then answer me."

"Yes, ma'am."

She looked at the rum, then held the glass out to him so he could smell it. "Do you like rum, Berean?"

"I do."

"You may go now," she said, but didn't move aside so he could pass. He hesitated. "Go to work!"

He sidestepped past her, not looking back as he headed for the front door.

"Berean!"

"Yes, ma'am," he said, turning and standing still, his eyes downcast.

"You brushed the hem of my skirt. Don't ever touch me again, unless given permission."

"I won't, ma'am. I beg your pardon. May I go now?"

"You may go."

That night he found she had left a bottle of rum in his room. He drank it. Except for a few forbidden, stealthy drinks, he had had nothing since he was arrested. It deadened the nighttime fears, allowing him to pass out and sleep until morning. His head throbbed, and he felt sick the next day.

That seemed to please Rebecca. "My father always said a man who couldn't hold his liquor was no man at all. You a man, Berean? Or are you simply a brute with intelligence?"

He had no idea what Rebecca wanted him to say. She could have him flogged if she felt like it, and with that punishment would go the hopes he had of her giving him some time to himself. Rebecca's eyes glittered as she waited to jump on whatever he said. He tried to look at her and couldn't. "I'm a man."

"We'll see," she replied, smirking.

The bottle of rum was in his room each night. For whatever reason, she wanted him to drink it, and he did, not because she wanted him to, but because it brought oblivion.

Every time she approached him outside the confines of his work, she seemed to poke at him, testing for some point in his character, or lack of it.

Occasionally, when he'd sit down to eat, she'd stalk up behind him. "Stand up when I enter a room!"

He stood. It was what she wanted—that or for him to lose his temper, which he found progressively hard to control as the season for the whalers to come to Hobart drew nearer.

Sometimes after she had done this, she would tell him to sit down and continue eating. At other times she would leave the room, standing near the doorway so she could watch him. The third time it happened, she left him standing so long he thought she had forgotten him. He sat down to complete his supper. She had him flogged for insubordination.

Without a word she had handed him the note designating the twenty lashes he was to be given. She sent him to deliver the message to the commandant, and then doubled his work load for the following three days.

There was no way he could win with Rebecca, no rationale that he could see. He groped through her maze of oddities, obeying the slightest or most ridiculous command she gave him, carrying wood from one end of the yard to the other only to be told to put it back from where he had taken it. He never knew what she wanted.

Had he not read Stephen's letter promising freedom, he believed he would have beaten Rebecca to death to insure his own end.

Then one night the bottle of rum wasn't in his room. That night the walls closed in again, worse in some ways for now he was craving the rum as well as having to fight away the awful dreads and apparitions. He paced the hours away, his fist tight against his teeth as he waited for morning.

Then just as suddenly and apparently irrationally as she did everything else, Rebecca announced the following morning, "You have earned an hour to yourself this Saturday afternoon."

"Thank you, ma'am."

"That's all you have to say?"

"Yes, ma'am."

"You may walk around the front yard during that hour."

"Thank you, ma'am."

She began to laugh. "I do believe, Berean, I have you so well trained that should I tell you to balance one-handed on the chimney, you would do it."

"I would if you asked it, ma'am."

"Perhaps I will do that one day for my own amusement; but this time your free hour will take you wherever you wish to go. However, bear in mind, should you try to escape, most bolters die of starvation or cannibalism. It would not be a pleasant death, I assure you, Berean. And should you be recaptured, which is likely, I will make you wish you had died so kindly. Keep that firmly in mind."

"Yes, ma'am."

"You have one hour. That is precise. Should you be so much as one minute late, I shall consider that gross disobedience. I needn't tell you the consequence."

"No, ma'am. I know it well," he said quietly.

"Then as a guide to what you can expect, think in terms of twenty lashes for every minute's tardiness."

He went elatedly bewildered to complete building her fence. He was trained and like all good dogs had been rewarded. Her mention of the lashes had little meaning to him. He had been threatened too often to pay attention until he was actually on the triangles. He thought only of Rebecca and the self-assured way she assumed he was a brute with intelligence, as she said it. In a sense he admired it in her. At least she was clear in her thoughts; she didn't claim to want to rehabilitate him, nor did she feel called upon by some version of God to convert him to her brand of Christianity. He was her faithful dog and she would treat him accordingly.

On Saturday he struggled with the apprehensions of having to go to the business section of Hobart. Everything was strange to him, but by the time three quarters of his hour had passed, he knew which tavern Tom Baker frequented, and that he was due in port soon.

He returned to Rebecca's house, presenting himself to her at the precise time she'd designated.

Rebecca was delighted. In her eyes Peter had come to heel without a lead. She had given him rum; she had kept him from it. Drunk or sober, free or confined, he obeyed. The man had not appeared, even under the influence of drink or the temptations of freedom. She knew what she possessed was an intelligent beast to work, watch, or serve for her on command.

Confident, she gave him more freedom. The door to his room was no longer locked, although he was to stay within its confines except when she designated. While she was at school in the mornings, he was given a list of jobs. She left him free to do them.

By the time Tom Baker arrived, Peter was sure, he'd be able to meet him.

Chapter 39

Tom Baker brought his *Hudson Lady* up the Derwent
for re-rigging as he always did before making his return voyage. This had been a disappointing trip. It
would not be profitable, and Tom worried about it to
the point of considering giving up whaling. He had
had too many unprofitable trips of late.

There was a time, not so many years ago, when he
netted forty to fifty thousand dollars with the sale of
sperm and whale oil. With the going market price of
sixty-five and a half cents per pound for sperm and
thirty-nine cents a gallon for whale oil, he needed no
more than an average catch to make money on the
voyage. But he entered Van Diemen's Land with only
fifty barrels of sperm and nine hundred barrels of
whale oil. He'd barely be able to pay off his men. He
spat disgustedly. They were hardly worth their pay.

The worse his luck ran, the harder it was to get seamen worth the space they took aboard ship. Almost
all his men were ignorant of the sea, which wasn't unusual on a whaler, but these were scrapings of the
barrel. He'd had to wet-nurse them all the way. A

couple more trips like this and he'd be out of the whaling business anyway.

Hudson Lady needed work, and Tom's equipment was old, some of it needing to be replaced. He hadn't any idea where he'd get the money, nor did he know where he'd find the means to pay the mortgage on the ship. He was glum and preoccupied when he entered the Bowsprit Tavern.

He greeted old friends, then retreated to a corner table to mull over his plight. He ordered ale, looking up to exchange pleasantries as the owner carried his mug to the table, bringing a mug for himself. The tavern owner sat down; then, without beginning their usual bantering gossip, he leaned close to Tom, speaking in a low rasp. It was unexpected, but not surprising, when the man told him Peter Berean had been in looking for him.

For the next three nights Tom came to the Bowsprit to sit and wait and hope that Peter would return. Stephen's words, "I'll pay anything . . ." kept turning over in his mind. It could be the answer to all his problems. And bringing Peter home sooner than Stephen expected should be worth a little extra.

He was impatient and more than a little worried. One never knew when a convict would be free to move about without his master looking over his shoulder. Saturday night was the usual time for convicts to be given free hours, but that was not always the case. Tom estimated he could put off his leavetaking for two more days at most.

It was with the greatest exercise of control that Tom didn't get to his feet to greet the tall blond man who furtively entered the tavern and sidled along the wall, his eyes darting nervously over the occupants. Tom remained seated, forcing himself to lean back and look relaxed and commanding.

Peter methodically made his way to the back where Tom sat. The whaler studied him. Tom had recognized him the moment he had walked in. He was of a height with Stephen, and while their coloring was different, the markings of brothers were strong. Both men boasted the same high cheekbones, the strong jaw, the mouth given to sensitivity, the indelible stamps of a single family. Beyond that Tom saw no similarity. Instinctively Tom's hackles raised. Before he'd even met him, he didn't like Peter Berean. He had the stink of a convict, and Tom did not like the convicts. There was something not quite human about them. He finally made a motion with his hand, drawing Peter's attention.

Tom gave him no help, but made Peter stumble through his request to return home on Tom's ship. He eyed Tom suspiciously, not truly certain he spoke to the right man, and knowing what it would mean to him if this conversation were ever repeated to Rebecca or the commandant.

Tom sat back, enjoying Peter's discomfort. Occasionally he shot a stream of tobacco juice in the general direction of the spittoon. He couldn't think of a single reason why Stephen should want this man freed. While he admitted that in his way Stephen had an engagingly honest way of speaking, Peter was tightly restrained and suspicious. His eyes never once met Tom's directly, and Tom had never met an honest man afraid to look him in the eye. There was no trace of the man Stephen and Jack had described to him in Poughkeepsie.

Curtly, Peter asked, "When does the ship leave?"

Tom laughed through his nose. The bastard was a convict down to his bones. Tom could smell it in the fear on his sweat, feel it in the cold impersonal way Peter talked, hear it in the nervous quaver in his voice. It eased his conscience about taking Stephen for more money than the trip was worth. This man would be a bundle of trouble to take back to New York.

Tom's jaw set hard; his eyes narrowed. There were no two ways about it: he didn't like convicts. Most of them deserved every bit of time they served. He didn't doubt this was true of Peter Berean. If he didn't need the money so damned bad, he'd leave the bastard to rot here where he belonged. His neighbors wouldn't thank him for bringing a murderer home to live right there on the Hudson. But he needed that money. "Be here at ten sharp Tuesday night," Tom finally said. "I'll take you to the ship. You're late and we sail without you."

Peter nodded with a taut jerk of his head. "I'll be here."

"See you are. To my thinkin' you belong right where you are. I'll be plain spoken, Berean. I don't like the stink o' you. I'm doin' this for your brother. But don't get it in your head that I'm runnin' a cruise ship for you. You'll obey the rules of my ship—no brawlin', no drunkenness, and you'll work alongside of my crew."

Peter's response was another tight jerk of his head. Nervously he asked the time, then stood abruptly and left the tavern. He ran the distance to Rebecca's house seconds before he was due in. She was waiting at the front door for him. "You're out of breath!"

"Yes, ma'am . . . I didn't want to be late. I'm sorry."

"Then you were careless. I've warned you such behavior will not be tolerated. Leave yourself time to get back here in orderly fashion. I won't have a convict of mine seen running through the streets! Did you think you'd get away with it! Don't you know I learn of everything you do?"

She locked the door to his room that night and handed him the slip of paper he would take to the commandant the following morning for the customary disciplinary flogging. He thought he'd go mad. He stared at the door for hours on end calculating his chances of breaking through it quickly enough so Rebecca could not get help to stop him. The thickness of the door grew as the night hours waned, and the escape that was so near at hand began to slip away like all the things he believed in and dared to place hope in.

He moved to the corner of the room, enclosing himself between the two wooden walls. With the promise of release as near as the tavern, and Peter blocked from it by the cruel turn of a key in a locked door, he again longed for it all to end. It was not that he should die, but that the unendurable should cease.

Peter returned from the triangles late the next morning. As usual Rebecca seemed pleased. She gave him another one of her lectures, accepted his apology with a noncommittal face, and told him she had committed him to work that day on the penitentiary stone pile, which meant he would spend the day in chains breaking large pieces of stone into smaller pieces while standing in the hot sun. However, when he was told to go to his room that night, she left the door unlocked. At first Peter didn't believe it. He thought it just another of those phantoms of hope that drew him out only to crush him again. Then he cried, praying that it would be unlocked the following night as well. What good would it do for a door to be unlocked to him on a Monday if it were barred on the all-important Tuesday? It was with a deep bitter agony that he found himself compelled to hope that the door would be open to him, while all his experience in prison made a cold despairing mockery of the naiveté of belief in escape.

Tuesday night, just before he was to meet Tom, he tested the door. It was unlocked, and he slipped out of his room. He walked quietly through the kitchen into the main room of the house. Rebecca looked up from the copy book she held in her lap. Peter froze.

"You dare come out of your room!? Where do you think you're going? One trip to the triangles in a week isn't sufficient for you, Berean?" she said as she got up, striding angrily toward him. "Get back! I'll have you back in irons tomorrow!"

Peter stared at the front door not four yards from where he stood.

"Get back in there!" Rebecca commanded.

He glanced down at her, hardly aware of who she was. She was between him and the door, screaming commands that he had always obeyed mindlessly because she'd owned him. She flapped at him with the copy book, trying to back him into his room. The key hung on a chain at her waist. When the book proved ineffectual, she dropped it, standing back fearlessly as she studied the dazed, desperate look on Peter's face.

"What have you been drinking? Where'd you get it?"

Peter stared without seeing her.

She drew back her arm, her hand swinging full force as she slapped him. He grabbed her hand as she reached back to hit him again. Anger flowed from deep inside; his dark brown eyes burned like hot coals in his drawn face. "Damn you!" He pushed her back as he moved toward the door.

"You're out of your mind!"

His laughter was a hard brittle sound. "Even dogs turn, ma'am."

Rebecca stepped away from him, reappraising, feeling both a sense of fear and the elated need to fight him until he was controlled. She glanced around, and finding no substantial weapon, she picked up the fire poker. Her eyes, bright with excitement, never left Peter as she stepped slowly to the side. Her lips drew back in a silent grimace. Gripping the poker with both hands, Rebecca lunged forward, thrusting it at him. She backed him toward his room. She began to laugh as he retreated through the kitchen. Awkwardly he dodged the poker, taking backward steps until he stood in the doorway to his room. The chain of keys at her waist jangled as she fumbled for the key to his room.

The front door was so close.

Rebecca found the key.

"No!" he said harshly. "I'm leaving here. Let me go!"

She laughed, sure of herself. "You're going into that room. Move back and do it now. I'll see to you tomorrow. This is a night you'll never forget!"

He put his hand on the door, holding it flat against the wall. "Move out of my way."

She aimed the poker at his head. Peter blocked the blow, grabbing hold of Rebecca at the same time. He threw her sprawling onto the kitchen floor, then ran for the door.

Rebecca got to her feet. "You damned animal!" she cried, running after him and bringing the poker down across his unhealed back. He spun around grunting in pain, his hands reaching for his back. She came at him again, the poker glancing off his shoulder. He hit her with his upraised forearm as he whirled to avoid the next blow. Rebecca let out a terrible strangled cry and lay still on the floor. Peter went out the front door, running through the streets toward the tavern.

He was late.

Tom was gone.

Everyone in the tavern knew Peter meant trouble. He was wild-eyed, frantic in his insistence that Tom had to be there. One of the settlers tried to calm him by offering a glass of rum. Foolishly, he cajoled Peter, insistently thrusting the glass into his face. Peter grabbed the glass from the man's hand, its contents spewing over them both. He hurled the glass, shattering it against the wall; then, shoving the man into the table, he raced back into the night again.

Tom's ship had just pulled free of its moorings. Peter ran down the street and along the quay. Alerted by the men in the tavern, guards appeared from everywhere. Peter dodged in and out among the packing crates and barrels. Warning shots were fired. Then, exposed to sight, Peter stepped up to the side of the dock. The guards shouted at him. He turned to stare at them, their guns leveled and ready. He looked back to the river, hesitating as he stared down into the dark rushing water that terrified him. Then he flung himself into its icy, rock-strewn depths.

Tom and the first mate of the *Hudson Lady* stood at the stern watching with interest the commotion on the dock. "Holy Jesus, it must be Berean. Crazy bastard. He'll never make it."

From the docks guns reported, the guards aiming into the darkness of the river. Along the shore and on the docks, torches flared, lines of them moving in march time toward the shore boats.

Once more Tom thought of the tidy sum he could expect if somehow he could manage to bring Peter home—even his body. "Send down a ladder."

The mate looked at him as if he'd lost his senses. "What for? He's gone."

"I gave you an order, Mister. Send a ladder over the side and make damn sure you keep an eye out for that man. If he's dead, haul his body aboard. One way or another, I want him."

The mate grumbled under his breath. "They'll stop the ship. Think they'll let him sail out of here?"

"You keep him on that ladder till we're clear and they'll never know."

The mate laughed. "You don't know the Limeys, Captain. They don't let nobody go. Onliest country I know will chase one escaped man 'round the worl' if they have to jus' so's they can watch him hang on English soil."

"Send over the ladder. They're about to lose one."

The mate smirked. "Aye, aye, sir; anything you say, sir."

Peter swam behind the ship, the frigid coldness of the river enveloping him. The choppy water heaved against his chest making a mockery of each stroke he swam. The ship remained a huge mass in the darkness ahead, his efforts never seeming to make the slightest difference in the distance. He ignored the rifle fire. He neither cared nor thought about it. He thought of nothing. His mind was frozen in fear of the water, and his eyes saw nothing but the ship's bulk. Slowly he began to gain a little on it, but his arms and legs were beginning to ache with the cold. His arms were leaden and his legs were cramping, otherwise he wouldn't have known they were there, for the cold was numbing him. He knew then he'd never reach the ship. He pushed himself harder, and thought he had come closer to it, but he couldn't keep swimming. He could hardly breathe, his chest hurt, and he was so frightened he was no longer sure where the ship was. Behind him the rifle fire began anew, and he heard a more ominous sound: the count of the oarsmen. The guards already had the longboats in the water coming after him.

Peter put his head down, his arms and legs moving leadenly. He wouldn't be taken back. No one would ever return him to Hobart Town or Sarah Island to labor or to hang. Water rushed into his mouth, choking him. As he coughed and swallowed more water, he had the insane desire to laugh. It was finally over. He felt a painful wrenching across his chest. He hurt and then he felt nothing more.

From the shore the guards shouted at the *Hudson Lady*, ordering her to drop anchor. Tom speculated that if he disobeyed, he'd never be able to bring *Hudson Lady* into Hobart again. He wanted no part of this, and his inclination was to run; but he shouted orders to drop anchor and prepare to aid a boarding party. Then he shouted for his first mate. "Did you get him?"

"He's danglin' at the end of a line off the stern."

"Alive?"

"Can't tell . . . don't look it."

"Get him aboard . . . we got no more than ten or fifteen minutes."

This time the man obeyed immediately without question or comment. Peter was dragged aboard. Three seamen picked up his dead weight and hauled him down the companionway to the hold of the ship. He was stuffed into one of the empty sperm oil barrels. With more men working now, the barrel in which he was hidden was put to the back of those barrels already filled with oil.

Tom greeted the captain of the guards and offered him free run of the ship in his search. Ten of the soldiers spread out over the vessel, opening hatches, tearing apart rolled canvas, searching the galley and the captain's quarters, opening sea trunks, poking into bunk rolls. They searched the hold, insisting that several barrels be opened, and all supposedly empty barrels be proven empty. Two hours later they left the ship, satisfied that Peter Berean was not aboard the *Hudson Lady*.

Tom headed the *Hudson Lady* out to sea, his attention on his charts because of the dangerous water ahead of them for the next hours. He felt a sense of satisfaction. Stephen Berean would have his brother, or what was left of him, and Tom would have his money and no trouble from a convict passenger.

Peter came to inside the barrel. He was cramped and twisted inside the vile-smelling container. His last memory was of a wrenching pain across his chest as he sank beneath the cold water. He choked, spitting out river water; then he tried to move. He began screaming at the darkness and the hard confines of his new world. Death could not be the same as living in the Grummet Rock cave. Insane with the horror of it, the hideous trickery that this could also be death as well as life, he thrashed, beating himself against the immobile walls of the secured barrel. He could see nothing. He knew nothing except that he was drowning and he couldn't find release from it. It went on and on and yet he didn't feel dead. He had to find an end to it. Somehow it had to stop. He continued to scream and beat against the hard blackness, the taste of blood flooding his mouth and choking him.

One of the seamen, sent below to check the fastenings of the cargo, walked down the lines of barrels. He stopped short, drawing in his breath as he heard the sounds. Young and morbidly superstitious, he ran wide-eyed for the mate.

"The barrels . . . sir . . . they're screamin'. They are, sir. I swear it. Oh, Jesus. It's the spirit of one of them animals . . . it is, sir . . . it's screamin'!"

The mate shouted to the night watch to follow him as he leaped down the rungs of the companionway. Hastily they broke the fastenings that held the barrels in place, thrusting aside one heavy container after another until they reached the one in which Peter had been hidden.

The mate pried the lid off the container. Peter threw himself against the side of the barrel, turning it over. He looked like a specter from the depths of Hades. He was covered with blood, his hair still wet and streaked with red. His eyes were tortured, swollen, red globes in his face. The mate dropped the crowbar and moved back, hesitating in horrified fascination as Peter clawed his way out of the barrel and gained his feet, staggering with his arms flailing madly. He ran erratically like a madman around the hold, leaping onto barrels and falling to scramble up again and jump from one to another.

The mate sent one of the crew to get the captain.

Tom Baker came into the hold, looked at Peter, and let out a stream of expletives that left no doubt as to his feelings about convicts in general and this man in particular. "Get him and lash the goddamned bastard to the mast. I thought you said he was dead," he shouted at the mate.

"Sir, I thought he was."

"You should have made damned sure!"

"But, sir, you didn't say—"

"I said get the son of a bitch, gag him, and lash him to the mast!"

Tom kept Peter lashed to the mast throughout the night. In the morning, he ordered him released and brought to Tom's cabin.

Peter hadn't been able to comprehend where he was. His confusion was so complete, little penetrated his mind. He hadn't yet figured out if he was alive or dead. Only the pain made him think of life; nothing else was familiar or made sense to him.

He was taken to the captain's cabin and thrust through the door. Tom jumped up from his chair, shaking his fist as he came at Peter. "What the hell was the meaning of that last night? Didn't I tell you I'd stand for none o' your friggin' convict tricks on this ship!"

Peter flinched at the burly fist bobbing about so near to his face; then he moved forward, his arms moving of their own accord, knocking away the fist, and his hands closed around Tom's thick neck.

Burly as Tom Baker was, he was no match for the terror-stricken power of Peter Berean. Tom bent backwards under Peter's onslaught. He brought his knee up into Peter's groin, breaking his hold long enough for Tom to shout for his mate.

Rubbing his neck, Tom, in a rage, ordered Peter thrown back into the hold until he could decide what to do with him. Livid with hate, Tom decided, as had so many before him, to flog Peter until he learned to respect and obey his betters.

Already close to senseless, Peter Berean was once again lashed to a mast and flogged. When it was over and he was cut free, he fell to the deck unconscious. Still not satisfied, Tom had him hung in the rigging to bake and bleed in the hot sun without water or food. He gained a modicum of appeasement when he heard Peter, barely able to talk, beg for water.

But Tom Baker wasn't finished with that man. He watched him hanging on the rigging, and felt a mystical sense of vengeance. That man had brutally killed his wife. He had tried to kill Tom. And being guilty of those sins, he had to pay. It was merely an accident of fate that it should be Tom Baker to whom it fell to extract that payment.

The crew looked on the proceedings with hard faces. They had experienced Tom Baker's discipline before. There were several men aboard who had spent their time lashed to the riggings. Most seamen had. The sea was not a tender mistress, and the men who lived their lives upon her back were not gentle men. They were hard and cruel, and expected their time spent here to be harsh.

Throughout the remainder of the voyage, Tom Baker watched Peter and brooded over the fact that if he lived to see New York, it would be Tom Baker who had set a murderer free. On occasion he wondered why Peter clung to life, and then decided that that too was a sign of his perversity. So he continued to have Peter flogged or lashed to the riggings for the slightest infraction of the ship's rules noticed or imagined by Tom.

New York and the Hudson River were still two months' voyage away.

Chapter 40

Stephen received Peter's letter from a packet ship about three months after Tom Baker had taken Peter from Van Diemen's Land. Stephen tore it open and read it aloud to Callie, his voice becoming more excited with each line. He read the many passages from the Bible, the references to the May house, and Hobart Town, and—significantly placed last—the quotation of the parable of the Prodigal Son. "This is it, Callie! Listen! It's Peter all over!"

Callie laughed and cried. Stephen hugged her, dancing her around the room, laughing uproariously over each pious note in Peter's letter.

Finally Stephen sank down on the sofa, catching his breath. "Tomorrow morning, first thing, we'll arrange to get him out. I don't believe it, Callie. He's there! He's in Hobart Town."

Stephen went the next day to all the places he would normally find Tom Baker. He was told Tom was on a whaling trip, but was expected back any day. In the process of asking questions as to how long it would be before Tom could ready his ship to take it out again, Stephen learned considerably more about Tom Baker himself.

During the ride home Stephen brooded. Tom Baker was a man who had little respect for the seamen who sailed with him. There were many who would not put out on the *Hudson Lady* for that reason. Stephen had learned enough about seamen to know they accepted discipline and punishment as part of their lives; but Baker had a reputation as a heavy-handed man who did not permit his crew to imbibe, but was known to drink heavily himself, fortifying an already nasty temperament. Floggings were frequent aboard *Hudson Lady*. Although Stephen had been assured that this was the case aboard most ships, Baker also practiced such things as keelhauling, lashing a man to the prow of a ship, and lashing him to the rigging. Again Stephen was told that happened on other ships as well, the difference being only the frequency of Tom Baker's punishments and his apparent enjoyment of them.

Stephen was faced with two problems. He needed a ship if he were to get Peter. And he needed a way to control Tom Baker. He had learned enough about Van Diemen's Land by now to know he didn't want to risk Peter's coming home with a ship's captain no better than a penal colony commandant. At least not alone. Stephen considered the one area in which he had the upper hand. It was in Tom Baker's greed, and Stephen was certain that the lust for money would overpower his desire to "discipline" his passenger.

When he told Callie that Tom Baker was somewhere at sea, he quieted her instant cries of disappointment by telling her he was expected daily, then alarmed her further by announcing that he had decided to sail with Tom when he hired his ship to go to Van Diemen's Land. He didn't tell her his true reason for going, but said instead, "I think I can help, Callie.

If they think I am a merchant, I should be able to move through the settlement quite freely. Hobart is always in need of supplies. I can ask many questions on the pretext of finding out what particulars they would like me to bring on the next voyage."

"You? But you can't."

"I am going, Callie."

"But Stephen, you know nothing about running a ship."

He laughed. "I won't be handling the ship, goose. The crew and Tom Baker will do that. I'll just be the merchant."

Stephen told her of his hastily conceived plan and went over with her the voluminous information he had collected about Van Diemen's Land over the past months. Last, he told her he would be going into New York to attend the dock auctions to bid on a proper cargo for Tom's ship. He wanted all in readiness when Tom returned to port.

"How long will you be in New York?" she asked.

"I'm not sure. Jack will look after things for me at the brewery, and Dick Adams can handle the farm, so you needn't worry about any of that."

"I wasn't."

He looked at her quizzically, then asked, "You're not afraid to be alone, are you?"

"Oh, no."

"Then what's wrong? You have something on your mind."

"There's nothing," she said lightly.

He put his hand under her chin, lifting her face to his. "Don't lie to me, Callie. What's wrong?"

She shrugged her shoulders. How could she explain to Stephen she was frightened. In spite of wanting Peter's freedom, she feared what his return would mean to her life. "Now that you're going to buy the cargo it all seems so near at hand and real," she finally said.

He looked hard at her, trying to tell what it was she was not saying. "And what we want. Callie . . ."

"But I don't want you on a ship going so far away and—"

"Nothing is going to happen to me. Either I go, or Peter will have to stay there until sometime next summer. Do you want that?"

"No! You know I don't. I'm just afraid of losing you both."

He shook his head, smiling. "Never that. You'll have us both."

He left for New York City at the end of the week.

Tom Baker brought his ship into the Hudson River the day after Stephen left for New York. He came into Poughkeepsie late that morning. Before he had the mate put Peter off the ship, he handed him a statement declaring that he had been a passenger aboard the *Hudson Lady* and had been brought to Poughkeepsie safely by Tom Baker. "Put your mark there, Berean," he snapped, pointing at the bottom of the paper.

Too ill to do more than he was ordered, Peter scrawled an *X* in the space Tom indicated. "Now go on, you son of a bitch, get the hell off my ship."

The mate helped Peter down the gangplank, then left him on the dock.

Peter began to walk in the direction the mate had pointed him. He no longer knew to what he was coming, only that he couldn't stop until he got there.

Callie had finished for the day in the dairy. She didn't want to go back into the house. It was unbelievably empty when Stephen wasn't there to fill it with his laughter and nonsense. She came 'round the side of the house to the garden and sat down on the stone bench. Though it reminded her of him, it wasn't satisfying. It was Stephen himself she wanted, not some thought of him. He was due back from New York in three or four days. If she was this lonely when he had left on a short business trip, what would it be like when he went to get Peter and would be gone for months? She got down on her knees, plucking the weeds that had grown in the past week.

Peter saw Callie in her garden as he walked the last bit of road to their gate. His head was swimming, and he walked unsteadily, but he kept looking at her. He had forgotten what she looked like. She was all milk and honey. It gave him an uneasy feeling to see her, so softly different from what his own dream images of her had been. The tight stirring of fright that was always with him wavered and rose, making his chest hurt.

He came up to the entrance of the gate and couldn't go any farther. He grasped the two gateposts, holding himself erect as he tried to breathe.

Callie glanced up, startled to see a man standing by the gate. He was raggedly dressed, his face nearly covered with a scruffy growth of beard. But his hair, his pale blond hair and the slashing dark eyebrows over his dark brown eyes—she mouthed his name, then broke into a wide, radiant smile. "Peter!" She ran down the path, her white work pinafore and skirts flying. She flung her arms around his neck. "You're home! Oh, thank God, you're home."

Peter kept both hands on the gateposts as hard and tight as if they had been riveted in place. He closed his eyes, still unable to breathe; the blood seemed to drain away from him. Callie, the house, trees, sky, all went spinning off.

Callie was aghast as he slipped through her arms to the ground. "Mary Anne! Mary Anne!" she screamed until Mary Anne poked her head out the upstairs window. "Run and get help—get Dick from the fields."

"Who's that?"

"Hurry! He's very ill."

"Why are you shouting, Callie?" Natalie asked as she came out the front door, peering curiously from around Callie's skirts. "Who is that? Is it Albert?"

"Go inside, Natalie. It's Peter."

Natalie let out a scream that petrified Callie. "For the love of God, Natalie!" she gasped. "Go inside." She took Natalie by the arm and led her back to the house.

"No! No! No! Make him go away. Make him go!"

"I called the men, Miss Dawson," Mary Anne called from the side of the house. "They'll be here any minute. What's the matter with her?"

"Do something with her. Hurry, before she begins screaming again. Take her to her room. Anything."

Mary Anne looked at Callie, then obeyed, taking Natalie with her.

Two of the field hands carried Peter upstairs. Callie, dashing ahead of them, frantically gave directions and told them where to put him. They laid him on his bed in his old room and then moved to the door to leave.

"Undress him for me," Callie said, handing Dick Adams some nightclothes. "He can't be left like that. He's ill."

She waited outside the door for what seemed an eternity until Dick finally stuck his head around the edge of the door. "Uhh—Miss Dawson?"

"Is he dressed?"

"Uhh, no, ma'am—don't seem right to do nothing about this back of his. Where'd you come by this fellow? I think you ought to be told, ma'am, 'specially with Mr. Berean out of town, this man ain't nobody for you to be havin' in the house."

Callie waved her hand to stop his talk. "Back? What's wrong with his back?"

"He's all tore up . . . been flogged looks like. Think I'd better call the sheriff?"

"No. Absolutely not!" Callie pushed past him. Peter lay on his stomach on the bed, his back a mass of open, infected tears and sores. The odor and sight of the purpled flesh among the scar tissue sent her retching to the water closet.

Shakily she sent one of the maids after buckets of hot water and her strongest lye soap. She washed his back until she was satisfied it was as clean as she could get it. She made a decoctation of spikenard, bacon rind, everlasting, and wool into a great steaming mass. She applied the poultice to his back.

He moaned as she worked on him, but he neither awakened nor moved. She replaced each cooling poultice with a steaming hot one, drawing the poisons from the infected wounds. After putting a fresh one on his back, and when she was fairly certain he would remain quiet and not likely to roll over onto his back, she went to find Mary Anne.

"What are you doing bringing a man like that into the house, Miss Dawson? With Mr. Stephen gone, and just the two of us here to protect Master Jamie, what business have you bringin' a murderer right in here amongst us?"

"Mary Anne, I want you to look after Jamie for me. I'll have to stay up there. He's burning with fever."

"Over my dead body! You aren't going near that brute, you hear me, Miss Dawson! You just let Dick pack him up and get him out of here."

"It's Peter," Callie said, bursting into tears.

Mary Anne gaped at Callie. "That's Mr. Berean? But I didn't know him . . . Dick said it was a murderer . . . marked with the sign . . . and . . . I didn't . . ."

"Just care for Jamie for me, and don't let him come into Peter's room. Not until he is . . . well," she said and went back to Peter's bedroom.

He was dreaming, murmuring about dogs when she returned. Then he fell into a restless, exhausted sleep. By late afternoon his fever rose and he was out of his head, thrashing about in bed. The cuts on his back opened again, bleeding as Callie fought to keep him on his stomach. He struck out at her, trying to push away the poultices on his back. "A man is no beast . . . no beast . . . no . . ." He tried to get up, his eyes wild and unfocused as he fought her and the air around him.

Mary Anne, hearing the noise and Peter shouting, took her rolling pin and went to Callie's aid.

"Put that thing down," Callie ordered. "He's out of his head. He doesn't know what he's doing!" Callie sprawled as Peter's flailing arms hit her again. "Help me, Mary Anne. Take his other arm!"

Mary Anne hung back.

"Take it! He's too weak to really hurt you," Callie cried, trying to hold him on the bed.

Mary Anne dropped her rolling pin, reluctantly doing what she was asked. "Mr. Berean will hear about this. He should be here."

"He isn't here. Get him on his stomach. He's tearing his back to ribbons."

Peter still struggled, crying in shuddering gasps over and over, "A man is no beast . . . a man is no beast. . . ."

"How're you gonna hold him there?" Mary Anne asked as Callie stretched across Peter so she could hold both his arms flat against the bed. "Seems like you're doin' it the hard way. Why don't you just tie his hands to the bedposts? That's what my ma did when Pa lost his leg in the carriage accident."

"I don't want to tie him."

"Well, you can't stay like that! It's not even decent. He won't know what's happenin'. Look at him. He don't even know who you are. What's he gonna care where his arms are?"

Peter broke loose from Callie again, turning to his back, clawing at the poultice.

"He sure don't like that poultice on him. You better tie him."

Callie picked herself up off the floor again. She looked at Peter turning and writhing on the bed, and then nodded to Mary Anne. "Tear one of the sheets. I don't want to put a rope on him; it is too harsh and biting."

"Sheets won't hold him."

"Then we won't tie him!"

Mary Anne tore the sheets into long strips, then braided them to make them sturdier. Periodically she glanced at Peter. "Leastways I'll feel a little safer with him tied to the bedposts. I just don't know what's got into you havin' this man in the house like this."

"Oh, Mary Anne, do be quiet!"

"Well, he's a murderer! I have a right to say what I think. Any man who can kill his own wife . . . there's no tellin' what he might do to you . . . or me . . . even Master Jamie!"

"Mary Anne, if you say one more word against him, I swear I'll send you packing tonight! If I didn't need you to help me with Jamie and Natalie, I'd do it in any case!"

"We'll see what's to be done as soon as Mr. Stephen returns. He won't put up with this nonsense of yours! Neither will the people around here. Dick Adams already tol' me if Mr. Peter comes back to the fields to work, he'll quit. He won't work for no murderer."

Callie looked at her furiously. "If you feel like that, why do you stay? Why don't you just leave?"

Mary Anne raised her head, her long face serious and lined with prim dignity. "Because someone has to look out after Master Jamie's welfare and Mr. Stephen's. Looks like I'm the only one who will."

"Why you miserable hypocrite! You don't . . ." Callie turned quickly as Peter cried out, thrashing wildly in the bed. She grabbed his arms and held them against her until he quieted, then got him back onto his stomach.

Mary Anne moved quickly. As Callie rolled him over she grabbed his left hand and lashed it to the bedpost, then hurried to the other side, tying his right hand securely. She stood back, satisfied. He wouldn't turn over again or strike out to hit Callie or anyone else. Then she jumped, clutching at Callie. Screaming, Peter arched his back so his chest was off the bed, fighting and straining at the binding sheets. Though he had been restless before and had thrashed about, there was no question that his struggles were different now. There was a frenzied desperation in his movements. The man was terrified, and his fear could be heard in his voice and seen in his movements.

"Oh, my God, Mary Anne! What have we done? Cut him loose! Hurry—oh, cut him loose!" she yelled, working at one of the knots. Peter pulled so hard against the restraints that Callie's efforts were in vain. He tightened the knots with every wrenching pull he made on the sheet ropes. His voice filled the room as he screamed for it to end.

Mary Anne ran to the sewing room and came back with Callie's shears; then she stopped at the entrance to the room.

"Hurry! Give them to me!" Callie shouted above Peter's impassioned cries.

"Don't cut him loose, Miss Dawson. Don't do it. Somethin' awful will happen. He's a madman . . . he . . ."

"Mary Anne! Give them to me!"

His hands released, Peter lay quiet, shaking and trembling. For a moment Callie was afraid to touch him, not knowing what any movement she made might bring on. She had no idea if it was the fever that had brought on the outburst, or if the sheet ropes in some way had hurt him, or if it was something she didn't understand. She suspected the last, but anything that could cause such a deeply fearful outcry as he had made was beyond Callie's knowledge or experience. When she decided to try once more to do something to bring him comfort, she brought her chair near the bed. She replaced the poultice, only to have him roll over on it. This time she didn't try to move him, but wiped the perspiration and tears from his flushed, fever-hot face with cool vinegar water. "Lie still, Peter," she whispered as he continued to shake, murmuring in a low frightened voice.

Throughout the night Callie sat, talking to him constantly, replacing the poultices as often as she could get him to stay on his stomach long enough for her to accomplish it. She worried, not only about the infected wounds, but also the fever that would not break or subside.

Through the long hours of the night she poured her attention on Peter and longed for Stephen's return. If only he were there; together they could manage. Alone she was afraid, and fought back the tears of giving up and knowing Peter wouldn't survive.

Repeatedly he went through his series of nightmares, crying out in terror and pain.

Just before dawn he was quiet for a time, sleeping almost normally. As she wiped his brow with the cold cloth, he opened his eyes. He lay still, looking at her. Then he turned over on his back, not violently, but to see her better. "Callie?"

"Yes, Peter," she said softly.

"What are you doing here?"

"You're home, Peter. It's all right. You're home."

Suspicion and cunning came into his eyes as he listened to her. She reached out to touch him. He pulled away from her. "You'll go away."

"No. I'll be here. I'll stay as long as you need me."

He watched her hand as a cat does a bird before it springs. He grabbed hold of it, a look of disbelieving triumph on his face. It was the first time he had ever been able to capture one of the air people. Without looking at Callie he rolled over on his stomach, her hand tucked beneath him, held close to his mouth as a child holds his nighttime doll. He slept, and Callie sat doubled over as he held fast to her hand.

Mary Anne brought her breakfast into her the following morning. "It's not decent you stayin' in here with him. He any better?"

"A little, I think," Callie said wearily. "His fever doesn't seem quite so bad."

"Well, come along and eat. You got to keep your strength up. Come along . . . what are you doing all hunched over like that, Miss Dawson? Your food is gettin' cold."

Callie began to giggle in tired hysteria. "He has my arm," she said, still unable to stop laughing.

"All night! You let me fix that!"

"No! Let him be. He'll wake up soon."

Mary Anne gave her a look of disgust. "You're too soft-hearted . . . and soft-headed for your own good. He doesn't even know you're there. Breaking your back for a fellow like that. It isn't gonna do him a bit of good."

Callie looked tenderly at Peter, touching his hair with her free hand. "Maybe it is I who is being done some good."

That day was much like the first, and while Callie had seen some slight improvement in Peter, it was very little, and he didn't seem to progress beyond that. His fever remained high, the nightmares continued to plague him, he slept restlessly, and those few moments when he seemed to awaken, he appeared not to recognize her or any of his surroundings. It was as if he remained within the bounds of the nightmare awake and asleep.

Callie sat through the long idle hours as he clung to her. Yet it was only her hand he accepted. Callie herself might as well not have been in the room, for to Peter she was not. But she left his side only when he seemed to be sleeping quietly.

She couldn't look at him and not remember him as he had been when she first saw him in London. She stared at the scarred, beaten man lying on the bed and heard long-ago echoes of his jubilant laughter as he went along the hop rows collecting the baskets from the pickers, joking and showing off. She thought of the man who had come to Poughkeepsie filled with visions and hope for the future. He was a happy man, proud of all the things he had done and owned in Poughkeepsie. The bright red sled, ornate and fancy, that he had used in the races on the Hudson in winter still sat as he had left it. It all seemed a lifetime ago, and surely the man she remembered could not be the same man she now nursed.

Mary Anne popped in from time to time throughout the day. "What's he dreamin' about anyway?"

"He dreams the same things over and over again," Callie said dispiritedly.

"You sure he was in prison? Sounds to me like he was in a zoo—dogs, beasts, whales, oxen, horses—it's all he talks about. What kind of a place was this Van Diemen's Land?"

Callie shook her head. "I don't know."

"Well, Mr. Stephen is due back some time late tomorrow. He'll know what to do."

"Tomorrow," Callie breathed.

"I'll sit with him for a time. You go rest. You haven't been to sleep since he fell through the gate. You're about to fall over, Miss Callie."

Callie looked up, noting the softening in Mary Anne's attitude. She was not only volunteering to watch over Peter, but she had called her Miss Callie rather than Miss Dawson. "Thank you, Mary Anne. I don't need the rest, but I would be thankful to be able to change my clothes and wash up a bit."

Callie stepped out of the room. She was too tired to chance lying down. She leaned her back against the cool wall, letting her eyes close for a minute. Shortly, she sighed, opening her eyes to go change clothes and wash her face. Natalie stood in the hall opposite her. "What is it, Natalie?"

"Is *he* in there? They said he was back."

"Yes, Peter's here, but he isn't well."

"Is he dead yet?"

"No!" Callie said harshly, then calmed her voice. "He'll be all right. He's going to be well again."

Natalie stood mutely, shaking her head in wide-eyed negation. "No, I don't want him well. I want him to die. He'll die, Callie. I . . ."

"Go back to your room, Natalie. Just go!" Callie said, hurrying toward her own door. Natalie followed after her.

"You can't let him get me."

"He wouldn't even recognize you. Does that make you happy?"

"He hates me."

"Go away, Natalie. I can't listen to you anymore. Just go!"

As soon as Callie came back, Peter groped for her hand.

"Now one thing I'm not gonna let you do, Miss Callie, is sit there all hunched over like that again tonight. He don't need your hand. I'll get him one of those old dolls Jamie had when he was a baby. Though what a grown man needs a doll to hang on to for is beyond me."

Callie shook her head.

"You can't stay like that. He's a grown man. He should have the sense not to ask it of you."

"He hasn't asked."

"I surely do hope he's worth it to you! It's gonna cause a lot of trouble an' a lot of talk. Mr. Stephen won't put up with this sort of nonsense." Mary Anne marched from the room intending to tell Stephen to do something about that as soon as he came home. It was sinful!

Both Mary Anne and Callie watched the windows anxiously waiting for Stephen. They waited in vain, for the only person to come to the house that evening was a messenger bearing a note from Stephen saying he would be delayed.

Callie ordered Mary Anne to set up a cot for her in Peter's room. Mary Anne bristled, lecturing Callie about propriety and how angry Stephen would be. "That man could get up any night, and Lord knows what he might do to you, Miss Callie. Think of it. You know the sort that kind is. Why, he might—"

"Set up my cot, Mary Anne, and keep your thoughts to yourself."

"I will not! Mr. Stephen—"

"I am sure Mr. Stephen is going to find your opinions enlightening."

Callie stayed in Peter's room. Sometimes she felt she'd never again be anywhere else. Infection still raged in him. The fever remained high. The nightmares tortured his sleep. He was not getting any better. Nothing she did seemed to help. During the next two days and nights, however, she began to understand that his nightmares were not the stuff of ordinary dreams. They followed a pattern: they were always the same, and occasionally he would call out a name—John the Pocket, Walter, the commandant, a guard named Gene, someone named Roush. Peter was not dreaming of horrifying fantasies, but of people and experiences he had known and had. She could make little sense of it for his words were too garbled; but she did know he had lived what he dreamed, and she suspected he no longer knew the difference between the nightmare and the reality. It nearly choked her when she began to fully realize that in fact there had been no difference, except perhaps the reality of his life had been far worse than what he now dreamed.

Late in the afternoon of the fifth day, Callie sat quietly looking at the sky through the window across the room from where she sat. She heard the first sounds of thunder roll and reverberate down the channels of the distant mountains. The Hudson Valley sky darkened, becoming strangely iridescent as she watched it turn the room dusky and then dark. She lit the whale oil lamp at the side of Peter's bed and sat down again in her chair by his side.

The wind and the rain began pelting the windows.

Peter stirred in his sleep. Callie liked the sound of the storm. She sat back peacefully as it picked up tempo, the wind blowing with a furious intensity. The windows rattled in their casements. Lightning flashed, illuminating the room with eerie brilliance.

She replaced the poultice on Peter's back. He lay rigid under her touch. As the thunder crashed again and the windows rattled, he spun in bed, sitting up, staring at the dark side of the room. He cowered at every rushing clap of thunder.

The whale oil lamp flickered and lowered in the blowing drafts which crossed the room. He reached out, protecting the fire as he had done his fire on Grummet Rock. As he bumped the lamp, black and amber shadows danced and squirmed crazily in writhing configurations on the walls and ceiling.

"Peter, lie back. You're dreaming again," she said gently, putting her hands on his shoulders to push him back down onto the pillows. He stared straight through her as though she weren't there.

"Peter . . . Peter! Look at me!" she said more forcibly, moving his head so he faced her. "Peter, I'm here with you. You're at home. Peter! Listen to me."

He looked at her, and as he had the only other time he had spoken to her, he said her name in the same dreading, bewildered way. "Callie?" Tears streamed down his face; his features were distorted with anguish.

"I'm right here. Keep looking at me, Peter. I'm here."

He shook his head, emitting an unintelligible sound of fright.

"You're home. You're safe. No one will hurt you here," she kept repeating in the same soft, gentle voice she had learned to use always with him.

He looked at her with tortured eyes, holding his

breath. A sob burst from him. "Don't leave me," he whispered.

"No, I won't leave. I'm right beside you, Peter. I won't leave. Touch me. I'm here, Peter."

He raised his hand, slowly moving it toward her face, but not touching her. He wouldn't risk that. Too often he had reached out for images of her only to have them vanish into thin air, leaving him alone again. "Don't leave me," he repeated, barely audible. He was trembling, not able to hold back the flood of hope that always tore at him. Once more he lunged for her image. This time it was solid and warm. Peter felt as though everything inside of him had been ripped and torn in that moment. He felt a greater pain than ever before when finally, this one time, the abysmal longing for the touch of another human being in kindness had been granted to him. He buried his face against her. His arms were wrapped so tightly around her they hurt. "Oh, please, God, don't take her away. Don't leave me here," he cried, pressing his face harder and harder into her. She put her arms around him, bending down to kiss his head. She caressed him, holding as tightly to him as he did to her.

"Oh, my dear love, what have they done to you?"

He kept on praying and pleading his single prayer. "Oh, please, God, don't leave me here alone."

Chapter 41

Mary Anne ran up the stairs to Peter's room. "He's home, miss! I heard the carriage. Mr. Stephen is home!"

Callie glanced over at Peter sleeping. "Sit with him, Mary Anne, and call me if he awakens before I come back. I don't want him alone."

Mary Anne made a face and sat down. "Hurry up, go see Mr. Stephen. I won't let any bogies get our bogie man."

Stephen came in the front door just as Callie left Peter's room, dropping his luggage and gear on the floor. "Callie!" he shouted happily, then saw her coming down the stairs. "I did it! We've got the biggest cargo of silks and laces and calico you've ever seen." He put his arms out for her to come to him.

Callie hesitated, a step away from tears. "Oh, Stephen," she cried and went to him.

He kissed the top of her head. "Why tears? Everything is good news."

Once started and feeling safe, she couldn't stop crying.

"Weren't you able to get my message to Tom?" he asked. She shook her head against him. "Don't let it upset you. Tom stays in Poughkeepsie for some time between trips. As soon as he rests his greedy eyes on the cargo, he'll do whatever I want. Cheer up, Callie. Everything is going to be all right. We'll be on our way to get Peter in less than a month. No more tears . . . it's almost over."

"Peter's here," Callie choked out.

"What?"

"He's here . . . upstairs."

"He got here on his own?"

"Yes, but Stephen . . ."

"Well, I hope you want a lot of calico dresses. You've got a whole shipload of the stuff." He laughed, hugging her.

"Stephen . . . please . . . Peter . . . he's so ill."

Stephen looked at her closely for the first time. "He's ill? My God, you're not far from it yourself. What's happened?"

Still crying, she began to tell him.

"Never mind, Callie. I'll find out. I want you to rest now."

"No—I've got to get back to him, Stephen. I can't leave him alone. You don't know . . ."

"Callie, you're ready to drop. I'll see to Peter."

"No! No, I've got to be there for him . . ."

"Listen to me, I'll care for Peter just as carefully as you."

"Oh, Stephen . . ."

"Go to bed now. You'll be fresh and able to be with him when he needs you. I promise."

Stephen walked upstairs with her, leaving her at her door. She looked back at him, still reluctant.

"I love him too, Callie," he said softly and walked down the hall to Peter's room.

Peter was asleep when he went in. Stephen stood quietly at the foot of the bed gazing at his brother. Peter's hands and forearms were scarred from innumerable logs hurtling down the slide to gouge into him, from the lumber he handled at the sawmill, and from the lash of the driver's whip. Stephen turned his head away when he first saw Peter's back. His stomach rolled uneasily, and he drew in a deep breath wondering how Callie had managed alone, before he looked back.

Mary Anne, drowsing, opened her eyes, getting to her feet. "Mr. Stephen!"

He put his fingers to his lips, frowning in warning. "How is he?" he whispered.

"Oh, he's gonna make it. Only the good die young. The fever's nearly passed, but you shoulda been here. That Miss Callie's worn herself to nothin' . . ." Mary Anne turned to point accusingly at the cot near Peter's bed. ". . . even slept in here, she did. She won't listen to me. You're gonna have to do somethin' about it."

Stephen's eyes remained on Peter. "I will," he said absently.

"Then I'll just stay put and look after him while you tell her to get herself to bed and stop all this nonsense about him. He doesn't need her being here. She hasn't seen the bedsheets since he fell through the front gates. Why, the way she caters to him you'd think . . ."

"I'll be staying with Peter, Mary Anne. You go on—Jamie has been looking for you."

Mary Anne's lips pursed; she shook her head disapprovingly as she watched Stephen take the place Callie had last sat in. Stephen smoothed Peter's hair back from his forehead; then he took his brother's hand. Mary Anne left the room muttering to herself.

Stephen stayed with Peter throughout the day and night. The first night he went through the same horrifying nightmares with Peter that Callie had gone through. He watched his brother writhe in fear and pain on the sheets while he stood by helpless to break through the veil of horror that enclosed Peter. Then as Peter fell into an exhausted sleep, Stephen slumped into the chair and wept for Peter, for Callie, and for himself.

At dawn of the second day there was finally a change in Peter's condition. The fever broke, and for hours Stephen changed bedsheets and mopped at his brother's wet body. When it was over, and Peter's forehead was cool, he slept, a natural sleep for the first time.

In the morning Peter opened his eyes without the fevered haze of distortion. He glanced furtively around the room; then he saw Stephen sitting in the chair beside the bed. Quickly he glanced at his brother, then lowered his eyes as he had been brutally trained to do, not daring to look Stephen in the eye.

Stephen spoke softly, his voice cheerful. "Welcome back."

Peter glanced up again, a look no longer than a blink. The gnawing pain was deep in his vitals, and his throat was thick. "Stephen?"

"Yeah. You look better . . . you feeling better?"

Peter nodded, still looking perplexed and frightened. He examined every part of his brother, daring to raise his eyes as far as Stephen's chest, but not to his face. Then he looked about the room. The pain grew stronger, tightening around his chest. His clothes hung in the cupboard as they always had. The clock on the mantel was there. It looked as though it hadn't been touched in the entire time he had been gone, but it was strange to him. He could no longer tell reality from dream. Many times he wasn't even sure if he was alive or dead. Nothing made sense any longer, and he hadn't the strength or the courage to examine anything very closely. He startled at the sound of Stephen's voice although he spoke softly and with an overtone of love that Peter hadn't remembered a man's voice could hold.

"You gave us quite a scare for a while."

Peter longed to ask him if that meant he was really here, and it wasn't another phantom of a tortured imagination; but he dared not. He kept his eyes down.

Watching him, Stephen felt his own stomach tighten, but he forced an easy-sounding laugh. "You don't remember? Well, believe me, big brother, you gave Callie the battle of her life."

For the first time Peter looked up and met Stephen's eyes for a moment. "Callie? I thought . . ."

"She was a dream?" Stephen smiled. "Well, I don't blame you. Waking up and seeing Callie is most likely to make any man think he is dreaming. But she was no dream. She was with you day and night."

Peter's face twisted; he laid back against the pillows, his eyes closed holding in the tears that burned.

"Would you like to see her? She's waited a long time for this moment."

Peter remained still with his eyes closed, the tears slowly trickling from his eyes.

Stephen went to Callie's room, knocking gently on the door. She opened it immediately, looking anxiously at him. "You shouldn't have let me sleep like that, Stephen! All day and . . ."

"He's going to be all right," Stephen said quickly. "He's clear-minded and awake—I think he'd like to see you."

Callie ran from the room only to be halted by Stephen's voice. "Callie . . . don't expect too much from him. Not yet."

She shook her head. "I won't." She ran the rest of the way to Peter's room.

Daring something he had not dared in over a year, and risking what he didn't know, Peter watched her as she walked toward him, never taking his eyes from her. She meant everything good to him. She had meant hope when there was none. Somehow when everything else became terrifying Callie had remained the one safe harbor in his mind. He had lost his courage, his sanity, his faith in everything but her. He had clung to the thought of her through everything, and he couldn't, no matter what it cost him in pain or punishment, take his eyes from her now. Slowly he moved his hand up to his chest to cover the brand.

"You look better today," she said, suddenly shy, faced with him awake and looking at her in naked wonderment.

"You were here? All the time?"

"Always," she smiled.

It was like seeing the sun come out. It blinded him. He looked down at her hand, remembering her touch, but not moving his own from the brand.

"There's nothing to hide, Peter. Give me your hand," she said softly as she put her hand out to him. "I have washed you and cared for you. There is nothing on the outside that I don't know about. Don't hide from me."

He took her hand without looking at her and brought it back against his chest. Callie sat on the edge of his bed as near to him as she could. Moving his hand slightly, she touched the brand. "Do you know what it stands for?"

He turned away from her, roughly putting his hand back in place over it. Again his muscles drew up involuntarily, his stomach taut and hard and hurting. She was so full of softness and forgiveness. Would she remain so if she knew the brand was a symbol of truth now? What would she do if she knew about Walter Wheeler and John the Pocket? Would she then hate him as others did, as he sometimes did himself?

"No, Peter, not what you think. Look at me." He couldn't do it. He was suffocating from the need to have her near, and terrified her nearness would somehow tell her of his own hideous depravity. Somehow she'd begin to sense what he was. He moaned with a physical ache as he thought of keeping her near only to watch her turn from him as everyone else did, or of putting her away from him now and never knowing her touch again. He was so tired he couldn't think any more.

He closed his eyes, shivering as she ran her sweet-smelling hand down the side of his face. "Look at me, Peter," she repeated softly. As he turned, she smiled, and again it hurt him deep inside. "Mine," she said, again tracing the scar of the brand. "That's all it means now. Welcome home, Peter." Before he could move or react, she leaned down to kiss him. Peter lay still for a moment, his chest tight, unable to breathe. Then her lips touched his eyes, and he put his arm around her, sobbing. He tangled his fingers deep in her hair as again he smelled the fresh scents of the lemon and herbs she used. "Callie," he murmured over and over. "Touch me . . . just keep your hand on me," he breathed, his face rubbing against hers until he found her mouth. "You won't ever . . ."

"I'll never leave you. As long as we both live, you'll never be alone again," she whispered, then sat up, kissing him quickly. She looked down at the brand again, drawing his attention to it once more. He tightened, flinching away from her gaze. "No, Peter, don't," she said so softly he wasn't sure he heard. She traced the outline of the letter. "Now, my own, I want you to sleep, and get well. Soon it will be time for you to think of Jamie and your hop yards. There's a whole world waiting for you, Peter."

He listened to her, and when he heard her words he wondered if perhaps there was such a thing as the world he so vaguely remembered and so poignantly distrusted. He watched her carefully as she stood, straightening her hair and dress.

She gave him a look of dismay, smiling and shaking her head. "You have no faith, silly. I'm not going anywhere. I'll be right here," she said, sitting down and taking his hand again.

Peter closed his eyes as she wanted him to, but he didn't sleep. He'd do nothing to displease her, nothing to make him lose the treasure of her hand in his, but as soon as he was sure she was no longer watching him, he opened his eyes, looking at her with naked longing. How he wanted the touch of her hand against his chest again, to feel her hand soothe his face, to feel her breath on him, to kiss her.

To Peter a regulated day had no reality. He lived in a limbo where no new pains were inflicted on him except those of longing and the fear of loss, and unknowingly he put enormous demands on Callie. He had once thought, the first time he had been sent to the triangles, that he knew what it was to want to die. He hadn't known then, but he did know now. All that represented life to him was bound up in Callie and his fantasy of her. She was his door to living, and without her he knew he not only did not want to live, but would no longer know how. He began to exist in desperate fear of losing her. If she wasn't by his side when he was awake, he felt closed in and terrified. If he awoke from sleep and she was gone, he was certain she had only been a dream. He wanted her with him day and night. He longed for her touch with a passion that went far beyond the mere needs of sex. To him she had become life. She was the only person in whom he believed; where she was, he was safe.

Callie responded to his need of her with amazing constancy. She was exhausted, but she refused to compromise or try in any way to lessen the time she spent with him. Though Stephen begged her to think of herself at least part of the time, he didn't pressure her, for he knew as well as she did why Peter clung to her. And Callie had slowly begun to learn certain ways of easing the pain and the nightmares that still racked him. In the middle of the night when he'd awaken the entire household with frightened, agonized screams of being closed in on the Rock and left alone, she had learned that all she need do was to move as close to him as she could, to warm his shivering cold body with hers, and slowly he'd awaken, understand where he was, and quiet again.

Weeks went by, a month, then two. Stephen and Callie watched as his body began to heal. The fever was a thing of the past; the infected lacerations were healing; his general state of debilitation was abating. Daily they expected him to become restless and take up his old life again. That there were some problems, they understood. Peter was a wanted man and would remain so all of his life. Any man escaping from a British penal colony was under the death penalty. Should he ever be seen or sought by a British officer, he would be taken back to England and hanged, so they would always have to be careful. But Stephen felt that Peter was safe in Poughkeepsie, and he would do all the traveling so that Peter could remain in the background as much as he thought advisable. In a few years, Stephen was sure, it would all be forgotten.

Peter listened to him and spoke agreement with whatever Stephen suggested, but the running of a brewery and a hop yard and a business were so far removed from Peter as to have no meaning. Stephen spoke in terms of years, while it required all of Peter's concentration and courage to live through hours.

What Peter wanted was for everything to stop long enough for him to rest. He didn't want to "get on" with his life. He didn't yet know what his life was, and he was too tired and too frightened to challenge anything. He just wanted to stay where he was for a time. For the first time since his arrest, Peter felt safe and comforted in Callie's care. For these past few weeks there had been no decision to make or problem to face, no punishment to come from looking her or Stephen in the eye or from speaking to them without first being granted permission. These were the things neither Stephen nor Callie thought about or would ever truly understand; but for Peter, breaking down the fear of flogging and isolation in order to do the simple things the rest of the world took for granted was a monumental undertaking. Most of the time he felt too weak and too confused to try to be "normal."

But Peter was aware that this interlude would have to end whether he was ready for it or not. It would last only as long as the healthy people accepted him as being ill. And when that time was over—and it was nearly so now—he would have to try to enter life as he had once known it. He saw it narrowly, as though there were only two choices: being what Stephen told him he should be, or going back to Van Diemen's Land. He never thought in terms of what he wanted, only in terms of what others might demand of him. He began to listen carefully to the noises of the household.

Stephen was like a fresh spring colt, romping

through the house with Jamie, teasing the servants, and playfully loving with Callie. But Peter was aware of more than that. Stephen was the central core around which the rest of the household moved. Mornings began when Stephen opened his eyes. The quiet broke as he strode from his room and then into Peter's room, tousled, hair wet from washing, and more often than not laughing as Callie ran behind, scolding his abominable habits.

Peter waited this morning as he did every morning for Stephen's appearance at the bedroom door.

"Good morning!" Stephen said, and then with only a towel wrapped around his loins, he sat in the chair near his brother's bed and told him of what was to be done that day in the yard and the brewery, and at what point the harvest was. Then he stood up, a smile on his face full of life and deviltry. He roared at Callie as he left the room, barely able to suppress his laughter. "Where'd you hide my shirt?"

"In your drawer."

"Not so!"

"It is—have you looked?"

"Drawer's empty!"

He held the shirt behind his back as she ran up the stairs, then followed her down the hall putting it on. He laughed as she turned around, scowling and hitting him.

Peter couldn't imagine being like that again. He could stay as he was, receptive and wanting, but to be able to sing and laugh as Stephen did for sheer good humor was something locked tight inside Peter. Van Diemen's Land was thousands of miles away, but it didn't matter because the prison was inside him, and that made everything else unimportant.

* * *

As Peter continued to stay in his room upstairs, Callie and Stephen worried, knowing that he didn't want to be well. "He can't lie up there tucked away from everything but us forever," Stephen said firmly one evening at dinner.

Callie ate slowly. This was something she didn't like to talk about, because she didn't like thinking about it. There seemed to be no answer. She finally said, "He needs more time."

"He's had time. It's only going to get worse the longer he puts it off. I'm going to tell him to come to dinner tomorrow."

"And if he refuses?"

"He won't refuse. Peter does what he is ordered. It is all that he does. God, Callie, he must have lived through hell, but if ordering him is the only way I have of bringing him back, I'll order him. I'll order him to laugh if I must."

"Stephen, that's cruel!"

"What choice have I got, Callie? Those scars he carries aren't only on the outside. What else can I do?"

"I don't know, but . . . oh, Stephen, he still has those awful nightmares. I know he has to get over them before he's better. I don't know what they mean exactly, but . . ."

"I've heard him too. But it doesn't matter; he has to get up and begin to—unless he makes a future for himself, Callie, he's always going to be trapped by that past. He'll never forget them unless he begins living and has something new to replace those old memories. And it's time he saw Jamie."

"He doesn't want to. It is the only thing he has expressed his own wishes about. He doesn't want to see him."

"Peter doesn't want to do anything. That doesn't mean that's the way it should be."

"Don't be angry with me. I'll take Jamie to see him tomorrow. Then you put off the dinner for a couple of days—all right?"

"All right, but only if he sees Jamie tomorrow," Stephen said, still angry with her, partly because she was so willing to spend the days and half the nights with Peter, and partly because he wanted Peter well, and he would never be until he tried.

The following morning Callie went to Peter after he had bathed to bring him his breakfast. "I want you to see Jamie today," she said as he finished eating.

"No."

"Peter, he's your son. He hasn't seen you since he was a baby. He needs you."

Peter laughed bitterly, but said nothing.

"Mary Anne will be bringing him here any minute now," she said firmly.

When Mary Anne knocked, Callie went to the door without looking at Peter. Jamie stood waiting. She took his hand and brought him fully into the room.

Peter stared at the child as he walked holding fast to Callie's hand. He was tall for his age and straight of body. He looked at Peter through eyes the same dark brown as his father's. His hair was like ripe wheat. Tears formed in Peter's eyes as Jamie smiled. And Peter knew Jamie was his son, not Albert's.

"That's Papa?" he asked, looking up to Callie.

"That's your Papa. See what a fine handsome man you'll grow up to be?"

"How do you do, sir?" Jamie asked as he climbed up on the bed with Peter, studying him with the minute attention of a five-year-old child.

"Can you make things like Uncle Stephen can?"

"What sort of things does Uncle Stephen make?"

"Almost everything."

Peter laughed. "I don't know if I can make everything, but perhaps something."

"Well, that would do for a start. Could you make me a new caboose? Mary Anne stepped on mine and—"

"Jamie! Enough of your nonsense. That's very rude to be asking for things."

Jamie looked regretfully at Peter, but slid off the bed. "I'm sorry, Papa."

"Don't be sorry," Peter said softly as though he didn't want Callie to hear. Jamie started to leave. "Must you go so soon?" Peter asked.

"Uncle Stephen is waiting for me. I can come back—if you want."

Peter glanced uncertainly at Callie. She was smiling her approval to Jamie.

"He looks just like you," she said in satisfaction as Jamie left; then she turned to Peter, frowning. "And he's just as naughty. I'll thank you not to encourage him to be asking for everything he fancies."

"Is it so wrong to want things?"

"No, but—no, it isn't wrong, Peter, but Jamie has to be taught to value things of value, and not yearn for the worthless."

Peter stared down at his hands, wondering how anyone knew something of value when it came. So many times he thought he had, and never had it been real.

"Stephen wants you to come to dinner tomorrow night. I'll have your clothes laid out for you. We eat at six," she said and stood up.

Peter wasn't listening to her. His eyes were studiously cast down, and his breathing was rapid and shallow. Finally he spoke, his voice tight. "You're angry with Jamie."

"No, I'm not angry . . ."

"Will you punish him?"

Callie looked indignant for a moment; then she

went quickly to the bed. "He's already been punished and forgiven." She took Peter's hand. "I'm sorry, Peter, I keep forgetting that I don't always see things as you do. Jamie has never been harmed in any way. We have no need for switches or paddles, and never will. If you are concerned about your son, the best thing you can do for him is to get well and teach him the things you believe in. I told you Jamie had to learn to recognize value. He will find it in you, if you allow him."

Peter came down to dinner the next night, feeling awkward and self-conscious in the clothes he hadn't worn for so long. They were crisp and fresh, clean and distinguished looking, but they covered a man who was none of these things. He sat nervously at the head seat Stephen had vacated when Peter entered the room. He was unsure as he tried to recall the intricacies of table manners long unused. He almost laughed trying to think when he had last used a fork, or when he had been allowed so close to such a weapon as a table knife.

He had difficulty eating, he was so tight and apprehensive. Nothing was the same here as it was in the warm little world of the sickroom. Callie was bright and cheerful, laughing and talking of people and hops and her dairy in a way that invited crisp, easy repartee. Stephen responded as he always did. But Peter, as he had realized while he lay in bed listening to that outside world go on, could not. He was silent throughout the meal, speaking only if addressed directly.

After supper he went upstairs. He stood in the hall for several minutes, wanting to enter his son's room as he heard sounds of childish laughter and questions. He went several steps in the direction of his own room, then turned back and entered Jamie's nursery.

He watched quietly as Mary Anne gave the little boy his bath and prepared him for bed.

"Why don't you talk much, Papa?" Jamie asked as he got into bed.

Peter smiled, shrugging. "I haven't much to say, I guess."

"How'd you get those scars on your hands?"

Peter's stomach tightened as Mary Anne stared at his hands along with Jamie. "Felling trees," he said.

"You felled trees?"

"Yes."

"Tell me . . ."

Peter glanced at Mary Anne's disapproving face and saw what neither Callie or Stephen would ever understand. Mary Anne didn't see Peter Berean when she looked at him; she saw the convict, and only a man like Peter could recognize that look. He stepped back nearer the door and spoke softly, "In the morning. You come wake me up."

"But Callie makes me go to lessons," he groaned. Then: "I'll come before school."

Peter nodded, hesitated, then quickly reached out, tousling Jamie's hair.

Peter's early mornings with Jamie became a habit. Those hours were the heart of his days, holding no threat or barrier of fear that he couldn't overcome. Beyond that nothing was easy for him.

The more he tried to please Callie and Stephen, the more they demanded of him, accepting each new thing as a sign of progress, never knowing that it took Peter half a sleepless night to calm himself enough to even try to do as they asked. Stephen tried to tempt him with books from the library in his study. Callie asked his assistance with small chores around the house. These things he could accomplish. He was used to working, but what was impossible for him was the lighthearted conversation, the laughter, the ideas they expected from him. Those things were too bottled up inside, driven too far by fear for him to retrieve. Once more the hard-learned habits of protection slipped back into place. He couldn't accept normal anger or irritation without reacting to the threat it implied. Refusal translated itself into disapproval and deprivation. No matter how hard or often he reasoned through the range of emotions that occurred in any given day, he couldn't break away from the constant expectation of punishment.

In his room was a mass of small items he had stolen from all over the house. Mostly they were worthless little things—pencils, quill pens, handkerchiefs, napkins, silverware. In one of Callie's large butter molds he kept food he pilfered from the pantry. He had not known a hungry day since his return home, but the dread of that day lingered. Each time the food in the butter mold spoiled he threw it out, replacing it immediately.

One afternoon, months after he had come home, Peter looked at the spoiled food in the butter mold. He didn't need it. He knew he didn't need it. As Callie had told him repeatedly, he was home and safe.

For the next few days he took the butter mold out every afternoon, repeating these assurances to himself, until finally after a week he emptied the mold, washing it in the marvelous bathing room that had been installed while he was in prison. He put the mold on the rear shelf of his closet, promising himself never to refill it. But he kept the mold.

After lunch that same afternoon, Stephen looked at him long and pensively. "You feel up to taking a look at the new field we're clearing?"

Peter looked away, then thought of the empty butter mold upstairs in his closet. He was inordinately proud of that empty container. Then he thought of Jamie. If he had taken one step, he could take two. Stephen would be with him. He was home and he was safe. "Yes," he said finally.

"Good! I'd like your opinion. It's not as good a soil as the rest. I'm not so certain we should even try putting it in hops. I've been thinking of making it the home garden, but no one knows soil better than you. I'd like you to tell me what it's best to plant."

The field lay just beyond the east boundary of the original tract of land Peter had bought. It was in the process of being cleared.

"Doesn't look too bad, do you think?" Stephen asked, waiting, hoping, half expecting to see Peter bend down to feel the soil and work it in his hands, smelling it as he used to.

Peter was rigid, holding firmly to the fence rail. "It seems all right," he said tensely. He shook his head, biting his lower lip. Perspiration stood out on his brow and lip.

Stephen put his hand around Peter's tight, cramped shoulders. "Are you all right? You're not ill?" He followed the direction of his brother's gaze, but saw nothing out of the ordinary. In the center of the new field Dick Adams drove a team of horses as they took a large tree stump from the cleared land. "Peter?"

"I'm all right," Peter said, then repeated it under his breath.

"Mr. Berean!" Stephen turned as one of the men from the brewery rode up. He dismounted and handed Stephen a sheet of paper.

Stephen read the message his foreman had written; then he smiled grimly. Tom Baker was waiting for him at the brewery. "I wondered how long it would take that greedy son of a bitch to show up." He folded the note and stuck it into his shirt pocket. "A little business matter has come up," he said to Peter. "I'll be back in fifteen or twenty minutes. This will be short and to the point."

Peter shook his head woodenly, still watching the team of horses struggling in the wet earth.

Stephen went back to the brewery with the messenger while Peter stood for nearly half an hour gripping the fence rail until his hands hurt and he was trembling. Dick Adams drove the team, cracking his whip behind their heads as he shouted, urging them on. The smaller of the two animals went down on its knees in the mud, snorting as it struggled to regain footing.

Peter squeezed his eyes shut, then put his hands over his ears to block out the sound of the man shouting commands to the horses. He began to walk away, fighting the feelings that were rioting inside of him. He kept saying to himself that this was normal. It was the way of things. They were horses, not men. This was home, not prison. But he couldn't keep his eyes off the sight in the field, and he couldn't help but flinch and feel all his muscles tighten every time a command was shouted, every time he heard Dick Adams's whip snap. He looked back to the field.

Adams brought his whip down on the small horse's flank, and the animal whinnied, struggling for footing in the mud. Peter leaped the fence, running across the field. He threw himself at Dick Adams.

As Stephen rode up, Peter was on the ground, hitting Dick with the handle of the whip. The horses pawed and pranced in fear, making more headway with the stump than before.

Stephen turned his horse, giving it room to make a run at the fence. He was beside the struggling men in seconds. He leapt from the saddle shouting Peter's name. Peter paid no attention. With clenched teeth he muttered, "No beast . . . man is no beast . . ." each time he struck Dick. Stephen tried to pull him away without success. Then with one hard motion, carrying all his strength and weight, he hit Peter, knocking him off Dick.

Stephen got Dick to his feet, groggily shaking his battered and bloody head. "Tha' man's a killer. He come outta nowhere, Mr. Berean. I'm tellin' you I was mindin' my own business an' here he comes a flyin' at me. I never seen him till he had me on the ground beatin' the hell outta me. I'm sorry about this, Mr. Berean, 'cause I allus liked workin' for you, but I'm not stayin' here as long as he's around. Find yourself a new man."

Stephen talked to Dick, trying to calm and reassure him. He made little headway. Dick stalked from the field, leaving the horses where they stood.

Stephen turned angrily to Peter still sitting on the ground. "What the hell got into you? You've lost me the best man I have."

Peter kept his eyes downcast.

"Get up on your feet, damn it! Help me with these horses. They can't be left out here in harness."

Peter hesitated, and Stephen yelled at him. "Get up!"

Peter got to his feet, the whip still in his hand. He held it out, handle end to Stephen.

Stephen stood staring at the whip, then he looked at Peter. Peter stood with his eyes cast down, looking at the ground. "Don't use the whip on them," he said so softly that Stephen wouldn't have heard him if he hadn't just realized what had caused Peter to attack.

He wanted to reach out and comfort him as Callie had done, but knew for him it would be wrong. That was Callie's place, and as he looked at Peter he knew that was where she ought to be. Callie would remain with Peter, and Stephen would do as he had always done—be there, love her, love them both.

For Peter he couldn't change a threatening world, but he could keep safe the small world of the farm. It was becoming clear to Stephen that Peter would never leave here. This farm, a safely contained and protected world, was the only possible world Peter might ever be able to handle, if that.

"Unharness them, Peter," he said, taking the whip.

Peter went obediently to do as he was asked. When they took the horses back to the stables, Stephen handed the whip to Peter. "Destroy it. Destroy them all. Remember one thing; this is our farm, Peter, no one else's. We do as we want here, and you're the boss. You always were."

Peter didn't appear for dinner that night, and Callie looked up in concern when Stephen said, "Let him do as he likes. It's been a bad day."

Callie remained seated. Neither of them ate. When it was time to retire and Peter had still not made an appearance, Callie stopped by his room. Peter wasn't there.

She found him sitting in his study, looking out the window that overlooked the Hudson. A half-empty bottle of rum sat on the desk beside him.

"I wondered where you were," she said, coming into the room. "Are you hungry? I'll fix something for you if you like."

"I'm not hungry."

"Stephen said you had a bad day. Will you tell me about it?"

"No."

"Peter, talk to me, please."

"There's nothing to talk about," he said edgily.

"You're unhappy."

"Let me be, Callie," he pleaded.

"I can't. I want to know everything that concerns you."

"You can't do anything, Callie."

"If I knew what to do . . . just talk to me, Peter."

He stood up, putting his glass down on the desk. The rum was doing no good tonight. The memories were razor sharp, and no amount of rum seemed to dull them. He looked at Callie, then away, not able to bear looking at her. The greater his longing grew, the more repulsive he found the idea of her ever really being with him. He couldn't think of her by his side without hating what he had become. He didn't want her, by her nearness, ever to learn the things he had learned in prison. When he finally managed to look at her again, his voice was unsteady. "I . . . can't talk to you. I don't *want* to talk to you." His voice rose and quivered with emotion. "I don't want you to know. Can't you understand that!? *I don't want you to know!*"

Chapter 42

Natalie had not spoken to Peter since his return. She stayed in her room, going out only to watch Jamie play. If Peter came near or tried to talk to her, she fled. He seemed to accept her peculiar behavior as he did everything else. After awhile he paid little attention to Natalie, but Callie began to.

Natalie had done nothing toward Peter that Callie could put her finger on, but she had begun to talk to Jamie about Peter.

"Aunt Natalie says Papa is a rake-hell. What's a rake-hell, Aunt Callie?"

"It's a very naughty thing for Aunt Natalie to call your papa."

"Are you going to get mad at her?"

"I certainly am."

"Will you wash her mouth out with soap?"

Callie grinned at him, then laughed. "It's not such a bad idea."

"What is a rake-hell?"

"Someone who is wild and bad."

Jamie wandered around the kitchen, coming back

to poke his fingers in Callie's bread dough. "What did Papa do?"

"Nothing bad."

"Then why do so many people say he's bad?"

"Who?"

"Aunt Natalie, and sometimes Mary Anne."

Callie stopped kneading the dough. She looked at Jamie and then away, unwilling to allow him to see the depth of her anger. Without realizing, her hands began to pummel the dough revealing what she wouldn't permit her eyes to do.

Jamie watched her hands in fascination and went on, "Some of the kids at the schoolhouse say they know all about Papa. I'm not allowed to play with some of them. I don't know why they know if I don't."

"What do they know?"

"That he's bad."

Callie forced herself to move slowly, talk softly. "How bad? What did he do?"

"I don't know."

"That's what they know too. He did nothing bad. Now think what you do know. Is he good to you? Does he love you? Is he kind?"

"Lots of yesses."

"Then that's what you know, and yours is better."

Callie went to Natalie's room late that afternoon. She knocked at the door and waited what seemed a long time for Natalie to answer. "Who is it?"

"It's Callie. I want to talk to you, Natalie."

"Are you alone?"

"Of course, I'm alone. Open the door."

Natalie opened the door a crack, peeking out to see if Peter was near. Satisfied, she let Callie in, closing the door and locking it.

"I've just been talking to Jamie, Natalie."

Natalie tested the door to be certain it was secure.

"Did you hear me? I know what you've been up to. I won't have it. I am willing to put up with all your other nonsense, but not this."

"Shhh."

Callie took her shoulders and roughly turned Natalie to face her. "Listen to me! You *may not* talk badly of Peter. Not ever! I mean it, Nat!"

"Peter's going to die." She nodded her head earnestly. "I saw it. I've been watching and I've seen it."

Callie rolled her eyes in exasperation at Natalie's favorite evasive tactic. "You're not going to get out of this with one of your dreams, Natalie. If you dare say one more word, just one single word more to Jamie against his father, I'll move you right out of this house. I mean it, Nattie. I'll get you a room in Poughkeepsie, or send you back to Kent."

"No . . . no . . . not me . . . I'm not the one who did it. He did! They said he did!"

"Don't try to test me, Nat. I'll do it."

"But you can't! Everything will be all right again as soon as Peter . . . is gone. It will be just like it was."

"Peter isn't the one who will go. It is you. Don't say any more. Not to me or to anyone else."

That evening after supper Callie told Stephen about her threat to Natalie. "Where's Peter?" she asked, making sure he wasn't in the room as she entered.

"Upstairs with Jamie. He gets along well with Jamie."

"No thanks to your sister!"

Stephen looked up from his newspaper. She sat across from him frowning. He put the paper down on his lap. "Well . . . ?" he asked, when she remained silent.

"You won't like what I've done, but it's done and I mean to stick to it."

"Am I supposed to guess?" he asked, grinning.

"It isn't funny. I've told Natalie I'll put her in a rooming house in Poughkeepsie if she ever says another thing to Jamie about Peter being bad."

"You want her to leave?"

"Yes."

"She can't manage on her own."

"Then she'll have to change her ways."

"You're becoming quite a little dictator, aren't you?"

Callie looked hurt, then defiant. "It doesn't matter what you think I've become. She cannot behave as she has been."

"All right. I'll talk to her."

"I already have."

"Well, if you've handled it and made your decision, why bother to tell me? Or do you want me to do your dirty work for you, and put her out?"

"It was mean of you to say that, Stephen."

"No meaner than your thinking it."

"You used to understand and help me."

"We used to do things together, Callie. I don't like being your second Mary Anne."

"Well, there's no talking to you! I can see that."

"No, there isn't. I'm going to visit Jack," he said angrily.

"Oh, Jack," she scoffed. "Why don't you just say what you're going to do. Why always—Jack?"

"Because, my stiff-necked beauty, it would turn your face bright red to hear what I'm going to do called by its proper name," he said nastily and stalked out of the house.

After Stephen left, Callie sat alone in the parlor as long as she could stand it. She was angry at everyone. Peter stayed as much to himself as possible. Natalie got worse by the day, and Stephen was spending more time with Jack than he was at home.

She went to the kitchen for lack of anything better to do.

"I don't need any help, Miss Callie. Everything's all done," Bea said as she came in.

"Did you find my bread knife?"

"No, ma'am. I've looked everywhere. It just ain't here."

"Well, it has to be here," she said and pulled all the knives from their holders and drawers.

"It's not. I've been all over this kitchen looking. It ain't here!" Bea insisted, cleaning up behind Callie.

Callie moved angrily toward the pantry.

"Don't you mess my pantry, Miss Callie. It ain't there neither. Why don't you go ask Mr. Peter. If anyone knows, it'd be him."

Callie glared at her.

"Don't blame me. I don't know what he carts all that stuff off for, but he does. All kinds of things up there in that room of his. Ain't no business of mine, but when Ginnie and Penny clean up they tell me about it."

"Well, it's his house. He can do as he likes."

"That's what I'm tellin' you. It ain't my business, but if you want your bread knife, I'd look there."

Callie stormed from the pantry back into the parlor. The longer she thought of Bea, the knife, and Peter, the angrier she got. She went upstairs to his room.

He was standing by the open window looking out into the night.

"Peter!"

He turned around smiling tentatively, walking toward her. Then he stopped. "You're angry . . . what have I done?"

"Do you have my knife?"

"What knife?"

"You know very well what knife. My bread knife. Did you take it from the kitchen?"

"I took nothing."

"Don't lie to me!"

He stepped away from her. "I didn't take your knife."

Callie put her hands out helplessly. "Knives don't just disappear."

Peter's face was pale. "Why did you accuse me? Why not Stephen?"

Nonplussed, Callie stared at him. He continued to move away, putting the expanse of the room between them. "You . . . you bring things up here sometimes," she stammered.

"Not knives."

"No. I never really thought you had," she said deflated and ashamed. She walked over to him. "Will you forgive me?"

"Forgive you?"

"I don't know what's wrong with me these days. I've managed to snap at everyone in the house today. It isn't you, Peter. It's me that's all wrong."

He stood looking at her, not knowing what to say. He didn't like to see her blaming herself for anything. Without her they'd all be at a loss, and yet he was afraid to say anything for fear it would bring her back to an accusation of him.

"I don't know what to say, Peter."

"There's nothing you need say."

"I guess not," she said and turned to go. She walked to the door, thinking only of going to her room and closing herself inside. She didn't know what was wrong with her. It wasn't really the knife, although it did worry her, and she had wanted to know what had happened to it. It was mostly Stephen she was angry with. She couldn't get near him anymore. He was always around and never truly there.

"Callie."

She turned, surprised to hear Peter call her name. He so seldom initiated any conversation. "Yes?" she asked and went back to him, waiting.

He looked at her, indecisive and tense, then shook his head. "Nothing."

"Oh. Well then . . . good night, Peter," she said, standing on tiptoe to kiss his cheek.

He went back to his window, and Callie having had enough of a bad day went to bed.

Stephen and Jack had begun with the nearest tavern and were continuing their prowl of the village. By the third tavern, Stephen wanted broader horizons. "Let's go somewhere else. Poughkeepsie is too quiet."

"Way too quiet," Jack agreed. His driver wisely took them back to the first tavern they had visited.

Stephen laughed as they entered. "We've been here before. Hello, everyone! Good-bye, everyone!"

Jack sat down. "Let's rest here for a minute and catch our breath. Are you having fun, Stevie? You said you wanted fun when you came bangin' at my door."

The waiter brought them glasses and a bottle without being asked.

"No. I'm gonna leave," Stephen said morosely.

"Wait till we finish the drink."

"No, I mean I'm gonna leave the house."

"What house?" Jack asked, looking around and concentrating hard.

"My house—Peter's house—our house—everybody's house. I'm gonna leave it all." He sat quietly for a moment. "I don't want to be there."

"I told you, you should marry Agnes. I think I'll marry her since you won't."

"You marry her. I don't want her."

"She won't marry me."

"Callie won't marry me either."

"Oh, God, Stevie, we're a sad pair. Nobody will marry us," Jack said sadly. "Why don't you move into my house and then we can be nobody will marry us'es together."

"That's a good idea," Stephen agreed happily.

"What are you gonna tell Callie?"

He shrugged.

"You should tell her fancy. Go out in grand style."

"She wouldn't care."

"We'll give her a party."

"A party?" Stephen asked, interested.

"Yeah! A going-away party—for you." He laughed, belching and choking himself. "Sure—we'll go home and sing and dance and tell her you love her and you're going away. She'll like that. All the girls like that. Look! June! Come over here," Jack called to the bargirl. She came over to the table, putting her arm around his shoulders. "Tell Stevie you like parties."

"Sure I like parties. Who doesn't?"

"See? I told you. And dancin'?"

"You want to dance, Jack?" the girl asked.

"Dance with Stevie. He's the one we got to cheer up. He's got a party to give to Callie."

June took Stephen's hands, drawing him to a clearing among the tables. Before long everyone was watching, clapping and stamping feet, laughing as Stephen continued to drink and began to sing merrily in his husky baritone, parading and clowning with everyone in the room.

By the time the tavern owner was ready to close

and Jack's driver was falling asleep on his barstool, Stephen was feeling quite up to anything—including taking his party home to Callie.

At three thirty she was awakened by the raucous, very inebriated voices of Jack and Stephen singing loudly on the front porch. She sat up groggily, then lay back down again, thinking he would eventually find his own way into the house and to his room.

"Callie!" She imagined his voice carrying for miles in the night air. "Callie!"

She got out of bed and ran down the stairs. Mary Anne, nightcap askew, stood barefoot in the hall trying to fasten her robe. "Should I let them in?"

"Lord, yes! He'll have the whole neighborhood up. Listen to him, will you!" Callie scolded and opened the door herself.

"Hello, Callie darlin'. We're bringin' you a party," Jack crowed.

"Hello, Callie," Stephen parroted and stumbled through the door.

"Go home, Jack. Is your driver outside?" Callie asked, trying to turn him toward the door as she watched Mary Anne squealing and playing dodge 'em with Stephen in fine fettle.

"Driver's drunk. Can't trust anybody." Jack grinned.

"If he got you this far, he can get you the rest of the way home." Callie pushed Jack into the doorway. "Mary Anne, walk him to his carriage . . . see that he gets in it too." Callie released her hold on Jack to grab hold of Stephen's arms so Mary Anne could get past him. "Hurry up!"

"In my nightclothes!" Mary Anne gasped.

"Come kiss me, Mary Anne," Stephen said, lurching open-armed toward her. Mary Anne dashed over to Jack who was placidly being propped up by the wall. "Come along, Mr. Tolbert. You're goin' home."

Stephen turned his attention to Callie, having a difficult time keeping track of the three figures who bobbed in front of him. He pulled her down on the steps, unbraiding her hair as she slapped at his hands and scolded him.

"Mmmm," he said and took the long strands, coiling them around his neck until he had drawn himself to her. "You can't blame me for what I do now. I'm tied."

"You're drunk." She laughed, untangling herself. She got up, taking his hands and pulling him to his feet. "Come on. Party's over. It's upstairs with you now."

"Come dance with me, Callie. We haven't danced. You always say no to me. Don't say no tonight. Dance with me." At the top of his lungs he began to sing. He grabbed her around the waist and began twirling wildly through the hall.

They were both lying on the floor when Mary Anne came back in, Stephen feeling very ill and Callie laughing so hard she was crying.

"Oh, mercy!" said Mary Anne.

"Help me get him upstairs."

Together they got Stephen to his feet, not quite so lively as he had been. As they went up the stairs, he recovered somewhat, singing again. "Everybody loves me . . . nobody loves me . . ." In turn he kissed Callie and Mary Anne.

"Oh, mercy, Mr. Stephen," Mary Anne breathed. "He is affectionate when he's in his cups, ain't he?"

Callie giggled and shoved as they maneuvered him toward his room. They stood him at the edge of the bed. With one finger on his chest, Callie pushed, sending him over laughing and grabbing the air as he reached for her.

"Let's take his coat and boots off. He'll do till morning if we get him that far," Callie said and began to take his boot off. "Help me, Stephen," she yelled as he stiffened his foot making it impossible to remove the boot.

"Stand over his leg like the men do," Mary Anne prompted. Callie straddled Stephen's leg, tugging at the boot. Laughing and enjoying the sight, Stephen let her struggle before placing his left foot on her hind end and pushing.

"Oh, damn you, Stephen Berean!" she shouted as she sprawled.

He sat up on the bed. "Come to me love," he half sang, half said, and flopped back, reaching for her. He got a fistful of Mary Anne's nightdress. As it rose to indecent heights, Mary Anne scrambled to keep up with it, landing partly on Stephen and partly on the bed. "Oh mercy! Mr. Stephen!"

"Oh, mercy! Mary Anne!" he roared, laughing. Nose to nose he looked cross-eyed at her. "Do you care, Mary Anne? Callie doesn't. Maybe I'll marry you."

"Miss Callie!?" Mary Anne asked close to panic. "What should I do?"

Callie took Stephen's hand from inside Mary Anne's nightdress, only to find herself entangled in his other arm. He let out a cry of triumph. "I've gotcha now!"

Callie squirmed around, trying to free herself, pounding at his chest and arms, making him laugh. He wrapped his arm more securely around her. She was pressed tight against him. "Calliekissme callie kiss me calliecallie kissme," he said until it was a gaggle of sounds he found hilarious.

Mary Anne looked over at her and then at the tangle of the three of them on the bed. "Miss Callie . . . he won't let me go."

Callie put her head down, and Stephen began kissing her hair and her temple. "Just lie still for a minute. He can't last long," she said giggling.

Stephen turned his head, kissing the one eye of Callie's he could reach. "You think I'm going to pass out," he said happily. "I won't."

"What do you think you're going to do then?"

He chuckled evilly.

"Thoughts like that will bring you shame in the morning," she said, suppressing laughter.

Mary Anne wriggled out of his grasp as he turned his full attention to Callie. He got up on one elbow. "No, they won't," he said, shaking his head vigorously at her. "I'm going to make a grand exit," he said magnificently, and then wished he hadn't moved so quickly. He felt sick and very dizzy.

Mary Anne looked on fascinated, then she said, "Uh oh! He's gone green. Get the mop!" She laughed and ran past Peter in the doorway to get the mop.

Stephen's moment of lively exhibition was over. He lay still and pale, completely unknowing as Callie easily removed his boots and loosened his shirt, belt, and tie. He was snoring when she finished and looked up to see Peter. "How long have you been there?"

Peter leaned on the door thinking of what he had witnessed, and of what a blind idiot he had been not to have seen it sooner. "A while," he said.

She laughed, glancing back at Stephen. "You might have helped."

"He didn't seem to need help," Peter said strangely, and she realized he had been drinking too.

"I didn't mean him," she said.

Peter followed her down the hall to her room, stopping there, looking at her pensively. "He loves you, Callie."

"He loves everyone when he's drinking," she said. "Good night, Peter."

Peter shook his head. "You weren't listening to him, Callie." He walked slowly toward his own room as

Callie stood watching and wanting to cry for all three of them.

Callie didn't expect to try to awaken Stephen. He wouldn't be fit company for bears all day. She was better off with him sleeping past noon, and beyond if he would. She went to the kitchen. Perhaps by dinner, with a blueberry pie to bribe him, he might be tolerably tempered. She looked up amused and a little surprised to see Jack Tolbert mincing his way through the back door. He slithered in one long motion into a chair.

"What's the matter, Jack? You don't look too well."

"Oooh," he moaned. "Callie, darlin', have you a sling for a broken head?"

"You'd do better with a sling for your bendin' arm."

"Umm. Where's Stevie?"

"Still asleep. I haven't seen him all morning."

"Asleep nothin'," Bea chimed in. "He come through here an hour ago snarlin' and bitin' at everyone. You want me to call him? Though I don't see why anyone'd want him."

"Yes, please, Bea."

Bea went out back, first calling Stephen and then clanging the bell they used to call him from the fields.

"Ohh," Jack groaned, getting up. "Stop! You're breakin' my head."

Callie shrugged. "If he doesn't answer that, then I don't know where he is."

"Doesn't matter. Tell him I brought his horse home. He left it at my place last night. I'll see him later. I think I'll go home and die some more."

Callie finished her pie and stuck it in the oven. "Watch it for me please, Bea. I think I'd better go see where he is," she said, grabbing her shawl and going out.

"I'd steer clear. He's not his lovin' best," Bea shouted after her.

Callie laughed. "He was last night."

She looked in all the sheds and the outbuildings, and then feeling stupid for not having thought of it first, went down to his favorite spot by the stream.

He was lying on the ground, his head propped up by a log. He played aimlessly with his hand in the water.

She looked at him, coming up quietly behind him. The November sun came through the last tenacious leaves on the trees, making bright spots on his face and hair. But Stephen looked tired and unhappy.

She sat down on the log, putting her fingers in his silky, sun-warmed hair. He smiled, his eyes still closed. "Jack was here."

Stephen remained silent.

"Didn't you hear us calling you?"

"I heard."

"Why didn't you answer?"

"I didn't want to."

"What's wrong, Stephen?"

"I'm atoning for my sins."

"It's no wonder; but there's more than that. You never act like this."

"There's nothing else."

"Why are you out here alone like this if there's nothing? Aren't you cold?"

"Nothing is wrong!" he said, wincing as he moved too quickly to get up. He went to a tree across from the log on which Callie sat. He reached up, breaking off a dead twig and snapping it into bits. One by one he threw the pieces of twig into the stream.

"I didn't mean to make you angry."

"Oh, for God's sake, Callie, let go of it. You're like a

dog with a bone. Nothing's wrong. I just wanted to be alone for a while. Do I have to report to you?"

Callie got up, wiping her hands against the big apron that covered her dress. "Well, I can't say Bea didn't try to warn me."

"Callie—I'm sorry," he said earnestly, coming over to her. "I didn't mean to hurt you." He pulled her against him.

"I know you didn't, but you're unhappy, and I . . . I wanted to know why."

He pushed her away from him so he could look at her face. He was grinning; the merry twinkle that she counted on was in his eyes. "I drink too much."

"Are you feeling better now?"

"Not much."

"Well, you should have seen yourself last night!"

"I probably would rather not have."

"My word, I thought we'd never get you to bed. You tried to take Mary Anne in with you."

"I must have been drunk if it was Mary Anne."

"You were."

"I think I still am. Three heads should mean something," he said and cupped his hands over his ears.

"Why don't you come in and lie down for a while?"

"I want to stay here."

"It's cold."

"Not that cold, and I like it here."

"I'll call you in time for supper."

"Why don't you stay here with me?" he asked, coaxing.

"I have a blueberry pie in the oven. You wouldn't want it burnt."

"Burnt berry pie would be just as good," he said earnestly, pulling her toward him again.

She laughed, pushing him away. "I'll call you."

He hesitated for a moment, then said, "I won't be here for dinner tonight."

"Oh?"

"I'll be staying at Jack's for a while."

"Jack didn't mention it."

"Does Jack have to tell you everything?"

"Stephen? Why?"

He shrugged, raising his hands in surrender. "Ah, Callie, what do you want me to say?"

"I want you to tell me the truth."

He laughed. "Sometimes Callie, you make me want to choke you."

"I love you, Stephen."

He turned to face her angrily, hearing her no more than she had heard him the night before. "I know, but not the way I love you. I want you in every way a man can want a woman. So let it go. You have your truth, and I'm leaving. You've got Peter and that's the way it should be. But don't ask me to stay. I can't."

Chapter 43

Stephen packed his clothes that afternoon. He told Peter that he would be helping Jack with some problems he was having with the farm. It seemed easier and wiser to tell him he was leaving in stages, rather than try to think up a plausible substitute for the truth. He was gone from the house before dinner.

In the days that followed Callie found an emptiness in everything she did. All the things she had always loved doing became chores so bothersome and tedious she had to force herself through each day.

She knew Stephen went to the brewery daily, and she knew that he was at the farm some part of every day, but with four hundred acres it was easy for him to avoid her.

Alone and faced with the responsibilities of Jamie, Natalie, and Peter, Callie divided her time among them, unsuccessfully trying to hold a worsening situation steady.

Natalie was her main concern. Believing Callie would really have her put out of the house and therefore away from Jamie, Natalie said no more to Jamie about Peter; but she was in such an excited state Callie often found herself wishing for the return of the verbal abuse. At least she had known what Natalie was thinking.

With Callie closing her off, Natalie took to her own irrational defenses, slipping through the house like a wraith, keeping track of Peter's every move. Whether she believed she could move unseen or not, Callie didn't know, but Natalie's figure could be seen flitting down the halls or emerging from the draperies at any time. It was nerve-wracking and frightening.

As Callie went to the parlor, mending in her hand, Natalie darted out from behind the grandfather clock in the corner of the room. "I have him fooled! He doesn't know I watch."

"Don't jump at me like that, Natalie—please!" Callie gasped, her hand pressed against her throat.

"I thought it was *him*."

Callie picked up the sewing she had dropped. "Peter?"

"*Him*. Peter's dead. I always know where *he* is."

"Natalie, stop it!" Callie cried, putting her hands to her temples. "Stop!"

In desperation Callie locked Natalie in her room and went to Sam Tolbert's wife. Mrs. Tolbert was one of the few people Callie could turn to. The rest of the neighbors, fed by gossip and curiosity, regarded the Bereans as freaks. Several hate letters had arrived at the house. Notes were shoved under the front door condemning them for harboring a murderer. But Sam's wife had remained a friend, as had Sam and Jack.

"I don't know what to do with her anymore," Callie cried. "She gets worse all the time."

"I'm sure you realize she is completely mad, or you wouldn't be here," Mrs. Tolbert said.

"Of course, I know, but what do I do about it? I keep her confined to her room as much as possible," Callie said fretfully. "But I can't keep her in there forever, and she manages to get out anyway."

"You could have her put away."

Callie rubbed her forehead. "I have thought of it, but Mrs. Tolbert . . . those places . . . there's nothing any doctor can do for them and . . . they are let to live like animals . . . chained and dirty . . . and . . ."

Mrs. Tolbert fidgeted with her handkerchief, then refilled both their tea cups. "I don't know what should be done, Callie. It's too easy for me to sit here and tell you she belongs in an institution. If she were my child . . . or cousin, I don't know that I could bring myself to put her in one of those godforsaken places either. I'm no help to you at all with Natalie. Perhaps if I took Jamie for a time? Sam is going to take our boys to the mountains in a few days. Jamie is welcome to come."

"Oh, he'd love that. And it would help. These spells of Natalie's have never lasted too long before. Mostly she is content to stay in her room. It's only been lately that she won't. Perhaps by the time Jamie comes home she'll be all right again."

"Natalie will never be all right, Callie. It's time Stephen did something about her. What is he doing living with Jack anyway? You'd better get him to come back where he belongs and begin mending his fences. I don't know what should be done about her, but something must. You can't manage this alone and he shouldn't be allowing you to."

"Stephen doesn't know about it, Mrs. Tolbert. I haven't told him," Callie said, shifting uncomfortably in her chair. "When may I bring Jamie?"

"When are you going to tell Stephen? And why haven't you? She is his sister."

"I'll tell him."

"When?"

"Soon . . . tomorrow. Tonight, if I see him. When may I bring Jamie?"

Mrs. Tolbert studied her, worried and dismayed, then decided it was futile to say more. It had been said; if Callie would listen at all, she already had. "Friday will be fine. Early afternoon is best. It will give the boys some time to visit before supper. Oh, and don't forget to send his heaviest clothes. There is already snow in the mountains," she added. "It's going to be a snowy winter this year."

Mrs. Tolbert walked with her to the door. "Take care, Callie, and don't hesitate to come see me. I don't seem to be much help, but I can listen."

Callie went home. She looked up at the house, its windows glowing soft amber from the lights within, promising the warmth and happiness that had once been and was no more. She turned away toward the woods. If Stephen were ever to come to her again, she was certain it would be in that clearing by the stream.

She had been going there daily since he left. She pulled her cloak more tightly around her as she sat down on the log at the stream's edge. She remained there looking into the water, wishing he would come and hoping he would not. She loved Stephen, but she knew as well as he that no matter how often they met or how deeply they loved, she'd return to Peter and Jamie.

At nightfall she walked slowly back to the house, feeling she had left behind at the stream's edge the joy of life, the laughter, the quiet joyous peace that lived tranquilly inside her, making each day bright as long as she knew he was nearby.

Supper was over. No one had eaten at the table because she hadn't been there to see that they did. Jamie had eaten in the playroom. Natalie was closed within her rooms. Peter sat alone in his study as locked away by his terrifying memories as Natalie was by her phantoms.

"Hello, Peter," she said as she came from hearing Bea's account of the afternoon. "Bea said you didn't eat. Would you like something now?"

"You look tired, Callie."

"It's been a long day. Sam Tolbert asked after you."

"How is Sam?"

"He's fine. He's going to take Jamie with his sons on a trip to the mountains."

"I should be taking him," Peter said quietly. "I don't know how to do the things I want . . . it's always there with me . . . stopping me. I . . ."

"You will."

Peter leaned forward against the windowsill, staring blankly at the barren trees robbed of their autumn colors, sapless and dormant in winter stillness.

"I was just going up to tell Jamie about the trip. Perhaps you would like to tell him."

Peter shook his head, remaining at the window.

Callie went to Jamie's room, prolonging her visit. Jamie happily repeated the stories Peter had told him of England and of the Cantii that had first lived roaming the Weald and the chalk hills and the forests. He blissfully mixed the Kentish countryside in atrocious confusion with bits of information about New York and the Hudson valley. He chattered incessantly, interspersing questions about the coming trip with Sam. Callie smiled as he listened. However Peter failed to free himself, he was building in Jamie an awareness of a bright world filled with promise and expectation.

Callie stayed until Mary Anne stood cross-armed and stern-visaged at the side of Jamie's bed. "How long are you going to keep this child from his rest?" she scolded.

Callie got up, still smiling. "We've been naughty, Jamie," she said, kissing him and helping him into bed. "Sleep well."

"Aunt Callie?"

"Yes?"

"How long till Friday?"

"Three days. Three little days that will pass before you know it."

Peter spent most of the night in his study. In the morning he was tense and pale when he came to breakfast with Callie. She hadn't seen that look on his face for a long time, and she didn't know what had caused it. It was the same expression of dreading determination he had had when Stephen had first told him he must join them at supper.

When Jamie joined them, Peter's tension eased as though some great milestone had been passed. He told Callie he'd be taking Jamie for the day—out of the house. Callie approved, and Jamie had the good sense not to mention school if the adults did not.

Peter spent most of the next three days with Jamie, walking the farm, hunting in the woods, and fishing in the cold streams.

"I think you'll be showing Mr. Tolbert's boys a thing or two on this trip," Callie said as they both came home slightly damp and very cold the third evening.

Jamie danced in place, warming his feet. He had his secret smile all over his face as he kept his hands behind his back, guarding his surprise between himself and Peter. "Papa knows everything," he announced, beaming up at Peter. "He can catch fish with a spear—and I did too! See!" he chirped, thrusting the half-frozen fish at Callie.

"Ohh! It's a lovely fish. The loveliest I've ever seen caught with a stick."

"A spear," Jamie corrected.

"A spear, indeed. Suppose I tell Bea to cook your fish for supper?"

Jamie looked at Peter, smiling at the nodded assent given.

"Then get over to the fire. I'll get you dry clothes, and then we'll tell Bea to cook your fish."

"We'll go up," Peter said, getting down on his haunches so Jamie could climb on his back for a ride up the stairs.

Callie told Bea to fry the fish, then followed after Peter and Jamie.

As Peter turned to go down the upper hall to Jamie's room, Natalie stepped out of hers. "Put him down!"

Peter stopped as though an invisible leash had tightened. He glanced over his shoulder at his sister. She was hardly recognizable these days. The elfin charm was lost in the soft-fleshed distortion of her features. Only her hollow, burning eyes had any familiarity, and that of a terrible night in Kent when James Berean had died. Peter put Jamie down, then picked him up again, holding him securely in both arms. "What do you want, Nat?"

"Put him down! He's mine! Put him down!" Natalie said, crouching slightly and edging toward Peter and Jamie.

Callie heard Natalie's last screamed command. She ran the last of the steps, calling to Peter to take Jamie to his room. Peter turned hurriedly with Jamie.

Natalie ran down the hall, grabbing hold of Jamie's leg and arm. Jamie cried out in fright, pulling his arm free of Natalie and taking a strangle hold on Peter's neck.

Peter struggled, holding fast to Jamie with one hand

and trying to break Natalie's hold on his leg with the other. Callie ran down the hall, taking hold of Natalie from behind. Between them they freed Jamie momentarily.

"Hurry, Peter!" Callie cried as she saw him hesitate, not knowing whether to help her or take Jamie to his room.

"You're evil!" Natalie hissed, lunging after Peter.

"Get in your room!" Callie grunted, dragging Natalie a step at a time back down the hall.

"I'll get her," Peter said as he ran back to Callie. Natalie flailed, clawing and writhing as he tried to pick her up.

"Get her to her room," Callie panted as Peter dodged Natalie's clawing nails until he got hold of both her hands. He carried her to the bedroom.

"Don't wait!" Callie cried, pulling at him. "Get out." She slammed the door shut, holding fast to the knob as Natalie pounded in fury from the other side.

Peter looked dazedly at the door, then at Callie. "How long has she. . . . Has she been like this ever before?" he asked breathlessly.

"No. No . . . never this bad. It's been getting worse recently. I don't know what to do anymore."

"She's insane," he said disbelievingly. "I always thought I had been the cause of . . . I mean I never believed her when she'd tell me . . ."

"That's why Jamie is going on the fishing trip," Callie said quickly. "I had to do something. I'm afraid. I never know . . . what could happen."

Peter moved slowly toward Natalie's door. "Don't! Don't go near her. Not until I've had a chance to talk to you about her, Peter. Please. I've got to see to Jamie now, but stay away from her until we talk. Promise me."

He glanced at Callie, then at Natalie's door. "I'll be downstairs."

She stopped before entering Jamie's room to be certain Peter went downstairs as he had promised.

Mary Anne had Jamie calmed, warm, and in dry clothes when Callie came in.

"What was goin' on out there? This child was scared out of his wits!"

"Keep Natalie away from him, Mary Anne—all the time. Don't let him near her for any reason."

"Miss Natalie? Why, she dotes on the boy. What harm—"

"Keep her away from him!" Callie said shrilly.

Mary Anne's lips tightened in disapproval. "Whatever you say, miss."

Callie rubbed her head. There was no use. "Only for a day or two, Mary Anne. Please. I can't manage alone."

Jamie sniffed. "I don't like Aunt Natalie when she's mean."

"I don't either, Jamie." Callie hugged him, then asked quietly, "What name does she call you, Jamie?"

"I'm not supposed to tell," he said, shaking his head and glancing at the door. "She said I couldn't—not ever."

"Is it Bertie?"

"I didn't tell!" he howled, his face puckering up.

Callie closed her eyes, letting him climb up onto her lap. "Jamie . . ." she said softly. "You must always tell me things like that, because what Aunt Natalie did was very wrong. Did you know it was wrong?"

"Aunt Natalie said I wasn't allowed to tell you."

"It is wrong to keep secrets from people you love, Jamie. No matter what anyone says, you always tell me when something is wrong."

"But she said pretending was all right. We were pretending . . ."

"Oh, Jamie . . ." Callie breathed, sitting back limply as Jamie told her of their pretenses of Albert and Natalie and Bertie, and of the evil man who wanted to steal Bertie away. She held him close until he fell asleep.

When she came downstairs, Peter was waiting for her.

"Is he all right?"

"Yes, he's all right." She looked worriedly at Peter's anxious face. "Peter, don't go near her."

"You don't need to protect me from my own sister, Callie."

"No, no, you don't understand," she said urgently and explained to him what had begun in Kent with Natalie's miscarriage. They talked about Albert's and Rosalind's death and what Peter's thoughts had been at the time and Callie's and Stephen's. Finally she told him about the violence and hatred that seemed to have come alive in Natalie again as soon as Peter had returned home.

Both Peter and Callie fell into a deep, pensive silence, going back over the years. Then Peter said, "She's been like this since you left England?"

"Oh, no—no. It's only when she thought you were coming home. She is afraid you'll take Jamie . . . Bertie . . . I don't know what she thinks really. She is far beyond me now. I can't keep her in her room, nor can I calm her this time."

Peter sat rigidly tense, staring past Callie, seeing what she couldn't imagine. "You'll put her in an asylum," he murmured.

Callie got up, nervously adjusting the figurines on the tables, dusting with the tip of her apron. "You and Stephen will have to decide," she said finally, her lips tight. "I'm going to send a message to him at the brewery tomorrow after I take Jamie to the Tolberts'.

He can come to dinner and then . . . then you two
will have to decide . . . what will be done."

"Locked in an asylum," Peter murmured in revulsion.

"Peter, I went to the asylum . . . to see if it was as
horrible as . . . I know what it's like! Do you think I
want to see her there! We brought her here with us to
keep her from one in England. I don't know what to
do! I don't want to put her there, but she can't stay
here."

He said nothing. Biting on her lip, feeling guilty at
the thought of coldly locking Natalie away for the remainder of her life to slowly rot away, Callie looked
beseechingly at him. "Am I wrong? Do you think it is
safe for her to be near Jamie . . . or you?"

"No, I don't want her near Jamie!" he said in agitation, then calmed slightly. "We'll take her away. But
not to one of those places . . . not . . . one of those
places."

Next morning Callie packed the bundle of clothing
Jamie would need for his trip. The last thing she did
before leaving for the Tolberts' after lunch was to
check the lock on Natalie's door.

Natalie worked at her door, sticking into the lock
anything she possessed, including a large assortment
of keys she had taken from all over the house. One by
one she tried them without success. Then she began to
work on the hinges, trying to remove the hinge pins.
Two she removed easily. The third was frozen in
place as the weight of the door pulled the hinges out
of alignment. She went back to the keys, trying them
with less haste and a diabolical concentration. Succeeding, she took Callie's bread knife from under her
mattress and slipped out through the door hanging
crazily on one hinge.

She edged down the hallway to Peter's bedroom. Enraged to find it empty, she slashed at the bed, tearing the coverlet and pillow to shreds.

Peter finished his coffee. He left the dining room having decided to walk to the brewery to see Stephen himself. There was no need to send a message, and it was time he spoke to Stephen about Natalie, and about his prolonged absence from home. He started up the staircase, preoccupied, trying to plan the simple trip to the brewery to find Stephen in an orderly fashion. He felt as he had the first time Rebecca had let him free to go into Hobart Town alone. He had been terrified; but finding Tom Baker had been important enough to override his fear. Today Callie and Stephen and Jamie were important enough for him to try again.

Natalie slithered along the wall, quiet and intensely alert to every sound in the house. She crouched at the corner of the wall where the steps reached the top landing—waiting, controlling the laughter and the moment of intense triumph that was so near.

Peter came within four steps of the second floor when she flew at him laughing maniacally, the knife held firmly pointed at his throat.

His arm went up, and Natalie hit him at the same time. They both fell with uncontrollable force down the stairs.

Mary Anne ran from the back of the house. She saw them both at the base of the stairs on the hall floor. Peter's arm was soaked in blood where the knife had gouged him. Natalie lay beside him, a broken doll. The knife was on the floor.

Mary Anne screamed at the top of her lungs, quivering in shock.

Peter dazedly opened his eyes, grimacing and holding his head. Her screaming cut through him. Then he moved quickly, getting to his feet, staring in glassy-eyed horror at Natalie. He put his hands out, his eyes imploring Mary Anne. She cowered away from him, finally breaking her fright to run from the house shouting to the field men to get the sheriff.

Peter was still huddled against the stair wall shaking and staring down at Natalie when Callie came up the front walk from having taken Jamie to the Tolberts'.

She stepped inside the foyer, taking off her coat and hat, hanging them neatly and straightening the others before she entered the main hall.

She swayed, her eyes growing dark as she looked at them. She compelled herself to cross the hall, going down on her knees beside Natalie, knowing before she touched her that she was dead. "Why? Why didn't you stay away from her?" she asked in anguish.

Peter began to shake his head mindlessly. "No . . . No . . . I didn't . . . I . . ."

Callie looked at him in shocked understanding. "I know you didn't," she said. "Oh, Lord, Peter, it wasn't you. I know that." As she looked at him and felt his bewildered pain, she began to gather her senses. She got up, coming around Natalie to him. She took his hand, felt the hot moistness of the still bleeding wound, and led him to the study.

"I didn't want her to be hurt. I tried to catch her," he said, looking at Callie. "She . . . she threw herself at me . . . she . . ."

"Drink this," she said and handed him a glass of brandy. She began to clean and dress the knife wound.

Though it was quite some time, it seemed they had no more than a few seconds before the sheriff and several men from the fields burst into the house led by Mary Anne hysterically babbling her story.

Peter laid his head against the back of the sofa, all expression drained from his face. If the taut look of despair hadn't been imprinted on his features, she would have thought him asleep. She stood between him and the door to the hall. She heard the voices of the sheriff and the other men mixed with Mary Anne's high tremor.

"Watch yourselves. He's got to be here somewhere. Don't take no chances."

Callie heard the sheriff's instructions and stepped out into the hall, leaning against the closed door to the study. "Sheriff . . ."

"It's all right, Miss Dawson. Don't you worry none. We'll get him."

"Sheriff . . . Natalie tried to kill Peter. He did nothing to her."

The sheriff looked at Mary Anne. Mary Anne looked sorrowfully at Callie. "I don't know about that. But it's Miss Natalie who's dead, and he was with her."

"Natalie tried to kill Peter," Callie repeated, fighting to keep control of her voice. She stood as she had been, her back to the study door, guarding it.

"Were you here too?" the sheriff asked, confused and no longer certain.

"She was at the Tolberts'," Mary Anne said.

"Then how do you know what happened?"

"I know."

"He tell you?"

"He didn't need to tell me, but he did."

The sheriff nodded to his deputy and two of the men from the fields. "Well, he'll get his say at his trial. You just step aside, and we'll get this over with just as quick as we can."

"You don't need Peter! He did nothing!" she said, her voice rising. She pressed harder against the door.

"Step aside, Miss Dawson," the sheriff said firmly.

"You can't take him." She was pleading now.

"Step aside, Miss Dawson."

"No! No! I won't let you. You can't do it!" she cried, cornered and frantic. The sheriff took her arm, pulling her away from the door. "You're blocking me from doing my rightful job, Miss Dawson. We'll find out if he's guilty or innocent of this, but either way, he's a wanted man by the English. I got to take him. Now you stand aside or I'm going to have to see you do."

The other man opened the door to the study. Peter sat where he had been, unmoving, his eyes closed. "Callie!" he said in alarm as she broke free of the sheriff.

She darted into the study, trying to block the men. "Get out of my house! You have no right to come in here!"

"Take her out of the way," the sheriff said to Mary Anne.

Callie ran forward shoving at each of the men in turn. "You can't take him! You can't! He's done nothing! Why don't you believe him? Why won't anybody ever believe? Oh, please! Please!"

"Callie, don't," Peter said, trying to get to her.

Both the field hands from the farm grabbed hold of him. "Let go of me! Let me go to her!"

"Get him outside."

Callie ran after them. "Let him go! Let him go!" She clawed at them. Peter turned back, struggling now with a desperate strength wanting to get to Callie.

The sheriff said quietly to Callie, "I told you he's a condemned man by English law. I'll shoot him if I have to. Nobody's gonna care. I'll get thanked for it. So unless you want to see that happen, Miss Dawson, you quiet down and let me do my job the right way, or I won't be responsible."

Callie looked at him with horror. "Is your job to condemn the innocent? He's done nothing. Why? Why are you doing this? You wouldn't if he were someone else."

The sheriff unsheathed his gun as Peter pulled free of the two men who held him. Callie leaped forward, throwing herself against Peter. He put his arms around her, ignoring the confused, angry voices of men uncertain now how to take him yet determined to do it.

"If you care for her, Berean, you'll come quietly," the sheriff said, alert now, ready for another struggle.

Callie clung to him, sobbing as he held her. "Callie, let me go," he said gently, his face buried in her hair.

"Berean," the sheriff said, moving closer.

Peter unwound her arms from around his neck, holding her at arm's length. "Don't let them hurt you, Callie, please," he begged. "Just let me go with them now."

"You've done nothing. They have no right."

"Callie . . . please. Don't fight them anymore." Peter released her, backing in between the two men who had held him before. He walked out the door guarded by the deputy and the two field hands.

The sheriff watched, following slowly after. He stopped at the front door. "He'll get his trial."

"I told you he was innocent! There can be no trial when you believe him guilty," she screamed, once more looking frantically to where Peter was climbing into the carriage. Mary Anne came up, putting her arm around Callie's waist.

"Come sit down, Miss Callie. Let me get you something to make you feel better."

Callie rounded on her, pushing her away. "Damn

you! You knew Natalie and still you condemned him!"

"Miss Natalie, devil that she was, was a tiny woman . . . she wasn't going to be doing any harm to that big brute. You know that as well as I do, Miss Callie. He was a violent man. He'd murdered before . . ." Mary Anne came near her again.

"Don't you touch me, you Judas."

"Miss Callie!"

Callie's voice was cold and flat. "Get out, Mary Anne."

"Out?" Mary Anne said weakly. "But . . . Master Jamie—"

"You'll never touch his son. Get out, Mary Anne. Get out now!"

Mary Anne packed her things, making one last unsuccessful attempt to talk to Callie before she left. Callie sat numbly in the study, uncaring that she was now alone in the house, or that Natalie lay unattended on the floor in the hallway. She sat in darkness and thought about Rehoboam, the son of Solomon. Rehoboam, the young and tender-hearted against whom the wicked children of Belial strengthened when he could not withstand them. And who were these children of Satan, who strengthened time and time again with their eyes blind and their ears deaf to all goodness, if not the very people with whom she had lived all her life? Were they not Rosalind turning from him to lust after another; Natalie coveting his son; Mary Anne, who knew him only by the brand on his chest; Frank, whose jealousy caused him to deny his brother's existence rather than risk his own pride?

If those were the legions of the Satan Belial, where was hope?

Chapter 44

Once in the carriage, Peter didn't speak again. He went as docilely and with as little interest in his destination as the sheriff had ever seen in a man. As long as Callie was left alone and the wary attention was on him, Peter was quiet.

"You want your brother told?" the sheriff asked as he locked the iron cell door behind Peter. Peter walked to the cot along the wall, lying down without saying anything or indicating that he had heard at all.

"Send for his brother," the sheriff said to the deputy. "Should be able to find him at the brewery. If not, try Jack Tolbert's place."

Stephen rode directly to the house. All he knew from what the deputy told him was that it hadn't been Callie who'd died. He saw the pitch-dark house, fright rising inside him. He burst through the front door. "Callie!"

He didn't hear a sound—no movement, no answer, not even the ticking of the clock. He lit the candelabra in the hall. Natalie still lay at the foot of the stairs.

"Oh, God!" He raced up the stairs, calling her name, "Callie! Answer me. Callie!" He came back downstairs, going from one room to the other. He opened the door to the study. The light from the hall fell across her, sitting motionless on the sofa.

"Callie . . ." he said softly, coming into the room. He sat down beside her feeling a sick relief to know where she was, and yet afraid to touch her looking as she did. "Speak to me, please."

"Natalie has finally killed him. She killed him, Stephen. She killed him and we're guilty," she said, emotionless and staring.

"He'll have a trial, Callie. It won't be like England. Things have changed."

She laughed senselessly in the dark. "Things never change. There'll be no trial. There'll be no justice. There is nothing!" she said shrilly, crying again.

Stephen touched his forehead to her shoulder. She kept on laughing and crying. "Should I give him another code? Another May house, Stephen? Should I tell him to believe? Should I? Believe in what? What is there, Stephen?"

The painful wrench he felt made him catch his breath. "Oh God, Callie, don't talk like that. Not you."

Stephen went to the hall, picking up Natalie to carry her to her room. He had never prepared a body. He had no idea of what should be done. He arranged her on the bed, trying to make her look whole and straight. Then he went back to Callie. "Where is Mary Anne?"

"Gone."

"Bea?"

"Gone."

"Callie . . . something has to be done for Natalie," he said helplessly.

She sat, unchanged in frigid stillness.

Stephen moved toward her then stopped, not knowing what to do or say. He wanted to go to see Peter; he couldn't leave Natalie as she was; and dear God, he didn't want to leave Callie this way. "She's my sister, Callie. Please. Peter . . . Peter wouldn't want her left like that . . . not even now. Do it for him. Please. She's dead."

"She killed herself trying to kill him, Stephen. And you ask me to do it for Peter?"

"I ask it for him, Callie . . . and for myself."

When she didn't answer, he said, "I'm going to see Peter. I'll bring someone from the village for Natalie."

Callie sat quietly as she heard his horse canter down the road in front of the house. Then she got up and went upstairs to Natalie.

Peter got up from the cot as soon as he saw Stephen approaching the cell. "Is Callie all right?"

The gaoler let Stephen inside the cell. Stephen looked at Peter, hesitated, and then embraced him as the whole of Peter's thirty-two years passed between them.

"When does it all end? Isn't there ever enough?" Stephen asked, holding Peter and seeing nothing ahead for any of them but the endless tragedy-torn years that dogged them.

"Is she all right?" Peter asked again as he and Stephen sat side by side on the cot.

"She'll be all right," Stephen said, trying to believe it himself.

Peter sat quietly thinking for a long time; then came a long damned up flood of words and feelings. He began to talk to Stephen of all the things he wanted to leave behind for Jamie.

Over Stephen's protests about the trial, which this time had to be fair, Peter laid out his plans to insure Jamie's future. When he finished he turned to Stephen and said, "Go to her, Stephen. If there is any sin I need atone for more than others, it is knowing you loved her when . . ."

"There is no sin, Peter. Callie loves you."

"Yes . . . and Jamie . . . without her I would have died long ago. She was hope to me. Where Callie stood there was light," he said and paused. He got up and walked to the window. He held fast to the grille, pulling against the bars. "Stephen—I don't want to die taking that away from her."

He came back to Stephen's side. "She gave me love . . . but she loves you. She's not the same without you. She needs you, Stephen. She always has. Promise you won't leave her alone. You won't let that happen to her."

Stephen looked at Peter through a haze of tears, unable to speak or promise anything.

He went home having forgotten to hire someone to tend to Natalie. The house was as dark and unnaturally quiet as it had been before. Again he felt the air of uneasy fear. He looked in the study. Callie was no longer there. He walked through the house and up to her room. She wasn't there either. He went to Peter's bedroom and all the others without finding her. Finally he pushed aside the broken door to Natalie's room. She lay prepared, candles lit around her. She looked as natural as if she had been sleeping. But Callie wasn't there. Fear mounting, he went to Jamie's nursery. Last, he opened the door to his own bedroom.

Still dressed, she lay across his bed, asleep.

Without waking her he lay down on the bed beside

her, knowing as he did that only unknown and in sleep would he be able to come near her. What he had seen, and Peter had not, was the despairing emptiness the day had cast on her. He could not keep his silent promise to Peter because the brightness of Callie's faith in God and man had gone out that afternoon.

He lay beside her, touching her hair, placing his fingers gently to her parted lips. As dawn crept into the sky and Callie's sleep lightened, Stephen left.

Peter was tried and sentenced to hang the following week.

Callie's visits to him were brief and unsatisfactory. She could no more face him than she had been able to face what had happened.

Peter thought through the years, going back before he had ever met Rosalind. There were no fears left in the memories. All his fears went toward the future as he saw Callie coming daily, struggling to be cheerful and reassuring when she couldn't accept what would be.

The morning before he was to hang, Peter waited for Callie to come. She wasn't there at the time he had learned to expect her. He paced the cell, anxiously returning to the grilled window that let him see the street outside.

When she came in he took the two steps across the room to her before the gaoler had closed the door. "I thought you weren't coming," he said, laughing in relief as he held her.

"You have no faith," she said, painfully cheerful.

"Come sit beside me."

"All right." She sat down on the cot beside him. "I brought you a pie," she said. "They have it in the outer room." She burst into tears.

Peter held her. "Don't cry for me, Callie."

"Oh, Peter, I don't know what to do. I pray there has to be something, and there is nothing."

"There's the world, Callie. You and Stephen and Jamie."

She shook her head, unable to speak.

He kissed her tears. "You told me to tell you when I began to believe again," he said softly. "I do, Callie. Look at me. I remember the May house. It's real, Callie, and I know it."

"I can't."

"After all these years, will you turn away from me now? I need you now more than ever before. Don't turn from me, Callie."

She looked up at him. "I haven't turned from you, Peter. I just don't know what to do."

"Love Jamie for me. Dream for him as you did for me. Believe . . ."

"Oh, Peter, please . . ."

"No. Listen to me. I'll never be able to say it to you again. Jamie's just beginning his life now. I want him to know who I am, Callie, not what I've done or where I've been. Keep Jamie safe for me. Teach him to believe. Oh God, Callie, I don't want him to be as I was for all those years. If I hadn't known you were there somewhere . . ." He turned from her.

Callie felt as though she were being crushed beneath her helplessness. She'd had nothing of value to give years ago, and she had less now. But she said what he wanted to hear. "Peter, I will. Jamie will know you. And I'll dream and . . ." she said brokenly until she couldn't say any more.

"Time to leave, Miss Dawson," the gaoler said, clinking his keys against the bars.

"Peter," she cried.

He took her in his arms, kissing her long and tenderly. "Keep him safe for me."

She backed to the door and stood staring at him. She blinked through her tears, trying to smile.

Jamie was still at the Tolberts', Mrs. Tolbert wisely keeping him until it was over. Callie was alone in the house. All this week she had taken a desolate satisfaction in the emptiness. Tonight, after she left Peter, she noticed the lifelessness for the first time. "There is the world . . . you and Stephen and Jamie," he had said. And there was Peter, all the things he might have been, and all the things he now would never be.

She walked up to Jamie's room, looking down at his empty bed, going from one cupboard to another, touching the toys Stephen and Peter had made for him. She sat down near the window, looking out onto the cold bleakness of a frozen earth, the soil deathly gray in frost, the trees barren, reaching denuded black arms into a lightless sky.

As she watched, letting the dry dormancy seep inside her, the snow that was to fall all night long in heavy, soft, moist flakes began, soaking into the hardened earth. *"There is the world . . . you and Stephen and Jamie."*

As the warming blanket of white covered, shielded, and nurtured sleeping roots and seeds to begin life anew, Callie's thoughts turned to the brown-eyed, blond-haired little boy who would be so like his father were Peter not destroyed by emptiness.

The snow fell and Callie prayed, groping her way back through the haze of hates and fears and judgments that had been brought down on Peter by others, blighting his life without reason or justice. She had had neither the power nor the wisdom to be able to help him, but she had enough for Jamie, if Stephen were by her side. With Stephen to keep her strong, and the world filled with the loving promise his father had given him, Jamie would grow up to be what Peter might have been.

The gaoler brought Peter out into the bright morning sun. He squinted against the glare it made off the fresh snow. Beside him stood the black-garbed minister who had been with him all night.

In many ways it reminded him of the long horrible time on Van Diemen's Land, where chains and preachers had the same meaning of endless captivity, and yet it was different.

The minister walked at his side, reading from the black leather-bound Testament he balanced perfectly on his palm. "They came to a small estate called Gethsemane, and Jesus said to his apostles, 'Stay here while I pray.' Then he took Peter and James and John with him. And a sudden fear came over him, and great distress. And he said to them, 'My soul is sorrowful to the point of death. Wait here and keep awake.' And going on a little further he threw himself to the ground and prayed that, if it were possible, this hour might pass him by."

Peter raised his eyes and saw Callie standing off and alone. He knew she'd be there without looking, but he wanted that brief final glance that would tell him of Jamie's future. He felt the tension in his body relax as he read it in her face. There were no tears in her eyes, only the loving smile he had learned no amount of cruelty or debasement could change.

The minister's voice went on slowly and reverently in Peter's ears as they walked through the snow to the gallows, which looked clean and newly built.

" 'Abba!' He said. 'Everything is possible for you.

Take this cup away from me. But let it be as you, not I, would have it.'"

Perhaps that was all the difference there was between this time and the time spent in Van Diemen's Land. She was there. And she was stronger than anyone he had ever known, because she believed in God.

"He came back and found them sleeping, and he said to Peter, 'Simon, are you asleep? Had you not the strength to keep awake one hour? You should be awake and praying not to be put to the test. The spirit is willing, but the flesh is weak.'"

Stephen was there as well. Not near Callie as he should be, Peter thought. But he was there. Too much could not be asked at one time. Stephen would never trespass in Peter's life. It was best that he die now. His life was over, and Stephen's couldn't begin until he was gone.

"Again he went away and prayed, saying the same words. Once more he came back and found them sleeping, their eyes so heavy; and they could find no answer for him."

Peter wondered if he, sinner that he was, repentant that he was not, could leave his blessings on the three people he loved. He thought it better he did not. Perhaps the blessings of a damned man would damn them as well. And then he thought of Callie's unquenchable trust in good, and he blessed them, waiting with a pounding heart to see if God heard.

Peter stood at the top of the gallows looking at Stephen, pleading with his eyes for Stephen to go to Callie, praying to God to be given this sign of absolution.

Stephen's eyes met Peter's. He walked toward Callie. Peter watched as Stephen hesitated, unsure, waiting for some sign from Callie. She moved toward him, and Stephen's arms closed around her. Peter knew the tears that hadn't been in her eyes before were there now, healing and soft.

"He came a third time and said to them, 'You can sleep on now and take your rest. It is all over. The hour has come.'"

Then Peter prayed. Silently, lips firmly closed, but unafraid, at long last within himself at peace.

The wormwood cup was emptied.